A COMPLICATED
LEGACY

Robert H. Stucky

Printed in the United States of America

First Printing, 2014
ISBN-10: 0692218602
ISBN-13: 978-0692218600

Eastcliff Editions
Baltimore, MD 21209
contact: eastcliff.editions@gmail.com

Graphic Designer: Jennifer S. Marin

About the cover: The magnolia and the cotton boll are quintessential symbols embracing the social polarities of the Ante Bellum South. They are a sort of leitmotif throughout the novel, and thus appear in the design of the book, as does the 19th century map of Barnwell District, South Carolina, where the majority of the novel takes place.

To my father,
William McDowell Stucky
Dramatist, journalist, lover of the English language,
And storyteller extraordinaire.

ACKNOWLEDGEMENTS

Every author owes a debt to those who inspired and supported him in the process of giving birth to the book. My particular thanks to Alanna Dennis, who first told me of Elijah and Amy Willis, and to her son, Elijah's and Amy's descendant, whom she hoped to inspire with the story; and to numerous friends and colleagues, black and white, who have been reading regular installments of the manuscript and giving me invaluable feedback as I churned them out; to my brother Bill for his extremely helpful criticism and for believing in me; to my wife Pitina and son, Franciso, who have both supported me and put up with me in the arduous process of writing this book; to Amanda DeStefano, who with great insight did the copy editing; Jennifer Marin, who designed the final book and its cover; Jay Perry for his unfailingly helpful artistic advice; and to Mark Twain, and the authors of *Fathers of Conscience, The Help, The Butler, Lincoln, Twelve Years a Slave, A Time to Kill, Mississippi Burning, To Kill a Mockingbird, The Blind Side, Amistad, Crash,* and numerous other books and films that attempt to shed a more human and honest light on the complex realities of race relations and their evolution in America over the past few centuries, right up to the present. They show both how far we have come, and how far we have yet to go.

As we celebrate the Sesquicentennial of the Emancipation Proclamation and the passage of the Thirteenth Amendment, I hope this book contributes something useful to our collective efforts to understand and more fully appreciate our complicated legacy, and Mr. Lincoln's exhortation for us to strive to "form a more perfect Union," in freedom from mutual fear, hatred and distrust.

Robemore

ACKNOWLEDGEMENTS

Every author owes a debt to those who inspired and supported him in the process of giving birth to the book. My particular thanks to Alanna Dennis, who first told me of Elijah and Amy Willis, and to her son, Elijah's and Amy's descendant, whom she hoped to inspire with the story; and to numerous friends and colleagues, black and white, who have been reading regular installments of the manuscript and giving me invaluable feedback as I churned them out; to my brother Bill for his extremely helpful criticism and for believing in me; to my wife Pitina and son, Franciso, who have both supported me and put up with me in the arduous process of writing this book; to Amanda DeStefano, who with great insight did the copy editing; Jennifer Marin, who designed the final book and its cover; Jay Perry for his unfailingly helpful artistic advice; and to Mark Twain, and the authors of *Fathers of Conscience, The Help, The Butler, Lincoln, Twelve Years a Slave, A Time to Kill, Mississippi Burning, To Kill a Mockingbird, The Blind Side, Amistad, Crash,* and numerous other books and films that attempt to shed a more human and honest light on the complex realities of race relations and their evolution in America over the past few centuries, right up to the present. They show both how far we have come, and how far we have yet to go.

As we celebrate the Sesquicentennial of the Emancipation Proclamation and the passage of the Thirteenth Amendment, I hope this book contributes something useful to our collective efforts to understand and more fully appreciate our complicated legacy, and Mr. Lincoln's exhortation for us to strive to "form a more perfect Union," in freedom from mutual fear, hatred and distrust.

Robert H. Stucky
February 28, 2014
Baltimore

DEDICATION

When I was nine, my family and I spent three weeks camping in total privacy on a tiny island in the upper end of Lake George, in Upstate New York, accessible only by our little wooden rowboat, and its five horsepower outboard motor. We lived in three Army tents on wooden platforms- one for my parents, one for my brother and me, and one was a cook tent for bad weather. In the middle of that triangle, facing the lake, was a stone ringed campfire and a picnic table.

There was a paddle-wheeled steamboat that used to ply the length of the lake, taking tourists up and down. At night we would hear it coming and watch it chug by, its lights aglow, twinkling and skipping on the waters of the lake, happy voices on the way to somewhere else floating out from it, echoing and fading through the pine trees, until they disappeared in the general flow of life around us, like the wake of the boat from whence they came.

With that as a backdrop, by the light of a kerosene lantern and the campfire, my father would read to us in his gentle Kentucky drawl, *The Adventures of Tom Sawyer and Huckleberry Finn*. A year later he died, but the combined magic of his voice, the setting, and the story, awakened in me both a love of storytelling and a social conscience that has stayed with me ever since. Unexpectedly, more than fifty years later, as I wrote this book, I realized my father's voice still spoke softly to me, over my shoulder. I hope this story does him justice.

There was a comforting rhythm to the churning of the paddle wheels, the twin steam engines huffing along with a steady down-beat, the water cascading off the paddles back into the current. The lapping of waves against the bow echoed the music of the cascade, sliding along the hull to join the frothing wake, fanning out across the river's surface astern like a cheerful wave "good-bye" to all that lay behind. It was May, 1855, and Spring was at its peak in the Ohio River Valley. The newly built steamship, the *Jacob Strader*, richly appointed and elegantly furnished, chugged purposefully up the river from Louisville toward the dock at Cincinnati, carrying cargo and 400 passengers past rolling hills and verdant grass-lands, limestone outcroppings, blooming orchards, farms and fields, to the bustling port. It was barely past sunrise as Cincinnati came into view from the balustraded decks of this floating, gilded palace, and the new dawn seemed redolent with symbolism in this booming land of new possibilities.

Cincinnati was a gateway to what Henry Clay of Kentucky had dubbed "the New United States"- the rapidly expanding Western territories that were forging a nation teeming with opportunity, beyond the staid confines of Colonial America east of Appalachia. Along with its thriving commerce, Cincinnati was also a hotbed of anti-slavery sentiment. She opened a welcome door not only to the prosperous and the entrepreneurs, but also to the fugitives from oppressive servitude even just across the river, granting those whom their masters chose to free instant emancipation by the mere act of setting foot on Ohio soil. And for those fleeing without their masters' sanction, there were many in Cincinnati who would help them on their way to safety in Canada. Everyone on board, no matter what his or her status, seemed to share in the energy such social and economic opportunities portended.

The symbolism of a new dawn was not lost on one family in particular on board the steamboat, for on this journey the *Jacob Strader* was carrying some passengers a bit different from the usual. A wealthy South Carolina planter, Mr. Elijah Willis, was heading North with his family. Nothing odd about that, except that his family members happened also to be his slaves- at least until they set foot on the North shore of the Ohio River in Cincinnati. Elijah's wife, Amy, her mother, Momma Celia, her seven children- Elder, Elleck, Phillip, Clarissa Ann, Julia Ann, Eliza Ann, and little Elijah (nicknamed Savage for his impishly rambunctious nature), were all passengers on this trip. Elder, Elleck and Phillip were not actually Elijah's own offspring, having been born of Amy's earlier marriage to a slave of her former owner. But Elijah considered them his own, not because he owned them, but for love of Amy, and treated them all with fatherly affection.

Of course, there were some on board who looked at them with raised eyebrows, pursed lips, and slightly stiffened spines, protectively pulling their children closer to them whenever the Willises drew near, disconcerted by this well-dressed family whose color ranged from fair to dark. Amy and her mother were a rich honey brown. Elder, Elleck and Phillip tended toward deep mahogany, and the younger four, Clarissa, Eliza, Julia and little Savage barely had what the ruling class sneeringly called, "a touch of the tar brush", looking almost as fair as their father, but for their mother's eyes and smile.

Ignoring the censure of fellow passengers, and hopping with anticipation, Clarissa, Julia, and Eliza chattered excitedly about the adventure that awaited them in Cincinnati. Little Savage, no more than a toddler, looked with wide-eyed delight at the river and shores teeming with life, pointing to each new discovery with insistence, demanding his parents' acknowledgment and confirmation that yes, it was indeed a wonder to behold. Meanwhile, the older boys, more aware of the difficulties they might encounter, pondered whether their new life would lead them to making new friends. They were shy, small-town teenagers who'd only been outside of rural South Carolina once before, on a trip to Baltimore. As they stood on the deck craning to see the city up ahead, they were eagerly fantasizing about exploring the wonders of a Northern city, even furtively glancing at the pretty girls onboard, realizing they'd soon be free to marry. Papa was going to buy them a farm, and he promised them they were all going to get good schooling, so they could hold their own in a free society when they were old enough to make a life for themselves!

Amy drank in the scenery, taking pleasure in the animation of her children, the lively sights, pulsating sounds, and stimulating smells of the river and the shores. They seemed to course through her veins, imparting new strength to her as she breathed in deeply of the fresh Spring breeze, reveling in the sunshine on her face. The strains of their carefully planned and daring departure from Carolina seemed to ease with every turn of the *Jacob Strader's* paddle wheels, and Amy indulged herself in the joy of the moment.

Elijah too, worn from the effort to orchestrate the legal and logistical coup of their relocation, soaked up the vibrancy surrounding them with a heavy sigh, yearning to put behind them the long, torturous, and exhausting road to a new life once and for all, and feel at last that all his efforts had been fulfilled. As the *Jacob Strader* headed East toward the landing, the sun almost seemed to rise up from the city itself, as if it were a beacon of liberty, welcoming them, rewarding their love, courage, and determination.

With each passing mile, the reality of starting a new life of freedom had been sinking in more and more. Even the richly varied landscape seemed to offer new possibilities- a refreshingly far cry from the dull, flat, dusty fields of the South Carolina lowlands. But for all their hopefulness, they were hardly naïve about the risks they ran. As they drew near the dock, Elijah and Amy looked at each other with a mixture of relief, cautious excitement, and trepidation. Elijah had put his fortune on the line to bring his family to freedom, against the full force of South Carolinian social disapproval and legal opposition. Despite his carefully laid plans, they both knew they were taking a leap into the unknown.

They had already attempted this once before, with their trip to Baltimore a few years ago. But, though there were certainly economic opportunities in that great port city, and a sizable population of free blacks too, Elijah had been dissuaded of the wisdom of relocating there. Maryland lay just South of the Mason-Dixon Line, and though proud of its heritage as a haven of religious tolerance, the Willis family found that Maryland was rather less inclined to racial equality than they had expected. There were well established racial attitudes there, dating back to colonial times, that made it clear that Maryland would not be as hospitable to a mixed race family as they had hoped. Maryland-born former slave, Frederick Douglass, was gaining a reputation as an eloquent voice for emancipation, but was feared as much as admired in the stylish parlors of the Mount Vernon district and Bolton Hill, where Baltimore's wealthy had built their elegant mansions. Elijah and his family had returned to South Carolina disappointed, but with renewed determination to find a way to circumvent the lynching noose of South Carolina's increasingly repressive laws tightening around them, and bring the whole family to a freedom assured by both legal emancipation and future inheritance.

Ohio definitely seemed to offer a more hopeful future than Maryland. It was a bastion of the Abolitionist Movement, and, as part of the new frontier, was unencumbered by Colonial attitudes. Cassius Marcellus Clay, passionately outspoken anti-slavery son of one of Kentucky's wealthiest slaveholders, had been publishing his emancipationist newspaper, The True American, across the river in Cincinnati, at least until he was commissioned as an officer to fight in the War with Mexico. Thanks to the Nationalist legislative efforts in Washington engineered by his still more eloquent elder cousin, Henry Clay, since even before the Compromise of 1850 Ohio had been proud to help impede the further spread of that "pernicious institution" to California and the Northwest Territories. In Cincinnati Elijah had easily and quickly secured the services of pro-abolition lawyers James M. Gitchell and John Jolliffe to write a new Last Will and Testament to replace the one he had written back in 1846, before he had fallen in love with Amy.

By social convention, he had originally and dutifully planned to leave his estate to his numerous immediate (white) relations, though truth be told, he was not overly fond of any of them, nor they of him. They struck him as entirely too eager to get their hands on his assets- especially his young nephews- and largely lacking in affection for him as a person. He considered them undeserving of his largesse for any reason other than the bonds of family loyalty. Falling in love with Amy and having children of his own, though at a more mature age than expected by the standards of the day, had given Elijah both a new lease and perspective on life- a life that no longer felt at home in the stuffy social confines of the rural South.

In his new will Elijah made it clear to Mr. Jollife that he did not want so much as a single penny to go to his avaricious white relations, but rather, his estate in its entirety was to go to Amy and her children. This was a sizable fortune for the time, amounting to more than three thousand acres of land valued at upwards of $150,000, not including cash and furnishings. This very fact alone was a monumental statement as to how far he was willing to go for the woman and family he loved. It was also a measure of how far he had departed from the Southerners' feudal obsessions with their Revolutionary War family lineages, and the sense of inherited privilege to which the descendents of the colonists and veterans of the Revolution believed it entitled them.

Elijah Willis was an intelligent man who was cautious by temperament, with a woman who was both shrewd in the management of her family's and household's affairs, and discreet in knowing how and when to play her role appropriately in the presence of others. Elijah and Amy had therefore taken great pains not to inform any of the Willis relations of the existence or the contents of his new will. Though there were a few in whom Elijah had confided his plan to take the family North and settle there, the particulars were a well-guarded secret until time necessitated otherwise.

Now, at last, the enormous strain of trying to pull all this off seemed to be lifting from his shoulders. His decision to make a complete break with his Carolina roots, though arrived at gradually and reluctantly, was beginning to feel liberating. True, he still had to return to Carolina, once he got the family settled, in order to sell his holdings and bring Amy's brother and his family, and his other remaining slaves North too, but with the rising May sun on his face, the happy chatter of the children, and the prosperous bustle on the wharves coming into view, Elijah felt he could permit himself at least a moment of satisfaction. Amy looped her arm through his and they gave each other a squeeze of grateful reassurance and anticipation.

Momma Celia, Amy's mother, was not so persuaded. A lifetime of slavery, despite the more recent years of kindness from Mister Elijah, made her distrustful of their impending freedom, uncertain of how these Northerners would treat her and her family, abolitionism notwithstanding. Out of respect for Mister Elijah, and not wanting to dampen Amy's spirits, Momma Celia chose to keep her own counsel, and said nothing. She kept a wary eye on the other passengers, however. Some of them seemed to welcome them openly, but others seemed to seethe with judgment against this anachronistic band of mixed race, as if their very existence were a reproach to the cherished values of genteel society.

As the steamboat pulled up to the landing, it blew its whistle to announce their arrival to one and all, the crew shouting orders and throwing lines to scurrying dock hands, who secured the *Jacob Strader* to the wharf. When the gangplank was lowered to the dock, Elijah and Amy marshaled their brood together. Elijah ordered the older boys to gather up their luggage, count the bags and steamer trunks, and make sure none were left behind, while Momma Celia ushered the younger children down the gangplank. Dockside, there were friends and relations of passengers waiting to greet the arrivals. Porters were rushing forward to vie for the opportunity to gather the passengers' luggage and carry it to the appropriate transportation. Private carriages and hacks for hire lined up expectantly across the street to convey the travelers to their respective lodgings, whether residents or visitors. The scene overall was one of happy, cacophonous pandemonium.

As Elijah stepped onto the gangplank, he felt light-headed and a little weak in the knees, as if the energy had suddenly drained out of him. His heart was fluttering. He broke out into a sweat. Dabbing his brow, willfully refusing to recognize the warning, and promising himself he would rest once they were safely in their hotel, he shook it off, chalking it up to the stress of fatigue, long anticipation, and the enthusiasm of the moment. Amy grabbed his arm tightly in excitement, unaware of his momentary vertigo. Energized and grounded by her touch, he regained his footing, and they headed down the ramp with his family, jostling through the crowds of fellow passengers and their friends and relations greeting them onshore.

Once on the wharf, Elijah quickly hailed a carriage to take them to Dumas House, a Negro owned boarding house in the city. Clearly, though theoretically emancipated upon setting foot on the Cincinnati shore, Elijah was not fool enough to assume that he could simply waltz into The Broadway Hotel where he had formerly lodged, or into any of the finer white boarding houses in town, with his colored family in tow, and not meet with disapproval, if not downright outrage. Not wanting to cause them or himself such discomfort, he had already made arrangements with the Dumas House accordingly, well assured of its comforts, and eagerly anticipated by its sympathetic owners. His family were not, after all, the first people of color to seek freedom in Ohio, and the Dumas family did a tidy business supporting such folks as managed to make it that far North.

Down on the wharf, Elder and Elleck helped the driver load the steamer trunks, valises, various bags, and hat boxes onto the carriage. It was a sizable load, as one might expect of a large family not merely visiting, but relocating to a new home. While the older boys loaded everyone's belongings onto the back and roof of the carriage, Phillip tried to herd his younger siblings inside. Momma Celia followed behind the family, shooing her younger grandchildren along, watchful and unsure.

Elijah bent down to pick up little Savage and lift him into the carriage, and suddenly let out a grunt of pain, clutching his chest. Amy, alarmed, instantly bent down to catch her husband as Savage managed to clamber into the carriage. Elijah was known to suffer from apoplexy- having had what they called "minor attacks" before.

"Elijah, is it your heart again?" she inquired anxiously, her face creased with concern, and her mind racing as to what to do.

Elijah nodded yes, breathing heavily. To Amy's horror, before she could even call out for help, he winced, let out two gasps, and fell like a sack of flour by the side of the carriage, his fixed gaze looking up at her, remorseful and wrenchingly apologetic, as if in his final breath he could see the difficulties his sudden departure would inflict upon his beloved family. She stifled a wail of desperation, her mind racing but her body frozen, half bent over her husband's lifeless figure at her feet.

Passersby, realizing that something was amiss, stopped and stared, uncertain of how to respond to the drama unfolding on the wharf. Some debated whether to call the authorities, others whether to approach the unknown family to offer aide. Virtually everyone, whether family or onlooker, seemed, at least momentarily, in the grip of a paralysis, followed by various people shouting out the news of a white man's collapse in the midst of what appeared to be his colored relations. All Hell then seemed to break loose in a frenzy of curiosity on the wharf.

Momma Celia felt a cold panic well up within her like the approach of death itself, suddenly terrified that the gift of freedom, so long-awaited and dreamed of, might suddenly be snatched from their grasp by Elijah's final heartbeat. Someone asked her with a demanding, suspicious and challenging voice, "Who are you?" She froze with fear, unable to find words, or even open her mouth. The questioner then rudely threatened to kick her into the river, if she didn't answer!

William Cullum and his wife, sympathetic fellow passengers in whom Elijah and Amy had confided their plans, had just debarked, and pushing through the crowd, immediately realized the danger the family faced. William grabbed Momma Celia by the arm gently, but commandingly, and drew her to her daughter's side. Mrs. Cullum then leaned forward in an apparent embrace of condolence, and whisperingly urged Amy to empty Elijah's pockets, before any authorities arrived on the scene. Upon receiving this wise counsel, Amy was instantly shocked out of the initial agonizing stupor triggered by Elijah's collapse, and back into the sharp focus of reality.

With steely determination not to lose their dream, and be forced back into slavery by this tragic blow for failure to act decisively, the distraught Amy immediately composed herself and, eyes on the growing crowd, protectively gathered her family with her back to the carriage, like a she-wolf defending her pups, ready to bare her fangs if necessary. She owed it to herself, to them, and to Elijah, not to let this tragedy rob them of their dream.

"Momma, Elder, Elleck, come on over here" Amy commanded quietly. "Phillip, keep the girls and your little brother in the carriage."

Before anyone in the crowd of onlookers could notice, Amy knelt by her husband's limp body, tenderly cradling his head in her arms, seeming to others to express no more than the tearful bereavement natural to such an event. In the shelter of her mother and older children surrounding and protecting her from the prying eyes of the crowd, Amy deftly took the money from Elijah's wallet, his gold watch, and most importantly of all, the Last Will and Testament he guarded in his left breast pocket- its safekeeping over his heart betokening its importance to him and his loved ones.

"Boys, help me get your father into the carriage." Amy calmly ordered as she stood up, smoothing her skirts.

With some effort, for he was a big, heavily-built man, Elijah's body was carefully loaded onto the carriage to the stunned silence of the older boys, and the bewildered and frightened sobs of their younger siblings. Having identified herself and her husband, and the address of their lodgings to those at hand and to the driver, with a crack of the driver's whip, the shaken family drove off to Dumas House, the staccato clattering of the iron wheel rims and horseshoes of the carriage on the cobblestones momentarily drowning out their muffled sobs. In the shock of riding with her entire grief-stricken family and the body of her husband through unknown streets, Amy's mind was racing as to what to do next. Could she really trust Elijah's lawyers to help them, sight unseen? Knowing not a soul in Cincinnati, what other choice did she have? She would have to notify them immediately, and take that leap of faith. Their future hung in the balance.

II

Upon arrival, the boarding house staff unloaded the carriage. Momma Celia escorted the younger children upstairs to their quarters, while the older boys and a clerk carried Elijah's body into a back parlor of the Dumas House. Amy immediately sent word to John Jollife, the abolitionist lawyer who had helped draft Elijah's will, to come and identify her husband to the authorities. She knew she would need all the help she could get when confronted with the inevitable inquiry into Elijah's death, and the nature of their visit to Cincinnati. Despite Elijah's assurances that their emancipation would be a fait accompli by the very act of their setting foot on Ohio soil, Amy was not ingenuous enough to think there might not be those who would challenge or question their freedom. In fact, even on the dockside, there had been some who tried to compel her and her family to get back on board the Jacob Strader until the authorities could arrive to sort things out. Realizing that departing Ohio soil onto the steamboat could unintentionally result in their deportation back to South Carolina, and permanent slavery under the hands of Elijah's dreaded relatives, Amy wisely had insisted they go on to their lodgings, where, for the sake of the children, they could await the authorities in more comfort, and in greater safety from inquisitive by-standers, as they faced their terrible loss.

It did not take long for John Jolliffe to arrive, accompanied by his law partner, James Gitchell, and another companion, Edward Harwood, one of the Ohio abolitionists initially willing to serve with Jolliffe as the executors of Elijah's will. Solicitous of the family's well-being, and, despite the sad circumstances, happy to finally meet those whom he had worked so hard to help free, Mr. Jollife introduced himself, Mr. Gitchell and Mr. Harwood with a gracious bow.

"My dear, it is an honor to finally meet you, and a great sadness to me that it has to be under such unfortunate and untimely circumstances. Allow me to present my partner, Mr. Gitchell, and my friend, Mr. Harwood, who, as you may know, had agreed to serve with me as executor of your husband's will." Amy acknowledged the introduction with a slight curtsey and a nod.

Jolliffe, sensing her underlying anxiety, quickly added, "Please, do not fear for your safety. My colleagues and I assure you we will do all that is necessary to make sure you, your mother, and your children are secure, and want for nothing."

"That's very kind of you gentlemen, and I surely do appreciate it. Lord knows, we shall need your support to get us through this loss, and the ordeals that may yet lie ahead because of it," Amy responded, conscious of the need to speak with a certain formality so as to assure these gentlemen of her competence.

Jolliffe was impressed with Amy's bearing and well-spoken response. She was truly a lady of even more formidable character and refined presence than he had expected. He couldn't help but wonder how she had come by such manners, given her upbringing as a slave.

The police inspector, a beefy faced gentleman intent upon discharging his duties as promptly as possible, and with far less decorum, arrived shortly thereafter, accompanied by the coroner, Dr. Menzies, and Mr. Ball, a local lawyer. The constable began the inquest, officiously asking questions as to the identity of the deceased, the circumstances of his demise, the reason for their visit to Cincinnati, and the identities of all those traveling with him.

"What is the name of the deceased?" asked the inspector.

"Elijah Willis, sir", answered Amy.

"And who was traveling with him at the time of his demise?"

"My mother, our seven children and I" answered Amy. At the use of the words "our seven children", the inspector paused for a moment, an expression of mild surprise on his face, before asking the obvious question, "And what was your relationship to the deceased?"

Amy too paused. She knew she and Elijah were not legally husband and wife, though they both felt they were, in the eyes of God. Yet, especially since her legal status had now changed with their arrival in Ohio, she was loathe to refer to herself, her mother or her children as slaves, on principle. She knew that in South Carolina, mutual expression of commitment was deemed sufficient proof of marriage, requiring no documentation, but she also knew that such commitments were only considered valid between partners of the same race. She had no idea what familiarity the constable might have with South Carolina law. Trusting that he would not demand she produce legal proof of marriage at this point, but also knowing that she was referred to as a slave in Elijah's will, she decided to simply say, with quiet pride and devotion, "He was the beloved head of our family, sir."

At this point, James Gitchell deftly intervened to prevent the constable from pressing the issue any further.

"Officer, the deceased was a client of ours. I can vouch for both him and his family, as they are personally known to me. In fact, both Mr. Jolliffe and Mr. Harwood are executors of his will," stated Mr. Gitchell. The constable's expression changed from one of suspicion to one of mild surprise.

"If I or my associates can be of any assistance to you, sir, rest assured we should be only too happy to provide any information necessary. Could we perhaps expedite the completion of this inquest, so as to let the family get some much needed rest after the shock of the sad events of today, and the terrible loss that has befallen them?" added Mr. Jolliffe.

"Of course, Mr. Jolliffe. Anything you say, sir." responded the constable, who then proceeded to finish his interview with Amy. Having answered each of the constable's questions with a clarity and quiet firmness belying her well-concealed anxiety and grief, Amy then produced Elijah's will in proof of her explanations. As Mr. Ball read Elijah's will, revealing that Amy and her children were the sole heirs to his fortune, and along with her mother, were to be emancipated, Mr. Jolliffe affirmed, with seasoned authority, that it was an exact copy of the will he had brought in a sealed envelope from his office. Mr. Ball and the constable then compared the two documents and confirmed that they were, in fact, identical.

While Mr. Jolliffe and Mr. Gitchell were speaking with the constable, the coroner, Dr. Menzies, a long-faced, gaunt and lugubrious fellow with a sallow complexion like beeswax, dressed in the customary black cut-away coat and high collar, examined Elijah's corpse, and made a few dispassionate inquiries of Amy as to his past medical history.

"Did the deceased have any medical problems that you were aware of?"

"Yes, sir" Amy replied, "He had some trouble with his heart. The doctor told him he was prone to apoplexy, and he had suffered a few palpitation spells in the past, but nothing too serious, and last Fall he had a mild stroke." The coroner allowed as how Elijah's condition was not uncommon in a man of his age.

Mr. Harwood confirmed that the deceased was known to suffer from apoplexy, and that it had been one of the motivating factors in his decision to seek the services of Messrs. Gitchell and Jolliffe, so as to provide for his family's emancipation and inheritance, in the event he should not survive to see such accomplished.

"It's more than likely that the strains of the long journey triggered the attack that took his life!" Dr. Menzies observed, almost as if speaking to himself, and with utter disregard for the emotional impact such a statement might have on the bereaved Amy. With bony fingers and squinting eyes, he then examined Elijah's corpse, by now in a state of incipient rigor mortis, noting the color of his nails and tongue for any indications of poisoning, and seeing no wounds or indication of foul play, pronounced himself satisfied that Amy's account was true and accurate.

Thanks in no small part to the assurances of Messrs. Jolliffe, Gitchell, and Harwood, who were eminent citizens and well known in Cincinnati, the authorities, being thereby satisfied that this was no more than a tragic loss due to natural causes, offered the family their condolences. The coroner issued a death certificate. With a doff of their hats, they bade Amy, Mr. Jolliffe, Mr. Gitchell, and Mr. Harwood farewell.

Upon consultation with Mr. Jolliffe and his companions, the now widowed Amy asked that a local undertaker, who catered to colored families, be notified to come retrieve the body and prepare it for burial, and a messenger was sent from Dumas House to that effect.

After considering the possible alternatives with her advisors, Amy decided that Elijah should be interred in a Negro cemetery there in Cincinnati, rather than sending his body back to Carolina for burial in the family plot. It would spare her and her family the expense of attempting a return for his funeral, and the inevitable confrontation with Elijah's relatives that would ensue, and probably result in their being returned to their former servitude. It would also be making a permanent statement of Elijah's abiding sympathies. The very thought of how powerful a testimony to their love that was, made Amy have to force back her tears, not wanting to be unseemly in the presence of the good gentlemen who had so chivalrously and promptly come to her family's aide.

"Do not fret, dear lady, about the costs or the arrangements for your husband's burial," said Jolliffe, "There are many here in Cincinnati who would willingly help defray the expenses. There is time enough to work out your finances, after we have had a chance to begin the probate process of Elijah's will."

"I am much obliged to all three of you gentlemen, Mr. Jolliffe, but I must make it clear that we did not come all this way to become wards of the State, but to enjoy long-dreamed of and hard fought freedom. I am well persuaded that that freedom always comes with responsibility, and I and my family intend to fully live up to that responsibility and not depend on charity to do so, however honorably intended your generous offer." Amy looked earnestly into the eyes of John Jolliffe, saying pointedly, "Such indebtedness would be to us but another form of indentured servitude, which, as I'm sure you can appreciate, for all the world we would not exchange for our freedom, no matter how difficult." She then turned to address the other two gentlemen as well. "I do have some $530 in cash and several notes and due bills amounting to another $3000 or so on hand, which I hope, with frugality, will see us through til such time as we are able to gain access more readily to the assets my husband has bequeathed us."

"You truly do your husband and family credit, ma'am," Jolliffe replied, impressed by her clear headed business acumen, "And I feel certain that the trust he put in you was more than justified. I do not doubt you in the slightest, and want you to understand that I meant no offense by my offer!" He was genuinely aggrieved that Amy might have felt insulted by his offer, but also was well aware that the probate of the will and settlement of Elijah's estate would take time, and Amy and her family might well need help to sustain themselves in the interim. He and his associates were truly eager to help. "Still, should you need to avail yourself of it for a time, until we have been able to work out the logistical details of your finances, do not hesitate to make your needs known to us. We can and shall provide for them without reservation, and you may reimburse us as time and liquidity allow."

Mr. Jolliffe and his companions once again reassured Amy they would help her with all the necessary arrangements for burial, and suggested they meet the following morning to proceed with the funeral, and to discuss how best to handle the probate of the will, the provision of living expenses to sustain them during that process, and the many other details that would certainly arise as the reality of this turn of events sank in, and reshaped their lives. All that could wait until tomorrow, however, and in deference to the family, they took their leave, insisting that Amy and her family get some rest, so they could better deal with what lay ahead.

By the time the family had settled into their quarters, and Elijah's body was laid out, awaiting the services of the undertaker, it was late afternoon. Momma Celia had already seen to the children and was putting the younger ones to bed. They were exhausted from the long day and the trauma they had all suffered. She kept her thoughts to herself, praying silently with a stern resignation, born of long experience and much suffering, that God would somehow provide. Downstairs, Amy sat numbly in the parlor where her husband's body lay, awaiting the undertaker. There, for the first time since they had landed early that morning, she could have a moment to herself- though she kept looking at Elijah's body, half imagining that he was only sleeping and would soon awake.

Amy's thoughts, like her mother's, suddenly filled with worry and doubt, sought comfort from Divine Providence. "Oh Lord," she sobbed, "How are we gonna get through this? What am I gonna do? What if Mr. Jolliffe can't get the will through probate? How will we all survive? And what if Elijah's family comes after us, and tries to take us back? Lord, I just can't even bear the thought of that! Please, God, help us! For Momma's sake, for my babies' sakes! Elijah," she said, turning tearfully to her husband's corpse, "I don't want your death to be in vain, honey! I can't bear that God's taken you from us, right when we were about to fulfill our dreams!" Her sobs were almost convulsive now, as the sense of desperation welled up from deep within her. " Lord, Jesus, I know you suffered, and I know you overcame that sufferin to show us we could too. But I'm scared, Lord! I'd rather die myself than see my family become slaves again!"

As she remembered all they had fought for, she felt overcome with a mixture of deep gratitude to Elijah for his love and his gift of freedom, devastating sorrow that he would never see them enjoy the fruits of that freedom he had risked everything to give them, and uncertainty as to just how free they would really be with him no longer there to protect them. As she poured out her soul in supplication, her heart aching with sorrow, she dissolved in a wave of tears of despair and loss. Salty rivulets streamed down her cheeks, dripping onto her lap, leaving darker patches on the dark green taffeta of her skirts, until, eventually subsiding, she felt infused with an unexpected sense of relief and calm assurance.

Her prayer had been cathartic, and now her mind felt a limpid clarity as it looked at their situation. Somehow, though she surely didn't know just exactly how, she felt with immediate certainty that they were going to be alright. It came to her that, in some mysterious way, in the very memory of the long sequence of events that had led them thus far, lay the key to their future survival. It seemed strangely important, even urgent, that she remember everything clearly and in great detail, so the telling of their story might tilt the scales of justice in their favor. With the clarity of intellect that had enabled her to manage Elijah's business affairs so well and prosperously for years, she began to take a mental inventory of the events and people that had brought them to this juncture.

Her mind wandered back to South Carolina and the plantation they had called home just a few short days ago. The whole evolution of this saga seemed to unfold before her memory's eyes, as she recalled the day Elijah had first confided to a friend this grand scheme to achieve the gift of freedom, not only for his colored family, but in truth, for himself as well.

III

It was about five years ago, during what they called the "dog days" of July, when the air hung so hot and heavy it left the dogs' tongues hanging out like wet laundry dripping on a clothesline. Summer in the South Carolina lowlands had a way of slowing everything down, and those that could sought shelter from the midday heat to sip cooling lemonade, iced sweet tea, or something stronger, in the shady recesses of wide verandas or high-ceilinged parlors.

The Willis plantations occupied some 3,200 acres or more between Barnwell and Williston. Though not as elegant or large as some, Elijah Willis' home, nevertheless, was comfortable. A Greek Revival, gable-fronted house with peculiar Victorian Gingerbread trim, the columned portico was flanked by outside twin stairways to the upper porch. It had generous, if somewhat stumpy proportions, well suited to family life. The planter earned a goodly living from his lands, not only supplying his own needs and those of his fifty-odd slaves, but enough timber, cotton, corn, meat, poultry, and vegetables to take to market and provide a steady income to increase his coffers.

Tall, strong, and industrious by nature, and single-mindedly intent upon building his fortune, Elijah had never married. Having inherited some property from the division of his father's estate among his siblings, he had shrewdly and continuously increased his holdings. By now in his mid-fifties, he was well past the age when young men of good family normally sought a wife. Not given to the ostentation of his wealth, or the social frivolities of some of his ilk, his determination was evident, for unlike some planters who seemed prone to a life of indolent leisure at their slaves' expense, Elijah was often seen working in his fields, side by side with his slaves.

Though subject to the judgments of his acquaintances as such a seemingly unconventional bachelor, there was a tacit nod and a wink among those who knew him that confirmed his marital status was not, at least, the result of any more than the usual preference for male company so typical of the landed gentlemen of his day. It was hard to say just why Elijah never married, but presumably, he never found anyone in his small world of white agrarian privilege to whom he felt attracted enough to want to raise a family into that closed society of Barnwell District.

It's not that he was really anti-social. He was well liked and admired as a man of upstanding character. He was a good steward of his lands, dealt fairly in his business, and was kind to his slaves and neighbors alike. But, to the chagrin of his peers, he seemed not to identify with the elitism and racial superiority of his white acquaintances and numerous relations. This, in itself, set him apart from the power structure of polite society in the South of his day, with all the unwritten "natural" laws of behavior and social intercourse that ruled his class and clearly separated the races. Mister Elijah was perhaps just a bit odd. Gracious and courtly in his manners, as befitted his station, he was nonetheless a very private person, keeping his thoughts and opinions to himself unless necessity demanded otherwise. In an era that admired the rhetorical skills of those who would pontificate on the proper order of things- in politics, and in society- Elijah Willis was decidedly disinclined to wax eloquent on such matters. He had left that to the great orators of the age, like fellow South Carolinian John C. Calhoun, Daniel Webster of Massachusetts, and Henry Clay of Kentucky.

He had no bones about expressing his views when he wanted to, it's just that he seemed not to want to do so with many, outside a select few long-standing friends whom he had known for years. Whether this was a matter of a more introverted nature, or simply the discretion born of realizing the possible dangers or futility of voicing unpopular opinions too loudly within earshot of those more prone to being swayed by hot-tempered ideologues, was hard to tell.

Perhaps it was a bit of both- for the permissiveness of his views regarding race, though not entirely unique, were far from normal for his day and place. Consequently, maintaining some standing in the community, in spite of his unusual home life, could not have been easily achieved without a measure of both discretion and inner stamina. For, though he had never married, it was not to say that Elijah Willis' life was loveless- far from it. It was simply that the love of his life, Amy, and their children, happened also to be his slaves- an uncomfortable technicality he bore far more lightly than his disapproving peers.

Amy had not been born on the Willis plantation; Elijah had not always owned her. She had belonged to William Kirkland, another planter in the area who had allegedly run on some hard times and been compelled to sell off some of his lands and slaves. He had sold Amy's husband and sent him off further South, but allowed her mother, Celia, her three sons, and her brother to stay with her in Carolina. Elijah Willis bought them all from Kirkland, and they settled into the Willis plantation.

Amy caught his eye. There was something undeniably attractive about her keen intelligence, her quiet, self-assured manner, her solicitous care of her family, and her skill in managing household and plantation affairs. Her mother, too, known for her excellent cooking, had a bearing that distinguished her from the average domestic with whom Elijah had thus far come into contact. Something set the whole family apart, and made Amy in particular distinct, not only from other female slaves but from any of the women he had known of his own race and social standing. They were clearly not just ordinary field hands. Elijah felt that Amy and her family deserved the privilege of service in the big house. Much to his surprise, having shunned marriage until well into middle age, he soon realized he was smitten. Though he may have owned her body before he won her heart, in truth, it was not long before she owned his as well.

Of course, the rules of propriety governing his class made his affections for Amy somewhat problematic. In a culture that carefully scrutinized and judged the bloodlines of horses and people alike, and set great store by them, racial intermarriage was not only illegal, but considered a pollution that would destroy one's reputation irrevocably. To some extent, as has ever been the case, notable wealth could trump social disapproval, but in the very small world of Barnwell District, South Carolina, even Elijah Willis' wealth could not completely prevent others from commenting on his atypical living arrangements. Having a female slave serving in the master's house was not forbidden, of course, it was to be expected, so for a time Elijah and Amy were able to mask their affections from others on those relatively rare occasions when someone came to call. But as is in the nature of love, and perhaps more eagerly so for having been deprived of it until so late in life, Elijah's affection for Amy began to show in the bulge of her belly, and the successive arrival of four children whose complexions were closer to their father's than to hers.

Though Amy was twenty years his junior, and according to the bias of some white observers at least, "not a handsome woman," Elijah Willis not only loved her, but clearly doted upon their children, and extended his affections equally to Amy's mother, her brother, and her three other children born before he acquired her family from Mr. Kirkland. In Elijah's case, such permissiveness was not a matter of a master having trysts at his convenience with a woman in the slave quarters, as some of his peers clearly did. Elijah did not assume that ownership granted the master sexual privileges as well as the fruits of others' labor.

Yet, paradoxically, having been born into it, Elijah seemed none too conflicted about owning slaves in principle. For many years he had certainly not given others any indications of being categorically opposed to the institution. In fact, it would have been impossible for him to be so, given his dedication to making his considerable acreage profitable. Without slave labor he could not have prospered nearly as much as he did.

By now, Amy and her children, however, openly shared the big house with him, living clearly as a family, to the mixed jealousy and admiration of the other slaves on the plantation and the whispered rumors of the white population in town. Amy, in fact, seemed to serve a dual function of mistress of the house and plantation manager. She looked after the other slaves and helped advise Elijah in the effective management of his business. Only those few friends of his inner circle understood and sympathized with Elijah- though even they sometimes felt the discomfort of reconciling their friendship with him and his illicit family with the mores of their class. After all, keeping secrets in a small town isn't easy, and people do talk. It's long been a favorite pastime in both small towns and big cities alike, and certainly was part of what wove together the fabric of that community.

One such long-standing friend, with whom Elijah could speak openly, was now coming to call- driving a horse and buggy up the long dusty road to the main house, past fields of blooming cotton, stands of long-needle pine, up under the shade of a grove of live oak, ash, and maple trees, and past colorful crepe myrtles and luxuriant magnolias, whose light, lemony scent wafted up to the front of the house in the muggy summer heat.

Dr. Joseph Harley and Elijah Willis had known each other for many years. As was typical of country doctors in his day, the medical needs of the local community gave the good doctor not only the opportunity to observe the private lives of all classes and conditions of humanity, but perhaps too, a more compassionate perspective on the social differences and emotional needs of both the ruling class and those they ruled. Dr. Harley had an admirable ability to refrain from judgment of others, and was well disposed toward Elijah Willis as a man not swayed by the hypocrisies, pretensions, or cruelties that often plagued white men living in close contact and interdependence with people of color.

As Dr. Harley pulled his buggy to a halt in front of the main house of the Willis plantation, a good looking Negro boy, about 13 years of age, came out of the house.

"Momma, Papa, Dr. Harley's here!" the boy called over his shoulder, as he headed out to greet the Doctor and tend to his horse.

"Thank ya, Elder," Dr. Harley said to the boy with a smile, "Give him a good drink will ya?" referring to his gelding, "Even he's feelin the heat today!"

"Yes sir, Dr. Harley, I'll be glad to." Elder held the gelding by the bit and gently stroked his nose, waiting for Dr. Harley to get out of the buggy, so he could lead him to water at a trough under one of the live oaks.

As he brushed the dust off his trousers before heading to the house, Dr. Harley could make out indistinct voices inside and the sound of heavy footsteps approaching the front door from the entrance hall. One of the double doors swung open, and a large man, wearing well-worn boots and a somewhat tattered, unbuttoned waistcoat and shirtsleeves, appeared beaming on the front porch.

"Joseph! It's good to see you! Come on inside out of this heat, my friend, please! We have much to talk about."

"Hello Elijah! Good to see you too! Looks like Amy and Momma Celia have been feedin you well!" the doctor said with a mixture of appreciation and mild reproach. There was no doubting that Momma Celia was one of the best cooks in Barnwell District- a talent some seemed to feel was wasted on the somewhat reclusive Mr. Willis, who was not prone to hosting the glittering parties that well-to-do folks up in Columbia or over in Charleston so enjoyed. The good doctor, however, could hardly blame Elijah for indulging, even though his medical mind also knew that caution was advisable, for reasons of health.

"Well," admitted Elijah, "I suppose I have put on a few pounds lately, but I'll surely work em off in the fields before this year's crops come in and the timber's cut!"

The two men walked amiably into the house, where shuttered windows kept out the worst of the heat, but cast a Victorian gloom on the high ceilinged parlor inside, relieved only by the brightness of the sunlight framing the shutters and sneaking through the slats.

"Amy, Joseph Harley's here to visit! Could you bring him a cool drink please?" Elijah called out towards the kitchen in the back of the house.

The sound of movement and the clink of glasses was heard in the distance as Elijah ushered Dr. Harley into the parlor.

"Have a seat, Joseph. Amy'll be right along with some refreshment." Elijah sat down a bit heavily in a winged back chair near the fireplace, propping his feet up on a low footstool. Dr. Harley lounged comfortably on the settee facing him, placing his high hat and gold-knobbed ebony walking stick by his side, and the ubiquitous black surgeon's bag of his profession on the floor.

"So now, tell me Elijah, what's so doggone important that you need to be callin me out here in the heat of the day? Is one of the children sick? Or Momma Celia? Or Amy? Or are you havin those chest pains again? You know I told you to cut down on some of that good food of Momma Celia's, now." Joseph Harley was affable, but also concerned, sensing something serious was afoot.

"No, Joseph, Amy and the family are all fine! I admit, I get a little out of breath sometimes, but that's the price I pay at my age for trying to make my land produce enough crops to support us all!" Elijah laughed a bit drily, displaying the stoic rejection of any intimations of his own mortality, typical of so many hardworking men for whom occasional aches and pains were thought to be no more than an expected nuisance, not to be coddled.

Dr. Harley looked at Elijah with a diagnostic eye, and then, satisfied that there was no immediate medical crisis at hand, relaxed and said, "Well, what then?"

At that moment Amy appeared through the parlor door from the hallway extending to the back of the house, carrying a silver tray on which sat two china plates laden with slices of cured ham and biscuits, and two tall tumblers of iced lemonade, each artfully decorated with a sprig of fresh mint. She nodded politely toward Dr. Harley as she placed the tray on the table before the settee, and offered him a well-pressed linen napkin and a small plate, on which she served him a portion of ham and a biscuit. She placed the lemonade on a silver rimmed crystal coaster on the end table by the arm of the settee, then proceeded to serve the same to Elijah, smiling warmly, but almost shyly.

"Thank you, my dear," said Elijah politely. "I thought it time to discuss my plans for the future with Joseph," he said with a knowing look that indicated far more than was said.

Amy looked quickly at Dr. Harley, then back to Elijah, and nodded slightly.

"Well, I know Dr. Harley is a good listener, so I'll leave you two gentlemen to your conversation. I'll be out back with Momma and the children if ya'll need me for anything."

Amy nodded again to Dr. Harley, and discreetly left the parlor, revealing not a trace of the butterflies she was suddenly feeling in her stomach. What if Dr. Harley didn't understand? What if he tried to convince Elijah his idea was a bad idea, or impossible, or worse, what if he decided to tell all the white folks in the area? "Oh Lordy, please don't let that happen!" she thought, suddenly uncertain whether she had spoken out loud. She deliberately slowed and softened her steps, stopping, in the hopes of being able to overhear Elijah's conversation without it becoming apparent that she was eavesdropping.

Once Amy had left the parlor and the social niceties had been customarily dispensed with, Elijah turned his full attention to his friend.

"Joseph, I need to talk to ya about a most important matter, but before I go into it, I must ask ya to swear not to divulge anything I am about to tell ya without my knowledge and consent. Do I have your promise?"

Dr. Harley, long accustomed to the confidences of his patients and their families, was only mildly surprised by the importunate tone of his friend.

"Well of course you have my word, Elijah. You know I'm no friend of gossip!" Dr. Harley's half-truth gave Elijah no pause. Though privy to all the gossip of the district by virtue of his office, by dint of the principle of patient confidentiality, as well as by temperament and natural inclination, Joseph Harley could keep a secret better than most men. Elijah felt sure he could be trusted with the information he was about to reveal. Moreover, being a pensive man, and given to scientific reasoning, Elijah felt equally sure his medical friend would render him well-reasoned, thoughtful advice. That was, in fact, the primary reason he had asked him to come calling.

"Look Joseph, you know I'm not fond of playin social games- though Lord knows I've learned how to, just to survive around here! But I can't keep that up any longer!" The comment was delivered with a tone of exasperation that harrowed the soil for what was about to be planted. "So I'll get straight to the matter. You know that Amy and I have become a family. Lord, you've delivered our children! And, as God is my witness, as much as it peeves my relations, I love the woman, and all her children- even the ones that aren't mine by blood!" He paused before continuing, as if deciding whether to go on. "The longer we're together, the more unbearable it is for me to think of any of them in terms of slavery. I want them to be free, more than anything else in this world. But I feel stuck. I don't know how I can achieve this, given the political situation down here in South Carolina these days. I need your advice, and maybe your help too- though I won't ask of ya anything more than ya're comfortable doin, of course." Elijah looked at his friend imploringly, temporarily at a loss for more words.

Unsurprised by this revelation, Joseph Harley took a thoughtful draught of his lemonade and munched on a biscuit before answering.

"Before I make any specific suggestions, Elijah, I need to ask ya some questions. A good doctor gathers all the data he can before comin to a diagnosis, or plan of treatment. So let's lay this situation out in all its known dimensions, shall we?

"We'll start with what we know: You're a well-to-do white planter and slave- owner in Barnwell District, South Carolina.

"The local economy is largely maintained through slave labor. Negroes actually outnumber us whites around here these days!

"Most of the white population is persuaded that people of color- any shade other than lily white-" (this he said pointedly to include Elijah's fair skinned children by Amy) "are inherently and irredeemably inferior, except in regards possibly to physical strength- hence their usefulness to our agricultural production."

Dr. Harley paused to take another sip of his lemonade and another bite of biscuit, wiping the crumbs from his lips with the linen napkin before continuing.

"Now, you know that, in theory, intermarriage is absolutely against the law in this state, and no court here will allow otherwise. So whatever your feelings for Amy may be, by no definition recognized by the State of South Carolina is she your wife, even by common law.

"You also know that in practice, you are far from the first white man to have a family with a colored woman! In fact, there are so many that some white folks have felt it incumbent upon them to make sure laws were passed in the General Assembly that make it damn nigh impossible to emancipate a slave in this state." The doctor took another sip of lemonade. "I'm told that, though it was not always so, the only recourse to emancipation now is by petitionin the General Assembly. As I'm sure you can imagine from the public fulminations over the years of the lately lamented Senator Calhoun up in Washington, not to mention our good representatives in Columbia, the chances of legislative approval of any such petitions grow slimmer every day."

Elijah had sat leaning attentively toward his friend, hanging on every word as he laid out the argument, hoping it would lead to some helpful conclusion. But his patience was wearing thin.

"Damn it Joseph, I know all that! But I can't believe there's not some way around the legal mess that's bein created up in Columbia and over in Charleston! Every time I see my nephew James in that store he runs, he looks at me like I'm a Christmas ham he's eager to stick his fork into!" Elijah's face began to flush as he spoke. "I tell you, it makes my blood boil to see my own kin look at me with that mixture of greed and contempt because of whom I love and how I choose to live! What the Hell good is it to have worked to build all this," (he gestured around him as if to indicate the entire plantation) "if I can't then do with it as I choose?" By now Elijah was nearly shouting, breathing hard, and sweat was beading his brow. He picked up a palmetto fan from the table and began fanning himself energetically.

"Calm down, now, Elijah. Have a sip of that good lemonade Amy brought ya. I'm not sayin there's no solution. But this is somethin we have to think through carefully, for if we do not, greater damage than good may come of it! Be patient with me, my friend, and let's continue." Dr. Harley's use of the term "we" was not lost on Elijah, despite his agitation. He realized his friend was thereby implicitly consenting to help him find a viable solution, and felt a bit calmer.

"Well, alright then! I'm no lawyer, but it seems to me we would do well to secure some well-informed legal advice before determining how best to proceed. The issues, as I see them are these:

"First, under what conditions, if any, do you have a reasonable chance of emancipating your family here in South Carolina? From the looks of things these days, my guess is there are few, if any.

"If that is the case, then under what conditions, if any, could your family be emancipated somewhere else, and would that emancipation be recognized here in South Carolina in such a way as to permit them to reside here in freedom? That too seems unlikely, but these are essential facts we must ascertain before determining any other possible course of action."

Elijah interjected a third issue. "I agree with you on that score, Joseph, but there's another issue that vexes me almost as much, and is perhaps just as problematic." His formerly dismissive tone concerning his weight and health now shifted to one of unvarnished frankness.

"You and I both know that I am neither young, nor without some health issues that could take me to my Maker sooner than I'd like. That bein the case, emancipatin Amy and the family alone may not be enough, for if I die, they must have some sort of provision in perpetuity, or circumstances could force a return into slavery upon them, and that I could not bear!" Elijah took a deep breath before announcing, "So I have decided that I want to leave my entire estate to her and the children, and not let any of my other relations get their hands on so much as a dime of it!"

Joseph Harley looked at his friend with slightly raised eyebrows, as the enormity of this statement sank in fully. He was not exactly shocked by this revelation, and well understood the measure of love it indicated for Amy and her family. But he was equally aware that such a move would be seen by the local white population as the ultimate insult, a breach of the most fundamental of social contracts assuring civic stability by the time-honored vehicle of inheritance. This was an expectation by which everyone, rich and poor alike, set great store. Legacy was the very mortar by which the building blocks of Southern society were held in place, and to violate that structure, for some, would be simply unthinkable, an unforgivable betrayal of his class and race.

"Well now! I imagine all Hell will break loose here in Barnwell District once that little bit of news becomes known!" Harley chuckled with some measure of appreciation at the image of Elijah's shunned relatives pitching a conniption fit when they found out they'd been cut out of an inheritance they'd done nothing to deserve, other than having the coincidence of shared blood. But the smile faded as he pondered the darker side of the uproar this could trigger, both in Williston and beyond. It had been his sad task on more than one occasion to treat the wounds of those beaten for such betrayals- not to mention having to cut down more than one lynched slave who dared attempt to violate the State of South Carolina's antipathy toward emancipation. It was unnecessary for him to point it out, as Elijah's expression, too, had grown grimmer at the implications of his own announcement.

"You asked for my advice, my discretion, and my help. I have already given ya my word as to our confidentiality. As for my advice, it is this: Do nothin rash, inform yourself well. Make your plans in secret, and as thoroughly as possible, before takin any action. For once these wheels are set in public motion, Lord only knows how quickly things may unfold, and how urgently you may be in need of a greater help than I can provide." Elijah shifted uncomfortably in his chair, well aware of Dr. Harley's intimations.

"However, on that last point, trust me, my friend, I will do anything I can to help ya realize your plans safely. It could be that my standin in the community may be of some future service to you and your family, and if so, I am glad to offer it." Dr. Harley paused and smiled reassuringly at his friend. "And now, I must be going. Arey Wooley's come down with the ague, and I promised I'd look in on her down the road before dinner."

"God bless ya, Joseph!" Elijah said with deep sincerity, "I knew I could count on ya for sound counsel. I shall try to make some inquiries as to these legal matters, and think on your point of whether emancipatin the family somewhere outside of Carolina might be an option. If you, in the meantime, are able to gain any insight into these matters, I'd be much obliged if ya'd let me know."

"Rest assured that I shall, Elijah. Rest assured that I shall." With that, Dr. Harley arose, gathering his hat and cane, and Elijah, handing him his bag, remembered himself and called out, "Amy! Joseph is leavin! Tell Elder to fetch his carriage!" Amy, startled from her eavesdropping, smoothed her skirts and moved toward the front hall as if coming from the kitchen, just as Dr. Harley and Elijah emerged from the parlor. Elijah however, realizing she had been there all along, gave her a reassuring smile, as Dr. Harley turned to her and with characteristic Southern charm said, "I surely do thank you for the lemonade and biscuits Amy. And my compliments to your mother as well!" He doffed his hat with genuine respect, and headed out the door to where Elder awaited, holding the reins of his carriage.

As Dr. Harley mounted the buggy, he turned to Elder and said quietly, tilting his head in Elijah's direction, "I hope you realize what a good man he is, and how much he cares for you!"

Elder recognized immediately that this was no white man telling a slave boy to respect his master, but a friend of the family telling a teenaged boy to respect his adoptive father.

"Yessir, Dr. Harley, I surely do! Thank ya, sir!" Elder grinned. He was suddenly aware that he had been acknowledged as a member of Elijah's family, worthy of respect, and not treated with the disdain or indifference which most white planters, and even their poorer relations, showed towards anyone of color. It made him feel proud.

IV

After Dr. Harley had left, Elijah went back to the kitchen with Amy. The smells of Momma Celia's cooking surrounded him like a comforting embrace. Amy sat down with a bowl of string beans in her lap, and began deftly stripping the stringy fiber off the length of each bean, as if the mechanical action would somehow help ground her, and calm her nerves.

"I imagine you heard my conversation with Joseph? Did you hear it all?" Elijah asked, without reproach.

Amy nodded.

"Well, I think he's right about one thing, at least. I need to get some legal advice, but I need to do it without tippin my hand. Folks around here can get mighty nosey, and Joseph urged caution in the plannin of all this."

Amy responded, "You know he's right on that account too, Elijah. If your family gets wind of what you're plannin, they could make it a whole lot harder for us to do this." Amy started stripping beans at a faster pace, revealing the stress she was feeling at the very thought of Elijah's nephews or siblings. She could imagine them storming into the house to confront Elijah. She was worried, both for the strains to Elijah's health that could produce, and the intense discomfort she would feel in her awkward position as both illicit lady of the house and as de facto overseer of the plantation's business. She would be wanting to defend her husband's choices without it simply appearing self-serving to Elijah's avaricious relations, but saw there was little chance his family could possibly see it as anything else.

"Well," Elijah chuckled drily, "I imagine James, Michael, and Eliza (and that Polish husband of hers) will raise a ruckus when they find out they'll have to earn their own fortunes, rather than walk off with mine, especially since my brothers and sisters have less than I do to leave to them in the first place!" There was no sympathy for his nephews and niece in his tone. "As for legal advice, if I recall correctly, old Angus Patterson defended David

Martin years ago, when David wanted to emancipate Lucy and their two daughters, Eliza and Martha. Seems to me he ended up takin them up to Kentucky and managed to emancipate them there. I'd best see if I can have a talk with Angus."

Amy placed the bowl of string beans on the table, and stood up, facing the man she had grown to love. Momma Celia quietly took the bowl over to the cookstove and poured them into a cast iron pot of boiling water, adding in a large pinch of salt, while listening attentively.

"I heard tell that when ole man Martin died, he managed to leave property to Lucy and the girls." Momma Celia said softly, wanting to make a point, but fearful of appearing demanding to the son-in-law who owned her.

"Don't you worry, Momma Celia," Elijah said reassuringly. "As Amy already knows, I have every intention of doing the same. Ya'll've got no call to worry for your security."

"No call to worry? Mister Elijah, with all due respect, you been drinkin more than lemonade?" Momma Celia had turned from the stove to look at her son-in-law square on. "I wish I had the faith in white folks you do! Seems to me we got a whole lotta call for worry, given the way folks around here been talkin." Momma Celia's eyes looked care worn, yet her face also exuded an ageless strength that had weathered fears and disappointments before. " But I know you a good man, and I know they's a whole lotta love in this house. What you already done for us is no small thing. Bible says 'God is love,' so I figure with all this love around us, we also got reason to hope." Momma Celia choked back tears that made "hope" sound as much like a plea as a statement of assurance.

Amy looked at Elijah in a way that conveyed not only the worry and the hope, but also a sense of determination they were going to find a solution. She turned to her mother and put a comforting arm around her shoulder, and said gently, "Come on now Momma, everything's gonna work out. No need to cry- you don't want your string beans to get too salty now, do ya?"

Momma Celia looked at her daughter and smiled through her rheumy eyes with a mixture of gratitude for her comfort and admiration for her strength. Wiping her tears away with her apron, she set herself back to cooking, shooing her daughter and Elijah out of the kitchen.

"Go on, now, you two. Ya'll got more important things to do than worry about this ole woman." Momma Celia had recovered herself and, in the comfort of the kitchen she ruled with absolute authority, she directed her attention back to the task at hand, saying, "Amy, send the girls on in here to give me a hand. Time they learned more of my cookin secrets anyway. Slaves or no slaves, won't be long before they'll be havin they own extra mouths to feed!"

Elijah winced slightly at Momma Celia's reference to his daughters as slaves, but he knew it was true, and the truth did not sit well with him at all. He was also more aware than ever that it didn't sit well with the people in his household either. Though a certain instinct for avoidance of confrontation made him reluctant to fully acknowledge it, in his heart he knew he was going to have to take some definitive action to free and safeguard his family, and it would have to be soon. There was no more time for dawdling.

Amy stepped out on the back porch to call the girls to help their grandmother. Clarissa and Julia were playing hide and seek under the clothes lines hung with freshly washed linens, shrieking and laughing as they dodged between the flapping bed sheets, shirts, bloomers and petticoats. Elijah followed Amy and put his arm around her waist gently as they watched their daughters gamboling about.

"Your Momma's comment just now hit my heart. I know she didn't say it to hurt, but truth is it does. Every passin day, the thought of ya'll being enslaved to me, or by me, or for me, just gets harder and harder to bear!" He paused for a moment. "You do realize though," Elijah said, as much to himself as to Amy, as he looked out past the children to his fields and beyond, "that once we set this thing in motion, we've gotta see it through to the end, or things could get a whole lot worse for all of us?"

Amy nodded. "I know, sugar, but what other choice do we have? People're already talkin about us now, even though we try not to give them cause. That horse has already left the barn!"

Elijah sighed deeply, turning to Amy to give her a kiss on the neck. "Well, alright then!" he said with resolve. "Guess I'd best be callin on old Angus Patterson and see what I can find out."

He called out for Elder, who by then was out back in the barn. "Elder! Fetch me my horse and help me saddle her up, will you? I've got an errand to do in town!"

Elder stuck his head out of the barn door and called back, "Yes sir! I'll be right there!" He disappeared back into the dark of the barn, and the muffled sound of voices and horses' hooves on the straw-strewn floorboards indicated that Elijah's mare would be out directly.

As he was leading the mare out of the barn, Elder called back to his brother Elleck, who was somewhere inside, "Hey Elleck! Bring Papa's saddle out from the tack room- we've gotta saddle up Beauty, so he can go into town!"

Elleck whined grudgingly, reluctant to exert himself in the blistering heat. "Alright! Don't have to be so bossy!" But, by and by, he came out toward the house, a lean and sweating eleven year old, lugging a well-polished saddle smelling of leather, saddle soap and neatsfoot oil, and a handsome burgundy wool blanket for Elijah's mare, Beauty.

The horse was well named, a good sixteen hands tall, with a white slash on her forehead, a black mane and tail, and the rich chestnut brown of her neck and flanks deepening to a dark coffee on her fetlocks - she was magnificent. Though Elijah may not have been socially ostentatious, he had a good eye for horseflesh, and was of the opinion that a good horse not only was the mark of a gentleman, but also was one of the more useful investments a man could make. He loved that mare, and made sure the boys kept her well fed and well groomed at all times. Her saddle was of English leather, and the bit on her bridle and the stirrups were of finely chased and brightly polished steel.

While Elder and Elleck were saddling Beauty, and bringing her around to the front of the house, Elijah had stepped back inside to change. Though he would have preferred riding into town in shirtsleeves, given the extreme heat of the day, he was well aware that a landed gentleman, such as himself, would be looked at disapprovingly if he were to go calling on a lawyer in town dressed like a field hand. Much as it irked him, he was smart enough to know they didn't need any more disapproval from folks around there than they already had- especially if his plans were to be carried out without raising local suspicions.

The boys were waiting with Beauty near the trough by the live oak when Elijah came out, choosing to leave from the upstairs porch down the outside stairway to the left, rather than from the double front door on the ground floor. Amy stood on the upper level, wiping her eyes with a small embroidered linen handkerchief, forcing herself to smile and wave to her husband, as he looked up to the balcony before turning Beauty and cantering off down the road toward town. Elleck noticed his mother's handkerchief, and realized something was bothering her.

"Hey, Elder, why's Momma cryin? What's goin on? Things have felt a little strange here ever since Dr. Harley left."

Elder looked up toward the balcony, but his mother had already disappeared back inside the house. "I dunno. I know Papa and Dr. Harley talked for quite a while. I was sittin out here waterin Dr. Harley's horse, and I could hear Papa raisin' his voice, but I don't think he was hollerin at Dr. Harley. I couldn't make out what they were sayin with the shutters closed." Elder reported. "When Dr. Harley came out though, he and Papa were all smiles. And then he said somethin no white man has ever said to me before. He looked over toward Papa and said, 'I hope you realize what a good man he is, and how much he cares for you!'"

"Dr. Harley told you that?" Elleck looked a bit doubtful. "Why'd he go sayin somethin like that?"

"I dunno", responded Elder pensively, "but he said it like he meant it, and really wanted me to know. Somethin's definitely goin on. Maybe Momma Celia knows what this is all about! Let's go ask her!"

The boys agreed, and set off toward the kitchen to find their grandmother, going around to the back of the house, so as not to track in any muck from the barn and raise their mother's ire. She was insistent on keeping the house immaculate, and even quarreled at times with Elijah for his lacksadaisical attitude towards the finer points of domestic orderliness. She frequently reminded him that no children of hers were going to be raised with a bad example of how to behave properly- even in the privacy of their own home. Though as a long-time bachelor, he had been set in the ways of his disregard for such matters of decorum, he would sheepishly apologize, and promise to amend his behavior, for the sake of the children- at least until the next lapse, from force of habit.

V

On the main road into town sat the General Store of James Willis, Elijah's nephew. James sat on the veranda fanning himself from the sweltering heat, when he heard the muggy-muffled sound of a horse's hooves, syncopating with the chirping of crickets in the otherwise sultry silence of the afternoon. He looked up and saw his uncle cantering toward town, and only slowing briefly to a trot to call out a greeting to his nephew. "Hi there, James! How's business?" But he did not stop to chat, or even wait for a response, and resumed his canter once he had passed the store.

James thought to himself, "What's that ole man up to? It's not like him to be off the plantation this time of day- and dressed up in this heat!"

James' brother Michael came out onto the veranda with a drink in his hand and noticed his uncle disappearing into the distance. He took a long swig, and nodding in his uncle's direction, asked his brother, "What was that all about?"

"Not sure, but somethin feels funny. He didn't stop to talk, and barely said hello as he rode by. I don't like it. Smells to me like that colored woman he's taken up with is behind this!" James' suspicion and disapproval was unmasked. Michael snorted his agreement, and took another drink. "I may call her 'Aunt Amy' to her face, but she ain't no aunt a mine!"

A few minutes later, Elijah rode onto a tree lined street in Williston, and dismounted. He tethered Beauty in front of a handsome brick house with well-painted black shutters, and a wide front door with a graceful fan shaped transom. As indicated by an elegantly lettered sign hanging on one of the twin pillars framing the entrance, it was the home of Angus Patterson, Sr., Attorney at Law. He gave the mare a loving pat on the neck before climbing the porch steps and lifting the heavy polished brass knocker to announce his arrival. A man about the age of Elijah's nephews answered the door. It was Angus Patterson, Jr. the good lawyer's son.

"Well, hello there, Mr. Willis! What brings ya'll to town on such a hot afternoon?" Angus asked graciously, but not without genuine curiousity.

"I hope I'm not interruptin anything, son, but I wondered, if your father is at home, whether I might not have a word with him?" Elijah said with equal graciousness, without wanting to appear too urgent.

"Well of course, sir, come on in! I was just fixin to go out myself, but I'll go call Pa. Why don't ya'll have a seat in the front parlor? I'll be back directly." Angus, Jr. showed Elijah to a seat in the parlor and disappeared down a hall to fetch his father.

Shortly, Elijah heard footsteps returning, punctuated by the slow hollow thump of a cane on the floorboards. An elderly gentleman with silver hair and goatee entered with his son watchfully at his side. He was dressed in a doe colored cutaway coat, cream colored linen breeches, and a gold brocade waistcoat, looking the worse for the wear and rumpled in the heat, rather out of fashion, but still dapper. Angus, the younger, helped his father ease into a chair. His father looked up at him with a weary smile of appreciation. "Thank you, son. That'll be all- ya'll go on now, so Mr. Willis and I can chat in private."

"Alright, Pa. You sure you'll be all right? If ya'll need help before I get back, you call Mary out from the kitchen. Promise?" The younger Mr. Patterson seemed genuinely solicitous of his aged father.

"I'll be fine son. You worry too much!" He smiled affectionately at his son before adding, "Before you go, why don't you offer Mr. Willis some of that good sippin whiskey over there on the table. And pour me a glass too, while you're at it!" The old man paused while his son poured the drinks and brought them over to his father and Elijah. He nodded approvingly and said, "Now go on, and close the door behind ya, please!"

The younger Patterson politely accepted his dismissal with a tip of the hat he had just put on, and on his way to the door, he turned and said to Elijah, "Nice to see ya again, Mr. Willis. Give my regards to Michael and James when ya see em!"

"I'll do that, son!" Elijah forced a smile, but felt a sudden discomfort at the thought that the younger Patterson might somehow be closer to his nephews than had occurred to him, and might share their points of view. He chose not to reveal any misgivings to the elder Patterson, and said affably, "Your son's care of ya does both of ya'll credit, Angus."

The old man nodded appreciatively. "Angus is a good boy. A little hot-headed sometimes, but he's still young!" he said with the knowing way of fathers sharing the realities of an older generation's perspective on their unseasoned children, hopeful they would mend their ways, in time.

"I'm glad to see ya, Elijah!" Angus Sr. said, taking a sip of the whiskey with a smack of relish. "It's been a while! I must admit, though, I'm a bit taken by surprise. What can I do for ya? You know I'm retired now, so if this is a legal matter, I'm not sure how much I can help ya."

Elijah sniffed the amber liquid in his glass with pleasure, before taking a sip. "Well Angus, I appreciate your time- and your whiskey! I'll surely try not to tax your energies. I don't need legal representation exactly, but I was hopin you might share the insights gleaned from some of your long years of practice, that could touch on a matter of great concern to me. I'm happy to provide a retainer in exchange for your wisdom."

"Oh nonsense, Elijah, that won't be necessary! Not even sure if what I have is wisdom, or maybe just a heap of experience! But I'm happy to share my thoughts with ya if they're of any help. Hell, I knew your daddy, it's the least I can do!"

Given Elijah's increasingly frequent intimations of his own mortality, it was a sobering but encouraging thought to realize that the counselor was almost of his father's generation and still sharp of mind, if a bit enfeebled of body. For though movement was clearly labored for the old man, his eye had the piercing clarity of a hawk's, and his mind seemed undimmed by his years.

"Is it safe to assume, then, that you could guard the matters discussed here in the spirit of attorney-client confidentiality, even without compensation?" Elijah didn't want to put too fine a point on it, but was increasingly aware of the need for a degree of secrecy in the formulation of his plans, at least in their initial stages.

"It most certainly is, my friend. You can count on that! Though I may not be taking new clients these days, let's just treat this as a long-standin relationship, for your father's sake, which would, by implication, assure that confidentiality." The old man paused, looking toward the door. "Truth be told, that was why I insisted on my son closin the parlor door on his way out, despite the heat. God knows I love him, but I'm no fool- I'm well aware that some of my views don't sit well with him, even though he still respects me enough not to say so to my face. And I'm not about to let a youngster like him meddle with my affairs, or tell me whom or what causes I should or should not defend!" The energetic delivery of this last statement was punctuated with a thump of his cane as an exclamation point. It seemed to indicate this was not the first time such an issue had been discussed in this household.

"So now, tell me, what brings ya here? Surely not social niceties on a day this hot, and this far from home?" The elder Angus appreciated the fact that it generally took some matter of importance to get Elijah into town at all, except when bringing crops to market or dealing with his business.

Satisfied that the old lawyer's discretion was unimpeachable, and he could be trusted to provide good counsel, Elijah prefaced his petition by saying, "If I recall correctly, you represented David Martin years ago in his attempt to emancipate his colored wife and daughters, didn't ya?"

Immediately picking up on the reference, and fully prepared for its associative connection to Elijah's situation, the old man simply nodded and said, "That's right. I did! And very successfully, I might add!" This last was uttered not without a little pride in his voice. A lawyer pleading such a case in rural South Carolina and still retaining a successful law practice thereafter was an accomplishment clearly justifying that pride, given the racial tensions growing in the region. It spoke well of both his legal skill and his social acumen to maintain such high standing in the community, despite its disapproval of some of his positions. Angus Patterson was unbiased in offering his legal services to rich and poor alike, and had earned the respect of the entire community for doing so.

Elijah then proceeded to lay the matter before Angus as best he could. He reiterated the key questions Joseph Harley had identified earlier that afternoon: namely, how and where his family could be legally emancipated; whether, once done, they could safely reside in South Carolina; and how their future could be assured in perpetuity through the inheritance of his entire estate. The old man listened politely and attentively, and without interruption, sipping on his whiskey pensively.

"So you want to know what ya should do?" asked the old man after a thoughtful pause. "I can't tell ya that, sir. But I can help ya look at the legal ramifications of what ya may do, as well as what ya can and cannot do! The decision of what ya ultimately will do lies in your hands alone!"

"Point well taken, Angus, and spoken like a true lawyer! But that's why I need someone of your experience to help me be more certain to make a well-informed choice! Walk me through my options, will ya?" Elijah suddenly felt a surge of indecision and inner conflict. He loved Amy and the children, but he didn't relish the idea of setting off the whole town against him. And, though he felt a little ashamed to admit it, he even wondered briefly whether maybe there was any other way out of this predicament that didn't even require emancipation!

The elder Mr. Patterson sensed the conflict, and it was not unknown to him. He'd lived long enough to know that human foibles being what they are, no matter how much one railed against the suffocating shackles of tradition, when push comes to shove, most people opt to remain in the bondage they know, rather than leap into the freedom they don't. He smiled at Elijah understandingly, and for a moment adopted an almost fatherly tone, despite the fact that they were less than a generation apart in actual age.

"Well, sir, there's a lot you'll have to sort out for yourselves as to what you actually want to do, but, as it happens, I do know somethin of the struggle ya'll're facin." He leaned forward toward Elijah, and in confidential tones proceeded, " Neither you nor David Martin are the only men to have faced these issues, so I can surely tell ya somethin of the legal precedents and obstacles that exist, how South Carolina has adjudicated these matters in the past, and at least how some other states have dealt with the issues of late."

"I'd be much obliged to ya if ya would, Angus. Truth is, I don't know where else to turn around here, and I know I'm dealing with a potential powder keg that I don't want set off, if it can possibly be avoided!" Elijah thought to clarify his concerns by sharing, "Joseph Harley was out to my place today. He is one of the few in my confidence these days, and I shared this matter with him. It was he who recommended I seek some legal advice, but also cautioned me against rashness, or makin' my decision public until necessity might require it, for the very fear of the repercussions that could back-fire on us."

The older man nodded appreciatively. "I understand, Elijah. Always did admire Joseph for his good sense. He was right to tell you so. So then, let's take a look at this situation legally, shall we?

"I'll be honest with ya. It would be neither easy, nor in my opinion, advisable for ya to attempt to petition the General Assembly for the emancipation of Amy, her mother and the children. God knows, it wasn't easy to attempt thirty years ago, but matters have frankly gotten worse since then." The old man shook his head, as if in dismay, "More and more planters have been havin mulato children they want to legitimize, and seems their own white offspring and other relations resent it. You know how folks around here judge things in terms of their acreage and slaves. Start messin with their holdins and their inheritance, and ya're apt to end up with an ugly fight on your hands!"

Though no great surprise, it had never really occurred to Elijah that the younger generation was an even greater threat than his own, for their sheer jealousy and greed, born of their sense of innate privilege as heirs of the ruling class. It made sense though- confirming his own suspicions of his nephews. Now that he thought about it, they had always been more overt in their hostility toward Amy and the family than his own siblings had.

"Well then what can be done, Angus?" asked Elijah pointedly. "Didn't David Martin manage to succeed in emancipatin his family and leavin em property?"

""Yes, Elijah, he did. And that's common knowledge, and a matter of public record- no breach of attorney-client privilege for me to tell ya so. But it surely wasn't easy, or inexpensive!" he added. "It cost him a great deal of time, money, and effort- as it also cost all the others who have walked down that road, whether successfully or not!"

Elijah took all that in. He weighed his next words very carefully, "So, in your legal opinion then, what would be the most defensible path to emancipation and inheritance, and what are the chances of its success?"

Angus parsed the question with lawyerly skill. "A question well put, or rather, two questions well-put. The answer to the one, however, may not necessarily be congruent with the other."

Elijah looked at the lawyer quizzically, uncertain as to his meaning. "How's that?" he asked.

"Well, I suppose it depends somewhat on what you mean by 'defensible'. Legal defensibility and moral defensibility are, sadly, not always synonymous. Legally, as things currently stand in the great State of South Carolina, the most defensible path to emancipation is one, and only one: the petitioning of the General Assembly, as there is no other recognized legal means of emancipation available." He looked at Elijah with disarming frankness, "Unfortunately, that also seems to be the least likely to succeed, since there have been no successful petitions for emancipation to pass the muster of legislative approval in years- a fact which some, at least, consider morally indefensible!"

"So where does that leave us, Angus? Surely there must be some way to accomplish this?" Elijah felt the reality of the futility of petitioning the legislature like the blow of a mule's kick. It temporarily knocked the wind out of him, and left him at a loss for words. His heart sank and his expression grew glum.

"Hold on now, Elijah, just because petitionin the General Assembly may be beatin a dead horse, doesn't mean there's no solution possible!" Angus reassured his friend. "Just means you'll have to think a little more creatively to find it!"

Elijah brightened slightly. "Got any ideas? I'm all ears."

"Well sir, much as we Carolinians tend to act as though the whole world lies within the borders of the Carolinas, there are thirty other states in this Union. I rather imagine that, in the annals of jurisprudence, there ought to be some alternative points of view in at least some of those states that could be useful in your situation!"

Angus stood up with difficulty, but steadying himself with his cane, walked over to a bookcase filled with leather-bound tomes with gilded lettering on their spines, and began to run a gnarled finger along the shelf searching for something. Finally, finding the object of his search, he turned to Elijah saying, "Give me a hand with this will ya, Elijah? I'm not as steady as I used to be, and these are a bit on the heavy side."

Elijah strode over to the bookcase and finished pulling the massive cordovan volume from the shelf, carried it over and set it on a table near the window, Angus by his side. The lawyer opened the book, almost caressing the leather affectionately, and began leafing through its gilt-edged pages. He peered attentively at the chapter headings and case numbers, and the names of plaintiffs and defendants, humming to himself softly. Uncertain as to what, precisely, Angus was looking for, Elijah was left to stand by expectantly, at the mercy of the old man's perusal.

Finally, Angus looked up excitedly. "Here it is!" he announced with the exuberantly declarative tone of a cock crowing, waving his index finger in the air as if calling down a witness from on high. "The case law I was looking for! Lookee here!" He pointed out several headings. "These are the cases tried in South Carolina for and against manumission- the emancipation of slaves. But as you can see, they're full of references to other case law as well, from outside the State, and even outside the United States- from as far away as England, and includes the precedents of English Common Law throughout her colonies." The old man smiled triumphantly, as if he had just clarified the matter definitively, but Elijah felt completely in the dark as to the old man's point.

"So, what do they say, Angus? Is there a precedent for emancipation and for leaving an inheritance to anybody of color, or not?" he blurted out with exasperation.

"Well yes, of course there is!" replied Angus, "But I'm afraid your solution is not quite that simple. You see, some of these cases go back quite a ways- to 1804 and even earlier, to Colonial times. Unfortunately, the laws governin these matters in South Carolina have changed in the intervenin years, so the existence of a precedent, in and of itself, is not necessarily an indication of a currently viable defense."

The old man, a bit unsteady on his feet, perhaps as much due to the whiskey and the heat as to his general frailty, tottered back over to his chair and sat down with a sigh.

"I'll continue to give this some thought, Elijah. It's a complex matter, and I don't want to lead you astray down a hopeless road. But I'm sure we can figure out some means for ya to realize your objective, though it may take some time." The old man looked at his nearly empty glass and, changing the subject, asked, "Would you mind pourin me out another finger or two? I'd almost forgotten how good this old sippin whiskey is!" he said with a cheery smile.

Elijah, realizing that the usefulness of the conversation was coming to a close, poured the old man another drink, and then took his leave.

"I surely do thank ya for your time, Angus, and would appreciate any additional insight ya might provide. Why don't I check back with ya sometime next week, and we can have another chat?"

"That'd be just fine!" said the old man, his voice thickening a bit with the additional infusion of bourbon. "I'll look forward to seein ya. Does me good to keep my mind active on such matters!" he said with genuine enthusiasm. "Give my best to your family, won't ya?"

"I surely shall, Angus. And thank ya for the drink too!" Elijah smiled. Angus raised his glass in salute before taking another sip, as Elijah saw himself out, shut the front door, mounted Beauty, and cantered off back toward home again.

VI

Elijah's mind was now churning with questions and doubts. Whatever the legal precedents might be, if they couldn't be implemented in the State of South Carolina, what good were they? Where could they be implemented? Would recognition in another state transfer to recognition in South Carolina? Was it more important to free his family, or provide for them? What if he couldn't do both, which should he choose? Which was more easily achieved? Was he being unrealistic to even try? Was the social stranglehold of white supremacy unbeatable? Would he end up losing everything, rather than gaining?

He was so absorbed in thought as he rode past his nephew's store, that he made no attempt whatsoever to appear even causally interested in any social exchange. In fact, he didn't even notice that James and Michael were sitting on the porch drinking with Angus Patterson, Jr.

"Hmm!" commented Angus the younger, "That's odd! I saw your uncle a while back at our house, and he was just as cordial as could be. Funny he didn't slow down to say hello just now!"

James Willis perked up his ears at this tidbit of news. "He was at your house? What for?"

"I don't know exactly. He just said he wanted to have a word with my father. They go back a ways, and I know Pa told me he'd done some legal work for the family in the past. Maybe it was somethin to do with your uncle's business. I didn't make much of it, truthfully. Seemed like a couple of old men havin a drink and a chat."

To the suspicious James, however, Angus Jr.'s assessment of the situation seemed either hopelessly naïve, or downright foolish. "I tell you what, Angus, if our uncle shows up again to talk to your Pa, do us a favor will ya, and see if you can find out what he wants to talk to him about? Somethin don't feel right about this! I think he's up to somethin- and it has to do with that nigra woman he's living with!"

"What makes you think that James?" asked the lawyer's son. "You boys seen anything in particular to make ya'll think somethin's wrong?"

"Wrong? Hell yeah!" chimed in Michael. "The fact that he's got that slave in his house and she keeps havin more children, for starters. She already had some when Uncle Elijah bought her, but she's got a couple more now- and it's not too hard to figure out their daddy's no nigra!"

"Sweet Jesus!" Angus said with a low whistle. "I didn't know that! Damn! You mean he's been sleepin with his slave woman and lettin her pickaninnies have the run of the place?" This thought seemed to disturb Angus out of his assumptions about Elijah's social visit, though the real motive for the visit still had not occurred to him.

"Like about to kill Daddy! They may be brothers, and blood is surely thicker than water, but Uncle Elijah's taken this thing too far!" blurted James. "Family always has been disappointed he never married. But hey, that's alright with me", he said with a sly, avaricious grin, "cause with no wife or children, he'd most likely leave at least some of all that land and those slaves a his to us!" James pointed to himself and Michael, making it clear they expected to benefit independently from anything their parents might devise. "But when Daddy found out that woman was pregnant, after movin into Uncle Elijah's house, well let me tell you, he set to cussin a blue streak about Granddaddy turnin over in his grave to see such a thing happen in his own family!"

"That's the truth!" agreed Michael. "He and Uncle Elijah had words, for sure! Hardly set foot in Uncle Elijah's house since. Said he couldn't bear to see the memory of his family tainted by that woman actin uppity, like she owned the place!" Michael spat off the porch in disgust, the spittle kicking up a little puff of dust as it hit the dry ground.

"Well boys, I had no idea!" said Angus. "I heard my Pa had a client once- some planter over in Barnwell years ago. Fella wanted to free his nigra woman and mulato daughters. Even wanted to leave em property. Can you imagine? But I thought that was ancient history.

"Good Lord!" Angus paused, as if suddenly stricken by an epiphany, as the dawn of understanding seemed to rise in his whiskey fogged mind. "Ya'll don't suppose your uncle Elijah's fixin to try somethin like that, do you?" The unimaginable had suddenly become imaginable.

"He'd better not be, is all I can say! Lest he wants to have a real fight on his hands!" James said pugnaciously. "He'd have to be crazy to even try it!"

Michael nodded energetically in agreement. "That's for damn sure!"

he interjected, with the bravado of many a country boy with a whole lot more opinion than knowledge or understanding. It never occurred to either James or Michael that, even if his uncle was crazy enough to want to leave his mistress something in inheritance, it could possibly be more than a cabin and a few acres. But even that was too outrageous to contemplate seriously! They were pretty well sure their uncle was just besotted with this slave woman and not thinking straight, but they needed to discover any misbegotten plans he might be cooking up, in order to save the family honor from the scandal of it all.

"So Angus, you see what you can find out, will ya? If Uncle Elijah's tryin to turn on us, we wanna know about it! Daddy told me he'd written a will back in '46 leaving everything he has to the family- his *real* family, that is! He'd best not be plannin to go back on his word!

"I promise you both, I'll do what I can. Pa can be pretty tight-lipped. Always goin on about attorney-client privilege, or some such thing- that obliges him to keep secrets. But his tongue sometimes loosens with a little sippin whiskey, so maybe I can wheedle somethin useful out of him. If I do, y'all 'll be the first to know, I swear!"

The three young men, unanimous in their sense of outrage at the very possibility of Elijah freeing slaves or leaving them any property, sealed their pact by passing around the bottle of whiskey and each taking a long swig. They thereby fortified their resolve to get to the root of Elijah's peculiar behavior, and to prevent any dynastic tragedies from occurring. Especially any that might deprive the Willis boys of property, both material and human, that might permit them to avoid the further necessity of the hard work of making their livings by the sweat of their own brows!

VII

Angus Patterson, Sr. was ruminating about Elijah's dilemma. He began to pore over his legal records, and even old newspaper articles he had saved. He remembered, from his own experience, the great debates over the issue of the abolition of slavery that had been argued, both in South Carolina and up in Washington, for decades. They seemed to have been waged with greater and greater intensity in recent years. He knew the issue was not going to go away, and that more and more good people were suffering for lack of its resolution. He decided that, retired or not, he wanted to do what he could to help Elijah, both as a friend, and for the sake of the larger issue of seeing justice done for all.

When he had defended David Martin back in the 1820's, the debate had been raging in Washington about the Missouri Compromise- whether to allow Missouri into the Union as a slave holding state or not. The Compromise, arrived at reluctantly, was to admit Maine as a slave free state, and Missouri as a slave holding state, thereby maintaining a precarious balance of power between the vested interests of the North and the South, to prevent the entire Union from splitting apart.

The rhetoric of the Compromise, though it had succeeded in preventing a regional partition of the Union, at least for a time, had hardly settled the issue. South Carolina's Senator Calhoun, though initially dedicated to the preservation of the Union, insisted 'til the day he died that slavery was a positive good, not a necessary evil. Much to the chagrin of his rivals, Kentucky's Senator Clay and Massachusetts' Senator Webster, the chief architects of the agreement, the Compromise in fact, seemed to have served to simply increase the Southern determination to reinforce what had become the mainstay of its economy.

The South was insisting on preserving the availability of plentiful slave labor that permitted Southern planters to make sizable fortunes selling ever-greater quantities of cotton to the textile mills of industrial New England

and Great Britain. The North accused Southerners of immorality for getting rich through slavery, while the Southerners accused the Northerners of hypocrisy for criticizing them while depending on the slave-harvested cotton to make their own fortunes in the textile mills of the North.

Angus saw that since then, the country had been clearly growing more and more divided. Even some of the politicians, like the aging Senator Clay, who, though a slave owner himself, was sincerely attempting to abolish slavery, felt compelled to do so only gradually. They feared destroying the Union by having to enfranchise an entire new class of liberated blacks, uneducated and unprepared for the responsibility of freedom. Though Northern politicians wanted to prevent the expansion of slavery and move towards its definitive abolition, they knew that move could not come at the expense of destroying the entire agricultural economy of the South. Nor could the opponents of abolition impose slavery on the North or the Western Territories. It was a conundrum that angered both the slaveholders and the abolitionists. Moreover, as more and more settlers moved westward, drawn by the discovery of gold in California in 1849, the balance of power between slave and free states became a matter upon which the very survival of the Union ever more tenuously depended.

The dirty reality of politics being what it is, idealism alone could not carry the day in Washington, let alone in State Capitals across the land. In order to prevent a definitive schism from rending the nation asunder, the anti-slavery faction was forced to accept what they saw as a draconian measure of repressive pro-slavery protectionism in the passage of the Fugitive Slave Act, championed by South Carolina's own late Senator, John C. Calhoun, who died shortly after its passage. That was the condition for the Southern states' acceptance of the Compromise.

Slave owners in South Carolina, and throughout the South, were fearful, and not without reason, that there would be an influx of slaves attempting to flee their masters. They worried that somehow fugitives would make it to safety in one of the slave-free states, assured that local ordinances would prevent their masters from tracking them down and returning them to bondage. With the Fugitive Slave Act, slave owners were empowered to run their slaves to ground, no matter where they went in the Union, and bring them back, kicking and screaming if necessary, to a servitude from which there was little hope of escape, and, as Angus was already aware, with often harsh punishment in reprisal for their "disloyalty."

Needless to say, the abolitionists did not take this "Compromise" omnibus bill of 1850 lightly, the golden oratory of Washington's senior statesmen notwithstanding. The argument was not only raging in Congress. The Abolitionist Movement became a galvanizing force throughout the Northeast and the newer states to the West of Colonial America, polarizing them against the Southern states. Former slave Frederick Douglass of Maryland shifted his allegiance from William Lloyd Garrison's commitment to a diplomatic solution, toward John Brown's increasingly activist, even militant attempt to force abolition on the nation as a whole. Cassius Marcellus Clay, first in Lexington, then in Cincinnati, had mounted a careful legal and constitutional argument against slavery in his newspaper, *The True American*, clearly arguing that it was a matter of national patriotism to abolish the entire institution, and that to do otherwise was downright un-American, even treasonous! Cincinnati was rapidly becoming a nexus from which that battle was being fought.

Harriet Beecher Stowe, also in Cincinnati, wrote Uncle Tom's Cabin, creating a literary and political sensation whose popularity far exceeded the author's wildest expectations. It was immediately adapted to the stage, and performed in New York and cities throughout the North, moving audiences to tears of righteous indignation against the cruelties of the villainous slave owner, Silas Legree. And while the politicians, orators, and writers argued their case for abolition in public, Harriet Tubman and countless others ran what they called an underground railroad, working courageously and in secret to prevent slave-owners from succeeding in capturing fugitive slaves, and saw them to safety across the border in Canada. Though a lawyer in a small town, Angus's thirst for knowledge and love of the laws shaping the nation had kept him well informed of the great issues of the day.

Even the backwater of Barnwell District, South Carolina, was not immune to the machinations wracking the young nation. At times, it seemed questionable whether the vision of the founding fathers would survive another generation, at least in Barnwell. Folks in South Carolina, as Angus well knew, were talking more and more about the Southern states seceding from the Union altogether, and creating their own Confederacy-one that would protect their economic interests and the primary institution that made them prosper. The younger generation, brought up on their grandparents' tales of the Revolutionary War and the War of 1812, seethed with righteous and rebellious fervor against what they felt was the increasing oppression of the federal government, as if it equaled the tyranny of the British Crown. They argued with the braggadocio of the young about States' rights, and the freedom to run things as they saw fit, Washington be damned!

Angus understood the economic argument in favor of slavery, for the South's one crop economy of dependence on the labor-intensive production of cotton had the entire region over a barrel. And the legal needs of planters had, after all, had helped provide him with a comfortable living for many years. But only a few realized that the greed for cotton profits was creating an economy of diminishing returns, slavery or no slavery, for it was drastically depleting the soil, and making it less and less productive. This, ironically, made cotton production require more and more acres and slaves to keep up with the growing demand. Moreover, the planters were essentially obligated to find higher yielding strains and improve efficiency to compensate for the soil depletion, in the face of increasing manufacturing demand from the North and abroad. Their solvency depended upon it.

Angus had often wondered how much longer cotton would be King in the South. Neither he nor anyone else, of course, realized that one day, many years in the future, a former slave from Missouri named George Washington Carver would advance the principles of crop rotation and the soil-replenishing properties of crops like peanuts, soybeans, and pecans. But it would take more than the emancipation of slaves to renew the agricultural vitality of the South, freeing it from its own inherent bondage to a failing system.

Aside from all the political and economic arguments, however, Angus remained unconvinced by the pro-slavery position. His profound commitment to the dispensation of justice took seriously the Declaration of Independence's premise that all men are created equal- the paradox of there being slaveholders among the founding fathers belying that equality, notwithstanding. He no longer owned slaves himself, preferring to employ free blacks as servants to run his household- whose help had become even more valued since his wife's death. He had long been convinced, by his own experience, that color did not define personhood or humanity, and therefore should not be a defining characteristic of the equality of freedoms bestowed by citizenship.

There was no doubt in Angus' mind that people of color should be treated like people and full citizens, and not like property or livestock. Moreover, his own life experience convinced him that, unlike the opinions of politicians like Clay and others, the existence of free Negroes in the society did not pose a threat or problem requiring their return to an ancestral Africa which most of them had never known, and was more alien to them than any state in the Union. Still, he was not feeling very optimistic about the chances of Elijah emancipating his family, at least, not in South

Carolina. He pored over his documents for hours and hours, trying to see his way clear to a possible solution.

Mindful of the urgency of not stirring up attention to Elijah's situation, Angus decided he needed to discreetly consult with his colleague, John Bauskett. John was an attorney who had filed a manumission petition for another planter, William Dunn, and had also served with him as co-counsel on behalf of Lucy Martin, David Martin's emancipated colored wife. Perhaps John could shed some helpful light on the possibilities. He sat down at his desk and penned his colleague a letter:

To John Bauskett, Esquire,
Attorney at Law,
Barnwell, South Carolina

My Dear friend John:

I have a matter of legal and personal interest concerning the current and probable future state of affairs in our fair State, and indeed the Nation, vis à vis the issue of the emancipation of slaves, and the possibility of them being granted rights to inherit property.

I would dearly love to have your insight on these issues for the sake of some research I have endeavored to undertake. Sadly, age and infirmity are beginning to limit my mobility, or I would happily call on you to discuss them, but my mind and heart are keenly interested in understanding more thoroughly the history of jurisprudence on these matters, and I thought your experience might prove enlightening

If you are able, I'd be much obliged if you could stop by and pay me a visit sometime next week. I can certainly offer you some fine sippin whiskey, good food, and good conversation for your pains.

Hoping to see you in the days ahead, I am most gratefully your friend and colleague,

Angus Patterson, Sr.,
Attorney at Law.

After signing the letter, he carefully folded it, wrote John Bauskett's address on the back in an elegant hand, and sealed the fold with a daub of bright red sealing wax into which he imprinted the mark of the heavy gold signet ring he wore on his right ring finger. Satisfied with his work, and actually energized by the prospect of a stimulating exercise in the law that he had loved for a lifetime, Angus called his son to deliver the letter in person to Barnwell, rather than having him hand it to William Beazely, the local postmaster in Williston.

"Now son, I want ya to ride over to Barnwell for me and deliver this in person to my old friend John Bauskett. Tell him I'd be grateful if he could send me a note in response before you leave, so I can have it right quickly."

"Sure thing, Pa. I'll be glad to. But what's so important that you need to send it in person, rather than just taking it to Mr. Beazely at the post office in Williston? It's a lot closer and easier!" replied the younger Angus, unnecessarily reminding his father of the obvious. However, truth be told, after his conversation with the Willis boys, it dawned on him this might be an opportunity to pry his old man for information he could pass on to James and Michael. Having nothing better to do in any case, he did not, in fact, feel at all inconvenienced by his father's request, and was genuinely eager to comply.

This, of course, his father read simply as filial piety, and a cause of paternal satisfaction, not suspecting the ulterior motives that fed his son's enthusiasm. Still the lawyer in him, by long habit, chose not to share his reasons openly with his son, for fear that in his youthful indiscretion the information might fall into unwelcome hands, and complicate the endeavor to which he was now feeling committed. Even the wording of the letter itself, he hoped, had been sufficiently ambiguous in its meaning that, in the event his son should see it while his friend John was reading it, the real motivation of the letter would remain obscure. Of course, he was not aware of his son's recent epiphany concerning Elijah and Amy's relationship, or he might have felt the need for even greater secrecy.

"Oh, it's nothin much. I just took a fancy to the idea of seein my old friend, and since I can't get around myself too well, I thought I'd invite him to drop by for a visit." said the elder Patterson.

A little disappointed, but hardly surprised that his father remained tight lipped about his own affairs, Angus Jr. realized that if his father wouldn't tell him anything, perhaps Mr. Bauskett would, in the process of sending his father a response. So he cheerfully took the letter from his father, and promised to set off for Barnwell straight away.

VIII

Dr. John G. Guignard and Mr. F. W. Matthews were concerned. This business of Elijah Willis having a family with that slave woman of his had gone beyond a little sexual dalliance from which folks could discreetly look the other way. Word had gotten out there were a couple of more children in the house that looked a lot like Elijah and called Amy "Momma!" Nor could they ignore the fact that Elijah had actually come into town with her once in his carriage, as if she were his wife! When Elijah had to go out of town occasionally on business, he had left Amy in charge of the plantation-and she had even come into town by herself to buy supplies, placing large orders on credit, or even sometimes with substantial amounts of cash to pay the bill.

According to Will Beazely, who owned the store by the train depot where Elijah shipped off a lot of what he produced on the plantation, Amy had come in on several occasions, on Elijah's instructions, placing large orders for goods, and then when Elijah came back from his business trips, he'd come in and settle up. The shopkeepers in the area knew that, strange as it seemed to see a colored woman dressed up and buying large, like she was white, they had no need to doubt that her money was good, and that Elijah would pay in full for whatever she ordered. However, it did seem rather scandalous, all in all.

The two men liked Elijah, but they feared that this eccentric behavior was ruining not only his own reputation as a planter, but that of his entire family! That was a clear violation of the cherished Southern code of family honor. Moreover, it gave the town a bad name too. They and their peers didn't cotton to the idea that Williston might become a place where good Christian ladies and gentlemen could not depend on folks maintaining the proper order of things- and that certainly included, in their minds, protecting the purity of their values and their race from the polluting influence of improper contact with people of color! Something definitely ought to be done about this!

So they decided to try to save Elijah from himself, and from the danger to his standing in the community being done by his inappropriate alliance with his slave woman. There was really nothing for it but to set out for the Willis plantation, and try to talk some sense into Elijah before the damage to his reputation became irreparable. After all, they had a moral responsibility, both toward Elijah and the community! Bolstered by their Christian assurance that scripture itself demanded no less, they set out together to pay Elijah a call.

Elleck and Phillip were the first to see the dust cloud kicked up by the carriage horses way down the road to the main house. The carriage betokening unannounced and unexpected visitors, the boys immediately ran to find Elijah and warn him of the impending arrival of a vehicle of unknown provenance. Though the younger Willis children were of too tender an age to fully appreciate the tensions gathering around their family situation, the older boys had been informed by Elijah and Amy to keep a sharp lookout, and to be very careful of their own behavior when in the presence of others, especially those not familiar to them. Elleck and Phillip and Elder already knew well enough that most white folks were not like Dr. Harley, and that they'd best be careful when anyone came calling. They hated it, but they knew to act submissive, and be as invisible as possible when any of Elijah's relations or folks from town came by.

Amy was over in the slave quarters, talking with her sister-in-law and brother, when she too saw the dust cloud approaching. Sensing it like a storm heading their way, she quickly went up to the main house to prepare for whomever was descending upon them, attending to the needs of her husband's hospitality while also being a more immediate witness to whatever was afoot.

Elder was sent out to tend to the arrivals, just as Dr. Guignard and Mr. Matthews drove up to the front of the house. Their Negro driver climbed down from his seat and opened the door for the gentlemen to descend from the carriage. Neither Dr. Guignard nor Mr. Matthews paid the least attention to either the driver or Elder, for the both of them were merely doing what was expected. They were simply doing tasks necessarily performed by menials to assure the smooth and efficient functioning of their masters, hardly deserving of any undue recognition. It was as if their color made them invisible, like the black clad stage hands in the Kabuki theaters that travellers to Japan had reported seeing.

By this time, Elijah had been alerted to the arrival of unannounced guests. Reluctantly pulling on his coat to receive them, he stood in the doorway sizing up the probable cause of the visit. Both irritated and disquieted by his suspicions, he forced himself to exude graciousness, resolving to dispatch with his callers as quickly as possible.

"Gentlemen, to what do w, ah, I owe the honor of your visit?" Elijah caught himself from saying "we" instead of "I", aware that including Amy in his query might only highlight the issue he suspected was the motivation for their arrival, and exacerbate what he devoutly hoped would be no more than a brief courtesy call. He pointedly did not invite them inside, but gestured graciously to a grouping of wrought iron chairs ranged around a table in the relatively cool shade of the veranda. "Won't you please sit down?" He turned to Elder and called out, "Elder, tell your mother to bring out some refreshments for my guests."

Well-schooled as to how he must behave under such circumstances, Elder simply nodded his head politely, answering "Yes sir. Right away, sir!" and quickly disappeared into the house, where his mother stood listening, just out of sight of the visitors. Elder looked at her anxiously, sensing the veiled hostility of the visitors. She smiled reassuringly and said quietly, "Go on baby, go ask your grandmother to get a tray ready, and I'll be back shortly to fetch it out." She clearly did not want to miss any more of the gentlemen's conversation than she could help.

As Elder went on to the kitchen in the back of the house, Amy could hear Elijah going through the motions of Southern hospitality, asking after the family and well being of each visitor in turn, with feigned interest. Knowing her husband well, Amy could detect a slight tone of impatience in his voice, eager for the arrival of the refreshments, so as to provide the appearance of normalcy and the fulfillment of social obligations that he was certain his guests were awaiting with a critical eye. She was equally certain he was even more eager for his guests' departure than for the refreshments.

Dr. Guignard spoke first. He had been out to the plantation before, and was aware of Elijah's family. In fact, on one occasion several years go, before the girls were born, when Dr. Harley had been out of town, it had fallen upon Dr. Guignard to pay a house call on Amy, who had a miscarriage. Fortunately, there were no complications, and she had recovered fully, but Dr. Guignard had noticed that Elijah seemed far more distressed about the loss of the child than one would have expected of a slave-owner accepting that one of his slaves had not bred successfully. These things happened, and no one who lived on a farm and dealt routinely with the reproduction of livestock would grieve such a loss unduly, but rather, simply hope for a more successful mating next time, as an expected return on their investment.

Though he did wonder whether the child Amy lost had been sired by her owner, neither Elijah nor Amy spoke of the parentage, and Dr. Guignard was initially left with his suspicions officially unconfirmed. But the deliverance of other successful children, and their indisputable resemblance to Elijah in both coloring and features, had disquieted those few who were privy to their birth, and they were murmured about in parlors and slave quarters throughout the area. Hence the clear need for Guignard's visit today.

"Elijah", said Dr. Guignard, "I've known you for a long time now, and have always admired ya for your industry and business integrity." The doctor was trying to ease into the matter as diplomatically as possible.

"I appreciate that, Doctor. That's very kind of you. I certainly try to handle my own business with integrity", Elijah responded, with a humorless smile and the slightest hint of emphasis on "my own business," as if to sound a subtle warning to his guests not to stick their noses into it.

Ignoring the warning, Mr. Matthews chimed in, "And we respect ya for that, Elijah, we truly do, but we've come here today to voice a concern, with your best interests in mind."

Elijah repressed a desire to snort in derision at Mr. Matthews' disingenuous and presumptuous notion of what the Willis' best interests might be. He decided to wait for his visitors to come out with the reality that they were more concerned with their own best interests than his, before he gave them a piece of his mind.

"Elijah," Dr. Guignard continued, "I don't know if you're aware of it, but some folks around here are beginnin to talk." Guignard inflected this last word meaningfully.

"Why, Doctor Guignard, it seems to me they've been talkin ever since I've known em. I've lived here in Williston all my life, and I'm not aware of any mutes in the community, are you? But if there are any, and they're now beginnin to talk, that is certainly noteworthy. And if they are doin so under your medical care, I imagine that must make ya right proud! Why it's an almost miraculous achievement that should be celebrated!" Elijah's repartee made Dr. Guignard and Mr. Matthews squirm uncomfortably, precisely as he intended.

Mr. Matthews, more blunt spoken than his companion, blurted out in frustration, "Come on now Elijah! You know that's not what we're referrin to, don't ya?"

Elijah leveled his gaze coolly on his visitor and said evenly, but with a quietly menacing undertone, "Well then, Frederick, if you're so concerned for my well-bein, why don't you just come right out and tell me what the nature of your concern is? I'm sure I'd like to know!"

Before either visitor could answer, the front door swung open and Amy appeared, carrying a tray of refreshments. Elijah looked at her with a mixture of gratitude and warning, to which, instantly understanding, Amy simply nodded submissively. She offered refreshments to her husband and his guests without a word, placed the tray on the table, and discreetly returned to the dark interior of the house. She positioned herself in the shadows near an open window in the parlor so as to better hear the conversation outside, without her presence being detected.

Dr. Guignard and Mr. Matthews looked at each other quizzically before answering, as if to determine who should better deliver the thrust of their concern, their argument momentarily disrupted by the arrival of Amy, the very object of their discontent.

Distrusting the diplomatic skills of his companion, and sincerely convinced of their own good intentions, Dr. Guignard spoke up. "Elijah, I'm not a man to pass judgment on others, but frankly, your relationship with your slave woman is gettin people around here riled up! Hell, I don't mind you havin your way with her, if you've got a cravin for a little brown sugar, now and again." Dr. Guignard's leer suggested a measure of hypocrisy on his part, as if he himself were not immune to such "vulgar" attractions, "But you must realize" he continued, "that havin a family with her, and worse, havin em live in your house as if they really were your family, has got a lot of folks around here feelin that the good reputation of the Willis name is bein severely marred." He sighed in frustration before continuing, "I don't have to tell ya this town is named after your forebears, and people look up to the Willises. Always have! Now what kind of message do ya think your behavior sends to folks around here who expect the planters to uphold the moral values of our society?"

Without giving Elijah even a moment to respond, Mr. Matthews jumped in,

"Elijah, for the love of God, and the sake of your family and friends, and the other planters in the district too, couldn't you at least just send em all back to the slave quarters, where they belong? It's not too late to restore your standin in the community, but to do so, ya really need to keep your nigras in their place!"

Elijah was furious. How dare these men come into his home and try to tell him how to live his life, or whom to love, and insist that social conformity to their selfish standards was more important than taking care of the people he loved most? Fighting to control his temper and not run them off at gunpoint, Elijah took a deep breath before responding.

"First of all, John," he said, deliberately dropping all titles of respect, "it seems to me that you are bein less than honest with yourself, or with me, if you expect me to believe you are truly not a man to judge others. For that is precisely what it seems to me ya're doin." His withering gaze then turned to Mr. Matthews. "And Frederick, your notion of who belongs where is your own opinion, to which, I'll grant ya, ya're entitled, but it does not in any way conform to my own judgment on the matter!" Mr. Matthews visibly shrank under Elijah's gaze.

"I appreciate your intentions to save what ya'll construe my family's honor to be," Elijah continued, "but frankly, I find it more honorable to respect and care for those whom I love, and who love me back, than to worry about the opinions of people who've got nothing better to do than gossip about others, and whose affections for me have never been more than superficial in the first place!" He resisted the temptation to add, "and God knows, there are none among your boringly prim and proper, straight-laced ladies of Barnwell District who can hold a candle to my Amy!'

"So, if that's all ya have to say, gentlemen," he concluded, "I thank ya'll for your time, and bid ya'll good day. Now, if you'll excuse me, I have other matters to attend to." Without waiting for their response, Elijah pushed back his chair, stood up, and unceremoniously walked into the house, leaving the erstwhile saviors of his social standing gaping like catfish out of water. Dr. Guignard and Mr. Matthews regained their composure and returned to their carriage, albeit flustered and incredulous that Elijah should be so mule-headed, and downright rude, in response to their good intentions. Their driver, however, overhearing the exchange, climbed down from his seat to open the carriage door for the gentlemen, discreetly hiding a smile of appreciation for Elijah's boldness in putting them in their place. That was something not many colored folk had ever seen, or would even believe!

As the carriage rolled off down the road in a cloud of dust, with the driver silently chuckling to himself, Amy came out of the parlor and threw her arms around Elijah, giving him a big kiss. "I am so proud of you!" she said, as she looked up into his eyes. "That was one of the bravest things I've ever seen!"

"Well, I don't know if it was brave or foolhardy, but whatever the repercussions may be, I just couldn't sit there and listen to them spoutin off about propriety and the family honor, and keepin slaves in their place, and actin like you were some sort of brood mare I'd bought! Made me so mad I wanted to shit in their hats and pull em down over their ears!" The unusual and satisfyingly graphic image made them both guffaw.

Recovering herself, however, Amy said, "Elijah honey, you can't really blame em. They don't know any better- in fact it's all they do know. If white folks actually believe colored folks are less than human, then we really are just livestock to them! As long as they don't see us as real people, they don't have to deal with our feelins, or recognize our intelligence, or see anything in us other than what serves their purpose." Amy looked at Elijah directly in the eye, and added, "And sugar, can you honestly tell me you didn't see me and my family as an investment when you bought us from Mr. Kirkland? I know you've come a long way, and I love ya for it, but don't act like you've never shared any of their thinkin in the past!"

Humbled by his wife's observations, Elijah sighed. "God love ya, Amy, you certainly know how to keep me honest! Ya're right. But that's part of what makes me so damn mad! I may have been ignorant, but coming to know and love ya'll as I do, and seein how much richer my life is for it, I get more and more frustrated that others still have such blinders on, and don't even know it!"

"I know, sugar, but ya can't go around stirrin em up against us if we're ever gonna find our way out of this mess. If I can appear to be your submissive slave, you're gonna have to try a little harder to appear to be my master. It may be play-actin to us, but all our lives just might depend on it!" As always, Amy's sober grasp of reality had a way of bringing Elijah back into focus on the task at hand.

IX

Over in Barnwell, Angus Patterson, Jr. knocked on the door of John Bauskett, his father's friend. It was Mrs. Bauskett who answered the door.

"Afternoon, ma'am", said Angus, remembering to take off his hat. "I have a message here from my father, Angus Patterson, over in Williston, for Mr. John Bauskett. Is he in, by any chance?"

"That would be my husband, and you've no need to identify yourself to me, young man, for you're the spittin image of your father when he was your age! How is he?" Mrs. Bauskett answered with sincere interest.

"Oh, he's fine ma'am. He has some trouble with his knees and can't get around too well, but his mind is as sharp as ever!" Here Angus' genuine admiration for his father shone through.

"Well, I certainly am glad to hear that. My husband always said your father has one of the best legal minds he's ever known. Please, come on in. Have a seat in the parlor while I go get John. Could I offer you a drink, or somethin to eat? You must be thirsty after your journey over here from Williston."

"Thank you ma'am, I'd like that very much." Angus fidgeted with the letter his father had given him, not sure whether to hand it to Mrs. Bauskett, or not. He decided to wait to give it to her husband in person, so he could see what the lawyer's reaction was, even if he couldn't look over his shoulder and actually see what his father had written.

Shortly after Mrs. Bauskett left the parlor, her husband walked in to greet his guest. "Well I'll be blessed, I'd know the son of Angus Patterson anywhere! How are you son? It's a pleasure to see ya. What brings ya here to grace us with your company? Is your father alright, I hope?"

"Oh yes sir, and thank ya for your hospitality! Pa asked me to come over and give ya this message in person, and, if ya don't mind, he asked me to wait for ya to write him a note in response. He's eager to see ya."

"Is he now?" The lawyer looked curious as Angus handed him the letter. "Well of course I'll send a note back with ya, but let's have a bit of refreshment first. I can't be sending ya out the door to ride all the way back to Williston on an empty stomach now, can I? What kind of way would that be to treat my old friend's son?"

Angus had stood up when Mr. Bauskett had entered the room. His host signaled him to be seated again. "Please, make yourself comfortable. My wife will be along directly with a bite to eat to help make your journey home more enjoyable. Now excuse me a minute, won't ya, while I have a look at what your father has to say?"

Angus took a seat, thanking his host, and trying to position himself to observe the expression on John Bauskett's face as he read his father's letter, hoping to find in it some clue as to its content. The lawyer, however, turned toward the window to better read the message, frustrating Angus' attempt, and making him wonder whether all lawyers had some sort of fraternal agreement to be secretive!

"Well," said Bauskett finishing the letter, refolding it, and carefully stowing it in his waistcoat pocket, "your father certainly hasn't lost his keen interest in the law, has he?" Angus wasn't quite sure how to respond, and was dying to ask what the letter had said.

"Uh, no sir, he hasn't. I doubt he ever will! He still reads all those law books all the time, as if he were tryin a case, even though he's retired." Angus hoped to spark a response from his father's colleague that might give him some indication of just why his father did seem more interested in poring through legal records and such than he had for some time.

"Well, son, when you've dedicated your life to the study of the law for as long as your father and I have, I suppose it becomes a force of habit, even when you've no more cases to try. It's kind of like a preacher always lookin for inspiration in the scriptures. But your father has an exceptionally keen mind, and, though he doesn't say exactly why he's studyin so much, I imagine he has a good reason, and it's not just out of old habit!"

That seemed to be as much as the gentleman was willing to reveal. "Damn!" thought Angus. But John Bauskett had deftly made it clear that Angus could expect no more.

Mrs. Bauskett entered with a basket filled with some chicken, cornbread, and molasses cookies. She also handed their visitor a tall drink of mint tea. "I hope this will see you safely home, Angus."

Angus took the tea and drank thirstily. He then accepted the basket, but looked uncertain as to whether he was to eat it right away.

"Oh, don't worry, honey, you take that with you. No need to rush and give yourself indigestion! You can have yourself a little picnic on the way home!" Mrs. Bauskett smiled sweetly. In the meantime, her husband had walked over to the tiger maple secretary by the window, sat down, and wrote a response to his colleague. He too folded and sealed the message before handing it to his messenger.

"Well, I put it in writin, as your father requested. But you can certainly tell him I'll be happy to provide any information or insight I can. I'll be by to see him next Thursday, as I have to go over to Williston on some business of my own anyway."

Angus thanked Mr. and Mrs. Bauskett politely, and, picnic basket in hand, mounted his horse and set out for home, frustrated that he knew little more than when he started. Perhaps there was a slight clue, insofar as Mr. Bauskett had promised to offer information and insight, but to what, he had no idea! That was no help at all. He felt bad about going back to James and Michael empty handed, but what else could he do? He would have to stay on the lookout for Mr. Bauskett's visit next week. Maybe he could find out more then.

X

The summer heat bore down on the Willis plantation house like a hammer on an anvil. Even though the lingering twilight dropped the temperature a few degrees, the humidity hung so thick and motionless it was nearly suffocating. Elijah and Amy sat on the upper porch looking out over the property, hoping to catch whatever whisper of a breeze there might be, their skin glistening with perspiration. The children had gone to bed, stripped down to their undergarments, which clung damply to their sweaty backs and thighs. Out on the porch, their parents saw huge clouds forming in the distance, piling higher and higher, glowing with gold and orange highlights at their peaks from the setting sun, and darkening to slate grey on their pendulous bottoms. They seemed pregnant with rain, like a woman whose waters were about to break.

"Elijah?" Amy broke the muggy silence. "Do you think Angus Patterson will really be able to help us?" Her voice sounded tremulous, catching on the last words, and her eyes welled up as if, like the gathering clouds, they might soon release a downpour of their own.

Elijah turned to look at his wife, instantly sensing her anxiety, even though the gloaming light hid the moistness brimming in her eyes.

"I believe he will at least make clear what our options are here, in South Carolina," he said in a calmly reassuring voice. "I know he feels the issue keenly, for we are not the first to come to him for help in seekin justice." He paused for a moment in reflection. "And funny thing is, even though he represented David Martin successfully, he's helped out so many other folks around here that he has the respect of even those who would rather see you and the children in the slave quarters than sittin here with me! That may help, if things heat up over our attempts to live freely as a family."

"Lord, I hope so!" said Amy fervently. "But we can't rely on just one old lawyer to get us out of this! Isn't there anyone else you can think of who feels kindly towards us? When I go into town or to the depot, I can feel people's eyes on me. Not everybody gives me looks, but it feels like some are judgin me and the children, and even you, just lookin' at us! You can see it written all over their faces!" Amy's tone shifted slightly as if disturbed by a sudden recollection.

"There are some who make my flesh crawl when I feel them lookin me over, like they were undressin me, and tryin to figure out whether makin love to a colored woman is any different. But then there are folks like the Wooleys down the road, who've never said an unkind word, or been anything but nice to me and the children!" She paused, as if searching for the words to unburden her heart. "It worries me, cause since I can't tell how many we can really trust around here, it makes me distrustful of just about everyone. It's not a good feelin, or the way I want to live, but I can't help it."

Too hot and sweaty to want to embrace her, but moved by her anxiety, Elijah responded by gently taking her hand in the palm of his, and with the other, tenderly caressing her fingers, their pink tips entwining in his. He looked into her face, darkening as night fell, and lifted her hand to his lips, brushing them softly against her smooth dark skin.

"I know, darlin, I feel the same way, and I don't like it either. We do have to be careful, but I don't think we have to distrust everyone. There are some people of good will who are sympathetic to our situation. I don't know how all this is going to play out, but I do know that my own determination grows daily to find a solution for us all." He clearly felt enslaved by the emotional atmosphere surrounding them, like a force threatening to invade the safety of the plantation, just as he felt engulfed by the suffocating summer heat, and was yearning for a release from both.

"Well, you need to do it soon", Amy said with unexpected urgency, "because it's gonna get a whole lot harder to hide from the folks who disapprove of us!" Elijah took her to mean no more than the fact that rumors were clearly circulating in judgment of their living arrangement, and that would likely lead to increased social pressure on Elijah to disavow her and the children publicly.

There was a rumble of thunder in the distance, promising the relief of a downpour rapidly approaching. "Elijah, honey, I'm not just talkin about the rumors," (she seemed to have read his thoughts) "I'm gonna have another baby!" Amy blurted. Elijah lifted his head from her hand with a start, instantly recognizing the impossibility of hiding the physical evidence of their love from everyone. A flash of lightening lit up the porch, showing the mixture of joy and alarm on his face. "Oh, honey, that's wonderful news!" he said, though his mind instantly felt concern as well.

As if on cue, Amy burst into tears, just as the heavens let loose with a gully-gusher. The air started to move and cool as the storm swept toward the house, and the next flash and crash of lightening and thunder brought the children out of bed, and running to the door to the porch, Clarissa and Julia shrieking. Even the boys looked uneasy. Not wanting to show weakness, they were trying to mask their fear, but shared in their sisters' desire for the comforting company of their parents.

Amy turned to see the children staring at her tear stained face. "Momma, are you cryin?" asked Clarissa Ann.

Wiping her tears from her eyes and cheeks, and forcing a smile, she decided not to share her news with the children just yet, or her concerns for their future. She said, "I'm fine, baby girl, I'm just so glad we're finally getting some rain! Come on out here, children, it's alright. See? Look! God is blessin us with this rain, cause He knew we just couldn't stand this heat anymore!" Elijah and Amy signaled the children to join them.

The thunder was soon receding in the distance, in the way of Summer thunderstorms racing by, but the rain continued with pounding force, playing a syncopated rhythm on the gable roof above them and running off the edges in great sheets. The children came out on the porch, the boys standing at the top of the twin stairs on either side, daring each other to let the rain wash over them, laughing with delight and the sheer joy of relief from the heat. The girls, no longer afraid, reached out in glee to feel the big warm drops splash on their arms and trickle though their fingers.

Suddenly the subtle lemony sweetness of the magnolia blossoms began to intensify, and as the rain diminished, and the earth seemed to exhale in a sigh of gratitude for the blessed refreshment, the intoxicating scent rose up and engulfed them all. The clouds began to disperse, revealing the glowing disk of a full moon, buttery gold and low on the horizon, rising enormous above the long needle pines and filtering through the live oaks, whose dripping garlands of Spanish moss, swaying gently in the dying breeze, cast serpentine shadows that undulated on the wet ground.

In the magic of the moonlight, the seven of them gathered closely together, little Julia climbing onto her mother's lap and Clarissa onto Elijah's. Even the boys, Elder, Elleck and Phillip, drew close and stood behind them, feeling their love for both their mother and for their adoptive father. It was awkward for them to show it, being nearly adolescents who were in that precarious stage caught between yearning for family closeness, and yearning to be independent. But, for now at least, all eyes were on the rising moon, in quiet wonder at its beauty and in intimate communion with each other in this rare shared moment, punctuated by the slow drip, drip, drip of the last of the rainfall spilling off the roof. For that brief interval, there was no slavery, no fear, no resentment, no racial or generational imbalance of power among them. It was one of those experiences whose memory can keep you going when things get rough, and doubt and fear close in on you, almost making you forget what really matters. It was a spell of pure love, and joy, and peace.

After the children were finally put back to bed and all their goodnights were said, Elijah turned to Amy, her honey brown face framed by the brilliant white cotton of the pillow. It was, perhaps, ironic that the cotton surrounding her burnished bronze features like a halo, expressed to Elijah the tension between the source of his material prosperity, and the emotional wealth bestowed on him by her love. "This news about the baby just strengthens my resolve to find a solution. There are others who support us, I am certain of it, though most are reluctant to speak openly, for obvious reasons. Perhaps it's time I shared our thinkin with some of them, discreetly, and build that support somehow. We may need it when it comes time to take definitive action- whatever that turns out to be."

Amy was pensive, rubbing her belly gently as if to reassure her unborn child of a better future. "Be careful, Elijah. They may not be ready to hear it just yet. And we still don't even know what that action will be, do we?"

"No, we don't," Elijah admitted, "but by now old Angus Patterson has had enough time to do a little research, and I promised I'd pay him another visit this week. I don't want to send one of the boys to give him a message, for fear of raisin folks' suspicions – too clear a connection between you and me." Elijah's voice began to thicken as sleep crept in. "But I could send one of my foremen- one who's helped me take the cotton to market, Jason or Julius, perhaps- to alert Angus, and see what day would be most convenient to him for me to come callin."

"That's a good idea" responded Amy sleepily, "Just don't send my brother, Gilbert. There are some in town who know we're related, and we can't risk provokin their curiosity any more than we already have just by bein who we are!"

In the now dark silence, the tree frogs and cicadas outside their bedroom window chanted a loud "Amen," as Elijah and Amy drifted off to sleep at last, and a soft mist arose from the wet ground, luminescent in the moonlight, as if to surround their home with a tenuous cloud of peace.

XI

When John Bauskett arrived at the Patterson's house in Williston on Thursday, he was greeted by Angus, Jr. at the front door.

"Well, hello there, Mr. Bauskett! Nice to see ya again! Pa's been waitin for ya in the parlor, come on in! He's been as excited as a little boy at Christmas about you comin, sir." The younger Patterson, though attempting to be ingratiating, was not exaggerating. His father had, in fact, been dressed and waiting all morning in eager anticipation of the visit.

"Why thank ya son. I don't know as I deserve such a welcome, but I'm glad of it anyway! I've been lookin forward to seein him too. We go back a long way, ya know."

Mr. Bauskett took off his hat and entered the house with the younger Patterson hovering behind him, announcing his arrival to his father, "Pa, Mr. Bauskett's here!"

"Bless my soul John, it's good to see ya!" The elder Patterson was standing in front of his favorite chair in the front parlor, with a broad grin and arms outstretched in welcome. The two men gave each other a brotherly hug with mutual pats on the back in happy reunion. Like a couple of war veterans eager to reminisce about their exploits together in past battles fought, they held each other at arm's length, beaming with satisfaction, relishing the renewal of their long interrupted camaraderie, in the certainty that time had diminished none of their mutual affection and friendship.

"Have a seat, John, please!" The elder Angus gestured to his friend to be seated, as he cautiously lowered himself into his own chair. "I can't tell ya how glad I am to see you again. It's been too long! I hope you'll stay to eat? We've got some slow roasted hog meat, turnip greens, hoe cake, and even peach cobbler and ice cream for dessert!" he enthused. Angus Sr. was positively animated, and before John could even respond, turned to the younger Patterson and said, "Son, go tell Mary to set another place at the table for our midday dinner!"

John couldn't help but smile, seeing the question of staying had been entirely rhetorical, for the foregone conclusion was that he had no choice. He was happy to acquiesce to the invitation, but couldn't resist nudging his old friend. "You don't mean to tell me you wanted me to come all the way over here just to see how your Mary's cookin compared to my wife's, do ya? You know my loyalties, not to mention my marriage vows, will always require a preference for hers!" He laughed mischievously.

Angus retorted, "Why that's most un-lawyerly of ya, John! I thought you'd be bound by your commitment to justice to examine the evidence thoroughly before comin to judgment! However, I'll acknowledge you may be obliged to a Fifth Amendment plea of *no lo contendere* on the subject of preferred cuisine, for the sake of domestic tranquility!" Both men were thoroughly enjoying their banter, but Angus then became more serious. "But you are also quite right, I did not invite ya here just to enjoy the conviviality of breakin bread together again after such a lengthy respite! I am truly most eager to hear your views on the legal matters I mentioned in my letter to ya." Once again Angus, Sr. applied restraint to his elliptical communications in his son's presence, to the younger Patterson's annoyance, who by now had returned to the foyer from delivering the message to the kitchen to prepare an extra setting for dinner.

"Mary said alright, Pa." Angus Jr. interjected, "She told me to tell ya, dinner'll be ready at one." Angus nodded, appreciatively.

"Thank ya, son. You go on now. Mr. Bauskett and I have some important matters to attend to, and I don't want to be disturbed!"

The younger Patterson, feeling stung by his father's dismissiveness, excused himself from their company and left them in the parlor to talk, feeling he had been treated like a child rather than like the man he already was. Why couldn't his father ever treat him more as an adult? Why wouldn't he ever share much of his legal knowledge? Was he so sure his son would not be able to understand? His father's all absorbing obsession with the law had often made him distant. It had driven his mother to distraction, and, Angus thought bitterly, his father's indiscriminate choice of clients and unpopular causes maybe even contributed to driving her to an early grave! Brooding on his conflicted relationship with his father, whom he genuinely loved, but whose brilliance often left him feeling inadequate, he was yearning for someone, at least, to take him more seriously. Never given to study, and well enough to do that work was not really a necessity, the younger Patterson was a bit adrift, in search of an identity that defined him as more than just "the lawyer's boy."

Angus, Jr.'s resentment made his thoughts turn to the Willis brothers. At least they seemed to understand him. He knew they shared a kindred feeling in regards to their elders. He repressed the urge to go find them straight away to vent his frustrations, realizing it would be better if he could first manage to glean some information about his father's doings, and whatever connection they had with Elijah Willis. He still wasn't sure that John Bauskett's visit and Elijah's were related, but knew for certain that his father seemed equally intent on both. Not being totally bereft of any inheritance of his father's intellect or deductive reasoning, he presumed both Elijah and Mr. Bauskett were consulting with his father for the same reason. He just needed proof.

The younger Patterson heard his father in the parlor say to his guest, "John, I hate to trouble ya, but would you please shut the parlor door?" He heard Mr. Bauskett stand up and start toward the door, and quickly realized his father knew he was still lingering in the hallway. So as not to embarrass himself, he quietly walked down the corridor toward the dining room, wanting to appear like he was on some logical errand of preparation for their meal, rather than hoping to eavesdrop on their conversation. He recognized that mealtime would be his only possible opportunity to prompt any useful hints from either his father or Mr. Bauskett, so he went on to the kitchen and out into the back yard to think about how he might do so.

Back in the parlor, Angus Sr. and John Bauskett were engrossed in conversation, keeping their voices low as they dissected the complex history of manumission in general, and the possible strategies that might lead to a solution for Elijah Willis and his family, in particular.

"What have you found, my friend?" asked Angus, with the eagerness of a hound dog catching a scent.

"I was able to do some investigation of my own after I received your letter, Angus," announced Bauskett. "The issue has clearly been buildin in the past thirty years. Even before you represented David Martin, back in '27, William Farr over in Union had petitioned for emancipation back in '23; Henry Ravnel, over in Berkely District, as his uncle Paul's executor, successfully emancipated Else and her children, Beck, Harry, John, James, and Nancy, as well as Beck's child, William;" Bauskett's tone became slightly somber, "But George Bellinger, of Colleton, was unsuccessful in his attempt to emancipate three of his infant slaves. And I myself represented William Dunn right over in Barnwell, but we were unfortunately also unsuccessful in emancipatin his mulato son, William."

He paused, as if suddenly remembering an important point to add. "Now, we're not just talkin about white planters here, either! There was a Jeremiah Dickey, a free black, who got married and then bought his wife's daughter, Jinsey, by her former master, hoping to emancipate her. There's not a very encouragin track record of success, either in the efforts at emancipation, or even the bequest of property- especially in more recent years! In fact, the Act of 1841 has negated the validity of emancipations achieved outside South Carolina for slaves still livin' in this State- thanks in part to your success with David Martin!" He fell silent for a moment, stroking his chin pensively, before concluding, "I'm afraid I see no easy path for your friend Mr. Willis and his family."

Angus was discouraged, but not defeated. "Well, John, I've already said as much to him myself, though I admit I was hopin, with your knowledge of such cases being a bit more current than mine, you might have found some chink in the wall that some of our South Carolinian brethren have been buildin around this issue, that might allow us to help my friend dig his family's way out to freedom!" His passion for justice overcoming his disappointment, he offered, "Well, there's more than one way to tree a 'possum. We're just gonna have to look a little further afield for the solution, that's all."

John Bauskett, like his senior colleague, was not one to give up lightly. They agreed they would each endeavor to look into the policies of neighboring states, and those North of the Mason-Dixon Line, or West of Appalachia as well. They were bound together in their certainty that there had to be a legal way for Elijah to achieve his goal of both emancipation and inheritance for Amy and her children. Like soldiers on campaign, they each pledged to pursue their respective missions of recognizance, and report back to headquarters as soon as possible. And on that note, the dinner bell rang, summoning them to the dining room.

Angus presided at the head of a handsome Sheraton mahogany dining table with brass clawed feet supporting gracefully turned pedestals at either end. The sideboard sported a pair of heavy silver candelabra and a large, pale green porcelain soup tureen, decorated with delicate floral arabesques in rose, red, yellow, dark green and lavender. On the damask draped table, elegant china and gleaming silver set the places for three diners. In the center, on a silver platter, sat a piping hot mound of succulent pork, framed with baked apples, spiked with cloves. Around this savory centerpiece were ranged various bowls of vegetables, breads, and condiments. It was truly a feast. The elder Patterson had spared no effort for his guest, for since his wife had died, it was not often he had the opportunity to entertain friends. As they took their seats they were joined by Angus Jr., who had come in from the garden, out back. He was attempting to look nonchalant, but was eagerly awaiting his chance to engage his elders in any conversation that might reveal something of the object of their colloquy. After grace was said, and his father and their guest had been served, he spoke up.

"Well, Pa, did you and Mr. Bauskett settle the legal problems of the great State of South Carolina?" Angus Jr. asked playfully, helping himself to a heaping serving of the pork.

"Well, son, I doubt our conversation has settled much of anything, I wish it were that easy! But we certainly did have an enjoyable time in stimulatin conversation, didn't we John?" The elder Patterson turned to his friend with a wink.

"Yes indeed, Angus." John replied. "You know son," he said, turning to the younger Patterson, "Stimulatin conversation, and the opportunity to plumb the depths of justice, are mother's milk to us lawyers, and I know no one better than your father with whom to engage in such discussion!"

The younger Patterson was sensing their evasion, and grew restive. His impatience getting the better of him, he responded, "Well, I sure wish that he'd share his insight with me sometime!" Meaning to sound light-hearted, instead he came across as sounding petulant.

"Now, son, you know ya could ask me anything, and I'd do my best to respond," said his father, placatingly. "It's just that ya've never really seemed to show any interest in my work, so I figured it best not to impose it on ya!"

"Well, Pa, every time I ask you anything, like when Mr. Willis came last week and I wanted to know what it was all about, you just told me that attorney-client privilege didn't permit ya to tell me!" he said with a bit of a whine.

"And it doesn't!" snapped his father emphatically, pounding his hand on the dinner table and causing the water glasses to tremble. There was a brief intimidating silence, as Angus Jr. shifted uncomfortably in his chair, feeling bullied by his father. Bristling at first, the elder Patterson then softened his tone and continued, "There's a difference, son, between askin me a question about the law- which I would happily share with ya any time- and askin me a question about someone else's business that doesn't concern you, nor are ya entitled to know."

His father was now feeling a bit testy, seeing that his son's mention of Elijah made it clear he was more interested than he ought to be in the Willis's issues. Duly forewarned, he shot his guest a quick glance of alert, and sought to defuse the tensions at the dinner table.

"Son, when I was studying law at the College of William and Mary, Judge Wyeth, up in Virginia, once commented to me that part of bein a good layer was knowing how to ask a question in such a way as to get the kind of response you wanted. In my experience, that has proved to be sage advice, for many a trial has hung on the issue not only of what questions were asked, but how they were put to a witness or a jury. So I pass that advice on to you, and hope you'll take it to heart."

The younger Patterson was temporarily taken aback. On the one hand, his father was actually sharing something of potentially great importance with him- and he was grateful to finally be permitted access to his father's considerable wisdom. On the other hand, it still felt like he was being shut off from the information he was so eager to discover.

At this point, John Bauskett sensed the direction in which the current might lead them, if left unchecked. Angus Sr.'s glance of alert when the younger Patterson had mentioned Elijah Willis had not been lost on him. He had instantly understood the warning. Like a riverboat captain having the pilot steer clear of sunken logs or hidden shoals, the two elders sought to guide the conversation in a safer direction, and avoid running aground.

"That's good advice, son, your Pa is absolutely right! It reminds me of a case of mine years ago, when I was a young lawyer comin up. I was defendin a client for allegedly stealin a neighbor's chicken." Like all Southerners worthy of the name, Bauskett loved to tell a good story. "Now, the prosecution was tryin to maintain that findin chicken feathers in my client's yard was clear and convincin proof of him havin taken the chicken, whose wings, he was certain, had flapped so much in protest, that it left a trail of evidence leadin straight to the alleged culprit's kitchen door!

"That's when it struck me, that rather than askin my client if he had stolen the chicken, I could ask him more effectively if he himself had any chickens, and whether they occasionally molted, or fought, and dropped feathers in his yard. I knew perfectly well that he did have." Bauskett looked as if he was stating the obvious to a jury who would immediately grasp its truth, "As anyone who has ever owned or seen chickens knows, the answer was obviously 'yes.' Since the neighbor had no other evidence to offer in proof of the alleged theft, the jury had to rule the accusations unsubstantiated, on the grounds of the scantiest of circumstantial evidence!" After delivering this triumphal judicial coup de grace, Bauskett demurred with a healthy dose of self-deprecation and amusement at the arrogance of his youth, "I, of course, bein young and inexperienced, thought I had achieved a historic victory in the halls of justice!" Angus Sr. laughed heartily, both at the aptness of the story, and at the success of his friend's adroit intervention to deflect his son from pressing the Willis matter any further.

Clearly defeated in his efforts for the time being, the younger Patterson was left to ponder the implications of his father and Mr. Bauskett's advice. He was determined to find a way to apply it to his quest for information about what he and James and Michael deemed Elijah Willis's suspicious behavior, and turn the tables on his father for once as well!

XII

There were around fifty slaves living on the Willis plantation. As on other plantations, there was a certain multi-layered hierarchy among them, between men and women, between house slaves and field hands, skilled and unskilled. What made the situation a little different from most other plantations, of course, was that, on the Willis plantation, the house slaves were related to the master, and some of the field hands were related to the house slaves.

This was a reality that alternately helped and hindered the cohesive functioning of the work force, and created simultaneously a trust and an intermittent jealousy between the residents of the Willis plantation. Some of the slaves, who had grown up on the plantation, resented Amy and her family, who were more recent arrivals, yet had risen quickly to the top of the social hierarchy of the plantation's slaves. On the other hand, Elijah's love for Amy and her family had a beneficent effect on the treatment of all the slaves, for Amy had become the virtual overseer of the entire estate. She could be trusted to advocate for their needs to her husband, diminishing the resentment natural to being enslaved. Momma Celia, less authoritarian than her daughter, nevertheless also commanded the respect of the other slaves, not only by her position of privilege in the big house, but by her practical wisdom in the ways of both slaves and whites. Yet Amy's brother Gilbert lived with his family among the others in the slave quarters.

Amy was not the first woman in her family to have had children with her white master, for she and her brother were themselves the result of a similar liaison between Momma Celia and William Kirkland. Momma Celia knew only too well what slave owners who loved their slaves were up against, and that not all would make the same choice to support their families that Elijah was making. Her former master, William Kirkland, was married to a loveless white woman, and had not been able to face the social pressures against him for loving Celia. Divorcing a white wife and remarrying to a colored one was both unthinkable and illegal. He found the best solution was to sell Celia and her children, rather than live with his shame and discomfort.

He did so under the pretense that hard times had befallen him, obliging him to sell off some of his property. Only a few realized that the hard times were, in fact, the pressure put on him by his wife and his white relations- not by any economic difficulties, given the booming cotton business. The property he had to sell to stave off the crisis was Celia and her family, not his land. Momma Celia didn't talk about it much, but her pain at the betrayal ran deep, and she struggled continually between her desire to trust Elijah, and her mistrust born of the disillusionment she had suffered at William Kirkland's hands. At least he had the decency to sell them to an owner who was kind to his slaves, saved Amy from an abusive husband by selling him apart from the rest, and had let Celia and her children and grandchildren remain in the same familiar area that had always been home.

If "a touch of the tar brush" tainted the mixed race children of white planters in white society, its corollary was that it ironically enhanced their status within the slave community. The lighter skinned slaves generally had higher status on the plantation, and were treated marginally better in the outside community as well. Of course, things were not so carefully stratified in South Carolina as they were in New Orleans, with their Creole hierarchy of mulatos, quadroons and octoons, but Amy and Gilbert did have an inherent advantage due to their genetic mix that the darker slaves on the plantation did not. This advantage was not limited to those in service in their master's house either. Gilbert, though not living in the main house, was, like Amy, not only seen and respected by the other slaves as favored, but was intelligent, hardworking, and a naturally good leader.

Elijah initially had set him as a foreman over the field hands working the cotton fields. It was back breaking work, tore up your hands til they bled at harvest time, but Gilbert was skillful in getting his crew to work with a minimum of complaining, and Elijah's plantation routinely got their crop in ahead of the others, demanding the highest price. He also had a talent for analyzing and developing news strains of cotton. This was a source of pride for everyone on the plantation.

In addition to cotton, Elijah had a substantial business in timber, with his own lumber mill, and another entire plantation dedicated to providing lumber from his stands of yellow and long needle pine for the rapid growth of the nation. He shipped lumber both North and West on the railroad, rafting timbers down river, and sending the sawn planks by train, allowing for a steady income even when the cotton was not in season.

Elijah was not a mean-spirited master. He rewarded his slaves' productivity generously with comfortable living quarters, knowing full well that people work better when they feel appreciated than when they feel threatened. They also work better when not overworked- a gang working together could get more done in a day than individuals working unorganized could do in a week. So Elijah worked them hard, but for shorter periods, and let them rest. Moreover, given their consistent success at harvest time, his slaves clearly earned such benefits. Elijah fed and housed them well, cared for them when they were sick, and was supportive of them socializing and having time for rest and relaxation. The slaves respected him, not so much out of fear because he owned them, (though that was inevitably in their minds), but because he didn't lord his ownership over them, and treated them as nearly as equals as any white man dared in South Carolina. The fact that he seldom asked of them anything he himself would not join with them in doing won him a grudging admiration from even those slaves who chafed hardest under the burden of their bondage. He was not a master prone to using the whip as a work incentive- for he knew too well the strains his slaves bore, and respected them for their efforts. They in turn rewarded him with a certain pride of team spirit and willingness to work, as both their accepted lot in life, and their obligation.

So life for the slaves on the Willis plantation, though socially rather complicated, and emotionally always overshadowed by the loathsomeness of being in permanent bondage, was no more physically painful than for many whites struggling to make a living in town, or on their own small farms. There was a tacit recognition of this among many of the working class whites, and the slaves from other plantations, and even the few free blacks in town, whose paths would cross in the course of engaging in the routine activities of local commerce- the buying and selling of supplies, bringing crops to market or to the train depot for shipment elsewhere, even the purchase and breeding of livestock.

For not all coloreds were nameless chattels in the community. As in any small town, people got to know one another, and greeted each other by name. Sometimes, at market, or major social events between planters, where some of their slaves would accompany their masters as a retinue charged with the performance of essential tasks, slaves from neighboring plantations would have an opportunity to meet and talk with each other, as well. And sometimes, although separated by transfer of ownership by gift or sale, family members even lived and worked on neighboring plantations for different owners.

This complex reality, of course, added another dimension to the challenges Elijah and Amy faced. Could they not only keep up the charade of discretion in the presence of whites, but also control the tongues of the other slaves from wagging indiscretions about their lifestyle and family make-up to the slaves of other planters, or to the tradesfolk in town? Both Amy and Momma Celia had spoken to Gilbert to keep a sharp eye and ear open for any such rumors spreading around the slave quarters. As an incentive, Amy hinted to the other slaves that compliance might be eventually rewarded by being included in a future emancipation. Of course, she didn't immediately tell Elijah of this, thinking it best to bring him to it gently, almost as if he had come to that commitment of his own free will, as the logical and inevitable extension of his plans to liberate those in his immediate household.

Momma Celia was not naïve enough to think that, despite their best intentions, word would not get out about Elijah and Amy's children, especially since Amy often had to go into town or the depot on her husband's business, and could not forever hide her pregnancy. But she was hoping they could prevent Elijah's legal inquiries and estate planning from being discovered by anyone outside the main house, at least until there was a definitive plan in place. When she learned that Amy had hinted at possible emancipation for the other slaves, Momma Celia was alarmed, and angry!

"Amy, child, now why'd you go sayin somethin like that in the slave quarters? Ya'll know the one thing even more likely to cause talk than a master beatin his slaves is a master thinkin about freein em! Do you honestly think everybody on the plantation is gonna be able to keep they mouths shut after danglin that temptin bait over them?" She lowered her head and looked at her daughter through knitted eyebrows, accentuating her reprimand with the recitation of a folksy maxim, "Don't you know that even the smartest catfish will go for a hook if he's hungry enough? Shoot, if anyone here lets some fool on a neighborin plantation know about this, it'll expose us, and stir up such a ruckus, Mister Elijah won't even know what hit him! They'll be all over him like flies on manure!" As if the very thought of it was too much to bear, she added, "So you'd best be sure you make it clear in the slave quarters there will be a severe punishment to anyone who lets word leak out of this plantation! And if Mister Elijah won't beat em for it, I'll make sure that Gilbert will!" Momma Celia was exasperated. Having been stung so badly by disillusionment herself, she didn't want to see history repeat itself, either for her family, or for any of the others slaves.

"Oh Lord, Momma, I never even thought of that!" said Amy, with a remorseful shock of realization. "I thought it would give them all incentive to keep the secret, not share it!" Amy's voice was tinged with both regret for her ill-considered message, and sudden anxiety about what its unintended consequences might be. "I'll talk to Gilbert and the others right away, before this has a chance to get out of hand!"

Recognizing the fear motivating her daughter, and satisfied she had driven the message home, Momma Celia returned to her cooking, muttering, "Child shoulda knowed better! I ain't been through all I been through to raise no fool!"

Meanwhile, Amy realized her plan to ease Elijah into the idea of emancipating all his slaves might backfire if she did not act swiftly. She decided that, rather than take a chance that he might hear talk among the slaves on his own, and feel manipulated by her, it would be better for her to just come clean with him, and tell him the truth. She resolved to speak to him as soon as he came in from the fields. She was also eager to hear whether he had sent a message to Angus Patterson about meeting with him again. She hoped he'd remembered to tell Jason to bring an answer back from the old man himself because, having heard Elijah's account of the younger Patterson, she shuddered at the thought that his father might send that son of his to deliver it, even though she was pretty well persuaded the elder Patterson was smart enough not to do that.

XIII

Amy went over to the slave quarters to find her brother, but he was out in the fields working. She found Phillip feeding the chickens, and told him to go find his uncle and tell him she needed to talk to him right away. Knowing it would take a while for Phillip to deliver the message and return with his uncle Gilbert, Amy returned to the main house, worried about what she might have set into play. There was nothing she could do at this point, so she decided she would just have to face the consequences as best she could. She wasn't sure which worried her more though, the possibility of slaves' gossip reaching beyond the confines of the plantation, or Elijah's possible upset that she may have compounded their situation and be trying to obligate him to free all his slaves, rather than just his immediate family.

When Phillip finally found Gilbert, he was a goodly distance from the house. His uncle was examining the cotton, comparing the growth of the four different varieties they had planted- Louisiana Creole black seed cotton, Sea Island cotton, Tennessee green seed cotton, and some new Mexican black seed cotton that was very promising. Gilbert was making careful notations in a large cloth-bound ledger provided by the enterprising Mr. Thomas Affleck-The Affleck Plantation Journal and Account Book- designed for just such a purpose and sold to planters as a business aid. Elijah was mindful that developing better, more productive strains was crucial to his success, and was working on breeding his own variety that would combine high yield of Creole black seed with the Tennessee green seed's ease of ginning, the Sea Island's long fiber, and the Mexican's resistance to disease and ease of picking.

Elijah kept careful track of his plantings, yields, varieties, cross breeding, and the volume picked per day per slave at harvest time. The ledger was laid out with the names of all his pickers listed, the pounds picked per day and per week at harvest, as well as all his annotations about varietal yields, characteristics, and disease or pest resistance. He had already succeeded in doubling the yield per picker by his attention to the merits of different varietals, as well as by organizing pickers into gangs. He also knew that, once his fields were fertilized with manure and planted, the work gang's efficiency at hoeing weeds and keeping the soil open for the cotton roots to grow better was key to continuing to produce a bumper crop and to bringing it in to market first.

He relied on Gilbert to keep the crew in line. The sad truth was, it was easier to plant and grow cotton than harvest it- and without his slave gangs working effectively, there's no way he could bring in anything like the same yields. He didn't think he could have done it with freedman paid labor, much less afford to do it! As it was, even with slave labor, he was having a hard time keeping up with the steadily increasing demand for cotton.

"Uncle Gilbert! Uncle Gilbert!" called Phillip, "Momma says she needs to talk to ya right away! She's waitin for ya over in the big house!" Phillip was breathless from running to find his uncle.

Gilbert was annoyed. He could ill afford to stop his work. But he also knew his sister was not likely to send a message out to him unless it was really urgent. Not wanting to take his annoyance out on his nephew, whom he loved, he dipped a copper dipper into a bucket of fresh water nearby and gave it to Phillip to drink. "Alright, son, tell your Momma I'll be along directly. I just need to make sure Julius understands how to fill out this ledger." He called to Julius, his second in command, to come over from supervising the field hands hoeing, and explained what observations needed to be written down, and where to write them in the ledger. Julius could read and write, but not too well, so Gilbert wanted to be sure he knew what to do before he left. Phillip, meanwhile, ran back to the house to let his mother know the message had been delivered.

Some of the field hands by now had stopped hoeing, curious as to what was going on that would make Mr. Gilbert rush off toward the plantation house in the middle of work. Leaning on their hoes, they were grumbling in the heat.

"Lord, I'm sick and tired of workin in these cotton fields!" said one.

Another agreed, saying, "My back hurts from bendin, an hoein these damn weeds. My hands are raw from pullin em!"

A third piped up, "There's gotta be a better life than this! I heard Miss Amy say we might be freed if we keep our mouths shut and don't tell nobody bout her and Mister Elijah!"

"That'll be the day!" said the first. "Mister Elijah's a good master and all, they's no denyin that. But you think he's gonna let us all go free, when he needs us to work his fields so he can make all that money? You a fool if ya believe that!"

Some of the others muttered an "Amen!"

Gilbert stepped in, "Alright ya'll, that's enough talk, now! Ya'll got work to do! Julius- I'm puttin you in charge til I get back. I gotta go over to the plantation house for a bit, and I need ya to keep the gang workin while I'm gone. And Julius, make sure they doin it right, will ya?"

"Alright, Gilbert, you go on then. I'll handle this here." Julius replied, telling the leader of the work gang to set the pace with a field holler, urging them back to work, as Gilbert wiped his hands on his trousers. Gilbert knew he could rely on Julius, so he headed off toward the main house.

When he got to the plantation house, Amy was waiting for him in the kitchen. Gilbert came on in, still a little annoyed at being called in from the middle of work in the fields, but eager to know why. "What's going on Amy? Phillip said ya needed to see me right away!"

Momma Celia interrupted, "Son, is that how I raised you, to come waltzin into my kitchen without so much as a 'hello,' or 'Mornin Momma?' Come on over here and give me some sugar!" Six foot four and over two hundred pounds of muscle, Gilbert suddenly looked like a little boy embarrassed by his mother. "Yes ma'am, I mean no ma'am, I mean, Mornin, Momma!" he stammered. He bent down and gave his mother a kiss on the cheek. Mollified, Momma Celia gave her son a hug and then dismissed him to talk with Amy, saying "Go on now. Amy got somethin important to tell ya- and ya'll'd best listen careful and take it serious, or you'll answer to me!"

Duly alerted, and no longer bashful, Gilbert reassured his mother, "Yes'm. If it's all that important, you can count on me to do whatever's needed."

"I know I can, baby, and I do. This touches all of us, and we're gonna have to rely on you to hep, if we're gonna get through what lies ahead." Momma Celia offered no more, but everybody knew that even when she seemed to be focused on her cooking, she had the ears of a bat, and didn't miss a thing.

Amy spoke up with urgency in her voice. "Gilbert, I may have done a terrible thing, and I need you to help make sure whatever damage I've done goes no further than this plantation!"

"What you talkin about, Amy? What kinda damage could you have done? You run this place better than any white person I know around here- except for Mister Elijah. The slaves respect ya, Mister Elijah loves ya. And we all need ya!" Gilbert was unabashed in his admiration for his sister.

"Well, ya know, Elijah's tryin to figure a way to free us, and to leave us this plantation when he's gone? But he doesn't want anybody- I mean NOBODY but NOBODY- knowin about his plans too soon, cause things're heatin up around here in terms of the white folks' attitudes about freein slaves, or allowin em to own anything!" She paused, as if to let the message sink in.

"Honey, Elijah and I're gonna have another baby, and Elijah's already had a couple a visitors- that Dr. Guignard and Mr. Matthews- come to tell him to send us all back to the slave quarters 'where we belong' and save his reputation!" She blurted this last word out like Elijah's reputation was somehow tainted, not by her, but by the racist attitudes of the whites that presumed to care so much about it.

"It's gettin harder and harder to play slave and master instead of husband and wife! And each new child makes it harder still, cause it's not difficult to see, lookin at the children, who their father is!" She smiled affectionately at the recollection of their two beautiful daughters, in spite of herself. "We realized, though, that it's not just a matter of stoppin the white gossips around town. We may have just as big a problem with the black ones! Momma says if any slave lets word leak out of Elijah's plans, there'll be Hell to pay!"

Gilbert took all this in, but still didn't quite connect it to any damage Amy had done. "I know you're right, Amy, but I don't see how you've done any damage- unless ya're thinkin white, and believe that you lovin Mister Elijah has made matters worse. Don't look that way to me- we're all livin better because of him."

"It's not because I love him, Gilbert, it's because I so want us all to be free that I told some of the other slaves to keep quiet about us here when they're in town, or when they see other slaves, to help keep us all safe- and then stupidly thought to say that if they did, they might get freed too! Momma pointed out that was a sure fire recipe for people to talk!"

Momma Celia chimed in, "What I *said* was, 'You know the one thing even more likely to cause talk than a master beatin his slaves is a master thinkin bout freein em!'" She leveled her gaze on her son, and continued sternly, leaving no room whatsoever for any doubt as to her demand for his compliance, "An I told Amy you gotta make sure nobody talks outside this plantation, or they'll get beat within an inch of they life- and if Mister Elijah won't beat em, you will! Last thing we need right now is some fool openin his mouth and stirrin up rumors bout plans on the Willis Plantation! Things're hot enough as is without pourin no oil on that fire!"

Gilbert shifted uncomfortably, realizing for himself what the potential dangers might be to them all. He remembered the grumbling comments overheard just before coming over to the plantation house, even though the offer of freedom had not been taken seriously by everyone, given Elijah's reliance on his slave labor for his prosperity. He was reluctant to even mention the slaves' comments, for fear of upsetting both his mother and sister, as well as opening himself up to being commissioned as the enforcer of discipline on a level he did not relish and would rather avoid. But he also knew the danger was real, and that avoidance was not an option, if they didn't want all Hell to break loose in Barnwell District.

He heaved a sigh, nodding his acquiescence, and said, "I'll see to it. There are a few talkin about what you said already, but most don't actually believe it. Still, it's not worth takin any chances. I'll make it clear to everyone that if they want to stay on this plantation, freedom or no, instead of bein sold off somewhere, they'd best keep quiet as a tomb about all this!" As if to further reassure them, he added, "I'll tell Jason when he gets back from deliverin Mister Elijah's message to Mr. Patterson too- though Jason's no fool, and already has sense enough not to let on to anything without Mister Elijah's say so!"

Amy's anxiety was not fully assuaged- especially when Gilbert admitted some of the slaves had been talking about her comment of possible emancipation. But there as nothing for it but for the whole family to be vigilant, and to trust God that things would work out somehow. Momma Celia, at least, seemed satisfied for the moment that Gilbert would be able to keep things in check.

"Well, alright then. You'd best get to it, b'fo they start talkin any more than they already have. And if you hear anything troublesome, you let me know right away, hear?!" Momma Celia knew her daughter was worried, and with quiet but firm maternal authority, intervened on her behalf. "We'll face whatever comes, but it'd sho hep to have any warnin possible, so we be ready!"

"Yes, ma'am." Gilbert promised. He leaned down and gave his mother a kiss good-bye, before heading back out toward the fields. As he walked away in the bright morning sunlight, the midday heat fast approaching, sweat ran down his chest and back in rivulets, making his shirt stick to him like a second skin. He moved with the supple muscularity of a black panther. Momma Celia looked out the kitchen window, admiring her son, and feeling proud she had borne such a big, fine, strapping man.

She turned to Amy and said, "Well, what's done is done, and what's said is said. We all in this together now! I know you worried, but as God is my witness, we gonna do whatever it takes, and we gonna be alright. But you gonna have to tell Mister Elijah, now, 'cause he needs to know, and be prepared!"

"Yes, Momma." Amy responded, not knowing what else to say, but she knew the knot in her stomach was not the baby in her womb. She was dreading facing Elijah and telling him the truth- not only about her ill-considered comment to the slaves, but the reality that she was no longer content to simply hope for her family's emancipation. With each passing day she felt more strongly that the institution of slavery itself was simply unacceptable, and something had to be done to free all those they could. She hoped that Elijah would see it that way too, but she knew that his own vested interests made him conflicted in facing this truth, and accepting it would put him and his business at risk.

As she went to the study to go over the plantation accounts while waiting for her husband's return, she prayed fervently to herself "Lord, give me strength, and show me the way! We can't just try to free the family, and let everybody else stay enslaved! You teach us to love one another- not to be selfish. How can I pray for my husband's help, only for me and my family? Please help me to help him understand!"

XIV

Elijah came in late for midday dinner, wiping the sweat from his forehead and neck with a handkerchief. After washing up, he came to the dining room and sat down at the head of the table just as Amy and Momma Celia came in carrying food from the kitchen. The children had already been fed and were off doing their chores.

"Sit down, ya'll." Elijah said, in a calm but firm voice. Unaccustomed to sitting in the dining room, Momma Celia immediately picked up on the signal that Elijah had something important to say. Different as Mister Elijah was from other white men she'd known, a lifetime of slavery made her antsy at even the thought of sitting down at a white man's table, especially outside the safety of her kitchen. Just didn't seem right. Amy looked at her anxiously, but her mother simply took her seat as she was told, and waited to hear what it was Elijah needed to communicate. Amy meekly followed suit, still wrestling with her uneasiness about having to come clean with Elijah about her comment to the other slaves.

"Jason came back from deliverin my message to Angus Patterson- he found me over by the creek where we planted that new Mexican black seed. He tells me Angus wants to see me right away, and that he allowed as how he'd been talkin to another lawyer friend of his over in Barnwell about the questions I asked him." The two women shifted expectantly in their seats, wondering whether there was something more he wanted to say, and suddenly anxious that the issue was already spreading beyond Williston, even if in confidential communications between lawyers. "So I'll be headin over to Williston after dinner. Angus didn't want to say anything more than that to Jason- he always has been careful that way- so I don't make much of his silence. But Jason said he got the feelin the old man wanted to say more."

Momma Celia looked at her daughter meaningfully, clearly signaling her with a slight nod and tilt of her head in Elijah's direction, not to avoid the issue of talking to her husband. He needed to know before he left for Williston, as it might make a difference to his discussions with Angus. Amy looked back at her mother, uncertain. Elijah picked up on the silent signaling and said, "What's goin on, you two? Is there somethin I ought to know about?"

Amy cleared her throat nervously. Momma Celia started to excuse herself, but Elijah signaled her to stay, saying, "Momma Celia, you're part of this family too. If Amy's got something to say, chances are it affects you as much as it does me, so there's no point in you leavin the table, just to put your ear to the door anyway." Elijah was no fool, and knew perfectly well that house slaves had a talent for eavesdropping on their master's business. In fact, it was almost a silent agreement on which the master depended, an integral part of making sure everything ran smoothly with the confidence that the slaves knew what was going on, and were prepared to deal with it. Not waiting for a response from Momma Celia, he turned to Amy and said, matter-of-factly, "So, sugar, what's got you worked up? Is it the baby? Or somebody makin comments about us? Or what?"

Amy couldn't stand it any longer, and the floodgate of her guilt burst with a rush of apologies. "Elijah, honey, please don't be mad at me, but I may have done somethin real stupid, and I feel awful about it, but I've already taken care of it, and Gilbert's gonna make sure it stays under control!"

Needless to say, Elijah had no clue as to the actual nature of her supposed crime. Not unlike Gilbert's reaction earlier, he responded, "What in heaven's name are you talkin about? You're the smartest woman I know. What could you possibly have done that was so stupid that it gets ya'll this riled up?"

Amy then recovered herself, realizing that the man she loved would not hate or reject her for the uncomfortable truth- and that was one of the many reasons she had come to love him so. She then proceeded to explain her slip to the other slaves, Momma Celia's reprimand, and Gilbert's revelation that some of the slaves were already talking about it. She also reiterated Gilbert's promise to keep the slaves in line, and even Momma Celia's insistence that anyone who opens their mouth about this outside the plantation will be beaten severely. Elijah listened pensively, without interrupting, though he looked uncomfortable and furrowed his brow at the threat of beatings. Finally he spoke up.

Much to Amy and Momma Celia's surprise and relief, he said, "Well, darlin, I'm glad you told me before I left for Angus Patterson's place. Don't beat yourself up for this- it doesn't surprise me. Probably wasn't the wisest choice you could have made, but the truth is, it was bound to come out sooner or later, and maybe it's better it come out now, so we have time to deal with it before things come to a head." He smiled at her affectionately and reassuringly, "I didn't fall in love with you because you were perfect, and besides, I've made my own share of ill-considered remarks too. I let on to Reason and Ary Wooley the other day that I wished I could find a way to stay prosperous and end slavery at the same time.

"Maybe it's God's way of keepin us humble, or maybe it's His way of leadin us to the truth He said would set us all free!" he said with an unexpected ring of veracity. "After all, it's not like the thought has never occurred to me. How could I love you, and be comfortable keeping everybody else enslaved? Maybe that worked for Mr. Jefferson up in Virginia, but I admit I'm feelin more and more conflicted about it myself every day. I'm just not clear yet on what the solution to the problem is," He looked almost apologetically from his wife to his mother-in-law, "cause every one I can come up with involves loss as well as gain- and both may involve a considerable amount of pain before we're done!"

Amy felt like the weight of the world had lifted from her shoulders, and Momma Celia sat back in admiration, realizing how different Elijah really was from William Kirkland, who had let social conformity and self-protection trump the truth of what he claimed his feelings were.

Not one to indulge over-long in sentiment, Elijah said, "Well, we gonna eat, or just watch the food get cold? Come on then, pass me the greens!" The intrusion of the ordinary had a grounding effect on all three of them, and they proceeded to eat dinner without belaboring the issue further. The conversation turned to the daily issues of the plantation- the crops, the livestock, the weather. Knowing her husband, however, Amy was certain this was not the end of the conversation, but the beginning of a more serious dialogue about how to confront the burning reality. It was not just the servitude of her family that was untenable, but the very system and beliefs that made that servitude possible in the first place. Neither she nor Elijah fully realized that they were, in fact, part of a sea change sweeping the nation that would turn their Southern conventions on their heads, and at great cost and pain, reshape both their lives and their whole society drastically. They, and everyone else in Barnwell District, were on the long road to that transformation, whether consciously and willingly or not. In any event, from where they sat, it already looked like the journey that lay ahead would most likely be a bumpy one.

XV

Elijah once again tied up Beauty in front of the home of Angus Patterson. He had chosen to go by a different route this time, avoiding his nephew's store, and hoped that the younger Patterson would be out and about somewhere, so as not to be able to spy on him. He didn't like feeling so secretive, but he knew that caution was of the utmost importance in what appeared to be an increasingly volatile situation.

As luck would have it, Angus Jr. was, in fact, away. The door was answered by Mary, the Pattersons' colored housekeeper. She seemed to be expecting him. "Good afternoon, Mister Elijah, please come on in! Mister Angus is waitin for ya in the parlor, sir." She greeted him warmly. Elijah's reputation for kindness to his slaves was well known among the free blacks in town as well, so most colored folks felt predisposed to liking the man, in spite of him being a slave owner.

"Thank you Mary," Elijah said with equal warmth, always courteous to those who served. He removed his hat and entered the parlor to find the elder Patterson awaiting him, bright-eyed and attentive.

"Thank ya for comin so promptly, Elijah. Seems Jason lost no time in deliverin my message to ya! He's a good man, and does ya credit. Thinks the world of you, ya know? No cringin or fawnin there either. I liked that! Says a lot about ya both."

"Thank ya for that, Angus, and thank ya for invitin me to come so soon. Jason tells me you've been consultin with some lawyer over in Barnwell. That wouldn't be John Bauskett, by any chance?" Despite his appreciation for Angus' compliments to him and Jason, he was eager to get to the point of the visit. Elijah knew of Bauskett's reputation, and heard he had been unsuccessful in representing a client in a manumission petition, but thought highly of him for even being willing to try.

"Well, as a matter of fact it was!" smiled Angus. "I was not aware you knew of him. John's a very fine lawyer with whom I have worked on a number of cases. Naturally, we did not win them all- no lawyer ever does- but his knowledge of the matters that concern you is extensive, and somewhat more current than my own, so I thought it best to include him in our exploration." Angus gestured to Elijah to be seated, as he continued, "He came over for dinner the other day, and we talked for quite some time about your situation, and the legal options that may be open to ya'll." Once again, Angus spoke as if his benevolent and courtly delivery of this information actually clarified the situation, yet Elijah was left uncertain as to what they had concluded.

Before Elijah could speak in response, Mary entered the parlor with a tray holding a silver coffee pot, sugar bowl, creamer, and a pair of white porcelain coffee cups and saucers with gilded edges. She silently poured them each a fragrant cup of coffee, offering cream and sugar to Elijah (she knew from long experience that Angus Sr. preferred his coffee black). Elijah helped himself, and thanked Mary. She smiled back at him and quietly withdrew. He wondered if it was perhaps symbolic of what was to come that he was being offered sobering coffee rather than the sippin whiskey of his last visit, but said nothing.

Angus, meanwhile, seemed to have realized he had not clarified the matter, and proceeded after sipping his coffee thoughtfully.

"I'm afraid we have not come up with any good options for ya, Elijah, at least not in South Carolina. There's quite a checkered history of manumission petitions here, but the trend has clearly gotten more and more negative toward them in recent years, and I see no way for you to make such a petition here successfully at this point." This was hardly news to Elijah, who had already concluded as much.

"However," continued Angus, "there have been a few, like David Martin, who successfully emancipated their families via their wills, and having done so, could thereby bequeath them property as well. Seems emancipation is the necessary precondition for a legal bequest. The law is not entirely settled on this point, however, and there are many currently in power who are insisting that any such post mortem bequest is also illegitimate, especially since the legatees would have to first be emancipated to qualify for a bequest. Besides, in your case I assume you are not looking to establish Amy's and the family's liberation only after you're dead and gone, are you?"

Elijah suddenly felt uncertain. Of course he wanted them to be free, and wanted to see that freedom in his lifetime, but then again, maybe it would be safer to arrange for it solely through his will? That would perhaps make it easier to deal with the other planters and his white relations, and avoid the confrontation that would ensue if his intentions became known in the community.

"What do you think, Angus? Can I do this through a will?"

The old lawyer, sensing his conflict, sighed. "Well, like many things in the law, the answer is yes, and no. Since the General Assembly passed the Act of 1841, South Carolina law will not allow you to emancipate your slaves, or leave them any bequest of property via a will written in the State of South Carolina. However, all may not be lost! For since the jurisdiction of South Carolina stops at her borders, it may be possible to have a will written outside of South Carolina that would have to be recognized here!" Angus seemed right proud of himself for coming up with that clever option.

Elijah visibly brightened at this idea. Suddenly, the impossible seemed like it might be within reach after all. He immediately started to ponder the possibilities and to determine exactly where he might be able to get such a will written.

"From what you know of the law outside of Carolina, what do you suggest might be the best option for me?"

Angus took another sip of his coffee before responding, seeming lost in thought. "Well sir, I don't exactly know, to tell ya the truth. John Bauskett and I are tryin to get a hold of more information for ya on what other states have to say on this matter. But I know one thing, if you try takin your family out of State before you know whether ya can settle this for certain, it may stir things up for ya'll here, and make ya have to face something ugly if ya'll have to return." The old man paused in contemplation, and then, brightening, continued.

"Perhaps ya could find a way to make such a move, as if temporary, so it appeared to be business related, and thereby assuage local suspicions? That way, should ya'll have to return, it would seem perfectly natural and set off no alarms." Angus had not reached his advanced age, nor achieved his high status, by being stupid. His mind was ever examining different approaches to the question, and trying to anticipate the consequences of each possible choice, like an avid player in a game of chess, looking several moves ahead toward checkmate.

"That's a damn good idea, Angus! Let me think on that a while, but I'm sure you're right! By the Good Lord's grace, my holdins are big enough, and my business extensive enough, that it shouldn't be too hard to create a believable scenario to convince folks around here there's nothin suspicious about what I'm doin. I've been sendin some of my cotton up to Baltimore by train lately, where they then send it on to England by ship. Perhaps I should think about takin the family on a trip up to Maryland!"

Angus thought about this for a moment. "Well, that might work, but before you do, ya need to think about the legal questions you'll need to answer up there. Maryland is still a slave state, but their laws, if I remember correctly, are rather different from ours. Seems to me slaves themselves can petition for manumission up there- or at least they could- but they had to then leave the state, if it was granted." He paused in thought again. "I'll be happy to provide a letter certifiyin your good character, in case the authorities of Maryland demand it for for bringing slaves into that State. That may or may not solve your problem. They've also been trying to enact new laws up there about runaways. That fella Frederick Douglass been causin quite a stir! Seems he escaped by train, and has become the darlin of William Lloyd Garrison and some of the other abolitionists. Right eloquent speaker too, I'm told." This seemed to be a point of fascination to the old man, who thoroughly enjoyed entertaining the possibility of an articulate Negro making the case against slavery.

After a moment's lapse, another idea occurred to him. "I'm aware that Senator Clay of Kentucky has also been wrestlin with this matter for some time now. You know, he and Senator Calhoun didn't exactly see eye to eye on the slavery issue. Seems that, though a slave owner himself, Mr. Clay has never really felt comfortable with the institution of slavery in the first place." The old man continued to ruminate. "He has certainly worked hard to prevent it from spreadin to the new states and territories, and, I've heard, has already made provision for the emancipation of his own slaves as well."

Like a lawyer seeking to defend a point from the recorded discovery, Angus rifled through a pile of papers by his side, apparently looking for a reference. "Seems to me I read somewhere Senator Clay's response to the pro slavery claim that the Negroes' alleged intellectual inferiority gives us white folks the right to enslave them! Where is that reference?" he muttered to himself, continuing to leaf through his papers.

"Aha! Here it is! Listen to this! He said,

'If that were true, then the wisest man in the world would have the right to make slaves of all the rest of mankind! And if true, that fact alone would require us not to subjugate or deal unjustly by our fellow men, who are less blessed than we, but to instruct, to improve, and to enlighten them!'

Angus shook his head. "Much as it may have peeved Senator Calhoun, that man has a brilliant and a subtle mind, and a gift for arguin a point, no doubt about it!" Angus could not hide his admiration.

"Bein that he's still one of the leadin legal minds of this country, might not be a bad idea for you to send him a letter, and ask his advice on how ya might best proceed. His insight into the matter might be most useful as ya move forward with your plans!"

"That's an interestin idea, Angus! I'd never thought of that, but you may be right. Certainly can't hurt to try!"

Elijah, now animated at the thought he might find a solution that would both free his family and preserve his fortune, or even increase it, was reluctant to discuss the issue raised by Amy and Momma Celia about the possibility of emancipating all of his slaves. But he thought the better of it, and decided to seek the old man's advice on that matter too.

"Angus, I know this may be stretchin things, but I need to know your feelins about another related issue. What would you say to the possibility of me freein all of my slaves, not just Amy and the children?"

Angus' coffee cup clinked slightly, as he carefully set it down and looked at Elijah square on. "Well sir, my thoughts and my feelings on that subject may not quite agree with each other. It's both a noble and a dangerous thing you're proposin, Elijah, and I won't deny either." Angus sighed. "I'm an old man, and may not live to see it happen, but my heart tells me your proposal is exactly where this nation is headin, sooner or later."

He looked over to the wall, where Elijah noticed for the first time a framed copy of the Declaration of Independence. As if pondering anew its proclamation as self-evident truth that "all men are created equal," his gaze turned back to Elijah and he continued. "I honestly can't see it happenin as fast as you or I might like, but I suspect it's gonna have to happen before too long. This institution, in my view, aside from being immoral, (no offense to you as a slave owner intended) is no longer sustainable. That may sound treasonous to some, but it is my carefully considered opinion, nonetheless."

Like a lawyer giving a summation to the jury, he then added in a declaratory voice, "It may be that servitude will de facto remain the lot of many colored folk for years to come, even if all the slaves are emancipated de jure, but I know if it were I, I'd feel differently about my own such servitude if it was not enforced by someone who claimed ownership over me, to be bought and sold at his whim as if I were no more than a beast of burden!"

His tone then warmed and softened as he went on. "I believe a change of heart can and will come, at least to most folks. I've often been moved by that hymn, "Amazin' Grace"- seems to be gettin more and more popular these days. Touched me to my core to learn that John Newton, the fella that wrote it, actually had been indentured into the British Navy, and then became a slave trader himself." He paused to reflect on the wonder and improbability that often made truth stranger than fiction.

"I'm told that then, overwhelmed by the suffering he saw, he turned to drink, before he finally turned his life around, and ended up a clergyman. Remarkable story! It reminds me that the Good Lord's grace can accomplish miracles, and that there's goodness and forgiveness even in the hard-hearted, though it may be hidden too deep for us to always see." He lowered his eyes, almost as if searching for any signs of hardness in his own heart, and then brightened.

"My advice to you? Pray for the hard of heart, for your family, for your slaves, and for a miracle! In the meantime, do your homework and find out what Maryland law will and will not let ya do. We'll just have to take it from there, and play our cards close to the chest in the meantime."

Elijah too was moved by the story of John Newton. He had often heard the hymn- both at church and in the slave quarters- but had never known the story behind the beautiful lyrics and melody. "That's a powerful tale, Angus, I had no idea! You're surely right about one thing- what we're gonna need is no less than a miracle! But you have restored my hope that there is a viable solution, and for that I am deeply grateful."

Elijah started to gather himself to get up and take his leave. "I'd best get on home and talk this over with Amy, but I will certainly keep ya informed as my plans unfold. And please thank John Bauskett for takin' the time to look into this for us, will ya? That's right generous of him, and I surely do appreciate it. Lord knows, we need all the help we can get to get through this!"

Angus smiled with that quasi-fatherly affection. "John's a good man, Elijah, and so are you. Times like these, the good need to stick together! Give Amy and the family my best regards, and let me know if there's anythin else I can do. I'm happy to help." The old man, deciding to impart one more piece of his wisdom, added,

"And Elijah," he cautioned, "it's clear that the younger generation is less than charitable toward this issue. Much as I hate to admit it, that's why I made sure my son was not here when you arrived." The old man suddenly looked a touch melancholy. "It's come to my attention that he's become quite friendly with your nephews, James and Michael. The boy has a chip on his shoulder, and tends to blame me for his mother's death, and for his failure to amount to much. Pains me to see him so!" Angus sighed and then, ever the optimist, went on. " I'm hopin that he'll have a conversion like John Newton, cause I know there's good in him, but he's bitter. He thinks I don't see it, but I do. And bitterness loves company. Seems he's found it with your nephews. Just thought ya should know, in case ya didn't already."

Elijah realized how hard it must have been for Angus to share this with him. It was time for him to reciprocate Angus' kindness. "I'm truly sorry to hear that Angus, both for him, and for you. Point taken. And I appreciate your confidence in tellin me," he said with heart-felt compassion.

He started toward the door, then turned to add, "Truth be told, I had already feared as much. Fact is, I even avoided comin past James' store on my way over here, just in case. But it's a lot easier to deal with the threat ya know than the one ya don't. So we'll just take things one step at a time, and do the best we can to see nobody gets hurt. Like you said, 'you're a good man, and times like these, the good need to stick together!' That goes for you too!"

Bound by their mutual respect and affection, the two parted company. Mary smiled as she showed Elijah out and closed the door. She didn't have to be a slave to know the value of eavesdropping. Folks like Mister Elijah didn't come calling every day, and it did her heart good to see Mister Angus was not alone in his feelings that the days of slavery were numbered- even if neither he nor she would see them actually end.

XVI

Elijah was excited now. For the first time he felt there was a way out of their predicament that included both freedom and prosperity, and he couldn't wait pursue it. He galloped home across his own fields as soon as he could leave the main road to take the short cut to the plantation house.

Amy heard the pounding hooves from a distance, and came out front to see who was coming at such a speed, her heart in her throat. When she saw it was Elijah, and that he had a grin on his face, she felt a huge wave of relief sweep over her, and ran to greet him just as he reined Beauty to a halt by the veranda and called for Elder to take her out to the stable. "Cool her down first son, she's been runnin' hard and worked up a sweat!" As Elijah dismounted and tossed Elder the reins, Elder looked at his adoptive father with a mixture of surprise and curiosity- he hadn't seen Elijah so animated in a long time. But Elijah didn't seem to be ready to let Elder in on the secret just yet, and instead wrapped his arms around his wife and gave her a big kiss.

"Well, sir!" Amy said as coquettishly as any Southern belle who ever wore a hoop skirt, "Am I to assume you bring good news? That was quite a greetin'!" Amy held her husband at arm's length and smiled up at him affectionately, now filled with curiosity.

"Indeed I do, my dear, indeed I do. Come on!" he said, hooking his arm in hers. They strolled towards a nearby magnolia and stopped next to the tree. He leaned over to smell the delicious scent wafting up from a low-lying blossom, like some rare elixir in a dazzling white porcelain bowl of exquisite delicacy, framed by the shiny dark green leaves. With a romantic glint in his eye, he picked it and handed it gallantly to his wife.

"Well, don't keep me in suspense for heavens sake! What did Angus Patterson have to say that put such a spring in your step?" Amy insisted.

"Well, fact is, it's not all good news, but for the first time I see a real possibility that emancipation and prosperity don't have to work at cross purposes! The bad news, such as it is, is that Angus is pretty well convinced there's no chance of emancipating you and the family in the State of South Carolina, or of leaving you any bequest here. But we had already figured that." Amy's face fell, and she pulled away to look at her husband as if he'd betrayed her.

"So what, in the Good Lord's name, are you still grinnin' about? That sounds like terrible news to me!" She blurted, with a wounded tone in her voice.

"I know, sugar, but there's another way out! And it may be even better!" Elijah animatedly recounted to Amy his entire conversation with Angus: the idea of making a trip out of State seem like no more than a business venture; the possibility of the family traveling to Maryland, where he already had business dealings in Baltimore; and even the warning about his nephews and Angus, Jr.

In Elijah's mind's eye, a trip to Baltimore seemed a natural fit. It had the beauty of being logical, sensible, and consistent with his existing business affairs, so it would be unlikely to raise undue suspicions around Williston. In his enthusiasm, however, he glossed over the need to find answers to various legal questions from the perspective of the Maryland statutes, painting a hopeful picture of a prosperous and free future for them all.

Amy warmed to Elijah's enthusiasm and dared herself a moment of cautious optimism. Yet something was telling her not to count her chickens before they hatched.

"Elijah, honey, that does sound promisin, but are you sure Maryland law will allow you to free us? I heard they're gettin stricter about such things up there, too."

Elijah was mildly put out at the dampening affect of Amy's caution, but experience had taught him to trust her instincts. She'd never been wrong so far. But he himself desperately needed to believe there was a solution, if only for a while, so as not to feel defeated already by the negativity he felt closing in on the plantation like some silent, malicious shadow.

"Well darlin, I guess we won't know for sure until we go there and find out. But tryin beats sittin here feelin like the walls are closin in on us, doesn't it?" he asked almost plaintively.

Amy heaved a sigh and nodded, "Well, that's true. I suppose it does! I'll go on and tell Momma then, and you go tell Gilbert, Julius and Jason what they have to do while we're gone. We have to make sure this place is runnin smoothly in our absence too, or folks will start to wonder what's goin on. We'll need to book passage on the train for us all, as well as find a place in Baltimore where we can stay. That may not be so easy."

Ever the voice of practical reason, it was not the first time Elijah felt admiration for Amy's sense of grace under pressure, and her ability to sort through the tangle of emotions to see what was functionally important in the moment. They agreed to set about making the arrangements as soon as possible, and to say no more than necessary to anyone else about what their plans really were.

The next day, Elijah rode over to the depot with Amy in the carriage, on the pretext that she had some shopping to do, while he inquired about the train tickets for the family's journey north. Mr. Beazely was a little surprised that Elijah was planning on taking the whole family, not because he was unaware of the family relationship, or even particularly judgmental of it, but because usually Elijah left Amy in charge when he went away on business. As Elijah was one of his best customers however, he said nothing about it, and handed him eight open-ended tickets, as asked. Elijah thanked him and chatted affably about his business, hoping to deflect Mr. Beazeley's curiosity about the family accompanying him.

"I heard that there's a new style of clipper ship bein built up in Baltimore. They say they're as fast as anything on the seas today, and folks are even talkin about buildin ships powered by both sail and steam! So I figured I might look into shippin my cotton to England from there, instead of from Charleston or Savannah. The cost of sendin it all the way up to Baltimore by train may be a little higher, but if I can get the cotton to England ahead of my competition, I figure it'll be worth the extra expense!" Elijah grinned at Mr. Beazely conspiratorially, knowing that it would serve Mr. Beazely well to be responsible for the shipping of all that cotton to Baltimore too. Mr. Beazeley was, as always, impressed with Elijah's business acumen. Elijah seemed ever eager to be ahead of the pack- in breeding cotton, in finding new markets, in running his plantation efficiently. Mr. Beazeley had to admire him for that, since some planters seemed to think all they had to do was keep on doing what their granddaddies had done, and everything would work out just fine.

Satisfied that he had made a persuasive case for their trip to Baltimore that would not cause undue curiosity or talk, and having planted the story, moreover, with one of the major sources of information in the community,

Elijah helped Amy load her purchases into the carriage, and they went off home, as if it was just another day doing business in the community.

Elijah wanted to send a letter to Angus, apprising him of his plans, but thought the better of it, for fear it might fall into the younger Patterson's hands. He'd have to find a way to let Angus know in person before they left, but driving through town with Amy in the carriage to pay him a visit seemed too impolitic, under the circumstances. So they went on back to the plantation. He would just have to ride back to town at some later point, before they left for Baltimore.

Feeling less fearful now that they finally had a credible plan, both Amy's and Elijah's mood lightened. They decided it was time to let all the children know officially what their intentions were. That evening at supper, with all the family gathered and the candles burning brightly at the table, Amy spoke first.

"Momma, children, Elijah and I need to tell ya'll about somethin real important, and before we tell ya anything more, I need y'all to swear you'll not talk about this to anyone else without our permission, cause things could get awful difficult for us if this information gets into the wrong hands. Do we understand each other?" Momma Celia, already knowing what this was about, gave a stern look to the children, to further underscore that failure to comply would be on pain of severe punishment. The children nodded their assent, mumbling in staggered chorus, "Yes ma'am."

The girls were only aware that whatever it was, it must be important, but the boys all suspected the nature of the news. They had been piecing things together ever since Dr. Harley's visit- Elijah's sudden departure into town, the visit from Dr. Guignard and Mr. Matthews, Jason carrying messages to and from Mr. Patterson, Uncle Gilbert rushing over to the house in the middle of work to talk to Momma…

By now too, they knew that Momma was going to have another baby. It would have been clearly visible to everyone, even if they hadn't already been told. Momma and Elijah seemed both happy and worried about it at the same time, but the boys weren't sure why. Of course, as adolescents, the idea of Momma having more babies took some getting used to. Living on a farm where animals bred openly, the boys had figured out the mechanical facts of life, but found it a little uncomfortable to think of their mother and adoptive father engaging in such activities. Nevertheless, they knew their parents loved each other, so they guessed another sibling would just add to the family love. However, they also knew for certain that something else was up, in addition to the new arrival, something that would affect them all, and they sensed both danger and adventure in the air. In short, they were all ears!

Elder spoke up first, "What's goin on Papa? Ever since Dr. Harley came to visit, seems like you and Momma have been sorta, I dunno, different- like you're nervous about somethin."

Elijah was impressed by Elder's perceptive observation. "Well, son, you're right about that, we have been, and that's why we want to talk to everybody now." He looked at Amy, uncertain where to begin. Amy just gave him a nod and said, "Go on, tell em!"

Elijah took a deep breath, gathering his thoughts. "Ya'll know I love ya, don't ya?" They all nodded, expectantly. "And ya'll know that it's real uncomfortable for your mother and me that ya'll're not only my family, but also my slaves, don't ya?"

The boys nodded. Having been born on another plantation with a different experience of slavery, and already aware of both their own discomfort and Elijah's at their having to "play submissive" when white folks came to call, they had a much clearer idea of how onerous slavery could be. The girls, on the other hand, being born here and seldom leaving the plantation, mostly just knew the love they had experienced in the Willis household. Being younger and less aware, they shifted in their seats, looking a little confused and uncertain.

Elijah went on, "Well, your mother and I have been talkin a lot about that, tryin to find a way that I can free all of ya, and to leave ya'll this plantation and everything I own when I'm gone." Clarissa, not concerned with issues of property and ownership, but very concerned about the father she loved, looked at Elijah, alarmed, and said, "You're not gonna die, are ya Papa?"

Elijah, taken aback, responded, "Well, we're all gonna die someday, sugar, but I don't expect or intend to die myself anytime soon! God willin, that's still a long way away from now. No, baby girl, it's not about that!" His daughter's innocence and affection moved him. Though she had, in fact, picked up on one of his own fears, he would not, for all the world, frighten her or the others by admitting it.

"It's about not wantin anyone to ever be able to tell ya you're not as good as they are because of the color of your skin, or who your parents are, or that ya don't have the right to live as ya choose, and marry who ya love, and do the work God inspires ya to do, and use the gifts the Good Lord gave ya, as you see fit." He paused for a moment, then added, "We may not be able to end slavery in South Carolina, but I'm tryin to do everything I can to end it in this family, and with the Almighty's help, on this plantation too!" Amy looked up at her husband with surprise, since it was the first time Elijah had actually admitted that was his goal for the other slaves as well, and voluntarily at that!

Amy then joined in. "Children, ya know how some white folks look at ya'll when we're in town, and sometimes seem to be talkin about us behind our backs?" Even the girls nodded to this. "Well, there are some folks who feel a white man and a colored woman should not love each other, or have children together!"

Little Julia piped up, plaintively, "But why not, Momma? That's mean! You and Papa love each other, and have us. Does that mean there's something wrong with us? Are we bad?"

Momma Celia could not keep silent. She turned to her granddaughter and said insistently, "No, honey child, there is absolutely nothin wrong with you! And none of us is bad! The folks that think that are the ones who have somethin wrong with them, they mean spirited, cause they can't see how wonderful and beautiful ya'll are!"

Elleck joined in, "Papa, if we were free, wouldn't people still just look down on us? I mean, the girls maybe not, cause they're near as light as you, but Elder and Phillip and me are darker than Momma. Seems to me the darker ya are, the worse most white folks treat ya!"

Both Amy and Momma Celia nodded slightly at this, and looked to Elijah for a response.

"Well son, I can't promise ya you'll never have to deal with other people's attitudes. Bein free doesn't eliminate others' ignorant ways, unfortunately. But bein free at least allows ya choices ya'll don't have now." He looked around the table at his family. "Ya'll have been born here, and grown up in South Carolina, but there's a bigger country and a bigger world out there, and it may be we can all be happier somewhere else. If ya're free, ya'll could at least choose where ya wanted to be!"

Clarissa looked pensive. "Papa," she asked, "if we moved somewhere else, would I be able to go to school?"

Elijah brightened, grateful that the children were starting to consider the possibilities that might lie before them. "I'm glad you asked that, honey, cause one of the things that ya need for freedom to really work is an education. I want all of ya'll to learn to read and write, and cipher, and study bigger things, so when ya'll grow up, you'll feel ya can not only earn a livin', but follow your hearts and minds wherever they lead ya!"

The children sat solemnly, taking all this in. Then Amy spoke up. "Children, ya'll already know that whether you're black, white, or brown, you gotta work hard in this life. But Elijah's tryin to make sure that we'll have whatever we need, so that nobody else can tell us what work we have to do or how we want to live. You can't put a price on that!"

Elder then asked, "So Papa, if we were to leave South Carolina, where would we go?"

Elijah responded immediately. "Well, I'm not certain, but I've been thinkin a lot about that, and tryin to figure out whether there's a way to move and keep the plantation runnin too. Since I've been doin some business up in Baltimore, I thought we should all take a trip up to Maryland and explore the possibilities there."

The idea of the whole family taking a trip outside of South Carolina caused a general stir around the table, and overrode any questions that might have occurred to them about how he could be thinking of freeing all the slaves, but still run the plantation. Momma Celia looked a little worried.

"I can't guarantee it'll work, or we'd be any safer up there, but it's worth lookin' into. I've already bought us train tickets. When we get up there, I'll have to talk to my business associates in Baltimore and also get some legal advice to find out how their laws differ from ours down here."

Amy interjected, "And if it turns out that the atmosphere there is inhospitable to our goals?" The family all turned to Elijah expectantly.

Elijah responded, "Well, havin set this up as nothin more than a business trip, it allows us to come back home without havin raised any suspicions here in Barnwell District. And then we'll just have to find another solution."

Momma Celia spoke up. "I know you thinkin we can keep what others around here think bout us under control, but seems to me they's bound to be folks who start addin two and two if we all go runnin off to Baltimore!"

Elijah looked at his mother-in-law, wanting to reassure her, but knowing full well she was probably right. "Well, Momma Celia, that may be, I can't deny it. We're already havin to stomp out brush fires around here just on the plantation, from what Amy and Gilbert tell me. But the alternative is to do nothin. I just can't see doin that anymore!"

"Besides, Momma," Amy said hopefully, "it just might work out up there in Baltimore, and we'd all already be there- except for Gilbert and his family. And we could bring them up later!"

Momma Celia remained unconvinced, but said no more for the moment. She was willing to be pleasantly surprised, but life had taught her to count on nothing.

"So, children", Amy continued, "ya'll need to understand that you mustn't talk about this in front of anyone else- not even the other slaves. Until everything's set, we have to make this our little secret. Agreed?"

At the word "little," Momma Celia muttered, "Hmm! If that's a little secret, I don't wanna know what you call a big one!"

Elijah had to chuckle at Momma Celia's candor. "Alright then, fair enough. It's got to be our BIG secret! But ya'll gotta swear to keep your mouths shut tighter than a snappin' turtle about this, understood?"

The children all nodded and said, "Yes, sir." Phillip added, "But we can talk to you and Momma about it, can't we?" He wanted to make sure if he had questions or doubts along the way, he was not going to be without recourse.

"Of course, baby," Amy replied, "you can always come to us if ya need somethin, or want to talk!" Amy's maternal instincts urged her to be ever available to her children.

Elder suddenly looked uncomfortable. He cleared his throat and asked Elijah, "What about the others?" He was obviously referring to the rest of the slaves on the plantation. Along with Uncle Gilbert and his wife and children, there were other boys on the plantation that he considered friends. Their future suddenly seemed in doubt. "You said ya were tryin to end slavery on this plantation. What's gonna happen to them?"

Elijah had been dreading this question, but knew he couldn't avoid it. He had to be honest with the children- especially because of the boys' earlier experience on the Kirkland plantation. "Well, son, I don't honestly know yet. Your momma and I are sort of takin this one step at a time. I've been talkin to Mr. Patterson, the lawyer in town, and to Dr. Harley for their advice." That immediately confirmed the boys' earlier speculations. "And I'm even seekin advice from some other folks who have been dealin with this issue for a lot longer that we have. A fella named John Bauskett- a lawyer friend of Angus Patterson's over in Barnwell, for one, and even Senator Clay up in Kentucky." Elder seemed impressed. "We're doin everything we can to find a solution for everybody, but truth be told, we have to start with the family. Then we'll see how best to help the others."

That seemed to make sense to Elder and Elleck. "Alright Papa, you can count on us! And we'll keep our eyes and ears open too- we'll let ya know if we see or hear anything!" The boys seemed eager to participate, sensing adventure and rising to the challenge.

"I knew I could count on you boys. But in the meantime, we still have to play-act like slave and master when anybody else comes to the plantation, or when we're somewhere off the plantation together, understood?" The boys frowned, but nodded their assent. The girls did too. They were not really conscious of the dark side of the game they had to play, yet even they could feel the negativity of Papa's relations, and some of the folks who came to visit, or who stopped to stare at Momma in town and whisper to each other as she walked by when they were with her.

"Well, alright then. Enough for now! Your Momma and I have a lot to do to get ready for the trip to Baltimore, so ya'll be sure to lend her a hand with whatever she asks, will ya? We'll let ya'll know as soon as everything's arranged."

After dinner, uncertain of any exact address but presuming that a man of such note would be known to the post office in Washington, Elijah sat down to write Senator Clay.

To the Hon. Henry Clay
Senator from Kentucky
The Capitol
Washington, District of Columbia

Dear Senator Clay:

Allow me to introduce myself. My name is Elijah Willis. I am a planter in South Carolina with sizable holdings- some thirty four hundred acres of arable land, planted in cotton and timber, and fifty-two slaves who work the property.

Despite the means of my livelihood, I am increasingly aggrieved by the institution of slavery, and having never married, found myself unexpectedly falling in love with one of my own slaves and having a family with her. I am most eager to emancipate my family, and wish to bequeath them my entire estate. Unfortunately, the mood in South Carolina is ever more insistent not only upon the perpetuation of slavery, but also upon making any escape therefrom nigh impossible. Such emancipations are possible only through the unlikely means of petitioning our General Assembly, and bequests are in all cases, by current South Carolina law, illegal.

My friend and attorney, Angus Patterson, Sr., of Williston, South Carolina, recommended I seek your advice as to a viable means of emancipation and legacy for my family. His thought was that it might be possible to achieve, if I had a Last Will and Testament written in a State that would permit such a choice. It would therefore have to be honored by South Carolina law, due to the laws of comity. He represented one David Martin, also of Barnwell District, back in the 20's, who brought his colored wife and mulato children to Kentucky and successfully emancipated them there, and, once they were freed, was thereby able to bequeath them property. I am uncertain, however, of what the current laws in Kentucky might permit, since, as they have in South Carolina, I suspect they may have also subsequently changed in your great State.

I have resolved to take my family to Baltimore shortly, to explore the possibilities there, since I already have some business dealings in that city. But I have been apprised that the atmosphere in Maryland in regards to slavery, emancipation, and miscegenation, may not be hospitable to our needs.

I throw myself on the mercy of your wisdom, as one dedicated to preserving our nation and, at the same time, working for the eventual emancipation of all slaves. I implore you to tell me how and where you would advise me to proceed, and whether, in your opinion, my desire is even an achievable goal or not.

Ever grateful for any advice or insight you may be able to offer, and trusting that my coming from the State represented by your political nemesis, the late Senator John C. Calhoun, will not render you ill-favored toward my petition,

I remain your humble servant,

Elijah Willis
Willis Plantation
Williston
Barnwell District, South Carolina

Elijah folded and sealed the letter, and placed it on the bureau in his bedroom until morning, when he could take it to Mr. Beazely to send off to Kentucky on the mail train.

He then remembered he also needed to send a letter to George Brown, apprising him of his intention to travel to Maryland, and inquiring about possible lodging for himself and several slaves. Mr. Brown was a banker-an excellent financial contact in Baltimore with whom Elijah was hoping to expand his business. They had corresponded by mail, but not yet met. Suddenly uncertain as to how such a request might be received, he was not sure whether to reveal the real purpose of his trip before arriving, so he merely identified his fellow travelers as slaves including two adult women and five children.

George Brown's Irish father, Alexander, had founded Baltimore's first international banking firm, and his brothers had opened branches in Philadephia and New York as well. Elijah was eager to pursue a possible alliance with Alex. Brown & Sons to assure continued growth of his cotton shipments to English mills- especially given that the tension between South Carolina and New England might threaten his domestic market. Alex Brown & Sons might, for that matter, also help him ship lumber to the growing towns to the West as well. After finishing his letter to Mr. Brown, he sealed it too, and placed it on the bureau with the letter to Senator Clay, resolving to take them both to the post office in Williston first thing in the morning.

XVII

When Elijah rode into town to mail the letters at the depot, he decided to swing by Angus Patterson's house and let him know of his decision even though he couldn't be assured that the younger Mr. Patterson might not be home. Now that the wheels were set in motion, he realized he would just have to deal with each situation as it arose and trust it would work out, so long as he remained vigilant. He knew, however, that it was increasingly unlikely that he could prevent all possible occasions for discovery of his plans. He would, of course, continue to keep his cards close to his chest, but the cards had already been dealt, and he intended to play his hand the best he could.

As luck would have it, when Elijah let fall the heavy brass doorknocker, it was Mary, not Angus, Jr., who answered the door. Mary flashed Elijah a toothsome grin of recognition, the bright white of her teeth fairly illuminating her aged face. "Well hello there, Mister Elijah! Nice to see ya, sir! Come on in! I'll go fetch Mister Angus right away! He's always happy to see you!" Mary climbed the stairs with some effort, her movements showing her age even more than her face.

"Mister Angus, Mister Elijah's here to see ya!" Mary called from the top of the stairs, slightly winded, and muttering under her breath about her old bones not being what they used to be.

Elijah felt a little guilty coming unannounced and for a moment there, standing on the Turkish carpet in the foyer, he feared he had come at an inopportune moment. But by and by, he could hear the thump of Angus' cane heading steadily and purposefully toward the stairwell, and the old man's voice calling down cheerily, "Well, Elijah! I didn't expect to see ya so soon, but I'm glad ya've come. Just bear with me while I negotiate my way down these stairs!" It was both a bit sad and a tad comical to watch as the elder Patterson was helped down the stairs by his equally geriatric housekeeper, who solicitously held his arm and cane while he worked his way downstairs, grasping the dark walnut banister, their progress punctuated by a series of grunts and winces. It was hard to tell who needed more support from whom, but eventually they both made it down with a smile of triumph as they reached the foyer without mishap.

"I'm sorry to barge in like this, Angus, I suppose I should have sent a message first, but I had to come in to the depot, and figured I'd just stop by to bring ya up to date on my decision." Elijah looked around to see if there was any sign of the younger Patterson.

Angus responded promptly, "Nonsense Elijah, no trouble at all! Glad ya came! I've been thinkin a lot about ya'll since we saw each other, and I'm eager to know how ya see things unfoldin. Come on into the dinin room with me. I'm afraid I'm not as early a riser as I used to be, and frankly, I haven't had breakfast yet. Join me for a cup of coffee while we talk, won't ya?"

"Well, I'd be glad to, if you're sure it's no trouble." Elijah responded, still a little uneasy that Angus, Jr. might appear in mid conversation. Angus picked up on his anxiety and reassured him. "Oh, don't worry, Elijah, we're quite alone, except for Mary here, so ya'll can speak in total confidence. Mary'd sooner die than let my son know anything he shouldn't, isn't that right Mary?"

Mary smiled and assured Elijah, "That's the Gospel truth, Mister Elijah. I may be ole, but I ain't no fool, an I know they's things that young Angus thinks and says that just ain't right, God love him, so even though I bout raised him, I ain't gonna risk tellin him nothin that he could use against folks like ya'll!"

It was clear Mary had some idea of what Elijah was facing, though given Angus, Sr.'s general circumspection, he wasn't entirely sure whether this was a matter of confidences shared between them, or perhaps between Mary and other coloreds in town. Once again, Elijah was struck with the challenge, if not the futility, of trying to keep anything truly secret in Barnwell District, South Carolina.

"Thank ya Mary, I appreciate that," was all he could think to reply.

Angus then interjected, "Well then, Elijah, where do things stand now, and what, if anything, have ya'll decided to do?"

"Well sir, I did take your advice to consult Senator Clay. In fact, it was my need to send the letter off in the mail that was the occasion for my visit to the depot and hence, my arrival here," Elijah responded. "Of course, I have no idea how long it may be before I receive a response, but I am at least consoled that I have taken that step toward clarifying my legal options."

Angus nodded appreciatively. "I'm glad to hear of it. Well done! By reputation at least, I'm told Senator Clay is attentive to his correspondence, and I would imagine that as he has spent so much energy himself on this issue, your letter will neither go unnoticed nor unanswered. Did ya send it to him in Washington, or to his home in Kentucky? Hard to say where he might be at present."

"I sent it to him in Washington, but I assume it will be forwarded to him if he is to be away for any length of time. Perhaps I should have copied it and sent it to both places, but truth be told I did not have an address for him in Kentucky, so I pray it will find its way to him from the Capital, if in fact it doesn't find him there."

"No doubt it will, in time. And what, if anything, have you determined concernin the possibility of makin a 'business trip' out of State?"

"Well, I have taken some steps on that front as well. I have sent a letter to George Brown, a financier in Baltimore with whom I have had some contact, apprisin him that I shall be visitin Baltimore shortly, and will be accompanied by seven slaves." Angus raised an eyebrow in curiosity at this, but did not interrupt. Elijah explained, "Not knowin Mr. Brown's views on emancipation, I decided it best not to reveal the nature of my relationship to those accompanyin me until such time as I could ascertain the climate for such a discussion in safety."

Angus nodded, "Probably a wise choice, though it may be cause for some initial discomfort upon arrival in Baltimore when, no doubt, the physical evidence of the nature of your relationship is apt to be immediately apparent, and duly noted." He was clearly referring both to the natural affection visible among his family members and the physical similarities the girls undeniably shared with their father. "I recommend you let Amy and the children know this, so they are properly prepared!"

Elijah felt a slight discomfort at Angus pointing out the obvious, and realized that he walked such a fine line between his love for his family and the need for great caution, that he might appear duplicitous to them. The thought disturbed him greatly. Angus, long practiced in the art of reading people by their demeanor, seemed to understand Elijah being ill at ease. "Forgive me for sayin so, Elijah, but are you sure you're ready to take this step? I am well aware how difficult a task you have set yourself to accomplish. It is a journey fraught with many a danger, and will demand the utmost strength of purpose, patience, and perseverance of you all, if it is to be accomplished. I mean no rebuke, only concern for your well bein."

"I'm truly grateful for your concern, Angus. Fact is, it feels like things are already movin at a pace I can no longer fully control, and that does, I must admit, make for some rather uncomfortable situations." Elijah paused for a moment, as if to verify in his heart what he was to say next. "Nevertheless, I am firm in my resolve to go ahead, wherever it may lead me, in the conviction that our cause is righteous in the eyes of the Lord. But He surely does know how to test our faith, doesn't He?"

Angus chuckled, "Yes, indeed He does, my friend! But I'd like to think that bein tried for a time in the flames of the Hell of fear and hatred will burn out the dross of bitterness in our hearts and leave pure gold. Given what God put his own Son through, I see no reason why we should be exempted from our own trials and tribulations, so long as Resurrection is the promised reward!"

"Sagely put, Angus. I'll have to remember that!" Elijah responded. "At any rate, I wanted to let ya know where things stand. Amy and I are makin preparations to head on up to Baltimore as soon as we can. I will, of course, keep ya informed of any developments as they unfold. Should you gain any fresh legal insights that might be of use in the meantime, please let us know." Elijah finished his coffee, and set his cup and saucer carefully on the highly polished mahogany dining table, there being no damask table cloth this time, but rather, only a linen place mat set out for the old man's less formal breakfast. He pushed back his chair and made ready to leave.

Angus looked up at his friend with his usual kindly glint in his eye. "God bless ya, Elijah, I surely will." He reached into his pocket and pulled out an envelope. Handing it to Elijah he said, "Here's the letter of good character I promised ya. I took it upon myself to get Colonel Hargood, the Barnwell Commissioner of Equity, and various other notables in the area to sign too. I hope it will be of some use to ya'll. And, should Maryland prove inhospitable, though that seem a misfortune, I shall at least take solace in the happy thought of seein ya again upon your return." There was a melancholy note in the old man's voice, as if he was suddenly uncertain whether he would live long enough to see Elijah's ultimate success.

Elijah fell silent, feeling his friend's intimation, and sought to reassure him, "Well, however things turn out, either in the short or the long term, I will always be grateful for your friendship and comfort in our time of greatest need. It means an awful lot to me and my family. Such support is mighty hard to come by. Rest assured we shall remain in contact the rest of our days, wherever the good Lord may lead us."   As if by finely tuned intuition bordering on telepathy, Mary quietly came back into the dining room, un-summoned, and handed Elijah his hat.

"Besides," Elijah added before following Mary to the front door, "I still owe ya some good sippin whiskey as a token of my appreciation! Of course, we'll need to taste it together to make sure it measures up, now, won't we? Maybe I should have asked Senator Clay to send us a bottle of that good Kentucky bourbon along with his letter, so we could toast his health and our future!" The old man brightened at this thought and waved his blessing to Elijah with one hand, his fork spearing a sausage with the other, as he continued eating his breakfast, nodding and smiling to himself at the pleasure of such a thought.

XVIII

Henry Clay, the elder statesman, much worn by his long efforts to preserve a union in increasing peril of division, sat pensively in the handsome octagonal study of his estate. The mansion, designed by Benjamin Latrobe, the architect of the Capitol in Washington and a friend of the Senator, was gracefully proportioned, and set in a lovely park on the outskirts of Lexington. The high-ceilinged study was paneled in the wood for which the Senator had named his beloved Ashland, and now, at the end of his long and illustrious career, it was to that place he called his "piece of the Promised Land' that he had retired for some much needed rest from his heavy labors. The recent battle over what was already being called the Great Compromsie of 1850 had sapped him of his energy, yet, once again he was being called out of retirement to head back to Washington, despite his advanced age and increasingly poor health.

His valet, Levi, appeared in the study carrying various letters just retrieved from the Lexington Post Office. Levi had once escaped his bondage and fled to Cincinnati, only to think the better of it and return to his master voluntarily. It said much about both men that he had chosen to do so, and was warmly received. Such was the loyalty and affection that the great man inspired in many. Even his political foes acknowledged the attractions of Clay's keen intellect, eloquent charm, and graciousness.

Long accustomed to attending to his master's needs, Levi deftly sorted through the letters so as to place them in order of probable priority. As he flipped through them, checking their return addresses, there was one which caught his eye. It was from a Mr. Elijah Willis in South Carolina, a state the Senator's late nemesis, John C. Calhoun had represented. It was not often that Mr. Henry received mail from South Carolina.

"Here's the mail for ya, Mister Henry." Clay looked up, shaken from his reverie as he looked out over the circular drive and the grove of ash trees in front of the house.

"Anything interestin, Levi?" he asked, somewhat distractedly.

"Well sir, there is one letter that could be. It's from a Mr. Elijah Willis, in South Carolina. Been a long time since ya got mail from down there!" Levi grinned, knowing full well Mister Henry's rivalry with Senator Calhoun had been one of the more stimulating relationships of his very long political career. Fact is, Mister Henry had enjoyed having a worthy adversary in debate, and the often pyrotechnical chemistry between him and Senators Calhoun and Webster had been both a source of inspiration for much crucial legislation, and of much entertaining oratory to the voting public. Levi had been right worried that since Senator Calhoun had recently died, it made Mister Henry start feeling more like his time had come too.

Levi's mischievous grin had been just the tonic to liven the old man's mood. Senator Clay took the letter, opened it, and read it with increasing interest. When he finished, he looked up and said, "Well imagine that! I'd wager old John Calhoun would turn over in his grave if he read a letter from one of his own constituents asking me advice on how to emancipate his slaves!" Mister Henry laughed out loud at that probability, but it set him into a fit of coughing, and it took some time for him to regain his composure. Even the annoyance of his ravaging cough, however, could not wipe the smile off his face at the thought of his old rival's presumable reaction to the letter he held in his hand.

Feeling too weakened by the coughing bout to get up and go to his desk, he turned to Levi and said, "Levi, pull my card table over here and fetch me pen and paper, will ya? I think this letter deserves an immediate response. Not only does it touch on a subject of burning importance still pressing on my heart, but to contemplate the calumny it would have provoked in John has given me the first laugh I've had in days! I'm grateful for both!"

"Yes sir, Mister Henry!" Levi dutifully carried over a mahogany card table from its place against the wall to his master's seat. The rectangular top swiveled and opened to a square of matching richly grained panels on a graceful cylindrical pedestal, with four carved lion's paws upholding a rectangular plinth supporting it. The Senator caressed the wood affectionately, remembering fondly the countless poker games played with political colleagues around this table. He had never been averse to a wager with either a friend or a foe, and found it often helped secure a vote for a bill he proposed, or help to block some opponent's. The art of poker, he reflected, was much like the art of politics. You had to play the hand you were dealt, but knowing when to hold the cards, when to fold them, and when to bluff your opponent was where the fun and excitement lay, and where the game was won or lost!

The old man looked back out the window a bit wistfully, well aware that he had little time or energy left to gamble. Levi then reappeared carrying a tray with writing paper and an elaborately chased brass desk set containing pen, ink, blotter, sealing wax, and Mister Henry's own seal.

"Thank ya, Levi. That'll be all for now. I must sit and consider my response, and hope the blank page will inspire in me some helpful insights for this gentleman. I'll let ya know when I've finished, and then you'll see to it that it gets posted, won't ya?"

"Of course, Mister Henry. Right away, sir!" Levi smiled with satisfaction to see the old man enjoying himself again, however weakened his health might be. Meanwhile, ever the orator with an ear to his wording, the Senator began to compose his response as if composing a symphony, with distinct movements leading to a satisfying climax and finale. As he starting putting pen to paper, just as when he stood before Congress, or in the Senate Chamber, or a crowd of admirers, words flowed from him as naturally as breath; in fact, given his consumptive condition, even more naturally than breath. He wrote thoughtfully and intently, with a candor, and even humility, born of his realization that there would be few such occasions remaining where he might yet exert some positive influence for a cause he had so long championed, yet despite his gifts of persuasion, with such limited success:

Mr. Elijah Willis
Willis Plantation
Williston
Barnwell District, South Carolina

My Dear Mr. Willis:

I received your letter today, as I was not in Washington when it arrived some weeks ago, and it was forwarded to me at Ashland, my home in Lexington. Though lately called back out of retirement to take my seat in the Senate once more, the vicissitudes of old age and poor health have obliged me to take some much needed repose in the place I most dearly love, in the hope that Providence will soon restore me to sufficient energy to fulfill that duty, while yet I may. I do apologize for my unwitting delay in responding to your queries, and regret any inconvenience that may have caused you.

I greatly appreciate the trust you have placed in me to advise you on the issue of the emancipation of slaves, though I must confess my surprise at receiving such a query from a South Carolinian. You have restored my conviction that my old rival and recently deceased colleague, Senator Calhoun, did not necessarily speak for all in that great State, and that there are sensible men even where the institution of slavery seems most deeply rooted, who are eager to see it end. This gives me hope for our great nation's future survival, despite being currently mired in the throes of such turmoil over this very issue.

As you surely are aware, I've spent much of my political and professional life striving to accomplish the goal of universal emancipation, though it continues to elude us as a nation so severely divided. At times, I confess, my love of our noble country, and my unshakable belief in the imperative importance of preserving its Union, has overshadowed my distaste for the institution of slavery, and I have felt compelled to make compromises that I would have preferred not to make, to that end. I pray the good Lord will forgive me if I have failed to achieve all my heart and mind have prompted me to do.

As a slave owner myself, I, like you, am keenly aware of the importance of treating the Negroes with dignity, and providing for their comfort and good health. As it happens, I have a number of slaves who are no longer able to work, due to advanced age or infirmity, whom I am pleased to maintain in comfort til the end of their days- at considerable expense, I might add. And though I have already emancipated a few slaves, such as my long time valet, Charles Dupuy, like you, I find myself in the awkward position of being unable to maintain my farming enterprise without their service. I am also mindful that to simply set them all free without the means to preserve that freedom would be a cruel gesture, condemning them to penury and to far more suffering than ever they endured in their bondage to my service. So I have provided not only for their emancipation, but their financial preservation and education, in my Last Will and Testament, thereby not only granting them their freedom, but also granting myself the peace of mind of having done right by them, at long last.

As a lawyer, I see your issue as a complex one, for the matters of manumission, inheritance, and miscegenation have distinct characteristics, moral implications, and legal parameters. As you may have heard, I personally have been of the opinion that emancipation should be accomplished with the ultimate goal of colonization, that is, permitting the Negroes to return to their native Africa, from which they were so untimely ripped, in freedom and peace. I am not only a founder, but have been for many years, and continue to be still, the president of the American Colonization Society. We have successfully been able to send a great many Negroes back to Africa, where they have founded a democratic society suitable to their own needs and culture, in the new nation of Liberia, in West Africa. That is not to say, however, that free blacks have not been, or should not now continue to be able to live in peace and dignity within our own borders, as you clearly intend for yours, at least until such time as their repatriation might be achieved.

Concerning the issue of emancipation, though I continue to defend the right of each sovereign state to determine its own policies on this matter, I would prefer there to be a national solution to the problem, and fervently pray we may yet achieve the same, even if not in my lifetime. However, since my own mortality, as I am lately aware, is likely to come to a close sooner than I might hope or expect, due to ill health and advancing age, perhaps the achievement of universal emancipation is not as far distant as it once seemed, when I was still young enough to believe myself to be immortal!

My younger cousin, Cassius Marcellus Clay, is also ardently committed to this matter, though I must confess some consider him rather prone to being inflammatory on the subject, as you might have formerly read in his publication The True American. Even here in Kentucky the subject has been the cause of much dispute, and due to the uproar that periodical caused in my hometown of Lexington, my cousin was compelled to move its publication to the city of Cincinnati, in the slave free State of Ohio, before he went off to serve in the Mexican War. I do sense, however, that the times may finally be changing, and the definitive impetus for emancipation is clearly growing, even in some of the states where slavery is currently still permitted. Nevertheless, manumission in general being so difficult a challenge, I fear universal emancipation will likely come at an even greater cost on the national level than on the personal one.

I am mindful, however, that whatever we politicians may do or decide will inevitably take more time than you have at your disposal to find a solution to your own concerns. Any eventual political solution that may be achieved, will, in any case, not answer your immediate needs. So in the meantime, you will have to ascertain whether it would be more efficacious and advantageous for you to seek emancipation for your slaves in another slave-holding state, or in one where Mr. Calhoun's "peculiar institution" is not permitted at all.

To my way of thinking, however, and for whatever it may be worth to you, you may run a certain risk attempting to do so in a slave-holding state, even though it might currently have more flexible laws than South Carolina's. I am intimately familiar with the machinations of government, and its intrinsic response to the changing, and at times, capricious moods and perceptions of the people. Given the heated divisions rending our nation on this very subject, it is, therefore entirely possible that you may encounter additional roadblocks to your slaves' freedom and financial solvency being created through new legislation, even should you succeed in their initial emancipation. Such seems to have been the case already in your own home state, where as I understand it, the matter of emancipation has become steadily more difficult, and interracial inheritance has been utterly prohibited. Herein lies one of our most intransigent problems: the integrity of individual States' rights must be held in balance with the integrity of our Union, and at times, these seem to be contradictory ideals.

Yet, despite your Senator Calhoun's notion that States' rights allow each state the option to choose the selective nullification of any federal laws it finds onerous, such a notion continues to defy the very logic of the Constitution and the fundamental principles of the basic concept of our Union, and the comity between states. No state can simply pick and choose what of our national law or policy it finds agreeable and jettison the rest, while still claiming membership in the Union. Consequently, the issue of legal jurisdiction is pertinent to your situation, since one of our nation's fundamental principles is that the laws of the several states will be mutually honored and respected by each. New and evolving legislation therefore can present interpretive challenges in its applications, especially when the legislation becomes clearly partisan toward a particular faction or value, such as is the case in the issue of emancipation versus slavery.

That being said, it must be admitted that we are speaking speculatively, as such possible legislation within slave-holding states that retain some proviso for limited emancipation is, at this point, merely hypothetical, and I do not wish to dissuade you from your noble efforts in Baltimore or elsewhere.

As for the matter of inheritance, however, you are certainly right to want to provide for your slaves in any way possible, for emancipation without a means of sustenance would be no emancipation at all, and a cruel joke to play. I have had the same concern for my own, and therefore sympathize. Emancipation is, manifestly, the necessary precondition to providing a viable inheritance. By both law and common sense, any person living in freedom should be, by logical extension, free to inherit property. Such would be an obvious manifestation by which that freedom is known and enjoyed. Once an emancipation is recognized, the issue of inheritance therefore changes in nature, especially if each is handled independently of the other. If your family were to be emancipated prior to your demise, for example, and such emancipation legally recognized, even in another state, you might then well argue their right to inherit through your Will. However, in my own case, I have managed to provide for both, through my Last Will and Testament, and it will be upheld in the Commonwealth of Kentucky.

On the final point of miscegenation, however, I must confess I do not approve of the mixing of the races. I have never thought it advisable, as I fear, in the issue of such liaisons each race is diminished by the other. I realize that some folks may not agree with me on this point- I'd expect you'd be one of them. And there are certainly a sizable number of the residents of New Orleans, for example, a city I dearly love, where such mixtures have become commonplace.

However, I do not wish to stand in judgment of what is already a reality, for to do so would be to evade the question you have put to me, and thereby also evade my sacred responsibility to you as a life-long public servant. I am fairly well certain there are no slave-holding states, other than Louisiana, where such racial intermingling is well tolerated, but that would be an issue for you to determine in making your choice. As to whether the slave-free states are more amenable, I suspect there is no conformity on this issue even there, though in theory, perhaps, there should be fewer obstacles thereto.

You might consider consulting a friend of mine, John Jolliffe, of Cincinnati, for further insights into the jurisdictional issues of your particular case.

I realize I may not have offered much by way of solution to your problem, sir, but I do hope that sharing something of my own experience and understanding of the issue will help you in determining the best course of action for you to take. Were I a younger man, I might pledge to you renewed efforts on my own part in Washington to facilitate emancipation, at the very least, but I fear such energies as that would require of me are fast diminishing. Alas, I am forced to accept that I am coming to the end of my career, and it will be for someone younger than I to pick up the torch of this cause and carry it further. Perhaps my fellow Kentuckian, that promising Mr. Lincoln, now of Illinois, or some other young buck, as yet unknown to the public, will succeed where my generation has failed. I devoutly hope so.

Forgive the ramblings of an old man! I wish you and your family well, sir, and trust that by the grace of the Almighty, you will in fact find a solution to your problem, somewhere in these United States. I remain,

Your willing servant,

H. Clay
Ashland
Richmond Road
Lexington, Kentucky

Looking over his words pensively, as if in unexpected summation of a lifetime of thought on the subject, he was mentally gratified but physically exhausted from the outpouring of this missive. With trembling hands, the old man folded and sealed the letter, and convulsing in another bout of coughing, summoned Levi to send it off in the mail straightaway.

XIX

Amy was getting anxious. She was feeling the dual pressures of finding a solution to the means of her family's emancipation, and the physical and emotional pressures wrought by the steady progress of her pregnancy. Elijah had still heard no response from Senator Clay, but he had received a cordial letter from George Brown in Baltimore, welcoming their visit to Maryland and securing them lodging in the Admiral Fell Inn. The Inn, Mr. Brown informed him, was located on the corner of Thames St. and Broadway on the Fells Point waterfront- a convenient location for Elijah to explore first-hand the prospects of developing his business through shipping.

Amy was feeling the imperative of making the journey soon. She felt torn, for she did not want to be delivered of her baby away from home, but neither did she want to delay their progress in seeking a solution to their legal and financial future. Though they both would have preferred to head for Baltimore armed with the advice of the Sage of Ashland, as Senator Clay was sometimes called, Amy convinced Elijah they could no longer put off their departure for Maryland.

"Elijah, honey, don't you think it's time we went to Baltimore? This is the best part of my pregnancy to travel, unless you think we should wait til after the baby comes?" She wanted to have the baby at home, but she also didn't want to wait any longer to find out whether Baltimore held any promise for their future. Truth be told, she was doubtful on that point already, and in her mind, saw them returning to have the baby here on the plantation.

Elijah sensed the urgency in her voice, and like any husband accustomed to the matrimonial imperative of heeding such warnings, on pain of undesirable consequences, knew he must choose his words carefully in response.

"Well, I suppose that now we've heard from George Brown and have secured lodgings, we could go most any time. It'd be nice to have Senator

Clay's input before goin, but I have no way of knowin whether he even received my letter, much less when he'll respond. It's been weeks since I wrote him, so I figure he must not have been in Washington. By the time the letter gets to Kentucky and the response gets down here, several more weeks might pass!" Truth was, though he really was hoping for some useful instruction from the Senator, he too was feeling that time was wasting, and they needed to go ahead with their plans.

"Elijah, honey, I just don't think we should wait that long to go to Baltimore! Whatever Senator Clay may advise, if ya want to investigate the possibilities of relocatin to Maryland, we need to know what's happenin before my time comes. I am not goin through all that in the midst of havin the baby, if I have anything to say about it!" Elijah knew of course that this was a rhetorical hypothetical, whose real meaning was, "I'm tellin ya, it's time to go now, so pack your bags!"

Surrendering to the reality that Amy did not intend to discuss the matter further, and almost grateful not to have to make a decision on his own about it, he replied, "Alright, sugar, I'll let everybody know it's time to pack and get ready to go." Amy beamed at him gratefully, content that her husband was responsive to her needs, and rubbed her growing belly as if to reassure her unborn child that all was going according to plan.

Elijah went downstairs and found Momma Celia in the kitchen. "Mornin, Momma Celia. How ya'll doin?" he asked, not wanting to simply announce their decision point blank. Momma Celia, ever alert to the nuances of the family dynamic, and no fool, sensed that Elijah was trying to ease his way into something.

"You mighty cheery this mornin, Mister Elijah. Sounds like ya got somethin ta say." She never had been quite able to bring herself to call him directly by his Christian name without the honorific Mister, but refused to call him "master." Her candor, as usual, was a bit disarming, but Elijah actually appreciated not having to beat around the bush with her. Made things simpler. Still, being a man, he found it easier to put the responsibility for his message on Amy, rather than taking it himself.

"Well, Momma, I sure can't put anything past you, now can I? As a matter of fact I wanted to let you know that Amy thinks it's high time we should be headin up to Baltimore, so we can figure out what our options are before the baby comes."

Momma Celia looked at her son-in-law with a wry smile, "Oh she does, does she? And what do you think?" not wanting to let him off the hook for a decision about which she had her own misgivings.

Knowing he was trapped like a butterfly with its wings pinned to cork, Elijah shifted a little uneasily, but responded, "Well, ah, I agree! I think she's right!" He said, almost as if convincing himself, "We been talkin and thinkin about this for a long time now, and it's time to finally take action! So I need ya'll to help get the children packed and ready to go, and pack whatever you'll be needin, too."

Momma Celia looked at Elijah, as if wrestling with her fears and her hopes, and simply said, "Well, alright then. I'll see to it." After a brief pause, she added, "You'd best go tell Gilbert, as I spect you'll be leavin him in charge? We need to keep things runnin smooth here while we away, or we might end up with a whole mess a problems we don't need, specially with the baby comin, an all." She did not reveal any of her suspicions about the outcome of the trip to Baltimore. Nor would it have done any good to do so, as Elijah felt compelled to at least go through the motions of exploring their options in Maryland, despite his own unacknowledged intimations that the environment might not, in fact, be conducive to their relocation there after all.

"You're absolutely right about that, Momma Celia! I'll go find him straight away!" he responded, and set out back from the kitchen door to find Gilbert and alert him to their journey. He wasn't too sure how Gilbert would take the news, but wanted to assure him that he and his family were included in their ultimate plan. He wanted to make certain that Gilbert did not feel resentment about not accompanying them to Baltimore before they knew whether Maryland held any viable hope for them or not. He was praying that, being the skilled overseer he was, Gilbert's concern for the plantation and the crops would outweigh any expectation he might have of immediate liberation.

Elijah found Gilbert out in the barn. He had just come in from one of the new fields of Mexican black seed cotton, and he was enthusiastic. "Mister Elijah, that Mexican seed is doin real good! The plants are strong, they bloom profusely, and are loaded with bolls. If we cross em right, we might be able to get a long fiber like the Sea Island on a higher yield plant!"

Gilbert's enthusiasm was contagious, and Elijah couldn't help but grin, and responded, "That's wonderful Gilbert. Good job! If we succeed, we may be able to get an edge on the English market, since it seems they really love that long fiber!" The prospect was so appealing, Elijah almost forgot why he had come out to find Gilbert in the first place.

Remembering himself, and realizing this news provided him a perfect segway, he continued, "Gilbert, I've been thinkin of makin a trip up to

Baltimore to see if I can't take advantage of the shippin opportunities up there to send our cotton to England. I'm worried that with the political tensions heatin up between the North and South around here, our Northern market may get cut off." He was trying to ease his way into the "family" portion of the trip, wanting to get a sense of Gilbert's reaction first.

"That sounds like a good idea, Mister Elijah. I heard tell they buildin some mighty fast ships up there in Baltimore. I guess you figurin they may be fast enough to beat out our competition from Charleston an Savannah, am I right?" Gilbert was foreman for a reason. He had a great sense of business logistics, as well as the managerial and horticultural fine points of cotton production.

"That's exactly right! Not only that, Baltimore has built a new railroad all the way out to Ohio. They call it the Baltimore & Ohio Railroad, or B&O! Seems the B&O is sending a lot of goods out West. They say towns are poppin up all across the continent, and out in the plains they need lumber for buildin. We may have a lot of promisin opportunities up there! At least, that's what I'm hopin."

He figured now was the time to close in on the family trip, since Gilbert clearly grasped and was enthusiastic about the possibilities. So he continued, "But I can't be sure until I find out more about it. I've written to a fella named George Brown up there. He's been pretty successful financin international business opportunities, so I'm hopin to be able to cut a deal with him." He paused for a moment, searching for the right words. "And Gilbert, I'm not sure yet, but I'm lookin into the possibility that Maryland's laws might allow me to emancipate ya'll up there. I've decided to take Amy, Momma Celia, and the children with me, so we can get a sense of the possibilities."

Gilbert shifted a little uncomfortably. He knew he was still a slave, and had no right to question his master's decision or insist he be included in that process, but he couldn't help feel a mixture of hope for their future, and jealousy of his mother and sister. He forced himself to mumble a submissive, "Yessir," but his heart wasn't in it. He couldn't hide a tinge of disappointment in his voice.

Elijah, expecting as much, went on to say, "Look, Gilbert, I promise ya'll that once I find a place where the law will allow me to do what South Carolina law denies us, I'll bring you and your family to wherever we end up. I couldn't do otherwise and be able to live with my conscience! And you know Amy would never let me hear the end of it!" he grinned at this last assurance.

Gilbert looked at his master squarely in the eyes and could see he was speaking truthfully. He relaxed, and nodded his understanding, "I surely do appreciate that, sir, and I believe you will."

The tension easing between them, Elijah shifted tone. "I know Momma Celia told ya we're gonna need your help to pull all this off. So this is what I need ya to do. I need ya to keep doin the wonderful job you've been doin. Watch after the cotton, and the lumber mill, and keep the others in line and workin hard, just the way ya always do."

Gilbert already anticipated where this was going. "If ya'll are gonna be away then, we've got to look like everything's business as usual while ya'll are gone, lest folks around here start gettin suspicious. And forgive me for sayin so, sir, but I spect that means your relations in particular!" He couldn't help but point out the obvious, as they both knew Elijah's white relations looked on the plantation with an avaricious eye, and looked at Elijah's relationship with Gilbert's sister with disdain and resentment. Last thing they needed was to have some other Willis trying to come onto the plantation and take charge. Hard to say whom that would be worse for, Elijah or the slaves, but that was an ugly possibility neither man wanted to contemplate!

"Lord knows that's right, Gilbert! I've already put out word to Will Beazely at the depot that I'm makin a business trip to Baltimore, and takin Amy and the children with me." As if to underscore the point, he added, "As far as anyone else knows, this is just a business trip, period. And we need to keep it that way, so you keep a sharp ear out among the others. Any gossip from around here has got to be nipped in the bud, or we'll have Hell to pay."

"I understand, sir. Amy and Momma already made that clear. Ya'll can count on me!" Gilbert's commitment was genuine, as he knew his own future depended on it, as well as that of the rest of the family and of everyone else on the plantation for that matter.

Satisfied that he and Gilbert understood each other, and knowing he could rely on Gilbert to run things well in his absence, Elijah began to feel energized by the prospect of the trip North. When he got back to the plantation house, it was as if he'd walked into a beehive. Amy had marshaled the troops like a general, shouting commands from her headquarters in the bedroom. Momma Celia, the adjutant general, had the children bustling all over the place, fetching dried clothes off the clothesline out back, heating irons on the stove to press and fold the clothes, pulling things out of bureau drawers, and armoires, calling back and forth to each other about what did Momma want them to do with this, or did Momma Celia know where they could find that?

"Momma, can I take my dolly?"

"Clarissa, don't forget to pack your new petticoat!"

"Boys, polish your shoes, you gotta make the right impression, and not look like some field hand!"

"Hey Elleck, that's my shirt, not yours!"

"Is not, yours is over there!"

"Phillip, do those pants still even fit you?"

"Momma Celia, have you seen my black socks?"

As Elijah came upstairs he looked around in wonder. He couldn't have imagined that the entire household could have been galvanized into such a frenzy of activity by the mere decision to go ahead and pack for the trip. Amy, bent over a large steamer trunk, organizing its growing contents, stood up, her hand on her back, massaging it. Elijah noted with surprise that even the baby seemed to have grown suddenly, and realized all this activity could take its toll on Amy.

"Hey there, darlin, why don't you lie down for a spell? I know you're eager to get goin, but we don't have to have the entire household packed up by dinnertime! You keep this pace up, and the baby might just pop out on its own, wonderin what all the excitement's about!" He smiled affectionately at Amy, who realizing he was right, sat down on the edge of the bed with a sigh of relief.

"Elijah, honey, I'm glad you're here! Could you get my hat box down from on top of the armoire for me?" She asked, still in command mode despite her need for rest.

Elijah sighed with a mixture of amusement and exasperation, seeing clearly that getting Amy to slow down was easier said than done. He smiled at her, saying with a touch of sarcasm, "You do realize, don't you, that we're not taking the whole house right now? We need to take only what's necessary, so we don't look like we're movin, but only making the business trip we said we were! If we do end up stayin, we can have the rest brought up later."

Amy smiled back. "I know, sugar. I'm sorry. I'm just so anxious for things to go well, I guess I'm gettin myself a little too worked up!"

"Yes, you are!" Elijah agreed calmly. He was charmed by the reality that, despite her extreme competence, she was also still at least a little vulnerable.

It inspired him to love her more and more. "Everything's gonna be fine. Don't you worry. We'll just take things slowly and steadily, and we'll be fine." he said reassuringly. "I just spoke with Gilbert, and everything's set. I know things will be alright leavin em in his hands."

"How did he react when ya told him ya're takin us with ya?" Amy asked, suddenly concerned about her brother and his family.

"About as I expected. I think he was a little upset, or jealous maybe. But I assured him that as soon as we figured out whether I could emancipate ya'll legally up there, I'd bring him and his family up there with us. He seemed a lot more receptive after that." Amy felt relieved.

"He also understood completely that his role here is crucial to our success, because he's got to keep the plantations runnin smoothly so neither my other relations, nor anyone else around town starts gettin suspicious and tries to come over here and take charge of things. That absolutely must not be allowed to happen!"

Amy suddenly became anxious again. Perhaps her pregnancy accounted for some of the emotional volatility, but even without being pregnant, the fact was they were entering into uncharted territory, and she couldn't help but be a little scared. It had never occurred to her, for example, that Elijah's relations might actually attempt to take over the plantation if they were absent for too long. The very thought of it conjured some frightening images about what would happen to the other slaves, and especially to Gilbert, as part of her family. It was clear they considered her an interloper, so she could only imagine how they might take that out on her brother!

"Elijah, honey, how're ya plannin to handle the plantations if it turns out we could resettle up in Maryland?" Amy looked at her husband without reproach, genuinely curious as to how he saw the subsequent steps, assuming they could in fact be successfully emancipated.

The question loomed heavy in the room, for the truth was Elijah hadn't figured that out yet, and was torn as to how best to proceed. Having spent a lifetime building a prosperous cotton and lumber business, the thought of giving it up or changing to some other enterprise of which he knew little, was distressing. He wasn't sure he had the energy and strength to start over this late in life. On the other hand, he was also increasingly aware that if he were to honor his commitment to free the other slaves, there was little likelihood that he'd be able to maintain the plantations. The alternative would be to sell off all the property. They could certainly live comfortably on the proceeds without having to work, and the thought of that as a possibility was, for the first time, attractive. Having more time with Amy and the children and being able to take an active role in seeing they all got an education was a dream he had envisioned with increasing frequency. But for now there were just too many variables in the equation to tell which way things might go. Elijah sat thoughtfully, contemplating the issue before responding.

"God knows I wish I knew, darlin. Truth is, I don't, at least not yet. It may be we'll have to do things gradually. Keep the plantation runnin as is, for a while, until I can set things up to bring Gilbert and his family up with us, and figure out how to handle the rest of the slaves too." Amy knit her brows at this.

Elijah continued, " It doesn't seem likely that I can emancipate all of them without requiring them to leave South Carolina, and there may be some who won't want to do that, since they have family on neighboring plantations and all." It had never occurred to Amy that there might actually be some slaves who preferred bondage at home to freedom someplace unknown. The thought was disturbing.

Elijah went on, "I may be forced to sell the place, and maybe even some of the slaves- at least some who don't wanna leave South Carolina- and just take the proceeds to help us get a fresh start somewhere else. Fact is, none of the options I can think of seem ideal to me, and I can't see how to guarantee that the outcome will be equally satisfyin to everybody." Amy shifted uncomfortably; the baby kicking made her wince a bit as she lay back against the pillows with another sigh.

"Lord, Elijah, now that we're actually takin action on all this, it's lookin a whole lot more complicated that just choosin freedom! We gonna have to do a whole lot of prayin to find our way out of this mess without hurtin anybody along the way."

Elijah looked at Amy almost with relief that she had finally realized this, for the probability that some, at least, might be sacrificed in the process had been plaguing him, even though he saw it as almost inevitable. He wasn't looking forward to making the decision about who was most expendable.

Rather than point that out and add to his wife's stress any further, he simply nodded and said, "Well, we knew this wasn't gonna be easy, and we'll just have to take things one step at a time and do the best we can. In the meantime, you try and get some rest, I'll go check with Momma Celia and see how things are goin with the packin."

By now drifting off into a deep sleep, Amy nodded and murmured, "Thanks, sugar, I just need to put my feet up for a little bit. Tell Momma I'll be down shortly to help." And she was fast asleep before Elijah could even respond. He kissed her lightly on the forehead, caressed her belly gently, as if to also comfort their baby, and tiptoed out of the room, closing the door quietly behind him so the continued bustle of the household wouldn't wake her.

XX

As Elijah thought about their travel plans, he began to feel that because the rail lines were not direct and there would have to be several changes en route, rather than taking the train all the way up to Baltimore, they'd better take it as far as Richmond, and go by ship the rest of the way. They could take a Powhatan Line Packet down the James River to Norfolk and continue their journey on the Baltimore Steam Packet Company, popularly known as the Old Bay Line, up the Chesapeake Bay to Baltimore.

He'd heard that the new steamship, *The North Carolina*, was the wonder of the Chesapeake with imported Belgian carpets, velvet chairs, white paneling, and gilded moldings. Even though he was not pretentious himself, he did appreciate quality and enjoy comfort, so he fancied making the last leg of the trip in style, as a treat to Amy and the family. Besides, the fresh sea air would be good for them, and there would be more mobility for Amy on board a ship than on the train. Moreover, taking the packet right up the Chesapeake Bay to Baltimore, they could dock within a stone's throw of the Admiral Fell Inn. That would make the luggage transfer easier. It also dawned on Elijah that traveling with seven coloreds, they might have fewer prying eyes and attitudes to confront onboard a ship than traveling through countless Southern towns the rest of the way by train. Not being too sure of what they might be confronted with up in Virginia, or even Maryland, that in itself might make things a whole lot easier on all of them.

Gilbert and Jason helped take the family to the depot early in the morning. Jason drove Elijah, Amy and the children in the carriage, and Gilbert drove with Momma Celia and the luggage in a low-sided buckboard, following behind. The buckboard was weathered from much hauling, but the carriage was well-maintained, painted black with the wheels and spokes painted a golden yellow. It was intended for traveling in greater comfort and style. Once all had duly boarded, Julius saw them off, as he was left in charge of the plantation until Gilbert and Jason got back.

Everything went smoothly and without mishap. Mr. Beazely, already alerted to their plans, met them on the platform, solicitously mindful that his assistance might ensure that he would be entrusted with the increased business Elijah hoped to achieve as a result of this journey.

Amy, Momma Celia, and the children were all appropriately submissive and well behaved, as behooved them in public. There was no hint of resentment or rebellion among them, not even the older boys let on that this was anything other than a master traveling with his slaves, despite the fact that Mr. Beazely knew they were Elijah's family. There was total complicity among them, even if each had their own reasons. Even the girls understood they were not to call Elijah 'Papa,' but rather, 'Mister Elijah,' whenever others were around.

Amy and Momma Celia had seen the train come through many times, but this was a new experience for the children. The boys looked with wonder and admiration at the engine as it spouted steam from its pistons, and smoke and sparks billowed from the funnel-shaped smoke stack. "Lawdy, would you look at that!" shouted Elder as the train came into view. "Look like a dragon spoutin fire!" Phillip chimed in "Sho does- and that cow-catcher on the front end is like his teeth!" he grinned. "Yeah! And listen to that whistle! Like about to make ya deaf, it's so loud!" agreed Elleck, enthusiastically.

The girls, on the other hand, were more intimidated by the iron beast, little Julia clinging tightly to her mother's skirts, and even Clarissa, holding her grandmother's hand, squeezed involuntarily as the train roared into the station before hissing, gasping and spluttering to a stop.

Standing back on the platform when the train chugged into the station to avoid the steam and the soot, Elijah now herded the family and luggage on board. Unfortunately, protocol demanded he sit apart from the family, slaves being relegated to a section of the baggage car. This caused some momentary separation anxiety, especially for the girls, but as they were in the capable company of both Amy and Momma Celia, this was soon replaced by the simple fascination of actually boarding a train for the first time in their young lives.

As they pulled out of the station to the growl of the engine, the lurching forward of the cars, and the shriek of the whistle, the children stared out the windows wide-eyed, waving to Mr. Beazely on the platform, and watching him steadily shrink in the distance. Before long, rounding a bend, he disappeared, and all they could see was fields, and farms, and forests whirring by faster than they could ever have imagined possible. The steady clack of the wheels rocked them gently into a reverie of wonder at such an adventure.

Momma Celia, as was her custom, was ever watchful, and wary of relaxing too much, fearful that now they had left the safety of the plantation that they knew and controlled, anything might happen. There was no telling what calamities might befall them! Amy, on the other hand, sensing the depth of Elijah's resolve to make good on his promise despite the risks, felt a mixture of anxiety and quiet determination overcome her, as if the train carried them not just towards Baltimore, but to fulfill an uncertain but hopeful destiny.

Elijah sat absorbed in his own contemplation of future possibilities. His mind vacillated between his entrepreneurial hopes and his concerns for his family's future. Those great hopes seemed tempered by possible dangers, and although the rhythm of the train's steady progress lulled even him into an almost trancelike state, his contemplation was not entirely peaceful. He did not dare let down his guard, for their future clearly depended on being ever-vigilant until a clear solution was found.

As the miles dragged on, the wonder of the adventure changed to boredom and discomfort for the children. Amy and Momma Celia tried to comfort the girls and keep the boys from getting unruly. Clarissa and Julia took turns sitting on their grandmother's lap, Amy's belly by now being too large to easily accommodate them without considerable discomfort. Their brothers would occasionally consent to the girls sitting on their laps too, but their tolerance was generally short lived, and the girls would grow fidgety. Fortunately, they had brought some of Momma Celia's fried chicken, some cornbread, some beef jerky and a bag of oranges to eat along the way, and a couple of jugs of water, since they were not sure whether it would be possible to stop for food, and figured it unlikely the train would provide any dining, especially for slaves.

Elijah came back to visit periodically to make sure they were alright, but could not do so for long without raising suspicions among the white passengers. Day passed to night, and the darkened landscape made their reality shrink to the confines of the interior of the baggage car, stacked with valises, and trunks, and all manner of goods, pressing in on the benches allotted to them. It was stuffy and uncomfortable in the wavering light of an oil lamp suspended from the ceiling.

Amy began to experience the clacking of the wheels and rocking of the car as increasingly jarring to her and the baby, feeling each bump with growing intensity as they went on. There was no bathroom on board, just a chamber pot with a lid in a sort of closet in the corner to do their business. The smell made her nauseated. The train ride had begun like a trip to the Promised Land, but was becoming more like a trip through Hell, when finally, after what seemed an eternity of sporadic dozing and shifting positions in a vain attempt to get comfortable, the horizon began to lighten and the sun edged its way up over the Richmond skyline.

When the train finally pulled screeching and clanking into the Richmond station, Elijah immediately came back to gather the family and usher them to a carriage. They were all looking somewhat worse for the wear, including Elijah, who had hardly slept a wink, despite being in more comfortable seating up front.

Relieved to get off the train, the boys looked around and started to stretch their legs on the platform. Richmond had a distinctly different feel from the low country of South Carolina. It was not just because the land wasn't as flat, or the trees were different, this was a real city, and they were fascinated by the bustle of it all. The girls, on the other hand, had already had enough of traveling.

Little Julia cried out, "Papa!" Before she could add anything more, Momma Celia gave her a quick jab of the elbow, looking around nervously to see if anyone noticed what her granddaughter had called their owner. Julia, even in her exhaustion, caught herself, looking very apologetic, and corrected herself, "I mean, Mister Elijah, I'm tired!" Elijah too, looked around before responding in a low voice, "I know sweetheart, we all are. I'm gonna get us to the boat landin right away, and once we're on board, you'll be able to rest more comfortably.

The children, working hard not to grumble or cause a scene despite their inclination to express their discomfort, helped drag their luggage to a nearby hack and load it on board, the family piling in as best they could. The boys were grateful for the exercise after the confinement on the train. The journey to the wharf on the James River Canal was not overly long, and being out in the air and with Elijah again was a relief to everyone after the constraints of the baggage car. Elijah was apologetic.

He looked at Amy with concern. Clearly uncomfortable from the long train ride, yet uncomplaining, she seemed to grit her teeth in determination. "Are you alright darlin?" he asked her in a low voice, so the driver would not hear. She nodded stoically. Momma Celia grunted skeptically as if to say, "You believe that?" but she kept quiet, as usual. The children grumbled and whined amongst themselves, vying for seating space in the heavily loaded and crowded carriage, but they were remarkably united in being careful not to cause too much fuss, or draw the attention of others as they went by.

Arriving at the dock, they saw a flat-bottomed packet, more like a barge than a ship, moored to the wharf, with a gangplank to permit the loading of passengers and freight alike. Once again, the family faced a new experience, and headed up the gangplank with trepidation and surprise. They felt the boat's rocking slightly as people boarded. As it was their first experience of not being on solid ground, the sensation was disconcerting, if not downright frightening. Momma Celia's face set like stone in distrust, but for all the world she would not risk complaining, even though it made her want to give Elijah a piece of her mind. Frightening memories of her grandmother telling her about being on a slave ship troubled her, and she had to face her fear and force herself onboard. Amy looked a little green as she climbed on board, uncertain whether the ship's movement was going to make her sea sick. The children, however, found the rocking movement both surprising and entertaining, as they gradually found their footing.

The trip to Norfolk was not, in fact, as onerous as the train-ride to Richmond. As the weather was mercifully fine, the family felt refreshed by the sun, the breeze, and the lush landscape as they headed down the James River toward the sea. There were only a few other passengers and they paid little attention to Elijah and his family. The packet was mostly loaded with goods for shipment to Norfolk. They had managed to buy some food on shore before boarding, and there were benches on the top deck where they could sit and enjoy the view, almost like pews in a church looking up at God's blue heaven.

XXI

By the time they reached Norfolk, they had grown considerably more comfortable with the whole idea of travel by water, but they were unprepared for the reality of the last leg of the trip. As the packet docked in Norfolk, they looked across the wharf and saw a sight that left them awestruck. *The North Carolina* was the newest and most stately ship of the Old Bay Line. She was a floating version of a grand hotel, a glimmering vision of unimaginable glory to the children, and an offering of comfort to Amy that was desperately needed after their sojourn from South Carolina.

As they boarded, the clerks verified that the tickets of Elijah's traveling companions were valid, and that as his property they were all there with his permission. People of color were not permitted to travel unaccompanied in Virginia, for suspicion of being runaways. As he had done earlier, when crossing into North Carolina, and then into Virgina, Elijah had presented Angus Patterson's letter as further confirmation, which seemed to convince the authorities that nothing was amiss. Having dispensed with that discomfort, the family immediately began to explore the ship. As they found their way along deck to the dining room, they all marveled at the elegance Elijah had already described to them. There really were Belgian carpets and marble topped tables, velvet chairs and gilded white paneling!

Since the Old Bay line catered to both Northerners and Southerners, the staff was rather more tolerant of racial differences than folks of an exclusively Southern persuasion. Having already procured food before boarding, Elijah managed to secure a couple of staterooms for them to get some rest, as the trip would take at least twelve hours. The steamship company seemed not to care who the occupants were so long as they paid, and it was by then nearly sunset. They had only dozed fitfully since leaving Williston, so after supper, the whole family welcomed their bunks like a long lost loved one, and fell into the embrace of a deep sleep.

A channel buoy's deep-throated bong awoke Amy from her dream. She and Elijah had been standing arm-in-arm on a hilltop blooming with wildflowers, overlooking a lush green valley. The children were there, and had friends with them, playing. Momma Celia, and Gilbert, and his wife and children were smiling and pointing excitedly to the farmland below. Down the hill behind them, the other slaves on the Willis Plantation were climbing the hill, dressed like they were going to a church picnic. There were other folks too, both black and white. Old Angus Patterson, and his housekeeper Mary, and Joseph Harley, and John Bauskett and his wife, Will Beazely, and Reason and Ary Wooley, and others she could not identify.

Everything was bright, as if the sun had been fresh-scrubbed and glowed warmer and more beautifully than usual. There was a fragrance of flowers and new mown meadows in the air, and a breeze that caressed the skin like a lover's gentle kiss. As they all gathered on the hilltop and prepared to go down into the valley to their new home, there was suddenly a warning bell sounding an alarm!

Amy awoke with a start, the buoy's voice still reverberating in her ears and making it hard to tell what was dream, and what was reality. She felt disoriented, and unsure if the dream were an omen that their entry into their "Promised Land" of freedom and prosperity was to be blocked, or the warning bell was to ward off those who might be coming after them, and would block their pursuers from entering. A dim light entered the stateroom from the porthole, and Amy could make out a misty smudge of green wooded shores on the horizon. It was dawn, and they must soon be approaching Baltimore.

Out on deck people were astir. As Amy's dream receded and her mind refocused on her awakening family, she felt the baby kick as if to say, "Come on, Momma, time to get up and get goin!" Feeling rested after the grueling train ride, though disconcerted by her dream, she got out of her berth, dressed quickly, and woke the children. With Momma Celia, she set to getting them all washed up, brushing the girls' hair, and making sure all the children looked presentable for their arrival in Baltimore. Fresh-scrubbed and wearing their best clothes, Elijah and the family presented themselves in the dining room for breakfast.

The passengers being a mix of Northerners and Southerners reflected America's mood of the times. When the Willis family entered the dining room, some travelers looked at them with curiosity, others with disapproval, as they made their way among the tables to a corner where they could sit undisturbed.

"Well that's certainly a sight you don't see every day!" commented one passenger to his wife, with an ungracious, gravelly drawl. She looked up, munching on a mouthful of breakfast ham and biscuits with a bovine expression, like a cow chewing her cud. She raised her eyebrows in the midst of her rumination, and said, "He's got his nerve, bringin them into the dinin room like that! I thought this ship catered to people of a higher social standin!" She shook her head disapprovingly, her second chin jiggling and flapping like a cow's dewlap.

At another table, two well-dressed gentlemen also looked up. Frederick Law Olmstead, a journalist and landscape architect, and his brother John were returning from a garden tour of the South, animatedly discussing what had most excited them of what they had seen. Frederick had been designing public gardens and parks up North and was looking for new ideas to incorporate in his plans. He hoped to even create a great landscape garden in the middle of New York City one day, and was coming home filled with new observations and inspiration. Along with the sweeping landscapes and grand gardens of the Southern cities and plantations, during their Southern sojourn he and his brother had, of course, also observed the condition of slaves throughout the South. They were consequently feeling more convinced than ever that the country must move toward their emancipation.

Seeing Elijah and his family pass by, Frederick commented, "Do you suppose, John, that is a glimpse of the future?" He added wryly, "Not since New Orleans have we seen such a blended palette!"

John cast an appraising eye on the Willis family as he sipped his coffee. "Much as I'd like to see the slaves emancipated once and for all, I suspect we are a long way from real acceptance of such things. I must admit, however, I admire that gentleman for the courage to treat them with such dignity and familiarity in public!"

Amy and Momma Celia could feel the eyes upon them and tried not to listen to the comments, but rather, stoically continued to a table somewhat removed from the other guests and took their seats for breakfast. The children were still too sleepy to pay much attention to the others in the dining room. Elijah, however, also noticed the stares and caught snatches of the comments. He looked at the children with a stern glance to remind them of their manners, but gradually relaxed as he reviewed the breakfast menu, smiling appreciatively at the prospect of a satisfying meal after the paltry fare of the earlier leg of their journey.

The food on *The North Carolina* was famous for being a blend of the best of North and South, and was served in elegant style. The menu offered

Southern standards like ham and grits, fried eggs, sausage and bacon, corn bread, buttermilk flapjacks with blackstrap molasses or magnolia honey, local specialties like crab cakes from Maryland, and more Northern delicacies like Amish Sour Cream Friendship Cake and pastries from Pennsylvania, and a wide variety of coffees, teas, and even fresh fruit juices from New York. Being breakfast, the selections were not as exotic as the evening fare, but the children ate with gusto, with occasional reminders and admonitions from Amy and Momma Celia, punctuating their repast.

"Children, sit up straight!"

"Phillip, hold your knife and fork properly!"

"Girls, use your napkins!"

"Boys, chew your food well, don't eat like you're a hog at a trough on the plantation!"

Satiated after the gastronomic delights of breakfast, the family strolled on the deck, taking the morning air. The fresh breeze smelled of fish, and salt water, and promise. The children hung on the railings pointing and waving to other boats, large and small, sail and steam, crab fishermen, and oystermen, and pleasure seekers. They noted various landmarks along the shores, and looking northwest, could see more and more houses and other buildings, a clear indication they were approaching a city. They thought it must be Baltimore, but they overheard another passenger telling his companion that it was Annapolis, the State Capital. The fellow traveler pointed out the State House, explaining that it had briefly been the center of the Federal Government before the founding of Washington and the District of Columbia. It was soon clearly visible on the hilltop overlooking the harbor, and to its right downhill they could make out St. John's College, Maryland's oldest, and next to it the recently founded Naval Academy. *The North Carolina*, however, kept well off from shore and steadily sailed on heading north, past Gibson Island. As they churned along, eventually they spotted off in the distance the ramparts of Fort McHenry, where the British had been repelled back in the War of 1812.

As the ship rounded the point at Ft. McHenry, the children looked wide-eyed at the size of the city that came into view. It seemed enormous. Row after row of brick houses, large and small, with gleaming white marble steps, on tree lined streets covered Federal Hill to their left and Canton to their right. Off in the distance they spotted a large dome, flanked by twin domed towers. Perhaps due to her own condition, the domes reminded Amy of the breasts and belly of a reclining pregnant woman. Unbeknownst to her, it was, appropriately, the profile of the Basilica of the Immaculate Conception, the spiritual heart of this city named after Lord Baltimore.

According to the loquacious passenger nearby, who continued to regale his companion with a monologue on the region's history, Charles Calvert, the first Lord Baltimore, had been a Catholic nobleman who exchanged the religious tensions spurred by his unpopular faith in England for the prosperous and more tolerant opportunities in the New World. King Charles, perhaps relieved to have him more distant, had generously granted him much of what became the State of Maryland. Unlike some of the Puritan colonies to the north, Baltimore City had from the outset given safe haven to many faiths: Catholics, all manner of Protestants, Quakers, the famously middle-of the road adherents of the Church of England, (by now its American descendants, the Episcopalians), and even Jews!

Upon overhearing this, Elijah thought to himself, hopefully, "Well that may be a good sign. If Baltimore is so open to people of different faiths, maybe they're also open to people of different colors!"

Further uphill beyond the Basilica, the Willis family could make out an enormous column with a statue on top. It was the first monument erected to George Washington in the nation, and stood in the heart of a neighborhood where Baltimore's wealthiest tycoons had their homes. The whole family gawked in wonder at such a vision of prosperity. On par with Charleston to the south, and New York to the north, Baltimore was one of the greatest hubs of commerce on the Atlantic coast. In addition to her shipbuilding and shipping enterprises, she was also a birthplace of the promise of the future that would one day unite the coasts: railroads. Elijah's eyes were opened to a new sense of opportunity here, and he couldn't wait to explore the possibilities. The excitement infected the whole family, even the wary Momma Celia.

As *The North Carolina* headed up the harbor, they passed ships from all around the world: whalers from New England, clippers in the China trade, sturdy merchantmen from England, and France, and Spain, packets that plied the inland waterways, privateers that sailed the Caribbean, navy frigates and men o' war, and countless others. The harbor seemed a floating forest of masts, and yardarms, and rigging. Sailors shouted to each other across cargo-laden decks in a dozen languages.

Closer by, past Canton and Lighthouse Point, they spotted Fells Point, their destination. There appeared to be a large plaza by the wharf, with a wide boulevard leading from there inland and uphill, toward the interior of the city, church spires punctuating the horizon in all directions. There was a great deal of activity in the streets: carriages, wagons, street vendors, shopkeepers, sailors, merchants- all manner of folk going to and fro.

Once *The North Carolina* had docked, Elijah gathered the family. "Well children, here we are!" he announced. "We'd best be gathering our things and get ready to go ashore. Elder, I need you and Elleck and Phillip to handle the luggage. Momma Celia, keep a tight hold on the girls. Girls, don't let go of your grandma, now. Amy, watch your step goin down the gangplank, darlin. We don't want that baby gettin baptized prematurely!"

The family, filled with a mixture of excitement and trepidation, made their way amidships to debark, along with the other passengers, onto the busy wharf and the bustle of Thames Street. Elijah was about to hail a carriage when he saw diagonally across Thames Street from the wharf, on the corner of the plaza, a sign indicating The Admiral Fell Inn, their designated address.

"Well!" he exclaimed, "That certainly is convenient! I never imagined our hotel would be so close to the landin!" He called a couple of porters and indicated they should bring the luggage across the street to the Inn, while he hustled the family together and led them to their lodgings. Amy clung to his arm nervously. Momma Celia was looking every which way, like she was expecting disaster to strike at any moment, clutching the girls' hands so tightly they winced and whined, "Momma Celia, you're hurtin me!" The boys simply gawked in wonder and excitement at everything.

Hoping for gracious accommodations, Elijah was distressed to discover that the Admiral Fell was more a sailor's boarding house and tavern than what he considered a real hotel. They made their way across the plaza, through longshoremen, carriers, drunken sailors, and ladies with heavily rouged cheeks and tightly-laced bodices displaying the buxom welcome sailors dream of on a long voyage. The boys gaped in fascination, while Momma Celia shielded the girls' eyes from these dockside denizens.

The excitement they had felt at seeing the city from afar was quickly fading and being replaced by both a sense of danger, and a disillusionment that Elijah's business contact, Mr. Brown, would have thought these accommodations appropriate. Elijah wondered whether if he had told Mr. Brown the nature of his relationship with Amy and the children, another hotel might have been recommended? But there was nothing for it but to make themselves as comfortable as they could, at least until some better alternative might be found. Amy began to feel the warning bell of her dream was an ill omen, not a protection.

Elijah decided the first order of business was to get word to George Brown of their arrival. Not knowing Baltimore first hand, he felt somewhat at the mercy of his sole business contact- a problem he determined he must soon remedy by making as many inquiries as possible to learn more about the city, its virtues, vices, policies, and problems. He also wanted to find someone of reputable standing in the legal profession, through whom he could discover the nature of Maryland's laws concerning people of color, both slave and free. He sent an urgent message to Mr. Brown, and then began to prowl about to see what other resources he could find.

As it turned out, the hotel clerk, accustomed to new arrivals seeking business or information, happened to have in his possession a copy of *Matchett's Baltimore Director*, a useful compendium of the names, addresses, and professions of Baltimore's residents, along with an engraved map of the city, lists of institutions, businesses, banks, and even places of worship. Though a few years old, Elijah assumed that most of the addresses would be current enough that he could quickly track down the kinds of contacts he so desperately needed. Orienting himself on the map, he began to search for lawyers within easy access of his lodgings, and struck upon one, William H. Dorsey, Attorney at Law, on 3 Fayette Street, not far from the hotel.

Meanwhile, Amy and Momma Celia were trying to make the best of the lodgings allotted them. "Children, you are not to go out of this building without one of us with ya, do ya'll understand?" Amy told her brood. "Yes ma'am!" was the immediate response of the girls, who were feeling a little alarmed by the sheer number and noisiness of people outside, not to mention the fact that clearly some of them were not what Momma would call "proper." The boys, eyeing some of the voluptuous ladies who were serving as an impromptu sailors' welcoming committee on the street outside, blushed slightly, and seemed a little hesitant in their response to their mother, but muttered an unenthusiastic "Yes'm," wishing they could go out and explore on their own the fascinations of this newly discovered metropolis.

Momma Celia, noting her grandsons' wandering eyes, reinforced Amy's admonition, which she considered far too passive to register the proper warning in the minds of adolescent boys discovering their natural urges. "I see ya'll lookin out the window at them ladies out there, but they ain't no ladies. Don't' ya'll be gettin no ideas. God strike ya if ya'll go messin with them! Ya'll can get all kinda nasty sickness, make ya man parts blister an itch, and shrivel right up!" The boys looked with horror at their grandmother, not sure which was more alarming- that such a thing could happen, or that their grandmother would know about it. Their response to the warning, however, was the far more immediate and unequivocal one she had been hoping to elicit. "No ma'am, I mean yes ma'am. I mean we won't, we promise!" They all nodded emphatically, their hands in their pockets cupping themselves protectively, as if to reassure themselves nothing had fallen off by Divine retribution for their fantasies.

Once settled into their quarters, it was nearly midday, so Elijah and the family decided to at least explore the plaza and immediate environs for someplace to eat. The ground floor of the Inn had a dark and noisy, smoke-filled tavern, but there were other options available too. There was a distinctive aroma wafting across the square, a mixture of fresh beer, fried fish, and crabs, for which Baltimore was famous. Down Thames Street at the corner of Bond, they saw a crab shack along the wharf. People were sitting at long tables covered with brown wrapping paper. Every few feet along the length of these tables there was a huge pile of steamed crabs in the middle. Wooden mallets were ranged along what passed for place settings. There were knives, and bowls for the picked shells. Pitchers of cold frothy beer were passed back and forth, and customers sat on long benches, picking crabs and talking affably.

The Willis family concluded that this was the Baltimore equivalent of barbeque in South Carolina- an event as much about socializing as eating, but with memorable smells and flavors to enjoy. Crab picking seemed to be an egalitarian event, as there were diners of all descriptions and stations. Someone saw them eyeing the table and, recognizing them as newcomers, waved them over in invitation.

"Come on over, hon, give it a try. You don't want to miss our famous crabs!"

Elijah thought it might be a good idea to get a sense of how people reacted, so he nodded to the children, and despite Momma Celia looking even warier than usual, the family approached the tables. People scooted amiably down the benches to make room, and a little awkwardly, the Willis family clambered over the benches and sat down to eat. Elijah asked the waiter if there was any alternative to the beer, as it wasn't suitable for the ladies and the children. His only option was root beer- a beverage the children had never tried, but since it was free of alcohol, Elijah agreed.

Picking crabs is a messy business at its best, but for the uninitiated, it can be a maddening challenge to extract enough of the succulent meat to fill you up. Moreover, the crabs were steamed in a mixture of spices that made your mouth burn and your lips tingle. It also made you thirsty-which was the point, since the crab shacks made more money off the sale of beer than from the plentiful crabs themselves.

With scowls from Momma Celia, wrinkled noses from the boys, whines from the girls, and a few expletives muttered by Elijah as he cut his fingers on a recalcitrant crab claw, trying not to wince in unmanly discomfort at the sting of the spices in the cuts, they valiantly attempted to make their way through the meal, to the amusement of the regulars. The customer who had invited them over, patiently tried to show them how to coordinate the use of the knife and the mallet with surgical precision, to split open the claws and extract the juiciest meat without cutting themselves on the shells. Amy was finding the fishy smell difficult to stomach with her pregnancy, and trying to smile graciously, scarcely picked at her food, sending Elijah looks that indicated it was time to go.

Elijah thanked the waiter and their host, paid for their meal, and bade them all farewell, as he mustered the family troops and they continued their exploration of the area. Along with the lofts of sail makers, rope makers, and the shipyards, there was a flourishing variety of shops selling all kinds of merchandise, from shoes and clothes, to furniture, to fruits and vegetables. There was also a plethora of pubs, taverns, and liquor vendors catering to the steady influx of sailors on shore leave, as well as to the local population.

Their stroll took them past numerous brick buildings- warehouses along the waterfront, and mostly two and three story houses along the inland side of the street, often with a shop or eating or drinking establishment on the ground floor. They were built adjoining each other, side by side, with only an occasional dark alley or wrought iron gate separating them. The family walked east down Thames Street to the tree-lined Ann Street, inland and north to Aliceanna, west back over to the Square, across Broadway on to Bond Street, and then south back down to Thames, before returning at last to the Admiral Fell. Amy, unaccustomed to walking on cobblestones instead of the soft dirt roads of South Carolina, was feeling tired and much in need of rest, and took the children upstairs with Momma Celia.

Concerned for Amy and the baby, Elijah said, "I'm sorry about the food, darlin. I can see it didn't sit too well with ya. Folks around here surely seem to love their crabs, but seems like an awful lot of work for little reward to me. Give me a crab cake anytime over that!"

Amy readily agreed, "I suppose it might'n have been so bad if we were more rested and I weren't pregnant. I mean, the people were friendly and all, which was a pleasant surprise, but the smell of the crabs, the sea, and the beer, nearly gave me a case of the vapors!"

"I saw a market up on the square," Elijah answered, "Do ya need me to get ya'll somethin?"

No sugar, I'm fine, I just need to get off my feet a spell and rest. The baby's been kickin a lot, and I want to calm him down a bit." Amy held her belly protectively.

"Oh, him, is it? So you think it's a boy?" Elijah perked up his ears.

"It sure feels like it. He's a rambunctious little bundle, like to wear me out before he even gets here!" Elijah smiled at the thought he might actually have a son of his own. He loved the girls, and he had come to love Elder, Elleck and Phillip too, but a son of his own to carry on the family name, now that would really be something!

"Will ya'll be alright if I leave ya for a few hours? I'd like to see if there's any news from Mr. Brown, and I want to look up that lawyer fella too."

"I'll be fine. You go on then. We'll be alright," answered Amy.

Elijah kissed Amy on the forehead as she lay down to rest. He told Momma Celia he was going out and would leave word at the desk as to his whereabouts in case they needed anything, and asked her to keep an eye on the children in his absence.

Momma Celia promised to do so, but muttered under her breath, "As if I'd be doin anythin' else! I'm about as comfortable as a cricket in a chicken coop in this place. Lord knows I won't be takin no nap!"

XXII

Elijah went downstairs and inquired at the desk as to whether there was any response from Mr. Brown. He was told the courier had returned with a message from Mr. Brown's housekeeper that the gentleman was out of town. He had gone to Philadelphia and New York to discuss business with his brothers in the branch offices of Alex. Brown & Sons and would return at the weekend.

Disappointed and frustrated by this setback, Elijah decided to take it upon himself to pay a visit to the lawyer he had found in Matchett's Baltimore Director, William H. Dorsey up on Fayette Street. He let the desk clerk know and then, rather than waste time on foot, he hailed a carriage and headed off. The carriage arrived at a well-kept brick row house of moderate proportions, duly furnished with the immaculate white marble steps so typical of the homes in Baltimore. He paid the coachman and asked the carriage to wait, as he was uncertain of finding Mr. Dorsey at home and he did not want to be left alone and without transportation in this city he had never known.

As he mounted the steps, he tried to put his thoughts in order. He decided that he could wait to discuss the legal matters that might touch on his business, and get straight to the crucial point of discovering Maryland's laws concerning people of color. After all, he thought, if the laws would make emancipation and inheritance impossible here, there really wasn't much point in pursuing the business related issues anyway!

He raised the knocker and let it fall. It echoed down the entry hall with a sonorous thunk, and was answered shortly by the sound of footsteps approaching the door from inside. A pleasant faced, middle-aged woman answered the door with a smile. "May I help you, sir?"

"Good afternoon ma'am. My name is Elijah Willis. I've just arrived in Baltimore from South Carolina, and am in need of some legal advice. Is Mr.

Dorsey in, by any chance? I found his name in the Matchett's Baltimore Director and thought I'd take a chance he might be able to help me with some pressin matters I'm facin. I hope I'm not intrudin?"

The woman opened the door wider and showed him into the foyer. "How do you do, sir? Nice to meet you! Please come on in, it's no trouble at all. Mr. Dorsey is my husband, and I'm sure he'd be happy to speak with you. I'll just go call him. I won't be a moment."

"Thank ya ma'am, that's very kind of ya. I surely do appreciate it!" Elijah answered.

While Mrs. Dorsey went to fetch her husband, Elijah looked around the foyer, and noticed a framed handbill from the 1844 Presidential Election. It touted the virtues of the Whig Candidate, Henry Clay, and was signed by the senator with an inscription, "I shall be ever in your debt for your kind help and generous support, H. Clay." Elijah took it as a good omen that this Mr. Dorsey was a supporter of Senator Clay, knowing that the senator was an advocate of emancipation.

Next to the campaign poster hung a list of Colonial Families of Maryland, which, as Elijah scanned the list, he saw included the Dorsey family. Familiar with the Southern tendency to tout one's lineage, it struck him that Mr. Dorsey was, by these two wall decorations, establishing his credentials as a bulwark of the kind of nationalism that took pride in its Revolutionary roots, and in a heritage of tolerance as an integral element in building a diverse nation. That seemed to bode well.

Just then, Mr. Dorsey, a lean and dapper gentleman of about fifty, entered the foyer with a wide smile and an outstretched hand. "Welcome, Mr. Willis, nice to meet you! My wife tells me you've just arrived in Baltimore and have need of some legal counsel. I'll be happy to be of assistance." He noticed Elijah staring at the list of colonial Families of Maryland.

"I see you are of a noble lineage sir, in terms of our colonial heritage, of course. I too have roots going back to General Washington's family." Elijah commented, thinking that to tout his own lineage might establish a certain parity of credibility between the two men.

"Is that a fact? What a coincidence! You know, we have the nation's first monument to Washington here. Perhaps you saw the column from the harbor?" Elijah allowed as how he had. "Well, we are a young nation, and despite all the new immigrants arriving here, it's good to remember our roots, don't you think? Especially those to whom much credit is due for liberating us from British tyranny, and setting us on a course of a freedom that is becoming the envy of the world!" Mr. Dorsey eyed Elijah shrewdly for any response to his political manifesto, trying to size him up to see whether he was of sympathetic opinions, or held those more akin to the secessionist leanings of his fellow Carolinian, the late Senator Calhoun. To give himself more time to make his evaluation, Mr. Dorsey continued his genealogical reminiscences.

"The progenitor of the Dorsey family in Maryland was my ancestor Edward Dorcy, spelled D O R C Y, or perhaps D apostrophe A R C Y. Like many immigrants, his name seems to have undergone a certain metamorphosis over the past two hundred years, to arrive at the current spelling." Elijah tried not to look bored as Mr. Dorsey prattled on. Dorsey continued deliberately, as his motive in revealing the family history was to touch on the issue of freedom, and see what nerve it might strike in Elijah.

He resumed, "In any event, it seems Edward migrated to Maryland from Virginia in 1649. He acquired property in Anne Arundel County, southwest of Baltimore, and settled near the Severn River in 1650." He turned to look at Elijah as if an aside, "You would have passed the mouth to the Severn on your journey, if you came up here on the Bay." Elijah nodded.

Dorsey looked back at the list, as if consulting an oracle, and drove on, "Anyway, Edward Dorcy came to Maryland seeking refuge from "proscriptive laws against Nonconformists" which existed in the Virginia colony at the time. Edward apparently picked Maryland because it was known as a place of toleration where all Christian sects were treated with equality, and none were persecuted."

At this point Elijah lit up a bit, thinking perhaps it might be a doorway to getting to the point of his visit, but before he could attempt an entrance into that topic, the relentless Mr. Dorsey continued.

"Now over here," he said pointing to the campaign poster, "Is a memento of which I am almost as proud as my lineage." He paused for effect, eliciting in Elijah just the sign of interest he was hoping to see. "I had the honor of hosting the great Henry Clay when he came to Baltimore during his presidential campaign in 1844. I continue to think it is a crying shame he did not win the election, but I still firmly believe in the rightness of his American System, and his belief in uniting the nation through commerce and transportation, roads and railways, and the elimination of slavery!"

At this point, seeing clearly that his host would not balk at the discussion of emancipation, and moreover, would be sympathetic to his entrepreneurial commercial interests, Elijah could stand it no more, and felt compelled to broach the subject of his visit. "Well, Mr. Dorsey," he interjected, "it seems Providence has led me to you, for I doubt I could have selected a lawyer more inclined toward my interests and needs if I had a month of inquiries to support my choice!"

Mr. Dorsey, suddenly realizing that they were still standing in the foyer, and that he had not even invited his guest to have a seat or some refreshment, smiled warmly and gestured toward the door to the parlor. "I do apologize sir, I have forgotten my manners. Please come in and have a seat so we may discuss your concerns more comfortably. Martha dear!" he called toward the back of the house, "Would you please bring our guest something to drink?" He turned back to Elijah asking, "What would you like, a cold drink, a hot drink, or something a little stronger?"

Uncertain of the drinking habits in Baltimore beyond those of the inebriates of the harbor district, he was not quite sure how to respond, but in truth, with the strains of the journey, their less than ideal lodgings, and the pressing issues they were facing, something stronger sounded appealing. Not wanting to seem over-eager, however, he demurred and asked, "What are you havin sir? Whatever it is, I'll be happy to join you in it."

Dorsey, seeing the flicker at his offer of something stronger, called back to his wife, "Martha, hon, could you bring out that bottle of Rye Whiskey in the cupboard and a pair of glasses, please?"

Martha called back, "I'll be right there, dear!" Sounds of cupboard doors opening and shutting, glasses clinking, and general movement could be heard from the kitchen in the back of the narrow house.

Dorsey turned his attention back to Elijah. "Well then, why don't you tell me something about yourself, and what brings you to Baltimore?"

They entered a graciously proportioned, high-ceilinged parlor with emerald green walls and white trim, and sat down in matching wing-backed chairs upholstered in a heavy gold damask, ranged in front of a stately fireplace with a carved white marble mantle. There was a handsome fireplace set consisting of a wrought iron poker, shovel and broom with gleaming brass handles to the right. A brass studded set of bellows and large copper coal bin with brass straps and handles sat to the left of the fireplace, filled with firewood and kindling. To finish the ensemble, in front of the fireplace stood an intricately worked screen with a brass frame, to prevent sparks from popping onto the rich burgundy and azure Persian carpet, or onto the polished chestnut parquet floorboards. Everything in the room spoke of quiet elegance and good taste. Clearly, Mr. Dorsey made a decent living, even if his home was not on the scale of the country homes to which

Elijah was more accustomed. Elijah suddenly realized that, were he in the Carolinas, this tableau would not be complete without a compliment of Negro slaves in attendance. That's when he realized how far he had come, in more ways than one.

After Mrs. Dorsey had served them each a cut glass tumbler of whiskey, the two men settled from the mandatory social pleasantries into more serious conversation.

"Well, sir, I need some information about the laws of the State of Maryland concerning people of color- specifically governing matters of the rights of emancipation and inheritance." Elijah was hesitant to reveal the entire reason immediately.

Mr. Dorsey looked at Elijah piercingly, and asked, "Are we speaking in the hypothetical sense, or is there a specific, concrete issue whose legal dimensions you wish to explore?"

Elijah shifted in his seat, realizing it was time to take the plunge. "As a matter of fact, it is quite specific. I have a wife and family who are, most regrettably, also my slaves. I wish to emancipate them and leave my entire estate to them, but South Carolina law will not permit it, so I am determined to find an alternative solution."

Mr. Dorsey took all this in thoughtfully before responding. "I see, that is indeed a challenge. And may I ask why you chose to come to Baltimore to investigate this matter?"

Elijah decided it best to go ahead and explain his thinking, and how he hoped to combine his business interests with the liberation of his family. "I have extensive holdins in South Carolina, and a thrivin business in both lumber and cotton. My hope is to establish business relations here to ship my goods more efficiently to wherever they are needed- perhaps the lumber out West and the cotton to England? But I am also considerin the possibility of relocatin the family here to Maryland, if, in fact, the climate here is legally amenable to such a possibility."

Mr. Dorsey sat with his arms propped on his armrests almost as if in prayer, tapping his finger tips together reflectively. After a pause, he spoke:

"Perhaps it would be best if I gave you a sort of overview of the legal conditions here first, before voicing any opinion in particular.

"I'd be most grateful if you would sir," responded Elijah, eagerly hopeful for some good news.

Mr. Dorsey then proceeded to tell Elijah that Maryland was something of a paradox. It was, in some respects, quite liberal in its attitudes, and tolerant of certain differences, but that tolerance was more religious than racial. "The importation of slaves into the state has been prohibited for many years, yet slavery still thrives here. An unusually high percentage of the colored population here is free, yet the free blacks suffer many dangers, despite their theoretical freedom. Free blacks have to pay taxes, but cannot not attend the schools taxes pay for." He continued, "Free blacks, if they leave the State for more than thirty days, or without permission of the authorities, cannot not return. If they are not employed, they can be deported. Their children can be apprenticed by the Orphan's Court. If their spouse is a slave, the spouse can be sold away, and any children they might have would be slaves. If they are convicted of a crime, they can be sold back into slavery. If they incurred the wrath of the slave posse, they could be beaten. If they joined a secret society, they could also be returned to slavery."

Mr. Dorsey went on to say that both free blacks and slaves were prohibited from camp meetings or religious revivals, other than those sponsored by whites and the Methodist Episcopal Church or other white churches. He also explained that laws had been enacted to make it a criminal offense in Maryland to distribute or publish abolitionist propaganda of any kind! He told Elijah that free blacks had to pay fines for every transaction performed without a license, and the license had to be renewed yearly. Maryland, moreover, actively supported the deportation of freed blacks to Africa, and systematically was seeking to eliminate the colored population from the state thereby.

"So you see, sir," he concluded, "there are, unfortunately, quite a number of mitigating factors that you might find quite problematic, despite our reputation for tolerance."

Elijah took a swig of his whiskey, as if to dull the blow of what, clearly, was unwelcome and unexpected news. His mind was racing with questions, and he hardly knew where to begin. "Now let me clarify something, if I may. First of all, when you say the importation of slaves is illegal here, do ya mean to tell me that, if I moved here, I could not bring any of my slaves with me, whether family or not?"

"That's a good question, and you are right to ask it. The law refers to the issue of trade, that is, the introduction of slaves into the state for the purpose of sale or purchase. Slaves already in the service of their master may, of course, accompany their master, as they are in effect his property, and our national commerce laws permit the free transfer of property within the United States. However, once here, they would remain slaves."

Somewhat relieved, Elijah continued, "Touchin another point of great concern to me, I am very desirous that my children be educated, but it seems they are not permitted any public education in this State, is that right?" Elijah asked.

"There are some schools that cater to the colored, but they are not part of our public school system supported by the taxpayers." Mr. Dorsey affirmed.

Thinking that private education would not be beyond his economic means, he moved on to his next question, and it was a most pressing one, upon which the future security of his family would certainly depend. "I am concerned that, when I die, if my family were residin' here, even if emancipated, they might suffer great limitations to their freedom, which, from what you're tellin' me, seems more than likely. What about the matter of inheritance and the free exercise of wealth? Are people of color allowed to inherit property in this state?"

Mr. Dorsey saw that Elijah was an intelligent man who had given his matters a great deal of careful thought. He appreciated his careful deconstruction of the issues into specific points of concern. "Why Mr. Willis, you would have made a good lawyer, judging by the way you've framed your questions!"

"Let's just say that, under the circumstances, I've learned you can't be too careful, for the devil is truly in the details!" responded Elijah.

"Indeed sir, I quite agree!" Mr. Dorsey replied. "So let us examine those very details, and cast out whatever demons we may by naming them, shall we?"

He then began to elucidate that most of those who were free blacks, were so by emancipation either by the master's choice, by will, or by birth. Though in theory, a slave could petition a master for manumission, since the General Assembly of 1826, deeds of manumission had to be witnessed by at least two "good and sufficient" witnesses. That made it hard to find free people who would willingly vouch for the slave. Even more problematic, the execution of the deed of manumission was only possible for slaves between the ages of 10 and 45, making it extremely difficult for owners to allow their slaves to be freed. Moreover, though it was possible for a slave to petition for emancipation, if granted, the emancipated slave then had to leave the state.

Though there were more free blacks in Baltimore City than slaves, the laws clearly did not favor the free blacks either. Mr. Dorsey went on to explain that the general tone in the State among those who did advocate for abolition, was not to free the slaves so that people of color might become better integrated into the society, but rather, so that they would be free to return to Africa, where it was thought they would be better suited and happier (despite the fact that few of the slaves currently living in Maryland had been born in Africa themselves). To that end, the Maryland Colonization Society had energetically raised funds to help establish a colony of free blacks in West Africa- a colony which, in conjunction with the efforts of the American Colonization Society, supported by Henry Clay and others, had been absorbed into the new democratic nation of Liberia.

Elijah began to realize that this stratagem, far from fulfilling his dreams, was a form of racism thinly veiled in patronizing concern for the afflicted, designed to ultimately rid the land of people of color, and leave it entirely in the hands of whites, who deemed themselves better suited and more deserving of its control.

Mr. Dorsey, being first and foremost a dispassionate professional in his dealings, gave no indication as to where his own sympathies lay, other than his obvious political support of Clay, and his general statement in support of emancipation as being desirable for the nation's growth. How he actually felt about people of color as *people* remained unclear, and was perhaps beside the point.

The challenge for Elijah in the face of this disturbing revelation, was whether he might find a way to achieve his goals for his family despite these sad facts. It was not looking very hopeful from where he sat. Mr. Dorsey still had not answered his question concerning the matter of inheritance, and Elijah's mind clung stubbornly to the notion that the entire matter hung in the balance of that response, though in his heart he could already see that even if freed in Maryland, life might be very unpleasant for his family here once he was gone. He needed to ask the question, no matter what the answer.

"So, sir, am I to understand that free blacks and mulatos may inherit property here?" Elijah asked, point blank.

"Well, yes, but there are various restrictions, depending on the nature and use of the property, for certain types of enterprises are prohibited to people of color." responded Mr. Dorsey.

"And do I also understand correctly that if I were to attempt to emancipate my family, I could not include my younger children nor my mother-in-law, they being either younger than ten or older than forty-five years of age?" Elijah queried.

"Sadly, that is correct sir, however unjust it may be, it is the current law." Mr. Dorsey looked at Elijah with regret, realizing this was not the news he had been hoping to hear.

Elijah's heart sank. He felt really despondent at what appeared to be insurmountable obstacles to any possibility of relocating the family to Maryland. He finished his whiskey with a gulp and set his glass down on a side table.

"Well, Mr. Dorsey, I am truly disappointed to hear this. I had high hopes that Baltimore might prove to be a place where we might relocate, and had envisioned a number of economic possibilities to explore in the development of my business ventures."

Mr. Dorsey smiled sympathetically. "I am very sorry to be the bearer of bad tidings to you sir, and personally regret that the climate is not more hospitable to you and your family's needs. It would be dishonest of me to tell you otherwise, however, and I do not believe a lawyer should ever hold out false hopes as a means of enticing new business."

Elijah cleared his throat to hide his emotion. ""I am grateful to ya sir, for your candor. I certainly bear ya no ill will for the news, which you rightly and clearly have communicated. I am happy to compensate ya for your time and trouble, and will not take up more of it at the moment."

"That won't be necessary sir, I assure you. Should you need further information, I am happy to try to provide it, and, in the event that you might still wish at any time in the future to pursue the business opportunities of which you spoke, we can certainly come to an amicable arrangement for whatever fees might be commensurate with the efforts they might require. I am at your service, sir," he concluded, and then, seeing the crestfallen expression on Elijah's face, felt compelled to add, "and I am truly sorry I could not provide a better solution to the challenge you face."

The two men shook hands; Elijah bade Mr. Dorsey farewell and remounted the awaiting carriage for the ride back to the Admiral Fell, wondering glumly how he could break this news to Amy and the family.

Not ready to face them, Elijah instructed the driver to take him on a tour of the city before returning to the Inn. The carriage drove west on Fayette Street, up Charles Street, past the apse of the Basilica of the Immaculate Conception, to Mt. Vernon and the Washington Monument, then east on Monument Street and back down Broadway to Fells Point. Elijah bade the carriage stop at a pub a block from the Inn, and decided to drown his sorrows for a spell, hoping the alcoholic haze would take the edge off the bad news, and help him find the strength to break it to Amy.

XXIII

Back in Williston, there was a subtle but growing anxiety felt by the slaves on the Willis Plantation. Gilbert had already warned everybody not to discuss anything about the master and his family, and most especially about any possibilities of emancipation, to anyone at all outside the plantation. Yet the seed had been planted, and it was only a matter of time before it started to sprout in the form of open speculation.

Jason and Julius were both allies of Gilbert. Being the leadership of the plantation, and in fact, on a daily basis the ones most responsible for running the business, they were the ones most likely to have contact outside. They often tended to matters in town or at the mill, (always wearing a numbered amulet of permission, to prove they were not runaways) taking loads of lumber to the depot for shipment, and picking up supplies for the needs of the plantation residents and livestock. However, such duties were seldom a one-man job, and often they had to take other slaves along with them to complete their appointed tasks.

On one such occasion, Jason was taking a load of lumber from Elijah's saw mill to the depot for shipment and took two men with him, Joshua and Elias. Elias was only a teenager, and not able to do as heavy work as the men, but was learning about the business.

The three of them were unloading the lumber from the wagon to the train when Mr. Beazely called out, "Hey Jason! There's some mail here for Mr. Willis! Come pick it up before you go!"

"Yes, sir! Thank you Mr. Beazely, sir! I'll send someone over right now to get it!" Jason replied. He turned to Elias and said, "Hey Elias, go on over to the station office and pick up that mail for me, would you?"

Elias, thankful for a break from the heavy lifting, eagerly agreed. "Right away, Mister Jason!" he said respectfully. He felt good that Jason would trust him, and wanted to show he deserved the trust, hoping he would be able to eventually do more than just plain labor.

Elias went over to Mr. Beazely's office and was handed several letters. He had been taught to read, as Elijah wanted his slaves as educated as time allowed, and though many of the older ones still couldn't read or write, the children on the plantation were given some regular schooling in what little time was available for it so they could at least write their names and recognize ciphers.

Never having received a letter in his life, or even handled mail, Elias looked at the letters with great curiosity. He felt excited that he was able to make out the letters, and recognized Mister Elijah's name and address. Fascinated, he turned the letters over in his hands, noting the daub of sealing wax on each, with different seals stamped in the wax being a unique sign of the letter's author. He also realized that in the corner was another name and address, which he deduced must indicate who had sent the letter and where it had come from.

Most of the letters were from around Barnwell District, but one, he noticed, had come all the way from Kentucky. The return address of the author was scrawled:

The Hon. H. Clay
Ashland
Richmond Road
Lexington, Kentucky

Elias was excited, and began to wonder who the Hon. H. Clay might be, and why was he writing to Mister Elijah. "Mister Jason, Mister Jason! I got the mail! There's a letter here looks important!"

Jason set down his load of lumber and took the letters from the boy. "What you doin lookin through Mister Elijah's mail? Did I ask you to read it, or fetch it?" Jason teased Elias.

"No sir, I wasn't readin it, exactly, I just never saw no letter befo and wanted to see if I could make out what was on the envelope!" the boy responded with a mixture of embarrassment and pride. "See! Lookee here, it say Mister E-lijah Willis!" he pointed proudly to the address. "Willis Plan ta tion, Williston, Barn well Dis trict, South Carolina!" Elias beamed at his accomplishment. Excitedly, he went on, "An up here it say 'The Hon. H.

Clay.'" He turned to Jason puzzled, "What you suppose a Hon is?" he went on, "an it say it from Ken tuck y! Where that Mister Jason?"

Jason snatched the letter from Elias and peered at the address. Gilbert had told him that Mister Elijah was looking for advice about emancipating his slaves from Senator Clay, and that he was a senator from Kentucky. Trying not to betray his own excitement or curiosity, and wanting to encourage Elias' reading but discourage him from prying any further, he said, "Never you mind, now! That's not your business. Mr. Clay's just a fella Mister Elijah wrote to. Mister Elijah knows important folks from all kinda places. And it ain't 'Hon.' That's short for 'Honorable,' cause Mr. Clay's an important man." He carefully tucked the letters inside his shirt. "Come on now, hep us finish up here! Train ain't gonna wait all day for us to get Mister Elijah's wood loaded, and there'll be Hell to pay with Mister Gilbert if this shipment don't get out!"

Elias felt a little stung at the rebuke, and Jason, realizing this, added in a low voice- since reading was theoretically forbidden to Negroes- "But you done a good job a readin! You keep workin at it, son, and before you know it you'll be readin books!" He smiled encouragingly to Elias, who rewarded him with a grin of his own.

"Yes, sir! Thank you sir! I will!" And immediately he set himself energetically to helping with the loading of the lumber onto the train.

On the ride home, Jason felt almost as if the letter from Senator Clay was burning through his shirt. He had heard about Senator Clay being in favor of the general emancipation of all slaves, and the very thought of carrying a letter from him that might be telling Mister Elijah how this could be done made him want to break open the seal and read the letter himself. Of course, he knew he couldn't do that, and that Mister Elijah would be furious if he did- Mister Elijah was a stickler about handling his business affairs right. But he couldn't wait to at least tell Gilbert that the letter had arrived!

Elias, excited by the mail and his discovery that he was able to read the addresses, couldn't resist telling Joshua all about it. "Hey, Mister Joshua! Did you hear! Mister Jason had me pick up Mister Elijah's mail from Mister Beazely, an I could read the addresses! They's a letter come all the way from Ken tucky. Mister Jason say it from someone important Mister Elijah wrote to. Fella name a The Honorable H. Clay. Actually it say the Hon, but Mister Jason splained to me that Hon be short for Honorable!" Elias chattered enthusiastically.

Joshua too had heard of Henry Clay. In South Carolina, any news about a white man who wanted to free slaves ran like wildfire among the coloreds, slave or free. He looked at Jason, trying to sound casual, "That so?"

Jason decided he'd best try to stop this from going any further. He spoke in a low steady tone, so as not to draw attention, but his voice was filled with threat. "Alright now Elias, that's enough! I know you pleased with yasef bout readin an all, an that's fine, but Mister Gilbert told us not to talk about none of Mister Elijah's business outside the plantation or we'd get beat, and this be Mister Elijah's business- not yours!"

To underscore the urgency, he continued "So ya'd best keep your mouth shut tight! You go yammerin on about how excited you is bout readin, and showin off that you know the Hon. mean the Honorable, and that Mister H. Clay be somebody important Mister Elijah knows up in Kentucky- no telling who might hear ya! Anybody round here overhear ya, and we all get in trouble! Do you understand me?" He glared at the boy fiercely, which immediately resulted in the smile being wiped off his face, a look of fear filling his eyes, and his mouth snapping shut, as if to prevent any possible response from escape. He simply nodded vigorously to indicate he understood, almost bracing himself against the blows he might have incurred. Jason and Joshua exchanged looks of warning, mixed with excitement.

Back at the plantation, Jason immediately looked for Gilbert. He had just come back from cutting a stand of pine ready to harvest. He smelled of pine pitch, and his hands were sticky and stained with the sap, wood chips still clung to his hair. As Gilbert was washing up, fluffing his hair to shake the wood chips out and scrubbing his hands with pumice until his palms glowed pink, Jason came up to him, letters in hand, to break the news.

"Gilbert, Mister Elijah got some mail today," announced Jason.

"That so? Anythin interestin?" responded Gilbert.

"Could be. They's a letter here from Senator Clay up in Kentucky!" revealed Jason.

Gilbert spun around and looked at Jason square on. "You serious? Lemme see that!" Gilbert scanned the pile of mail and, seeing the letter from Senator Clay, read the return address and held it in near reverence.

"What you gonna do?" asked Jason.

"What you mean, what am I gonna do?" shot back Gilbert

"Well, ain't you curious bout what it say?" asked Jason.

"Well a course I am! But this here is Mister Elijah's mail! We got no right openin his mail. I could get shot for that!" insisted Gilbert.

"Aw come on now, he your brother-in-law. He ain't gonna shoot you!" Jason responded with a suggestive glint in his eye.

"Jason, look, he may have fathered my sister's children, but you know as well as I do that by South Carolina law and white folks' opinion, he ain't my brother-in-law, or my brother-out-law for that matter- though some folks might see him as an outlaw for the way he deal with us!" They both laughed at the joke, relieving the growing tension between them.

"I know it's temptin, but they's no way this letter is gettin opened by anyone but Mister Elijah. It would destroy the trust he has in me, and that trust may be our ticket outa slavery! Sides, I owe it to him for the way he treats us so decent."

This last point struck home with Jason too. He nodded in recognition. "Well, since you put it that way, I see you right. But Lawdy, I sho wish he'd get home, so we can find out what it say!"

XXIV

Elijah stumbled into the Admiral Fell Inn, clearly inebriated but trying to maintain his composure. The desk clerk looked up in recognition, not unaccustomed to guests under the influence.

"Good evening, Mr. Willis. I see you've had the opportunity to sample our local beverages!" He said with a slightly mocking tone.

Elijah straightened up, and trying to smile, replied, "Very observant of ya sir! In fact I have, indeed." He spoke with slightly slurred speech, and his eyebrows furrowed, as if trying to remember what he wanted to say. Then nodding to himself slightly and raising his eyebrows as if it might help him to see better, he lifted his head, leaned forward over the counter and asked breathily, "Are there any messages for me?"

A wave of alcohol wafted across the counter toward the face of the clerk, who stepped back involuntarily, and answered, "One of the colored boys you brought with you just asked if I knew where you were, and I just told him what you had told me, you'd gone to see Mr. William Dorsey on Fayette Street."

Elijah realized that Amy and the family might be worried about him, as it was dark by now. He wasn't sure even what time it was, and suddenly wondered if the family had had anything to eat. He fought his way through the fog in his head, with compunction for his delinquency, and then felt a new wave of remorse wash over him for failing his family even in the simple matter of making sure they had gotten dinner. He simply nodded to the clerk and turned to find his way up to his quarters.

The clerk realized that Mr. Willis had not been drinking in celebration, and seemed deeply troubled by something. Perhaps he had received some bad news from his visit to Mr. Dorsey. Concerned, and also wanting to avoid his guest having any accidents, he called out, "Mr. Willis, are you alright sir? Do you need some help?"

Elijah managed to turn waveringly back to the clerk. His first instinct was to try to be the courtly Southern gentleman and refuse, but the truth was, he needed help, and he knew it- even if what he really needed was more than the clerk could possibly give. He managed to respond, "Well sir, as a matter of fact I would be most grateful if ya'll could help me to my room, if it's not too much of an inconvenience?"

The clerk promptly came out from behind the counter and, looping Elijah's left arm around his shoulder, and grabbing Elijah with his right arm around his waist, slowly and patiently led him to the stairs and up to his room.

When he opened the door, the clerk was a bit surprised to find Amy and Momma Celia waiting for him. Amy looked up with alarm, and disregarding any pretense of maintaining a master-slave relationship, blurted out, "Elijah, sugar, where have you been? I've been worried to death about you!"

For the first time the clerk noticed Amy's pregnancy, and putting two and two together, raised his eyebrows slightly, letting out a soundless whistle from his lips, before seeing Elijah safely to the bed, and saying "Well, Mr. Willis, I see you're in good hands. Uh, sleep well sir!"

Elijah managed to say, "I do thank ya for your assistance, sir. Most kind of ya!"

With that he lay back on the bed and fell fast asleep, leaving Amy and Momma Celia wondering what in the name of tarnation had happened for him to go get stinking drunk like that. Amy's worry increased, but Momma Celia intervened. "Come on now, child, Mister Elijah'll be alright. Sometimes a man take a few drinks, like a medicine to ease a pain. He just need to sleep it off."

"I know, Momma, but it's not like him to get drunk, least not this drunk. Somethin must have happened with his meetin with that lawyer, and it can't be good!"

"Well, I never was convinced comin' up here was such a good idea in the first place. Somethin' just don't feel right. I know Mister Elijah tryin' hard to make things work out for all of us, an I appreciate that, but if ya ask me, anyplace where they love eatin' food that look like a pile of big ole spiders, an smell bad too, just ain't right for us!" She grinned and looked at her daughter, as if to cajole a smile out of her.

Amy's mood lightened. "You're right Momma. If Maryland is not hospitable, we'll just keep lookin til we find somethin better!"

"That's my girl!" smiled Momma Celia, giving her daughter a kiss on the forehead. "Child, never forget that as wrong as slavery is, if ya don't let it beat your spirit down, ya end up mighty strong. You strong. And Mister Elijah's a good man. He strong too- Lord knows I never saw no white man fight like he do for folks like us." She paused and then said, "I believe God rewards strength like that, and though I don't rightly know how, I feel it in my bones that we gonna be free, somehow."

Amy nodded, pensively, and looked her mother in the eye. "I do too, Momma, I do too, but the how and the when is what worries me!"

"The how and the when don't matter, baby. For your children, and they children, and they children's children, freedom matter a whole lot more than the how or when." Momma Celia was calm, but adamant.

Amy knew her mother was right, but she couldn't help wonder what Elijah had heard that prompted him to drink himself into oblivion, rather than just come home and tell her. She was angry at him, but at the same time she was touched that he wouldn't want to give her bad news after their long trip. Either way, she needed to know the truth. There was no point in trying to wake him from his stupor, for even if she roused him, she was in no mood for incoherent answers to her questions. She would just have to wait until morning.

XXV

Elijah awoke with a headache and a heartache, feeling sick with guilt and still uncomfortable about breaking the news to Amy of what he had learned from William Dorsey. Fortunately for him, by this time Amy's anger had subsided, and already having deduced and accepted the basic import of it, she was more concerned for his well-being than for the news he bore.

"Darlin, I am so sorry for last night. I feel like I abandoned you and the children, though I didn't mean to," he fumbled, massaging his aching temples.

Amy looked at him understandingly. "It's alright, sugar, I know ya didn't mean to." She paused reflectively, "I take it the news from Mr. Dorsey wasn't good?"

Elijah shook his head miserably. "No, it wasn't at all what I was hopin for! And I was so depressed by it, I just couldn't bear breakin it to ya, especially after puttin ya'll through that long trip up here!" His voice trembled with emotion.

Amy stroked his head soothingly. "It's alright baby, we just gonna have to find a better solution, that's all. Momma says she feels in her bones that the Lord's gonna help us find a way, and somehow we will be free."

Elijah nodded, more in acceptance that Momma Celia believed it, than in conviction of it himself.

"She also said that it was just as well, cause from her point of view, 'anyplace where they love eatin' food that look like a pile of big ole spiders, an smell bad too, just ain't right for us!'" Amy imitated her mother to perfection, with a giggle. Even Elijah had to chuckle at his mother-in-law's amazing ability to cut through to the basic truth of her experience in such an earthy, direct way.

"Well, alright then," he said, smiling gratefully. "How soon will you be up to travellin home?"

Amy stroked her belly and sighed. "Can you give me a few days? I think the baby felt the trip more than I did, so it might be best for me to rest some first, before we head on back. And that way you might still be able to talk to Mr. Brown when he gets back in town. Be a shame to come all this way and not even see if he could help somehow."

Elijah thought about this for a moment, and then perked up. "Well, I suppose that it wouldn't hurt to see if I can set up some business arrangement with him that could benefit you and the children. But from the sound of what Mr. Dorsey told me, even that might be a problem. I'll try to arrange a meeting with him, and in the meantime make preparations for our return to South Carolina."

Amy then asked him, "What do you want to tell Momma and the children?"

Elijah paused for a moment before responding. "Well, I'll just have to tell them that Maryland wouldn't be the right place for us to live, and not to worry, that I'm gonna find a solution, somehow." He struggled to hide the dejection in his voice as best he could, looking at Amy apologetically. What she saw in him, however, was not so much the pitiful failure he was so acutely feeling, but the courage and determination he had to keep looking for the solution. It made her love him all the more, and made her think that Momma Celia was right. She thought to herself, "God surely must reward people for that kind of faith and perseverance, mustn't He?"

The rest of the week passed uneventfully. Amy was able to rest, Momma Celia and Elijah managed to keep the children out of mischief, exploring the city, and Elijah was finally able to meet with George Brown upon the latter's return from New York.

Mr. Brown invited Elijah to call on him at his home on Monument Street, a large brownstone townhouse with majestic proportions, not far from the monument to Washington. The monument was a tall, massive limestone column, topped with a dome-like base, upon which stood a statue of the great man looking vigilantly out over the city toward the harbor. The neighborhood had been named after Mount Vernon, Washington's plantation in Virginia overlooking the Potomac. There was a certain irony that a white Southern planter, hoping to emancipate his enslaved colored family, was meeting with a banker in a neighborhood named after the slaveholding first president, whose phallic memorial proclaimed him the father of the nation.

Once inside the Brown mansion, Elijah having been offered a comfortable seat in the parlor, Mr. Brown smiled graciously and said,

"Well, nice to finally meet you face to face, Mr. Willis. I'm terribly sorry I was out of town when you arrived in Baltimore. I hope your stay has not been an unpleasant one?"

"Not at all, Mr. Brown. Thank you." Elijah lied. "It has been most, ah, informative."

Mr. Brown raised an eyebrow in curiosity. "Glad to hear it, Mr. Willis, glad to hear it. So, how can I be of service to you?"

"Well, Mr. Brown, I'm not sure, to tell you the truth. I'll allow as how I came here with mixed motives, only one of which was related directly to my business. The other was related to some personal family matters which, unfortunately have proven elusive of solution. That bein the case, my economic concerns may be a moot point."

Mr. Brown looked puzzled. He could sense a tone of defeat in Elijah, which, in his experience, did not bode well in a prospective business proposition. "Well then sir, I'm not clear on the purpose of this visit. Was there some specific business matter you wished to discuss?"

Elijah realized he had probably misplayed his hand, and that he should at least inquire about financing opportunities to build his business. "I am sorry, Mr. Brown, I didn't mean to be opaque in my communications. Allow me to clarify my situation."

He wanted to be careful, not knowing Mr. Brown's feelings about the emancipation issue. "I have extensive holdins in South Carolina, with a dual enterprise in cotton and lumber. Bein as how the tensions between the South and the North are increasin, but the market for cotton in England is also increasin, I thought we might discuss shippin possibilities to England." He paused for a moment, trying to assess his host's reaction. Mr. Brown was listening attentively. He continued, "But I also realize that the need for lumber out West is growin too, and there's a lot of buildin goin on out there, so it occurred to me that maybe I should also explore what ya'll are doin with the Baltimore and Ohio Railroad. Thought maybe I could strike a deal with ya about financin regular shipments and givin ya'll a share of the profits!'

Mr. Brown examined Elijah with an equally appraising eye. He couldn't help but wonder why Elijah had told him he was bringing seven slaves with him to Baltimore, yet none of them were attending to their master's needs on this social call. The business proposal was one that had clearly been thought through carefully and intelligently. It was perfectly true that there were sizable business opportunities, both with Great Britain and the nation's Westward expansion. The railroads were playing an increasingly important role in the national expansion, and there was clearly money to be made. But he couldn't help but wonder about the "family matters" that seemed to sap Elijah's interest from his otherwise intelligent business goals.

After an awkward silence, during which he pondered whether to broach the subject of the family matter outright, he responded, "Well, Mr. Willis, I'm certainly open to exploring business opportunities, and I must compliment you on your keen grasp of the current market trends. You are quite right that there are possibilities both to the East and to the West!" He paused, "But I am curious as to why you might think your business opportunities are a moot point? I see no economic reason to consider them as such, so I'm assuming there is some other factor that you have not yet mentioned."

Elijah decided that Mr. Brown's attitudes about emancipation really didn't matter in the long run, especially since it was already clear that relocating the family to Maryland was not a viable option. And the possibility was dawning on him that even a short-term business arrangement might allow him to increase his coffers, so that, when he finally managed to emancipate the family, they would have a larger legacy to assure their long-term well-being.

"Fact is, Mr. Brown, though I don't know your position on these matters, I might as well come clean and tell you the full extent of my dilemma. The seven slaves of which I told you in my letter are, in fact, my family- my wife, my mother-in-law, and our five children -with a sixth on the way!"

George Brown was not totally shocked by this, having suspected that there was more to the story of the slaves than met the eye. His business interests had made him rather apolitical and, if not callous, generally somewhat indifferent to the emotional involvements of his clients. He was not insensitive, however, to the difficulty Elijah must be confronting, and the emotional toll it would be taking. He also realized that Elijah was no longer a young man, and that too would be contributing to his sense of urgency. Approaching a similar age himself, he felt compassion for Elijah, and was moved to respond.

"Well, sir, I can well appreciate the difficulty you must be facing. I am aware that the laws in Maryland are not very amenable to your situation, so I doubt there is anything I could do to help you on that score." Elijah looked at him forlornly.

"As to your business affairs, however, I may be able to be of assistance to you. I am certainly willing to make arrangements to back your business ventures, and may be able to help you place the earnings in trust for your family, to which, if they were residing in a slave-free state, I believe Maryland law could not prevent them from having access." Elijah perked up considerably at this.

Mr. Brown continued, "Moreover, now that I think about it, since our family business has branches in both Philadelphia and New York, even if you opened an account with us here, it could be cross-registered with our Philadelphia and New York offices. I think we could thereby arrange it in such a way that access to the funds could be guaranteed, regardless of Maryland law!"

Elijah felt like he had just been granted parole, even if the sentence itself had not yet been fully commuted. He looked at George Brown with sincere gratitude. "How can I ever thank ya enough, Mr. Brown? You have just lifted me out of a crushin despair!" He stood abruptly, with outstretched hand. "That is a truly wonderful idea! Don't know why it hadn't occurred to me before. I would be most grateful if ya could advise me on how to proceed, so we can establish the trust as soon as possible. I have even made the acquaintance of a nearby attorney, Mr. William Dorsey, whose services I am certain I can easily engage, if necessary!" he enthused.

"Excellent! Alex. Brown & Sons does have its own lawyers, of course, but if you wish to engage Mr. Dorsey's services I would have no objection. I know the gentleman. He has an excellent reputation, and in fact he has worked with us on several accounts." Mr. Brown seemed impressed that Elijah had managed to locate Mr. Dorsey on his own, and so quickly. It confirmed his willingness to offer his support, clearly recognizing that Elijah had a shrewd head for business, and the determination to seek out whatever was needed effectively, without hesitation. This promised to be mutually beneficial.

"If it meets with your approval then, I shall draw up a proposal and send it over to Mr. Dorsey for legal endorsement, and we can settle the paperwork at your convenience." Mr. Brown offered.

"That is most kind of you, sir. I'd greatly appreciate it if you would. I'd like to get this settled straight away, before I return to South Carolina. As my wife is with child, I am eager to make the journey home while she is still able, since because of their slave status, a baby bein born to a South Carolinian slave outside of South Carolina might add yet another legal complication and a worry to our plight that I'm sure we don't need. Lord knows, we've enough to sort out as it is!"

The two men agreed, and shook hands. Elijah then departed George Brown's company in a markedly better state than he had left Mr. Dorsey's. All the way back to the Admiral Fell Inn, Elijah's mind was racing, suddenly enlivened by the discovery of a new piece to the puzzle of his family's future survival.

When he returned to the Inn, rather than stopping at the tavern, Elijah, in his enthusiasm, fairly bounded up the stairs to find Amy. The clerk raised his eyes in astonishment. His mouth opening to greet his guest, he was left gaping soundlessly, the message never uttered, as Elijah disappeared from view.

"Amy, darlin! I finally have some good news!" Elijah burst into the room. Amy looked up in surprise, her finger to her lips. Elijah stopped in his tracks and noticed his younger daughter snuggled blissfully in their bed, sound asleep.

"I just put her down for a nap," Amy whispered, looking tenderly at little Julia's angelic face in repose. "Momma's taken the boys and Clarissa out to get some bread, and cheese and fruit. She can't wait to get home and be back in her kitchen!"

Elijah smiled, well aware that his mother-in-law was never more comfortable than when in her own kitchen, doing what she loved best. "Well sugar, we'll be home soon, and she can go cook up a storm if she wants to! I just came from my meetin with George Brown, and he gave me an idea that gave me a whole new lease on life!"

"Well, for heaven's sake, what is it? Don't just stand there, tell me!" Amy replied.

Elijah proceeded to recount his entire visit with Mr. Brown, and their conclusion that he could perhaps provide for them in a way that neither Carolina nor Maryland law could prevent. Amy listened attentively and, ever one on the lookout for the Achilles' heel in a plan, responded, "That's a wonderful idea, honey, but there is one snag that remains." Elijah, accustomed to the wind being taken out of his sails by his wife's unrelenting gift for pointing out reality, looked at his wife quizzically.

"What do you mean?"

"Well," Amy answered, "didn't you say this would work if we were livin in a slave free state? That's fine, but don't you realize what that means, sugar? We're all gonna have to move to some other state! And we still have to figure out where. It's obviously not gonna be Maryland!"

This time, however, Elijah was prepared. On the carriage ride home he was pondering George Brown's involvement in the Baltimore and Ohio Railroad, and his recognition of the business opportunity to ship his lumber westward. As a Southern family, they might not be well received in Pennsylvania or New York, but Ohio might be a real possibility.

"Well, now, darlin don't go gettin yourself all worked up about that! I figured you might say that, and I think I have a solution." Amy looked at him, almost surprised that he had second-guessed her.

"What is it?" she asked,

Elijah smiled. "Ohio! It's a slave free state, without New England's attitudes about Southerners. It's at the other end of the Baltimore & Ohio Railway. Makes business sense and legal sense. Of course, I'd have to go there and find a lawyer to write me a new will first, but honey, I really think this could work!"

Amy sat thoughtfully. Little Julia stirred, and then settled back to sleep. Amy was almost afraid to believe it, but she too began to feel that a solution had been found. She looked hopefully at her husband. "Elijah, honey, do ya really think ya can pull it off?"

"Come Hell or high water!" he responded. "Amy, darlin, I think the Lord has finally shown us a way."

"Please God, let it be so!" Amy responded fervently, as much to God as to Elijah.

"Well, alright then! We'd best go home and start gettin ready! I'll have to locate a reputable and sympathetic lawyer in Cincinnati. I can take a steamboat up from Louisville to Cincinnati and make the arrangements, then come back for you and the family.

Amy felt the baby kick, and said, "Elijah, honey, could you wait to go to Cincinnati until after the baby's born? I don't want ya away when my time comes, especially with your family nosin about."

"Of course, darlin!" as if suddenly remembering that there would soon be another child in the family. He looked at Amy and caressed her belly. "The baby may not be born free, but as God is my witness, if I have anythin to say about it, my baby's gonna grow up free! Free and prosperous!" he added. He gave Amy a kiss, and she smiled up at him, feeling suddenly that these were no longer mere words, but a real possibility.

"Well, you'd best go tell Momma and the children. They're all gonna be mighty pleased we're goin home, big city thrills or no!" Amy said.

Elijah said, "Don't you worry, honey, everything's gonna be alright. You get some rest now with my baby girl. I'll go tell your Momma what she's been wantin to hear all week!" he grinned. With that, he softly shut the door and went off to find the rest of the family with a new spring in his step.

XXVI

Back in Barnwell District, life continued along, more or less as usual. Elijah had sent a telegraph to Will Beazely to send word to Gilbert to come and pick them up at the station. Mr. Beazely, short-handed, saw James Willis at the post office, and asked him, "Hey, James, my errand boy's momma sent word that he won't be in today- he's down with a fever- and I've got too much work to go myself. Could you take this message out to your uncle Elijah's plantation and give it to Gilbert for me, since you pass more or less that way anyways?"

James, far from being inconvenienced, willingly accepted the commission, realizing it would give him a legitimate excuse to snoop around. "I'd be glad to, Mr. Beazely, I'd be glad to! Didn't realize Uncle Elijah was out of town, to tell ya the truth. Where'd he go?"

"Went up to Baltimore with his whole household! Sorta surprised me, since he usually leaves Miss Amy in charge when he's away."

"Well, that is a tad surprisin, I agree! Never know what Uncle Elijah might do next, seein as how he's got so many irons in the fire with his business! Did he let on why he decided to take em all up there with him?" James tried to sound casual.

"No, not really. Just said something about lookin into business opportunities, especially for shippin his cotton and his lumber. Talked about railroads and clipper ships. Your uncle's got a mighty good head for business! Always lookin for new possibilities- I surely do admire him for that," said Mr. Beazely, naively unaware that he might be revealing confidential information. He assumed that as a member of the family, James would already be informed of such matters.

James set to thinking. It was not unusual for Elijah to leave town. He was an avid businessman with extensive contacts, both in South Carolina and further afield. But, as far as James knew, he had never taken any of his slaves with him, much less the entire household, including children. Immediately suspicious, he was consumed with curiosity as to the reason, and he was clear that this was not just a matter of negotiating shipping deals for his cotton and lumber! He resolved to keep a sharp eye out when he went out to the Willlis Plantation and do whatever he could to wheedle some useful information out of that brother of Amy's. There was no longer any doubt whatsoever in his mind that Elijah was up to something, but he still wasn't sure just what it was, and figured maybe he could force it out of Gilbert, or one of the other slaves.

As James trotted up the road to the plantation house, admiring the property with an envious eye and dreaming of what he hoped might someday be his, Gilbert saw the dust cloud from a distance and was immediately on the alert. It was not often that people came to visit, and especially with Elijah out of town, it made Gilbert nervous, wondering who it might be and why they had come. Wiping the sweat off his brow, he headed out to the front of the house to greet the unknown visitor. When he saw it was James, he felt a knot in the pit of his stomach and immediately felt suspicious. He hadn't seen Elijah's nephew often, but it only took once for him to realize he didn't like him, and that the feeling was totally mutual. "What's that fool doin comin round here?" he wondered to himself.

"How do, Mister James? What can I do for ya'll?" Gilbert offered in greeting.

James rode right up next to Gilbert and looked down on him. He deliberately didn't dismount, so as to maintain his superiority, since Gilbert was taller and considerably stronger than James.

"Mornin, Gilbert," he said with a condescending sneer, "How's things here on the plantation? You nigras still workin when my uncle's away, or are ya'll just lazin around til he gets back?"

Gilbert bristled, but controlled himself. "How in the name of God could this surly son of a bitch be related to man as kind as Mister Elijah?" he thought to himself, but what he said was,

"Oh we workin hard as ever, Mister James, cause Mister Elijah treats us so good, he deserves it! Sides, we got one of the best run plantations in the South Carolina lowlands, and we proud of the work we do!" He wanted to add, "and we run it better than your sorry ass ever could," but of course he didn't.

James, knowing full well Gilbert was right about the Willis Plantation being one of the most successful plantations in the area, was torn between the vicarious family pride of basking in his uncle's reflected success, and feeling bitter envy that this colored man was enjoying or deserving any credit for it.

"I wouldn't get too uppity bout that if I was you, Gilbert. Y'all know that property can change hands and fortunes along with it." He said with menacing innuendo and a withering smile, deliberately giving Gilbert a disdainful look as he enunciated the word, 'property.'

The threat was not lost on Gilbert, but he didn't flinch a bit. He thought to himself, "If ya'll think you're gonna inherit this place and us along with it, ya'll in for a mighty big surprise!" He inadvertently chuckled at the thought of the look that would be on James' face when he found out he'd inherited nothing! James, of course, took the chuckle as an insult.

"You sassin me, boy?" he asked threateningly.

"No, sir!" Gilbert responded immediately, with fervor. "I was just thinkin how proud it must make ya'll feel to be related to Mister Elijah, he bein so successful and all. I imagine he must be an inspiration for your own business too!"

Never one for subtleties, James missed the sarcasm. He puffed up with pride, neither willing to recognize that he himself was not successful, nor that Gilbert was also related to Elijah. "Damn right! I'm proud to be a Willis! This town was founded by my ancestors, so you might say I'm part of the rulin family!" This last he said with unmistakable emphasis, lest Gilbert think otherwise.

"Yes sir, you might say that." He was thinking, of course, 'and I might not', but didn't say so. "Well sir, I guess ya'll know Mister Elijah's away, so if you not payin him a social visit, what brings ya'll out here?" Gilbert was not about to let James go too far or start poking around.

"Well, as a matter of fact, I came as a favor to Mr. Beazely. He asked me to tell ya my uncle's sent a telegram sayin he's comin home tomorrow, and he wants ya'll to pick him up at the depot." James pondered whether to offer to get his uncle himself, so Gilbert would have to tell him the whole family went, but that would seem like he was doing Gilbert a favor, and he wasn't going to be beholden to any Negro, even for the sake of getting a reaction out of him. And in truth, the last thing he wanted was to have to be with Elijah's bastards and that woman of his, and have to act polite and call her "Aunt Amy!"

"Yes, sir. Thank ya sir! I'll be there, don't you worry! Mister Elijah say pick him up, pick him up it is!" Gilbert was in fact glad of the news and didn't have to feign willingness to comply with the request. In fact, he was eager to find out what had happened up in Baltimore. He had actually expected them to be away for longer, and wasn't sure if their early return was a good sign or a bad one.

James, realizing that Gilbert was too smart to trick easily, decided he'd had enough, and replied, "See to it that you're there on time, boy! It's not good for nigras to keep their masters waitin!"

Overcoming the impulse to drag James out of his saddle by the throat and squeeze the life out of him like wringing a capon's neck, Gilbert smiled coldly and replied, "I wouldn't keep Mister Elijah waitin for all the world, sir." And looking at James with a piercing eye that made the younger Willis squirm, added, "And I'll be sure to tell him you was kind enough to stop by and deliver the message in person!"

James, suddenly aware that Elijah might not be too pleased to know that his nephew was on the plantation in his absence, and having no doubt that Gilbert would leave out no details of their conversation, decided to end the discussion without pressing any further.

"You do that, boy!" was all he could think to say. Gilbert having faced him down, James turned his horse and cantered off, the gelding raising his tail, and letting his dung fly as he went, as if expressing his owner's attitude. The fresh, moist stench of the manure hung in the humid air, wafting slowly toward the house.

"That ain't the only thing smells like horse shit round here!" thought Gilbert as he gave a disgusted look toward the backside of James Willis as he disappeared down the road.

That night, after all the workers had come in from the fields and the mill, and everyone had had supper, Gilbert let Julius and Jason know that Elijah and the family were coming home.

"Why do you suppose they comin back so soon? Hardly been more'n a week!" asked Julius.

"Maybe there's such good news, Mister Elijah didn't wanna wait, and figured he'd just rush right home to let us in on it!" suggested Jason, hopefully.

"Or maybe it's such bad news there wasn't any point in stayin any longer," speculated Gilbert. "I have no idea. Could be anything."

"Well, whatever it is, I still believe Mister Elijah gonna do whatever he can to set us free," said Julius with ardent conviction. The other two men nodded in agreement.

"I only hope that 'whatever he can' will be enough for it to actually happen!" affirmed Gilbert.

"Amen to that!" said Jason.

"Well, I guess we'll find out tomorrow. And a good thing, too! That James Willis makes me wanna squirm like a night crawler on a fish hook, just waitin to get a bite took outa him," confessed Julius.

The three grunted in total agreement that James, under any circumstances, was bad news, and looking for trouble.

"I know that's right!" said Jason.

"Man truly makes my flesh crawl," reiterated Julius.

"I know he's lookin for trouble," continued Gilbert, "I as afraid he'd ask for Amy, and I'da had ta tell him she was away, or get caught in a lie. He snoopin around alright. Make no mistake bout that. Best be extra careful, especially in town. Ya'll don't know whose eyes and ears he might be borrowin for information, trying to stir somethin up with his uncle!"

"If that little weasel goes makin trouble for Mister Elijah and ruins his plans, and I ever get my hands on him, he'll be sorry he was ever born!" swore Julius.

"Damn, Julius, don't you go talkin like that, even here! Ya want to get us all killed? That son of a bitch would stop at nothin to take his revenge-uncle or no! I'm tellin ya, he mean, and vicious, and stupid, and that make him dangerous! Ya'll steer clear of him, ya hear me? Last thing we need is to give that miserable excuse for a human bein any reason to attack us!" Gilbert was adamant.

Julius calmed down, with Jason looking on, frightened at the possibility of the conflagration they were all convinced that James was capable of provoking. "Gilbert's right, Julius, Mister James ain't worth it, no matter how mad he makes us and how much he insults us, he trash, plain and simple. Don't deserve the Willis name. Let him be! God'll take care of him."

"Hmmph! Maybe so," muttered Julius, "but the Lord sure seems to take care of things a lot slower than He oughta, and in the meantime folks like Mister James keep walkin all over us!"

"Well, we'll just see what happens when Mister Elijah finds out his nephew been here! Lord knows they's no love lost between them two. And ya'll listen close for any talk among the rest. We gotta keep a tight lid on things, or we gonna have a real mess on our hands!" Gilbert concluded. "Ya'll go on an get some rest, now! Julius, you and me gotta get up early to fetch everybody from the depot. I'll see ya'll in the morning."

"G'night Gilbert." Answered Julius

"G'night ya'll," called Jason.

An uneasy silence fell over the plantation as one by one the lights went out in the slave quarters, and the big house sat dark and brooding, the shadows of the trees playing across it like ghosts hovering in the dim moonlight. Gilbert's dreams were far from restful. He and Amy, and the whole family, were in the chicken coop. Somehow they were also chickens, and there was a rabid fox trying to break in, and the fox was actually James Willis. He was pushing his nose through the wire fence and snapping his jaws at them, teeth bared in an ugly, drooling grin. Just then, Elijah came out of the plantation house with a Kentucky long rifle in his hand. He took a shot and it wounded James, who then turned on Elijah. Gilbert woke up with a jolt of fear, sweating, and lay there uneasy until dawn, when he finally got up and got ready to go meet the family at the depot.

XXVII

When the train finally pulled into the Williston Depot, Barnwell District had probably never seen eight travel-weary passengers more ready to get home. It was hard to say who was gladder to see whom, for Gilbert and Julius were happy and relieved to see the family back home safely. The children ran to embrace their Uncle Gilbert and even Julius, almost desperately, as if they were grabbing onto a life-preserver on the high seas. The girls hung around Gilbert's neck so hard they wouldn't let him go. Even Momma Celia wiped a tear from her eye at the sight of her son, and gave him a silently loving pat on the arm as he helped her into the wagon. Amy too was eager to see her brother, though cautious about saying too much in public. But the one Gilbert most wanted to see was Elijah.

Anxious, strangely disquieted by his dream about James, and eager for at least some glimmer of hope that Elijah's plans were in fact moving forward, it was difficult for Gilbert to refrain from any show of particular interest, much less any signs of affection for his brother-in-law. Elijah sensed this too, and spontaneously reached out and clasped Gilbert's hand firmly, as if to reassure him non-verbally by that manly gesture, as scandalous as even such limited physical contact or show of mutual respect between races might seem to some.

Mr. Beazely, of course, was also there on the platform, tending to his business as stationmaster, but likewise eager to glean news of Elijah's trip. Of course, Mr. Beazely's interest was economic, hoping for tidings about some great new shipping enterprise in which he himself might be allowed to profitably participate.

"Welcome home Mr. Willis! How was your trip, sir? Were ya able to make those profitable connections ya'll were hopin for?" gushed Beazely.

Elijah, feeling circumspect about revealing too much even to a friendly face, decided to deflect the inquiry by saying, "The trip was very informative, thank ya, Will! I see ya got my telegram. Thank ya for deliverin the message so Gilbert and Julius could pick us up on time. It's been a real long journey, and we're pretty worn out from it. It woulda been a shame to have to wait to get on home."

"Oh, no trouble at all, sir! Matter of fact, your nephew James happened to be here when your telegram arrived and was kind enough to take the message out to your plantation on his way home! As luck would have it, my errand boy was down with a fever, so your nephew did a true act of Christian charity by helpin me out like that!" Beazely smiled effusively.

At the mention of James' name, Elijah shot a quick glance to both Amy and Gilbert. Amy looked alarmed, but Gilbert shook his head almost imperceptibly to prevent her from speaking. Not wanting to alert Mr. Beazely, Elijah simply agreed, "Well that really was right Christian of him now, wasn't it?" knowing full well that James' motivation was nothing of the sort. "I surely do thank you, Will. Sorry to hear about your errand boy. Tell Johnny's mother I hope he feels better real soon. If he doesn't, let me know, and I'll ask Doc Harley to look in on him." Mr. Beazely was touched by Elijah's solicitude, and thanked him. Always had been kind to the folks in town.

"Ya'll enjoy your day now, Will. We'd best be gettin on home," Elijah concluded. He had no intention of providing the loquacious Mr. Beazely with any tidbits of information from his trip at this point, as the stationmaster was clearly naïve enough not to recognize the tensions between Elijah and his nephew. And until Elijah'd heard from Gilbert exactly what had transpired when James came out to the plantation, he wasn't about to take any unnecessary chances. They gathered up their luggage, loaded it onto the wagon and the carriage, and proceeded to climb aboard themselves. The children chose to go in the buckboard with Momma Celia and Julius, chattering excitedly about being home and leaving Elijah and Amy in the carriage with some privacy to talk with Gilbert.

Once out of the depot on the open road, Elijah advised Gilbert to take them by an alternate route, to avoid passing by James' store, feeling fairly certain his nephews would be on the lookout. He was just not ready to deal with the likes of them until he'd had a home cooked meal, a bath, a change of clothes, and maybe even a good night's sleep! Then he asked Gilbert with genuine concern,

"So what happened when James came out? Did he give you any trouble?"

"Well sir, he wanted to, but I didn't let him. I hate to say it Mister Elijah, he bein your family and all, but that man is just plain mean. An I know he suspects somethin, and is tryin hard to figure out what's goin on. But he's a coward too, and I think he's as scared of ya as he is jealous! I told him I'd be sure to tell ya'll he'd been by, and his face turned from nasty to scared in the beat of a hummin bird's wing!" To affirm the seriousness of the encounter, he added, "I made sure Julius and Jason know to keep an extra sharp eye out for Mister James and his brother, cause they don't mean you or us no good."

"I don't doubt that! I've seen him and his brother and young Angus Patterson starin and whisperin amongst themselves when I go by. All three of em are unwillin to work as hard as their fathers, but expect to live comfortably off their parents' earnins. It's a shame really. And a terrible waste."

Gilbert responded, "You a lot more generous toward em than I am. Sound to me like a white man's way of saying they lazy, greedy, and no account!" Gilbert grinned at Elijah, and Elijah, taken aback at first, returned the grin in recognition of the cultural difference between them in handling the same unpleasant reality. Amy stifled a chuckle.

"Well, I suppose you're right, Gilbert! But make no mistake, I know the boy's a weasel, and you did right to warn Julius and Jason about him."

There was an awkward silence before Gilbert was able to ask, "So, what dya find out up in Baltimore?" He knew the query was loaded, but his own anxiety wouldn't let him keep silent any longer in the passive choreography typical of master-slave relations, where the slave doesn't initiate any probing questions but simply waits for the master to bestow upon him whatever information he may choose to share. He wanted to talk man to man.

Elijah of course understood completely, and had no problem with Gilbert being forthright with him. "Well truth be told, it's a mixture of good news and bad news," he replied. "The bad news nearly drove me to despair at first, but the good news pulled me out of it, and I think we've found a solution to our dilemma at last!" Gilbert perked right up at that.

Elijah proceeded to tell him all about the trip to Baltimore, with special attention to the meetings with Mr. Brown and Mr. Dorsey. He elaborated on Mr. Brown's helpful suggestion about setting up a trust- perhaps even in the Philadelphia or New York branch of Alex. Brown & Sons- to which the family might have an access that neither Maryland nor South Carolina could deny them.

"But, what of the possibility of relocating to Maryland? I thought you was thinkin we might all just move up there instead of stayin here in South Carolina?" asked Gilbert, highly skeptical that the words "solution" and "stay in South Carolina" could possibly fit in the same sentence, much as he would regret leaving the more satisfying aspects of the work he was doing and learning on the plantation.

Elijah then came to explain what he had discovered about the draconian laws of Maryland, and the difficulty posed by emancipating only those over the age of ten and under the age of forty-five, the restrictions even on free blacks, and the requirement that slaves granted emancipation by their own petition then leave the state.

"So, unfortunately, Maryland would be barely more hospitable than South Carolina, and there seems to be no way the whole family- much less the rest of the slaves here- could be emancipated successfully there, accordin to Mr. Dorsey. I'll admit," he continued, after seeing Gilbert's expression change from enthusiastic to crestfallen, "I was mighty disappointed bout that, especially since when I walked into his house, I saw on the wall a campaign poster of Senator Clay from when he ran for President back in '44- signed by the Senator himself, with a personal dedication to Mr. Dorsey. Seein as how Mr. Clay has been supportive of emancipation, I was hopin for a better response from a lawyer who supported him!"

Before Amy could interject any comments about Elijah's drunken escapade, followed by her encouraging him to the more hopeful meeting with Mr. Brown, at the mention of Henry Clay, Gilbert suddenly remembered the letter that had come. He almost pulled the carriage to a dead stop for not having remembered it sooner. "Mister Elijah, I most forgot! You finally got a response from Senator Clay!"

Elijah and Amy both looked up with surprise. Amy squeezed Elijah's hand in anticipation. Gilbert continued, "The letter arrived a few days back. Jason was at the depot with Joshua and young Elias, loadin a shipment of lumber onto the train. Mr. Beazeley called out that you had mail, and Jason sent Elias over to get it. Dang if the boy ain't figurin out how to read! Discovered there was a letter from "The Hon. H. Clay in Kentucky" and started to get all excited, asking bout what a 'hon' was, and where Kentucky was, and who in tarnation was H. Clay. Seems he was all worked up about bein able to read the names and addresses."

Amy groaned in alarm, and Elijah, though smiling at the "hon" reference and patting Amy's hand reassuringly, asked evenly, "Anybody hear him?"

Gilbert answered, "Jason and Joshua set to calmin him down an shuttin him up right away before anybody overheard, so I don't think so. But Jason like about to tear that letter open hisself when he realized what it might tell us! Course I wouldn't let him. We both knew it was not for us to open your mail, but Jason had to admit, it most burned a hole through his shirt on the way back to the plantation. I hid it good and safe til you got back. I'll fetch it as soon as we get home."

Elijah responded, "Well, I'd been hopin it would arrive before goin to Maryland, but havin learned what we learned up there, maybe it's just as well. Question is, will he have anythin helpful to say now?"

The question hung in the air like a rhetorical challenge which none of them were sure they were ready to face, so they all fell silent for the rest of the ride home.

When the family got to the plantation at last, the children eagerly helped unload the luggage, delighted to be back home. Momma Celia made a beeline for her kitchen, and Amy went upstairs to lie down. She was feeling the pregnancy more than usual, and felt quite drained from the journey. After Gilbert had finished unloading, and had taken the carriage out to the barn, he went to his room where he had hidden the letter from Henry Clay under a loose floorboard for safekeeping and brought it back to the plantation house.

He found Elijah in his study and handed it to him saying simply, "Here it is."

Rather than then excusing himself, he lingered, hoping Elijah would open it and tell him what it said.

Elijah made no move to dismiss him, on the contrary, he invited him to have a seat while he read the letter out loud, commenting on it to Gilbert as he read:

Mr. Elijah Willis
Willis Plantation
Williston
Barnwell District, South Carolina

My Dear Mr. Willis:
I received your letter today, as I was not in Washington when it arrived some weeks ago, and it was forwarded to me to Ashland, my home in Lexington.

"Just as I thought, that explains why it took so long to get the response!"

Though lately called back out of retirement to take my seat in the Senate once more, the vicissitudes of old age and poor health have obliged me to take some much needed repose in the place I most dearly love, in the hope that Providence will soon restore me to sufficient energy to fulfill that duty, while yet I may. I do apologize for my unwitting delay in responding to your queries, and regret any inconvenience that may have caused you.

I greatly appreciate the trust you have placed in me to advise you on the issue of the emancipation of slaves, though I must confess my surprise at receiving such a query from a South Carolinian. You have restored my conviction that my old rival, and recently deceased colleague, Senator Calhoun, did not necessarily speak for all in that great State, and that there are sensible men, even where the institution of slavery seems most deeply rooted, who are eager to see it end.

"Let's hope he's right that there are enough of us to make a difference- to my way of thinkin, that remains to be seen! There may be a few of us, but not too many- at least not in these parts!

This gives me hope for our great nation's future survival, despite being currently mired in the throes of such turmoil over this very issue.

As you surely are aware, I've spent much of my political and professional life striving to accomplish the goal of universal emancipation, though it continues to elude us as a nation so severely divided. At times, I confess, my love of our noble country, and my unshakable belief in the imperative importance of preserving its union, has overshadowed my distaste for the institution of slavery, and I have felt compelled to make compromises that I would have preferred not to make, to that end. I pray the good Lord will forgive me if I have failed to achieve all my heart and mind have prompted me to do.

"Well, it's refreshin to hear I'm not the only slave owner feelin conflicted by havin to play along with the social pressures in ways I'druther not!"

As a slave owner myself, I, like you, am keenly aware of the importance of treating the Negroes with dignity, and providing for their comfort and good health. As it happens, I have a number of slaves who are no longer able to work, due to advanced age or infirmity, whom I am pleased to maintain in comfort 'til the end of their days- at considerable expense, I might add. And though I have already emancipated a few slaves, such as my long time valet, Charles Dupuy, I suspect that, like you, I find myself in the awkward position of being unable to maintain my farming enterprise without their service.

"I heard tell that his current valet, name of Levi, actually ran away to Cincinnati, but came back of his own accord, and the Senator welcomed him with open arms and not a word of punishment. Says a lot about em both!"

I am also mindful that to simply set them all free, without the means to preserve that freedom, would be a cruel gesture, condemning them to penury, and to far more suffering than ever they endured in their bondage to my service. So I have provided not only for their emancipation, but their financial preservation and education, in my Last Will and Testament, thereby not only granting them their freedom, but also granting myself the peace of mind of having done right by them, at long last.

"He's right about that too- that's why I want the children to all get schoolin!"

At this point Gilbert began to shift a little in his seat. He had mixed feelings about what the Senator was saying. On the one hand, it sounded patronizing and condescending. At the same time it sounded compassionate and even insightful. Gilbert could see for himself the dilemma of running a farm on slave labor that one might not be able to afford to run on paid labor. Gilbert had enough business sense to appreciate the conflict, while deploring the vacillation about its solution. Elijah continued to read:

As a lawyer, I see your issue as a complex one, for the matters of manumission, inheritance, and miscegenation have distinct characteristics, moral implications, and legal parameters. As you may have heard, I personally have been of the opinion that emancipation should be accomplished with the ultimate goal of colonization, that is, permitting the Negroes to return to their native Africa, from which they were so untimely ripped, in freedom and peace. I am not only a founder, , but have been for many years, and continue to be still, the president of the American Colonization Society. We have successfully been able to send a great many Negroes back to Africa, where they have founded a democratic society suitable to their own needs and culture, in the new nation of Liberia, in West Africa. That is not to say, however, that free

*blacks have not been, or should not now continue to be able to live in peace
and dignity within our own borders, as you clearly intend for yours, at least
until such time as their repatriation might be achieved.*

"I heard this same argument up in Maryland from that lawyer Mr.
Dorsey, and to tell the truth, it made me realize that at least some of the
abolitionists are working to free the slaves, not just to end a cruel injustice
or so they can be part of a balanced society, but to better get rid of all
coloreds by sendin em away, back to where some of the abolitionists think
they belong. It sounds generous at first, but in fact, it strikes me as racist
and self-centered in a different form!"

*Concerning the issue of emancipation, though I continue to defend the
right of each sovereign state to determine its own policies on this matter, I
would prefer there to be a national solution to the problem, and fervently
pray we may yet achieve the same, even if not in my lifetime. However, since
my own mortality, as I am lately aware, is likely to come to a close sooner
than I might hope or expect, due to ill health and advancing age, perhaps the
achievement of universal emancipation is not as far distant as it once seemed,
when I was still young enough to believe myself to be immortal!*

"That's too bad. I didn't realize he was in such poor health. I guess that
means we won't be able to call on him for much help in the future! Makes
me feel the urgency of our task all the more intensely! Let's hope there's
something in the letter that is of immediate usefulness!"

*My younger cousin, Cassius Marcellus Clay, is also ardently committed
to this matter, though I must confess, some consider him rather prone to
being inflammatory on the subject, as you might have formerly read in his
publication The True American. Even here, in Kentucky, the subject has been
the cause of much dispute, and due to the uproar that periodical caused in
my hometown of Lexington, my cousin was compelled to move its publication
to the city of Cincinnati, in the slave free State of Ohio, before he went off to
the Mexican War. I do sense, however, that the times may finally be changing,
and the definitive impetus for emancipation is clearly growing, even in some of
the states where slavery is currently still permitted. Nevertheless, manumission
in general being so difficult a challenge, I fear universal emancipation will,
nevertheless, likely come at an even greater cost on a national level than on the
personal one.*

"Well now, that's an interestin coincidence, since I figured out in Baltimore that Cincinnati might be the place for me to go, and it seems the Senator's cousin is not one of those wanting to free the slaves just to ship em back to Africa! If he was publishin in Cincinnati, sorta confirms my instincts that Cincinnati is likely the place for me to go next to sort all this mess out, as they seem to be friendly to our cause by general disposition up there!"

I am mindful, however, that whatever we politicians may do or decide will inevitably take more time than you have at your disposal to find a solution to your own concerns. Clearly, any eventual political solution that may be achieved, will in any case not answer your immediate needs. So in the meantime, you will have to ascertain whether it would be more efficacious and advantageous for you to seek emancipation for your slaves in another slave-holding state, or in one where Mr. Calhoun's "peculiar institution" is not permitted at all.

"Aha! You see. I was right! That settles it! We do need to go to a slave-free state! Pity that wasn't so clear before we went up to Maryland! Even though I suppose we could head up further North- Mr. Brown talked about his branch offices in Philadelphia and New York- I just don't think we'd be happy in a Northern city. Ohio still strikes me as our best solution.

To my way of thinking, however, and for whatever it may be worth to you, you may run a certain risk attempting to do so in a slave-holding state, even though it might currently have more flexible laws than South Carolina. I am intimately familiar with the machinations of government and its intrinsic response to the changing and at times capricious moods and perceptions of the people. Given the heated divisions rending our nation on this very subject, it is therefore entirely possible that you may encounter additional roadblocks to your slaves' freedom and financial solvency being created through new legislation, even should you succeed in their initial emancipation. Such seems to have been the case already in your own home state, where as I understand it, the matter of emancipation has become steadily more difficult, and interracial inheritance has been utterly prohibited. Herein lies one of the intransigent problems. The integrity of individual States' rights must be held in balance with the integrity of our Union, and at times, these seem to be contradictory ideals.

"Well, whatever the politics of it may be, he's right on the money about the problems it could still raise. Mr. Dorsey made that mighty clear too. So did Mr. Brown."

Yet, despite your Senator Calhoun's notion that States' rights allow each state the option to choose the selective nullification of any federal laws it finds onerous, such a notion continues to defy the very logic of the Constitution and the fundamental principles of the basic concept of our Union, and the comity between states. No state can simply pick and choose what of our national law or policy it finds agreeable and jettison the rest, while still claiming membership in the Union. Consequently, the issue of legal jurisdiction is pertinent to your situation, since one of our nation's fundamental principles is that the laws of the several states will be mutually honored and respected by each. New and evolving legislation, therefore, can present interpretive challenges in its applications, especially when the legislation becomes clearly partisan toward a particular faction or value, such as is the case in the issue of emancipation versus slavery.

"Question is, can we work our way around it? Old John Calhoun sure convinced a lot of folks around here that his notion of 'nullification' was just what the doctor ordered for slaveholders to keep control."

That being said, it must be admitted that we are speaking speculatively, as such possible legislation within slave-holding states that retain some proviso for limited emancipation is, at this point, merely hypothetical, and I do not wish to dissuade you from your noble efforts in Baltimore, or elsewhere.

As for the matter of inheritance, you are certainly right to want to provide for your slaves in any way possible, for emancipation without a means of sustenance would be no emancipation at all, and a cruel joke to play. I have had the same concern for my own, and therefore sympathize. Emancipation is, manifestly, the necessary precondition to providing a viable inheritance. By both law and common sense, any person living in freedom should be, by logical extension, free to inherit property. Such would be an obvious manifestation by which that freedom is known and enjoyed. Once an emancipation is recognized, the issue of inheritance therefore changes in nature, especially if each is handled independently of the other. If your family were to be emancipated prior to your demise, for example, and such emancipation legally recognized, even in another state, you might then well argue their right to inherit through your Will. However, in my own case, I have managed to provide for both, through my Last Will and Testament, and it will be upheld in the Commonwealth of Kentucky.

"This, right here, is the key of the matter! I need to tell Angus Patterson about this, as well as discuss it with a lawyer up in Cincinnati. There's gotta be a way for ya'll to be emancipated legally, and have it recognized outside of South Carolina. It's our only chance to make the case that ya'll'd then have a right to inherit!"

On the final point of miscegenation, however, I must confess, I do not approve of the mixing of the races. I have never thought it advisable, as I fear in the issue of such liaisons, each race is diminished by the other. I realize that some folks may not agree with me on this point- I'd expect you'd be one of them. And there are certainly a sizable number of the residents of New Orleans for example, a city I dearly love, where such mixtures have become commonplace.

"Well, that's disappointin. I woulda thought he'd be more acceptin. Guess he never fell in love with a colored woman, or he might think differently!" Elijah smiled at Gilbert.

However, I do not wish to stand in judgment of what is already a reality, for to do so would be to evade the question you have put to me, and thereby also evade my sacred responsibility to you as a life-long public servant. I am fairly well certain there are no slave-holding states, other than Louisiana, where such racial intermingling is well tolerated, but that would be an issue for you to determine in making your choice. As to whether the slave-free states are more amenable, I suspect there is no conformity on this issue even there, though in theory, perhaps there should be fewer obstacles thereto. You might consider consulting a friend of mine, John Jolliffe, of Cincinnati, for further insights into the jurisdictional issues of your particular case.

"Well, fair enough! He's probably right. So I guess we've got to determine how folks would react up in Ohio, but I don't see a lot of sense in goin' further North or further West than there. Still seems like Ohio'd be our best bet."

I realize I may not have offered much by way of solution to your problem, sir, but I do hope that sharing something of my own experience and understanding of the issue will help you in determining the best course of action for you to take. Were I a younger man, I might pledge to you renewed efforts on my own part in Washington to facilitate emancipation, at the very least, but I fear such energies as that would require of me are fast diminishing. Alas, I am forced to accept that I am coming to the end of my career, and it will be for someone younger than I to pick up the torch of this cause and carry it further. Perhaps my fellow Kentuckian, that promising Mr. Lincoln, now of Illinois, or some other young buck, as yet unknown to the public, will succeed where my generation has failed. I devoutly hope so.

Forgive the ramblings of an old man! I wish you and your family well, sir, and trust that by the grace of the Almighty, you will, in fact find a solution to your problem somewhere in these United States. I remain,

Your willing servant,

H. Clay
Ashland
Richmond Road
Lexington, Kentucky

Elijah finished reading, carefully refolded the letter, and sat there, pensive. Gilbert finally broke the silence.

"So what ya gonna do?"

"Well, one thing's clear. This letter confirms that I need to go up to Ohio and find a lawyer to help me set things up there," he answered, "but Amy doesn't want me to go til after the baby's born, cause she's afraid it'll come when I'm away and doesn't want to have to deal with folks around here findin out about it without me here."

Gilbert couldn't hide a look of disappointment at the prospect of having to wait still longer now that there seemed to be feasible plan.

"I think she's right about that Gilbert, much as I'd prefer to just go ahead and get it done- for everybody's sake! If Doc Harley comes to help with the baby, I wouldn't worry, but if he were indisposed and that Dr. Guignard were to come- sure as the sun comes up in the mornin he'd be tellin the other planters, and there'd be talk in town that we don't want to be dealin with!" Elijah continued, "So we'll have to wait a bit- but maybe I can get the names of some lawyers up there in Cinncinnati from Angus Patterson and start writin some letters to get things started!" He seemed to have forgotten or overlooked Mr. Clay's reference to John Jolliffe, perhaps not realizing Jolliffe was a lawyer.

"Lord knows I hope so Elijah, cause it's only gonna get harder to keep things a secret around here, and there's no tellin the trouble that might get stirred up amongst the other planters in these parts, not to mention your relations, if they find out what ya're doin, baby or no baby!" Gilbert agreed, with unexpected fervor. It was the first time he had dropped the honorific "Mister," and both men realized it, spontaneously denoting a fundamental change in the relationship where the two men were less master and slave and more co-conspirators in a plan that would shake Williston, South Carolina to its roots.

Gilbert's response struck Elijah as both insightful and appropriate. "There's no doubtin that, Gilbert, you're absolutely right, and we're all gonna have to be extra careful in the weeks and months ahead- and for however long it takes to get this done! It's not gonna be easy.

XXVIII

Since their return to Williston, Elijah and his family had settled back into the patterns of normal life- temporarily at least. This was both by natural inclination, and by specific design, so as to quell any suspicions that might have been raised by the inevitable discovery that they had all gone up to Baltimore. Things had been busy- so busy that Elijah had not found time to consult with Angus Patterson yet, and was eager to do so once things calmed down a bit after the harvest and the Holidays. The cotton harvest that year had been an exceptionally good one, the lumber business was prospering, and to those who didn't know any better, the Willis Plantation simply seemed to be just one more of many such highly successful and profitable enterprises throughout the South.

At Christmastime, Elijah had even managed to receive his brother and sister and their families- Amy, Momma Celia and the children all being well prepared beforehand to keep up the charade of their slavery. It was onerous for all of them, but Elijah felt that to avoid all family contact at the Holidays would make matters worse, especially at this delicate juncture in their process of moving forward with their plans. They tried to get through it without any major incidents, and Elijah kept the conversation as brief and superficial as possible, assiduously avoiding any topics that might trigger open conflict.

Of course, despite Elijah's and his household's efforts, James and Michael eyed everything and everyone critically, making the atmosphere most uncomfortable. Elijah's sister and sister-in-law cast covetous eyes on the silver and china, each looking around as if mentally measuring for new drapes, but managed to avoid making any overt comments. Amy, even though staying out of sight as much as possible, could not hide her pregnancy and could feel everyone's prying eyes not only searching her, but assessing every object, gesture or comment within eyesight or earshot throughout the entire visit. This, of course instilled in her a whole new level of loathing for them all, especially Elijah's nephews, who were the most invasive and least apologetic of any of them.

Elijah's brother and sister, out of family loyalty, seemed to be trying to avoid any conflicts, in the Holiday spirit, but the tensions were palpable, and when he picked up on his son James' prurient eyeing of Amy, Elijah's brother Jimmy, decided it was time for them all to be getting on home. Awkward goodbyes were mumbled, judgmental looks given, and any vestige of Christmas cheer seemed to be sucked out of the house with the opening of the front doors, and the last hollow wishing each other 'Happy Holidays,' as the extended family exited.

It was hard to say who felt more relieved once they had gone. The pretense of sociability was somehow maintained, against all odds, throughout their guests' departure. A heavy sigh of relief, however, was uttered by all in the household as soon as they closed the front door, after watching the other Willises trundle down the road to their respective homes, leaving little to the imagination as to the conversations they were having en route. The strain of the encounter had taken its toll on them all, especially Elijah. It had thrown into high relief the untenability of his relationship with his white relations quite definitively.

"Elijah, honey, I don't know how many more times I can stand to have your relations in this house!" said Amy in exasperation. "This game is just too hard to keep playin! The way they look at you with such judgment and resentment and the way they look at me and Momma and the children with such hatred, I just don't know if I can handle it any more!" Amy was on the verge of tears when suddenly, Elijah grew faint, nearly falling, and rubbed his chest as if to massage away a cramp. He grew very pale, and his forehead beaded in perspiration, despite the cool weather.

"Amy, darlin, I am truly sorry, but I'm not feelin well! Please send Gilbert or Julius to go fetch Doc. Harley right away!" Elijah gasped.

Amy, alarmed, called out, "Momma! Come quick! Hurry, I need your help! Elleck! Run an tell Gilbert to fetch Doc Harley immediately!" She turned to her husband, "Elijah, sugar, are ya havin chest pains?" Amy fought to keep down the panic welling up inside her.

Elijah was breathing heavily, but shook his head 'no' to the chest pains. "No, darlin I just feel really peculiar. Like I'd had way too much to drink, or somethin. My head was spinnin, I felt a flutterin in my chest, and my knees felt like the energy drained out of em, and then it was like everything went black for a second, and then the lights came back on!"

A clattering was heard in the kitchen, and suddenly Momma Celia came running from the back of the house to see what the matter was. She helped Amy get Elijah to lie down on the settee, ran to get him a blanket and a pillow to prop him up, and brought him a draft of whiskey which she insisted he sip like a medicine. The two women took turns wiping Elijah's brow.

Momma Celia called her grandson, "Elder, come here quick, child! I need ya to do somethin for me right now! Go out in the garden out back and see if they's any stalks of foxglove out there. You know the tall purple flowers like a cluster a bells?- they won't be bloomin now, but if theys any leaves or stems left cut me some and bring em to me right away."

"Yes'm!" answered Elder, suddenly worried, and already on his way out to the garden. Since the winter had been mild, he was in luck and found the foxgloves right away. He broke off a large handful of stems and wilting leaves and ran back to the kitchen with them, a chill wind blowing at his back and making him shiver involuntarily with dread. When he got inside, he called out to his grandmother, "I got em Momma Celia. Now what you want me to do with em?"

Momma Celia handed a cool compress to Amy, "Keep wipin his brow, sugar, I need to go make some digitalis tea. Phillip- go stoke up the fire- we gotta keep Mister Elijah warm!" With that she scurried off to the kitchen, leaving Amy to tend to Elijah and Phillip to tend to the fire. The rich smell of applewood smoke perfumed the room, blending with the smell of Holiday greens decorating the mantle. Elijah was breathing a little easier now but was still very pale. The girls, who had made themselves scarce during the visit from Elijah's relatives, came in now, frightened and worried. Their presence made him rally a bit, as he didn't want them to be alarmed.

Before long, Momma Celia came in with a piping hot mug of digitalis tea. "Come on now Mister Elijah, you got to drink this up. It don't taste too good, but it'll set your heart straight. Ya'll got yasef worked up with all your relations here, an all. You gonna be alright. Gilbert's gone to fetch Doc Harley an they be back real soon. You just rest easy now." Momma Celia's tender ministrations revealed a side to her Elijah had not realized before. He had seen her love for Amy and the children, of course, but had never felt he was on the receiving end of it himself, until now. He was deeply touched, reaching out to grasp her hand affectionately in return. Momma Celia just nodded silently to him in acknowledgement.

By the time Joseph Harley arrived, Elijah had more or less recovered, and was embarrassed he had interrupted his friend's holiday celebration.

"Joseph, I am so sorry to call you out here! I just felt so odd! But it's passed now. I'm sure it was nothin!" Elijah said hopefully, despite his instincts telling him this was a warning he should heed.

"Nonsense Elijah, think nothing of it! No trouble at all for an old friend! You let me be the judge of whether it was nothin or not! I just need to examine ya." Dr. Harley took out his pocket watch and felt Elijah's pulse, counting the heartbeats per minute. He detected a slight arrhythmia, but the heart did not seem to be racing too fast, which was reassuring. When he saw the tea he asked,

"Momma Celia, did you make that tea? And did you also give him whiskey?"

"Yessir!" she replied fearlessly. "Made out of foxglove- they calls it digitalis tea. Put a little chamomile in it too, for the blood. And the whiskey was to ease his pain."

Dr. Harley was impressed, since digitalis was the medicine of choice for tachycardia and cardiac arrhythmia, chamomile was considered a blood thinner, and alcohol was thought to be a vasodilator, helping circulation.

"How'dya know what to give him?" Unlike some white doctors who would have been annoyed and insulted at the presumption of a slave treating a white patient, Dr. Harley had the keen curiosity of a true scientist, and was genuinely interested to know where Momma Celia had come by this life-saving knowledge. Some whites would inflict severe punishment on someone like Momma Celia for fear that her knowledge of medicinal herbs and plants might be used to poison her master. Dr. Harley was neither so venal nor so foolish.

"My grandmother knew all kinda things bout herbs and plants, and made all kinda potions an teas, sir. Told me her father had been a medicine man back in Africa. She passed it on to me. I just did what I'd been taught."

"Well, I congratulate ya. Ya did exactly the right thing. I couldn't have done it better myself!" One of the things about Joseph Harley was that everyone seemed to feel valued by him. That was a rare thing, and Momma Celia blushed shyly at the compliment.

"Thank ya, sir." she mumbled, embarrassed.

"No, no, I thank you, Momma Celia. As I'm sure Elijah does too." Dr. Harley turned to his patient. "You're a lucky man, Elijah. Thanks to Momma Celia, ya managed to avoid a full-out fit of apoplexy. But I'm ordering ya to bed rest for at least the next twenty-four hours, and then I want you to take things easy for a few more days."

Elijah looked disgruntled but nodded in acquiescence, too weakened to offer any real resistance, and too disconcerted to want to try.

"And Elijah," the good doctor added as he was about to leave, "No more extended family visits- Doctor's orders!" Joseph Harley smiled knowingly at Elijah, confirming everyone's feeling that the charade had gone on long enough, and that contact with Elijah's "other" family was literally bad for his health.

XXIX

"Did you see that woman spyin on us from the hallway? Who does she think she is? Why I bet ya your brother even lets her eat off of good Willis silver and china! The very thought of it makes me ill!" blustered James' mother, highly distraught. James' father, though basically agreeing with his wife, felt a certain reticence to say so, however. Despite their widely divergent life styles and fundamentally opposite points of view concerning people of color, Elijah was after all, still his brother. Blood loyalties ran deep in Barnwell District, even when families sometimes feuded amongst themselves. It was a peculiar but common type of dysfunction that allowed the afflicted parties to say grievous things to and about each other, but could not abide anyone else from outside leveling like criticisms.

"Now Mother," Elijah's brother Jimmy said placatingly to his wife, "don't go gettin your knickers all in a twist about Elijah's peculiar tastes for company. He's my brother, for heaven's sake! He showed me himself the will he wrote back in '46, and it leaves his entire estate, includin his slaves, divided fairly amongst us!" The reminder of this fact only slightly mollified his wife.

"I don't like the company he keeps any more'n you do," he added, "but so long as the will is clear we got no cause to worry, and no need to be tearin him down, just because in his old age he felt a little lonely and decided to keep company with one of his slaves!"

Mrs. Willis did not seem convinced. James spoke up. "Daddy, he may be your brother and all, but I think Uncle Elijah's gone right off his head, actin like that nigra's his wife and havin children with her! Good God, what's got into him? And not only that- I can't prove it, but I'd bet most anything he's up to somethin with that woman and her family. Why'd he go takin them all up to Baltimore?"

Michael had come in on the tail end of this. "You ask me, she's got him bewitched! I heard that some nigras actually cast spells on folks- black magic they brought over from Africa! Friend of mine went down to New Orleans, and they say some of those creole nigras practice somethin they call VooDoo. Stick pins in little dolls of folk they don't like, and that person in real life gets sick, or drops down dead!"

"Oh now stop it, you two! Elijah may be peculiar, but he's not evil, and I don't believe that Amy woman's got any power over him beyond the power every woman has over her man! Nothin supernatural about sex for a lonely bachelor- even if he and I have decidedly different tastes!" He smiled affectionately at his wife, as if to reassure her that she was the flower of Southern beauty and his undeniable ideal of feminine charm. She blushed, slightly flustered at the reference.

"Besides, as a slave owner he has a right to take his slaves wherever he wants, no matter what the Yankees say! Fugitive Slave Act made sure of that!" he said with the confidence of a Southerner determined to ignore any Northern anti-slavery nonsense.

Elijah's sister-in-law seemed quite prone to agree with the boys, but for the sake of family harmony, and out of respect for the head of the family, they said no more. If not a peace, at least an uneasy truce was struck- a truce however, which left each one wondering, in the quiet hours of the night, if there was something more going on than met the eye.

The next morning, Angus Patterson Junior, stopped by James' store, and the boys set to talking about the most recent goings on.

"Mornin, Angus! What brings you over here today? You heard the news bout our Uncle Elijah's trip up to Baltimore?"

Angus allowed as how he had, but that wasn't the reason for his visit. "Thought ya'll ought to know an interestin little detail. May mean somethin." Angus immediately had James' and Michael's undivided attention. It didn't take much, since so little ever happened in Williston, even the slightest thing out of the ordinary monotony of life there counted as an event of considerable importance.

Angus, suddenly pleased by the power of his message to elicit the attention of his companions and thereby enhance his own standing with them, continued with the voice of someone 'in the know,'

" I was over the depot a few days back, while your uncle was away. Some of his nigras- Jason and Joshua and a boy name of Elias- were loading your uncle's lumber onto the train, when I heard Mr. Beazeley call out to Jason that there was some mail for your uncle. Jason sent the boy to fetch it, so I hung around, casual like, to see if I could find out where it was from."

He paused for affect, to make sure his next report would have maximum impact.

"Well?" James said impatiently, "did you find out anything, or not?!"

"Matter of fact, I did!" said Angus expansively. "I heard the boy soundin out the names and addresses on the letters- seems your uncle's lettin his nigras actually learn to read, which I think is a terrible idea, and I'm pretty sure is even illegal- but anyway, it sounded like he said one of the letters was from 'The Hon. H. Clay in Kentucky!'

"I asked Mr. Beazely, 'Did I just hear that boy readin off a Mr. Willis's mail?' and he said,

'Well, seems he's tryin!'

"So I just kinda played along, and asked Mr. Beazely, 'So did he really get a letter from some fella up in Kentucky?' and Mr. Beazely said, 'Sure enough did! I'm not too sure, a'course, but seems to me that 'the Hon. H. Clay' would most likely be Senator Henry Clay. Didn't realize your uncle knew him!' Mr. Beazeley was so eager to appear knowledgeable himself, and so taken by Elijah's business acumen that he was easily impressed by what he deemed the Willis sphere of influence in high places.

Michael and James exchanged looks, and Angus continued, "That Will Beazely really is a fool, but it's easy as pie to get him talkin bout who's writin who and everybody's business."

James and Michael were not exactly well versed in the ins and outs of national leadership, and didn't want Angus to know they weren't quite sure of who Senator Henry Clay was, even though the name rang a bell. Angus sensed another opportunity to enhance his reputation in the eyes of the Willis boys, further redeeming himself from his earlier failures to provide them any helpful information.

"My Pa told me Henry Clay was one of the greatest legal minds of the age. Seems that, though he's a slave owner himself, he's also a believer in what Pa calls "universal emancipation"- wants to see all the slaves in the country set free!"

James let out a low whistle, and Michael muttered a fervent, "Jesus!" as an expletive, not a prayer.

"Now why do you suppose your uncle is in correspondence with Henry Clay?" Angus asked, rhetorically.

James swore, "Christ! Isn't it obvious? He must be askin bout emancipation for that woman an her children! I knew he was up to no good!" The idea of not inheriting all of Elijah's slaves was so upsetting that it still didn't even dawn on him that slaves might not be the only thing Elijah was not wanting them to inherit.

Michael, usually one to readily agree, was so stunned by the thought of such a travesty that it bred an unexpected caution in him. "Hold on now James, we don't know that for sure! We got no real proof."

Angus, emboldened by his enhanced status in the Willis boys' esteem, chimed in, "Ya'll oughta tryn' get a hold of that letter, then- see what it's really all about!"

This daring proposal struck both of the Willis brothers momentarily dumb. It was unthinkable, preposterous! Actually steal their uncle's mail?

James started to look like he was seriously considering it. Michael, however, suddenly anxious and sensing danger, pointed out, "James, don't do it, James! Don't you dare do it! If Daddy ever found out, he'd tan your hide til you're blacker than a nigra!"

"Aw shut up Michael, don't be so yella! I ain't gonna steal the letter, I just gotta figure out a way to read it!" He smiled an evil, conspiratorial smile.

Though not without trepidation, the three co-conspirators then began to ponder how they might go about engineering such a coup, knowing that with absolute proof in hand, the Willis boys' father might finally take them more seriously. Their mother already did, and she might even be able to help.

XXX

Elijah, restored by Momma Celia's good cooking, some much needed rest, and the encouragement of Senator Clay, decided it was finally time to pay Angus Patterson a visit. He was by now feeling that so much had been set in motion by the trip to Baltimore and the letter from the Senator that he could no longer afford to worry too much about annoyances like Angus Junior. Though hardly throwing caution to the wind, he simply resolved to visit Angus Senior without resorting to clandestine attempts to arrange a meeting.

Elder had saddled Beauty and brought her around to the front of the house. "What you gonna tell Mr. Patterson, Papa?" he asked, as he held the mare while Elijah mounted.

"Well son, I want to share Senator Clay's letter with him, tell him about what I learned from our trip up to Baltimore, and then see if he or his friend Mr. Bauskett, can put me in touch with a good lawyer up in Cincinnati who'll be sympathetic to our cause. The baby'll be here soon, and once your momma's recovered I'm gonna head on up there and get a new will written."

This made sense to Elder, who was rapidly approaching manhood himself, and starting to have a deeper appreciation of the complexity of what Elijah was dealing with. He was also no fool when it came to spotting those who could be trusted, and those who couldn't.

"Be careful, Papa. I know ya'll're eager to get this done, but there's plenty of folks around here who'd tar and feather you- and maybe lynch us- if they found out what ya'll're fixin to do!" This unvarnished declaration struck Elijah as unexpectedly realistic from someone so young, and he simply nodded his agreement.

"Don't worry, Elder. I may be eager, but I'm no fool. Tell your mother I'll be back by suppertime," and with that, armed with the letter from

Henry Clay and the trust agreement written up by George Brown, he swatted Beauty on the rump with the reins, and she bolted off down the road towards Williston. Bearing Elder's admonition in mind however, Elijah changed course, deciding to go off road across the fields, now lying fallow waiting for the Spring plowing, so as to avoid running into James or Michael on the outskirts of town, hating all the while the necessity of doing so.

When he got to Angus Patterson's house, he tethered Beauty and marched right up the porch steps to knock on the door. Mary answered with her usual welcoming grin, but something in her demeanor suggested all was not well.

"Mornin, Mister Elijah, how ya'll doin this morning?" Mary asked, somewhat distractedly.

"Mornin back at you, Mary. I'm doin just fine. How bout you?" He responded warmly, but a little distractedly himself, as he looked beyond her to see if there was any sign of either Angus Senior or Junior.

"Come on in sir, please. I'll go fetch Mister Angus, but ya'll oughta know, he's feelin' right poorly, and I don't know how long he be feelin like visitin."

Elijah was immediately distressed. He was not so selfish as to be concerned only for his own need of advice, he had deep affection for the old man. He valued Angus' friendship highly, especially at a time when he was beginning to feel more and more isolated from his own kind. "Hold on a minute, Mary. I don't want to trouble him, if this is a bad time. Perhaps I should come back later?"

Mary stopped and thought a moment, then shook her head slowly. "Nossir, ya'll stay right where ya are. It may take a little while, but I'll get him to ya, cause I know he's eager to hear ya'll's news. Been askin me every day for weeks if I'd heard anythin. Might actually do him a world a good to see ya. Ya'll go on into the parlor an set a spell- he'll be along directly."

As Mary limped off arthritically, Elijah realized that Angus Sr. was not the only one upon whom time seemed to be taking an accelerating toll. He was vaguely uneasy, recalling the wistful tone in Angus' goodbye when last they'd met- a presage of his mortality perhaps? Elijah tried to shake off that thought, unwilling to even contemplate just yet the possible loss of one of his only allies. "Tempis fugit!" he muttered to himself with a sigh.

After what seemed an eternity he finally heard the thump of Angus' cane, far less emphatic than before, and with tentative, shuffling gait, the elder Patterson entered the parlor, Mary loyally and attentively at his elbow. With some difficulty, as much due to her own limitations as his, she was able to steer him slowly, like a heavily loaded barge fighting the current, toward his armchair, into which she gingerly lowered him with a sigh.

"There now, Mister Angus. You alright?" she asked.

As the old man settled himself, he looked up at her mutely and nodded, breathing a little heavily. Elijah had sprung to his feet in respect upon Angus' entrance, and was alarmed by his diminished appearance, but the old man seemed almost not to notice him at first, at least not until he was comfortably esconced in his accustomed seat. At that point, however, as if no longer hampered by the extreme concentration his physical arrival had required of him, his mind was now as free as ever to attend to his friend.

"Forgive my tardiness Elijah, I'm sorry to keep you waitin. Though I'm not planning on 'casting off this mortal coil' just yet, seems to me the Bard had some insight into the tedious burden our mortality can sometimes be. Had a gift for puttin it into words anyway, no mistake about that!" The old man smiled wearily, but with affection. Then he suddenly brightened.

Before Elijah could express his concern about his friend's unmistakable decline, and wanting to avoid being on the receiving end of any pity himself, Angus immediately continued in a voice with surprising vigor, "Now sir, no need to waste time on such borin matters as my deterioratin health! Such creepin decrepitude only afflicts those of us who've lived long enough for it ta catch up with us! Enough said! Now then, I want to know all about your trip to Baltimore and where things presently stand!" Remembering his manners, he called out to Mary, "Mary, fetch us a couple a glasses and my sippin whiskey. I want to drink a toast to my friend here!" Mary looked at Angus with one eyebrow raised quizzically, as if he was joking.

"Mister Angus, it ain't but eleven in the mornin! You sure you wouldn't rather have a nice cup a coffee or some sweet tea?" Angus shot Mary a look that left no room for debate.

"Jus a thought, Mr. Angus!" she knew better than to argue with him. "Lord Amighty," she confided in an aside to Elijah, "the man's more stubborn than my grandaddy's mule! Once he done made up his mind, not even the Good Lord Jesus gonna get him to change it!"

She turned back to the old man, "If ya'll want sippin whiskey, sippin whiskey it is, but don't ya'll go complainin to me if ya get too wobbly to get back to your bed! I'm too ole and tired mysef to pick ya'll up if ya fall down now, and young Angus ain't home yet to hep me!"

Elijah was touched by Mary's deep affection in the intimacy of this exchange. He was also delighted that it revealed he would not have to worry about the younger Patterson eavesdropping, at least for the moment.

Once Mary had returned with the glasses and the drinks had been poured, Angus asked her gently to leave them be. "And Mary, if my son arrives, try to steer him clear of us, if you can?"

"Yessir I will, best I can, but ya'll know he worried bout ya, and young Mister Angus awful headstrong, (gets that from his Pa)," she added pointedly in a stage whisper directed to Elijah, but clearly intended for the elder Patterson to hear. "He might just march on in here, no matter what I say!"

Angus Sr. nodded with a smile in recognition. "That's alright, Mary-you do the best ya can, and hopefully we can have us a nice chat before he gets back."

Angus raised his glass to Elijah and said, "To solutions, my friend!" They clinked their glasses together and each took a long appreciative sip of the golden liquid, savoring its aroma expanding in their noses and on their palates, smoothly sliding down their throats and warming as it went.

As if purified by this libation, Angus eyed Elijah keenly and asked, "What have you found out?"

Elijah proceeded to recount the details of his trip to Baltimore, his meetings with Mr. Brown and Mr. Dorsey, the realities of Maryland slave laws, and the possible trust fund for the family. He showed him the trust papers written up by George Brown.

"It's a good idea, Elijah. But bear in mind that, by South Carolina law, as long as your family continues in slavery, even though the assets come from outside of South Carolina, they would not be allowed to receive them here!"

Elijah said, "You mean to tell me there's no way to provide for them by trust so long as they're in South Carolina?"

"Not any more! At least not so long as they are still slaves. The General Assembly has prohibited it. And since they can't be emancipated here, as we've already concluded," Angus continued soberly, "seems like relocation is gonna be your only option."

Elijah responded with a heavy sigh. "I reckon I'd already figured as much," he affirmed a little morosely. He then elucidated the key point of the need to seek emancipation in a non-slave holding state, which he had all but concluded must be Ohio, since it could credibly dovetail into his business ventures with George Brown and the railroad as well. He also assumed it might be a bit more welcoming to the family than the Northeast, from a cultural point of view. He then brought out the letter from Henry Clay.

"When I got home, this was waitin for me."

Angus eagerly asked to see it himself, and handled it with extreme reverence, as if it were holy writ from on high. Clay had been a sort of legal hero to him for nigh on to half a century, and Angus was avid to plumb the thoughts of a legislator of such illustrious stature. He read with total absorption, interjecting an occasional "Hmmm," or "Aha!" as he went along.

"Well! That was quite a missive! And right interestin to see his way of thinkin, I might add!" affirmed Angus with satisfaction, once he finished his reading. Angus had a habit of ending a sentence on a note of contentment, while appearing to elaborate on it in the privacy of his own mind, without realizing that others were no longer privy to the communication. As was so often the case, Elijah was left unclear as to the lawyer's actual opinion of the content under discussion, and prompted him for clarification.

"So what do you make of it?" Without waiting for a response, he offered, "My sense is that the most promisin piece is his opinion that I might be able to emancipate the family in a slave-free state, as the necessary and effective precondition to them bein able to inherit from me. It concurs with what I learned in Maryland and seems my best, and maybe even my only option for success. What do you think? And how would I go about accomplishin that?"

"Well, I quite agree, Elijah. What regrettably remains unclear, is the precise mechanism for doin so, and unfortunately, I am not well enough versed in the laws of the Great State of Ohio to be able to tell ya that with certainty."

"I figured as much. But do you, or perhaps John Bauskett, know the names of any lawyers in Ohio? I thought I might just take a trip up there on my own, after the baby comes, and see about makin the appropriate arrangements."

Angus nodded thoughtfully. "Trouble is we're not exactly sure what the appropriate arrangements are, now are we? There're basically two approaches I see to the problem. One is emancipation by Last Will and Testament. The other would be by the grantin of some judicial writ or deed of manumission." He paused reflectively, before continuing, "I'm familiar enough with the first, but not too certain about the specifics of the latter in the State of Ohio. Each state has its own variants, so we will definitely need the advice of counsel in Ohio to accomplish this." Elijah was touched by Angus' use of "we," even though it was looking more than likely that the old man might not be around long enough to see the process completed. Identifying a specific lawyer seemed to be less of a concern to Angus than identifying the legal procedures necessary to accomplish Elijah's goals. He too seemed to have overlooked the mention of Jolliffe.

"Since we don't know what the specific instrument of emancipation in Ohio is," continued Angus, "I suggest ya start draftin a will with whatever provisos ya want to make as a startin point. Then take that up to Cincinnati with ya, and once ya find yourself a reputable lawyer, let him help ya sort it out. In the meantime, I'll see if John Bauskett knows anyone up there he could recommend. Of course, it would be preferable to emancipate them while you're still livin, and I know that's what they would prefer too."

Elijah nodded in agreement, then said, "But I've been thinkin, Angus. I've had a couple spells with my heart lately, and to tell ya the truth it's got me worried. Course I'd rather be able to emancipate my family while I'm alive, but I may not have that luxury, so it may be that I'd best do it by will, in case somethin happens to me." Angus seemed to appreciate the intimations of mortality on a personal level, and sat nodding sympathetically.

"It'd just kill me if I left them un-emancipated!" Elijah declared. Then realizing the odd word choice, he elaborated wryly, "That is, it would if I wasn't dead already!" Angus chuckled in recognition of the dark humor.

"I understand perfectly Elijah, and I think ya may be right. If you were to create a new will in a state where slavery is not permitted, even if you are, God forbid, unable to see them emancipated in your lifetime, ya would have managed to protect their future!" Upon reflection he added, "Provided, of course, that ya can at least get em out of South Carolina, and out of slave territory in general. The new Fugitive Slave Act that Congress passed may complicate things, and you'd need to see em safely away to even have a chance at success. I doubt even an executor in a slave free state could bring them up there successfully to emancipate em without a whole lot of resistance from your relations on the grounds that possession is nine points of the law. And that would surely be a misery for Amy and the whole family- not to mention the rest of your slaves!"

Elijah nodded. "It would surely be a comfort to my soul to see em freed!" he responded. But he felt a sudden pang of anxiety at the realization that he would need to see them safely out of South Carolina at the very least, and even that might not be enough.

"Seems our South Carolinian brethren wanted to make sure no slaves can make it to freedom just by leavin slave-holdin states, so that's a troublesome little detail we'll have to find a way around if you think ya might not make it yourself," mused Angus matter-of-factly.

"Well then, I guess I'll just have to resolve not to die until they're free!" Elijah muttered half to himself. Angus looked at him analytically, as if to assess whether that resolve were sufficient. Apparently determining that it was, he continued:

"Now then, what I reckon ya need to do is find out the particulars of Ohio law on the mechanism of manumission up there. Ya want to know how emancipation, or manumission, is legally defined there, what its criteria are and what are its restrictions or limitations." Angus was expert at identifying what was needed to build a case. "Ya also want to know how Ohio sees the rights of colored folks in relation to the issue of the inheritance of property, once they've been emancipated." He seemed to be checking off a mental list of factors, like a bricklayer systematically laying a foundation. He knew perfectly well the structure of the case had to be strong to withstand the inevitable challenges Elijah's family were likely to mount against it in the courts.

"You'd best be prepared for the other Willises to try to fight ya on this, even if ya got it all nice and legal, and make sure Amy understands too, in case anything should happen to ya- she'll need to know. For my part, I'll do what I can to help, but it may be that John will have a larger hand in this than I, due to the regrettably inescapable reality of my increasin decline." Angus elucidated this last observation in a matter of fact tone, without complaint or regret. It was a simple statement of fact needing no further commentary.

"Well sir, I don't doubt they'll try to block it, so I suppose I'd best get in touch with John then, and see what information he may have available." Elijah concluded.

"Don't you worry, I'll write to John myself, but it certainly won't hurt for you to do so as well. Senator Clay and I are, apparently, in similar states of disintegration, and gravity is pullin us steadily downward, if you'll forgive the sepulchral play on words. But I feel confident that we both may have provided some useful aid in helpin ya'll achieve your noble goal." Angus smiled with satisfaction and took another sip of his whiskey.

Elijah found his throat involuntarily choking slightly as he responded, "There can be no doubt of that whatsoever, Angus. I couldn't have made it this far without ya, and with all my heart I do thank ya for it! I feel confident that my family will be free, though Lord knows the road's a long one, and we're not quite there yet! I can't thank ya enough for all ya've done!" It was interesting, and perhaps revealing, that he continued to express that his "family" would be free, rather than all his slaves, despite the lengthy conversation he and Angus previously had on this subject. How conscious this was wasn't clear, but Angus took note of it, nonetheless.

"It's been my great pleasure, Elijah. As I already told ya, you're a good man, and ya'll deserve every happiness, as does your family- and as do all the rest of your slaves too, for that matter" he reminded him, with a faintly scolding tone. "May God bless ya'll abundantly, for He knows ya'll've certainly blessed me in allowing me the pleasure of helpin. It feels kinda like a curtain call on a good play for me. When the curtain finally falls, I may be a touch sad the play's over, but I'll certainly have enjoyed the show, and I'll take that with me when I go!" he concluded with unexpected poetry.

Angus raised his glass again, and both men drained their cups in mutual affirmation, smacking their lips with satisfaction. When Elijah rose to take his leave, as if on cue, Mary came into the parlor with his hat, surreptitiously wiping a tear from her cheek with the back of a gnarled hand, and trying not to sniffle audibly.

However frail of body, Angus was far from being feeble-minded, and noticing Mary's covert gesture, looked at her with affection saying, "Now Mary, don't ya'll go gettin all misty on me. We've already talked about this, and I'm at peace. Whenever the Good Lord decides to call, I'll be ready." Looking at Elijah with equal affection and grabbing his outstretched hand, with a spark of his old vigor, he added, "In the meantime, as long as I have breath in me, I intend to continue fighting in any way I can for what is just and fair. And especially for the people who continue to inspire me with their love and courage!" He patted Elijah's hand expressively, as if to seal his benediction into it.

Strangely, Elijah did not feel this was a final good-bye, despite the sensation that Angus was fading from his corporeal state like a mirage on a hot summer's day. As if to express that conviction he said, "I don't believe in 'good-byes' Angus. I prefer 'farewell' or 'until we meet again.'"

Angus, ever attentive to the meanings of words, and suspicious of this atypically maudlin expression of Elijah's, responded with lawyerly aplomb, "Are you aware that 'good-bye' comes from the Old English? It's a contraction of 'God be with ye'. Are you therefore certain ya don't believe in 'good-byes?'" he asked, as if interrogating a witness, "For I would have thought that with the faith ya'll've shown in Almighty Providence, endurin what ya have already, ya might feel differently!" He smiled wryly, always happy to score a point for the defense.

Elijah, slightly taken aback by this interjection of thought-provoking erudition, returned the smile and answered, "Point well taken, counselor! In that case, if it please the court, I would have to accede. I reverse my position, and acknowledge that by that definition, I most certainly do believe in good-byes, as there is not a man on the face of this good earth to whom I would more urgently and devoutly say 'God be with ye,' Angus Patterson. God be with ye always, my dear friend!"

In the emotion of the moment, as Mary fought back her tears and tried to smile her gracious grin at Elijah on his way out the door, neither Elijah nor Angus realized he had inadvertently left the letter from Henry Clay on the table in the parlor, where Angus had deposited it after reading.

Elijah mounted Beauty and, doffing his hat to Mary, headed off back toward the Willis Plantation. As he went through town, however, Angus Junior was heading home towards him from the direction of James' store. By then Elijah was far enough from the Patterson house that it was not obvious he had paid the elder Patterson a visit. At least, so he hoped. But then he suddenly realized he had left the letter!

A cold panic seized him like an icy claw in his gut. He wasn't sure whether Angus Junior had spotted him. Should he turn and gallop back to the Patterson's place and retrieve it? No, that would be too obvious. Could he trust that Angus Senior would realize he had forgotten it, and tuck it safely away from his son's prying eyes? Clearly the old man's mind was still sharp as a tack, and equally clearly, the father knew better than to trust his son in a matter of this delicacy. Elijah desperately tried to persuade himself that there was really no reason to fear, but he remained uneasy as Angus Junior approached and called out to him in greeting,

"Hi there, Mr. Willis! I hear ya'll went up to Baltimore a while back! Since I haven't seen ya since then, welcome home!"

Elijah fumbled for a response, desperately not wanting to give any evidence of having visited the Patterson household and thereby provoke the very kind of prying that might uncover the letter, even if as he ardently hoped, Angus Sr. had managed to squirrel it away before his son's arrival. It was clear, in any case that he would have to retrieve the letter somehow, no matter how awkward that might be.

"Hey there, Angus! It's a beautiful day, and there's no place like home! Always good to be back, thank ya son!" Elijah hoped this was specific enough not to pretend he'd not gone, and vague enough for Angus Junior to think it was no matter of great importance, and he was happy to be at home among his own. The two men trotted past each other with a tip of their hats, and each continued along his way.

Elijah's mind was racing as to how and when he could recover the letter. Angus Junior's was racing to figure out where Elijah had been coming from, and whether his father knew.

Back at the Patterson house, Angus Sr. was, in fact feeling slightly tipsy from a tumbler of whiskey on an empty stomach, but rather than going up to bed, as it was nearly mealtime, he asked Mary to help him to the dining room, well assured that some food would absorb the whiskey and he'd feel better. As she hauled him out of his chair with a series of grunts and groans from both of them, each one-pointed on the daunting task of mobility, neither of them noticed the letter on the table by the armchair. By the time his son came in through the front door, the elder Patterson was settled in his place at the head of the table, waiting expectantly for his meal and his son.

"Pa?" called out Angus Junior. "You alright Pa?" Whatever issues the younger Patterson may have had with his father, he genuinely loved him, and was very concerned about what seemed to be a steadily accelerating decline.

"In here, son! Go wash up and come on an have your dinner!" Angus called back.

As Angus Junior walked past the parlor toward the powder room to wash up, and then to go on to the dining room beyond, something caught his eye. He saw the letter, and instantly curious, stealthily walked in to take a look. His eyes lit up with excitement when he realized what he was looking at. The letter was long, and his eyes wanted to devour it hungrily, but voices further back in the house intruded.

"Come on now, son! Food's gonna get cold!" called his father, impatiently. Angus Junior knew he couldn't take the letter, or he'd be found out. He scanned it quickly, desperate to commit to memory whatever he could, but his unpracticed eye and untrained memory were not adept at picking out the essentials from the Senator's grandiloquent phraseology and florid script.

So absorbed was he in his urgent attempt to glean information, that he had not heard Mary's approach. Suddenly he looked up, and saw her staring at him as he was desperately trying to read the letter from Senator Clay. Caught red-handed, he had no choice but to stop reading, and try to cover his behind. "Oh, hi there Mary!" he stammered, "I, uh, I saw this letter, and thought maybe Pa had forgotten it, and it might be important," he bumbled lamely. Knowing all his ways since infancy, Mary was not easily fooled.

"Ummm, hmmm. Is that right?" she looked at him with one of those, "I wa'nt born yestiddy, so don't ya think you foolin me!" looks, but she didn't say anything. No need to. She held out her hand for the letter, and young Angus, like a child being caught with his hand in the cookie jar denying he'd done it, reluctantly handed it to her. Mary folded it carefully and tucked it in her bosom where the younger Patterson would never dream of intruding. "Now go on child, eat your dinner. Ya Pa's waitin on ya. Best not keep him waitin too long. I know ya'll don't wanna be upsettin him."

Angus Junior slinked to the dining room, cursing himself for getting caught before he'd had a chance to read the whole letter. When he got to the dining room his father queried him, "What took ya so long, son? Food's getting' cold! Come on now and set yaself down and eat this good cookin." Angus' body may have been getting feebler, but just as there was nothing wrong with his mind, ever the bon vivant, there was nothing wrong with his appetite either. Though he tended to eat somewhat less than usual these days, he continued to relish the flavor of Mary's food.

Mary walked quietly over to Angus Sr. and handed him the letter, saying pointedly, "Young Mister Angus found this in the parlor, and was worried you'd forgot it!" They exchanged knowing looks, but always the practiced lawyer, the elder Patterson simply replied, "Bless me, I had! Thank you son!" He smiled at his son in such a way that the younger Patterson couldn't be sure if he'd been caught out or not, but was pretty well certain that if his father hadn't already realized he'd read at least part of it, Mary would lose no time in telling him, once dinner was over.

Angus Sr. had always found it effective to leave some room for doubt in facing an opponent- helped keep him off balance, and made it easier to expose him when need be. Though he hated to think of his own son as an opponent, when touching the matter of Elijah Willis and his household, he harbored no illusions to the contrary.

The meal was passed mostly in silence. Angus Junior attempted to shift the focus by asking after his father's health. "How're ya feelin Pa?" It's not that he wasn't sincerely interested. He actually did care, but Angus Sr. was wily enough to know his son's motives, and wasn't quite ready to let him off the hook.

Choosing the high road, he decided to simply observe, "Well, to tell the truth, I'm feelin a tad disheartened. Ya know son, even when well-intended, it's actually against the law to read someone else's mail without their permission? I appreciate your concern, but keep in mind, you could find yourself in a whole lot of trouble not rememberin that! I'm just sayin, for your edification. I know ya think I'm too strict about these things, but people's lives can depend on such seemingly small matters sometimes, and I really want ya to understand that." He gave his son a piercing look that caused the younger Patterson to shift uncomfortably in his seat, feeling conflicted and guilty for disappointing his father, in spite of his commitment to aiding the Willis brothers.

"Yessir! Sorry, Pa." was all he could manage in response, realizing that the less he said at this point, the better chance he had of not digging himself a deeper hole.

Suddenly there was a knock at the front door. Mary hastened to answer before young Angus could get away from the table. He heard low voices in the front hall- a man's voice and Mary's- but he couldn't make out whose it was, or what they were saying. Footsteps approached, and Elijah stood in the doorway. He had decided that the best defense was to attack, and that there was a chance they could control the damage by appearing more transparent.

Angus Sr. immediately recognized Elijah's intent, and holding up the letter, said, "Aha! Elijah! Glad ya came!" Turning to his son, he deliberately handed young Angus the letter and said, "Son, would you please give this to Mr. Willis?" knowing full well it would fairly burn in his fingers, and hoping the lesson would not be lost on him. The younger Patterson felt like a drop of water on a hot griddle, dancing between his father, Mary's watchful eye and Elijah's outstretched hand, but tried to smile and handed Elijah the letter, saying as casually as he could, "Here you go, Mr. Willis."

"Thank ya, son." Elijah said civilly. Then turning to Angus, "Sorry to interrupt your dinner Angus- and sorry for the inconvenience!" he looked piercingly at the younger Patterson, implying the inconvenience was mutual.

"No trouble at all, Elijah. Nothin to fret about! Matter of fact, young Angus here and I were just talkin bout how important it is to respect the law, and how even little things like readin someone else's mail without their permission can be a serious offense. Good object lesson, wasn't it son?"

The younger Patterson blushed fiercely, hating his father's penchant for turning everything into a lesson, but he knew enough to mumble a polite, "Yessir. Sure was!" There was no doubt in anybody's mind as to the intent of the elder Patterson's summation. And there would be no hung jury in rendering a guilty verdict concerning the younger Patterson's implicit transgression, even though it remained unmentioned.

Turning to Mary, Elijah said kindly, "And thank you too, Mary. I can see myself out, no need to trouble yaself." Elijah bade them all farewell as casually as possible and left, his heart pounding erratically and his mind racing to assess the probable consequences of his momentary forgetfulness in leaving the letter.

As he rode home contemplating Angus Junior's malice, or jealousy, or insecurity, or whatever it was that was motivating him, for some reason Elijah recalled the Biblical story of Joseph and his resentful brothers, who sold him into slavery only to be rescued by him from famine in the end. Elijah saw the face of Angus Junior in his mind's eye, filled with emotions at war with each other- love, jealousy, admiration, fear, hatred- and suddenly, Joseph's words of reconciliation rang out, "You meant it for evil, but God meant it for good!" Strangely and unexpectedly he felt calmed by that recollection, though he was not able to see clearly any good in Angus Junior finding the letter. Nevertheless, some intuition bade him trust that the Almighty knew all things, and would lead him where he needed to go. His heartbeat now considerably calmer, he made his way back to the plantation, where he was greeted with open arms by Amy, eager to hear what had transpired.

XXXI

"How did it go with Angus?" Amy asked anxiously, as Elijah came in from the stable after unsaddling Beauty and putting her in her stall with an extra forkful of hay.

He greeted Amy with a kiss, and then took her by the arm and led her into the parlor where they could sit comfortably.

"Well, he agreed that the best course of action is to seek emancipation outside of slave-holding territory, and that Cincinnati may be our best bet." He proceeded to recount the details of the visit- including the problematic fact that even if he set up a trust for them with George Brown, so long as they remained slaves, they could not access those funds in the State of South Carolina. This made it definitive that they must ultimately relocate altogether out of the state. As he elaborated on the various factors and details of the plan as it stood presently, he decided to confess to Amy his concerns about his health, and the possibility it might interfere with those plans, even though she was already aware of that danger.

"I talked it over with Angus- thought he should know. He agreed that I should write a new will outside of South Carolina, and recommended I start workin' on it right away. But he pointed out that I would still have to get ya'll out of here for it to be valid, and that I need ya'll to get emancipated before I die, for the Fugitive Slave Act that Congress passed a few years ago would make it possible for my relations to chase you down and drag ya'll back here!"

"Oh my Lord! Elijah, that absolutely cannot happen! Please God! Do you have any idea what they would do to us if they owned us?" Amy's alarm was extreme.

"I don't even like to think about it, darlin! Unfortunately, I can imagine only too well, and the thought of it makes me sick with worry," he acknowledged.

"Sugar, you gotta promise me you'll take better care of yaself! We just have to see this all the way through!" Amy urged.

"I will darlin, I promise. I told Angus it'd kill me if I left ya'll un-emancipated- if I wasn't dead already!" His attempt at levity the second time around failed miserably.

"Elijah, that's not funny! You are *not* gonna die leaving us un-emancipated, you hear me?" Amy insisted,"Promise me?"

They both knew, of course, it was not in their power to guarantee such a promise, but figuring the Good Lord would hear that prayer and do His part to see it accomplished, Elijah nodded and said, "I promise darlin, as God is my witness!"

Elijah then realized he needed to let Amy know about the unfortunate incident with the letter from Henry Clay. He recounted the full sequence of events, Amy punctuating it with several gasps and groans and the wringing of hands. Elijah concluded saying, "I have to hand it to Angus for the way he handled it with his son- you should a seen the boy squirm! - But there is no way in Heaven or Hell that boy is not gonna let James and Michael know about the letter, even if he didn't manage to read much of it. All he had to read was the first two paragraphs to know it was about emancipation, so we'd best prepare for the backlash!" Amy sat silent, horrified at the contemplation of the probable consequences.

"I feel like such a fool for forgettin the letter in the first place, but truth be told I was just not at all prepared for how emotional my meetin with Angus would be. It caught me completely off guard! The change in him in just a few months is truly stunnin, and my heart is heavy with the feelin he won't be around much longer. He's been the truest of friends, and one of few I would really call by that name at all, at this point."

Amy, though angry at first, felt Elijah's sorrow and understood. She too, after all, felt quite alone. She couldn't talk with the women slaves as an equal, for many were jealous and resentful of her relationship with Elijah. They envied her living in the plantation house rather than the slave quarters, despite them being modestly comfortable and well kept. Nor could she talk with any white woman in town. Momma Celia was the only female support she could really rely on, and even that was sometimes complicated, just because she was her momma, and Momma Celia's own experience of white men and having their babies as a slave couldn't help but exert a marked influence on the way she perceived their current situation.

"I understand, sugar. I suppose it coulda been a whole lot worse! At least Mary caught him before he'd read the whole thing!"

Since the possibility that emancipation in a slave-free state could grant them inheritance rights was not mentioned until nearly the end of the letter, they agreed there was at least a possibility that Angus Junior had not fully grasped its import, and therefore could not convey that to Elijah's nephews. Elijah then shared with Amy his epiphany on the way home, remembering the Biblical reconciliation of Joseph with his brothers and his comment to them, "You meant it for evil, but God meant it for good!" Even though not particularly religious, Elijah had always felt open to divine guidance, in his own informal way. The very fact of Amy's love for him, and the joy she and the children had brought to his life felt like sufficient proof of God's existence and love, for him.

"Seems to me we oughta be holdin onto that story, and keep tryin to find God's purpose in all this for us. He led Joseph outa bondage because he was smart, and strong, and good, like you. We gotta keep prayin He'll do the same for us, and try to find His grace, even in the mess we're in!" Elijah urged.

"'Yea, though I walk through the valley in the shadow of death, I will fear no evil, for Thou art with me,'" Amy quoted. "Lord, help me remember that when your nephews start stirrin things up, as you know they're bound to!" responded Amy plaintively, as she felt her belly. She had gotten considerably larger, and just in the past few days it seemed she was carrying the baby lower. She thought the baby wasn't due for at least another month, but from the look of her it might come sooner.

"Elijah, honey, I know I told ya not to go to Cincinnati until after the baby's born, but I'm scared your nephews are gonna make trouble, either with your brother or the other planters, or folks like that Dr. Guignard and Mr. Matthews. I have this sinkin feeling that time is runnin out on us. Do ya think you should go on up there now?"

"Well sugar, I understand the feelin, but I still think it's best I stay til the baby's born- and for the same reason. Especially since we know Angus Junior knows about the letter from Henry Clay, and will most surely tell James and Michael, now more than ever, I don't want to go rushing off to Cincinnati while you have the baby, left alone to face my family's reaction without me here!"

"Oh Elijah, I'm so worried. Do you really think we're gonna be alright? Can we really do this?"

"We can, and we shall!" he insisted. "Don't you fret! Remember how your momma said she felt it in her bones? Well, I do too, even if I can't say for certain how or why."

Suddenly remembering the verse from the hymn, Amazing Grace, Elijah sang softly, as if humming to himself, modifying the lyric, 'Twas grace that brought us safe thus far, and grace will lead us home,' adding after a pause, "I refuse to believe that the Good Lord would have brought us this far with such amazin grace, only to deny us in the end! I heard a preacher say once that when all else is gone, grace remains, and will see ya through. I'm choosin to have faith, sugar, cause frankly we've got no other choice!

XXXII

Somehow they felt more assured that there was a viable legal solution to their predicament, and trusted that God would eventually help them accomplish it, despite their fears of what might have been set in motion by Angus Junior's discovery of the letter from Senator Clay and their worries about Elijah's health. After the holiday tensions, the Willis household had gradually settled back into the rhythm of daily life with few interruptions. The men continued to harvest timber and saw it into lumber, the cotton seed was sorted by variety in preparation for the spring planting, hogs were slaughtered, hams were hung in the smokehouse, eggs were gathered, the root vegetables harvested, plows were sharpened, harnesses were cleaned and oiled, ready for Spring plowing- in short life on the plantation, on the surface of things, went on like life on any most other plantation in the South.

Yet, after the trip to Baltimore, and all that it set in motion, life could never be really the same again. There was a subtle, but steadily increasing tension among all who lived on the Willis Plantation- a growing expectation of immanent and fundamental change that the normalcy of daily life seemed to refute. The fear of rumors, and the heavily emphasized need for secrecy to prevent serious conflict with the community had put everyone slightly on edge, and they were all trying hard to hide it, from the youngest child to the oldest of the slaves.

As Amy's time for delivery drew steadily nearer, Elijah set himself to work on a draft of his new will. He pondered long and hard about how to set things up, and whom to actually name as heirs. He realized he would also have to name someone his executor, and immediately thought of Angus Senior, but then realized he was too frail and in too poor health to be relied upon to serve. He then thought of possibly naming John Bauskett, whom he had come to admire and trust, but upon John's own recommendation, he recognized that his executor or executors would have to be from the state in which the new will was written. It was frustrating, but the truth was he couldn't name anyone until he first made a trip up to Cincinnati, and circumstances seemed to be conspiring to delay that journey.

Elijah was sitting at his desk one afternoon working on the draft when Amy came in to check on him. In his original will he had distributed specific parcels of land to each of his relations. As his mind wandered over each plot and parcel, with all its memories and associations, he recognized painfully that he had to rethink the entire will, rather than just scratching out and replacing names of heirs. Being steeped in Southern traditionalism, he also realized that part of him felt guilty about cutting his relatives out altogether, despite their loathing of Amy and the children, but in truth he saw it could be much simpler to sell everything and simply endow his family of choice. He couldn't help but mourn, however, the loss of the plantation he had spent his whole life making so profitable, and so to console himself for its eventual loss, he tried to convince himself he still had plenty of energy left to start anew in Ohio.

"Howya doin, sugar?" Amy asked, placing her hands comfortingly on his shoulders and leaning forward heavily to give him a kiss on the neck.

"Well, alright I guess. I've named you and all the children as my sole heirs, and made it clear that under no circumstances do I want any of my estate going to my white relations. I'm still wrestlin with how to word it, and want to identify my property clearly so there're no misunderstandin as to my disposition of it all."

"Well, that's a good start honey," she said, looking over his shoulder and scanning the draft, "but what about the rest of the slaves? How are ya plannin to emancipate and provide for them? Didn't Senator Clay insist that it would be cruel just to free them, and make no other provision for their well-bein?" Amy asked.

Elijah balked. It's not that he was intending for them to all remain in bondage, he just didn't see logistically how he could possibly take them all up to Ohio to emancipate them. There had to be another way. Traveling up to Ohio just with the immediate household- not even including Gilbert and his family- seemed to him to be a mighty long row to hoe! He looked up at his wife.

"Darlin, I just don't know how I'm gonna be able to do that!" he blurted.

Before he could elaborate upon his comment, or explain what his thinking was, Amy interrupted, "Elijah, you know how I feel about this! How can I let you free me and the children, and live with myself lettin everybody else live as slaves? I thought we'd come to an agreement about this!" Her voice started to rise in distress.

Elijah, instantly eager to appease his wife said, "We did, darlin, we did! And I'm gonna get it done- I'm just not sure yet how to do it legally and logistically! Remember how we talked about how we might have to do this in stages- get you and the children to safety first, and then bring Gilbert and the others? Well, that hasn't changed."

Amy, somewhat pacified, responded petulantly, "Well you'd best figure out how, and soon!" She strode out of the room leaving Elijah to wrestle with the matter and, to underscore the point by infant complicity as she went, she suddenly winced with a kick from the baby, as if it were saying, "Ya'll listen to Momma, Papa! She means business!"

Amy's distress might have been explainable in part by the emotional vulnerability due to her condition, but she was not the only one feeling testy. Despite Gilbert's best efforts to quell it, there was talk around the plantation. The folks in the slave quarters were starting to wonder whether Mr. Elijah was going to do anything about emancipating them or not. Months had passed and nothing had changed. Some grew hopeful, while others grew more skeptical. All began to feel restive, and long-standing fears and attitudes couldn't help but surface.

Those who had been born or grown up on the plantation long before the arrival of Amy and her family tended to be suspicious. Jealous of Amy's privileged status, and fearful that her intentions were to free her own and abandon the rest, they began to strain Gilbert's ability to keep everyone else in line. That affected the dynamic of the workforce- some slaves taking sides as to which faction was more deserving, or more likely to be left behind- and their bickering about it amongst themselves sometimes became a distraction to getting their work done. Eventually this also began to sour the generally positive feeling the entire plantation had felt toward Elijah.

As some of the slaves sat shucking the dried Indian corn one day so it could be cleaned off the cob for seed corn, some of the conversations got a little heated.

"Mister Elijah been a good master, far as that goes, but if ya'll ask me, it don't go too far- specially when a white man look at a colored woman and folks just think he randy and got a taste for dark meat. He can do whatever he want with her. But if a black man so much as look at a white woman, he a fornicatin son a the devil, and be hanging from a tree branch b'fo he can look at her twice!' said one of the slaves who had been bought long before Amy and her family came to the plantation. His views were in part colored by a deep distrust that Mr. Elijah could actually be as different from the other Willises as he seemed. He had been a slave on another plantation, and to him no white man, much less a planter, was to be completely trusted.

"That ain't all!" said one of the women. "If one of us looks at a white man, we evil, wicked women, got no right to steal no white lady's man! Now how you gonna call that stealin, if they women can't hold onto they man in the first place?"

She paused and added with a mischievous laugh, smoothing down her dress to accentuate her voluptuous figure, "Shoot, can't hardly blame a white man for lookin' at us, when all they womens is skinny, an thin-lipped, an act like they gots a pole up they backside!" She imitated the straight-laced stiffness of most white women, pursed her lips in a prissy manner, raised her eyebrows, and folded her hands primly in her lap, like she was protecting the holy grail between her legs. Her companions roared with laughter.

"True! True!" cackled another in agreement, "But white women sho can be just as mean as they men folk! Look what happened to Momma Celia with old man Kirkland! His missus found out bout Miss Amy and Mister Gilbert and like about gelded him- and then she made sho he got rid a her and hers, to keep the peace. Called Momma Celia all kinda nasty names b'fo Mr. Elijah come along an bought the lot of em."

"Ummm, hmmm. That's true!" affirmed another as they continued shucking.

"I heard tell that a slave over in Barnwell got hissef lynched just a few weeks ago. Wan't but a sixteen year old boy- no older than Miss Amy's Elder! They say his mistress come up on him in the stable one afternoon-surprised him playin' with his man parts all by hissef, as boys'll sometimes do- and she went an told her husband, and he had the boy strung up, and cut him like he was gelding a colt, to boot! Thought the boy got hisself all worked up over his wife, and it just made him crazy mad!"

"No! That's just wrong! Sick son of a bitch!"

"Dang! And the woman ugly as sin, at that! Ain't nobody, not even a randy young boy, gonna get hisself worked up over her! She probably thought about tryin some dark chocolate herself, wishin he had got worked up- cause ain't no way her husband would!"

"I know that's the truth! I seen her myself one time Mister Elijah and a bunch a us was taking produce to market." They chuckled to keep from crying at the horrific brutality of the loss.

After a pause someone muttered, "Sweet Jesus, what a cryin' shame, lose a good boy cause a some white fool's trouble with his missus!" The shucking went on unabated.

"D'ya'll hear about the two slaves over Barnwell got killed for helpin a couple a runaways?" asked another.

"Lawd ha' mercy when compassion get punished by death! Sweet Jesus on the cross wa'nt the only innocent one who suffered, that's fa sho!" someone commented vehemently.

As the stories of white malice, cruelty, and pure ignorant evil ran around the circle and the slaves felt the cumulative weight of them, a chill ran through the group at the reality that in their world, facts and fairness had little to do with their survival. They lived, and sometimes died at the pleasure of their masters. Period.

Except on the Willis Plantation. At least here, the master's pleasure was not a stranger to fairness or justice. For despite the grim realities of the world just outside the plantation boundaries, there was another reality on Willis land, and if not totally free or without problems, it was at least considerably more benign.

Henry, one of the oldest slaves, spoke up, "Ya'll can complain about Mister Elijah and Miss Amy all you want- but I ain't jealous or mad. Seems to me we lucky they loves each other, cause it heps make sho we get treated right. Every baby they have feel like another promise he can't just turn his back on us. Momma Celia had it hard, but it was cause Mister William was married. Mister Elijah bein a bachelor an all, him fallin in love with Miss Amy best thing that coulda happened for all of us, if ya'll ask me!"

The rest of the group began to nod in recognition, allowing as how that was probably true.

"Still don't mean we gonna be freed!" insisted another one of the old-timers, on principle not willing to completely cede ground on his discontent.

"Well, mebbe not- but at least the man's tryin to do right by us, which is more'n I can say for any other planter I ever saw. God hep us all if he don't succeed, an we end up in the hands of his relations when he's gone!"

There was a general groan of agreement from all.

"Ain't that the truth!"

"Amen to that!"

"You got that right!"

"I'druther be sold down the river!"

"Please, Lord Jesus!"

The tensions amongst them seemed to ease for a while, and the good will toward Elijah was fully restored. For some, it was restored out of resignation to the relative blessings under which they lived compared to those of most slaves; for others, out of a desperate hope that a better future for them lay in Elijah's determined hands. The festering boil of involuntary servitude being lanced and drained for a time, hopefully it would not become re-infected, and they could resume as workers with a common purpose- a purpose so ironically shared by the man who held them in bondage.

XXXIII

Angus Junior could not wait to talk to James and Michael, his father's "object lesson" not withstanding. Though he was not able to read what Senator Clay had actually advised Elijah Willis to do, or how to do it, there was no longer any doubt that Elijah was looking into the possibility of freeing some of his slaves- and it wasn't too hard to guess which ones! That was the momentous news that confirmed all their suspicions that he had been up to something. The Willis boys, he concluded, needed to know this right away.

Of course, it never would have occurred to Angus that Elijah in fact was considering freeing all of his slaves. Why would anyone do that? Least of all Elijah Willis- he was too good a businessman to lose that much valued property willingly. No, this felt personal- an insult to the family by those who would usurp their very identity of being related! Moreover, since Elijah was a bachelor with no children- at least none the law would recognize- his estate would go to his next of kin. James had even said his father had seen the will- and anything that might diminish that estate, such as the elimination of some of its chattel, was to Angus' way of thinking, virtually stealing the birthright of the Willises! It just wasn't right, or fair!

Angus was not so foolish as to rush out of the house right after lunch. He helped his father up to bed, made sure he was comfortable, sat with him a spell, and only once the old man fell asleep did he quietly slip out to find his friends. He even controlled his pace when leaving, so as not to raise suspicions with Mary, who would undoubtedly report his comings and goings to his father.

Mary did in fact hear him sneak out, and looking out the window, figured by his body language alone where he must be going, but she couldn't do anything about it. Her authority over the younger Patterson extended no further than the front porch or the backyard.

Once out of sight of the house, Angus picked up the pace and went galloping over to James' store. Barely taking time to tether his horse to the hitching post, he bounded up the stairs to the veranda, calling out, "Hey James! Michael! Ya'll in there?"

James and Michael were out back unloading sacks of flour and sugar, and other provisions they'd picked up at the depot.

"Hey there Angus! We're back here!" called out James. When Angus rushed through the store and burst through the back door from inside, James looked up at him, surprised.

"What's got you all worked up?"

"Ya'll look like you're about to bust wide open! What's goin on?" added Michael. Angus by now had their undivided attention.

"I found out what your uncle's up to! I actually saw the letter from Henry Clay!"

"No shit!? Seriously? Well what did it say for Christ's sake! Come on man, out with it!" responded James

"How in Hell did you get a look at that letter? I thought we were gonna have to come up with some plot to get our hands on it!" Michael proffered.

"Hold on, hold on! Let the man talk!" James interrupted.

"Well, fact of the matter is I was only able to read the first part of the letter. My Pa is not doin' real well- it's not like him to make mistakes like this- but seems your uncle paid him a visit and showed him the letter, and somehow left it on the table in the parlor by accident! I passed your uncle while I was comin' home for dinner, and wondered if he'd been by to see Pa. Course, he didn't let on that he had. Looked like I was not someone he was real eager to see though, so could be he suspects we're on to him. Anyway, when I come in the house, I spotted the letter in the parlor on my way in to dinner," Angus explained.

"Damn! That is surprisin- Uncle Elijah's always real careful about that kinda thing too!" offered Michael.

"Never mind how or why the letter got left on the table, damn it! What did it say? How do you know what he's up to? And why the Hell didn't you take it, or at least read the whole thing?" James fulminated, his voice rising.

"Jesus, James, calm down! Let the man tell us what he found out!" urged Michael.

Angus proceeded to recount in detail the how and why of the discovery, and the impossibility of procuring the letter for them to read.

To Angus' chagrin, Michael muttered "Chicken shit!" as Angus reported handing over the letter to Mary, but James realized that had Angus tried to keep the letter, Mary would have reported it immediately to his father, and in fact he had no choice but to surrender it. That reality was underscored by Angus' recounting his father's "object lesson" on the illegality of reading others' mail. Angus knew moreover, that his father, for all his love for his son, was not beyond pressing charges to teach him another lesson.

"Well, one thing's sure clear- we've lost the element of surprise now, since Uncle Elijah clearly knows you saw the letter. But he doesn't know how much of it you read, does he?"

Angus shook his head, "No."

"Well, that's somethin' at least! Maybe we can use that to our advantage- make him think we know more than we do. At least he'll be afraid of what we might know!" James mused, "So just exactly what did you read, Angus?"

Angus then came to the heart of the matter, and revealed that Senator Clay was offering advice on the issue of the emancipation of slaves. Unfortunately, since he'd been caught in the act before he could get to Mr. Clay's specific recommendations, he could only presume that some specific advice had in fact been given.

"Whatever it was don't really matter," pronounced James, to the others' surprise. "The point is, now we know definitively what he's tryin to do, we gotta do whatever we can to make sure he can't succeed!"

"Now how we gonna do that, James? They're his slaves, he can do anything he wants with em!"

"Not anything, Michael. The law says you can't emancipate a slave in South Carolina except by petitionin the General Assembly," corrected Angus. The Willis brothers seemed surprised that Angus actually seemed to know something about the law. They figured he must have imbibed it from his old man in spite of himself!

"Well then, seems to me there oughta be a way we can make sure the Genereal Assembly don't grant em emancipation."

"And how do you propose to guarantee that?"

"By lettin folks know- especially the planters- what Uncle Elijah's tryin to do. I'd betcha if we can get up a petition, or at least get some of the planters to write the legislators, we can pretty well make sure they'll turn down his petition for emancipation."

"I don't know, James. Remember, you start stirrin up a lot of talk about Elijah Willis, an it could drag our names in the mud just for bein related! A white planter agin slavery is a stain on the whole family's reputation! People might start to think we're guilty too, by association!" worried Michael.

"Not likely, Michael. Most folks round here know how we feel about the nigras. Ain't exactly a secret! We've expressed ourselves right out loud on the subject more'n once, that's for sure! Damn, but I wish I knew what Senator Clay told Uncle Elijah! Hell, I'm pretty sure he owns slaves himself so, unless he's a Yankee sympathizin hypocrite, maybe he told Uncle Elijah there wasn't much he could do," James pondered.

"I doubt that," said Angus. "I been reading newspapers Pa has collected, and there's a lot of talk about how Clay's been promotin a gradual but total emancipation for years. Seems he and our Senator Calhoun fought about this all the time. I just don't think he'd walk away from the question without offerin some sort of legal suggestions."

"Angus- do you think you could read up some more, and maybe figure out what Clay's most likely recommendations might be?'

"Well, I suppose I could try. If I show interest in Pa's work, he might even help me understand the law better. It's sorta what he's always wanted anyway- part of his disappointment with me was that I never really took a shine to it before." This spontaneous offer was revealing of Angus' ultimate driving force, making conscious for him his ongoing desire for his father's approval, despite their disagreement on the issue of slavery and racial equality. It might even be a way to grant his father's fondest wish before he died, so he could make peace with the old man at last.

"If you can learn somethin more bout the law, maybe we can find a smarter way to block this thing without having to drag the whole family through the embarrassment of having an uncle with such unconventional inclinations. Makes Momma near crazy to even talk about it amongst ourselves! Damn, almost makes me feel like a Yankee snuck into the family somehow!" avowed James.

"You may be onto somethin there James! Lord knows folks around here could get mighty upset- and then suspect us too, or be mad at us for not stoppin it! It'd be a whole lot better if we could fight this legal, instead of just stirrin things up directly with Uncle Elijah," affirmed Michael.

"I gotta admit, when I went out there to tell Gilbert to pick em up at the depot, I'd forgot how big that man is," acknowledged James. "Truth is, I wouldn't want to have to tangle with him in a fight- even if we have the law on our side! Man's a hoss, and solid muscle too. Bet he'd just love to tie into us- and if it was defending Uncle Elijah or his property, we couldn't even jail him. Daddy told me once that the law says that's the only time a nigra can attack a white man an get away with it! A slave's gotta defend his master!"

"Alright boys, I'll do what I can. It may take a little time. If I just go bargin in on Pa demandin he teach me all about slave law, he's gonna know right away why I'm doin it. And with him feelin so poorly, I also don't wanna upset him. I gotta play my cards smarter'n that, or I won't get much of anything outa him but another damn lecture!"

"Understood. Take all the time you need to make it work. After all, if Uncle Elijah was thinkin of this when he took em all up to Baltimore and then came back, probly means he had no luck up there. I doubt it'll be easy for him to find anyplace he can just walk in and emancipate slaves like that," James snapped his fingers. "So we may have time on our side. Specially since that nigra woman of his is about to drop foal again! Betcha Uncle Elijah's not too eager to be outa town just now!"

The three agreed that Angus would proceed with his plan, and report regularly back to the Willis brothers. They sealed the deal, as was their custom, by passing around a bottle of whiskey, and gradually the conversation shifted to other things as the boys resumed their stacking supplies for the store.

XXXIV

March had rolled in wet and chilly. Unlike the balmy downpours typical of the summer, this rain made you shiver and not even want to get out of bed. It had been raining for two days, and the grey sky showed no signs of lightening up. The only counterpoint to the gloom was the sudden profusion of bulbs, the bright greening of the fields, highlighted against the rain-blackened bark of the trees and the swelling buds of the quince, azaleas, redbud, dogwood and peach, preparing for their annual riot of color, promising that Spring truly was on the doorstep.

Amy was sitting in the kitchen, chopping spring onions for a stew Momma Celia was making. Her mother was pouring ingredients into a large cast iron pot, the rich smells arising from it like a comforting cloud, taking the edge off the dreariness of the day. As Momma Celia worked her magic, sniffing judiciously to make sure of the proper blend, she asked her daughter, "Amy sugar, can you fetch me some water over here for ma stew pot? I gotta keep stirrin' so it don't burn whilst I'm brownin' the meat."

Momma Celia heard Amy get up, and then there was the wet sound of liquid splashing on the floor. "Now child, why'd you go spillin the water" Don't you feel well?" Momma Celia asked, as she turned around. Amy was standing in the middle of the kitchen floor, clutching her belly, and grimacing with a contraction. Momma Celia immediately realized that the origin of the splash was Amy herself.

"Oh my Lord, your waters done burst! Hold on sugar! Elder, Elleck, Children!!" she shouted, "Come here, quick!! Baby's comin, and I need ya'll's hep!"

Momma Celia managed to take the stew pot off the stove so it wouldn't burn, and then helped her daughter sit down, taking care not to slip in the puddle on the kitchen floor. The children came running in from the various locations of their chores- the boys from the stable and the chicken coop, the girls from upstairs where they'd been changing the linens. They stopped in shock, worried expressions on their faces, as they saw their mother wincing in pain and a puddle of wetness on the floor beside her. Little Julia started to cry.

"Hush, child. It's alright. Your Momma's gonna be fine- it's just that the baby's done decided it's time to come out and meet ya'll! Elder- you go saddle up a mule and fetch Doctor Harley. Elleck, honey, you go find Mister Elijah. Phillip, you hep me get ya Momma upstairs to bed. Clarissa, you an ya sister clean up this mess, go fetch me some fresh water, and then bring me some clean towels." Momma Celia's calm authority was unquestioned, and each of the children rushed immediately to their appointed tasks.

"Phillip, honey, you go on an start takin ya Momma upstairs- I gotta hep the girls put some water on to boil first, an I'll be along directly to hep ya."

"Momma!" cried Amy, panting. "Somethin don't feel right! I'm scared!"

"Now hush, child, everything gonna be alright. You just breathe! No cause to stress yasef. Phillip an I'll get ya up to bed, an ya'll'll feel better in a minute."

The girls came in toting a bucket of water together from the well. "Bring that bucket over to the stove, girls," Momma Celia said. She lifted an empty cauldron off a hook above the stove. The cook stove was supplied with two lower burners on the side, and setting the cauldron on one of these, she had the girls fill it with the contents of the bucket while she opened the fire door, added some wood, and stoked the fire.

"Ya'll run along now and fetch them clean towels, an bring em up to ya Momma's room."

"Yes'm," the girls replied as they rushed off to get the towels.

Momma Celia took a quick look around the kitchen to make sure all was in order, and then headed upstairs to help Phillip. Phillip was struggling to hold up his mother, who had doubled over with another contraction half-way up the stairs, clutching the mahogany handrail with one hand and her belly with the other. Amy was so pale she almost looked white. Momma Celia looked at her daughter with alarm, but didn't want to let on, especially not in the middle of a stairway where any sudden surprise could result in a fall.

With effort, Phillip and Momma Celia managed to get Amy to bed before the next contraction. Momma Celia saw Amy was spotting, and discretely stepped between her and the boy, not wanting her grandson to be frightened by the sight of blood.

"Thank ya, sugar. Ya'll go on now, go see if ya can find out whether Mister Elijah or Doc Harley come yet, cause I ain't sure which direction they be comin from. Ya'll keep watch for me. Won't ya?"

Phillip nodded mutely, looking at his mother with worry written all over his young face. "It's alright, child. You go on now. This be women's work. Ya momma'll be fine once we get this baby out! Ya'll go find out what's keepin' the girls with them towels- and then go down to the kitchen see if the water's boilin' yet, and let me know when it does!" Momma Celia knew that the most helpful thing of all for her grandchildren at this point was to try to keep them busy and feeling useful, so they'd have less time to sit and worry- but the fact was, she didn't like the way Amy was looking at all, and could hardly blame the children for fretting.

Momma Celia kept Amy as comfortable as she could, wiping her brow and keeping her nether parts clean. It was, she knew, not only safer for the baby when it did finally come out, but also a good way to judge how much Amy was actually bleeding. She looked outside at the rain and felt the chill. When the girls came in with the towels she had them build a fire in the fireplace and then said, " Go check on Phillip and tell him to fetch some more firewood upstairs."

Before the girls could get downstairs, they heard Phillip shout, "Momma Celia! The water's boilin'! What you want me to do with it?"

Momma Celia told the girls to go downstairs, calling as they went, "Momma Celia says, 'Bank the coals, and just let it simmer. We don't need it just yet. Go fetch some firewood! And bring it on upstairs!'"

"Yes'm," Phillip called back. Clarissa, reaching the kitchen, realized that she and her sister couldn't carry the hot cauldron upstairs by themselves, so she ran to the washroom and grabbed a big stoneware pitcher. "Julia! You take this to the kitchen. I'm gonna take the basin upstairs to Momma Celia. I'll be right back to help you fill the pitcher an bring it up."

When Clarissa came upstairs with the basin, proud that she had thought of it, Momma Celia looked up in alarm, her hands covered in blood. Clarissa shrieked and almost dropped the basin at this macabre sight. Amy lay semi-conscious, groaning.

"Come on over here girl, no time for cryin! Ya Momma needs hep. Ya done real good bringin the basin, sugar. That was real smart."

Clarissa recovered herself quickly, sensing the urgency in her grandmother's voice. "I told Julia to put the big stoneware pitcher in the kitchen, Momma Celia."

"Good girl! Ya done right. Now I need one of ya'll to bring up some of that hot water- best you do it, cause Julia might spill, she so little. But tell her to fetch my scissors out my sewin basket, and bring em up to me real careful. Go on now, honey, hurry!"

There was still no sign of either Elijah or Doc Harley. By now Amy's contractions were coming closer together. It had felt like an eternity since Amy's waters had broken, especially with the dismal grey weather making the day seem almost like night. Elleck finally found Elijah over at the sawmill, instructing the men to cover the fresh sawn wood so it wouldn't warp in the rain. They were stretching big oilskin tarpaulins over the newly stacked wood, raised up on pallets to keep it out of the mud.

"Papa! Papa! Come Quick! Momma's havin the baby, and Momma Celia needs help! Elder's already gone to fetch Doc Harley!"

Elijah immediately called Jason, who had been helping coordinate the stacking. "Jason, take over here! Ya'll know what to do!"

"Yessir, Mister Elijah! Don't you worry, ya'll go on an take care a Miss Amy! We'll handle this! An Congratulations!" Jason grinned.

Elijah nodded in trust, untethered Beauty from her spot under a shed where she and her fine English leather saddle had been kept out of the rain, mounted up, and spontaneously reaching down, pulled Elleck up behind him. "Come on son, let's get home!"

Neither Elleck nor any of the slaves had ever seen a white man share his horse with a black man, or even a black boy for that matter. The workmen stood open-jawed in amazement and admiration.

"Good thing we ain't in town, or folks'd be buzzin bout that like someone kicked a hornet's nest!" observed one of Jason's co-workers.

"Lord, that's the truth! I dunno whether to admire the man for his generosity, or be scared that he's gonna get us all killed if he forgets and does somethin like that in front of the white folks in town, or in front a some other planter!" said another. "Sho is a sight though, see a white man and a black boy sharin the same horse!"

"Fact is, it's a sight to see a black boy on a horse at all!" agreed another. White folks around there considered a horse too good an animal for a slave. Slaves either walked, rode piled in a wagon, or sometimes were allowed to ride a mule- the sterile embodiment of their bondage, and from a white man's point of view, of the inveterate stubbornness of the Negro.

On the way home, cantering through the puddles and rivulets of the water-logged road back to the house, the rain pounding down on them and soaking them to the bone, Elleck told Elijah what had happened, even though he didn't fully understand.

"Momma Celia says Momma's waters broke. I dunno exactly what that means, but there was a mess on the kitchen floor, and Momma was cryin like it hurt real bad. Momma Celia called and set us all workin to help out."

"Your grandmother did well, and so did you son, and I thank ya." Assuming that from watching the farmyard matings, his son already understood the basics, Elijah did not feel up to the task of a full explanation of the birds and the bees, least of all in the wind and rain, galloping through the mud on horseback. Sensing the boy's anxiety however, he realized that he might be a little vague on some of the fine points, and need some clarification, so he managed to say, "You remember when Beauty dropped foal last year?"

"Yessir."

"And you remember how, before the foal came out, there was a sort of bag of water pushed out first and popped open, and wet the straw?"

"Yessir."

"Well that's nature's way son- all mommas go through that. The baby's in a sort of sac inside, swimmin around until it's time to come on out, and the bag's gotta pop open so the baby can get outside. So don't be scared." Elijah spoke as if trying to convince himself as well. Even though he didn't know Amy was bleeding, or Momma Celia was worried, and had no real reason to suspect anything was wrong, because of her past miscarriage, he knew there could be complications, despite what had appeared to be a normal, healthy pregnancy.

Elleck, at least, felt relieved. He remembered how Beauty had dropped foal about this time a year ago, and he and Elder and Phillip had watched in fascination as Beauty's bag broke and the colt's forelegs had first stuck out from between her hindquarters, followed then by the head and neck, and then finally the body and hind quarters. It had been messy, but amazing, and both the dam and the colt recovered quickly, the colt standing promptly on spindly legs as Beauty nudged him toward her teats, and he took his first drink.

Elijah had deliberately chosen to give Elleck the example of Beauty's foaling rather than the nightmare of a breach delivery, where sometimes the foal was still-born, the umbilical cord strangling it, or worse, when the mare had a placenta previa blocking the birth canal and bled to death before the foal could even be pulled from her womb. Elijah shook his head involuntarily, as if to banish the image from his mind, for fear of transferring it to Amy. Nevertheless, he had a knot in the pit of his stomach, remembering Amy's miscarriage, and prayed there would be no similar tragedy now. He also prayed fervently that Joseph Harley would be found in time and there would be no need to call that odious Dr. Guignard to come, along with all his negative judgment, as had been the case with the miscarriage. That was surely the last thing any of them needed, and would upset Amy no end!

When they finally got home, Elijah said, "Elleck, you go on and take Beauty into the stable, rub her down and give her some fresh water and hay. She worked hard carryin the two of us! I'm goin on in to check on your mother."

"Yessir. Don't worry, I'll take care a Beauty, Papa. Hurry on to Momma!" Elleck hadn't realized how anxious he still was until he blurted that out. Elijah looked at him for a moment, making sure the boy was alright before running through the rain to the house, to check on Amy.

As he came in through the kitchen, he could hear Amy screaming in pain upstairs. These screams sounded different from her previous deliveries. With a feeling of dread, he ran up the stairs, taking them two at a time. He was barely cognizant of looking out the window to the front of the house to see whether Joseph Harley's buggy was anywhere in sight. It wasn't until he reached the top of the stairs, breathing hard, that he saw the wet, muddy footprints signaling the doctor's recent and hasty arrival. Elijah opened the bedroom door, afraid of what he might find.

The room smelled of blood, sweat, wood smoke, and lamp oil. Amy lay exhausted in the bed, the sheets stained bright red with blood. Joseph Harley was examining her, trying to ascertain the cause of the bleeding. He listened to her belly intently with a sort of funnel-shaped brass tube, the narrow end of which had a flange, a bit like the mouthpiece of a trumpet, to which his ear was firmly pressed.

"The baby's heart is still beating!" he announced with relief. "But the baby's under a lot of stress, and if we can't get it out soon, we may lose it!." Amy moaned weakly, and Momma Celia wiped her sweat-beaded brow with unspeakable tenderness.

"Joseph, what can we do? Amy doesn't look like she's doin too well. I doubt she can stand much more of this!" Elijah said, alarmed at his wife's appearance.

"Well," said Dr. Harley, looking up at Elijah for the first time since he had entered the room, "We can either see if she can hold on a little longer and try to deliver naturally, or I can cut her open and remove the baby by Caesarean section. The thing that worries me is she's already lost a lot of blood and is getting steadily weaker. I can't tell whether the bleedin' is just some inner tear from pushin' so hard, or whether there's somethin' more goin' on inside we can't see."

Momma Celia spoke up, "Scuse me for sayin so, Doctor Harley, but this ain't no regular tearing- baby's head ain't even crowned yet. Sides, she was bleedin b'fo' you got here, and there wa'n't no tears on her outer parts. Either she done tore the after birth, or bust a vessel."

Momma Celia's observations, trained by long experience rather than medical schooling, were in fact confirming Dr. Harley's own fears. If Amy had a placenta previa, she would most likely die unless he operated on her right away. If, on the other hand, the umbilical cord had somehow torn, the baby would likely die from lack of oxygenation through the bloodstream. Neither scenario was very hopeful, and he did not want to choose which life was more important to try to save. He looked to Elijah for a response.

Elijah, realizing that the children were gathered against the wall, staring and frightened, said, "Elder, take your brothers and sisters downstairs please. Ya'll go get yourselves a drink a water or somethin while I talk with Dr. Harley. It's alright- your Momma's gonna pull through, but we got work to do!"

The children filed out mutely, Elder carrying little Julia, who was sobbing softly, and Elleck held Clarissa's hand to comfort her, but in truth it was mutual. Phillip looked dazed. Once they were out of the room and the door had been closed behind them, Elijah turned to the doctor.

"Give it to me straight, Joseph. What are their chances?" Elijah felt like his whole world was about to crumble, but he was not willing to surrender.

"To tell you the truth, Elijah, I think it best if I operate on her. She's too weak from pushin and loss of blood to withstand much more of this, and if I do a Caesarean, we might be able to save them both. If I don't, it's possible neither will survive."

Realizing there was no time for a leisurely decision, Elijah went to Amy's side. Grabbing her hand, he spoke urgently in her ear.

"Amy darlin, can you hear me?" She nodded weakly, but couldn't speak.

"Amy, sweetheart, you're gonna get through this. *We're* gonna get through this! You can't leave me! We're too close to freedom now! But I need ya'll to be real strong. Joseph says he's gonna have to operate on you to get the baby out, and stop the bleedin."

Amy did not respond.

"Amy, sugar, I know this is gonna hurt, but the hurt will get you better, and save the baby." Amy nodded almost imperceptibly.

That was all he needed. Like a general mounting a sudden attack, Elijah leapt from the bedside to the door, opened it, and called down, "Elder, Elleck, bring up some hot water!" He looked at Joseph Harley and nodded his consent. Joseph opened his black bag, which had gotten knocked onto the floor when Amy had suddenly kicked during one of her contractions. He began taking out various instruments, and then saw that with the fall, the bottle of grain alcohol he had had broken, the astringent smell of alcohol fumes wafting up from the floor.

"Damn!" he muttered softly, but not missing a step, and accustomed to improvisation, he continued his preparations.

"Momma Celia, I'm gonna need your help on this. Yours too, Elijah. Let me explain what we've gotta do. I'm gonna cut the skin right across here," he indicated a horizontal line across Amy's lower abdomen. "There's a layer of fat under the skin, and a band of muscle under that. I have to cut through all that, to get to the wall of her womb. I'll have to open the womb and get the baby out quickly, and then we have to sew her back up right away to try to stop her from bleedin too much."

Momma Celia nodded, understanding instinctively. "You gonna need extra hands! Somebody gotta hep hold her open, somebody gotta take the baby, and then we gotta hold her closed so's you can sew her up. Ain't that so?"

"That's exactly right! Elijah- I need alcohol- the strongest you've got. I need boilin water, and I'll need some more light in here to see what I'm doin."

Elijah called the older boys. "Elder, Elleck, you two come on and haul up that cauldron of boilin water from the kitchen now! Hurry up! Be careful, but be quick! Phillip, bring in another lamp! Girls, get some fresh sheets, and run and bring up the soap from the washroom. Hurry!" Elijah went to get the whiskey. Momma Celia removed the top sheet, trying to clean up the blood already shed, then gently washed Amy's thighs and belly, placing a towel under her to catch the blood. Dr. Harley checked Amy's pulse. It was weak but steady. She had dozed off, exhausted, as her contractions seemed to have slowed temporarily.

Elijah had thought about calling Gilbert's wife, or one of the other women in to help, but there was no time. Besides, it was clear the children, however upset they might be, were united in wanting to help, rather than being cast out to wait in fear. The family converged in the bedroom, each promptly bringing whatever was asked and ready to do their part.

Momma Celia set to cutting strips of cloth from a sheet to use for cleaning, bandaging, or whatever else might be needed. Dr. Harley took one, and rolled it up into a cylinder about six inches long and two inches in diameter. He handed it to Elder, explaining, "When I tell you, you need to put this in your Momma's mouth for her to bite down on. When I start cuttin, it'll keep her from bitin or swallowin her tongue and chokin." Elder nodded grimly.

"Elijah, wash your hands. You too, Momma Celia." Holding up a pair of pliers, and a curved needle, almost like an upholstery needle, he told them, "Take the needle in the pliers, hold it in the fire or over a candle for a minute, then dip it in the whiskey and wipe it off with a clean piece of sheeting. Do the same with the scalpel, but be careful not to cut yourself-it's real sharp." He showed them a thin-handled steel knife with a curved razor-like blade and a mother of pearl handle. Already having removed his coat, he now proceeded to roll up his sleeves, took off his tie, and scrubbed his hands and arms up to the elbows with lye soap, drying them with a strip of the clean sheeting Momma Celia had cut. Elijah and Momma Celia followed suit.

When all was prepared, the room now smelling faintly of whiskey and soap, overlaying the other smells, Elijah woke Amy gently. "Amy darlin, we're ready. I'm right here, sugar. We're all right here with ya. It's time for our baby to come out and meet the family! Joseph's gonna have to open ya up, but ya're gonna be alright!"

Amy opened her eyes and looked up at Elijah trustingly. She nodded and said softly, "I'm ready, and I'm not leavin!" She smiled at him with immense love.

Then she looked up at Elder, her first-born. "You alright, baby?" He nodded, not speaking to avoid choking up. "Thank ya for helpin me through this!" she told him. She nodded to Dr. Harley, and opened her mouth to receive the roll of cloth to bite down on.

Elijah asked her, "Do you want some whiskey for the pain?" She shook her head. Elijah wished he could have a few swigs, but didn't dare take the time at this point. Doctor Harley had given her some opium when he first arrived, but dared not give her more for fear it would affect the baby. Amy started having another contraction and moaned, the cloth muffling her cries.

"Momma Celia, take some strips and tie her arms and legs to the bed frame!" Dr. Harley ordered.

Momma Celia resisted, the very thought of tying up her daughter for any reason was unbearable. Realizing her resistance and the reason for it, Dr. Harley said, "Well, if you won't tie her, ya'll're gonna have to hold her down real still, 'cause she's gonna wanna flail about when I start cuttin. Can you do that?" He looked around demandingly at them all. They nodded back, and Elleck grabbed his mother's feet, Momma Celia one arm and Elijah the other. Elder stayed by her head, wiping her brow.

With surprising speed, Dr. Harley sliced firmly through the skin, fat, and band of muscles in her belly, exposing the wall of the uterus, warm, sticky blood streaming down her lower abdomen and drenching the sheets. Amy's screams could not be absorbed by the cloth she was biting. Her body tensed in spontaneous reaction, and then relaxed. The children winced, looking on with horror and morbid fascination as, the second she relaxed, with another steady cut by Doctor Harley, the womb seemed to burst open, and they saw the baby inside.

"Clarissa, come here darlin," Doctor Harley said kindly, but firmly, "Your gonna receive your little baby brother or sister. Grab that clean cloth over there to hold the baby- cause it's gonna be wet and slippery, and we don't want to drop it, now do we?" Clarissa shook her head emphatically, 'no.' "Ya'll need to wrap the baby up like your baby doll right away so it doesn't catch a chill, alright?" Clarissa nodded.

They all watched in amazement as Dr. Harley gently pulled the baby out, held it by its tiny feet, and gave it a single smack on its bottom to jolt it into breathing. It's tiny chest heaved, filling its lungs with the shock of fresh air, and it's cry filled the room with a sense of relief. It was alive- a beautiful little baby girl.

Elijah, having gotten used to the idea that Amy thought it was a boy, was a little surprised, but didn't care. She was alive. Thank God! But there was no time for sentimentality. Amy was weakening. Copius blood was now oozing from her vagina, mixing in dark pools on the stark white cotton sheets with the bright red blood dripping down from the incision in her belly.

"Amy sugar, it's a girl, she's fine and beautiful, just like her Momma!" Elijah pushed her sweat-dampened hair back and spoke into Amy's ear, as

Doctor Harley cut the umbilical cord, now assured of the baby breathing on her own.

Amy squeezed his hand weakly in acknowledgement.

Dr. Harley immediately readied himself for the task of sewing her up, but before he did, he wanted to look inside to see if he could figure out the reason for her bleeding.

"Elleck, bring that lamp over here and hold it steady for me, son. I need to take a look to see what's causin all this bleedin."

Elleck nervously edged closer, wrestling between his fear and his fascination. Though Dr. Harley was relieved to discover the placenta was not totally blocking the cervix, the lower edge of it was perilously close to it, and had ruptured with the baby's efforts to get into the birth canal. Rather than waiting for Amy to pass the afterbirth naturally, he removed it and stitched up the wall of the uterus where it had been attached, Momma Celia spreading open the incision with both hands, so he could get to it. She then took the afterbirth in a washbasin and put it under the bed. (Later she would bury it, to assure the baby's connection with her ancestors; even as a third generation African, some traditions ran deep).

Dr. Harley then closed the incision of the outer wall of the womb and, with Momma Celia pushing the edges of the belly together so they would make a clean seam, he patiently and deftly sewed up her abdomen, first the womb, then the abdominal muscles, then the skin, carefully washing the area, wiping it first with a cloth soaked in whiskey, and then wiping it clean with the boiled water (now cooled down, but sterile). Amy had passed out from the pain and was now in a deep sleep.

By now the baby had been cleaned up and stopped her crying, and was nestled in her big sister's arms, who first looked down at her in wonder, and then looked at her mother with a mixture of worry and awe. The five children had been forced to grow up fast that evening. In the after-shock of this life or death drama, unable to speak, but more deeply bonded than ever, all eyes were moistly focused on Dr. Harley, expectant.

He looked at Elijah, as he was washing the blood off his arms, and said with a tired smile, "Amy should recover fully. She'll be weak, and must have total rest. She's lost a lotta blood. It'll take a while for her body to recover, and there's still a danger of infection. If she's too weak to nurse, I expect ya'll can find a wet nurse on the plantation to help her out. I'm gonna give her some more opium for the pain. It'll make her pretty groggy, but that's alright." He then turned to Clarissa, holding her baby sister.

"Now, let me take a good look at this precious little girl!"

Clarissa gently handed the baby over to Doctor Harley. He carefully unwrapped her, at which point she awoke, annoyed at the sudden drop in temperature, and immediately demonstrated that if nothing else, she had a good set of lungs. Dr. Harley checked her from head to toe- her hands and feet, her legs and hips, her neck and ears and tiny eyes, her bottom, her privates- carefully examining her skin and scalp as well. He looked up and announced with a smile, "She's small, but she's perfect!"

Somehow this was the point at which everyone seemed to exhale a huge sigh of relief. Little Julia, who had been pretty overwhelmed by the drama, and had sat almost cowering in the corner to keep out of the way, timidly approached the side of the bed and leaning over, gently kissed her sleeping mother. She then turned to her sister Clarissa, and asked, "May I see her, too?"

All five children clustered around their new sister, touching her tiny fingers and stroking her little head, feeling the amazing, almost waxy softness of her skin and admiring her creamy coffee color - surprisingly a little darker than Julia or Clarissa, yet still a touch lighter than their mother.

Momma Celia came over and held her arms out to receive her newest grandchild. As she cradled her gently in her arms, she looked at Elijah and asked, "What ya'll gonna call her? Have ya picked a name?"

Elijah looked surprised. "Come to think of it, we haven't even talked about it! Up in Baltimore, Amy told me she thought it was a boy, and so I was sorta thinkin we might call him Elijah Junior. But seein as how it's a little girl, we'll have to come up with another name now."

Momma Celia thought a moment, and with a soft smile said, "Why don't ya'll call her Eliza? It's close to Elijah, an it's a real pretty name- ain't that right, baby girl?" She smiled lovingly down at her granddaughter and murmured to her, "My little Eliza Ann!" The baby seemed to smile as she nuzzled her grandmother contentedly.

XXXV

Amy's recovery was a slow journey back. Doctor Harley had told Momma Celia to make sure she got food that would help her recover her strength- red meat, calf's liver, spinach- lots of vegetables and fruit, and not too much rice, since it could bind her up. He didn't want her having to push to move her bowels, so as not to stress the incision.

Momma Celia was expert at caring for the wound, and knew to look for any signs of infection. Dr. Harley had come back a week or so after little Eliza was born to check on the mother and child. He was impressed with the look of the incision, which lay flat and pink and smooth. Even as he removed the stitches, there were no signs of the scarring being raised, darkened and bumpy, as so often occurred, especially with colored women.

After examining Amy, who was resting peacefully, he asked quietly, "Momma Celia, have you been puttin somethin on this wound to make it heal so well?" By now well aware that her knowledge rivaled his own, he treated her as a colleague from whom he was eager to learn.

"Yessir. Trick my grandma taught me. I got me a plant helps all kinda scars an burns heal. She told me it used to grow where her people come from, back in Africa, but it grow fine here, long as it don't get too cold. Cut the leaf, and a clear juice drips out like a syrup. You rub that on any scar or burn, rub it into the skin all round real good, and it'll ease the pain an make it heal clean. Got lotsa other uses too. My grandma called it alavera- but I don't rightly know if that's its real name. Told me it was even mentioned in the Bible!"

Joseph Harley's admiration for Momma Celia was immense. He knew that the ancient Greeks had used aloe vera, as did the Jewish physicians in the Bible, but was not expecting a slave woman of African stock to not only know about it, but to have grown the plant, and know how to use it effectively, as well.

"Momma Celia, you amaze me!" he said with genuine admiration. "Seems I learn something new from you every time I come out here! Ya're doin a wonderful job takin care of this family. There's at least three of em owe their lives to your doctorin! They're mighty lucky to have ya!" Momma Celia beamed back at this recognition.

"Thank ya, Doctor Harley, sir, I surely do appreciate that!" She wanted to let him know he was an inspiration too, both medically and personally. "Ya'll 're the only white doctor I ever met who don't put me down, or feel threatened by what I know. Makes me wanna learn from you, too! That cuttin ya did on my Amy, not too many white doctors woulda bothered on a colored gal, or done it so good! I truly do thank ya, sir. It's a pleasure to work with ya'll. May the Good Lord bless ya always!"

"Why, Momma Celia, I do believe that's the nicest compliment I've ever received in my entire professional life! God bless you too!"

Amy, roused from a semi-slumber by this enthusiastic exchange, spoke up. "Excuse me! Ya'll done? Didya forget that I'm right here listenin to ya'll expressin yourselves? Well I got somethin to say too!"

Dr. Harley and Momma Celia looked a little embarrassed, realizing that in fact, they had acted almost as if Amy hadn't been right there! Before either could respond or even attempt to make any excuses, Amy continued,

"Dr. Harley, Momma, now that ya'll 're done complimentin each other on what a wonderful job ya done, I need to remind ya'll that you forgot to mention that my Elijah, my children, and the Good Lord had a hand in this too!" She grinned in teasing. "The fact of the matter is," she said with a pause for effect, "I am truly blessed to have ya'll in my life, and I can't thank ya'll enough for what ya've done, each and every one of ya!" Her eyes welled up.

"Amy, my dear," said Dr. Harley, "I couldn't agree with you more that everybody had a hand in helpin ya, and they all deserve credit. I'm also quite convinced that the Good Lord has a plan for you- and wants ya to live to see your whole family free! I think He just chose to use each of us to help make sure that happens. It wasn't your time, that's all there is to it, and nobody goes before their time!" Momma Celia nodded in agreement.

"That bein said, however, I still think your Momma deserves a whole lot of the credit! Why, the simple fact of the matter is, with her knowledge and skill, if she were white and a man, she'd be considered to be as good a doctor as any I've ever met!" Momma Celia blushed with pleasure.

"With all due respect Doctor, I coulda told you that!" Amy grinned at her mother in affirmation.

Joseph Harley then proceeded to check little Eliza too. Amy had been trying to nurse, but was so weak she was not producing much milk yet, and unfortunately none of the slave women on the plantation were nursing at the time, so a wet nurse had not yet been found. Momma Celia had been feeding the baby with fresh goat's milk, dripping it into her through a piece of clean boiled muslin cloth the baby had been trying to suck on. But the goat's milk sometimes made her colicky. Eliza seemed alert, but was still very small, and Dr. Harley was a little concerned.

"Amy, dear, how're you doin with the nursin? Has your milk come in yet?"

Amy sat up in bed, her abdomen still very sore and weak. "I been tryin Doctor Harley, but Eliza don't latch on too well yet, and I get mighty full. Sometimes my breasts get hard and sore, cause she's not drinkin much."

Momma Celia interjected, "I been puttin hot compresses on her and rubbin her with lanolin." Dr. Harley nodded in collegial approval.

""Ya'll gotta keep tryin, before your milk dries up. Put her to the breast as much as ya can, an sorta tickle the corner of her mouth with your nipple-she needs to be coaxed, but she'll catch on. It'll also help ya keep producin. Your milk's the best thing for her, if ya can get her to drink it." Dr. Harley insisted. Trying to think of helpful suggestions, he added,

"So even if she won't latch on, ya can squeeze your milk out into a cup, and you or Momma Celia can give it to her with the muslin cloth, or drip it into her mouth with a spoon, little by little. Ya can also try puttin your finger in the milk, then put it in her mouth to try to get her to suck on it. Once she does, switch her to the breast right away. One way or another, she needs to put some weight on her!" He handed the baby to Amy in encouragement.

Almost as an afterthought, he continued, "Now that Spring is comin, it'd also be good to take her out into the sunshine some. Keep her warm, but let her get some sunshine. It'll do you both good!"

Amy and Momma Celia thanked Dr. Harley warmly. Amy decided to put Eliza to the breast to see if she could coax her to eat, while Momma Celia accompanied him downstairs to see him off.

"Doctor Harley," Momma Celia confided, "I'm a tech worried. Amy just don't seem to be comin back real fast like she usually do- she's still awful sore- an if she can't get little Liza to nurse, that baby's gonna do right poorly.

She's just not gettin enough milk. She don't like the muslin, an the goat's milk make her colicky."

Dr. Harley nodded in agreement. "I know. I'm concerned myself, but it's still early. Remember, Amy lost a lot a blood, and it takes time to recover from that. I'm not surprised she doesn't have much energy yet, and nursing can drain what little energy she does have. But the baby's gotta gain some weight, or she's gonna end up sickly- or worse. If Amy doesn't make the change to nursin successfully, ya'll 're gonna have to find the baby a wet nurse somewhere, somehow, and soon- even if Elijah has to buy one, much as I hate to say it!"

Momma Celia winced at the thought. Surely her granddaughter's survival was not dependent upon commerce! Though she loathed the idea of Elijah acquiring any more slaves, she would buy one herself if it would save her granddaughter. After Joseph Harley left, she went back upstairs to check on Amy and the baby. When she got there, the baby was crying, and Amy was getting frustrated that she couldn't console her.

Momma Celia took the child from Amy to try to calm her down. Laying her on her back, she firmly grabbed her granddaughter's legs and started pumping them alternately to distract her, pushing her little feet up toward her ears. Screaming at first, little Eliza suddenly let out a noisy fart and started smiling.

"Well, if that don't beat all! All that crying for a little wind? You little stinker!" Momma Celia chuckled. Amy looked almost as relieved as Eliza.

"I don't know why, Momma, but this birth was so different from the others. Maybe it was all the worryin about Baltimore, our future, and Elijah's health. I just never had a baby take so long to settle down!"

"That's alright child, every one's different. My little Liza gonna be just fine, but she gotta eat, that's all, wind or no wind."

"I just wish I felt stronger. I'm not used to feelin weak and worn like this, an it worries me that it puts more pressure on Elijah too. I'm scared it'll affect his heart again."

"The Good Lord gonna take care a Mister Elijah honey, just like He done took care a you. Sides, the children an I can take care of the both of ya'll just fine. So don't you worry. Ya'll just get your strength back, so Mister Elijah can go on up to Cincinnati and get that new will writ." Momma had a very clear sense of where the family priorities lay.

The reality was, Elijah was loathe to go to Cincinnati until he was assured that both Amy and the baby were safely out of danger and doing well, and neither had really reached that milestone as yet. The days passed into Spring, and the demands of plowing and planting now took over his full attention, for the crops waited for no man. Their collective survival depended on them getting it done within a narrow window of opportunity.

As the tilling progressed, Spring burst forth in full flower, and almost as if responding to new life all around them, Amy and the baby grew steadily stronger too. Eliza had finally figured out how much better her mother's warm and bountiful breast was than sucking on a milk-soaked piece of cloth, and was now feeding greedily and frequently. Amy's milk had also finally come in fully, as her incision healed and her abdominal muscles knitted themselves back into a functioning band. Though still taking it slowly and not able to do all she was accustomed to, she was by now at least getting up and out of bed, to everyone's relief. Momma Celia, thankful that they had not had to search for or buy a wet nurse, announced her satisfaction.

"Amy, sugar, God is Great an truly hears our prayers, don't you doubt it! Just think about it! We was worried bout you not bein able to feed Eliza, and that Mister Elijah might even have to buy a wet nurse, cause we couldn't find none here on the plantation. I couldn't stand the thought of him buyin one more slave, when he doin all he can to free the ones he already got! An see? Ya milk come in plentiful!"

"Ya're right, Momma. We have been blessed. I'm feelin better every day, and my baby's finally growin!" Amy acknowledged contentedly, admiring the chubby cheeks and plump thighs of her baby girl sleeping with innocent abandon in her arms.

As she looked affectionately down at her daughter, her thoughts turned to the future, and to her determination that Eliza, her mother, her brother, his wife, and all their children would soon be free. She wanted to urge Elijah to go on up to Cincinnati, but knew that he suffered from his own sort of slavery, as he was bound to the cycle of the Spring planting, and could not possibly leave until it was done. It would be futile to even try to make him go. Time seemed to be a cruel master, as, for all the hopefulness of Spring, the baby's growth, and her renewed energy, reality would not permit them to move forward as swiftly as their hearts desired.

XXXVI

The news came as an unexpected shock, despite the clear intimations from his letter that it might be immanent. Denial is a curiously powerful thing where matters we'd rather not face are concerned. Elijah was not quite sure why it affected him so, but the news of the death of Henry Clay felt like a deep personal loss, despite the fact they had never actually met. Elijah found himself lying awake much of the night that he heard the news, as if being carried by a current of personal memories, political arguments, his own hopes, fears, and dreams, and the attitudes of friends and foes alike. They eddied around his mind, like waves relentlessly washing over and around a rock in a riverbed, gradually wearing it down and reshaping it, all night long.

The newspapers were full of accounts of the Senator's pitiful last days, dying of consumption in the National Hotel on Pennsylvania Avenue, poignantly near the White House he had sought, but never managed to occupy. The President and leaders of Congress of both parties had come to pay him homage and to seek his dying wisdom, and when the curtain finally came down on the drama of his life, there was an extraordinary outpouring of national mourning that overcame all partisan animosity, in recognition that one of the nation's formative and guiding lights had been snuffed out, and all were bereft. Born in the year our nation declared itself independent, he was one of the last of his generation, the sons of the founding fathers themselves. Thousands lined the railroad tracks and streets where his funeral cortege passed by- in New York City, in Buffalo and Saratoga Springs, even in Springfield, Illinois, and Cincinnati.

It was telling perhaps that the earthly remains of this champion of national unity made a final tour of places he had often visited during his long political career- but, despite being a slave owner, his body traveled northward rather than southward before returning home. In Springfield, one of the last stops before returning to Lexington for burial, a fellow

Kentuckian whose star was clearly rising, and who would in fact achieve the emancipation of the slaves that Clay had long fought for, gave a lengthy eulogy in the State House on his political hero and inspiration. Little did he know that his own body, not many years hence, would lie in state in the same chamber.

In his eulogy, Abraham Lincoln specifically and emphatically endorsed Clay's views on the emancipation of the slaves. The papers quoted Mr. Lincoln as saying,

"The very earliest, and one of the latest, public efforts of his life, separated by a period of more than fifty years, were both made in favor of gradual emancipation. He did not perceive that on a question of human rights the Negroes were to be excepted from the human race. And yet Mr. Clay was the owner of slaves. Cast into life when slavery was already widely spread and deeply seated, he did not perceive, as I think no wise man has perceived, how it could be at once eradicated without producing a greater evil even to the cause of human liberty itself. His feeling and his judgment, therefore, ever led him to oppose both extremes of opinion on the subject."

Elijah had read Abraham Lincoln's eulogy on Henry Clay with mixed feelings. Having been inspired by the letter the Senator had written him, he had found new hope that he might in fact succeed in freeing his family. But Clay's death was also a reminder that time waits for no man. Though Mr. Lincoln might sing his praises, and some day follow in his footsteps on the issue, there was no guarantee anything of significance would happen in the foreseeable future that might facilitate or expedite the process- especially since the moderation Mr. Lincoln was exhorting the nation to observe seemed far from the minds of the folks here in South Carolina.

Elijah's heart, both physically and metaphorically, was telling him that time was of the utmost importance and in limited supply. But he took some comfort in Mr. Lincoln's insistence on the wisdom of Clay's views, and the nation's eventual need to follow suit on universal emancipation. That was a hopeful sign for the future. However, uncertainty of the timing continued to plague him in determining the practical implementation of his goals in the present.

Elijah took note of another detail of Mr. Lincoln's eulogy, and found it oddly encouraging. Perhaps because it mirrored his own rustic upbringing, and thereby struck a sympathetic chord, Lincoln acknowledged that

Clay's relatively humble birth and lack of formal education proved that in America, part of the treasure of freedom was that anyone willing to work hard could rise to eminence and make important contributions to the life of the nation. Elijah felt such an acknowledgment that humble beginnings do not define us was strangely hopeful and affirming for Gilbert, Elder, Elleck, Phillip, and the whole family. They too could in fact as freedmen have a bright and prosperous future- which was a driving force in his hopes for them all.

Unfortunately, Elijah was becoming all too aware that the atmosphere in South Carolina, as a whole, did not seem to endorse his hopefulness. The death of John C. Calhoun had left a power vacuum in the state, and the oligarchy of white planters vied with each other to fill it. Calhoun had attempted to broker a convention of Southern States to agree upon seceding from the union back in 1850, but his death just before the convention was to take place in Nashville, Tennessee, robbed it of its momentum. Moreover, South Carolina's threat to go it alone, if others did not accede to her initiative, had seemed arrogant to some, and offended the leaders of many slave holding states who still considered membership in the union to be valued, in principle.

The Compromise brokered by Henry Clay in 1850 had preserved the union intact for a time, convincing many, but not all Southerners they had more to win than to lose by remaining in the Union. The South Carolinians, however, more than all other Southerners, continued to disagree. Appealing to their pivotal role in the Revolution to throw off the yoke of the British crown, they began to equate Washington with the onerous control formerly exercised by the British monarch from London. In flagrant individualism, they claimed that espousing States' Rights was the preeminent value that trumped any encroachment by the federal government. The doctrine of States Rights, and Senator Calhoun's promulgation of the "right of nullification" of federal laws locally deemed onerous, were still seen as their most important guarantors of the carefully designed freedoms white South Carolinians intended to preserve and enjoy. That included, of course, the freedom to enslave and to reap the benefits of the servitude of all non-whites. Most folks in South Carolina- white folks, that is- saw the emancipation of slaves as a death knell to their entire society, and its cultural underpinnings- the tolling of which must be prevented at all costs.

Then this very year of 1852, the state legislature had held a convention up in Columbia, in which the delegates voted to affirm their right as a state to secede from the union. Judge Wardlaw had presided over that session, and John C. Calhoun's erstwhile successor, Robert Barnwell Rhett, from right here in Barnwell District, had been a prime mover of the resolution to insist upon South Carolina's fundamental right to secede from the union if she so chose. He proclaimed it as a matter of States' rights protected by the U.S. Constitution!

Elijah read in the papers that, for better or worse, depending on your point of view, the cooler heads of Benjamin Perry and James Orr had persuaded the Convention delegates up in Columbia to go no further than insisting on reserving that right, without actually exercising it as yet. Perry warned of the possible dangers to South Carolina of going it alone, insisting that it would be far better to first secure a coalition of Southern States, just as the late Senator Calhoun had intended, before taking the definitive step of secession. He rightly feared a backlash that might isolate South Carolina and end up starving its economy. But given the local planters' attitudes, it seemed only a matter of time before the separatist inclinations of the lowland gentry, the state's most powerful voting block, would win the day.

What was clear to Elijah, at any rate, was that white feelings were increasingly being galvanized to prevent any incursions against slavery whatsoever. Both the white folks and the coloreds felt it. He had heard it in snatches of conversation in town, at the depot, even right here at home on the plantation. He knew the reasons for the galvanization were mixed. In part they were pure economics- which is to say, greed-driven. The Southern economy was utterly dependent upon slave labor, and the perception shared by nearly everyone was that its abolition would be a crippling property loss and expense, from which the planters and agriculture itself could not possibly recover. Elijah had been struggling over that issue himself in trying to find a way to free his slaves and preserve his wealth at the same time. To most white folks' way of thinking, giving the slaves their freedom, and then having to pay them for their work on top of that material loss on the owners' investment was unthinkable, unless the government was able to duly compensate their loss. Such compensation, however, was economically impossible.

There were other, darker arguments, however, that also fueled the turmoil. There were both conscious and subliminal worries, which many white folks shared, but which Elijah largely avoided facing, because his love for Amy persuaded him they didn't really apply to him. The deep-seated fears of many saw any freed black as a potential threat, though the exact nature of that threat was only hinted at, and rarely articulated in polite society, thereby rendering it all the more frightening. In an area like Barnwell District, South Carolina, where coloreds now outnumbered whites, the threat was perceived as proportionately and increasingly more serious.

The growth of the colored population was, in itself, a persuasive reason, in the minds of Elijah's peers, for preserving white control through continued subjugation of all non-whites. Paradoxically, it simultaneously made it harder and harder for whites to do so, by virtue of being increasingly outnumbered. There was, therefore, an endemic fear of the risk of a black revolt, a take-over whose dangerous possibility, in the minds of whites, grew proportionately with the growing black majority. Elijah wondered, did his white peers fear black reprisals- a role reversal of enslavement, in terrifying revenge for centuries of white oppression and cruelty- or was it just that the notion of free, intelligent, and affluent people of color was such a contradiction of their paradigm that the possibility of it was simply untenable, too disturbing for most of them to even entertain?

Amy's comment reminding Elijah that he had, at least at one point, thought much like his white relations and the other planters, came back to haunt him. He himself began to plumb the depths of this complex reality that not only seemed to be unwinding, but which he realized he was actively involved in dismantling himself. Was he playing with fire? Was he, as some seemed to think, a besotted old fool, fallen under the Circe-like spell of a black sorceress, manipulating him with her sexual favors to gain her freedom and turn him into a swine? Or was he a noble hearted man who discovered that love could transcend race, class, culture, and all the stifling attitudes and priorities imposed upon him by his upbringing?

As he lay there, his mind churning with all the issues confronting them, he also faced another realization. Some of his own feelings, fears, and motivations that he seldom considered consciously, it occurred to him, might be a part of those darker arguments surrounding slavery. What about sex- that subject so skittishly avoided in polite society as a topic of conversation anywhere outside of a barn or a bedroom? Elijah enjoyed making love to Amy, as the birth of their three daughters helped attest, but in the solitude and dark of the night, as he lay there thinking about it, the rest of the household lost in sleep, he had to admit he had felt a bit insecure with her at first, until her responsiveness had showed him he had nothing to fear.

It struck him as a paradox that, on the one hand, black fertility was considered a valuable and highly sought asset, guaranteeing a handsome return on the slave owner's investment. Every slave owner welcomed the birth of healthy children among the slaves. It was a sort of bonus that spared them from having to purchase replenishments for their labor pool.

Especially since the African and West Indian direct slave trade had long been prohibited, this permitted a natural restocking of the workforce, and slave owners sought to breed slaves for specific attributes, such as strength, with the same keen interest with which they bred race horses or other prized livestock. On the other hand, their very success at this, resulting in the growing number of blacks- especially strong, well endowed, fertile black men- was subliminally feared as a sexual threat to the purity and virtue of white women and, if truth be told, though never acknowledged, a sexual threat to white men as well, who feared they didn't "measure up" by comparison.

In the South, and throughout the nation from colonial times on, and most definitely here in Barnwell District, the primordial value of puritanical propriety had always stood as a check against wanton sensuality. In fact, it became foundational to what was understood as being "the proper order" of things. Under the dominant influence of Protestant notions of virtue and morality, white society idealized the essential value of prim and proper behavior. They saw lust, beyond the acceptable titillating emotional foreplay of courtly flirtatiousness and romance, as a base desire, and a grave danger to the social order.

The Southerner's notions of the allegedly seductive powers and lustful libido of people of color, both male and female, were profoundly disquieting. They epitomized that threat to the social order, especially since white puritanical ideals often denied the physical reality of the natural urges of healthy men and women. Generally repressed, those notions danced around the edges of white awareness, alternately as a source of envy and dread, a cause of potential temptation and damnation. White men in particular, as an antidote to such dangers, sometimes felt compelled to affirm their masculinity by abusing their female slaves at their pleasure, simultaneously subjugating the women and making their male slaves feel impotent to stop them, thereby dominating them both.

Elijah wondered if, at first, he too had been trying to at least prove his virility, if not establish his dominance with Amy, especially after such a prolonged bachelorhood. The thought was disturbing, but so what if he had? By now it seemed a moot point, as the relationship had grown, and such insecurities had long since been laid to rest. But, he realized, he had never really asked Amy how she felt. Had she simply submitted to him out of duty? She wouldn't have to be black for that to happen, he mused, since it was clear to him there were any number of loveless white women in the community who nevertheless bore their husbands' heirs with dutiful regularity! But, since she couldn't legally be his wife, and therefore be subject to notions of marital obligation, he didn't want to think Amy had been merely dutiful as a slave. Much less did he even want to entertain the possibility that, as others whispered maliciously, she had serviced him simply as a means to gain her freedom.

Whatever the initial truth had been, what he felt in his heart for her was unquestionably love, and he felt that love reciprocated, both by Amy, Momma Celia, and her whole family- including her elder children, and even her brother Gilbert, for whom he felt a genuine affection. In Elijah's mind, there was no doubt where either his affections or his responsibilities lay. He had committed himself utterly to their care and liberation. There was no turning back.

Elijah knew he was not totally alone in this, of course, no matter how lonely he might at times feel, for he had known William Kirkland, and others who had relationships with their slaves, and some of those relationships, at least, were emotional as well as physical. He understood how difficult it was, and that most of them wrestled with at least some of the same issues of conscience he did. The majority of slave owners, deeming themselves good Christian gentlemen, were not devoid of conscience- however prone they might be to rationalizing the alleged justness of owning slaves in the first place, or to keeping their relations secret for propriety's sake. Even those who imposed male dominance on their female slaves felt unexpected repercussions, for the fruits of their liaisons confronted them with a moral dilemma.

The Bible (though notably not the words of Jesus himself), when selectively read, seemed to endorse the institution of slavery on the one hand, yet it also compelled the slave owner to deal compassionately with the slave, and particularly to care for women and children. This could be quite a quandary, for the sin of adultery was punishable by death in the Bible, but the sin of abusing a slave was also egregious, and few if any of his peers wanted to see themselves, or be seen by others as notable sinners. Local preachers had been getting more and more vocal in expressing both sides of this dilemma. Even William Kirkland had allowed as how he felt a "Christian" responsibility for Momma Celia, her children and grandchildren, whatever the truth of his domestic conflicts may have been.

Elijah, at least, consoled himself that as a bachelor, the sin of adultery did not apply to him. But he realized there were other repercussions of his choice of lover as well, in the impact of that choice on his blood relations. Was he violating the commandment to "Honor thy father and thy mother" by loving Amy? His relatives certainly seemed to think so! In that he was not alone either. For there were undeniably practical repercussions of the growing number of white planters having mixed race children, whether out of love or domination, sin or salvation. Legitimizing such children was resented profoundly by the younger generation of whites, whose fathers' marital disloyalties threatened their own inheritance, to which they invariably felt exclusive entitlment by the mere virtue of their white birth. Elijah realized, by his own nephews' behavior, that theirs were the voices most resistant to any and all emancipation, both in town and in the state legislature.

It dawned on him that there was a certain irony in South Carolinian planters' claims to freedom and independence, appealing to their colonial role in overthrowing royal tyranny. At the same time they seemed to believe themselves to be a hereditary aristocracy enjoying a sort of *droit de seigneur!* The irony, however, was apparently lost on most everyone in the white community. It was simply their lust for power and control, and their love of order- the "proper" social order, that is- that convinced them that slavery was an inescapable and necessary fact of life, and in fact, of the natural order. Their selective notion of freedom, however, applied only to themselves and not to their slaves, who should ever remain in their thralldom. In the minds of the younger generation at least, thus would the white population remain undiluted by the encroachments of any interlopers' attempts to break the chains of the slaves' servitude, or usurp the rightful inheritance of their white fathers' legitimate heirs.

Elijah began to understand, on reflection, that in the context of this complex web of social, economic, and religious beliefs and fears shared by the white folks of Barnwell District, the very fact of Elijah's love for Amy was far more disturbing and threatening to his family and peers than either of them had ever imagined. Unfortunately, on the conscious level, the true origin of that threat was barely understood by any of them. For Elijah and Amy, their love was the natural consequence of each recognizing in the other something for which they yearned, and allowing themselves to express it. It was, at this point at least, not about seduction or rape, or dominance and subjugation, or any form of power and control- at least no more power and control than was natural to any marriage in the give and take between the sexes. It was about mutual attraction and self-surrender, and deep companionship.

Though Elijah had not purchased Amy for love, he saw extraordinary qualities in her from the outset that made that purchase seem more than justified, even if he originally thought he had bought her and her family to help out a neighboring planter in distress. It was not until they had moved to the Willis plantation that he began to feel an unexpected attraction to Amy, which soon blossomed into a genuine love, surprising as that was. What did not fully register in either Amy or Elijah's awareness was that what now felt so natural to them was not merely socially unconventional or unacceptable, it was horrifyingly unnatural in the eyes of most whites in the area! Not only were there those who saw Amy as a conniving Jezebel, seeking the downfall of her white master as a road to freedom and power, there were people who considered Elijah's sin of shamelessly loving her as the utmost in moral depravity- so at odds with all they believed in, that they even considered it a possible proof of insanity!

As he lay there pondering, Elijah realized that, given the social norms that governed them both, having gradually come to see each other as people whose color differences were almost incidental to the substance of their relationship, he and Amy inevitably faced disapproval for their challenge to conventional propriety. The uneasiness in his relationship with his acquaintances and family, and the unambiguous loathing that especially James, and Michael, and his sister-in-law displayed toward Amy and her family, were not lost on him. They were making him understand more and more why the very thought of freeing a family of intelligent, skilled, and industrious slaves would be seen by most folks as tantamount to loosing a scourge upon the community- especially by those who were less talented and hardworking!

The ruling class implicitly feared that such a scourge was capable of "taking over," and forever upsetting what white Southerners deemed the "natural order" of society! In the minds of the local white population, and most especially of the landed gentry, to voluntarily allow such a choice was both unimaginable and inexcusable! Such emancipation simply could not be allowed to happen! Moreover, some, at least, were determined they would stop at nothing to assure that it didn't! His nephews, and people like Angus Patterson, Jr., Dr. Guignard and Mr. Matthews were making that quite clear!

Elijah lay in bed for hours anguishing over what, if anything, he could possibly do to dissuade them from their obstructionist efforts, short of denying his wife and children, and thereby also denying himself the happiness he had known with them? He knew that denial was definitively out of the question, so in the absence of stumbling upon any viable alternatives, and worn out by his mental churning, he finally fell into a fitful sleep.

XXXVII

As the balminess of Spring melded into the sweltering heat of Summer, the dog days began to sap the strength of even the strongest of the workers on the Willis plantation. The cotton was doing most of the work at this point, now that the plowing, fertilizing, planting, and hoeing were done. Gilbert still kept the work gangs after the weeds, but everything slowed down in the suffocating heat, and in that idleness, the slaves began to talk.

They were getting restless about Miss Amy's hint at their emancipation, for they had seen no progress in more than a year in that direction, and the heat didn't help their tempers. It might have been better if they had never been tempted with the idea, but now that they had, their expectations being frustrated did not sit well with any of them. Some even began to think that maybe they should help things along somehow, though agitation, they knew, could be dangerous for everyone. Others turned to religion to find a means of enduring their bondage, while still yearning for their freedom. The slaves were not alone in this, their owner too struggled to find a way to endure his own form of bondage – bondage to a system he no longer believed in, but in which he seemed inextricably tangled, at least until he could manage to free himself and them, once and for all.

Elijah was not much of a church-goer as a rule, but the combination of an urge to find spiritual comfort, and a pragmatic eye to keeping up appearances by not giving his white peers more fuel for criticism, found him contemplating attending services in the local Episcopal Church. The heir of the Church of England, and still South Carolina's established religion, the Episcopal Church had fallen into disrepute following the Revolution, and in recent years the Baptists and Methodists had taken by storm most of the local population, both white and black. Many of the lowland planters, however, still owed their religious allegiance to what was favorably seen by some traditionalists as the church of the aristocracy.

Elijah debated about whether to bring the family, knowing that if he did, they would have to be seated apart, for despite Jesus' unitive message, the local house of God was clearly segregated. He wondered whether even bringing them at all might not just trigger gossip, given the obvious physical resemblance his daughters shared with him. On the other hand, not bringing any of his slaves could be interpreted by some as a failure to fulfill his moral obligation to bring those benighted souls to the incalculable mercies of Christ. Apparently, that was the unique blessing and exclusive prerogative of whites to do! As usual, he sought Amy's input before making a decision.

"Amy darlin, I want to go to church on Sunday," he announced one morning at breakfast. Amy looked at him with mild surprise.

"You gettin religion all of a sudden, sugar? Or is it somethin else?" she asked, perceptively. "And I hope you're not thinkin of bringin us along with ya? That could be dangerous!" By voicing his own doubt out loud, she had confirmed his suspicion.

"I know you're right, but it feels wrong to leave ya'll. Part of me just wants to placate the other planters by tryin to seem normal, but the better part of me really wants God's help for all of us in this!"

Amy laughed. "Honey, you startin to go to church after so many years of not goin is hardly likely to seem normal to them, if they even notice! As for needin God's help, you've been askin for that in the privacy of your heart for years, and it seems to me He's been givin it openly all along! What's that scripture? 'When thou prayest, pray in secret, and thy Heavenly Father will reward thee openly'? Seems to me we're the livin proof of that!"

Somewhat abashed by the bracing reality of her ability to cut through his internal debates with her uncluttered faith, he chuckled in recognition that she was right on both counts. Still, something was actively drawing him to seek out some minister or preacher who might offer him inspiration in facing the multiple challenges confronting him, or maybe he just sought the comfort of the Anglican's silent confession and public absolution, without him having to reveal his alleged sins to anyone overtly.

"Well, alright then. You're probably right, but for some reason I can't quite explain, I think I'll go to services anyway. Maybe it's the Lord leadin me, in spite of myself!" He grinned. "They tell me that over in Barnwell, that Episcopal parish they founded a few years back, The Church of the Holy Apostles, is plannin to build a new buildin in what they're callin the 'Timber Gothic' style. Some English fella is the minister over there, the Reverend Edwin Wagner, and since England's already forbidden slavery, who knows?" He said hopefully. "He might be more inspirin than the preachers around here. Maybe it won't seem strange that a lumber mill owner from the area might show up for services, and offer to provide them some lumber!" He paused a moment in reflection. "Daddy used to keep a Book of Common Prayer by his bedside, and I'd read it when I was growin up. I don't know why, but somethin about the language touched my heart, and I'm kinda yearnin to hear it again.

"Well, you go on then, and do as you please honey, but don't drag me and Momma and the children into this. I'm sorry, but God's Amazin Grace or no, I can't help but feel that the less folks see us together in public, the better right now!" Amy insisted.

Elijah nodded his acceptance, and resolved to ride over to Barnwell on his own on Sunday. He might, it occurred to him, even run into John Bauskett over there.

The fact was that Amy too felt strangely drawn to seeking a community of faith, as an antidote to the isolation she was increasingly feeling close in on them. But rather than the measured orderliness and the cadences of the Golden Age of English literature infusing the Anglican liturgy, she felt more attracted to the sometimes raucous, but emotionally gratifying evangelism in which most of the slaves found expression, even if only in informal gatherings.

Whites had severely limited the rights of slaves and free people of color to worship without white supervision, but Elijah had always tolerated spontaneous expressions of faith on the plantation, and even occasionally invited Methodist circuit riders, or local Baptist preachers to lead services for the slaves in a clearing down by the creek, well away from the earshot of any neighbors.

The deeply emotive lyrics and rich, sonorous harmonies sung by the slaves spoke to Amy and her family powerfully, as did the rhythmic chanting of the circle shouts and ring chants that hearkened back to their African ancestors. She felt drawn to them, even though her presence at the slave gatherings made the less privileged among them a bit uncomfortable. It seemed that neither she nor Elijah could really be entirely at home any longer in the traditions of their upbringing, despite the primordial tug those traditions exerted on their heartstrings.

When Sunday rolled around, Elijah saddled up Beauty and rode on over to Barnwell, his father's Book of Common Prayer in his pocket. A strange and unexpected melancholy came over him as he rode along past the farms of neighbors, familiar roads and fields evoking a lifetime of memories.

He had a strong presentiment that whether the Lord took him before or after they moved to Ohio, there would not be many more such nostalgic rides ahead.

The Church of the Holy Apostles was on the far side of town, and as he rode through Barnwell, he passed by John Bauskett's house. To his pleasant surprise, just as he had hoped, John and his wife were getting into their open phaeton carriage and heading off in the same direction.

"Mornin, John!" he tipped his hat affably to them both. Realizing that John's wife had never met him, he added, "Elijah Willis, Mrs. Bauskett, pleased to meet you!" She nodded cheerily in acknowledgement as her husband responded,

"Well good morning, Elijah! This is a pleasant surprise! My wife and I are headin over the Holy Apostles for service. Eugenia," he turned to his wife, "This is Elijah Willis, Angus Patterson's friend I told you about," turning back to Elijah, "Elijah, This is my wife, Eugenia." Elijah nodded in acknowledgement.

"Are you headed our way?" she asked hopefully.

"Matter of fact, ma'am, I am! Mind I if I accompany you?"

"Not at all!" responded her husband enthusiastically, "in fact, why not join us in the carriage? You can tie your horse to the back, that way we can chat on the way!" John Bauskett instructed his Negro coachman to hold the carriage to let Elijah on board. Elijah had not realized Bauskett seemed to be a slave owner too. He felt a little awkward, instantly cautious about speaking too openly, as he did not know Mrs. Bauskett's view on the matter of emancipation, and did not want to risk the coachman hearing and passing on any sensitive matter that might crop up in their conversation, whether he was slave or free. But he realized it would be rude to refuse the invitation, so he dismounted, tied Beauty to the back of their carriage, and joined them. Something told him not to fear- chances were, after all, that if John was helping him with Angus, he was among friends.

The carriage trundled off down the road, the three of them in amiable proximity. Despite Elijah's uncertainties of Mrs. Bauskett's views and the coachman's confidentiality, he realized this was the first time he had felt comfortable in a social situation for some time. He contented himself with enjoying small talk, something he ordinarily loathed because it was from insincere people whom he distrusted deeply. But his respect for John Bauskett was profound, and in fact, he was grateful for the contact of someone he deemed a true friend. He also found Mrs. Bauskett a refreshingly friendly change from the judgmental women in his own extended family.

They eventually drove up to a comfortable looking house, which proved to be the home of the Rev. Mr. Wagner, Vicar of the Church of the Holy Apostles. A variety of carriages, wagons, horses, and mules were tethered in the adjoining field, and various people were making their way up the front porch into the house. Most seemed to be planters, or well-to-do merchants. Some were accompanied by a handful of slaves. Services were to be held in the drawing room, with the slaves delegated to the adjoining dining room, as befit the custom.

"The new church is going to be built over there," said Mrs. Bauskett enthusiastically pointing over to the nearby field. "We're still raisin funds for the construction, but it won't be long now, God willin!" The good woman seemed irrepressibly cheerful.

"Well, I'd heard about that, and in fact, thought maybe I could help provide some of the lumber!" said Elijah. "Be a fine thing to have a proper church over here, wouldn't it?"

"Oh, indeed it would, Mr. Willis! Indeed it would!" Mrs. Bauskett gushed, "That would be truly wonderful if ya'll could help! I must go tell Rev. Wagner right away! He'll be so pleased!" Mrs. Bauskett bustled off excitedly to find the Vicar, leaving Elijah and John a brief moment of privacy where they could speak more openly.

"Angus has already shared with me about your trip to Baltimore, Elijah, and shared the basic contents of the letter from Henry Clay too- pity he's just left us! It's kinda ironic we both end up goin to church together just after his passin, don't ya think?" John spoke in a quiet voice so as not to draw the attention of any of the gathering parishioners. He would smile and wave cordially as others passed by at a distance, but continued to speak to Elijah in confidence.

"I think you're right to go to Cincinnati, so I've taken it upon myself to seek reliable legal counsel for you up there. I found a law office in which both partners are sympathetic to the emancipation cause, and I feel confident would provide ya'll with good legal service. Their names are James M. Gitchell and John Jolliffe. Seems Jolliffe actually knew Henry Clay. I think you should contact them, and be sure to tell them Angus and I are well persuaded, from their reputations, that they are the best choice of counsel to help you out!" John pulled out a calling card and quickly scribbled the lawyers' names on the back of it, handing it to Elijah as if simply exchanging addresses.

"I can't thank you enough, John!" said Elijah, "I felt this almost inexplicable urge to come over here this mornin, and I truly believe the

Lord sent me right to you! This is exactly what I needed in order to make the next step! I'll keep you posted as things develop, but I'll send a letter off to these two right away, in the meantime!"

Elijah was struck that the name Jolliffe rang a bell. He suddenly realized that this name had been mentioned by Senator Clay in his letter!

"John! This must be truly Providential! I just remembered that Senator Clay mentioned your Mr. Jolliffe as someone who understood jurisdictional matters pertainin to the case. I don't know why I never thought to follow up on that, but I guess I didn't quite realize that he might not be a politician, but rather a lawyer who could actually help me write a new will!"

"Well then, there ya go!" replied Mr. Bauskett, "Maybe this is the Lord's way a tellin ya to get in touch with him, after all!" he smiled.

By now, Mrs. Bauskett was standing up on the veranda of the Reverend Mr. Wagner's house, the worthy cleric by her side, waving insistently for John and Elijah to come on up. Elijah felt there was no need to prolong their conversation, as John had given him a gift of unimaginable value without him having to explain or request a thing, thereby circumventing the need for further disclosure. Speaking in a louder voice, buoyed by this development, and no longer needing to be secretive, he said to his legal advocate, "Well alright then! We mustn't keep your wife and the Reverend waitin!" and with that, the two men strode purposefully up the steps to the eagerly waiting Mrs. Bauskett.

"Reverend Wagner, I'd like to present to you our dear friend Mr. Elijah Willis, a planter from over in Williston. Elijah, this is the Reverend Mr. Wagner, our Vicar!" Mrs. Bauskett fluttered.

The Rev. Mr. Wagner reached out his hand and grasped Elijah's warmly. "Awfully nice to meet you, Mr. Willis. Mrs. Bauskett here has just told me of your most generous offer to supply lumber to help us build our church. That is very kind of you, sir, very kind indeed, and would be an enormous help to our fledgling flock here in Barnwell!" He paused with a supercilious smile before adding with a sigh and a patronizing tone, almost as if chastising a wayward child, "It seems the Church has fallen on rather hard times in recent years here in South Carolina, and our good Anglican presence no longer so keenly felt as it was before that unfortunate conflict separated us. With your generous help, perhaps that might change, eh, what?"

Despite the Southern affinity for the social refinements of the British landed gentry, the Reverend Mr. Wagner's effete British accent, his affectation of the speech mannerism of the late King George III, of unhappy memory, who punctuated statements with a final rhetorical 'eh, what?,' and his disparaging allusion to the Revolution in which the locals took such patriotic pride, as 'that unfortunate conflict'- all struck Elijah as totally anachronistic, pompous, and even repugnant. Moreover, he was far from certain he knew exactly what the Reverend intended by reasserting the "Anglican presence", or whether he would agree on the desirability of doing so. Nonetheless, with John Bauskett's gift safely tucked in his waistcoat pocket, he was feeling magnanimous, and readily played along with the Vicar's prattling.

"I gather you have substantial holdings over in Williston. Am I to assume the town was named for the founding family?" The vicar raised an eyebrow in effete curiosity.

"Well, as a matter of fact that's right, on both counts. I have over 3200 acres, some in cotton, some in timber, plus my own sawmill. My ancestors built the town, but I built up the business."

The Reverend eyed Elijah appreciatively. "Well, we must certainly stay in touch then, by all means!" he said with a voice that hinted at the enthusiasm of a hungry man about to sit down to a free feast. Elijah couldn't help but feel the Vicar was opportunistically starting to tally up an estimate of what he might be able to persuade Elijah to part with. It faintly annoyed him, but couldn't totally dampen his raised spirits.

The Vicar's wife, a straight-laced, prim and rather dour looking lady, swathed in black taffeta and jet-sequined lace, then appeared on the porch to remind her husband that it was time for services to begin, thereby effectively putting an end to the conversation, as the last stragglers made their way inside.

"Do forgive my wife, sir, she's a stickler for punctuality!" the vicar said with an apologetic simper.

"Not at all, Reverend. Nice to meet ya! Ya'll just let me know what ya need when the time comes for buildin, and I'm sure we can work somethin out!" Elijah responded, grateful for the matrimonial intervention. "Thank the Lord!" he thought to himself, "Next thing ya know, he woulda been askin to stop by and pay us a visit! That's about all we need!" John Bauskett looked at Elijah as if he had read his mind and nodded, with raised eyebrows, and rolled his eyes with a slightly ironic, bemused smile.

As they walked into the drawing room, they joined some thirty-odd white parishioners, and noted around ten Negro slaves in the dining room, waiting expectantly for the service to begin.

The Reverend Mr. Wagner reappeared through the kitchen door at the back of the dining room, dressed in black cassock and a flowing white linen surplice, with a gold-fringed green silk damask stole, and walked in stately gait through the dining room, past the slaves, to the reverently awaiting parishioners in the drawing room. A few of the younger slaves hid smiles and stifled giggles at this strange apparition.

"Why dat white man wearin a dress?" murmured one of the children.

"Look like he got the sash from the drapes hangin round his neck!" giggled another.

"Look like he wrapped hissef in a bedsheet to me!" whispered a third.

The elder slaves poked their companions in the ribs in reprimand, glaring at them with furrowed eyebrows and pouting lips, and shushing them to avoid provoking their masters' displeasure.

The Vicar, oblivious to their tittering, arrived at the far end of the drawing room, where an impromptu lectern had been set up using a standing writing desk fashioned out of local pecan wood, upon which a white linen runner with lace borders had been draped. A pair of heavily chased silver candlesticks stood at either side, the smell of hot beeswax dripping off the burning tapers in the summer heat. Heavy red velvet drapes with golden tassles framed the window behind. The humidity was steadily mounting in the densely packed drawing room, the late morning sun approaching its zenith, and the tightly corseted and silk enshrouded ladies were already feverishly flapping their fans to keep from fainting, all the while smiling in sweet expectation of the Vicar's dulcet words.

The Vicar began to intone the service, and Elijah fumbled for the Book of Common Prayer in his pocket, leafing through it quickly, trying to find the right page, his sketchy memory, due to long disuse, adding to his delay.

"Blessed be God, Father, Son, and Holy Spirit," the Vicar proclaimed with a ponderous sing-song inflection, the last word rising almost like a question mark. It immediately reminded Elijah of why church had bored him as a child.

"And blessed be his kingdom, now and forever, Amen!" Dutifully responded the congregation, the women considerably more enthusiastic than the men.

The Vicar then recited a collect, "Almighty God, to thee all hearts are open, all desires known, and from thee no secrets are hid. Cleanse the thoughts of our hearts by the inspiration of thy Holy Spirit, that we may perfectly love thee, and worthily magnify thy Holy Name, through Jesus Christ our Lord."

The congregation muttered in response "Amen."

As the Vicar droned on through the familiar sequence of the confession and absolution of sins, and prayers of petition for the congregants, their livelihoods, the crops, the civil authorities and the governor (notably omitting prayers for the President), for the bishop and clergy, Elijah's mind wandered, pondering the opening collect.

"Lord, you know my heart. Give me the strength to see this thing through- and if I can't free everybody, at least let me succeed in freein Amy and the family!" he prayed ardently in silence.

As the vicar invited the congregation to join in the *a capella* singing of the Canticle, the rich harmonies of the slaves joining with the white parishioners in the cadences of Anglican chant struck him powerfully, and gave a whole new meaning to the lyrics of the song of Zechariah:

"Blessed be the Lord God of Israel,
For he hath visited and redeemed his people;
And hath raised up a mighty salvation for us
In the house of his servant David.
As he spake by the mouth of his holy prophets,
Which have been since the world began:
That we should be saved from our enemies,
And from the hand of all that hate us…"

The words hit Elijah as a sacred promise, renewing his hope in the righteousness of his cause.

"… That we being delivered out of the hands of our enemies,
Might serve him without fear.."

Feeling powerfully that the words of the service were in some mysterious way speaking to and confirming him in his hopes for Amy and the family, Elijah lost track of the rest of the hymn in his reverie, but was brought back by the voice of Mrs. Wagner, the Vicar's wife, as she read the appointed lesson from The Book of Joshua, Chapter 1. He missed the first few verses, lost in contemplation of the hope of deliverance of his family, but was struck by a few lines in the middle of the reading, when God spoke to

Joshua, exhorting him to cross over the Jordan and lead the people of Israel into their new inheritance saying,

"As I was with Moses, so shall I be with thee, I will not fail thee or forsake thee.

Be strong and of good courage: for unto this people shalt thou divide for an inheritance the land, which I sware unto their fathers to give them…"

Elijah couldn't help but wonder whether there mightn't be a big difference between the white parishioners' understanding and that of the slaves back in the dining room as to who was going to get the land of promise divided up amongst them! But he chose to take it as an affirmation speaking to Amy and his family of inheriting a new land, up in Ohio.

By the time the service finally ended, Mrs. Wagner invited everyone out onto the veranda for sweet tea or punch and some light refreshment before heading off home. As a clear indication of the Rev. Mr. Wagner's "High Church" leanings, the punch was generously laced with West Indian rum – a delight forbidden to the Baptists and Methodists that abounded in the region, and another reason for the popularity of the Anglicans with the landed gentry, who tended to be hard drinkers. Some even jokingly dubbed them Whiskeypalians. Elijah savored a glass of punch and chatted briefly with John Bauskett and his wife, thanking them for their companionship. Eager not to be cornered by the Vicar again, or queried by the other worshipers either, he soon made his excuses and bade them all farewell, cantering off on Beauty toward home, feeling surprisingly uplifted by the combination of the Spirit and the spirits.

Amy too had felt the urge for worship, and decided to take Momma Celia and the children to the clearing by the creek where the slaves gathered on Sunday mornings. The gathering was not highly structured, as there was no ordained preacher to preside, but some of the slaves who could read, (though in theory it was against the law), took it upon themselves to lead the worship, reading a passage from scripture, and then commenting upon it as the Spirit moved them. They would then offer up prayers for the congregation, and sometimes engage in a ring chant or circle shout, to end up with praise.

As Momma Celia, Amy and the children approached the creek, over the sound of the water they could hear someone reading.

"Sisters and brothers, the Lord spoke to me in my heart this mornin, and moved me to share a scripture with ya'll from the Book a Exodus. It begins in the Fourth Chapter at the 29th Verse:

'And Moses and Aaron gathered together all the elders of the children of Israel: And Aaron spake all the words that the Lord had spoken unto Moses, and did the signs in the sight of the people." There was a smattering of "Yes, Lord!" and "Thank ya, Lord!" and "Praise God!" uttered among the crowd gathered.

"And the people believed; and when they heard that the Lord had visited the children of Israel, and that he had looked upon their affliction, then they bowed their heads and worshipped." Most of the congregation found themselves bowing their heads and muttering heartfelt prayers for their own deliverance.

"And afterwards Moses and Aaron went in, and told Pharaoh, Thus saith the Lord God of Israel, Let my people go, that they may hold a feast unto me in the wilderness." The congregants began to affirm the scripture with "Hear us, Lord!" and "Please, dear Lord!"

"And Pharaoh said, "Who is the Lord, that I should obey his voice to let Israel go? I know not the Lord, neither will I let Israel go." There were moans and groans heard in the crowd.

"Brothers and sisters, we're like the people of Israel in bondage to pharaoh!" The people were nodding in agreement, "Even though we may be livin on a plantation where they treat us better than Pharaoh treated the children of Israel, we still slaves!" The crowd became noticeably more agitated, interspersing the reading with "Amen!" and "That's right!" and "Ain't that the truth?"

The leader continued, "Seem to me Pharaoh is like the whole system that allows white folks to keep slaves at all! But the scripture says the Lord heard the affliction of his people, and gave em Moses and Aaron to lead em to freedom." There was a chorus of 'Hallelujah,' and 'Praise God,' and 'Thank you, Jesus!' heard throughout the clearing.

By this point Amy and the family had arrived, and the people stood aside to let them in in deference. Some looked suddenly uncomfortable, fearful that they might be accused to the master of stirring up trouble. They knew that agitating for freedom could be punishable by death. The tension rose in the crowd, expectantly.

Amy, sensing the potential for the mood to shift and get ugly, decided to intervene.

"That was a mighty fine passage you read, Jeremiah. And ya'll 're right. Every single person here feels the burden of that bondage! We all do!" There was a ripple of 'Umm, Hmm's and 'I know that's right!' as she continued, "But as God is my witness, Pharaoh is not livin in the big house, or on this plantation at all! We're blessed here. We truly are. Remember, Moses was an overseer of slaves, and saw how Pharaoh's men were abusin em, and in anger killed one of Pharaoh's officers, an they put a price on his head, and he hadda get outa town. Only then did he meet the Lord, and get sent back to free the people."

Momma Celia, to Amy's utter surprise, chimed in, "Ain't nobody sayin Mister Elijah is Moses, an Lord knows we don't want him runnin off and killin nobody who's badmouthin us, leavin us here to suffer under the hands a his miserable relations! But ya'll need to trust in the Lord and have hope, cause he hears our affliction! He truly do!"

Though some had looked a little skeptical when Amy was speaking about how blessed they all were, even though the point about Moses' history was not lost on them, their respect for Momma Celia was immense, and her addendum really hit home.

Jeremiah, the leader, at first feeling threatened and then relieved by Amy's and Momma Celia's comments, responded.

"Praise the Lord! Miss Amy, Momma Celia, we sho do thank ya'll for joinin us this mornin, and for sharin your words with us in the Spirit! I feel a new song comin on! I heard it from a friend. Folks tell me it just come down here from up in Virginia! Lemme sing it for ya'll:

The Lord, by Moses, to Pharaoh said: Oh! let my people go.
If not, I'll smite your first-born dead—Oh! let my people go.
Oh! go down, Moses,
Away down to Egypt's land,
And tell King Pharaoh
To let my people go."

The congregation took up the melody and spontaneously set to harmonizing. They hummed a mournful cadence, and then began to repeat the words, over and over again, with growing fervor, gradually subsiding with a heart-wrenching final plea, Jeremiah's solitary bass voice bringing it on home:

"Let my people go!"

Amy felt the depth of the singing, but saw that, like the scripture reading and the preaching, it could get the people really worked up, and not necessarily for the better. She looked to Gilbert to start a new song. He nodded to her almost imperceptibly and began to sing with a rich baritone voice,

There is balm in Gilead,
To make the wounded whole ;
There's power enough in heaven,
To cure a sin-sick soul.

The congregation joined in, adding spontaneous verses, swaying to the melody, verse after verse, coming always back to the opening lines:

There is balm in Gilead,
To make the wounded whole ;
There's power enough in heaven,
To cure a sin-sick soul.

Finally, one of the women began a slow, plaintive opening of the hymn 'Amazing Grace.' Well known to them, the congregation immediately joined in, and though the first verse started off slowly and with utter sweetness, successive verses picked up the tempo, people started clapping their hands rhythmically, and dancing ecstatically, until by the last verse,

"When we've been there, ten thousand years, bright shining as the sun
They'll be no less days to sing God's praise, than when we'd first begun!"

There were Halleluiahs shouted as the crowd was jubilantly swaying, hands raised toward heaven, tears running down some people's cheeks, others sobbing in joy. The cantor brought the hymn to a close by repeating the first verse one more time with almost unbearable sweetness, slowing it down again, and drawing out the last phrase with a series of trills and flourishes in a rich contralto that left everyone totally speechless.

"Was blind, but now I see."

A deep silence fell on the gathering, which nobody wanted to break. The only sound was the flowing creek, the rustling of the leaves in the slight breeze, and the chirp of crickets in the grass. Judging by the number of moist eyes in the crowd, it seemed like most everyone could see a little differently for a moment, at least, and what they saw was hope, and the simple beauty of life itself.

The slaves all greeted each other with a heart-felt "Peace be with ya," or, "Peace of the Lord," and wandered back in small groupings of family and friends to their cabins for their midday dinner and rest, still reluctant to break the spell their worship seemed to have cast over them. Amy, Momma Celia, and Gilbert walked quietly together toward the plantation house. The children had run on ahead, happy to play with the other children and have a brief respite from their chores.

"That was a right smart thing you did, sugar," Momma Celia complimented her daughter. "And you done good too, son," she added to Gilbert. They continued to walk in silence.

"Momma, you never cease to amaze me!" admitted Amy, after a while. "I gotta hand it to you- I wasn't sure I was gettin through to them, but when you spoke up, I think it really drove the message home. When I said we were blessed, I saw some of em didn't understand what I meant. Some of em looked at me like I was crazy, like I meant it was a blessin to be a slave! I couldn't think what to do!"

"It's all right, honey, you served it up just fine. I just put the cherry on top!" Momma Celia smiled with satisfaction.

"Well, ya'll can feel good about what happened this morning, but that don't mean we should drop our guard. You could tell from the emotions in the singin that it don't take much to get people goin," remarked Gilbert. "It's like everybody's livin on the edge of something we can feel, but can't quite see yet. If y'ask me, it's gonna get harder and harder with people like Jeremiah there, cause he know he got a gift to preach, and his preachin could go either way if he gets worked up and feeds off the crowd's excitement!"

Momma Celia nodded. "Well sugar, you just gonna have to keep an eye on young Jeremiah, and do whatever you can to make sure it go the right way!"

Despite the fact that they all knew they were sitting on a powder keg, they couldn't deny that the service had moved them deeply, and even if the slaves lived in different quarters, the struggle belonged to everyone. Amy had spoken truth when she said everyone felt the burden of their bondage. Yet even so, she also felt such a presence in the singing that it made her own hope feel more real, as if the people, and even nature itself were corroborating it.

They finally arrived back at the house, and Momma Celia set to finishing the midday meal she had started to prepare before worship. Amy called the girls in to set the table, and the boys went to water the horses and feed the chickens.

Just as Amy was beginning to wonder what had happened to Elijah, and how his morning had gone, he came riding up to the house, rode around back to the barn, dismounted, and called for Elder and Elleck to unsaddle Beauty and let her out to pasture. Scraping a clump of manure off his boots at the back door on a wrought iron boot scraper fitted with coarse bristles on the sides, satisfied that he had thereby avoided incurring the displeasure of either his wife or his mother-in-law, he entered the kitchen with a smile.

"Mornin, ya'll!" he said cheerily. It made Momma Celia turn in surprise and brought Amy running in from the dining room, where she had been supervising the girls.

"Well, mornin to you too, darlin. Welcome back! What got you all full a smiles?" asked Amy.

"Look to me like Mister Elijah done got religion!" Momma Celia interjected with a playful smile.

"Well, Momma Celia, perhaps I have, perhaps I have! I don't rightly know, but I tell you what I did get, which might be even better than religion, is the names of two reputable, pro-emancipation lawyers in Cincinnati!" He held up John Bauskett's calling card and waved it in the air like it was a flag of victory.

"Watch yasef, Mister Elijah! Don't you be talkin like religion don't matter, disrespectin the Lord! Lord'll make you pay for that!" Momma Celia sniffed.

"Now Momma Celia, don't get yaself all worked up- I'm not critcizin religion at all, much less criticizing the good Lord! Fact of the matter is, I truly felt led by the Lord this mornin, and even though the preacher didn't inspire me, the words of the scripture and the singin truly did!"

He proceeded to recount all that had happened in Barnwell in detail, even affecting the Reverend Mr. Wagner's pompous British accent- to the giggles of Momma Celia and Amy alike. But he spoke with great sincerity about how serendipitous it was that he not only ran into John Bauskett, as he had hoped, but that the lessons all seemed so pointedly appropriate to their situation.

"And what about you all? Did ya'll end up goin to worship at the clearin by the creek?" he asked.

Amy proceeded to tell him her account of the service and how, for them too, the lessons and singing had struck a deep chord and spoken to their hearts. Just as Elijah had acknowledged that holy inspiration notwithstanding, he had felt the need for caution in talking to the Vicar, much less to any of the parishioners other than John and his wife, Amy shared their concerns about the slaves being prone to getting worked up. She shared that both she and Gilbert felt that Jeremiah was someone they should watch out for. She had seen preachers mistake their own gifts for speaking and working a crowd for the inspiration of the Holy Spirit, and knew the power to move others could be a heady wine for some of them.

Yet despite the reality that feeling God's presence, however briefly, did not obviate their need for caution, it seemed portentous to all of them that the scriptures at both services, though different, were so equally timely and poignant.

"The Lord truly does seem to work in mysterious ways, doesn't He?" Amy asked.

"Indeed He does, darlin. Indeed He does. I gotta tell ya, when John Bauskett gave me the names of those two lawyers, I felt like the heavens opened up and the angels started singin 'Amen! And Halleluiah!' For the first time in months, since before Eliza was born in fact, I feel like the Lord is leadin us steadily forward. We're gonna get this thing done, I just feel it in my bones!"

Amy looked at her husband with a mixture of affection and admiration. It dawned on her that going over to Barnwell for Church services and walking right into a group who might have treated him hostilely, playing along like one of them, despite the risks, was a bold proof of just how determined he really was to save them all.

That night, after the household was asleep, for the first time since before Eliza was born, they made love. It was slow, and tender, and gentle, and deep. Amy got over her embarrassment at her scar, and her fears that the surgery would leave her unresponsive. She had healed so well under Momma Celia's ministrations that the scar was barely visible, but she had, until that night, still believed it was glaringly disfiguring. Elijah, suddenly feeling years younger, covered her with kisses, even caressing and kissing the scar on her belly, a silent homage to her suffering and bravery, and a thanksgiving for her survival, and for their beautiful daughter Eliza. She playfully offered him her breast, still full from nursing the baby. He surrendered to her deft touch, surprising them both with his vigor, despite his age. And when they had both nearly swooned in climax, giggling at their attempts to stifle a shout of pleasure, for fear of waking the children, they lay silently and deliciously entangled, unable to tell where one left off and the other began, reluctant to withdraw into their separate selves, deeply content, drifting off into a peaceful sleep.

XXXVIII

Elijah quickly managed to find time to write a letter to Messrs. Gitchell and Jolliffe in Cincinnati, explaining his plight and inquiring as to their availability for him to come up to Cincinnati to get a new will written. He also made sure to ask what the laws in Ohio were concerning the procedure for emancipation and the legality of inheritance for free people of color. Moreover, he wanted to make sure that if emancipated there, there would be no impediment to them purchasing property, getting an education, running a business, or making a living of their choice. He did not want to repeat the same mistakes of his trip to Maryland.

He took the letter to the depot for Will Beazeley to mail. Mr. Beazeley took note of the address and inquired, "Well, Mr. Willis! Looks like your connections keep on growin! All the way out to Ohio!"

Immediately alert to the potential for gossip falling on the wrong ears, Elijah quickly responded, "Well, Will, I been workin on developin my shippin business for the lumber ever since I went to Baltimore and started talkin with folks up there about the B&O Railroad. Figured I'd best find someone to represent me on the other end of the line too, since the market for lumber out there seems to be growin steadily with the Westward expansion. Lotta money to be made, if I play my cards right!" he smiled with a conspiratorial wink.

Always swayed by his admiration for Elijah's business sense, Mr. Beazely nodded appreciatively. "Well sir, if anybody can do it, I'm sure you can! I wish ya'll the best of luck, then! We all stand to win around here with your success!"

Elijah left the depot hoping that if Mr. Beazely loosened his lips to any of Elijah's family, as he was wont to do, it would at least be with a credible tale of business building, rather than planting the suspicion of abolitionist activity! That was the last thing he needed!

Having contented himself that he had done all he could for the time being about securing legal services in Cincinnati, he contemplated paying Angus Patterson a visit, but gathering storm clouds on the horizon made him think the better of it, so he headed on back to the plantation.

As he was riding up the road to the plantation house, the wind picked up suddenly, and the skies opened, dropping hailstones as big as bantam eggs. Elijah spurred Beauty on to get out of the storm, praying that the hail would not wreak havoc on the crops. He could hear the hailstones exploding on the barn roof like artillery fire as he unsaddled the mare and patted her nose and neck soothingly. Spooked by the unaccustomed din, she stood trembling nervously in her stall as the noise continued, steam rising from her flanks from the melting hail. Elijah was hesitant to make a run for the house just yet, wanting to be assured that Beauty would not try to bolt. She was high-spirited, and could hurt herself if she got too skittish.

Elijah heard a door bang at the other end of the stable, and heavy footsteps came running towards him. "Elijah? Elijah!" Gilbert's voice shouted urgently.

Beauty jumped and whinnied in alarm at the shouting- already edgy from the steady barrage of hail. Elijah worked to calm her down again, as he called in response, "In here Gilbert!"

Gilbert reached the stall breathless and soaking wet. A large bump on his forehead swelled painfully from where a hailstone had hit him particularly hard.

"Good God! You alright? You look like somethin the cat dragged in! That's quite a goose egg ya got there!" Elijah said, looking at the lump on Gilbert's forehead.

Gilbert felt his forehead and winced, as if just becoming aware of it. "Elijah- the hail is smashing the cotton to pieces! That field of new hybrids we been workin on? Mostly flattened. Hail tore through the Sea Island and Mexican black seed too. Most of the Tennessee green seed's still standin, but overall the crop's taken a beatin!"

Elijah groaned. This was bad news at any time, but particularly bad timing right now. It was too late to sow new seed and too soon to harvest what they could. To salvage anything was going to be a challenge, but if they worked fast, they might be able to save at least some of the crop. Of course, that would mean yet another postponement of his trip to Cincinnati too, he thought with a pang of regret. By now the hail had stopped as suddenly as it had started, Beauty had calmed down, and pushing his worries about

Cincinnati aside in the face of a more urgent crisis, the two men went outside to look around.

"Damn!" was all either one could utter at first. The area looked like a war zone. Leaves and twigs were strewn about everywhere. Hailstones puddled in the warm soil, Amy's flower garden was looking ragged, and out beyond the slave quarters the corn and vegetables were bent –some virtually buried under piles of hailstones, and the cotton looked battered as Hell.

Like a general assessing battle damage, Elijah took a look around. "Well, we may still be able to salvage some of the plants. Get the crew together and gather up all the hemp twine and stakes we've got. If the branches are only bent, but not too badly broken, we may be able to tie and stake em up so they can recover. If the stems are split but not torn off, we may be able to splice them back too, by wrappin em with twine until they heal. We'll focus on the strongest lookin plants only. But we gotta hurry!" He thought for a minute. "Get Jason and Julius to get everyone together right now! We need every man, woman and child on the plantation who's not sick, too young, or too old to work. Best tell the women to start cookin, cause this is gonna be round the clock work to get it done! Tell em to bring the food and lanterns out to the fields, and we'll break in shifts to eat. I'll be out to help, directly."

Without a moment's hesitation, Gilbert set off to do as Elijah had instructed. Elijah headed for the big house to tell Amy and Momma Celia to prepare for a long night, and to get the boys fed so they could get to work too. They certainly weren't too young to help or to learn what it meant to run a plantation!

Every soul on the plantation knew how much depended on getting the cotton crop to harvest, so there was no grumbling amongst them, only grim determination. This act of God in fact united them all in purpose, and they rose to the challenge in surprisingly good spirits, proud of their history of getting the first crop in. It was almost as if they were eager to see whether they could laugh in the face of adversity and continue that history. Elijah knew, however, it would be like pulling off a minor miracle if they did!

The work was back breaking and tedious, for great care had to be taken, checking each plant for damage, focusing on the strongest branches with the most bolls forming, and not only tying up the damaged plants, but also not getting their hands torn to shreds in the process. On top of that, especially from dusk til dawn, the humid air fairly swarmed with mosquitoes, eager to feast on the sweating workers, adding to their misery. Momma Celia's salves and herbs not withstanding, there wasn't enough aloe vera or citronella leaves, or calendula from the marigolds in her garden to go around, if everyone ended up getting cuts and bites, and in the heat and humidity, the thorniness of the cotton bolls, and the sheer dirtiness of working their way through wet cotton fields, there was always a risk of infections.

By the grace of God and the teamwork of everyone on the plantation, within about a week they had managed to rescue a goodly portion of the crop, though some plants that had been particularly hard hit by the hail were clearly beyond saving. Now they could only hope, pray, and wait to see whether their efforts would actually result in the cotton ripening fully or not.

Elijah was feeling increasingly anxious about finding the time to go up to Cincinnati, but he clearly did not feel he could simply leave with the crop hanging in the balance. It's not that there was much more he could do, it's just that he felt responsible, as he had always been a careful steward of all under his sway and he felt that this was no time to leave either the fields or the slaves in the lurch.

Weeks went by, and most of the cotton seemed to revive, along with a good bit of the corn and some of the vegetables. Fortunately, the timber had not been severely affected, the hail serving to do no more than a sort of natural pruning of dead limbs.

As their hope seemed to be bearing fruit, Amy approached Elijah one morning in the kitchen after the children had eaten and Momma Celia was out in her garden picking herbs for her cooking. She seemed nervous, as if wanting to tell him something, but uncertain how he would react.

"What's goin on darlin? You seem sorta jumpy this mornin. Everything alright?" He asked with genuine concern.

Amy sat down at the kitchen table and took hold of Elijah's hand in both of hers.

"I'm alright, sugar." She suddenly felt a wave of nausea wash over her and started to retch.

Elijah was alarmed, thinking that perhaps she had come down with something.

"Was it somethin ya ate, honey? You're lookin a little flushed. What's goin on? Do you want me to send Elder to fetch Doctor Harley?" He felt her forehead for signs of fever.

"No baby, I'm not sick, and I don't need the doctor. I may need a little rest, but I'll be fine." She smiled as if holding an inner secret, and suddenly recognizing the familiarity of her symptoms, he looked at her piercingly.

"You're not…? Are you… ?" he didn't quite know how to ask without upsetting her.

Amy looked at him, then down at her belly, and simply nodded. She was several weeks late, and though she had taken a while after Eliza's birth to get back to normal, she had always been as regular as clockwork in her cycle. The nausea that came mostly in the mornings and then faded by the afternoon, and her craving for buttermilk biscuits were the confirmation that she was not just late for her period, she was in fact pregnant again.

Elijah looked at her in astonishment. "Are you sure? Are you really gonna have another baby?!" He grinned broadly, as secretly he was still hoping for a son, but had figured after the last pregnancy, given her surgery and his age, there would probably be no more children.

"Isn't it amazin?" she gushed, finally feeling free to smile back her pleasure. "I thought for sure after Eliza that there wouldn't be any more! But you remember that night?" she blushed at the recollection of their passionate lovemaking. "I was afraid you'd be upset, and didn't want to tell you, because it might mean another delay for your trip to Cincinnati!"

"Now how could I be upset with you when it was my doin too?" Elijah responded with a mixture of masculine pride and, simultaneously a disquieting recognition that in fact, this might delay their plans further. But after only a moment's pause, he continued with certainty, "Darlin, if God sees fit to grace us with this child, then seems to me we oughta be grateful, and just welcome one more to the family! But you gotta promise me you'll take care of yourself this time! We don't want you havin to go through the ordeal you went through with Eliza ever again!"

"I promise- but only if you agree you won't overdo it either! We can't have that big heart of yours givin out on us any time soon, you hear me? Your little boy's gonna need his Papa." She spoke with both affection and urgency, openly affirming his long held wish for a son of his own.

At that moment, Momma Celia came in from the garden carrying a basket of fresh cut herbs- dill, licorice, parsley, English thyme, marjoram, rosemary, oregano, basil, chamomile, and most fragrant of all, mint. Tying them in bunches and hanging them inverted on a rack near the stove, the smells perfuming the kitchen with a delicious medley of scents, she overheard the tail end of their conversation, and assured her daughter,

"Who said anything about Mister Elijah's heart givin out? I got me enough foxglove and chamomile to keep him in tea for a long time to come, hailstorm or no, so don't you worry!"

Elijah smiled, "God willin, I won't need your tea Momma, much as I appreciate it. You were right, it tastes awful!" he teased her.

"Mebbe so, but it sho kept you from leavin us, and don't ya forget it!" She countered with a playful twinkle in her eye. "Even Doctor Harley said so!" she added with pride, as if to trump any further doubt on the matter. "My grandma used to say, 'Don't have to taste good to be good for ya!'"

"Well then, ya'll's digitalis tea is the proof of that, Momma, and there's no denyin it!" Elijah acceded with a loving double entendre, proclaiming the curative powers of her nasty tasting tea.

Elijah turned to Amy with a quizzical eyebrow raised, cocking his head in Momma Celia's direction, uncertain whether his mother-in-law had heard the news.

Before she could even nod back, Momma Celia settled the matter.

"Now as happy as I am about ya'll givin me another grandbaby, both of ya'll're gonna have to be careful. Amy, sugar, after Eliza, this one might not be easy either, and ya'll need to save ya strength as best as ya can. You ain't no young girl no more. An Mister Elijah, sure as the sun come up, ya'll ain't no young buck!"

Elijah didn't know whether to flinch or laugh at his mother-in-law's inimitable candor reminding him of the passage of time but, pushing sixty, he knew she was right on both counts.

"As I see it (even if nobody asked me), ya'll'd best stay here, get whatever crop as grows to harvest, and rest up till the baby come. With all the ruckus round these parts bout South Carolina leavin the Union, and folks chasin after runaways with a vengeance, no tellin what might be brewin!"

Elijah and Amy's joy over the baby was instantly sobered by Momma Celia's surprising grasp of the political realities and their possible repercussions on the plantation. Elijah nodded in acknowledgement. "I suspect you're right about that, Momma, even though it galls me not to get on up to Cincinnati, at least to get the new will written."

"Time enough for writin wills later, Mister Elijah- ya'll got other things to tend to first! We all know ya want to get it done, don't ya worry none bout that- and we got faith that ya'll get it done too, but God got His own timetable, even if it don't match ya'll's! Best accept it!" she said with finality. There was no point in arguing. She was right.

XXXIX

Up in Cincinnati, James M. Gitchell was opening the morning mail in the law office he shared with his partner, John Jolliffe. One letter in particular caught his attention due to its unexpected return address. It was from one Elijah Willis, and the address was a plantation in Williston, Barnwell District, South Carolina.

"John! Have a look at this!" James exclaimed to his partner. John looked up over his glasses from perusing the morning paper, his eyebrows raised in curiosity.

"What's the surprise James? Mrs. O'Leary finally pay her bill?" he asked with a chuckle.

"No, of course not!" James replied with a mixture of ridicule and importunity. He thrust the letter over towards his partner, shaking it insistently until Jolliffe took it from him and began reading. Jolliffe's eyes widened steadily as he read. When he had finished, he sat back, the letter on the desk before him, took off his glasses, and rubbed his eyes.

"Remarkable!" was all he could think to say at first.

"Indeed it is! Monumentally so, in fact!" replied Gitchell. "Do you realize what this could mean? We might be able to assist in securing the liberation of an entire plantation's population of slaves!" He fairly crowed with enthusiasm.

"Clearly we must write to Mr. Willis right away, and encourage him to come see us at his earliest convenience!" agreed Jolliffe. "But we must be very careful not to scare him off by being over eager. I sense from his letter this is hardly an easy choice for him, and we must be sure he doesn't get cold feet because of an untoward word from us!"

Gitchell readily acknowledged his partner's superior tact, but could scarcely contain his pleasure at the prospect of helping not just a slave owner, but a slave owner in the most notoriously secessionist state in the nation, emancipate his slaves. The fact that some of them also happened to be his family made the case all the more interesting, and he rubbed his hands together in gleeful anticipation.

"Now James, I know that look in your eye! I forbid you to talk about this to our abolitionist friends! It would be a violation of attorney client privilege and a sore injustice to Mr. Willis, whom we have not even met yet, may I remind you?! Much as I realize how such a case could further the overall cause of emancipation, I really must insist! No press! No comments! At least, certainly not yet, not before we have even spoken with Mr. Willis directly!"

Mildly chagrined, but with enthusiasm undampened, Gitchell agreed. "Alright John. You're right, quite right, as usual. Forgive me, it's just that the odds of such a thing happening are so improbable that you must admit it is quite tantalizing to ponder the possible repercussions!"

Jolliffe nodded his head thoughtfully. "No doubt, but I for one am not entirely sure what all those consequences might be. Some may be unforeseen, and not necessarily what one might hope for. So let us take this thing slowly and carefully, and see what we can do to help our Mr. Willis, shall we?" He took out paper and pen and began composing a letter.

Mr. Elijah Willis
Willis Plantation
Williston, Barnwell District
South Carolina

My Dear Mr. Willis:

Thank you for your recent letter of inquiry expressing your interest in ascertaining our availability to help you in the drafting of a new will, with the purpose of the emancipation of certain slaves and the bequeathal to them of your worldly goods.

As you can imagine, such a request from a South Carolina planter is more than unusual for us; it is in fact unprecedented. In order to effectively provide you the services you require, therefore, we would like to make sure that we understand your desires thoroughly and accurately. It is also important that you understand the constraints of the law in the State of Ohio before you make a final determination to have the will written here, as those constraints will necessarily dictate the probate process following your eventual demise.

My partner and I would be more than happy to meet with you at your convenience to discuss the matter in greater detail.

As you will be traveling some considerable distance, no doubt you will be in need of lodging. Might we recommend to you the Broadway Hotel, here in Cincinnati? It is near our office, and we would be happy to make reservations for your lodgings in advance of your visit to spare you the inconvenience of having to search for them upon arrival. Simply advise us of your arrival date, and we will do the needful.

Very much looking forward to hearing from you in the near future, we remain

Sincerely yours,

John Jolliffe, Attorney at Law
James M. Gitchell, Attorney at Law

He signed the letter, and handed it to Gitchell for his counter-signature before folding and sealing it for posting.

"Well, this should be interesting! We'll see whether he follows through on it or not. I must admit, I'm quite curious to know the story behind this development. I never would have imagined such a request coming to us from South Carolina!" commented Jolliffe.

"The more I think about it, the more surprising it seems, given the furor that seems to be mounting among the acolytes of old John C. Calhoun, and their pro-slavery fulminations!" responded Gitchell. "I don't know when that racist son of a bitch finally died whether it was the merciful Lord who received him or the Devil himself, but God knows those whom he inspired certainly have taken up his cry for secession with a vengeance! I imagine things must feel pretty hot for a white man in love with a woman of color in that environment! Especially since our friend Mrs. Stowe's new book has stirred up so many passions!"

"No doubt. It must be truly dreadful for them- and for their children!" avowed Jolliffe, deeply aware of the human cost of such a dilemma. "One thing is clear though, with all due respect to Mrs. Stowe and the slaves she has interviewed, our Mr. Willis is no Simon Legree! He must be a man of considerable courage, fortitude, and heart to even attempt such a thing in the present climate. God willing, we will be able to help him achieve his goal!"

XL

Elijah received the letter from Messrs. Gitchell and Jolliffe with elation. He thanked the good Lord that another piece of the puzzle had fallen into place, despite the unexpected delays and complications. He resolved that he must share the good news with Angus Patterson, but his heart grew heavy at the thought of visiting hid old friend after their last encounter. The pain of watching Angus fade away was almost more than he could bear, so he found himself procrastinating about the visit, and yet longing for Angus' companionship and insight at the same time. Feeling the need to at least let someone in on the good news, he decided to share it with John Bauskett as soon as he was able, and the mere thought of the hale and hearty attorney in Barnwell helped assuage his anxiety over Angus Patterson's approaching demise, as if John would at least provide the continuity of empathy and understanding he so craved.

Such melancholy musings notwithstanding, Elijah swiftly fired off a grateful response to Messrs. Gitchell and Jolliffe in Cincinnati, affirming his determination to engage their services as legal counsel, but explaining that due to the unforeseen combined events of the hailstorm, the announcement that he was to be a father again, and the impending harvest, he was not yet in a position to make the trip Northward. He promised to keep in touch, and vowed that after the baby's birth he would most definitely head up to Cincinnati to see them and make the necessary arrangements. Expressing his appreciation for their attentiveness and their generous offer to make reservations for his lodging when the time came, he projected a probable travel time in the early Spring, and promised to keep them apprised of his plans and any new developments in the meantime.

His attention then turned to the annual ordeal of the cotton and timber harvests, and his desperate hope to fill his coffers against the probable costs and possible losses that his plans might entail. With the political climate becoming tenser by the day, he was increasingly fearful that a potential economic collapse brought about by a rash move by South Carolinians to secede from the Union could have a devastating impact on his ability to achieve the goals he and Amy had so assiduously set themselves to accomplish. He knew that if it came to a choice financially, he would have to opt for only providing for Amy and the family, rather than providing for any of the other slaves, and he prayed he would never have to justify such a choice to Amy.

Thanks to the hard work and quick response of everyone on the plantation to the hailstorm crisis, and their successful breeding of some higher yield plants, the cotton crop proved to be better than he had expected. His crew once again proved their mettle by getting the crop in before any other plantation, to everyone's delight. It was encouraging at least, that all their hard work had paid off, and once the last bale had been shipped off, Elijah gave everyone on the plantation a much deserved rest. Exhausted but content, he began to breathe a little easier, at least for the moment, and looked with hope toward the birth of another child. After three girls in a row, he couldn't help but pray it would be a boy.

XLI

On October 24th in Marshfield, Massachusetts, Daniel Webster, the last survivor of the triumvirate of statesmen that had helped define the young nation fell off his horse, smashed his head, and died of a cerebral hemorrhage. His end was fittingly dramatic, though cirrhosis of the liver might soon have taken him less sensationally anyway, after years of hard drinking. Mercurial and arrogant, he had been, nonetheless, incomparably eloquent when he wanted to be. The papers quoted his speech entitled "A Plea for Harmony and Peace" from March 7, 1850, given in defense of the Compromise he had worked so hard to confirm with his colleague, Henry Clay:

"Secession! Peaceable secession! Sir, your eyes and mine are never destined to see that miracle. The dismemberment of this vast country without convulsion! ... There can be no such thing as a peaceable secession. Peaceable secession is an utter impossibility... We could not separate the states by any such line if we were to draw it..."

Given the climate in Barnwell District and throughout the South, his words seemed to take on new and unintended meaning. South Carolinians took Webster's words, rightly enough, as a refutation of their beloved late champion, John C. Calhoun. The words remained the same now as then, of course, but the interpretation of them seemed to shift, as more and more Southerners appeared unfazed by the possibility that secession might not be attainable peaceably. It was attainable, nonetheless, and to most white folks in Barnwell, and throughout the South Carolina low country at least, that mattered more and more every day. In fact, it was starting to seem like a right good idea whose time had finally come, even if it might mean having to take a few blows to get it done!

South Carolinian white males had always been a bit prone to braggadocio. They tended to see themselves as the benchmark of virile independence, blended with the authority born of a long-honored tradition to which, curiously and paradoxically, they themselves seemed enslaved. So it was hardly surprising that men throughout the region, and most especially young men looking to prove themselves in the eyes of their families, sweethearts, and communities, showed no inhibition whatsoever in asserting their conviction that it was time to put both the coloreds and the Yankees in their place, once and for all. Such declarations were generally accompanied by generous infusions of whiskey and a great deal of enthusiastic whooping and hollering, which some were already designating with pride, "a rebel yell!"

Like the popular uproar at gladiatorial events in Ancient Rome, this boasting took on a certain sporting challenge, with bets being made over swigs of spirits as to how long it would take to whup the Yankee boys' asses and send them all packing back North with their tails between their legs, or more graphically with other body parts in their hands, or shoved somewhere the sun doesn't shine. Clearly, though the intensity of the boast was directly proportional to the amount of whiskey consumed, the value of the wager was in inverse proportion to the length of time projected for the victory to be accomplished.

Most naively agreed that it would be no more than a matter of weeks, or at most, a few months, before the secessionists triumphed by securing the safety of a new nation of Confederate States, dedicated to the preservation of the natural social order: the perpetual and inescapable enslavement of all people of color, and the endless bounty accruing to their white masters from their labors. For some reason they seemed to think this was a small thing, easily accomplished, that would simply allow them to continue the status quo. This would then assure their stability without any pesky interference from the North, who would presumably still need and buy their cotton as if nothing had happened at all, allowing the planters to continue to prosper!

Young ladies swooned in admiration for their handsome beaux's touted bravery, not to mention their dashing good looks in their imagined uniforms, and the whole area seemed to be just itching for the fight, as if it were preparing for a sporting event of epic proportions. In truth, these enthusiastic purveyors of what they deemed justifiable sedition in the name of preserving their Southern honor, were oblivious to the fact that Webster's words were already proving prophetic. The very convulsion of which he warned was, even now gaining momentum, like a tsunami too far out to sea to be noticed as anything more than a simple swell, but racing toward the oblivious shore with murderous and devastating speed, its impending damage unimaginable.

Elijah's nephews and young Angus Patterson wanted to stand up and be counted among the loyal defenders of South Carolinian values. They had grown up in political indifference, simply assuming themselves to be the inviolate presumptive heirs of all their parents and ancestors had accumulated to pass down to future generations, as if their private fiefdoms. It had only recently occurred to any of them that their assumption of birthright, if not totally ill-founded, was at least in peril. This constituted a rude awakening that clearly demanded of them some kind of action.

Living in rural South Carolina, with not a whole lot to do that wasn't already being done for them by menials in their parents' possession, these young men desperately needed a cause to give them a sense of identity beyond being the children of the ruling class. Secession, and the consequent opportunity to build a new nation more to their liking, seemed to fill the bill perfectly. After having resisted most schooling beyond learning their "three R's"- reading, riting, and 'rithmetic- they had developed a sudden interest in keeping up with the news, and flocked to Will Beazeley's store at the depot to get the most recent newspapers arriving from Columbia, Charleston, and even further afield.

Not only were they more interested in the news than ever before, it dawned on them that perhaps they should even get involved in politics themselves. The power of democracy- selectively limited to representing the ruling class of course- might actually provide them the means to thwart the efforts of people like Elijah Willis from shaking up the proper order of things, and altering the course of society in ways that it made them shudder to contemplate.

Angus Junior had been doing his homework. He had in fact succeeded in persuading his father, in his dotage, to begin to educate him in the law, and he had been assiduously reading the elder Patterson's volumes of case studies illustrating the complexities of its applications.

"Hey there, James," he commented one day when he and the Willis brothers were lounging on the porch of James' store, "I been readin up on the laws about emancipation here in South Carolina lately, like I promised."

He had James' and Michael's immediate attention.

"Did you know that it used to be fairly easy for a master to free a slave? Seems way back when, before we were born, some slave owners wanted to reward their favorite slaves for good service, and wanted to set em free! Give em a few acres to raise some food and live out their days!"

"Damn!" responded Michael. "What's the sense of that? If they served em so well, why not just let em keep servin? It'd be cheaper too! Slave gets the satisfaction that comes of doing somethin well, still gets fed til the day he dies, and the owner keeps his land!"

"Jesus, Michael, are you really that hard-hearted?" Angus asked, thinking of the love and loyalty of the aged Mary and how his father had freed her long ago, but she remained forever in his service by her own choice. James gave him a piercing look, not expecting what seemed to him such a nigra-lovin response, but said nothing.

"Hell, I'm just sayin, why deprive a nigra of the chance to do what he's so good at? It'd be like takin away the poor bastard's pride, wouldn't it?" Michael's mind was neither subtle nor deep in its understanding, but it was clever in devising plausible sounding excuses to justify the perpetual enslavement of those he considered born to be the property of his kind.

"Christ, Michael, you're missin the point!" exploded James, always the brighter of the two, and long frustrated by his brother's obtuseness. "So Angus-" he said, shifting his focus back to the younger Patterson, and curious as to where his argument was leading them, "you mean to tell me it's gotten harder to emancipate slaves?"

"Exactly!" answered Angus, "And, like I told ya'll before, the key is in gettin folks to petition the legislature up in Columbia to pass stricter laws. These days the only way to emancipate a slave in the Great State of South Carolina is to petition the General Assembly! So, logically the best way to make sure the slaves don't get emancipated oughta be to petition the General Assembly even more!"

"It's plain enough to see who'd win that battle, if we get folks round here to write their legislators! Hell, Robert Barnwell Rhett over in Barnwell is becomin a leadin voice for secession. If he can speak up, so can we!" proclaimed James.

"Damn right!" insisted Michael. "Why should he have all the fun!" he grinned. His smile had that disturbing mixture of arrogance and belligerent stupidity that seldom boded well for those disinclined to disturbing the peace.

"Seems to me," Angus interjected, aware of Michael's potential to be a loose cannon that could inadvertently end up undermining their efforts, "we should think this thing through carefully. It ain't enough to just make noise- we need a persuasive argument that will convince young and old alike, so we need to understand what's worked in the past- and what hasn't! We also need to find out who has the governor's ear, and start makin' contacts.

Maybe we should start over in Barnwell by contactin' Rhett himself?"

James might have been the instigator of the group, but it was rapidly becoming apparent that Angus was providing the brains. All of a sudden he seemed to be coming into his own, drawing on all that he had heard and learned from his father (which was considerably more than they or even he himself had realized). Lamentably, Angus seemed to be channeling it toward pure self-interest- a far less noble, but perhaps more easily attainable direction than his father's true love of justice. Happy to accommodate that trajectory, however, James quickly realized he needed to encourage Angus and yet keep him under his control too. Cynical by nature, he recognized Angus' thirst for approval, and understood instinctively that slaking that thirst was his best means of making sure the younger Mr. Patterson did his bidding.

"Why Angus, you truly amaze me! That's a Hell of an idea!" James extolled. Angus seemed to fairly glow with pleasure at this long sought sign of approval.

James continued, "I think you might really be on to somethin there! Why, we could start up a petition, or maybe even a local political party, and go around gettin everyone we know to join us- tell em we understand their feelins and values, and want to help make sure their voice is heard up in Columbia!"

Angus chimed in, "Yeah, I mean, if we actually do end up secedin, we'd be in a position to help set the right course! After all, our daddies aren't gonna be runnin the show forever! It'll be our turn soon. We'd best make the most of it!" Angus' insecurities revealed much about his yearning, having more to do with his relationship with his father than any political position or doctrine. But James and Michael, each in their own way, suffered from the same affliction, and so were readily in agreement with him.

Feeling bolstered by the prospect of securing their parent's admiration, they broke out a bottle of whiskey to celebrate their political debut. They pondered giving themselves a name befitting their revolutionary spirit, a name that would embody their energy, their values, and their roots.

"How about The Williston Wildcats?" suggested Michael.

Angus shook his head. "Sounds too much like a bunch a good ole boys on a binge. We need somethin more serious!"

"What about The Southern Sons of Liberty?" suggested James.

Michael objected, "With all due respect to Daddy, I'm sick and tired a bein just somebody's son!" Angus and James nodded in agreement.

"How about The Barnwell Tea Party?" offered Angus.

James objected, "Sounds too much like the Boston Tea Party, and I don't want us bein' associated with any damn Yankees, even if they did do a good thing helpin us some, back in the Revolutionary War." James' grasp of history was clearly geocentric and more or less limited to his conception of South Carolina as the center of his universe.

"What d'ya'll think about The Proper Order Party?" suggested Angus, by now the whiskey starting to slur his speech. The other two sat nodding, glassy-eyed, staring off the veranda, each imagining his own scenarios of political and social success awaiting them. James smiled, Michael belched softly. Unable to agree on a definitive name, but, thanks to the whiskey, no longer caring, the three ended up just drinking deeply, and feeling the pleasurable warmth of the whiskey infuse them with the contentment of embarking upon an adventure that might at last earn them fame and fortune.

At the very least, it would garner them the enthusiastic support of like minded folks in the area, who were scared to death that Yankee ideas of abolition might get to the nigras and lead to the eruption of a full fledged uprising they'd be hard pressed to stop. Some folks around Barnwell still remembered the horrifying news from Virginia twenty years back, when Nat Turner killed his master and led a rebellion that resulted in the deaths of at least fifty-seven whites. Even though Turner had been caught and executed for his crimes, the memory of the revolt hung like a nightmare, lurking in the shadows of the minds of the folks in Barnwell District like a bogeyman waiting to pounce on innocent children in the dark.

XLII

Harriet Beecher Stowe was a former school teacher from Connecticut who had moved with her family to Cincinnati, where her father became the head of Lane Theological Seminary. Just as the boyhood experience of river life in Hannibal, Missouri inspired the writing of Samuel Clemens, her more famous Connecticut compatriot from Hartford, Harriet's move to Cincinnati and her experience of the thriving life of the Ohio River's busy commerce throughout slave territory provided her much inspiration. It also gave her access to many abolitionists aiding the Underground Railroad, and to a number of runaway slaves as well. Her husband, Calvin Stowe, was an ardent supporter of the Railroad. There was a steady stream of runaways from across the river in Kentucky whom they helped on their way to freedom in Canada, for unfortunately, the Fugitive Slave Act had assured that fugitives could not merely stay in Ohio even though free by Ohio law, for the slave owners had been empowered to track them down even in slave-free states.

Harriet had interviewed Josiah Henson, a slave who had escaped from a tobacco plantation in Bethesda, Maryland and fled to Canada, where he willingly received fellow fugitives and helped them establish a new life there. She was always eager to hear the first-hand stories of others who had escaped this most odious condition too. Her growing passion for the abolition of slavery seemed to run in the family, for her father and brothers, all well-known preachers, frequently held forth on the evils of slavery and the Christian obligation to abolish such bondage forever as a necessary part of God's work of salvation for the whole human race.

Clothed in righteousness and sympathy for their tales of horrific suffering and inhumanity, and thereby moved to share these compelling stories of runaway slaves in the fervent conviction that it was part of God's higher purpose, Harriet conceived her novel.

Writing it in sections, in the unabashedly melodramatic style of the day- popular especially in what sophisticates deemed the "lesser" literature penned by female authors- Harriet had started publishing *Uncle Tom's Cabin* as a series in the *National Era*, a leading abolitionist publication, back in June of 1851. Unlike Cassius Clay's *True American*, which had promulgated gradual emancipation in emphatic tones, but with measured legal and constitutional argument, the New Era was shamelessly and fervently abolitionist, and made no bones about cravenly appealing to the emotional and moral proclivities of all those who would give ear to their cause. If tending to the inflammatory and histrionic, that was deemed no more than an appropriate expression of the publishers' righteous thirst for justice. The appearance of *Uncle Tom's Cabin*, to Harriet's surprise and the abolitionists' delight, was successful beyond all imagining and spread like wildfire, igniting the passions of supporters and opponents alike.

In March of 1852, a month before the last of the serial publication in the *National Era* came out, a New York publisher, John Jewett, issued 300,000 copies of *Uncle Tom's Cabin* that sold out quickly and took the bold step of reprinting it in a less expensive format to cash in on the book's outrageous popularity. This made Harriet's success an instant and unheard of phenomenon in the literary world, setting a precedent for the publication of first edition clothbound and subsequent paperbound volumes that would become a profitable norm. Who could possibly have foretold that less than a decade hence, the newly elected Abraham Lincoln, fighting to preserve the Union would ask her, "So you are the little woman who wrote the book that started this big war?"

If Harriet Beecher Stowe had quickly become the darling of the North with the best-selling book of the times, next to the Bible, the reaction to her writing in the South was the complete opposite. One bookseller down in Mobile, Alabama was run out of town for selling it. Harriet even received a threatening letter with a package containing the severed ear of a slave! Southern novelists issued rebuttals, penning revisionist responses as a sort of counter-novel to her damning narrative. It inspired her to publish a second volume, *A Key to Uncle Tom's Cabin*, an annotation in which she argued the cause more deeply. Southern writers were particularly incensed by what they deemed her utter falsification of Southern life- a life of which she had no personal experience whatsoever- and her flagrant disregard for the virtues of the institution upon which they depended. Passions were fanned into a fire of rage against this presumptuous Yankee, and a woman no less, who dared criticize their life-style. Nor was this antagonism limited to literary circles.

"Damn! Did ya'll hear about that Yankee woman writin a novel about the cruelty of slavery? Never set foot on a plantation in her life!" James remarked in disgust as he read a paper from Charleston one morning. He, Michael and Angus had stopped at the depot to pick up supplies for the store. James had become a regular customer of Will Beazeley's, as Will always received the shipment of newspapers from the capital, and all over the region.

"Who in Hell does she think she is?!" retorted Michael, who increasingly seemed to speak in one of two modes- bellicose or braggadocio. "It's bad enough a Yankee'd write such a thing, but a woman to boot? Now that's just plain wrong!"

"Well, wrong or not, her book's sellin like hotcakes up North! Some publisher in New York had 300,000 copies printed, and seems folks just can't get enough of it! Even been made into a play! They say people in the theaters are cryin' out loud to see the nigras sufferin' so!" said Angus with a mixture of irritation and admiration.

"Well it burns my ass to hear some damn Yankee goin' on about how hard the slaves got it down here. Shit! Look at Uncle Elijah's nigras! Hell, they live better than some white folks I know! Gettin people down here all riled up with her lies!" James swore incoherently to himself, fuming.

"Ya'll know if anybody round here's sellin it?" Asked Michael.

Barnwell District was hardly known as a hotbed of literary ferment, or a place of pilgrimage for bibliophiles, but that was not to say the population was entirely illiterate. There were any number of folks in the area, especially the well-bred young ladies with time on their hands, prone to wiling away the hours reading out loud to each other at barbecues or evening soirees. Ever fashion-conscious, they often looked for the latest publications, priding themselves on being up to date with popular literature.

James realized the potential danger in this. "Boys, I don't rightly know where folks get their books around here, not bein that much of a reader myself. I don't recall any bookstores in the area, but I'll tell you one thing. There's a lot of impressionable young ladies in these parts who should never be allowed to get their hands on such vile tales as this Miz Stowe's been writin'! We oughta do somethin to make sure they don't!"

Angus brightened. "James, why not use this as an opportunity to launch our new party's efforts? If folks come to see us as the protectors of their rights and values, Hell, we might even be able to get ourselves elected to the General Assembly!"

"Why bother goin to all the trouble of gettin elected? Shoot, we can just let folks know that readin Yankee trash like that *Uncle Tom's Cabin* is unpatriotic, and anybody caught with it might wish they hadn't been- if ya'll know what I mean!" said Michael with a vicious leer, far more ready to take on the role of the ruffian than the politician.

James thought a moment. "Both of ya'll got a point! We don't need to actually get elected to have an influence on what happens around here. But if all we do is rough up a few book buyers, that ain't gonna amount to much. What we gotta do is help people see how dangerous that abolitionist shit really is. So we need to organize a campaign- and Angus is right that if we do it in the name of our new party, we'll be killin two birds with one stone!"

Angus chimed in, "We can start by askin Will Beazely to keep his eyes open for anyone sendin away for the book to either New York, where that publisher fella is, or Cincinnati. I hear this Stowe woman lives up there, and been helpin runaways from Kentucky! So we keep an eye on the mail and keep our ears open for any rumors about anyone readin anything that might be considered abolitionist." James nodded approvingly, impressed with Angus' strategic thinking.

"That's a real good idea, Angus!" he affirmed. Angus once again beamed with pleasure at the recognition.

"And James," Angus continued, flush with his companion's encouragement, "my Pa told me that up in Maryland they passed a law makin it illegal to write, publish, or distribute any abolitionist ideas of any kind. Maybe we should see if the General Assembly up in Columbia's got anything on the books like that here, and if not, well, that might be another opportunity for us to get our voices heard!"

"Damn, boy, now you're really thinkin smart!" crowed James, Michael nodding enthusiastically in confirmation.

"Gentlemen, it seems we have a plan. Let's get to work!" James concluded.

XLIII

When James Willis approached Will Beazely to find out if anyone around Williston was writing to Cincinnati, he was not expecting to discover that his Uncle Elijah had. Mr. Beazely, of course, ignorant of the sinister intent of James and his companions, readily avowed his admiration for Elijah.

"That uncle of yours sure is a smart one! Told me he was makin business contacts to ship his lumber out West, to try to cash in on all the construction, as folks start settlin in the prairies. Figured as the end of the B&O Railroad line, it'd be a good idea to find someone to represent him there!"

This of course was total news to the Willis brothers, but it was plausible. Elijah had always shown a better head for business than anyone else in the family, and this sounded like a scheme he might well have cooked up. But knowing that he had at least been thinking about emancipating Amy and her family, James in particular suspected Elijah was not telling Will the whole story.

"Well, is that so? Leave it to Uncle Elijah to come up with some new idea of how to get richer!" James commented. "He didn't say anything about orderin anything from Cincinnati though, did he?"

Mr. Beazely looked puzzled. "Why would he do that? As far as I know, all he intends to do is sell his lumber up there!" Clearly James was barking up the wrong tree if he suspected Elijah of ordering a copy of Uncle Tom's Cabin, so he let it go.

"Will, did ya'll hear about that Yankee woman wrote a book against slavery?" Angus asked.

"Seems to me I recall seein somethin in the paper to that affect, but, Hell, I didn't pay it much attention, to tell the truth. I just figured no one round here would care about what some Yankee woman said, anyway!"

"Well, you're probly right about that, Will. But some folks round here, especially our women folk, shouldn't even be exposed to such trash! We wouldn't want to sully their Southern virtue, now would we?" James asked insinuatingly.

"Well, no! I hadn't really thought about that, but you're surely right, James! You don't suppose any of them are thinkin of orderin the book do you?" Will gave a little shudder in recognition that such venomous writings could inadvertently pass through his depot; the thought was disturbing.

"I don't rightly know, Will. Lord knows I hope not, but you know how the ladies can be sometimes, always eager to be up on the latest fashions and fads!" James continued. "I could see that in their innocence, they might send away for it, without realizin the damage it could do them. I mean, think of it! Who would want any of our women readin about the exaggerated cruelties this Yankee from Cincinnati has been spewin forth in that book! Why it makes my heart bleed for them, to even contemplate such a violation of their innocence, fillin their poor heads with her lies!"

By now Will was looking rather alarmed at the prospect, not only for the potential damage to the fair ladies of Williston, but for the disquieting possibility that he might be considered an accomplice in their downfall! It also struck him as disturbing that a man whom he admired as much as Elijah might be doing business with folks in a city where such a venomous book could be written. He had no idea that Cincinnati was not only a gateway to the West but also a hotbed of abolitionism, but surely not everyone there was so rabidly misguided?

Presuming that Will would play into his hands precisely as he had hoped, James then attempted to deliver his coup de grace, "So now, Will, you'll keep an eye out for such things won't you? For the sake of our community and our sacred values here in South Carolina, we need to keep an eye out on anything goin to or comin from Cincinnati or New York from here. We don't want any abolitionist trash poisoning the minds of folks here in Barnwell District!"

Despite the Willis boys' menacing innuendo, Will still could not bring himself to believe that there was any such serious danger, much less that Elijah would be involved in such a thing. His admiration for Elijah seemed better deserved than trusting entirely in the opinions of Elijah's poorer relations, who he could see had ulterior motives. He was not, in fact, such a fool as the Willis brothers seemed to think.

He also knew, both from seeing Elijah with his family and from his own experience of black folks, that hating or fearing them, especially when they had raised and cared for a good many of the white children in town, didn't seem to make much sense. But he did not want to alienate or aggravate the Willis brothers and Angus Junior either- for they were good customers and this was a small town, where one paid dearly for creating enemies, especially enemies who were clearly inclined to taking it out on the offender!

"Don't ya'll fret. If I see anything worrisome, I'll let ya'll know." He deliberately avoided defining for them what he considered worrisome, hoping that the ambiguity would satisfy them and let him off the hook.

Michael grinned his lupine grin, "I knew we could count on ya, Will!" and the newly minted and self-appointed Three Musketeers of Williston went off, assuming they had just struck a blow for the cause of preserving the virtue and purity of the women of Barnwell District. This, they deemed, was an important first step in their campaign to win the support of the local populace for their political ambitions.

Will Beazely watched as the three of them rode off and, feeling vaguely uncomfortable, wondered whether he shouldn't let Elijah know what they were up to.

XLIV

Much as the Willis boys and Angus Junior would have loved to get up a counter-petition and march it right on up to the General Assembly in Columbia in person to thwart Elijah's alleged intention to emancipate Amy and her family, to do so would first require Elijah to petition the legislature for his family's freedom. They needed to find out if such a petition had been filed, so Angus Junior took it upon himself to ask Robert Barnwell Rhett to ascertain this. To his and the Willis brother's surprise and disappointment, they found that Elijah had not yet petitioned the legislature for any such thing, (nor would he ever, realizing that it would be futile, though they had no way of knowing that).

Since no such petition had been made, they decided in the meantime it was best to focus on their campaign against the promulgation of abolitionist literature of any kind as the means to establish their political voice in the area. They decided to hold a rally to drum up support, and needed to find someone willing to help host such an event.

"I got an idea!" said James to his companions. "What about askin Dr. Guignard and that friend of his, Frederick Matthews? They're well-respected and would give the gatherin a feelin of legitimacy!"

Angus responded, "That's a good idea, James! Gettin some of the leadin citizens behind us will make folks take us seriously!"

"Oh, they're gonna take us seriously alright, and if they don't, they'll wish they had!" insisted Michael, gesticulating with his fists his usual preference for communicating his convictions.

"Aw, shut up Michael! Don't you get it? This ain't about some barroom brawlin! We're lookin to make ourselves a reputation that'll give us real power- power to do and change things around here!" James was not averse to unleashing his brother if needed, but knew that their ultimate success would depend on a lot more than big talk and muscle flexing.

"Shut up yourself, James! Think you're such a damn know it all! I'm not as dumb as ya think. I'm tellin ya'll, it's gonna take more than speech makin to get this done, and I'm ready, willin, and able to provide the muscle to back it up- that's all I'm sayin!"

"Knock it off, you two!" interjected Angus, with annoyance. "We need both of ya'll to stay focused, and stop yer bickerin. Jesus! Ya'll're like a couple of cocks fightin in a barnyard, and don't even get that if you're not careful, you could both end up bein someone's dinner, no matter which one wins!"

This surprising show of force from Angus caught both brothers by surprise. They realized he was right, though it sort of peeved James that his protégé had challenged him.

"Well damned if you didn't grow a pair, Angus! Never heard you speak up like that before! You're probly right though- we do need to focus on gettin this rally together! Why don't you go talk to Dr.Guignard, and I'll talk to old man Matthews. If we can get them to back us, they'll bring most of the other planters along too, I reckon," responded James.

"Before we go talkin to anybody, we'd best figure out what we're askin for. It won't look good if we look like we don't have any idea of what we're doin!" insisted Angus.

"We need to let them know we want to protect Barnwell District from any abolitionist ideas, and get up a petition to send up to Columbia for the legislature to make it illegal to write, publish, or distribute them here in South Carolina at all. That'll include trash like that *Uncle Tom's Cabin* and anything else any self-righteous Yankee do-gooder can come up with!" proclaimed James vehemently.

"Well, shouldn't we write up a petition then, if what we're askin is for folks to sign it?" observed Michael. Despite his bravado, he had a gift for pointing out the things that were so obvious they could be easily overlooked.

"You got a point there, Michael," James acknowledged, to appease his younger brother. "Angus, why don't you write up the petition? You're better with words than we are," James delegated. He hated having to admit his own inferiority, but his sense of power was such that he knew a good commander didn't have to know everything to be able to be effective, he just needed to know how to delegate to whomever was best qualified for the task at hand. Angus, of course, was thrilled to get the acknowledgment and eagerly agreed.

"I'll get right on it!" He decided to go home and look in his father's library to see how other petitions had been worded, eager to sound as legal and professional as possible to make the right impression both on the Willis brothers and on folks like Dr. Guignard.

"I think I'm gonna head on home and work on it- I'll see ya'll later!" he added. With that, he jumped off the porch and mounted his horse, cantering off towards town, wondering how he might get his father to help him without revealing his purpose. His father had even served in the General Assembly years ago, so he figured he could just ask him about how he went about writing up legislation in general, and that would give him all the clues he needed to write their petition.

When he got home, he immediately went to his father's library and began rifling through his law books to find examples of petitions. Angus Senior heard him rustling around and, his curiosity aroused, made his way slowly and painfully downstairs to see what the boy was up to. Angus Junior had been so absorbed in his search he didn't hear his father's labored steps until he was almost at the door. He looked up to see his father leaning against the door jamb, panting for breath.

"Pa! Are you alright?" he asked, jumping up, even more alarmed by his father's fragile appearance than by his unexpected arrival.

Angus wheezed in response, "What're you up to, son? I heard you rustlin around like ya were desperate for somethin, and it concerned me."

Angus Junior hastened to his father's side and led him gently to his chair. "Sit down, Pa, you're winded," he said solicitously. His father's question still hung in the air, unanswered. The younger Patterson desperately tried to think of a plausible answer.

"I didn't mean to disturb you, Pa! I just been thinkin about all the years you been lawyerin, and your service in the General Assembly too, and realized that I never really paid much attention to what it was ya did, or how ya did it. I felt kinda ashamed, to tell the truth, so I thought maybe if I studied more of your books here, I might be able to learn to make a difference myself!" His answer was at least partially true, and the old man softened to hear it. Fact was, Angus Senior had been longing as much for his son to want what he had to offer as the son had been longing for his father's approval. This seemed to be a watershed moment for the both of them.

"It pleases me to hear ya say that, son. Fact is, I've been wantin to pass my knowledge on to ya for a long time, but it didn't seem like ya were interested, or even ready. So what is it ya want to know?" the old man asked.

"Well, I was thinkin about how government and the law go hand in hand, right?"

His father nodded expectantly. "I don't quite understand just how that works. So let's say a group of people think there oughta be a law about somethin, but it's kinda local- not everybody in the State has expressed this idea. How do ya get the General Assembly to make a new law?"

"Well, that's a good question, son. There're a couple of ways ya can go about it. One way is to talk to your legislators directly. Try to get em interested, or persuade em that there is actually a need for such a law. If ya can do that, the legislator can propose a bill- usually after gettin at least a few others in the General Assembly to join him, to make it more persuasive." Angus Junior nodded attentively. "If it gets to the floor of both chambers and gets voted on and passed, it then goes to the governor, who has the final word. The governor usually signs into law any bill passed by both houses. Course, he also has the right to veto it- in which case it either goes back to the legislature for them to correct the parts the governor didn't accept, or it simply doesn't become a law."

"Well, I sorta figured that much, Pa, but you said there was another way too, didn't ya?" Angus Junior knew perfectly well that petitioning the General Assembly was a possibility, but didn't actually know how it was done.

"Yes, I did! It's possible for an individual or a group of interested citizens, to present a petition directly to the General Assembly. It doesn't necessarily mean the legislature will take it up, but if there is a pressing issue that requires government approval, or if there is a significant number of citizens advocating for a particular cause, it will generally be debated in the General Assembly and then voted on, either yea or nay. Sometimes it may even be put up in a referendum for all the voters in the state to decide at the next general election." Angus Junior continued to nod thoughtfully.

"So is there a particular form petitions have to take, or can folks just say, 'We want thus and such'?" he asked after a pause, hoping he would not seem too eager or obvious to make his father suspicious.

"Well now, generally speakin, it starts with something like, 'I (or we) the undersigned do hereby petition the General Assembly of the Great State of South Carolina for...' and then the petitioner or petitioners explain what they want the legislature to do, or approve, or prevent. It generally has to include some sort of well-argued reason for why the legislature should approve it- what are the benefits of approval, and what the negative impact of failure to approve it might be." He then added, "Then they sign it at the bottom, with a 'I/we do hereby set our hand and seal to this petition in such and such a place, on such and such day of such and such month, in the year of our Lord One thousand eight hundred and whatever.' And that's about it!"

"Thanks Pa! I gotta admit, it's pretty interestin when you start thinkin about what makes a government a democracy, and how the people's voice gets heard!"

The old man lit up enthusiastically. "Democracy is a powerful and a beautiful thing, son, and somethin to be cherished. But it isn't always easy, cause folks don't always agree on what the government ought and ought not do, or what laws should and should not be passed. It's somethin of a paradox that the majority in a democracy may win, but is not always right!" He let that hang in the air a moment before driving the point further home. "People can be sincerely wrong sometimes, and petition for the wrong thing, or pass bad laws. Time will tell. Good thing is, the law can be repealed or changed to adapt to changin times and situations. Sometimes it takes time for people to see that what's right and best for em isn't always what makes em comfortable!"

Angus Junior couldn't help but wonder if his father suspected what he was up to, and was trying to warn him before writing his petition. He felt a tad uncomfortable, to tell the truth, but his eagerness to make a reputation for himself, and to win the admiration of the Willis brothers – not to mention folks in Barnwell District- was overriding his conscience in listening to his father's advice. All he could think to say was, "Thanks Pa, for sharing with me. It means a lot to me."

Feeling that on some level at least, his son was telling the truth, and hoping he would take the lesson to heart, the old man was satisfied. Father and son then heard a shuffling in the corridor, and Mary appeared in the doorway.

"Mister Angus! What ya'll doin comin downstairs without no hep? I musta dozed off upstairs, but when I woke up and saw you gone, I like about to have a fit! Skeered the daylights outa me! I as worried you'd done fallen down the stairs or somethin! I couldn't ne'er fagive mysef if ya'll got hurt cause I wan't there to hep ya!"'

"Now Mary, don't ya go gettin all riled up. I'm fine. Truly! I was just havin a good talk with my son here." The old man smiled with pleasure. Angus Junior felt a little guilty about using his father, but at the same time genuinely savored the feeling that at last his father was pleased with him. He smiled too. Mary looked at them both and thought to herself, 'The boy's playin his daddy like a fiddle, sure as anything, but I ain't gonna upset Mister Angus in his condition by tellin him so! I just pray the boy don't break the old man's heart!' She said nothing to Angus Junior, who instantly felt the suspicion in her silence.

Mary turned to the elder Patterson and said, "Well, now that ya'll're down here, might as well head on into the dinin room for supper!" The old man nodded with pleasure and now allowed her to help him down the hall, Angus Junior trailing behind, his mind already intent on how to word their petition. Having been deflected from his reading of the South Carolina Statutes by his father's unexpected arrival, he had failed to notice that there was already legislation on the books dating from 1820, prohibiting the publication or dissemination of any abolitionist materials, rendering their petition, in fact, redundant.

XLV

As Christmas rolled around again, Elijah reconsidered whether to invite any family over, given the extreme discomfort they had all felt the year before and the growing tensions clearly visible with his nephews. Amy being pregnant again, he had the dual concern of not upsetting her unduly and of not being able to hide her condition from his judgmental family, if they were to stop by.

"Sugar, why don't you go pay them a visit this year? Ya'll can bring em a gift- say a ham, or something from the plantation. Ya'll can say your Merry Christmases, and we can avoid all that nastiness of them comin over here and judgin us all!" Amy suggested one morning, as Momma Celia was baking molasses and ginger cookies for the Holiday. The sweet smells of brown sugar, cinnamon, nutmeg, ginger, allspice and cloves filled the house with a delicious warmth.

"That's a good idea, darlin! Sure would make things easier on all of us!" Elijah responded willingly.

Momma Celia added, "Lord knows that's the truth! And that way maybe we can avoid ya'll havin another episode with your heart! We gotta keep ya'll from gettin all worked up bout your relations, Elijah. Best Christmas present you could give us!" Everyone noticed that for the first time, Momma Celia had called Elijah by his name without the honorific "Mister."

Amy and Elijah readily agreed. It was a relief not to have to prepare for the invasive presence of Elijah's relatives descending on the plantation, and everyone seemed to experience more Holiday cheer as a consequence of this decision. The girls were enthusiastically putting colorful bows on the garlands they were making from magnolia leaves and pine branches, the boys laid in extra supplies of firewood, Momma Celia was baking up a storm, and Elijah and Amy indulged in savoring the Holidays, unencumbered by outside social obligations. But it was a fragile illusion, like a beautiful soap bubble that would float delightfully for a while, and then suddenly burst, leaving nothing but a sticky hollow ring where it had landed as a reminder of its vanished beauty. Elijah suspected that by visiting his family, the bubble would likely burst.

Things had started well enough. His brother Jimmy greeted him at their door with seeming affection, no doubt made the more heart-felt by his relief that Elijah had none of his illegitimate family in tow. His sister-in-law made an effort to be courteous and invited him into the front parlor for mulled wine and holiday goodies before adjourning to the dining room for Christmas Eve dinner. Even James and Michael seemed to be on their best behavior, chatting affably with him, their sister, and her husband over glasses of mulled wine before the crackling fireplace.

The veneer of their civility, however, started to come unglued with every additional glass of wine, and the mean-spirited underlying attitudes of his relations, particularly his sister-in-law and the younger Willises, started to show like the cheaper, rougher wood underlying the polished veneer marquetry of a table top showing its wear and tear.

Elijah's niece, Eliza, had married A.P. Bogacki, a Polish immigrant eager to better himself, presuming that marrying into the Willis family would secure his future. He was by nature, opportunistic, a bit crass and, like her brothers James and Michael, over-fond of drinking. A.P. had by now consumed a copious quantity of mulled wine, and loosening his tongue, to everyone's horror, spoke up to Elijah in rapidly deteriorating English.

"So vat is like to fuck black voman, eh? Is better than vite voman?" he leered at Elijah with bloodshot eyes. Eliza turned beet red with embarrassment, not only at her husband's inappropriate questions, but at the unsettling thought that anyone, including her husband, might think such a lascivious thing was possible. She felt polluted by the very thought of it.

"A.P.! Well I never!" spluttered Eliza, looking desperately to her mother or father to intervene.

Michael and James started giggling uncontrollably, and took another generous swig of the mulled wine. Elijah blanched at first, stunned that his niece's husband could surpass even his own worst fears of social interaction with the family, as if expressing the question they had all secretly wanted to ask, but wouldn't dare. And then he felt the blood rise to his face in a fury that took his breath away and left him momentarily speechless.

His brother Jimmy, noting Elijah's color rise and attempting to salvage some dignity from the ashes of this debacle, spoke up. "That's about enough of that, A.P.! I won't have that kinda language in my house, you hear me? You gonna talk like that, you'd best go on home, and don't come back til you've sobered up!" Eliza was reduced to sobs of shame, feeling unfairly banished by her husband's blunder. Her mother was patting her soothingly, trying to reassure her everything would be alright.

"Now sweetheart, don't you fret! It was just the wine talkin, that's all! Mulled wine will go to your head! But isn't it just like a man to ask such things! After all, you can't hardly blame A.P. for being curious- I bet that question's been asked by a lot a folks! He shouldn't have said it, it was truly very rude, but I'm sure your Uncle Elijah will get over it in time!" She looked reproachfully at Elijah, almost as if it was his fault her son-in-law had committed such a gross breach of etiquette. After all, if Elijah hadn't taken Amy as his concubine in the first place, the subject would never have come up and ruined their Christmas!

James and Michael, quite drunk themselves by now, were actually disappointed that Elijah hadn't answered their brother-in-law's question. "Well, Uncle Elijah, it's a fair enough question. I'm sure we'd all like to know your answer!" declared James.

His father shot the boys a warning look, but it was too late. "That's right! Come on, Uncle Elijah, tell us what is it like with that nigra woman a yours?" echoed Michael with a surly edge in his voice.

At this point Elijah could stand it no more. He set down his glass on the mantelpiece slowly and deliberately, and glaring at the younger Willises, announced, "Well, I'll tell you one thing, not that it's any of your business, but it's a damn sight more pleasant than being with any of ya'll!" He could bring himself to say no more- to the horrified gasps of his niece and sister-in-law and the stunned disbelief of his nephews. He immediately hated himself for stooping to their level, but it also felt good to tell the truth, and stop playing this ridiculous game of avoidance! Elijah's brother, Jimmy, even more disquieted by his family's behavior than by his brother's revelation, was at a complete loss for words to mend the tear in the family fabric.

Elijah stood facing the family, looked at his brother and, forcing himself to control his temper, simply said in an even voice, "No need to bother- I'll see myself out!" He added with an acerbic tone to the rest of the family, gaping at him with open-mouthed incredulity, "Merry Christmas!" walked out of the house without another word, mounted Beauty, and headed back home.

As he rode home, his head and heart were pounding with the wrenching reality that, for all his attempts at maintaining some semblance of family peace, his white relations were truly poisonous. Silent tears ran down his cheeks, stinging in the winter night air. A wave of depression consumed him as he trotted up the long road to the plantation house. The lights inside, glowing in what should have felt like a warm welcome, failed to cheer him as he dismounted and called for Elder to take Beauty to the stable.

Elder came running out of the house, hearing a distressing tone in his father's voice. "Papa, you alright? What happened over at your brother's house? Was it that bad?"

Elijah looked at the boy, almost a man, and the contrast between Elder's solicitous behavior, and the cruelty and insensitivity of his brother's family, jolted him out of his melancholy.

"To tell the truth, son, it was worse than I could possibly have imagined!" was all he could manage to say before handing Elder the reins. "Take her out to the stable and unsaddle her for me, will you? I need to go talk to your mother."

Elder nodded silently, feeling Elijah's pain, and wondering whether whatever had happened was going to make things even harder for them.

When Elijah came inside, Amy was waiting for him. She looked up anxiously when he walked into the parlor, worry written all over her face.

"How did it go?" she asked, almost afraid to hear the answer, but knowing with one glance at her husband that it hadn't gone well.

"It was truly God-awful!" Elijah replied with a groan, as he slumped down onto the settee beside her. "It started off well enough, everybody play-acting at bein polite and all. But once the boys had drunk enough, the whole thing just went straight to Hell, and they started showin their true colors! *In vino veritas*, as they say!"

Amy shuddered involuntarily- having no trouble at all imagining the kinds of comments that must have spilled out.

"So what did they say, and what did you do? Come on, honey, get it off your chest!" she urged, after a pregnant pause.

Elijah proceeded to tell her about A.P.'s crude remarks, his brother's reprimand, his sister-in-law's defensive comments to Eliza, and the goading by James and Michael.

"So I ended up tellin em that being with you was a damn sight more pleasant than bein with any of them!" In the retelling, Elijah was able to feel a wry smile of satisfaction creep across his face as he remembered his family's scandalized reaction. "They like about to mess their drawers in horror at that little piece of truth! Then I walked out on em, plain and simple." Putting the tragi-comedic behavior of his relations in perspective, his mood began to lighten.

Amy didn't know whether to laugh or cry at the image of the Willis family sitting open-mouthed around the fireplace in shock that Elijah finally told them the obvious truth that had remained unspoken until then. What a blow that must have been to their precarious sense of self-worth, she thought!

"I gotta admit, I hurt pretty bad on the way home," Elijah confessed, "but you know what, darlin? I almost feel relieved now! It was sorta like lancin a festerin boil, and drainin out the pus. Much as it hurt, it made it real clear that I don't want to keep playin this damn game with them any more! The sad fact is, though my brother still harbors some trace of fraternal affection for me, and I can feel that, he hasn't the balls to deal with the rest of his family, and they're a bunch of cowardly, mean-spirited, poison tongued rattlesnakes who'd sooner strike than look at ya! I've had enough! I won't put myself or ya'll through that anymore!"

Amy put her arm comfortingly around her husband's waist and patted him on the arm reassuringly with her other hand. "Remember sugar, your real family is the one in this house, whatever those fools think or say, and we all love ya!"

Elijah turned to her, seeing the love in the light in her eyes, and hearing it in the warm timbre of her voice, that reality cleansed him of the filth of his encounter at his brother's house. Nodding in acknowledgement, he placed his forehead against hers, as if trying to absorb the healing goodness of her thoughts, a single large tear rolling slowly down his cheek in silent gratitude.

Recovering himself, he spoke up at last. "God only knows what they'll stir up now! But the devil take em! We just have to keep it together a little longer, til after the baby comes, and then I'm off to Cincinnati come Hell or high water!"

With that Amy took his hand in hers and placed it on her belly. The baby was kicking energetically, as if to say, "You tell em Papa!" She smiled up at Elijah, her head leaning on his shoulder and said, "This time I'm sure it's a boy! He's kickin like a little savage!"

They sat there by the hearth in silence for a while, Elijah letting the warmth of Amy and the fire engulf him, easing the pain, his thoughts turning to the happy prospect of the birth of a son.

Momma Celia appeared in the parlor door, reluctant to break their reverie. She seemed instinctively aware of what had transpired at Elijah's brother's house, and Elder had come in through the kitchen to confirm it after bedding down Beauty in her stall for the night.

"Ya'll hungry? I cooked us a dinner I know'd put anything ya sister-in-law come up with to shame! Come on now, put ya worries behind ya for a spell. This is Christmas! After all, if the Good Lord was born in a stable, and nobody wanted to let His family in, I figure we ain't doin too bad! Seems to me we in pretty good company!" She said with a grin.

"God love ya, and bless your heart, Momma Celia! Ya know, ya're absolutely right! We need to give the Good Lord thanks! Call the children and let's eat! And tell Gilbert to let the others know, nobody works tomorrow!" Elijah answered. Turning to Amy he kissed her on the cheek and said, "Merry Christmas, darlin! Ya'll're the best Christmas present I could ever have!"

XLVI

"Well boys," proudly announced Angus, "I got a little New Year's present for ya'll. My Pa told me how petitions get written, so I worked on ours and here's what I got:

'We, the undersigned concerned citizens of Barnwell District, South Carolina, in view of the potentially damaging influence of recent incendiary abolitionist publications, such as the book Uncle Tom's Cabin, by Mrs. Harriet Beecher Stowe, in which the cherished values and very foundation of Southern society are grossly misrepresented and heinously distorted, do hereby petition the General Assembly of the Great State of South Carolina to prohibit the sale, publication, or dissemination in any form of said book, or any other materials deemed to promote the cause of the abolition of slavery.

We make this petition on several grounds:

To protect our women and children from the deleterious effects of hearing such flagrant distortions and cruel misrepresentations of our way of life, assuring their sacred purity and innocence is thereby preserved, and the vulgar and abusive imagery and language used to describe the alleged horrors of bondage never offend their eyes or ears;

To prevent the fomentation of unrest and rebellion among the colored population of Barnwell District and the State of South Carolina, both free and slave, and thereby prevent the undermining of our economic and social stability.

To preserve the natural order of society, and fulfill our sacred obligation, endorsed by Holy Writ, to care for and uplift the benighted heathen souls of African descent, so that they might reap the benefits of a loving God through our benevolent patronage, and prosper under our care, without the burdensome expectations that might be laid upon them in their inferior condition, were they to have to fend for themselves.

To fail to prevent the dissemination of such literature and misguided notions of the proper social order would be to invite the violation of our women and children's innocence, the promulgation of violent uprisings by coloreds against their white masters, the disruption of the protection offered them by their owners, and their unrestrained indulgence in base and Godless lusts and desires, thereby undermining the stability of society, and the productivity of the economy upon which everybody's well-being depends. It would, moreover, constitute a violation of that sacred trust to which Scripture exhorts us, and thereby cause us to sin against both society and humanity itself, which would be offensive in the eyes of Almighty God.

To which petition we hereby set our hand and seal on this_____ day of the month of _____, in the Year of Our Lord One Thousand Eight Hundred and Fifty Three, in Williston, Barnwell District, South Carolina.'

Angus ended with a flourish and laid his petition before the Willis brothers with satisfaction.

"Well I'll be damned, Angus! That's a mighty impressive piece of work ya'll did! Sounds like it was written by a full-fledged, honest to God lawyer!" proclaimed James with genuine admiration. Angus beamed. This was music to his ears.

"Helluva good job, Angus!" chimed in Michael enthusiastically.

"Well, boys, now that we got our petition, I think it's time we set to talkin with Dr. Guignard and Mr. Matthews bout gettin that rally organized!" insisted James. "We need to get this out to everybody in Barnwell District, and do it soon!"

The three of them agreed to approach Dr. Guignard and Mr. Matthews and to start raising the issue among folks around town to build interest before announcing the actual rally.

"Way I figure it," reflected Angus, "if we start plantin the seeds of discord over this issue now, they're bound to take root and grow quickly, so by the time we actually announce the event of the rally, folks'll be itchin to sign the petition already!"

"I like the way you're thinkin, boy!" said James with a grin, already imagining themselves local heroes. "I'll go talk to Mr. Matthews today- you go see if you can find Dr. Guignard. He's got a real nice meadow by his house just off the main road, easy to get to. It'd be a perfect location to hold the rally. We could do a barbecue, and see if we can get Tom Stoddard to donate a barrel of that sour mash whiskey he's been makin!"

"That's a great idea, James! An maybe we could get some of the ladies to bake some pies or somethin for dessert!" added Michael, almost as partial to eating as he was to drinking.

"So, we turn it into an event that celebrates our society, see, and then we've set the stage for the speeches, where we'll scare em with the prospect of all this bein ruined by some damn Yankee literature and crazy ideas about nigras bein equal to whites! Hell, I'll bet ya'll five dollars everybody there'll sign the petition before they even finish their pie!" James went on. "But now we gotta figure out who's gonna give the speeches to get em all worked up?" Knowing he did not have the oratorical skills they really needed, and Michael couldn't possibly stand before a crowd and say anything effective beyond a rebel yell of support or conviction, James looked expectantly at Angus.

Angus was taken aback. It had not occurred to him to make any speeches himself, but he realized that secretly he had been hoping that this rally might launch him into public life somehow, and at least get his father's attention if not win his outright approval.

"You… ya'll want me to make a speech?" he stammered uncertainly.

"Well if not you, then who? Damn, Angus, if you could find the words to write that petition, you can certainly come up with what we need to tell the community!" insisted James, Michael nodding emphatically his agreement.

"Well alright then, I guess I could try!" agreed Angus. He thought for a moment, and added, "Alright with you if I work it out on paper first and practice with ya'll before I get up there in front of everybody? I don't want to mess it up, that's all!"

"Hell, yeah! That's a great idea- that way we can add things if we think you left out anything important!" James commented.

"You got yourself a deal!" added Michael. The three shook on it, and Angus then began to ponder what he should say, and how to say it so that folks would believe every word, and would eagerly agree to whatever they proposed.

"I've got a good feelin about this, ya'll. Yessiree! We're gonna start makin our mark round here with this!" He declared with relish, feeling like he might finally be coming into his own.

XLVII

Amy's pregnancy had proceeded without any noticeable problems. She felt good, her energy level was normal, her appetite was undisturbed, (other than a peculiar craving for mustard, potato and green bean salad, and buttermilk biscuits) and she was even sleeping well, despite the fact the baby truly did seem unusually active. Lying in bed, Elijah had seen the baby kick and punch like he was shadow boxing, causing Amy's belly to protrude in peculiar and sometimes comical ways.

"He really is a little savage!" Elijah observed. "That's gotta be a boy- or the toughest little girl this side of the Mississippi!" he laughed. "Stop beatin on your Momma, son! I know it's gettin cramped in there, but it isn't her fault! Don't worry, ya'll'll be comin out to see us soon, and we're all gettin excited to meet ya!" Amy smiled as Elijah bent to kiss the baby in her belly. The baby stopped kicking at that point, almost as if in response to his father's voice.

"I do believe he heard you, Elijah, savage or no!" she chuckled, caressing her belly affectionately. "Won't be too much longer now, little one," she murmured.

There was, to be sure, still the unspoken fear lingering from Eliza's birth that, even though all seemed normal now, something horrible could still happen. If it weren't for that fear, in fact, Elijah might well have gone on up to Cincinnati, but he just didn't dare. He knew he would never forgive himself if something happened and he was away.

In the meantime, he tried to find out more about the laws of Ohio so he'd be prepared when he finally did make the trip, and not have to stay up there too long before coming back to retrieve the family and bring them all on up there. He couldn't bring himself to ask much of anything of Angus, not wanting to tax the poor man's dying strength. Realizing that the enjoyment of Angus' company mattered more to him than his need for advice or his discomfort at facing his old friend's demise, Elijah contented himself with paying brief social visits to simply comfort his friend and pass an amiable afternoon with him from time to time, though the old man's attention span was waning. It was hard to tell whether Elijah's visits were more draining than helpful, but the old man was always happy to see his friend, and ever solicitous of his family's well being, never failing to inquire after the progress toward their emancipation.

Elijah was able to get more useful information from John Bauskett, and shared that with Angus too, to the old man's delight.

"Angus, John tells me that in Ohio it turns out that if a slave owner brings slaves into the state with a clearly expressed intention of emancipating them, they become free as soon as they set foot on Ohio soil!"

"That's good to hear Elijah, and important to remember! However, given the mean-spirited thinking toward such matters around here, I imagine your relations will claim no such intention can be demonstrated. They'll be thinkin the Fugitive Slave Act will let em simply march on up to Cincinnati and drag all your family back down here as their own property, unless you make it crystal clear and in writin to the contrary!" warned the old man, not too feeble to think through the legal challenges, even in his weakened condition. "It won't be enough to just tell someone that's what you wanna do- though you should tell at least some folks around here of your intentions before you leave, as a safeguard of witnesses for the defense! Your family will surely try to play the 'his word against mine' game on that one!"

"Well, won't that be established by the writin' of the will itself, Angus?" Elijah asked, suddenly concerned that he not overlook any crucial details.

"True enough it will, but Amy's gonna need access to that will, and the lawyer in Cincinnati should surely keep a copy on file in proof, lest your relations attempt to negate its existence by waving a copy of your old will in some probate judge's face! Be sure and tell Amy the names and address of the lawyers up there too, in case she needs to call on em to vouch for her and the family!"

Elijah took all this in thoughtfully, and concluded, "I reckon then that when I finally take them on up to Cincinnati with me, I'd best keep the will with me at all times, and make sure Amy knows where I've kept it too, in case anything happens!"

The old man nodded with satisfaction and then, unexpectedly nodded off. Mary came in to check on him and said, "He's like that most days now, Mister Elijah. He perk up like his old sef for a bit, and then the next thing ya know he sleepin like a baby. One time he woke up sudden like, and tole me he'd been talkin to some angels! Like about to skeer me to death, but I kinda believed it, to tell the truth!" Mary looked at Angus with unspeakable affection, mixed with profound respect.

Elijah heard her sniffle, and turning, looked at her straight on. "Freed me a long time ago, Mister Elijah- befo it became most impossible. I gots me a paper to prove it too! He tole me, 'Now Mary, don't you be losin this paper I'm gonna give ya, b'cause there may be a day when I ain't around no mo, when ya'll'll need to prove you don't belong to nobody but your Maker!' Truth be told, in my heart I still belong to him, but I feel like he belong to me too!" She wiped a tear from the corner of her eye and added, "Kindness be a powerful bond, Mister Elijah! An I reckon I's only a slave to his kindness now. I always hated slavery, but I never hated him, and fact is he made my life pretty good. But I spect ya'll already know that." She smiled, almost to herself, gently tucked a wool plaid afghan around the old man's shoulders to ward off any chill, and quietly limped out of the room. Elijah looked at the sleeping Angus in silent admiration, and tiptoed out behind her.

As he rode home, Elijah resolved to be sure and share with Amy Angus' sage advice, promising himself he would guard his new will with his life, and make sure that Amy was duly prepared to prove his intention should the unfortunate need ever arise, though it made him uncomfortable pondering his own death. For at this point, feeling a respite from the despondency that intermittently plagued him, with the baby on the way and their plan slowly but steadily coming to fruition, he earnestly hoped they would simply succeed at last, and enjoy years of prosperous freedom together in Ohio, or somewhere in the Northwest Territories!

XLVIII

Up in Cincinnati, John Jolliffe was pondering Elijah's latest communication. Elijah had shared Angus' advice with the good lawyer in anticipation of his upcoming visit.

"James, our Mr. Willis from South Carolina has written again to apprise us of some of his concerns pertaining to his visit. He feels a need that he and, if need be his family, be able to demonstrate proof of his intent to emancipate them, prior to their arrival in Ohio, in the unfortunate event that he is not able to see their deliverance to fruition in person."

"Well, clearly a rewritten will would establish such intent, would it not?" answered his partner.

"True, as he himself pointed out. However, it remains to be seen whether such a will would pass probate both in Ohio and South Carolina. I suspect there may be challenges, at least down there, if not up here. I wonder if this might not be a case where legal redundancy is actually advantageous. We might want to discuss with Mr. Willis the preparation of a deed of manumisson to be executed by whomever he appoints as his executors." Jolliffe went on, "It might be useful, even if the family makes it safely to Ohio, just so as to leave no shadow of a doubt as to his intentions, and thus thwart any efforts on the part of his white relations to renege on the emancipation of his chosen family, and claim them as their property on the grounds of them being legal next of kin by South Carolina law!"

"Excellent idea, John! Excellent idea!" responded James Gitchell. "All of this presumes, of course, that he can at least succeed in getting them out of South Carolina before he dies! Were he to die in South Carolina, I imagine it would be virtually impossible to extricate them from there to Ohio without a fight!" He pondered the matter for a moment and then added, "The question still remains, however, whether such a document might also be executed on behalf of any of his slaves who are unable to accompany him on his journey to Ohio? We don't yet know his full disposition on the matter, but I would certainly foresee the need to make some kind of provision for bringing the remaining slaves to Ohio, should he not be able to do so himself."

"Good point, James. It's true, that aspect continues to elude us, but presumably once Mr. Willis is able to meet with us face to face, we shall find the means to settle the matter. He informs me that his child will be born shortly, and that barring any further complications, he anticipates making the journey up to Cincinnati in the near future."

"That's wonderful news! I'm sure he must be more eager than ever to resolve this matter and get his family out of that nightmarish situation. I've read in the papers that the push for secession in South Carolina is more urgent than ever, and that their pro-slavery rhetoric is quite extraordinary for the inventive excuses they use to justify the inhuman cruelty being perpetrated upon that unfortunate race!"

"Pray God we succeed in alleviating at least some small measure of their suffering!" uttered Jolliffe with great sincerity. "This is truly a sacred challenge we face James, we must not fail them!"

XLIX

Angus Patterson, Jr. stood nervously on the doorstep of the home of Dr. John Guignard. It was an elegant whitewashed brick structure with a graceful portico on the outskirts of town. Turning off the main road, there was a tree-lined avenue approaching the house. To the right were the stables with white-washed fences enclosing paddocks where Guignard indulged in a passion for racehorses. He prided himself on breeding some of the fastest horses in the area, and in fact helped finance this addiction with the winnings from races across the state.

To the left of the avenue lay an open meadow, bordered by large trees. The land was extremely flat, so when mown, the meadow gave the impression of being an expansive lawn. It was here that Angus and the Willis brothers hoped to hold their rally, depending of course upon the good doctor's willingness to sponsor it! It was to that end that Angus had come calling.

The younger Mr. Patterson took off his hat, smoothed back his hair, and tried to make himself look as presentable as possible for this all important first impression as someone other than just his father's son. He raised the heavy door-knocker and let it fall three times to announce his arrival. Shortly, a glum faced, heavy set, middle-aged house slave appeared in a black dress, covered by a crisp white apron and a white headscarf.

"Yessir? May I hep ya?" she asked Angus as he stood in the open doorway looking past her to the expensively appointed interior of the house.

"Is Dr. Guignard in, by any chance? I'd like to speak to him for a few moments." Angus replied.

"Yessir, he's here. Whom shall I say is callin?" the woman replied in a well rehearsed and carefully scripted response. There was a trace of anxiety in her voice, as if she were afraid of not speaking correctly.

"Oh, sorry ma'am. Uh, please tell him that Angus Patterson Junior has come callin, and would like to ask for just a few minutes of his time." Angus immediately realized he had addressed a slave as ma'am, and wondered if some might find that unnecessarily respectful. Yet he realized too that it had been Mary, even more than his mother or father, who had insisted on his being polite and respectful to all people, when he was growing up.

The woman looked at Angus piercingly, as if she knew something about him, but said nothing other than, "Please wait here sir, I'll go inform Dr. Guignard that ya've come." Angus wondered whether she too had found his calling her ma'am surprising.

After several minutes of waiting awkwardly, standing with his hat in his hand and shifting from foot to foot, uncertain whether it might seem rude to sit down on one of the velvet upholstered rosewood side chairs ranged along the wall, Angus saw Dr. Guignard approach through a door at the far end of the foyer. He was dressed in an expensively tailored suit of white linen. A heavy braided gold watch fob hung from the pocket of a rich peacock blue and burgundy brocade waistcoat, and his boots were highly polished. His slightly graying hair was combed back in a luxurious mane, and though his face was tanned by the sun, his manicured fingernails made it clear this bronzing was not a farmer's tan achieved through hard labor, but merely from his leisure passion for riding and overseeing the training of his horses. His demeanor was refined, giving the impression of being more a man of the world than a medical practitioner. The fact of the matter was that though he would give medical care to anyone when asked, he preferred to limit his practice to the families of wealthy planters, who by the looks of things rewarded him amply for his services.

"Well, bless my soul, if it isn't the son of Angus Patterson! Welcome, son! Welcome!" Guignard said with an effusiveness that lacked real warmth. "How's your father doin? I hear he's been fadin lately. Sorry to hear that. Good man, your Pa." Guignard was quickly dispensing with the formal niceties by answering his own questions, leaving Angus little room or need for comment.

"Come on in and set down!" He gestured to a pair of high backed gold and burgundy striped arm chairs, with arched rosewood crests carved in a pattern of rose blossoms. "Sally!" he barked in command "Fetch my guest a drink!" He turned to Angus to ask, "What'd you like to drink son? Sweet tea? Rum cooler? A mint julep?" the question almost seemed like a test of Angus' manhood. He figured he'd best show he was a man and not a boy, so he asked for the mint julep.

Satisfied with the response, Dr. Guignard ordered Sally, "Bring him a mint julep, gal, and make it fast!" He turned to Angus in a loud explanatory aside, "She can be slower'n molasses in January if I don't make it clear I need somethin right away! You know how the nigras can be- if we don't show em how to do things right, they just don't get done!" Angus realized that his father's treatment of Mary was markedly kinder that Dr. Guignard's treatment of Sally, and suspected the doctor was that way with all his slaves. It made Angus a little uncomfortable, but he wasn't going to let it deter him from his mission.

Dr. Guignard watched to make sure Sally was bustling off with due haste to obey his orders, then turned back to his guest and assumed a sort of crocodile smile.

"So, to what do I owe the pleasure of your visit, son?" Guignard finally asked.

A bit flustered and annoyed by being repeatedly addressed as "son" rather than being shown the respect of "Mr. Patterson" as he had hoped, Angus took a deep breath and decided to push on to the purpose of his visit.

"Well, Dr. Guignard, as a matter of fact, I'm here on behalf of my colleagues, James and Michael Willis, in the hopes that we might persuade you to help us sponsor a rally to inform folks around here of the dangers of abolitionist literature invadin our fair district, and pollutin the innocent minds of our women and children with pernicious lies about the cruelty of slavery. We are particularly concerned that the book recently published by a Yankee woman, Miz Harriet Beecher Stowe, of Cincinnati, not be allowed to be sold anywhere in Barnwell District, or even in the Great State of South Carolina!"

Dr. Guignard's eyes had lit up at the mention of the Willis brothers and abolition in the same sentence. Perceiving that this might represent a possible opportunity to force Elijah to amend his perverted ways, so deleterious to the standing of all honorable citizens of the area, he pressed Angus for more information.

"Well! I certainly do applaud your civic-mindedness, Angus, and that of James and Michael Willis as well! Good to know that the younger generation of our town's founding family is as concerned for our fair community's well bein as you are!"

Angus smiled with relief that he had at least not met with outright rejection. The fact that Dr. Guignard had addressed him as Angus, rather than son, was a reassuring sign he was being taken seriously- even if he would have preferred hearing "Mr. Patterson." He'd settle for whatever he could get!

"Yessir, thank you sir, we surely are!" he replied gratefully.

"So what exactly is it ya'll're proposin to do?" pressed Guignard, not yet willing to concede his support without first ascertaining whether these young bucks had any good idea of what they were setting themselves to do.

Angus felt this might be his opportunity to show his mettle, and even plant the idea of a possible future candidacy for the General Assembly. He adopted what he deemed his most serious tone, and proceeded to explain:

"Well, Doctor Guignard, it seems to me that this whole abolition issue is startin to get outa hand. There's rumors of some folks talkin of emancipatin slaves, and who knows, maybe even tryin to leave em property! We just feel that's not only wrong, but a threat to the stability of our well-ordered society!"

Guignard was all ears, wondering whether the alleged rumors pertained to Elijah Willis. "So we thought it would be good to get up a petition that folks could sign, and we could take it up to Columbia to the General Assembly to see if we can't press them to enact stricter laws against the writing, publication or distribution of any such abolitionist ideas in the State of South Carolina!" Feeling now infused with enthusiasm he ended on something of a rhetorical flourish that was quickly deflated by Dr. Guignard's response.

"Son, there've been laws against abolitionist materials in this state since 1820! And it's not only nigh on impossible to emancipate a slave, it's already illegal to leave any property to one in any case! No need to petition for that!" Guignard replied in a matter of fact tone, eyeing Angus carefully to gage his response.

Angus, thinking quickly to try to cover his embarrassment and salvage his political future from premature defeat, answered, "Well, yessir, but since this book, *Uncle Tom's Cabin* came out, the issue seems to have been rekindled, and we want to make sure that whatever the law may currently be, the prohibition of Miz Stowe's scurrilous novel be enforced throughout the State, with specific punishment for those buyin, sellin or readin it! It constitutes a potential pollution of the virtue and innocence of our women and children, and we feel its lies must be stopped!" He paused before adding, "Never hurts to reinforce existing law when it comes to protectin our women folk!" hoping that his defense of the fair ladies of Barnwell District might overcome the bumbling impression his apparent ignorance of existing statutes must have created. He suddenly remembered he had brought the draft of the petition and handed it over to Dr. Guignard for him to see they were truly in earnest.

After reading the petition, Dr. Guignard was actually impressed with Angus' response. Not only had he proven he could write a cogent argument, he had shown an ability to think on his feet and cover his behind at the same time. These could be useful skills. Though he noted that, contrary to Angus' claim, there was no mention in the petition of specific punishments for the supposed crime, he chose not to raise that issue just now, knowing full well Angus had been trying to compensate for his mistake. He decided this was a horse to back in the race toward secession, and if he played his cards right, it might also be used to exert the specific pressure on Elijah that had eluded him and Frederick Matthews when they had visited the Willis Plantation.

He returned the petition with a smile and said, "I couldn't agree with ya more, Angus. Ya'll're absolutely right! So how can I help?" to Angus' huge relief.

Feeling encouraged, Angus plowed on ahead, "Well sir, we were wonderin if ya'll'd be willin to let us hold the rally on your meadow out front, and perhaps we could get you, and Mr. Matthews, and anyone else who's interested, to contribute some barbecue, drinks and pies for dessert. We we're thinkin we might get some of the ladies to contribute their favorite recipes (or their cooks' favorites, a course)!"

Guignard wanted to be sure Angus would feel duly beholden to him, and deliberately waited a moment, to keep him in suspense before replying, then said, "Well, I think that could be arranged! Ya'll got a particular date in mind for this shindig?"

"Well sir, we'd need enough time to get word out all around the District, so's to get a good turn-out, and most likely a Saturday would be best, so both the merchants and planters and their families could attend. Why don't you tell us what's convenient for ya'll, and we'll work around it!" Angus was perceptive enough to know it would be best to offer Guignard some say if he wanted his full support.

Dr. Guignard was hatching a plan of his own to try to help force Elijah's hand, and young Mr. Patterson and his companions played right into it, making his objective all the easier to attain. His pride had been badly wounded by what he had construed as Elijah's unforgivable rudeness to him and Frederick Matthews, and his longing for an opportunity to give Elijah his comeuppance seemed about to be fulfilled.

"I'll tell you what, son. I will personally invite all the planters in Barnwell District, and request that each plantation also provide a quota of slaves to help put this rally on. That way, we can not only inform the white folks, but make sure the nigras are put on notice, so they don't get any ideas about emancipation themselves!"

This struck Angus as a stroke of genius. "Why that's a wonderful idea, Doctor! I can't thank ya enough! With the support of folks like you, it's bound to be a big success! The Willis brothers and I will personally deliver any invitations you write, and will be happy to organize the event, to make sure folks see we're committed to makin sure their voices are heard up in Columbia!" Angus attempted to reassert himself as a promising political force and potential candidate, before Dr. Guignard could take the reins away from him and run the show himself.

Quite willing to let Angus think he was in charge, Dr. Guignard smiled benignly and said, "Well, that's just grand! I'll see to it the invitations are written by next week, and ya'll can drop by to pick em up and deliver em. I'll even give ya'll the use of some of my slaves to build a stage and set up tables to serve the food. Maybe ya'll could get the Willis boys' uncle Elijah to provide ya'll some lumber for the stage!" he suggested slyly.

Angus felt a knot in the pit of his stomach at this, knowing full well there was no chance in Hell that Elijah would provide the lumber, and they'd have to come up with it on their own without letting Guignard know, or he'd write them off as gutless. Guignard knew it too, of course, but was determined to push Angus and the Willis boys for his own ends, figuring he would win no matter what the outcome: he'd have a budding politician in his pocket and either be credited as a patron of this worthy cause, or succeed in pressuring Elijah into a recapitulation (thereby humbling Elijah for his misbehavior, and in so doing gaining a moral victory for the planters), or both.

Angus replied, "Well I'll be happy to convey that to James and Michael for ya, sir. And I surely do appreciate all ya'll's help. We'll drop by to fetch the invitations next week!"

"That'll be fine, son! You just let me know if ya'll need anything else now, won't ya?" he asked smoothly.

"Oh, yessir, thank ya sir, but I think we can handle organizin the rest. I truly appreciate your offer! Long as we can give folks food and drink, I reckon they'll be more'n happy to come!"

Dr. Guignard eyed Angus appreciatively, calculating the immense value of having an eager, aspiring young politician under his thumb. This could not only help assure his victory over Elijah, but be a useful tool in maintaining the proper order and his ability to influence it throughout Barnwell and beyond. He much preferred the role of puppeteer or king-maker to that of elected office, for politics was like horse racing, the outcome of a race didn't always depend on who had the best horse, but who had the smartest rider. When it came to public influence, Guignard saw himself as an expert jockey.

Dr. Guignard rose, indicating the audience was now over and his guest was free to leave. Angus jumped to his feet in response, quickly downing the mint julep Sally had wordlessly placed on the table by his side, and stretched out his hand to Dr. Guignard, saying, "We really appreciate this Doctor, and I promise ya ya'll won't regret it!"

"I should hope not!" replied Dr. Guignard cooly, slightly rattling Angus. There was a subtle trace of a threat in Dr. Guignard's tone that made Angus certain that if this rally were not successful, there'd be Hell to pay. The two men shook hands, and Sally silently held the door open for Angus to depart, a melancholy expression on her downcast face. As she closed the door behind him, Angus could hear the voice of Dr. Guignard barking orders at her again with the same edge of perpetual irritation and condescension, as if it was all he could do to endure the obstinate and willful incompetence of the inferiors under his proprietorship.

Angus winced to hear it, but then felt quickly overcome with the elation of his success in eliciting Dr. Guignard's support. As he rode down the alley to the main road and looked at the nearby meadow, he could picture the throngs of people, smell the smoke of the delicious barbecue, hear the cheerful clinking of glasses raised to toast their success, and imagined himself receiving the accolades of the crowd up on a stage draped with bunting. The effects of the guzzled mint julep quickly rising to his head enhanced the euphoria. He couldn't wait to tell James and Michael. They needed to talk this up all over town.

L

Will Beazeley heard rumors of the rally, and remembering the pressure James had tried to put on him to inform him of anyone attempting to send or receive any communications from Cincinnati or New York, could well imagine where this was headed. He was certain that Elijah was no rabble rousing Yankee abolitionist, and he felt bad for him and his family. He decided he should at least warn Elijah so he wouldn't be caught off guard by the upcoming event.

The next time Elijah came into the depot, Will drew him aside and said, "Mr. Willis, I think ya'll need to know about somethin your nephews are up to."

Elijah was immediately on the alert, already suspecting that it must have something to do with their having learned he was looking into the emancipation of his family.

Will proceeded to recount to Elijah the episode with James and Michael. He added, "I heard Dr. Guignard's sendin invitations to all the planters to attend a rally at his place, and is askin each planter to provide a quota of slaves to help put it on, to boot!"

Elijah swore softly to himself, "Son of a bitch!" immediately grasping Guignard's intent.

"Well, I surely do thank ya for tippin me off, Will. It's a sad day in Williston when families are pitted against each other, but I expect we'll be seein more of that before long. It's nothin but ignorance, fear, greed, and lust for power that feeds all this, and it's a cryin shame some folks don't just try to do better themselves, so they don't feel so threatened by the prospect of others' success!"

Elijah's comment hit home for Mr. Beazeley, as it put a finger on the reason he admired Elijah so. Will didn't see himself as a brave man, but he wasn't a fool, and knew full well he might be criticized, or even ostracized, if he failed to notify the Willis boys of "suspicious activity." But he knew in his heart that Elijah was a good man, and didn't deserve to be persecuted by relatives or neighbors simply because they resented his success and were offended by his choice of whom to love. He resolved to give Elijah whatever protection he could by keeping him apprised of the local gossip.

"Mr. Willis, I promise ya I'll let ya'll know if I hear of anything that might put ya'll in danger. This rally your nephews and young Angus Patterson are holdin just don't feel right, and I'd hate to see folks get riled up against you and Miss Amy."

"Ya're a good man, Will, and I truly do appreciate your offer. I can't say as this comes as a real surprise, but it'd surely help to know whatever else they're cookin up!" Elijah made a spontaneous decision to let Mr. Beazeley know some of the background so as go better asess the risk. "Things around here could get ugly if Dr. Guignard and his friends are sponsorin this. He's been holdin a grudge against me ever since he came over with Frederick Matthews to tell me I should send Amy and the family 'back to the slave quarters where they belonged,' and I told him where to go! I don't want to give those folks any cause to come out to my place and threaten us, especially with Amy about to have another baby!"

Elijah had not expected to reveal such personal information, and Will Beazely looked stunned by this revelation. He let out a low whistle at the image of Dr. Guingard and Mr. Matthews giving Elijah an ultimatum, and shook his head. He could well imagine how Elijah must have felt, for slaves or no slaves, Mr. Beazeley was of the opinion that a man's home is his castle, and no one's got a right to come into a man's house and tell him how to handle his personal relationships.

"Lordy, Mr. Willis, I had no idea it had gotten that bad! I sure am sorry to hear that! I promise ya, I'll warn ya if I get wind of anything else!" he swore.

Elijah nodded his thanks and headed for home. As he rode along, he began to contemplate his strategy for dealing with this unfortunate development. His natural inclination was clearly to boycott the rally and have nothing to do with those people, out of sheer disgust for their bigotry. But he wanted to beat that son of a bitch Guignard at his own game, and actually considered attending the rally himself, and bringing some of his most trusted slaves along, too. He figured it might be the safest thing to do, as it would temporarily shut the mouths of the other planters- who no doubt would be expecting him to boycott the event and thus become an easy target for their criticism and suspicion. But it would also allow him and his chosen colored companions to gather first hand information to prepare for what was coming. He knew it wouldn't be easy- either for him or whomever he took along with him. He also knew he'd have to talk to Amy about it, and began to worry it was going to upset her and the baby.

LI

Who's gonna take the invitation to your Uncle Elijah?" Angus asked, as he, James, and Michael were sorting the invitations, elegantly written by Dr. Guignard to all the local planters and their families, into three piles-one pile for each of them to deliver.

James and Michael looked nervously at each other and then back at Angus, clearly a little uneasy with the question. The fact of the matter was, much as they hated their uncle for what he was doing, they were also scared of him, for they knew he was not easily intimidated, nor was he afraid to tell people what he thought if the situation demanded it. His Christmas visit had made clear enough that he did not have a very high opinion of either one of them, and neither of them was eager for another tongue-lashing to remind them. And then there was James' vivid memory of Gilbert too, who he was pretty sure could make small work of both him and his brother in a fair fight. He decided he could side-step that unpleasant little possibility by using Angus as his messenger.

"Well, uh, actually Angus, we kinda thought it might be best if you took him the invitation, and asked him for a lumber donation too! Uncle Elijah respects your Pa a lot, so it might go down a little better comin from you," James informed him. "Besides, we don't exactly want him to think all this is just about him! We can't have folks around here thinkin this is just personal, or they might not take us seriously!"

"That's right, Angus! We figure you could give Uncle Elijah the message better than we can, cause you're such a good talker too!" agreed Michael.

Angus was not feeling convinced. He would much have preferred to dodge the bullet himself and let the Willis boys deal with their own family. On the other hand, he sensed that if they failed to invite Elijah, they would incur the displeasure of Dr. Guignard, and that might jeopardize their whole plan.

"Aw, Hell, alright! I'll do it, damn it! But ya'll owe me one for dealin with your own family for ya!" He was only half joking, and they knew it.

"Fair enough Angus, fair enough, but you really gotta do this for us, alright?" insisted James.

"I said I'd do it, didn't I? Now let me be! I gotta figure out how to present this so he don't get riled at me," Angus replied defensively. "Now, how'm I supposed to ask him for a lumber donation on top of the invitation? That Dr. Guignard's a fox, trickin us into this! He knows damn well your Uncle Elijah's got a family with that concubine of his!" fumed Angus, clearly identifying the primary reason the Willis brothers wanted to evade the issue.

"Well, fox or not, we can't afford to get on his bad side, cause we need his support to pull this whole thing off!" pointed out James, Michael nodding in agreement.

"Well it ain't gonna be easy to talk with ya'll's uncle. What if he tries to run me off his property?" asked Angus, suddenly worried that Elijah might have finally had enough, and take matters into his own hands. "Aw, now Angus, Uncle Elijah's not the type to shoot anybody! Worst that could happen, I figure, is that he might yell some! You'll be fine! Sides, it'll be good practice- arguin with folks who disagree with you is part of politics, ain't it?" James said reassuringly.

Angus looked at the Willis brothers with annoyance, but took his pile of invitations and headed for the door. "I'll see ya'll later, and let you know what happens!" he said, accepting the challenge.

"You're a good man, Angus! Good luck!" James and Michael echoed with relief.

LII

What d'ya'll think I should do?" Elijah asked. Gilbert and Momma Celia had joined him and Amy in the kitchen at Elijah's request. Elijah had broken the news to them about the rally, and figured he didn't want to be the sole voice making a decision that could impact them all intensely.

"Lord, Elijah, I was afraid somethin like this might happen!" said Amy, a combination of anxiety and fatigue coloring her voice.

"I know, darlin, so was I. I figured it was only a matter of time, but it sure feels like just when things seem to be easin up a bit, we get faced with another crisis! I'm sick and tired of the games people are playin around here, but I don't see any easy way out of it either!" Elijah admitted in frustration. "When I first heard about this rally business, I figured I'd ignore it and stay as far away as I could get from those folks. But then I started to wonder whether that wouldn't just play into their hands?"

Gilbert sat grim faced for a moment, and then spoke up. "Well Elijah, forgive me for sayin so, but I don't think this is somethin we can just run away from. Amy told me about you tellin off that Dr. Guignard and his pet dog Matthews. Five'll get you twenty he's still lickin his wounds over that! That can't be good! An it's not likely to be forgot any time soon, with folks around here gettin all agitated about the abolitionists!"

Momma Celia decided to weigh in too. "Gilbert's right about that! That Dr. Guignard's got a mean streak in him, and a pride big as all outdoors. I seen that man plenty a times over the years, even b'fo we come over here. I know how he treat his slaves, and the man's got ice in his veins, he so cold. You done wounded his pride, an he can't forgive that. He gonna look for a way to humble ya, if not worse. An he'll bide his time 'til he find it- then he'll strike like a rattlesnake, mark my words! Question is, what ya'll want to do bout it?"

Amy, Gilbert and Momma Celia all looked at Elijah expectantly.

Elijah sat thinking, and then with a sigh said, "Much as I hate the idea, I think the smartest response is to play along for a while. I stay away from the rally, or run Guignard's messenger boys off at gun point from deliverin his "invitation", and I'll be playing right into his hands. That's what he wants me to do, so he can call me out!"

Gilbert nodded in agreement.

"He won't be expectin me to show up, much less to bring any of my slaves along with me!"

"But sugar, if you take Gilbert with you, don't you think Dr. Guignard'd try to pounce on ya'll just because he's my brother?" worried Amy, assuming Gilbert would be the best choice to go along with him to the rally.

"Could be. I don't rightly know. God knows I'd feel better with Gilbert by my side, though." Elijah smiled honestly at his brother-in-law, and Gilbert grinned back.

"Mebbe so," commented Momma Celia, "But with or without Gilbert, I guarantee you ole Dr. Guignard'll stick ya wherever he can. He might expect ya'll to bring Gilbert, but he won't expect ya to bring nobody else. What about Jason an Julius? They loyal to ya, an smart too! Give ya plenty a ears to listen up for comments, both among the white folks and the slaves!"

"You're right, Momma! We need to play our cards right, but we might just be able to turn this thing to our advantage if we're careful," Elijah responded. Turning to his brother-in-law he asked, "Gilbert, tell me the truth, do ya'll think the three of you can pretend well enough not to let on anything about emancipation, even if Guignard and his people try to bait you into revealin somethin? He's gonna try to get a rise out of us one way or another- that's for sure! Question is, can we refuse to give him that satisfaction, without feelin like were sellin our souls to the Devil to do it?"

Gilbert looked his brother-in-law in the eye and said, "Elijah, we learned a long time ago how to make white folks think we're passive and stupid- as a matter of survival! Ya think we can't do it now, when ya'll know damn well that's what they all wanna believe anyway?" He laughed a mirthless laugh. Then he nodded, his face deadly serious. "We'll play any role we have to if it means gettin us closer to freedom!"

Elijah looked at him thoughtfully. "Well, alright then! I need you to let Jason and Julius in on this, but I don't want the others to know. Can't afford any loose lips around here, and some of ya'll could get carried away and let slip information nobody needs to know just yet. We're gonna have to plan this out carefully if we're gonna beat that bastard Guignard at his own game and keep my nephews off my back as well."

"Well, what d'ya want us to do? Did ya'll get the invitation to this rally yet?" asked Gilbert.

"Not yet. I heard James and Michael and young Angus Patterson are deliverin the invitations to folks all over the area. I imagine James and Michael are none too eager to show up here just now, after my comments to em at Christmas, and I'll bet they're scared to death of you, Gilbert, since you faced James down a while back when he came out with the message to pick us up at the depot on our way back from Baltimore!"

Gilbert chuckled at the recollection of the cowardly James flinching when he had said "I'll be sure to tell Mister Elijah you was kind enough to deliver the message in person-" and James' horse's shit had been the perfect expression of how Gilbert had felt about the rider!

"Guess that means it'll be Angus who comes callin on ya then?" Amy interjected.

Elijah nodded. "More'n likely, that's right! So, I want ya'll to show young Angus every courtesy. As far as ya'll're concerned, he is an honored and welcome guest. You let me know as soon as ya'll see him comin and we'll give him a proper reception. It'll probably catch him completely off guard, so he might just open up and let some useful details slip. I want to be able to show up at this rally fully prepared- loaded for bear, but not lettin it show."

"Sounds more like playin possum to me!" remarked Momma Celia. "But that's alright. More'n one possum done escaped bein dinner by pretendin to be already dead!"

Now that he had been forewarned, Elijah was almost relishing facing his opponents, for at least it made him feel like he was actively doing something, rather than just passively waiting for disaster to strike. He didn't know how long he could or would have to keep up the charade, but he figured he had no other choice at this point.

Amy spoke up again, revealing her worry. "Elijah, honey, what're ya'll gonna do if things get nasty? You know they could easily get ugly, and any angry crowd can get dangerous!" Momma Celia and Gilbert looked at him attentively, waiting for his answer.

"Well sugar, I know that's true, and I surely don't intend to do anything to set em off on purpose, but if it comes to protectin you and the family, I'll do or say anything I have to ta keep things under control." He turned to Gilbert and added, "And let me be clear, that even under the hateful laws of South Carolina, you and Jason and Julius are legally allowed, and even obliged to protect me with force, if necessary!"

Gilbert looked at Elijah and grinned, "God knows I don't want nobody to take a poke at you, Elijah, but if they do, I promise ya they'll wish they hadn't! Would give me the greatest of pleasure to have permission to give those folks a lickin they'd never forget!"

"Careful, son. Don'tya be goin there to pick no fight just to get ya anger out! We got too much dependin on ya'll to let it get outa control like some barroom brawl. Right or no right, I guarantee, you boys start throwing punches at white folks, and there'll be no end of Hell to pay!" Momma Celia exhorted him.

"Momma's right, Gilbert," added Amy, "We need ya'll to keep Elijah safe, but not put yaselves in harm's way unless there's no other way out!" Amy held the baby in her womb protectively. "Elijah, I'm scared! Are you sure goin to this thing is the smartest choice?"

"Well darlin, the way I see it, there are no good choices for us that are comfortable. But if it comes down to livin with my conscience, it'd be a whole lot easier to go, and feel like I have some control over the situation, than to sit around here hidin like some coward, waitin for them to come and get me!" Elijah insisted. Momma Celia and Gilbert were both nodding their agreement.

Momma Celia spoke up, "Just remember, ain't no need to seek vengeance on them fools. God'll take care of em sooner or later. Bible says 'Vengeance is mine; I will repay, saith the Lord'."

"True enough Momma," answered Gilbert, "but if I remember rightly, it goes on to say, 'Therefore if thine enemy hunger, feed him; if he thirst, give him drink: for in so doing thou shalt heap coals of fire on his head!' Can't hardly blame us for wantin to at least light the coals for the barbecue!" He grinned mischievously at Elijah.

"Now don't you be twistin the Lord's words, just so's ya'll can get some satisfaction agin that mean ole Dr. Guignard, son! He ain't worth it! Too many folks could get hurt if it goes wrong! Book a Romans ends that passage sayin 'Be not overcome of evil, but overcome evil with good'!" Momma Celia was adamant.

Elijah had listened to this Biblical repartee, remembering how his experience at Holy Apostles, Amy's experience at the creek, and young Jeremiah's experience preaching had all been sincere, and all been different, and all been their own interpretation of scripture. Cognizant that subjective experience could work for or against you, he decided, "Momma's right, Gilbert. The hardest thing of all is gonna be not lettin our enemies' hatred and fear get under our skin and infect us. We gotta keep our heads and hearts about us, or we'll really be in for trouble. These folks are scared, and that makes em dangerous. What I need you and Jason and Julius to do is just be my extra eyes and ears, and give nobody cause for suspicion. No more than that!"

Gilbert thought about this, and responded, "Alright Elijah, we can do that. We'll help ya learn everything we can about what folks are sayin and thinkin. Maybe that'll help us see how best to finally get out of all this!"

Elijah answered, "Thank ya, Gilbert, I'm countin on ya'll to do just that!" He fell silent for a moment. "I remember somethin my granddad told me when I was a boy. He'd fought back in the Revolutionary War, and told me he once heard a general say he'd read a book about warfare back in ancient times. Seems the book talked about how to be a successful warrior, and it insisted that if you know your enemy and yourself, you won't be imperiled, no matter what the battle. But he also said if you didn't know your enemy or yourself, you'd always be imperiled!"

"Makes a lotta sense, don't it" Gilbert replied. "So I guess this rally's an opportunity to get to know our enemies and ourselves a little bit better, don't ya think?"

"That's exactly right, Gilbert! Exactly right!" affirmed Elijah. "And who knows? We may be surprised by what we learn!"

Amy had been listening pensively to the entire exchange. "Promise me one thing, both of ya? Whatever it is you learn about either our enemies or yaselves, ya'll won't go runnin off doin anything stupid! I don't want my baby bein scared outa me by some vigilantes poundin on our door!"

That possibility was a sobering reality, given the circumstances. Both men readily agreed. Elijah said, "Darlin, we're gonna do everything we possibly can to make sure you and the children- all the children, and Momma too, and everybody on this plantation- stays safe and sound, so we can move forward with our plan without any interference from those folks! I swear!" Gilbert nodded in agreement.

"Well, alright then," concluded Momma Celia, "Ya'll best let Jason and Julius know what ya'll are fixin to do, so nobody gets caught with they pants down! Ya'll gotta be ready for anything!"

"Amen to that, Momma!" they agreed. Gilbert got up to go find Jason and Julius.

Elijah called after him, "Gilbert- once I get the invitation, and I see exactly how Dr. Guignard has worded it, we'll need to sit down together again to see how best to prepare ourselves. In the meantime, tell Jason and Julius that 'mum's the word', for now!" Gilbert nodded, and went out the back door toward the slave quarters to find his companions.

"Mister Elijah said what?!" asked Jason, incredulous.

"Is he gone plumb crazy?!" echoed Julius.

"You heard me, he said we gonna have to go with him to this rally his nephews and that Dr. Guignard are cookin up, and play act like we against abolition, and Elijah freein us is about as far away from our minds as you could get!" affirmed Gilbert.

"Damn, Gilbert! Now how we gonna be able to do that? Ya know it's a lie!" said Julius.

"Course I know it, and so does Mister Elijah, but the way he figures it, if we avoid the whole thing, it plays into their hands an they can call him out for it. But if we go and act like we obedient slaves, an like Mister Elijah got no intention of freein nobody, it may buy us time for him to go on up to Cincinnati and get that new will written that will free us all at last!" He paused, then added, "Besides, I told him we all experts at pretendin we don't mind bein slaves, just to stay alive and not get beat! Not that he ever threatened us, but we know plenty who do! Ya'll know how to play that game!"

Jason and Julius shook their heads in amazement. "Mmmmm, mmm, mmm! I don't know, Gilbert, sounds mighty risky to me. You know how Mister Elijah can get! Somebody starts bad mouthin Miss Amy or the children, and he gonna see red, and then it's over! The jig is up, and the next thing ya know, we facin an angry mob of white folks!" said Jason.

"No tellin what might happen then!" agreed Julius.

"Well, ya'll may be right, but Mister Elijah's askin for our help, an it seems to me, since he's layin everything on the line to get us to freedom, we got no choice but to do what we can to hep him!" insisted Gilbert. "He figures we can go, an the three of us'll keep our eyes and ears open for anything- from whites or blacks- that might help him stay clear of trouble long enough to get us out. Let's face it, if we fail, life gonna get a whole lot worse for all of us once he's gone, an we ain't got all the time in the world to get this done. The man ain't young, and his health ain't what it used to be!"

"Well he may not be young, but he's still mighty strong, fatherin children at his age!" Julius said, admiringly.

"That don't mean squat, Julius. I heard tell a men younger than him dyin on top of some woman, and she still ended up pregnant!" swore Jason.

"Look, fellas, all that don't make no nevermind. Ya'll in with us or not? We gotta make some decisions here right now, b'fo it's too late!" urged Gilbert.

Julius and Jason looked at each other. "We're in, Gilbert! We can do this! Ain't gonna be easy, but we can do this!"

Gilbert smiled in relief. "That's good! Ya'll're right, I believe we can! So here's what's gonna happen: once Mister Elijah gets the invitation from Dr. Guignard, we all gonna sit down and make a plan." Jason and Julius were listening attentively. "Probly gonna be young Angus Patterson deliver it, so Mister Elijah wants us to be sure to treat him nice, so he don't get suspicious. After all, his daddy's the one been helpin Mister Elijah get the legal answers he needs, so we got no cause hurtin the boy, even if he is hangin out with Mister Elijah's ornery nephews."

"I swear, if I live to be a hundred, I never will understand how that boy turned so mean with a daddy like ole Mr. Patterson. He been helpin black folks for years, and done a lot for Mister Elijah an Miss Amy. Why his son go so nasty?" wondered Julius, who had delivered messages to Angus Senior and knew Mary as well.

"Hard to say. I agree it's mighty strange, but folks say he's bitter about his momma dyin and blames his daddy. His daddy loves him, but I get the feelin from Mister Elijah he don't think he'll amount to much. Probly makes his son mad his daddy feel that way," observed Gilbert.

"Just the same, I wouldn't count young Angus out just yet," insisted Julius. "I heard tell Miss Sally, Dr. Guignard's house slave, claimed that he the one pitched this rally to ole Dr. Guignard in the first place! He may be a heap smarter than he acts when he drinkin with Mister Elijah's nephews. Best not take him for granted, he could be trouble!" The others nodded in agreement.

While Gilbert, Julius and Jason sat speculating about the upcoming event, they looked up and noticed the dust cloud of approaching hooves down the road. Sure enough, it was Angus Patterson Junior, coming to deliver the invitation.

"Oh Lord! I betcha that's him comin now! Looks like it won't be long b'fo we find out just what we up against!" commented Julius.

"I'd best head out front to receive our guest!" smiled Gilbert, who, like Elijah, was at least feeling some satisfaction that they were actively facing the issues, rather than waiting in fear. He was sort of looking forward to it!

Gilbert stood on the veranda, shading his eyes with his hand as he peered down the road to the approaching rider. Angus Junior was clearly nervous. He was fidgeting in the saddle and seemed to be talking to himself, like he was rehearsing for his imminent meeting with Elijah. He was determined not to make it confrontational, but wasn't any too sure Elijah would share the same determination, from what James and Michael were telling him.

"Afternoon, Mister Angus!" Gilbert called out cheerfully as Angus approached the front of the house. "What brings ya'll out here to visit? Your daddy alright?" Gilbert was setting a perfect tone to avoid any possible flare-up.

"Afternoon, Gilbert! Nice to see ya! Oh, yeah, Pa's holdin on, I guess. Best as can be expected, anyway. Thanks for askin! Uh, is Mr. Willis in? I came out to deliver an invitation to him from Dr. Guignard." Angus immediately worried he had already revealed too much, but Gilbert appeared unfazed by this revelation.

"He's here, somewhere. Let me go find him for ya. Why don't ya'll have a seat here on the veranda, an I'll be right back!" Gilbert responded.

"Thank ya, Gilbert. Much obliged!" Angus dismounted and led his horse over to the trough by the live oak to give him a drink before taking a seat on the veranda. Gilbert went into the plantation house to look for Elijah, and sent Clarissa Ann out to bring Angus a drink while he was waiting. He coached her to call Angus, "Mr. Patterson", and told her to be extra nice and polite with him, figuring the younger Patterson would feel flattered to be treated respectfully. Once at ease, by the time he talked to Elijah, he might open up and reveal something useful about this rally and its purpose.

"Would ya'll like some lemonade, Mr. Patterson?" Clarissa asked sweetly.

Angus was pleasantly surprised, for he had been prepared to be met with hostility. "Why thank ya! I believe I would!" he answered, still nervous, accepting the tall glass being offered him as he took a seat on the veranda.

"If there's anything ya'll need, just call, sir. Mister Elijah be out shortly!" Clarissa smiled.

Angus smiled back. "Thank ya, sugar, I'm fine." He realized that, having heard about Elijah's illegitimate family, this was the first time he had actually talked to any of the children. It struck him that the child was both well dressed and well mannered, and far from the image of the unruly, slovenly pickaninnies that James and Michael had painted them out to be. He realized too that, unlike some slave children he'd seen, there was nothing cowed or subservient in Clarissa's bearing. She was merely being gracious, without fear of reprisal if she failed. This slightly troubled him, though he wasn't prepared to recognize why, for it would have required him seeing he was becoming a pawn. He had more than enough self-doubt as it was, without opening himself to reconsider his course of action. He convinced himself that, despite his mixed feelings about coloreds, his future depended upon following through on his commitment to the Willis brothers and Dr. Guignard.

After a few minutes, Elijah came out the front door of the house, hand outstretched in greeting. Angus jumped to his feet, nearly knocking over his glass of lemonade, and shook Elijah's hand.

"Well, nice to see ya! Welcome to my home, Angus! How's your father doin?" He paused, but before Angus could answer added, "It truly pains me to see him in decline, but he never ceases to amaze me with his wisdom, knowledge, and carin. Must make ya right proud to be his son!" Angus was caught off guard, not sure whether Elijah was just admiring the father, or subtly criticizing the son. He knew he had to be careful how he responded.

"Thank ya for your kindness, sir. He's holdin on still, but he's goin downhill, no doubt about it. It's hard on all of us; that's a fact. But since ya mention it, I am right proud to be his son, and I'm trying to learn all I can from his knowledge and wisdom while he's still around. I gotta admit, I'm gonna miss him like anything when he's gone. Don't even like to think about it!"

"I can imagine," Elijah responded sincerely. "But I'm sure glad ya're tryin to learn from him. Couldn't ask for a better teacher! I know he sure has taught me a lot over the years!" Elijah thought it interesting that Angus had chosen to reveal he was trying to learn from his father- assuming that meant he must be learning something about the law and how to use it. A useful tidbit, under the circumstances.

"Gilbert tells me you've come out to deliver an invitation to me. That's very kind of ya. What's the occasion?" Elijah asked innocently, changing the subject. This was the moment of truth, testing Angus' ability to the fullest. Both men knew a lot hung in the balance of how he chose to answer now.

Angus hesitated, as if searching for the right words, suddenly unsure of himself, and even of the whole point of the rally. Realizing he had Dr. Guignard's written invitation in his hand, he held it out to Elijah in offering.

"Well sir, Dr. Guignard asked me if I'd bring this out to ya, and wondered if he might also prevail upon your generosity to contribute some lumber to set up a stage for this event," Angus said, a little too breathlessly, as if trying to make sure he got it said before Elijah could discover the purpose of the rally and get mad.

Elijah opened the invitation and read it carefully, showing no reaction that Angus could decipher.

To Mr. Elijah Willis
Willis Plantation
Williston, Barnwell District
South Carolina

My Dear Elijah,

You are cordially invited to a social gathering at my place on Saturday next, beginning at noon. We will be offering barbecue, desserts and beverages, and an opportunity to meet in a friendly environment with friends and neighbors from around the district to discuss some matters of concern to the entire community. In the spirit of community in which we are gathering, I am happy to provide the refreshments, but am requesting each plantation provide at least one or two of their slaves to help in the preparation and serving, as a show of mutual good will, civic pride, and conviviality.

Please respond by way of my messenger. We are hoping for representation from all our families in the district.

God willing, we shall see you on Saturday.

Most sincerely,

John D. Guignard, M.D.

Elijah calmly folded the invitation and returned it to its envelope. He decided to play Angus a bit before giving his answer.

"Interestin! Been a long time since anybody's thrown a shindig around here to 'discuss matters of concern to the entire community.' I wonder what they are?" Elijah asked in feigned ignorance. He watched Angus keenly for a response.

Angus shifted his weight uncomfortably from one foot to the other, looking down at his boots. It suddenly struck him that he had forgotten to polish them, and he became acutely engrossed in observing the film of dust covering the toes of both boots.

"Any idea, son, of what the Doctor's got in mind?" Elijah queried.

Angus felt panic twist and tie his stomach in a knot. What should he say? Should he tell the truth? Should he lie? Should he play dumb? Thinking fast he blurted, "Well sir, uh, I think Dr. Guignard feels there's been so much talk about things that've been goin on up in Columbia and in Washington and all, that it's created a lot of anxiety, so, um, it might be good for folks just to have an opportunity to express how they feel about it, and, uh, that way we could all let our representatives know where we stand, so's they can represent the will of the people accurately in this great democracy of ours!"

Elijah eyed the boy critically. Like his nemesis, Dr. Guignard, he was impressed by Angus' ability to think fast and talk his way out of a tangle. "Is that a fact? And how do you feel about what's been goin on around here?" he asked pointedly, without deigning to specify to what he was referring, to see if Angus would figure it out, or throw up a smoke screen. Angus started to perspire, desperately trying to weasel his way out of the trap Elijah was deliberately laying for him. He decided he needed to take a stand without specifying the key issue of emancipation and inheritance.

"Well sir, my own feelin is that, uh, if this is truly a democracy, we need to be sure the people's voice is heard and duly represented in our government, so that the decisions we have to make for our safety and future truly reflect the people's will! And I, for one, am willin to speak up and help others do the same, to that end!" He hoped this sounded impressive without tipping Elijah off or opening the door for him to lash back.

Elijah stroked his chin pensively, as if pondering the wisdom of Angus' response.

"Spoken like a true politician, son!" he made it deliberately unclear as to whether this was intended as a compliment or a criticism. "Why, I do believe you might just have a future in politics yourself, with a speech like that!" He meant of course that Angus would fit right in up in Columbia, or maybe even Washington, where saying a lot of words while utterly avoiding the truth of the matter was the name of the game, if not a blood sport. But Angus was so relieved, he chose to take it as a compliment.

"Why, thank ya, Mr. Willis! Am I to take it then that you'll come next Saturday, and bring along some of your slaves to help?" he asked quickly, before he lost his nerve.

"By all means! Tell Dr. Guignard that I shall be pleased to attend, and shall provide a compliment of three of my best slaves. I'll even send a wagon-load of lumber over to his place so ya'll can set up your stage. Sounds like a most informative and right entertainin event. Wouldn't miss it for the world!"

Angus was stunned, and for a moment could hardly believe his ears. Looking uncertain as to how to respond, Elijah teasingly added, "Somethin wrong, son? You will give Dr. Guignard my message, won't ya?"

Angus snapped out of his stupor and falteringly stammered, "Well, yessir! Of course, sir. Ya'll can count on it, sir! And thank you, sir! We surely do appreciate it, sir!"

He immediately felt foolish for repeating 'sir' so many times, but couldn't think how else to respond.

Elijah, rather enjoying the young man's evident astonishment and nervous discomfort, drove a final nail into the coffin by saying, "Good Lord, son, one 'sir' is plenty polite- five makes ya'll sound like some groveling Englishman, tryin to ingratiate himself to a nobleman! Can't be havin that kinda foolishness if you're thinkin of headin up to Columbia or Washington some day! Hell, we Carolinians fought the British in two wars so's not to have to do that!" He smiled playfully at Angus who, intensely uncomfortable, was uncertain whether he was being scourged or teased.

"Yessir, I mean, no sir, I mean thank you, Mr. Willis!" he winced at his own bumbling.

Elijah chuckled without malice and said, "It's alright son, I was just playin with ya. Ya'll go on back and deliver my acceptance and thanks to Dr. Guignard for me now, won't ya?" Angus decided to keep his mouth shut at this point, for safety, and just nodded energetically. Elijah dismissed him saying, "Bye now! And please give my warmest regards to your Pa and Miss Mary for me, too!" He deliberately included Mary to observe Angus' reaction for tell-tale clues. He knew Mary had raised the boy, and there was real love between them. He figured as long as Angus could be continually made aware of the truth of his experience of colored folks, there was still a chance he might not sell his soul and turn rabid against them.

Angus stood there, shook Elijah's hand in thanks, and then headed for his horse, saying, "I sure will, Mr. Willis. And I'll see ya'll on Saturday!"

Recovering himself, he tipped his hat politely as he mounted, settled into his saddle, and then spurred his horse to a gentle canter, not wanting to look too eager to escape, but feeling a wave of relief wash over him with every hoof beat. He figured he had dodged a bullet of possible confrontation, but Angus hadn't even felt Elijah deftly cut open and expose some of his underlying motives with all the skill of Doc Harley's scalpel when he was delivering Eliza by caesarean.

As Elijah watched the boy ride off he turned and called out, "Alright Gilbert! Might as well come on out with Jason and Julius! We got some plannin to do!" Gilbert opened the door to the veranda with a sheepish grin. He realized Elijah had been aware that he and Julius and Jason had been eavesdropping by the parlor window through the entire exchange. Jason and Julius followed behind, looking slightly embarrassed.

"It's alright boys! I knew ya'll were there all along, and in fact that's exactly what I need for ya'll to do next Saturday. Position yourselves so ya'll can see and hear as much as possible without it being obvious you're doin it!" He chuckled, "Angus Junior was so nervous just now, he about peed himself. I almost felt sorry for him! I think he was afraid I was gonna pull a gun on him or somethin! Shoulda seen the look on his face when I told him I'd be glad to come, and bring some slaves, and even send over a load of lumber for their stage!"

"Wonder what Dr. Guignard'll make of your reply?" Julius commented.

"Doubt he was expectin an acceptance without at least some sorta fuss!" added Jason.

"Maybe not," answered Elijah, "But he's a snake, and like Momma Celia said, he may lie coiled up for a while, but he'll strike as soon as he gets a chance! And he's smart enough to reposition himself strategically with this unexpected change in plan. He figures to win, no matter how it plays out. We gotta do all we can so that doesn't happen. The less fuel we give for that fire, the better."

Gilbert spoke up, dropping the epithet 'Mister' as if speaking to his brother-in-law in private, though Jason and Julius didn't seem to notice or mind, "Elijah, you may beat him for a while and buy some time, but I promise you, long as that man has breath he's not gonna forgive or forget it! Best be careful you don't rub his nose in it too much. Not now!"

"Gilbert's right, Mister Elijah. We gotta be real careful how this plays out! But buyin ya'll more time right now is exactly what we need to do. Once we can all get out of here, ole Dr. Guignard can stew in his own juices, and it won't matter no more! In the meantime, we got work to do!" offered Julius. All four nodded in agreement and, pulling out the invitation to look at its clever wording, set to planning how they would deploy themselves to handle the rally.

Dr. Guignard! Dr. Guignard!" Angus called out eagerly as he spied his mentor by the paddock fence, watching one of his grooms put a two-year-old colt through his paces.

"What is it son?" answered Dr. Guignard somewhat distractedly, absorbed as he was in assessing the potential for his prized animal.

"I just thought ya'll oughta know that I got Mr. Willis to agree to come to the rally, and even send over a wagon-load of lumber for the stage!" Angus announced triumphantly, as if this had been achieved by his own diplomatic prowess, rather than by Elijah's wileyness.

Dr. Guignard spun around and looked at his young protégé with sudden acute attention. "Did ya now? Well, that's just grand! Thank ya son, for the news!

Dr. Guignard seemed lost in thought. This was an unexpected development, to be sure! He had assumed Elijah would choose to boycott the rally, thereby providing him the perfect opportunity to call Elijah out for his subversive and anti-social behavior. Elijah's acceptance of the invitation, and even his agreement to provide the lumber for the stage, was a reminder to Dr. Guignard that Elijah was more than capable of challenging his assumptions, and even of repeating his insulting behavior in direct confrontation. This called for a tactical reassessment at the very least, if not an ouright change of strategy. He had to figure out a way to expose Elijah's moral depravity publicly, without actually seeming to do so, so that Elijah couldn't confront him without seeming overly defensive and culpable.

The best victory, of course, would be to get Elijah to simply renounce his family and behave as society demanded without any fuss. Dr. Guignard, however, was not sure whether this acceptance of his invitation was an indication that Elijah was finally coming to his senses, or whether he was a sly fox playing for time. As he pondered this development, Angus still stood there somewhat awkwardly, uncertain as to whether he should wait for further instructions or simply take his leave.

"How did Mr. Willis seem to you, Angus? Did he seem aggravated or in any way upset by the invitation?" Dr. Guignard.

"No sir! Not at all! Tell the truth, I thought he would be, but he was real cordial. Kinda surprised me! And me askin if he'd be kind enough to donate some lumber for the stage didn't seem to faze him at all. He agreed to it right away!" Angus replied.

"Interestin," responded Dr. Guignard pensively. He realized he couldn't afford to simply take Elijah's acquiescence for granted. He wanted to be prepared for any eventuality, so as to be able to maintain the upper hand, securing thereby both Elijah's social compliance and the revenge he was owed for the unpardonable insult of Elijah's behavior at their last encounter as well.

"Do me a favor, Angus. Keep an eye out for the lumber delivery and a sharp ear open to any comments made by Mr. Willis' slaves, would ya?" Guignard was hoping to smoke Elijah out, but he would need Angus' complicity to acquire further clues as to Elijah's real motives in attending the rally. Perhaps something useful could be gleaned from his slaves.

"Sure thing, Dr. Guignard! We'll be glad to keep our eyes and ears open." Angus answered on behalf of all three of them. "Never know what you might pick up from the nigras' small talk!" he added. Dr. Guignard smiled and nodded his appreciation, then turned back to observing his promising colt in the paddock, calling out instructions to the groom as if Angus no longer existed.

"Oh, and Angus," Dr. Guignard suddenly added, "be sure and let me know when the wagon arrives. I should like to be on hand to express my appreciation for the donation in person!"

"Yes, sir! Whatever you say, sir!" Angus replied, eager to please the man whose coattails he hoped to ride into political power, and into his own idea of independence.

Seems he and everyone else in this drama wanted freedom of one kind or another- to be free of parents, or masters, or the need to suffer fools and inferiors, or rivals. How you saw freedom all depended on where you sat, yet each one's dreams were inextricably interwoven with the others- as were their fears- and each was unfolding in ways that were not always predictable.

LV

Now listen up, boys!" Elijah counseled. "When ya'll take the lumber over to Dr. Guignard's, ya'll'd best be on the alert. That man's gonna do anything he can to try to get information out of ya he can use against us. Be on the lookout for his slaves too. There's no guarantee that they're all loyal to him, given the reputation he has for treatin em hard, but there's also no guarantee some of them won't spy for him. Ya'll know perfectly well that some masters'll use all kinds a dirty tricks to make their slaves obey. Trust no one, but be courteous to everyone! Understood?"

Gilbert, Julius, and Jason all nodded their assent, mumbling "Yessir!" The wagon was piled high with rough sawn planks and enough saws, hammers and nails to put together a decent sized platform. The three men clambered up onto the wagon- Gilbert and Julius in the driver's seat and Jason behind them in back, making sure nothing fell out on the way. Elijah waved to them as they slapped the reins on the mules' backs and started off down the road.

"Ya'll be sure and report back to me anything and everything ya see or hear! The Devil's in the details! Even if it doesn't seem important, it might be!" Elijah called after them.

"Don't worry Elijah, we know what we gotta do!" Gilbert shouted back with a wave.

Elijah sighed as he watched the men drive out of sight, bracing himself for what might lie ahead. Uncertain of what to expect, but fairly well assured that whatever it was, it was not going to be easy, he turned and went into the house.

As he opened the double front door, he saw Amy coming downstairs, her belly now quite large since her due date drew near. Her steps were slow and a bit labored as she held firmly onto the mahogany handrail. When she reached the bottom of the stairs, she too let out a sigh, her right hand still clutching the rail and her left hand massaging the small of her back. "Have they gone?" she asked, panting, knowing full well where Gilbert and the others were headed.

Elijah nodded. "I'm not sure how this is gonna play out, darlin, or exactly what's been set in motion, but as sure as those wagon wheels are turning, I can feel us being carried forward in our plan, one way or another," he averred. "Are you feelin alright?" he asked, suddenly aware that Amy was breathing a bit heavily.

"I'm fine sugar, it's just carryin this baby is getting tiresome. It's almost time for him to come out!" She smiled hopefully. "Doctor Harley made me promise to call for him at the very first sign of any activity- even if my waters don't break."

Elijah nodded in agreement. Joseph had exacted the same promise from him too, assuring he'd come immediately if called. Elijah offered Amy his arm as they strode down the hall toward the kitchen. "Lord, I hope this time everything goes smoothly. I can't bear the thought of ya goin through the agony ya went through with Eliza again! I was scared we were gonna lose ya!"

"I know sugar, I hope so too, but that's in the Good Lord's hands now, not ours! I remember Doctor Harley insistin it wasn't my time back then, and that he was convinced the Lord had a plan and wanted to see us all free. I'm holdin onto that! Every day!"

"So am I, darlin, so am I," Elijah confessed. They found Momma Celia in the kitchen, as usual. Elijah ushered Amy to the same chair where she had been chopping spring onions when her waters broke and Eliza had announced her arrival. Momma Celia smiled at them both.

"Ya'll set down and have some tea. Calm ya nerves," she offered, as she pulled a brightly burnished copper tea kettle with an ebony and brass handle from the cookstove. Wisps of steam puffed cheerfully out of its spout. There was a plate of fresh buttermilk buiscuits on the table, a crock of fresh churned butter, and a stoneware pot of magnolia honey from their own bees, too.

This idyllic scene of family tranquility and warmth felt in stark contrast to the drama that seemed to be unfolding in Williston. Elijah was conflicted. On the one hand, he wanted to indulge in this warmth, wrapping all of them in it like some protective shield, separating them from the currents of fear and hatred and suspicion that seemed to swirl outside the plantation like the branches of the creeks that flowed through and around his lands.

But another part of him felt like building a barricade and arming his slaves in preparation for a full-fledged attack. He was worried that the rally on Saturday would make those political waters overflow their banks and threaten the safety of the plantation. Yet he knew he had to exercise restraint too, for he still had not been able to get to Cincinnati, and until he could go up there, come back, and return to Ohio with the whole family, their entire plan could still fail.

"How do you suppose Doctor Guignard's gonna handle your presence at this rally?" Amy asked, sipping her tea, her gaze fixed on Elijah over the edge of her teacup.

"Well, I imagine he's tryin to figure out whether, by acceptin his invitation, I'm concedin and complyin with his expectations that I amend my dissolute ways and send ya'll back to the slave quarters- OR, whether I'm playin for time! The man's an arrogant ass, but he's not stupid, and I expect he'll figure out it's the latter and not the former, before too long."

"Ummmm, hmmm!" interjected Momma Celia, "An when he do, we gonna all have to be prepared for him to do whatever he can to call ya out!"

"I'm sure you're right Momma Celia, but him callin me out isn't what worries me most. I'd face him any day- already have, though it made him mad as Hell. It's how far he's willin to go to stir up the community against us that is the bigger problem!"

"It's because ya already did face him that he's determined to get back at ya now!" responded Amy, "Even though I thought it was real brave of ya at the time."

"Yeah, and do ya remember I told ya I wasn't sure whether it was brave or foolhardy?" responded Elijah. "Well I'm still not, but it is what it is, and that's what we're gonna have to deal with!"

"True, but Doctor Guignard's wiley enough not to lose control with you face to face- least of all in public," opined Amy.

"That may be, sugar," said Momma Celia, "but he's also enough of a weasel to find a way to use them boys, like Angus Junior and Elijah's nephews, to do his dirty work so he can still come up smellin like a rose! An they too foolish an too needin somebody to pay attention to em to realize what he's doin!"

Elijah, as usual, was impressed by the keen insight of his mother-in-law.

"Momma's right, sugar. This rally is gonna be like walkin into a snake pit. No tellin where the strikes will come from!"

"Elijah, I'm scared! Do ya really have to go to this thing? What if the boys get liquored up and start workin up the crowd? It could get real ugly, and I just can't have you gettin hurt- especially not now!" Amy started to sob softly. Momma Celia put a comforting hand on her shoulder, and Elijah took Amy's hands in his.

"Darlin, if I don't show, Guignard's gonna make a big deal out of it, for sure! The question is, can I go for long enough to be seen, but not stay throughout the whole event? I'm just not sure, and will probably have to play it by ear."

"Alright, but you promised me ya'll wouldn't do anything stupid! Ya simply mustn't let them get to ya- not doctor Guignard, or that fool Mr. Matthews, or the boys, or anyone in town!"

"I can handle em, darlin, don't you worry! You'll see! Everything's gonna work out," he swore, "somehow!" he added softly, as if to himself.

Momma Celia looked at her son-in-law with trusting eyes. He had already proven himself incredibly faithful to all of them repeatedly- in Baltimore, in confronting his family, in confronting Dr. Guignard and Frederick Matthews. She felt confident nothing would change that.

"You do what ya'all feel ya gotta do, Elijah. We got faith in ya!" Momma Celia avowed.

"Thank ya, Momma. I truly do appreciate that. Ya'll know I only want what's best for all of us. I just gotta be sure to buy us enough time before this pot of anti-emanicpation feelin boils over around here, and we all get scalded! The first chance I get after the baby's born, I'm headin to Cincinnati at last!" He downed the rest of his tea in punctuation, grabbed a biscuit, slathered it with butter and honey, and got up from the table.

"Now, where dya think ya're goin, droppin crumbs all over my kitchen like that?" scolded Momma Celia, lovingly. Amy smiled in appreciation- it was rare her mother spoke in such a motherly tone to Elijah, but she felt comforted by it, as if it further cemented the family bond.

Elijah sheepishly cradled the buiscuit with one hand, trying to catch any other waywards crumbs from falling, and licked the honey off his fingertips with the other, as he headed out the back door. "Sorry Momma! I got work to do! I can't just sit around here waitin for news from Gilbert and the others, or I'll go crazy!"

Both women smiled in recognition of his honesty. "Probly best you go then, or you'll be drivin us crazy too!" responded Amy, patting her belly, "an I just don't need that right now!" Elijah blew her a kiss, grinning as he went out the back door.

LVI

Angus Junior was riding past the paddocks when he saw the lumber wagon coming up the road toward the meadow and ran to find Dr. Guignard, as he had promised. He found him giving orders to his groom about the feeding of that promising colt. Dr. Guignard was quick to respond to the news and headed directly for the meadow, showing up with Angus eagerly in tow just as the wagon was turning off the road and coming to a stop.

""Mornin, Doctor Guignard, Mister Angus!" Gilbert tipped his hat respectfully to them both. "This here's the lumber ya'll asked for to build the stage for ya'll's shindig on Saturday. Our master Mister Elijah tole us to bring it to ya, and build whatever ya'll wanted us to build, wherever ya'll tell us to build it!"

"Well thank ya, boy! Tell your master that I surely do appreciate that! Ya'll do him credit!" Doctor Guignard was not one for complimenting slaves, and Gilbert, Julius and Jason knew it. They were instantly on their guard.

"Thank ya, sir, but ain't no special credit in doin what we told! That's just our job!" Gilbert was not about to fall into Dr. Guignard's trap.

"Indeed it is, boy, indeed it is! Pity more nigras don't see it that way," Doctor Guignard responded flatly, eyeing all three of them coolly for any sign of response.

"Yessir!" mumbled Gilbert, his eyes downcast in what he hoped was a convincingly submissive manner. Julius and Jason eyed Dr. Guignard furtively for any clues as to his intentions or probable next step.

"Angus! Come on over here, son!" Dr. Guignard called to his protégé. "Tell em where ya'll want your stage built. Ya'll can use some of my nigras too, if ya need em."

Angus, slightly uncomfortable under the gaze of Gilbert, replied, "Right away, sir!" He then turned to Gilbert and said, in a tone he hoped expressed to Dr. Guignard the proper level of authority, "Bring the wagon over there, an I'll show you where to build it!" He didn't want to sound too bossy and offend Gilbert, but he didn't want to sound overly friendly with Elijah's slaves either, for fear that Dr. Guignard might think him weak. Dr. Guignard seemed to lay great store by what he called "observin the proper social boundaries." Angus looked at Gilbert almost apologetically.

Gilbert, of course, was fully prepared to deal with Angus Junior, and really had no problem going along with this charade with him. To Gilbert's dismay, however, out of the corner of his eye he noticed that James and Michael Willis were riding toward the meadow, apparently wanting to be in on the preparations, or at least take the credit for them. Gilbert was certain they would be wanting to order him around, almost as if being on Dr. Guignard's property gave them dispensation to be ruder than usual. He shot a warning glance to Julius and Jason to prepare them for some ugliness.

"Mornin, Doctor Guignard!" James and Michael both called out in greeting to the host of the event they hoped would boost their social standing. "Fine morning, ain't it?"

"Mornin boys! Yes, indeed it is! Nice to see ya! Thanks for comin over to help out!" Dr. Guignard responded amiably. "Your uncle's sent over a load of lumber for ya'll to build yaselves a stage and some tables. Ya'll can tell his nigras what ya want. This is your event, boys! Best get goin!" Dr. Guignard turned to head back to the house, deliberately leaving the Willis boys to figure out how to set the whole thing up. Hardly experienced at staging such affairs, they sat slightly stupefied before realizing that Dr. Guignard had just given them the authority and the manpower to make of it what they would.

Spotting Angus over by the wagon full of lumber, James called out, "Mornin Angus! We're here to help!"

"Mornin James, Michael!" Angus called back, waiting for them to offer some actual assisance. "Well don't just sit there, come on! We got work to do!" he insisted.

The Willis boys rode their horses over to the wagon at a slow, liesurely walk, looking around the field to get a sense of what had to be done. When they got to the wagon, James said to Gilbert with a snide drawl, "Well I gotta admit, this is a surprise! Didn't really expect Uncle Elijah'd send his nigras over here to help – much less send a load a wood! Mornin, Gilbert!"

Gilbert held himself back from bristling at James. He loathed the man, but was determined not to let it show.

"Mornin, Mister James," he replied calmly. He offered no more, waiting to see what the Willis boys would do. However, they did nothing, yet, for Angus immediately deflected their attention.

"Come on, James! Help us unload the wagon so we can get to buildin' the stage!" urged Angus.

James looked at Gilbert, Julius, and Jason with a surly smile and answered, "Why should we help unload? Ain't that what the nigras're for?" He turned to his brother and grinned.

"That's right, Angus! Ain't no need for us to unload- we just gotta tell all these coons what to do. That's what they're here for!"

Angus was uneasy. He actually liked Gilbert and the others, and saw them as human beings even though he felt duty bound to maintain a social distance from them. James and Michael on the other hand, were clearly unencumbered by any humanitarian notions of dealing with people. They simply related to the coloreds as if to livestock, livestock with a utilitarian purpose at their disposal. Gilbert and Jason and Julius all watched this dynamic unfold in silence.

"Jesus, James! At least help me figure out where to put the stage then, and how big we should make it!" Angus said in exasperation.

"What's got you all worked up, Angus? Ya'll got a problem with telling slaves what to do? Doubt Doctor Guignard would like to see that!" James said with a vindictive edge. He was clearly jealous and resentful that Angus seemed to have ingratiated himself to Dr. Guignard, implicitly relegating James and Michael to a secondary role. He was conveniently forgetting that it was he himself who had insisted Angus was the better qualified to broach the subject of the event with Dr. Guignard in the first place.

"No, I don't have a problem givin orders, James, so I'm gonna give you some!" Angus retorted, "Get your butt movin and help me get this thing organized! Don't you get it? Doctor Guignard's testing us three, and we'd best past the test or our political future's gonna look mighty dim!"

"Angus's got a point there, James!" chimed in Michael, ever ready to see his brother knocked down a peg or two instead of being on the receiving end of criticism himself. "Let's stop wastin time bickerin, and figure out how and where things need to get set up, so Doctor Guignard don't feel like we're wastin his time and money!" he urged.

"Well, alright then!" said James, looking around, trying to regain some control and look like he was in charge. "Let's see, if folks're gonna be comin into the meadow from over there, we'd best set up a row a tables for the food and drink over here." He gestured toward the shade of the trees lining the edge of the field. "And then over there, out in the meadow facing the entrance point, is where we oughta put the stage. That way folks can come in, get somethin to eat or drink, and be socializin in the space in between. And anyone arrivin late will see us up on the stage, facin the crowd to welcome them!"

The other two nodded their agreement. The plan made sense, and James' irritation with Angus seemed assuaged, for the moment at least. Listening to all this, Gilbert was torn. Should he simply set to work putting James' plan into action or wait for orders to do so? If it were Elijah announcing the plan, he would already be on the move to make it a reality, but he was as wary of looking overly cooperative as he was of appearing deliberately recalcitrant with James and Michael there. He hesitated.

"Well, go on boy! Ya'll heard what the man said, didn't ya?" Michael barked at Gilbert, wanting to share in the feeling of authority, and deliberately calling him 'boy' even though Gilbert was his senior.

"Yessir," Gilbert replied submissively, "But how long ya'll want to make the tables, and how big do ya'll want the stage to be?" he asked innocently.

The Willis brothers and Angus looked at each other uncertainly. Gilbert could tell perfectly well they had not thought this thing through, and hadn't even figured out how many people were likely to come. He suspected they also wouldn't even think of where to build the fire pits for the barbeque- or know to make sure they were downwind from the crowd, so's not to get smoke in everybody's eyes, but he wasn't about to point any of this out. He was actually rather enjoying their bumbling competition, and was more than willing for them to make fools of themselves. Julius and Jason both surpressed smiles as they watched the three companions muddle about, trying to look authoritative and figure out what to do at the same time.

"The stage has gotta be big enough for several people – with a row of chairs in back and room for someone to stand in front to give speeches. And steps! Be sure ya'll build it with some steps, so folks can get up there in a dignified manner!" insisted Angus, clearly more focused on his anticipated moment of glory than on the requisites for the Southern hospitality for which the region was famed, and of which the locals would clearly expect to partake. Gilbert nodded, signaling Julius and Jason to help him with the lumber so they could get started.

"Best make the tables long enough to serve at least a hundred people!" interjected James, now starting to get a feel for what was actually needed. Not that he had an accurate head-count of who had been invited, but a hundred at least sounded like a respectable turn-out.

"Michael, could you go on up to the big house and ask Miss Sally, Doctor Guignard's housekeeper, to send down the red, white and blue bunting we ordered from Will Beazely at the depot to decorate the stage and the tables?" Angus asked.

Michael grumbled, "I ain't no nigra to do your biddin, Angus!"

"Aw come on now Michael, it ain't like that; it's just that I can't go cause I gotta make sure Gilbert builds the stage right, and James is over there trying to pace off how long the make the servin tables. Everybody's gotta pitch in, or we won't get it done in time!" Angus pleaded.

"Oh, alright then! Miss Sally, did ya say? But I ain't haulin yer cloth down here. Doctor Guignard said we could use some a his nigras, so I'll deliver the message, but they gonna have to do the work!" Michael responded, put out as if the very idea of him having to work was a contradiction of the whole reason for the rally.

Julius almost felt pity for Michael. He saw a man with no skills, desperately wanting to be in charge of something, but without a clue as to how to even take charge of himself. Indolence, a distorted sense of privilege, and a society that reinforced them both had made him a slave to his own lethargy and stupidity. Julius started to understand for the first time why the Willis brothers made Elijah as sad as they made him mad.

Upstairs at the plantation house, Dr. Guignard was actually watching the whole scene through a spyglass from his bedroom window. He chuckled to himself as he observed the faces and gestures of the Willis brothers and Angus working out what to do. He was also interested to observe Elijah's slaves who, though outwardly submissive, seemed to be giving each other covert signals belying their apparent passivity. He also noted the skill, speed, and dexterity with which they promptly set about laying out the stage, once given the command. Much as he resented it, he had to admire Elijah for having slaves who actually knew how to work. It seemed an anomaly to him, and never occurred to him that perhaps his own slaves were deliberately less willing or skilled, simply because he treated them so much worse than Elijah treated his slaves.

Satisfied that his protégés were at least meeting the task set before them, Dr. Guignard decided to come downstairs and start to take charge himself.

Calling out to Sally as he reached the bottom of the richly carpeted, elegant spiral stairway, he strode toward the front door just as Michael reached the portico. "Sally! Bring that buntin we ordered, gal! Mister Willis is gonna need it, and I want ya'll to send some of the young gals down to help him with the decorations!"

As the doorknocker fell, echoing loudly through the foyer, Sally appeared from the back, sighing and huffing as she trudged in with the same glum expression as the day Angus had first visited. "Yassuh!" was all she mumbled as she stopped, torn between fetching the bunting and answering the door. This seemed yet another source of exasperation for Dr. Guignard.

"Oh for the love of God, woman! Don't just stand there like you were dumber than a bag of hammers! Go on! I'll get the door. Get a move on!" snapped Dr. Guignard as he opened the door and assumed his crocodile smile to greet Michael. "Well hello there, Michael! What can I do for ya?" he asked, to Michael's surprise.

"Uh, excuse me Doctor, but Angus sent me up to ask that the bunting be sent down to the meadow, so's we can decorate the stage and tables."

"Don't you worry son, I've already ordered Sally and the gals to bring it down and help ya'll. I'm glad ya came though, cause I wanted to suggest that ya'll build the barbecue pits to the east of the stage and servin tables. That way the smoke'll blow away from the crowd. We don't want any hickory smoked planters at our event, now do we son?" Dr. Guignard smiled an ingratiating smile at his own weak joke, and just as he intended, Michael was unaware of being manipulated like a puppet.

"That's a great idea sir! Thank ya for your help! We surely do appreciate it!" Michael answered enthusiastically.

"That's alright son, I'm glad to be able to support such fine young men in doin their civic duty!" Dr. Guignard replied smoothly. He, of course, had a vested interest in the outcome, counting on successfully garnering both the community's admiration and the means by which he could finally exact his revenge on Elijah Willis. He wasn't about to let Angus' and the Willis boys' inexperience undermine the success of the event. After all, as the host it would reflect poorly on him, and that was simply not acceptable. As he put a congratulatory arm around Michael's shoulder, as if to bestow upon him his approval, Sally headed out with two slave girls carrying yards and yards of bunting, lumbering heavy-footed down to the meadow to where Angus, James, and Elijah's slaves awaited them.

Dr. Guignard resisted the tempation to run upstairs and watch them through his spyglass, but he was pretty well certain there would be some sort of exchange between his slaves and Elijah's that wasn't just about hanging bunting or setting up tables.   He pondered whether it would be worth dragging it out of Sally when she came back to the house or whether he'd just let things play out as they would. Perhaps it was best to let Elijah's slaves think he was unaware. He knew if need be he could always count on some of the other planters' slaves to spy for him too, and chuckled cynically to himself at the thought of how easily he could secure their collusion by crossing their pink palms with a little silver.

LVII

Amy was sitting in a rocking chair on the upper porch enjoying the late afternoon breeze when she saw Gilbert and the others heading up the road to the plantation in the wagon, which was now empty of lumber.

"Elijah honey, they're back!" she immediately called inside to her husband. Elijah appeared on the porch directly, to join his wife and await the report from Gilbert of the day's events on the Guignard plantation. As the wagon drove into view, Elijah called down to Gilbert, "Come on up, ya'll. We're eager for ya news!"

Gilbert pulled the wagon to a stop and set the brake as Julius and Jason clambered down. The three of them headed over to the water trough to rinse some of the sawdust and dirt off before climbing the stairs to the upper porch. Jason and Julius held back, as they were less accustomed to being in the big house and felt a little uncomfortable, in spite of Elijah and Amy's welcome.

"Well boys, how'd it go? What news?" Elijah asked with the alacrity of a general demanding a report from the enemy front, eager to out-strategize the opponent.

Gilbert and his companions proceeded to recount the day's events, blow by blow. There was little that could be called news exactly. The tensions between the Willis brothers were long known to Elijah, but he found Angus' ascendancy over James as an authoritative voice both revealing and a touch surprising. Julius and Jason confirmed that Sally had told them about Angus having initiated the rally. Sally had been surprised by that because she knew Angus Sr. and admired him. Wouldn't have expected this of his son. She also revealed that Angus Jr. sought Dr. Guignard's support to get people to sign a petition against abolitionist behavior of any kind, which they planned to take up to Columbia and present to the legislature in person. She even mentioned the ban of the sale or reading of *Uncle Tom's Cabin* as the pretext.

The most interesting tidbit, however, also came from Sally. She tipped Gilbert, Julius, and Jason off that Dr. Guignard had invited Robert Barnwell Rhett to speak at the rally! Rhett was a particularly strident voice against emancipation, who some felt was too extreme to be reliable as a real political leader despite him seeing himself as John C. Calhoun's successor. Elijah was a bit alarmed by this, as the potential for inflammatory rhetoric at the rally would be greatly enhanced by Rhett's presence. Moreover, it would quickly overshadow Angus' and the Willis boys' amateurish pretentions to political involvement, unless they played their cards as Rhett's acolytes.

That was a disturbing development indeed, for it seemed unlikely anyone could walk away from the rally without having signed the petition and not face the ire or reprisals of Rhett and his minions. Elijah realized that Dr. Guignard was not taking any chances of relying solely on Elijah's nephews and Angus. He wanted to make sure to extract some kind of retribution from Elijah come Hell or high water, and chose to use his considerable influence to set things up to assure his success. Elijah was also virtually certain that Rhett's invitation was unknown to Angus and his nephews and would come as a rude surprise to them too, even if for different reasons.

"Damn!" he uttered in exasperation. "Guignard's clearly playin for keeps! This is definitely not good news! That heartless son of a bitch wants his pound of flesh, no doubt about it! I said he was a snake, but seems he's more like a spider, weavin a web to catch us all, and doesn't even care if his own pawns, Angus and James and Michael, get tangled up in it on the way by!"

"Whether a snake or a spider, he's poisonous either way, Elijah! I'm scared!" Amy blurted.

"Which is exactly what he wants us to be! The man uses fear as a weapon to intimidate people. He's nothing more than a bully in fancy dress. I'm not gonna give him that satisfaction!" insisted Elijah.

"That's all well and good Elijah, I'm with ya on that, but there's a difference between being brave and being reckless. Ya'll can't go to that rally unprepared, or they'll try ta eat ya alive!" cautioned Gilbert. Amy, Jason and Julius all nodded their agreement. Elijah sat there listening and taking in their responses. After a pause, he asked,

"Amy, remember I told you, that night you told me you were pregnant with Eliza, that there were well-meaning folks that supported us?" as if lost in thought.

"Yes I do, an I also remember you said maybe we'd need to solicit their support at some point." Amy replied.

Elijah nodded. "I'm thinking maybe this is that point! If not everybody who goes to that rally is all het up to go on an anti-emancipation rampage, we might be able to keep tempers cool enough that the powder keg we're sittin' on doesn't explode!" Elijah proclaimed.

"I dunno, Mister Elijah. Might be playin with fire to go around tryin to drum up support at this point, when you haven't even been able to get to Cincinnati yet!" Julius offered

Gilbert nodded in agreement, "It'd be one thing if everything was in place already, and we just needed to keep things calm long enough to get away, but we don't know how long that's gonna take, and things look mighty close to a boilin point right now!"

"Not only that Mister Elijah, but it's askin a lot of folks to put their own selves at risk facin Doctor Guignard and Mister Rhett, with such a long way to go still!" chimed in Jason.

Julius spoke up, "I know they's a lotta folks around here who like and respect ya, Mister Elijah- specially colored folks, and white folks like the merchants ya'll do business with. They know you honest and treat everybody fair. But if they get the sense that Mister Rhett or Doctor Guignard want to rout out and punish any 'sympathizers' with ya'll's cause, they might be too skeered to speak up!"

Elijah heaved a heavy sigh. They were all right, of course. Yet the situation did not permit just hiding out at Willis Plantation as a viable option. He desperately wanted to believe that not everyone in the community was hateful, and that there were enough people who recognized the coloreds as human beings, not so different from whites, to stem the corrosive tide rising throughout the region. But the fact was, he wasn't sure there were, and was even less sure of what that might mean in terms of his own choices and options.

Once again, the scripture came to mind, "You meant it for evil, but God meant it for good!" He looked around at everyone- a swirl of brown faces glowing in the late afternoon light like the varied tones in the rich grain of hand-rubbed mahogany, looking expectantly to him for some wisdom, or at least a clear choice and plan of action.

"Well the way I see it, I gotta be true to myself and to the promise I've made to ya'll, or I just can't go on any further. I'm gonna go the rally just as we planned, do what I can to keep tempers from flarin, learn what I can about people's current sympathies, and get the Hell out of there as soon as possible without givin anybody cause for criticizin me. The rest is up to God!" He paused for a moment, and then added, "Actually, maybe it's all up to God! I keep coming back to Joseph telling his brothers, 'You meant it for evil, but God meant it for good,' and I feel like I got no other choice but to trust in Him at this point! I just don't know what else I can do!"

Amy felt the baby moving like a boxer throwing punches. The ferocity of the movement startled her out of her anxiety about the rally, reminding her that whatever might happen, she still had a life and a family to take care of, and a child seemingly eager to make his entrance into the world. "Well, your son at least seems to agree with you!" she smiled up at Elijah, and her smile scattered the clouds of doubt he felt closing in on him.

"Thanks for the report boys. Why don't ya'll go on an get some food and rest? It's been a long day, and ya'll've done a good job. I'm sure with ya'll's help we'll be ready for whatever comes on Saturday. I knew I could count on ya!" Elijah smiled appreciatively at the three of them. They nodded their acceptance back and headed for the stairs.

"One more thing, Elijah," offered Gilbert, pausing before heading downstairs with the others to take the wagon out to the barn and unharness the mules before supper, "We figured if one of us stations ourselves at the servin table, another at the barbecue pit, and the third somewhere near the stage, we should be able to pick up on most of the conversations runnin round there at the rally. That leaves you free to mingle with whoever ya'll need to, and should give us a real clear idea of who's who an what's what."

Elijah nodded. "Good idea; that'll do fine Gilbert! Thanks for your help!"

Gilbert nodded to Elijah, smiled reassuringly at his sister, and headed on downstairs.

"Two more days, sugar, just two more days, and we'll be over this particular bump in the road!" Elijah said, trying to comfort his wife and calm her anxiety.

"I know you're right about havin to go an all, and about trustin the Lord too, but God Almighty, this stress is just awful! I'm worried about your heart, and the baby, and Gilbert, and the boys…"

"You worry too much!" Elijah answered. "Has your worryin ever changed anything?" he asked bluntly, trying to make the point that surrender to reality was the only viable option.

"Course not!" Amy readily admitted, "But at least it makes me feel like I'm not just sittin here doin nothin about it!" She grinned in a flash of self-recognition, and found that in fact her tension was eased by realizing there wasn't much they could do but stay alert, be careful, and let things play out as they would.

"Mmmm, hmmm! I thought so!" replied Elijah, smiling back at her. "Come on darlin, let's get you downstairs to supper, or I'll have to face something far more fearsome than the wrath of Robert Barnwell Rhett or John Guignard: your mother!!!" He looked at her bug-eyed in mock terror.

Amy laughed and offered him her hand to help her up out of the rocking chair. Heaving her baby-bulk out of the seat and steadying herself, leaning slightly backwards to compensate for the forward thrusting change in her center of gravity, with the splay-footed waddle of all women in late pregnancy she accompanied her husband inside and downstairs for their evening meal.

LVIII

Saturday dawned fair and balmy. It seemed like heaven itself was smiling down on the Guignard plantation. Dr. Guignard had been up since dawn, ordering his slaves to finish the preparations. Lavers of savory snacks, bowls of punch- with and without rum (a concession to the ladies)- and various plates, bowls, and trays of goodies converted the trestle tables into veritable groaning boards of bounty. From the east side of the meadow the succulent aroma of roasting meat- chicken, pork, and even beef- wafted across the field and out onto the road. The bunting rippled attractively in a slight breeze, lending a decidedly festive air to the scene as Dr. Guignard, Angus Junior, and the Willis brothers surveyed the area in anticipation of the arrival of the first guests.

"It's a fine day, boys! Ya'll oughta be right proud! Ya done a real good job! This looks grand!" announced Dr. Guignard with satisfaction. Whatever his political or social motives, being a dyed in the wool Southerner, he deemed the fine points of hospitality the mark of a true gentleman, and he had spared no effort in making sure that the event would duly impress and be remembered by all those who attended.

"Yessir! Thank ya sir, but we couldn't have done all this without ya'll's help!" acknowledged Angus, seemingly unaware of just how much of all this was due to Dr. Guignard.

"We surely do appreciate ya'll hostin this for us!" added James sincerely, with Michael nodding his agreement by his side.

"Well boys, I'm happy and honored to help such upstandin young men in our community! After all, our future depends on folks like you boys steppin up! Ya'll got your petition ready for signin? No point in gatherin all these folks together and then forgettin what ya'll called em here to do!" Dr. Guignard reminded them.

Michael suddenly looked panicked. In the hustle and bustle of setting up everything, it dawned on him that he had absolutely no idea where the petition even was. James, picking up on his brother's anxiety, looked almost as uncomfortable, making it clear that he didn't have the petition either but was terrified to admit it. To their immense relief however, before their ignorance could be discovered, thereby shattering Dr. Guignard's presumed confidence in them, Angus responded,

"Yessiree! I got it all set up on a table near the entrance, with an inkwell and quills all ready, and a paperweight to keep it from blowin away in the breeze!" He paused, "And thank ya, Dr. Guignard, for the list of all the folks we invited, so we can check em off as they sign. That was a real good idea! I even set Gilbert at the table to remind folks to sign and check off their names on the list!"

The brilliant irony of assigning this task to Gilbert, whether by design or by dumb luck, seemed to amuse Dr. Guignard and actually provoked a chuckle from him. "Did ya now? Well isn't that just grand?!" he said approvingly.

Dr. Guignard seemed not the least bit perturbed that that meant Gilbert might be in a position to overhear numerous conversations on the topic of the petition's content. Being convinced of the intellectual inferiority of all people of color, it seemed not to occur to him that Gilbert might find such information somehow useful. It appeared to be more a matter of whether Dr. Guignard thought or cared whether such information might make Gilbert uncomfortable. It was hard to say, however, whether Dr. Guignard's indifference to Negro humanity led him to think Gilbert's possible discomfort simply unimportant, or whether his underlying cruelty and jealously relished the discomfort such conversations would cause Gilbert, who would nevertheless be duty bound to remain there despite his distress.

Michael and James, unaware of Dr. Guignard's inner thoughts or twisted machinations, simply looked with relief and gratitude to Angus for saving them from the embarrassment of being caught unprepared in such a glaring way. They now contented themselves with officiously surveying the field to be sure there were enough slaves on hand to serve all the participants. The event in fact seemed unusually well-supplied with servants, due to Dr. Gignard's clever insistence in the invitation.

Julius had stationed himself by the serving tables, having dressed in his Sunday finest to help serve the guests. Jason meanwhile, was attempting to decide between placing himself by the barbecue pit or near the stage, and concluded it would be best to compromise, so he placed himself in between the two, trying to look useful and readily obedient to the needs of any of the white attendees.

By late morning, the first guests were starting to arrive, especially those who had come from further away, not wanting to be late for the big event. Dr. Guignard stationed himself to greet each of them as they came in, cordially gesturing to the tables laden with food and the barrel of whiskey at the end, around which James, Michael, Angus and the young bucks of the region were already cheerfully gathering like eager gamblers to a poker table.

Elijah chose to come on Beauty rather than in the carriage. He had considered coming in the wagon with Gilbert and the others, but realized this would only give folks more cause for 'nigra-lovin' talk, which he studiously needed to avoid, despite his proletarian preferences. He dismounted near the entrance to the meadow and tethered the mare to a tree where she could graze contentedly.

"Well good day to you, Elijah! So nice of ya to join us! And thank ya for both your lumber, and the use of your slaves!" Dr. Guignard said effusively but without warmth, eyeing Elijah like a hawk looking for his kill.

"Hello, John! Happy to oblige! Never was one to shirk my civic duty to a town my own family founded!" Elijah answered, pointedly. He noticed that pulling social rank as a founding family member rankled Dr. Guignard ever so slightly, for it was indicative of a status he himself could never attain. No amount of wealth or influence could ever grant him Elijah's inherited status. Clearly knowing this, Elijah smiled at him with satisfaction, which the Doctor found irritating but ambiguous enough that he could not afford to call him on it.

"So, what exactly are the 'matters of concern' ya'll are thinking of addressin today?" Elijah asked cheerfully. "The risin cost of sour mash whiskey?" he grinned,

"We should probably be teachin the younger generation how to distill it, or they'll drink us dry, from the look of things!" Elijah looked over to the end of the serving tables where James, and Michael, and their peers were eagerly partaking of Mr. Stoddard's donation.

Dr. Guignard forced a smile, and replied, "Perhaps so! No doubt that is a matter of concern to at least some of our community!" His smile froze, his eyes growing cold as if in response to their chilling proximity to his mouth. "However there are more pressin matters for us to attend to- but all that'll be explained once everyone's assembled. Now if you'll excuse me,

I must continue to greet our other guests. Why don't ya'll go on over and help yaself to some refreshment?" With that, he seemed to dismiss Elijah, either in the hope of playing one up on him, or simply to be freed by the distraction of the next guest, from the overwhelming desire to throttle the man and have done with it, for his insufferable impudence.

As Elijah worked his way down the serving table, most of the slaves smiled at him in recognition, serving him the choicest morsels. Elijah smiled back, always thanking each, often by name. A few guests in the line gave mild looks of surprise at this seemingly excessive and unneccessary courtesy, as did some of the slaves who did not know him, but blacks and whites alike refrained from making any comments. Elijah was not unaware of these responses, but felt it imperative to remain true to himself as much as possible. He knew the slaves, in particular, would notice it immediately if he acted otherwise. Whether discreetly discussed amongst themselves, or reported clandestinely to Dr. Guignard, they would not fail to comment on it.

While seeming to be simply helping himself to the delicious repast, Elijah kept a wary eye on Dr. Guignard, and checked regularly to see who else was arriving. Having been raised in Barnwell District he knew most everyone by sight at least, if not by reputation. As he surveyed the crowd, he made a mental tally of friends and foes. There were some, like Dr. Guignard and his yapping lap dog Frederick Matthews, who were clearly his opponents, but there were also some he trusted not to join any mob mentality, should the speakers manage to raise the tensions to a fever pitch. He saw Will Beazely, for one, looking slightly uncomfortable and very much on the alert. He was also relieved to see Joseph Harley, who spotted him and waved with a cheerful smile. John Bauskett and his wife Eugenia were there too, yet so were his own brother Jimmy and his sister-in-law, smiling graciously as they greeted friends and acquaintances. Even Reason and Ari Wooley, his nearest neighbors, had shown up with some other townsfolk, wondering what all the ruckus was about. It seemed that pretty much everyone around had shown up for this- either out of conviction or curiosity.

As Elijah was reaching the end of the table with a well-laden plate, he happened to notice a particular flurry of activity at the entrance to the meadow. Several of the local belles were suddenly lacey fans all aflutter, like a veritable cloud of brightly colored butterflies, and their husbands were doffing their hats respectfully. The crowd then parted like the Red Sea before Moses, and it became clear whose arrival had caused such a stir. It was none other than Robert Barnwell Rhett, scion of the founding family of Barnwell, and the leading political figure of the region.

Elijah took note with some amusement, of the startled and disconcerted expressions on the faces of Guignard's three protégés, whom the good doctor had apparently not deigned to inform that Mr. Rhett would be in attendance to upstage them as keynote speaker! He could see the anxiety on their faces- especially on Angus Junior's- as if the bubble of their self-promoting political fantasies was brushing against the pin of Rhett's sharp-toungued reputation, ready to burst at any minute. "What a fox Guignard is," thought Elijah to himself. "This should be interestin!"

"I wonder how that's gonna play out!" murmured Julius in Elijah's ear, glancing in Rhett's direction as he offered him a delicacy to add to his plate.

Elijah signaled Julius to keep silent, but with raised eyebrows and pursed lips, he hunched his shoulders slightly, and gave him a look that mirrored Julius' curiousity.

As he enjoyed the finger-lickin delicacies on his plate, Elijah circulated through the crowd, greeting friends and acquaintances in his most courtly fashion. The social graces did not come easily to him- he had had to work to acquire them, and often felt them to be phony- but the realities of local life had long since taught him that they were of immense value when applied judiciously. Folks in Barnwell District valued their independence, especially the freedom of property owners to live life as they pleased, so they tended not to mind much what others did, so long as they behaved in a genteel manner. Folks in Barnwell District set great store by style and delivery. Wasn't so much what you said that mattered, but how you said it! They also tended to take the words of the town's founding families as having weight worthy of serious contemplation. Knowing this, Elijah set to planting his own seeds, in the hopes they might arrest or even choke out the growth of whatever Guignard and Rhett might be sowing.

"What d'ya'll suppose Dr. Guignard's trying to accomplish here today?" he would ask one or another, innocently.

"I heard that Robert Barnwell Rhett got so worked up at that Southern Convention in Nashville a few years back, that even the other secessionsists felt he was goin too far!" he would say casually to another.

"I wonder who put a bee up my nephews' butts to get involved in politics? Seems a little outa character for them!" he would comment off-hand to another smilingly, and then move on.

By and by, when the number of new arrivals had trickled down to nothing, and everyone seemed to have partaken of at least one serving of barbecue and other delights, Dr. Guignard ushered Mr. Rhett onto the stage, followed by James, Michael, and Angus. They ranged themselves in back along the row of red velvet chairs brought down from the plantation house for the occasion. To the astonishment of all, Dr. Guignard gave a signal, and seemingly out of nowhere- from somewhere behind the stage- appeared a group of musicians with a horn, a drum and a fiddle. They struck up a lively tune with a martial beat, immediately grabbing the attention of all, which after a ripple of delighted applause at the surprise, rendered the assembly expectantly silent.

The tune finished, Dr. Guignard took to the podium.

"Dear friends, neighbors, and fellow residents of Barnwell District! I bid you welcome!"

The crowd, duly sated with good food and well plied with strong drink at their host's expense, jovially shouted back and clapped their enthusiastic thanks for the welcome.

"It is a great pleasure to see ya'll here today! Ya'll do me honor comin on such short notice, and I thank ya! I truly do appreciate that nearly all of our leadin families are present, along with a goodly number of townsfolk, and that most everyone has also provided the support of their nigras to make sure ya'll's needs are duly met!"

There was another round of generally appreciative applause.

"It also gives me great pleasure to see the younger generation gettin involved in matters of civic pride, for truth be told, this event was not my idea!" There were murmurs of surprise rippling though the crowd. "No indeed!" he said for dramatic effect, "This event was conceived and requested by these three fine young gentlemen sittin here behind me, Mr. Angus Patterson Junior; Mr. James Willis Junior; and Mr. Michael Willis!"

Mrs. Willis, to James' and Michael's embarrassment, waved and called out rather too energetically to her boys as more raucus applause followed, several of the Willis brothers' peers mocking their mother's enthusiasm in drunken amusement. There was also a considerable number of comments of surprise, mostly whispered behind fluttering fans or tilted hat brims, that the owner of the general store outside of Williston and his do-nothing brother should have proven to have more substance than anyone realized. A few speculated as to why Angus Junior was present and his well-known father was not. But many realized that the elder Patterson was in poor health, and thereby absolved him of the expectation of participating in this momentous occasion, which they assumed would make the father proud, in any event.

"It also truly gives me great pleasure to welcome one of South Carolina's leadin politicians, and a clarion voice callin us to a bright future, a man who many thought would fill the shoes of our late and lamented champion, Senator John C. Calhoun, only to realize he had a vison of his own to inspire us: none other than our local favorite son, and like the Willis boys here, the descendent of one of our illustrious foundin families, Mr. Robert Barnwell Rhett!'

The planters' wives and daughters in the front all clapped their gloved hands energetically with a patter of happily muffled applause, or waved their fans coquettishly, hoops skirts and ruffled petticoats swaying, their powdered and corseted décolletage smiling up at him on the stage. Mr. Rhett smiled back at them charmingly, his well trimmed graying beard and mustache lending him an irresistibly dashing air, doffing his hat and waving to the gentlemen, who cheered their approval vociferously.

Dr. Guignard felt the crowd duly prepped and decided to hand the proceedings over to his protégés, with the certainty that even should they fail to inspire his guests, Robert Barnwell Rhett was more than competent to rescue the situation. He would assure that the rally ended on a high note, virtually guaranteeing that one and all would eagerly sign Angus' petition. Of course, Guignard's check list would also make it possible for him and his delegates to do whatever "follow-up" might be necessary, in the event that it was noticed that some had failed to affix their signatures to the document, as requested. He would not be averse to the judicious application of pressure on the reluctant, if necessary. He smiled with satisfaction that Elijah would not be able to easily depart without signing, and would therefore be forced to eat the humble pie Dr. Guignard had been so carefully preparing for him for so long.

Dr. Guignard continued with a flourish of false modesty, "So rather than undeservedly hoggin all the attention myself, bein just a simple, honest citizen tryin to support our boys here in a worthy cause, I'm gonna hand the proceedins over to our up and comin young civic-leaders-to-be! I wanna ask them to come forward now, and share with ya'll what it is they think we oughta know and do, to keep our fair district safe and sound from the unseemly agitation that appears to be seepin southward like some sort of poison, contaminatin the very groundwater of our good Southern society!"

Dr. Guignard figured he had by now set the stage for them about as well and eloquently as anyone could, and turning, applauded the Willis boys and Angus, signaling them to come forward, as he stepped back to join Mr. Rhett on the dais chairs. Mr. Rhett and Dr. Guingard leaned together, smiling, and exchanged a few convivial words out of earshot, making Elijah wonder just how much of this whole event his nemesis had managed to stage.

As Dr. Guignard insistently urged the boys to step forward, Michael looked at James, terrified. He was not expecting to have to speak, and got a major case of cold feet. Having imbibed a substantial quantity of Mr.Stoddard's sour mash in his excitement and enthusiasm about the event, he now sat there paralyzed, hiccupping nervously until James, only slightly less nervous and inebriated than his brother, realized that he couldn't just let Angus walk away with the whole prize. Shufflingly, he got to his feet and stepped forward. He wanted to make sure people understood that the three of them had political aspirations to represent their guests. They wanted to be an effective voice against liberalizing change, and against the pollution of not only the district, but of the white race, by subversive Negro influence or by the dangerous collaboration of unscrupulous whites like their Uncle Elijah, who threatened the very continuity of their social system and privileged way of life.

"Howdy, ya'll!" he declared falteringly, uncertain of just what he should say, "It's, um, it's mighty good to see so many of ya'll turned out for this rally!" He was still fumbling to find his voice. "Uh, let me tell ya'll why we've invited ya here! Me and my brother, and Angus, have been gettin worried about changes we see takin place around here- changes that could threaten our whole way a life!" He was desperately hoping for some positive response from the crowd to endorse him, but none was forthcoming as yet. There was nothing for it but to drive on. "So we figured we couldn't just sit around and hope somebody would do somethin about it. We needed to take the bull by the horns and do somethin ourselves, to make sure our representatives in government- whether up in Columbia or Washington- truly understand our values and needs, and make sure we're protected from these negative influences!"

There was finally general, if tepid, applause in agreement, despite the fact that James had avoided spelling out what those negative influences really were. Folks at least seemed ready to believe that whatever they might be, being negative influences, they surely didn't want them. Much as he would have loved to pour out his pent up invective against his uncle, driven by his fear of being disinherited in favor of his colored aunt and cousins, (whom he refused to recognize as relations), something told him it would not help his political career to make too personal an attack on Elijah at this time.

Elijah, Gilbert, Julius and Jason all waited with baited breath from their respective vantage points, watching not only the speakers on the dais, but the crowd as well, for any building signs of either support or agitation. Would the speakers really dare to launch a full frontal attack, or would they keep beating around the bush? Elijah gave his nephew a stern look.

Seeing his uncle's look, his muse suddenly abandoned him. James fumbled for a moment. But quickly recovering under the critical eye of Dr. Guignard, he saw a light at the end of the tunnel through which his rhetorical train of thought was chugging and turned with a smile to invite Angus forward to rescue him, saying graciously, "My colleague and friend, Mr. Angus Patterson Junior, is gonna tell ya'll now about a petition we're askin ya'll to sign. It's our intention to deliver this petition in person to the General Assembly up in Columbia, to make sure ya'll's voice is truly heard and our cherished society is preserved in its Proper Order. You might say we see ourselves as a sort of Proper Order Party! Angus, come on up an tell the folks what we've got in mind!"

The crowd clapped politely, still uncertain as to just where this was heading. Some began to mutter to each other that there'd better be more to it than this. Others said that at least the barbeque was good, so their time wasn't really wasted, and it had been good to catch up with friends and neighbors, and wasn't it nice to see the younger folks getting involved. As he stepped forward on stage, Angus sensed they were losing the crowd. Many had decided to return to the serving tables or the whiskey barrel, rather than stand in no longer rapt attention before the stage. Desperate to recapture that attention and win their admiration, Angus spoke up.

"Citizens of Barnwell District, we must unite!" he shouted a little too energetically, sounding almost panicked rather than persuasively stentorian, as he had intended. The people stopped and looked up from their amiable foraging to see what the fuss was about.

"There is a shadow bein cast over South Carolina!" he went on ominously, proud of his suggestive allusion to the darkness of the Negro problem, "And we are concerned about that darkness overtakin the light that assures the safety of our families and the purity of our wives and daughters!" Angus was stretching here, since he had neither wife nor daughter, but he had managed to catch the peoples' attention. Anything that appeared to threaten the well being of the ladies (other than the abuse by their own husbands, protected by the laws of matrimony and not spoken of in polite society, of course) was automatically and universally deemed a matter of great concern. Feeling relieved that he had prevented the crowd's outright defection to more sociable pastimes than listening to his speech, Angus now felt emboldened to continue.

"Folks up North want to see us put an end to slavery! They want to see all the coloreds set free and able to inherit property, like anyone else!" Angus blurted- with none of his planned finesse, going straight to the core of the matter. The crowd shouted, "Boo!" and "Hell No!" and "Damn Yankees!"

Every slave in the meadow froze, as did a goodly number of the white folks, their eyes now riveted on the stage. As Angus looked out at the crowd, he realized he'd better measure his words carefully. He did not want to provoke any violence, for if any slaves got hurt in such a fracas, he might be held liable for property damage! He only wanted to keep the crowd's attention. He then rembered the original premise of the petition, and the publication of *Uncle Tom's Cabin*, and decided he'd best return to that theme, rather than stir the pot of inheritance or the fear of Negro rebellion too much just yet.

"Now, I know we've already got laws against manumission and colored inheritance. Hell, you can't even try to free a slave without petitioning the General Assembly, an everybody knows the General Assembly ain't gonna approve any more petitions! So that shouldn't be our concern at this point!" He noticed a ripple of nods of agreement pass through the crowd.

"However, Miz Harriet Beecher Stowe, a Yankee woman livin up in Cincinnati, has written a book that's taken the North by storm, and we are concerned that this book should never be sold or read anywhere in Barnwell District, or even in South Carolina, for it is full of pernicious lies and gross misrepresentations of our Southern way of life!" There were loud shouts, jeers, and boos at the name of the author, indicating clearly that a goodly number in the crowd were already well aware of the book and its author (though no one would readily admit to having read it).

"Why, I'd wager" Angus continued, encouraged by their response, "that most of us would not recognize a single grain of truth in her version of the evils of slavery. Nor should we, for the woman's never set foot on a plantation in her life, and doesn't know what she's talkin about!" The reality that Stowe had interviewed numerous slaves escaping along the Underground Railway was a fact he would not allow to cloud the issue.

There were more boos and cat calls, and from the drunker younger generation, some lewd allusions to Miz Stowe's rightful membership in the world's oldest profession, which were quickly shushed by their more proper elders.

"Now I don't know how ya'll feel about it, and not bein a married man yet, I suppose I can't fully know myself, but I surely wouldn't wan't my wife or daughter, or fiancée if I had one, to suffer the indignity, the rude violation of her tender sensibilities, the viscious assault on her inviolate innocence, by readin or even hearin the contents of Miz Stowe's book- or any other such foul, abolitionist Yankee lies!

The crowd now roared its approval.

"So all we're askin ya'll to do is to sign our petition, so we can take it on up to Columbia, deliver it to the General Assembly, and make sure our representatives pass laws that reinforce our sacred values and protect the innocence and purity of our families!" Hugely relieved to have turned the tide and elicited a positive response from the crowd, Angus decided to quit while he was ahead rather than attempt to wax eloquent elaborating on the theme and thereby run the risk of losing their attention again. "Thank ya'll for listenin, and may the Good Lord bless ya and keep ya!" he concluded.

"… far away from us!" muttered Elijah in fervent punctuation, under his breath.

Dr. Guignard was now on his feet, clapping enthusiastically and grinning at Elijah with steely eyes. Gesturing for the crowd to quiet down, he spoke.

"That was a mighty fine speech son, delivered with real heart! It certainly does inspire us to hear a young man express so eloquently the dangers of abolitionism and the Negro pollution of our race!" Turning to the crowd, he urged, "Let's give em another round of applause, what d'ya'll say folks?" The crowd responded readily. Mrs. Willis' tightly corseted bosom heaved with such emotion and pride as she saw her sons and Angus take a bow, that her husband feared her stays would burst, and the true generosity of her unbounded proportions would be revealed to one and all!

Dr. Guignard then turned to the final figure on the platform and signaled for him to approach.

"Now before ya'll finish off the barbecue, the punch, and the whiskey" (he grinned mischeviously at the young men around the whiskey barrel) "…it's alright boys, I was young once too!" the older generation chuckled in amusement, " I'd like to ask our former Senator and now the owner of the influential paper, *The Charleston Mercury*, Mr. Robert Barnwell Rhett, to come forward and give us his blessin on our young men's efforts. Robert, come on up here, would ya?"

The crowd clapped respectfully, and Mr. Rhett finally took the podium.

"Good people of Barnwell District! How about that? How about that? Weren't they somethin?!" he turned and initiated another round of applause as he offered his accolade to the Willis boys and Angus Junior, who swelled like parched plants drinking in a summer rain.

"It surely does my heart good to see such young men step forward to help shoulder the load of leadership, for these are truly troublin times we're livin in! Very troublin times, indeed!" Elijah could feel his stomach tighten and his pulse become erratic in the anticipation of whatever was next to spill forth from the mouth of a man he knew embodied everything he disavowed and loathed about his own society.

"I am proud to have listened to our young men's speeches, and I want to urge all of ya'll to be sure to sign that petition! Why, it'd be unpatriotic, a virtual heresy not to! Moreover, I will personally promise you boys to do everythin in my power to see to it that ya'll's petition is taken up by the very next session of the Genreal Assembly. I would be pleased and honored to help ya'll find legislators who will sponsor such a bill and turn it into law!"

James and Michael grinned their excitement. Angus was a little less enthusiastic in his response, sensing that what Rhett was really saying was that he was intending to take the credit for their effort, lest their fledgling Proper Order Party usurp his own Southern National Party of so-called Fire Eaters. Angus did recognize, however, that just as he had needed Dr. Guignard's sponsorship for the rally, cultivating Rhett's patronage was likely a necessary next step in his political aspirations, especially as Rhett was not only a leading voice of secessionism, but a man with his very own newspaper, able to promote his views to a wide audience.

Rhett, having dispensed with the niceties of casual patronage, began to warm to the opportunity to speak to a crowd- something he had not done since his resignation from the U.S. Senate in frustration that his views were not persuasive in Washington. He was on home turf now, with his yearning for a South freed from Northern agendas or controls, rooted in the fundamentality of the slave economy. He was even hoping to remove the prohibition of the slave trade, so as to embrace a trans-Caribbean nationhood of his own devising. It made him thirst for working up the crowd to a fever pitch of enthusiasm for his own agenda.

"Now when I was in the Congress and the Senate up in Washington, I heard a lot of stuff n nonsense about the alleged 'evils' of slavery! And I came to realize that reasonin with the Yankees about the matter was a waste a time, for they are truly deaf, dumb, and blind to the reality of this most essential of our Southern institutions!" Rhett roared. He was just warming up, fixing to launch into a diatribe against the selfishness and stupidity of those who would promote emancipation. "Now, everbody here knows that slavery is the best thing that's ever happened to South Carolina, and the very source of our prosperity! Anybody wantin to put an end to it oughta have his head examined!" There were twitters of laughter and nods of agreement running through the crowd.

Willingly playing off his audience, Rhett continued, "Why, I'd wager our good Dr. Guignard here would be happy to declare any such fool as certifiably insane!" Dr. Guignard grinned and nodded, and most of the planters laughed out loud at this patently obvious truth.

Rhett continued, "Moreover, all that Yankee foolishness about cruelty and injustice, just like young Angus said, is clearly nothing more than a pernicious lie! Why, just take a look around here! Most of ya'll brought some of your slaves with ya, and they're as clean and well dressed and well behaved a bunch of niggers as anyone could ever ask for! They do ya'll credit! Clearly they are not sufferin any cruelty! Why, I'm sure we don't even mind if they share some of the left-overs (on their own plates of course)!" he laughed a mirthless laugh as he scanned the crowd looking for dissenters.

The slaves looked at each other nervously, especially the ones like Miss Sally, who had suffered constant cruelty and emotional abuse, but it was clear that not even all the whites were warming to this argument. John Bauskett took his wife's arm discreetly and casually started edging toward the entrance to the meadow. Many of the townspeople, who did not themselves own slaves, began to give each other looks, uncertain as to how far they wanted to express their agreement with Mr. Rhett, for some of his postitions, even in this conservative district, seemed just a tad too extreme for their tastes. Not surprisingly, the planters and their families on the other hand, stood mesmerized and adoring, and regularly punctuated his points with energetic shouts, and clapping, and general expressions of approval.

Elijah was worrying about how far Rhett would push the issue, wondering how he was going to manage to get away without having to choose between being coerced into signing the petition or publically refusing to do so, when suddenly Joseph Harley grabbed him by the elbow, saying quietly but urgently, "Come with me! Right now!"

Taken aback by this unexpected accosting, Elijah looked toward the entrance to the meadow and saw Elder standing nervously, holding the reins of the mule in one hand and Beauty's reins in another. Immediately, Elijah realized something must be wrong at home. He felt a wave of panic surge through him, deafening him to any more of what was going on on the platform, until he realized Joseph was saying something to him.

"Elijah! Elijah! Listen to me! It's alright! Amy's goin into labor, that's all, and she knew she'd promised to let both of us know as soon as anything started happenin! But we've gotta go, now!"

Recovering his wits, Elijah realized he should not take Gilbert, Julius and Jason with him. It would be playing right into Guignard's plans, because it would cause too much of a stir, and that could be read as untimely and deliberate dissent. He realized he actually wanted them to stay, because he needed their eyes and ears to be there until the end, so they could report back to him whatever it was that Rhett was about to unload on the crowd, and, more importantly, how the people responded to it.

"Wait a minute Joseph, let me just alert Gilbert!" Elijah pleaded.

Dr. Harley nodded as he headed for his buggy. "I've asked a friend to take my wife home. She's well accustomed to such emergencies. So I'll meet you at the house, but don't dawdle- we don't want to take any chances!" Joseph said quietly. Several guests noticed him making haste for his buggy and, accustomed to the realities of a country doctor's life, simply assumed there was a medical emergency somewhere and thought nothing of it.

Elijah found Gilbert by the petition table, as stationed. "Gilbert, stay here and keep an eye on things," he said softly, out of earshot of the guests who were drawn like a moth to a flame by the rhetorical fireworks Mr. Rhett was fixing to display. "Amy's gone into labor, and I have to get back to the house. Now listen, this is important! Pay attention to the rest of the speeches, and then afterwards, to who signs and who doesn't. They don't know you can read- best keep it that way! And be sure to offer my apologies to Dr. Guignard! Tell him there was a medical emergency on the plantation that required me and Dr. Harley leaving early. Tell him that I thank him for his hospitality, and congratulate him on his efforts!"

Gilbert smiled wryly and nodded. "Lord sure loves you, Elijah!" he said, now grinning, "This is about the only way ya'll coulda gotten outa here without signin that damn petition! Now hurry up, cause if Doctor Guignard sees ya'll talkin to me, I'll catch Hell for not makin ya sign it before ya'll left! Go on, get outa here, and tell my sister we all with her in spirit and will get home soon as we can! And God bless ya!"

Elijah nodded, took Beauty's reigns from Elder, and mounted his mare without waiting for Elder to mount the mule. As he did so, he noticed John Bauskett taking in what was happening, and nodding to him subtly in support. Elijah nodded back gratefully, tipping his hat with a slight tug at the brim, and with that, feeling a mixture of relief at escaping before any outburst and anxiety about Amy and the baby's condition, he cantered off toward home, Elder hurrying along behind him.

From up on the dais, to his considerable annoyance and frustration, John Guignard caught a glimpse of the exchanges at the entrance to the meadow and spied Elijah cantering off toward home. The timing of this departure just before the climax of Rhett's speech and his own intended final remarks made Dr. Guignard furious not to have been able to deliver his long dreamed of and eagerly awaited coup de grace to Elijah publically. He was, moreover, desperately curious to know the cause of Elijah's departure, for he knew he had to be careful not to criticize Elijah openly without first knowing the reason for his escape. After all, Elijah had shown up, he had provided his lumber and the service of his slaves, who were still in attendance. To all appearances, Elijah had done everything he had been asked to do and was behaving in a manner appropriate to his station. There were many who would take it amiss if he were to be unfairly criticized, and might hold it against Dr. Guignard personally. After all, though he was as wealthy as any other planter, the very fact that he was not at least a fourth or fifth generation resident of Williston made some of the longer established planters see him as something of an interloper, aspiring to the status of the older families. Misbehavior on his part would not be tolerated and would assure that status would continue to elude him.

Guignard sat fidgeting on the dais, his hands tied, fuming that he could not move from his seat to find out why Elijah had left without disrupting his keynote speaker's address. It would be considered unforgivably rude by both his guests and Rhett himself- a man whose control of the press and propensity for targeted vitriol, made him someone who it was very much in Guignard's interest to keep on his good side.

Since the timing of this sequence of events had been serendipitous, or some would say Providential, rather than by human design, Elijah, of course, did not even realize what was happening to Dr. Guignard, and so unfortunately could not derive any satisfaction from it. He had other more pressing things on his mind by then.

Dr. Guignard, nevertheless, was left there to 'stew in his own juices,' as Jason had put it, too self-absorbed and unaware to even realize that Elijah's black proxies, at least, were observing his discomfort with interest and even a certain flush of satisfaction. Once again, this self-appointed arbiter of white supremacy was thwarted in his attempt to exact retribution from Elijah for what he deemed his unpardonable sins against Southern Society, his alleged betrayal of his race, and his personal affront to the Guignard honor! Dr. Guignard couldn't bear that, for all his efforts and clever planning (not to mention expense), Elijah had managed to add another insult to compound Guignard's injury with his untimely departure, and had thereby completely avoided the chastisement he so richly deserved! No doubt about it, it was positively maddening! From Guignard's point of view, Elijah's failure to sign the petition that would either seal his redemption and Guignard's moral victory, or document a hypocrisy that the Doctor would be only too happy to use against him in the future, was truly exasperating.

Gilbert, Julius, and Jason, on the other hand, felt a thrill of vindication, despite the poisonous rhetoric that continued to spill out of Rhett, still bloviating from the platform to an increasingly restive and disinterested audience. They noticed with relief that, though the planters continued to listen, more and more of the townspeople were showing signs of having heard enough and wanting to get on home. They were just politely awaiting the conclusion of the speech so they could thank their host and take their leave. A few even started wandering back toward the entrance to sign the petition as a courtesy and as a signal to the speakers perhaps that it was time to call it a day, but there was hardly a stampede of eager supporters rushing to do so.

LIX

By the time Elijah and Elder got back to the house, Joseph Harley had already arrived. Elijah dismounted quickly and threw the reins to Elder.

"Take care of her for me, will ya son?"

Elder nodded, nervously. He was not sure what to expect after the trauma of Eliza's birth the year before. To their mutual relief, Momma Celia greeted them at the door and smiled reassuringly. "Don't ya'll be gettin yasevs all worked up, now! Everything's alright. She's upstairs- go on!" She looked at Elijah and nodded sideways as if to indicate the route. Elijah took the steps two at a time, eager to confirm his mother-in-law's assessment.

When he got upstairs, there was none of the tension or fear that had greeted him at Eliza's birth. No blood, no panic-striken faces, no heart-wrenching screams of agony. Everything seemed to be running like clock-work. The children, now seasoned veterans after last year's trauma, all knew exactly what to do, and seemed to be carrying out their respective duties at an almost casual, yet efficient pace. Amy lay propped up in bed, smiling.

"So, are you really havin the baby, or are you just play-acting to get me out of that awful rally?" Elijah asked, only half in jest. Amy laughed, but before she could answer, Joseph spoke.

"Oh, he's comin alright! It's no act!" he said, looking up from his examination. "She's fully dilated. Her waters haven't broken yet, but he should be making his appearance real soon!" He too smiled at Elijah, confirming that this was not going to be a repeat performance of the life-threatening scenario of Eliza's birth. Elijah noted that Dr. Harley seemed as convinced as Amy that it was going to be a baby boy, though there was no clear reason why.

Elijah came over to the bed and leaned over to give Amy a kiss. She patted the bed beside her, indicating he should sit by her side.

"Do ya'll need anything?" he asked, solicitously.

"No, sugar, I'm fine. Just sit here with me! Dr. Harley, Momma and the children have got everything under control!" she responded, almost dreamily. Elijah could hardly believe their luck. Suddenly he felt almost stress-free- at least for the moment.

"So tell me, how did it go at the rally?" she asked, holding his hand in hers.

Elijah proceeded to recount his experience of the rally step by step, as Amy listened attentively. His narrative, however, was punctuated and interrupted by an occasional tightening of Amy's grip as her contractions gradually became stronger and closer together and her breathing heavier.

When Elijah got to the point of telling about Rhett's allegation that anyone in favor of emancipation must be considered insane, and that Dr. Guignard nodded and grinned at Rhett's assertion that he would happily certify as much, Amy looked alarmed. "Oh Lord Elijah, do ya think they'd really try to claim you're crazy as a way to take control over us?"

Elijah merely laughed, refusing to let himself experience that chilling possibility, and saying lightheartedly, "Well Hell honey, they may be right to think I'm crazy! Sometimes I do too! But who cares? I'd rather be crazy than sane by their definition any day! Let's face it, the case could be made that it takes a madman to do what I'm tryin to do, but that doesn't mean it's wrong, or won't work, or can't be done!" His good cheer helped assuage her anxiety just in time for a particularly strong contraction to effectively change the subject and put an end to all conversation.

The afternoon passed into evening as Amy's labor gradually intensified. Unlike the last time, there was no haemorrhaging and no terrifying pain- compared to a normal birth at least! And based on Dr. Harley's frequent application of his brass ear trumpet stethoscope to her belly, there was no indication of fetal distress either- despite the fact that they could occasionally make out the clear shape of a tiny fist, or foot, or knee pushing outward and distending Amy's belly impossibly far in unpredictable places as the baby worked his way downward into the birth canal.

Everything went so smoothly that Elijah finally told the girls to go to bed, promising to wake them if they were needed or at least let them know when the baby came. Julia, with little Eliza straddling her hip, climbed up on the bed to give their mother a good night kiss between contractions, and trundled off sleepily to the room they shared down the hall under Momma Celia's watchful eye and gentle encouragement. But Clarissa seemed reluctant to go. Perhaps her vivid memories of Elizah's birth were haunting her, making it hard to trust that this delivery might be completed without danger. But finally, as midnight drew near, her eyes too became heavy with sleep, and under Momma Celia's loving embrace she was ushered at last to her bed, tucked in, and fell fast asleep.

Even Elijah, worn out from the tension of the rally and his anxiety about the baby, unintentionally dozed off as he sat at Amy's bedside holding her hand leaving Momma Celia and the patient Dr. Harley to keep vigil over Amy's contractions. Shortly before dawn the quiet was shattered by the piercing crow of a rooster in the chicken coop out in back of the house, followed promptly by a fierce sounding animal grunt from Amy pushing the baby out. They startled Elijah wide awake. As he looked up, at first uncomprehending and disoriented from sleep, he saw Joseph Harley pulling a wet, wriggling little boy from between Amy's open legs. Momma Celia smiled encouragingly at her daughter saying, as the child's first lungful of fresh air caused him to let out an exuberant cry, "Sugar, you were right! It's a boy, an he's beautiful and strong like you!"

"And like his Papa!" Amy insisted, turning her head toward Elijah with a weary but triumphant smile. "Mornin, sugar. I got a little present here for ya!"

As his head cleared from the fog of too little sleep, Elijah looked with wonder at the son he had so long dreamed of having. Momma Celia had wiped him clean and was wrapping him in a soft blanket. Joseph Harley also grinned with satisfaction and relief.

"Congratulations, Papa! Well done to ya both!" He went over to the bureau where there sat a large wash basin and a pitcher of water from which wisps of steam gently rose. He filled the basin, splashed his face, and began to scrub his hands and forearms to remove the bodily fluids of childbirth from them. Momma Celia showed the baby to Elijah, pride written all over her face, and then, having received his father's blessing, tenderly laid the baby on Amy's chest, where he promptly nuzzled against her warm breast and fell asleep, worn out from his efforts to join the family.

Momma Celia was covering a basin containing the afterbirth with a clean cotton towel, and placing it aside for later burial, when the patter of feet hurrying toward the bedroom was followed by the door bursting open. The three girls bounded in excitedly, little Eliza's arms and legs wrapped around Clarissa's neck and hips tighter than a jocky riding a hunter in a steeplechase. The older boys were not far behind, peeking in anxiously at first, then grinning broadly as they took in the scene and realized the baby had been born with none of the drama of Eliza's birth. They began chattering all together,

"Can we see him?" Can I touch him?" "Gosh, he's big!" "He looks like Papa!" I think he looks like Momma" "Does not! But he's got Momma's eyes!" "What're ya'll gonna call him?" "Are you alright, Momma?"

With all the chattering, the baby awoke and began flailing his arms as if to say, "Quiet down, ya'll! Can't ya see I'm tryin to sleep here?"

Momma Celia chuckled. "Well ain't you a little savage!" she said to her newest grandson. "Look at him lettin everybody know to hush up. Child's got a strong spirit! Gets that from both his Momma and his Papa!"

"Yeah he does!" agreed Elder and Elleck. "Maybe we should call him Savage! Suits him, don't ya'll think?"

Elijah, a little put out that the naming of his first-born son should be usurped by the children and treated in such a cavalier fashion, decided to assert himself. "Well, I had always wanted to name a son Elijah Junior!"

Amy looked at all her children gathered together and smiled conspiratorially. "That's a nice name, sugar! Of course you can name him Elijah Junior, just like you always wanted!" but then looking at her older children with a wink, added michievously , "but we're all gonna call him Savage!"

The children all nodded in agreement, laughing delightedly, taking the wind out of Elijah's paternal sails only for a moment, for the baby then kicked his blanket vigorously as if to affirm the family choice. Elijah couldn't help but laugh in acceptance. "Fair enough, so be it!" he declared.

As Momma Celia herded the children downstairs to help her get breakfast, Joseph Harley turned to the happy parents.

"Well, I must admit, I am a bit tired, but I certainly found this a whole lot more satisfyin than that God-awful rally! Thank you little man, for your exquisite timin!" He leaned over and gently caressed the child he had just helped deliver, smiling broadly at his parents.

His face becoming more serious, he went on, "Don't worry, Elijah, if Guignard asks me, as I'm certain he will, I'll simply confirm that there was a medical issue with one of your slaves- which is of course technically true- but there's no reason he should know the name of the patient or the nature of the medical issue. Given the distressin heat of Rhett's toxic rhetoric in particular, I'll do all I can to deflect attention from here." He paused, "I assume Gilbert, Julius, and Jason are safely home by now, and will give you a full accountin of whatever happened after we left?"

Elijah nodded gravely. The euphoria of Savage's normal birth was clearly tempered by the uncertainty of what had followed their departure from the rally, and he realized he needed to get that report from Gilbert as soon as possible, at least to know what they might be facing.

"Why don't ya'll come on downstairs and have some breakfast, and I'll send one of the boys to go fetch Gilbert so he can fill us in?" Turning to Amy, who was starting to doze off, exhausted, he asked her, "You don't mind if we leave ya'll for a little while so's you can get some rest, do ya darlin?"

Amy shook her head sleepily, the baby snuggled in her arms. Dr. Harley suggested the baby be laid in the cradle beside the bed, so Amy would not have to worry about the child, and said as Elijah gently laid his son in the cradle, "I'll be back to see you soon, my dear. Well done, and congratulations!"

Amy smiled and nodded her head weakly, already more asleep than awake, mumbling, "Thank ya Dr. Harley, and God bless you too!"

Father and friend walked out of the room and gently closed the door behind them. Once downstairs, they headed to the back of the house, where there was bustling activity as Momma Celia and her five oldest grandchildren set to making a celebratory breakfast for all to feast upon. Little Eliza sat on the floor in the corner, playing with a sauce pan full of dried lentils.

Elijah sent the boys to go find their uncle- both to share the news about Savage's birth and to ask him to come over and give them the report on what happened in the rally after their unexpected departure. Meanwhile, the girls kept on helping their grandmother with the attention and efficiency of nurses assisting a surgeon.

Within no time at all the boys were back with their Uncle Gilbert, who showed up with Jason and Julius in tow as well, knocking on the kitchen door. Elijah had told Momma Celia to set the table in the kitchen, rather than the dining room. After being up all night without washing or shaving, he thought it a little ridiculous to set a formal table under the circumstances. Dr. Harley was not the least put off by sharing his breakfast in mixed company in the kitchen. In fact, he seemed to welcome not having to bother with the usual social graces after his long night- not to mention the long day at the rally.

"Have ya'll had breakfast yet?" Elijah asked, as Gilbert and the others stepped into the kitchen.

"No sir," they answered.

"Well pull up a chair and set yourselves down!" Elijah insisted magnanimously. "You don't mind do ya, Momma Celia?" he asked, remembering suddenly it was his mother-in-law who was doing the cooking, and she'd been up all night helping deliver the baby too!

"Course not, but thank ya for askin!" she smiled at her son-in-law. "It's nice to share the news and a meal with everybody. It's a big day! Not everyday such a fine strong boy's born into the family!" She was clearly almost as thrilled as Elijah that the baby was a boy- but not in a way that belittled her granddaughters, who were in eager attendance, helping her set the table.

"Lucky number seven, Elijah?" Joseph Harley asked, teasingly.

"And likely the final addition to the family! We're gettin too old for this!" Elijah said, half jokingly. Everyone knew it was probably true, but that didn't diminish their joy any.

"How's Amy doin?" Gilbert asked a little anxiously, despite the fact that everyone else seemed far too cheerful for there to be anything important amiss.

"She's doin fine, Gilbert! Everything went smoothly, and she'll be up and about in no time!" Dr. Harley affirmed.

"Your sister has proved again that she's the most amazin woman I've ever met. After all the Hell she went through with Eliza, this time it seemed as easy as rollin off a log."

"That's easy for you to say- you slept right through the hardest part!" teased Momma Celia. "Just like a man to think 'labor' don't mean what it say, cause they ain't the ones doin the work! They calls it that for a reason you know! It's hard work! But you right about one thing, my Amy did a real good job, and the Good Lord musta knowed she couldn'a handled another one like Eliza! So my little Savage just come on out, mostly by hisself!" She smiled with satisfaction to be the matriarch of such an accomplished daughter and considerate grandson.

Joseph Harley grinned, and added teasingly, "Well now, come on Momma Celia, much as you did last night, ya'll gotta admit some of us men had a hand in the work!"

Momma Celia laughed. "Lord knows that's true, Doctor, I just didn't want Elijah thinkin that just cause he had somethin to do with makin the baby, don't mean he unnerstands the work a deliverin it!"

"I am not gettin into any family arguments now at a time like this, Momma Celia! And we all know how hard he worked to help save Amy's and Eliza's life last year, so I think we can cut him a little slack this time, don't you?"

Everybody nodded and chuckled in agreement, as Momma Celia happily plied them all with sausages, bacon, eggs, grits, flapjacks, molasses, biscuits, jams and jellies, and a seemingly endless supply of hot coffee. The entire household dove in hungrily to their meal.

After the children had wolfed down enough food to feed a small army, catching Dr. Harley's eye- and sensing that he was much in need of getting on home himself- Elijah said, "Children, why don't ya'll tiptoe upstairs and see if your Momma's awake and wants anything to eat. She might be hungry after all that work! An I'm sure she's gonna be eager to see ya'll too!"

The children readily excused themselves, clearing away their dishes, and promised their grandmother they'd be back shortly to help her clean up so she could get some rest too.

Once the children were out of the kitchen, Elijah turned to Gilbert, Julius and Jason. "It's alright boys, Dr. Harley here is in my confidence so ya'll can speak freely. We're both right eager to hear ya'll's version of yesterday's events at the rally- especially what happened after we left!"

Jason began, "Well sir, when ya'll left with Doctor Harley an Elder, the expression on ole Doctor Guignard's face coulda bout stopped a train!"

Julius chimed in, "That's the truth! Looked like he coulda spit bullets, he was so mad!"

Jason continued, "But, since Mister Rhett was still up there spoutin off about what a good thing slavery was, and how grateful we all should be, an how it was only ignorant Yankees like that Miz Stowe, and fools who thought of freeing their slaves who could fail to see the truth of the matter, Doctor Guignard couldn't even get up off the stage to find out why ya'll'd left!"

Gilbert interjected, "Ain't no doubtin that made him mad as Hell, but he didn't dare say anything about it. Kinda felt like he'd been intendin to finish with a show a pro-slavery, anti-abolitionist fireworks and ended up with not much more'n a firecracker!"

"So what did he do once the speeches were over?" asked Elijah eagerly.

"Well sir, after Mister Rhett finally shut up, Doctor Guignard invited everybody to help themselves to more food and drink and not forget to sign the petition on the way out." answered Gilbert. "Course he came up to me as soon as he could without bein impolite to Mister Rhett. He was dyin to know why ya'll'd left, but me and Julius and Jason hadn't gone with ya."

"What d'ya'll tell him?"

"I told him just like you said, 'There was a medical emergency at the plantation that demanded your and Doctor Harley's immediate attention, and that you was really sorry to have to leave early, but wanted to thank him for his hospitality and congratulate him on his efforts!' I added on my own that you'd told us to stay there and do as we'd been told." Gilbert added with a wry smile, "Figured he'd like that!"

"And how did he take it?" asked Dr. Harley.

"Well, he sorta paused like he was thinkin, and then just said, real cold like, to tell ya'll he was sorry to hear that there was an emergency, and he hoped everything was alright at home. And that us nigras did ya'll credit by bein obedient, like we sposed to."

"Mmmm hmmm, I bet he did!" answered Elijah, to no one in particlar. "Wonder if he took 'congratulate him on his efforts' as a compliment or as mockin him for his efforts havin failed – with me at least?!"

"Elijah, did Guignard know Amy was pregnant again?" asked Dr. Harley.

Pulled back from his abstractions, Elijah responded, "I don't rightly know. Perhaps not, but it wouldn't take long for him to find out if he didn't. He may have put two and two together and figured out what the nature of the medical emergency was- or he may not, at least not yet- but I suspect he'll try to find out as much as he can." Elijah paused again, thinking.

"What else happened? Did my nephews or Angus say anything worth rememberin? And what about the crowd's reaction at the end- was there a heap a cheerin and a rush to sign the petition, or was the response sorta mixed?" He pressed for more details.

Julius responded, "I heard Mister James and Mister Michael and Mister Angus talking afterwards. Mister James and Mister Michael was all excited Mister Rhett'd promised to get their petition read up in Columbia. Mister Angus seemed eager to get Mister Rhett's attention and try n talk with him alone, but all the planters' wives and daughters was makin such a fuss over him, Mister Angus was hard pressed to get more'n a word or two in edgewise."

"The way he's been courtin Guignard's favor, Angus knows which side his bread's buttered on, but he didn't look all that thrilled when Rhett was making promises of what he was gonna do. I expect Angus's smart enough to realize Rhett's not likely to share power willingly with any upstarts, so he's gonna have to figure out how to play his cards now that he's beholden to both Rhett and Dr. Guignard!" Dr. Harley observed.

"That could end up puttin him in a bind!"

"Hmmmm," thought Elijah. "Should be interesting to see how that plays out! We need to keep a sharp eye out on all three boys, but my money's on Angus Junior for the smartest and therefore, possibly the most dangerous of the three."

He went on, "What about the petition? And the general reaction of folks? It seemed before we left that a goodly number of the townsfolk were less than impressed by Rhett's blusterin. Did ya'll sense that there might be some, at least, who wouldn't jump on Guignard's band wagon?"

"Yessir, I spect you're right about that!" replied Julius. "Seemed to me that more'n a few were sorta luke warm when it came to rilin folks up against the Yankees, or pushin to secede from the Union. But most everyone seemed in favor of banning Miz Stowe's book, or any other abolitionist writin, even though not everybody signed the petition."

"I dunno, hard to say," interjected Jason. "Mister Bauskett an his wife, Mister Beazely from over the depot, Mister and Miz Wooley down the road, and more n a few others kinda looked like they'druther not have to listen to no more political yammerin. I seriously doubt they'd wanna get involved in tryin to stop ya'll, but that don't necessarily mean they'd all support emancipatin slaves or leavin em property!"

"An judging from the reactions of the other slaves, who were jumpier n a bullfrog bein watched by a heron when ole Mister Rhett started goin on about how wonnerful slavery is, they's more'n a few who'd love to revolt against they masters, but are skeered to death of the vengeance they master's'd take out on em if they tried!" added Julius.

"And with good reason!" interjected Momma Celia, unexpectedly. She had been listening intently to the conversation in silence, and the others had just about forgotten she was even there. "When I was a girl, before even comin to the Kirkland plantation, I seen a master kill his own slaves for resistin him. He was so brutal, skeered me half to death! It was ugly, so ugly it gave me nightmares for years!" she added with an involuntary shudder of unexpected vehemence, reminding everyone that she had a depth of experience that explained much of her wisdom and even more of her cautious skepticism when it came to dealing with white folks.

Dr. Harley spoke up with unusual candor, given his general tolerance of most everyone. "Guignard's a vindictive son of a bitch, but he's too smart to come after ya'll personally without the support of a significant portion of the planters, at least. He'd need more than his puppet Frederick Matthews, that's for sure! He's not likely to get too many of the townsfolk backing him- he's too arrogant for the likes of most of the folks around here. And some of the other planters, at least, would probably balk at attackin ya directly, out of respect for ya'll as part of the town's foundin family, as well as outa admiration for your success as a planter!"

"As ever, Joseph, I truly appreciate your perspective. You're probably right- which hopefully will buy us at least a little more time to try to accomplish our plan before things blow up around here- but I can't shake the feelin that they will sooner or later, no matter what we do. This thing is bigger than any of us!" Elijah affirmed.

"Well, I don't imagine there'll be any mobs comin down your road with pitchfolks and torches any time soon, but I'd still keep as low a profile as possible if I were you. And be very careful about who ya'll let know that Savage has joined the family!" Dr. Harley added. "I'll keep my eyes and ears open and let ya know if I catch wind of anything troublesome! Now, if ya'll'll excuse me, I'm sure my wife must be wondering where in blazes I've been all night, so I think I'd best be gettin on home. Ya'll take care now, and tell Amy I'll drop by to check on her and the baby within the next few days."

With that, Dr. Harley pushed back his chair, and everyone stood up out of respect, thanking him and shaking his hand repeatedly for being such a good friend and a good doctor. On this last point, Dr. Harley winked at Momma Celia and said, "Well, I got a mighty good colleague here to help me out, so I know ya'll're in good hands! Thank ya Momma Celia for all your help, and thank ya for the delicious breakfast too!" He grinned, and Momma Celia beamed back at him wordlessly but expressively, her skepticism about white folks temporarily eclipsed by the genuinely mutual respect they had for each other.

LX

Damn boys, we did it! We actually pulled that rally off and got Mr. Robert Barnwell Rhett himself to promise to help us get our petition read by the General Assembly!" exulted James incredulously.

"That's right! Who knows where we might end up? With backin like his, we could really go places!" chimed in Michael enthusiastically.

"Well, we got Rhett's endorsement, alright," responded Angus soberly, "but there was more'n a few who didn't sign the petition. It wasn't just your uncle Elijah! I gotta admit, I thought there'd be a bigger turn out and more folks signin up right away!"

"Hell, Angus, you worry too much! It don't really matter, anyway! The important thing is that now folks know who we are and will take us more seriously!" James insisted.

"That's right! Didn't ya'll see how different they look at us now? Like we was worth listenin to? Felt good, didn't it?" Michael enthused.

"Ya'll may be right, but now that we got folks' attention, we're gonna have to do somethin to keep it and earn their trust, or it won't amount to more'n a fart in a gale!" Angus declared. "I was watchin Mr. Rhett's face when you mentioned us as the Proper Order Party, James, and he didn't look any too pleased. The man's got his own agenda, and I don't think he cottons much to competition, no matter what he may say publicly."

"Who say's we're competin with him?" asked James. "Hell, I just called us that to make us sound more impressive, not to take anything away from Robert Barnwell Rhett!"

"Maybe so, but he don't know that! I think we gotta play our cards real careful with him. He thinks by makin us a promise, we're beholden to him to do his biddin, an when he starts talkin about a Caribbean Empire, I'm sorry ya'll, but that is not why I'm in this! Feels like Guignard kinda set us up, not tellin us Rhett was comin- like he didn't trust we could get the job done!" Angus's suspicion of Rhett and his assessment of Guignard were both visceral and well-founded.

James, ever quick to make a course correction if it seemed to put him in a better light, responded, "You may be right there, Angus, come to think of it! We need to keep our focus on stoppin Uncle Elijah from doin anything foolish right here in South Carolina and make sure his nigras can't get their thievin hands on anything when he goes. We shouldn't let ourselves get distracted with slave trade in the Caribbean or other such nonsense."

"Speakin of Uncle Elijah, did you see Dr. Guignard's face when Uncle Elijah left before the speech was over? Looked like he took it real personal- as if Uncle Elijah was deliberately tryin to upset him," observed Michael.

"Now, why would he think that? Is it just because he doesn't approve of your uncle's livin arrangements, or is there some bad blood between em?" wondered Angus. None of them, of course, realized the grudge Guignard was holding against Elijah for not complying with his insistence that Amy and the family be sent back to the slave quarters, as he felt propriety demanded. They probably would have agreed with him if they had, but Guignard would never suffer the embarrassment of openly admitting his hurt feelings- especially directly to Willis family members.

"I dunno, but I noticed he made a beeline over to Gilbert to find out why Uncle Elijah had left." Michael responded.

"And what did Gilbert tell him, d'ya'll know?" asked Angus.

Both brothers shook their heads. "We were too far away to hear, what with people comin up to congratulate us an all," replied James. "An I, for one, don't fancy tryin to ask Gilbert about it!"

Michael nodded his agreement. "James is right- that'd be barkin up the wrong tree for sure! Gilbert ain't about to tell us nothin if he can help it. He's too loyal to Uncle Elijah."

"He's not only big and strong, he's smart too," observed Angus. "Best not mess with him!"

"I saw Doctor Harely drivin away in his buggy just before Uncle Elijah left, but from where I was sittin on the stage the crowd kinda blocked my view, an I couldn't really tell what was goin on or who was involved," James observed.

"Me neither, but I did see a nigra boy following Uncle Elijah on a mule. Couldn't make out which slave it was, but it was definitely one a Uncle Elijah's nigras," declared Michael.

"Well, it sure would be helpful to find out what was behind all that, and just exactly what was goin on at your uncle's plantation that would make him have to leave in such a hurry, if he wasn't just bein rude or tryin to make a statement about what he thought of the rally!" Angus commented. "And somehow, from the way he spoke to me when I delivered the invitation, I think he's too smart to have decided just to be rude or make a public statement like that! Why would he want to deliberately make Doctor Guignard mad at him?"

"Besides," agreed James, "if he'd wanted to make a big show of it, he'd a called his nigras to come home with him!"

"Or woulda boycotted the whole thing from the get-go!" added Michael.

"Seems to me we need to find out what called him home, and if it was a medical emergency, who was the patient, and why'd they need a doctor? Question is, how we gonna find out without stirrin things up?" Angus concluded. "Ya'll're gonna have to keep your eyes and ears open for any gossip or rumors round town that might give us a clue. It makes a difference if this was just an ordinary problem on the plantation, or whether it involved his nigra woman and her children."

"Why's that, Angus?" asked Michael obtusely, somewhat bewildered by their own machinations and uncertain he understood why they should be so concerned.

"Because if he's rushin home to deal with a family that shouldn't be his family, he's violatin the code, and it might give us a clue as to what else he's planning to do for em. We can't accuse him of violatin any law or breachin any kinda contract without hard proof that he's doin anything more than fuckin his slave woman!" explained James in exasperation, immediately grasping the thrust of Angus' point. "And fuckin her may be morally wrong, but it ain't illegal- since he can do what he wants with his own property!"

"Except emancipate em and leave em an inheritance!" corrected Angus.

"Yeah! Except that!" repeated James.

Michael suddenly seemed overwhelmed by the complications of the whole situation. "Well, if he can't emancipate em or leave em property in the first place, why're we getting ourselves all worked up about him thinkin about it, or tryin?"

"Because, though he can't do it here legally, in South Carolina, there is a chance he could find a way to pull it off somewhere out of state! Like up in Baltimore, or Cincinnati maybe!" informed Angus.

"Well, now, how's he gonna manage to do that when he ain't even left the state since he went up to Baltimore last year?" demanded Michael.

"I dunno brother, but Angus's right, that's what we gotta try n find out!" responded James. "Angus, don't your Pa have anything in those law books of his that might tell us how to get around South Carolina slave laws? I know he's helped some folks get free in the past."

Angus looked pained. It was not clear whether it was the pain of betraying his father's commitment to freedom for all, or having to dig around in the books with his father not feeling well, or being embarrassed that his father had defended manusmission cases, or simply not knowing, and therefore disappointing James and Michael. Or maybe it was the discomfort of spying on people in order to further his own goals that pricked his conscience as somehow dirty or dishonest. He was after all still his father's son.

"I'll, I'll look into it- might take a while to find out, but I'll try." Was all he managed to say. That assurance seemed enough for the Willis brothers- for now at least- so they sealed the deal, as was their custom, passing around the ubiquitous bottle of whiskey.

LXI

Sally stood terrified before her master. Dr. Guignard was livid. "I know you spoke to Elijah Willis's slaves. You'd best tell me what you said to them, or ya'll're gonna regret it!"

"I ain't hardly said more'n hello to em, Doctor, I swear!" she answered tremblingly.

Regardless of the public's generally favorable reviews of the rally, Dr. Guignard was still licking his wounds from what he seemed to feel was his defeat. He had failed to exact his revenge on Elijah which, Angus' and the Willis boys' political aspirations notwithstanding, had been his primary motive in hosting the rally in the first place! He was deperate to find a scapegoat for that failure. He suspected it must have been caused by one of his own slaves betraying him by warning Elijah, and that was why Elijah had left early. Sally was the scapegoat of choice because she knew too much about her master.

Sally knew the price she'd pay if she told Dr. Guignard that she had warned Gilbert, Julius, and Jason about Robert Barnwell Rhett coming, and how Angus had been the one to come ask for Dr. Guignard's help, and how it had been Dr. Guignard's idea to keep a check list of all the signatories of the petition, invite all the planters, and demand they send their slaves. He'd done all that as an attempt to either smoke Elijah out, or, if he didn't show up for the rally, to use his boycott of it as an excuse to attack him. She also knew perfectly well her master couldn't abide the thought of Amy and her children living in the plantation house as Elijah's family, or that he could not only live with them, but actually love them and prefer their company to that of any white person. Elijah's whole living arrangement was so wrong on so many levels that it made Dr. Guignard crazy just to think about it- not to mention how insulted he still felt that Elijah didn't immediately acquiesce to his insistence they all be sent back to the slave quarters!

The truth of the matter was that Guignard, along with his many other character flaws, was a hypocrite. In fact, he was fundamentally jealous of Elijah, and Sally knew it. Once married but now widowed and childless, for all his affluence and power, Guignard's loveless emotional life left nothing but pain and suffering in its wake. He had forced himself on more than one of his own slaves, and when one of them responded to his advances with disgust, he had felt his manhood humiliated and nearly beat her to the edge of her life in revenge for his impotence. His anger unsated, he then took it out on the woman's son, feeling suddenly aroused by his perverse fury, threatening the boy that he'd kill his mother if he didn't satisfy his master's lust.

Unfortunately, Guignard, was paranoid. He was afraid that all his slaves might be plotting against him, and rightly suspected that Sally knew this. That was dangerous, for she knew it would take next to nothing for him to turn his rancor on her. Being fundamentally both narcissictic and sadistic, Guignard was convinced that her demeanor was expressive of loathing for his impotence, and so he found it unbearable when she looked at him with what he saw as a slack-jawed, beetle-browed, heavy-lidded expression. It would take little for her loathing to become punishable.

He was right of course, that she detested him, but it had nothing to do with his sexual prowess or proclivities. Such attributes were simply byproducts of her justifiable hatred. It was his fundamentally bitter, joyless soul and mean-spirited, hard-hearted, abusive treatment of them all that was the root cause of her loathing. This was a lingering reality that poisoned virtually all of their communications, and contributed not only to his cumulative annoyance with her every action but also to the increasing inertia against which she struggled, and the depressing cloud of negativity and misery that hung over her every time he asked her to do anything. She had learned over the long years of her servitude, that playing stupid was only sometimes an effective strategy against her master, for if over-played, it could provoke him to explode with a chilling cruelty that was a cause of dread and horror to all the slaves on the plantation.

"Don't you lie to me, gal! I was watchin from upstairs, and I could tell you said more'n hello. D'ya take me for a fool? D'ya'll think you and all the other darkies on this plantation can pull the wool over my eyes so easily?" Dr. Guignard's expression was clearly menacing.

"Naw sir, I know you ain't no fool, sir! I ain't trying to pull no wool over ya eyes, sir! As God is my witness, when I seen Mister Elijah's slaves, I said 'Hello, how ya'll doin? Nice to see ya! Doctor Guignard sent us down here to help ya'll with this here buntin. What can we do to hep?' I swear, Doctor Guignard, I as just obeyin your orders, sir, just like ya'll told me to!"

All of this was perfectly true, so Sally was confident the Lord would not strike her down for lying. Even if she had failed to add what else she had told Elijah's slaves, her conscience was clear she had truthfully answered her master's question. By the grace of God, that confidence prevented Dr. Guignard from detecting anything out of the ordinary in her body language that might have revealed the reality of what else she had disclosed.

Obedience always being a source of satisfaction to Guignard, especially when rendered to him, he was somewhat mollified, and his anger abated. Suddenly uncertain whether someone had actually tipped Elijah off, or whether his opponent was simply even smarter than he'd realized, Dr. Guignard found himself in something of a quandry. Try as he might, he couldn't shake the feeling that Elijah was mocking him and was plotting something, but he was hard pressed to figure out how to discover and expose the plot once and for all. He wanted incontrovertible proof. He just wasn't sure how he could get it.

"Well, alright then! You'd best be tellin the the truth or there'll be Hell to pay!" Dr. Guignard concluded, "Now go on n get your fat black ass outa here! I need to think about this Elijah Willis situation, and I don't want anybody disturbin me, d'ya hear?"

Relieved to be dismissed despite the insufferable rudeness with which it had been communicated, Sally managed a "Yassuh!" before beating a hasty retreat, grateful for getting out of her master's presence relatively unscathed. She left Dr. Guignard brooding over what he was convinced was Elijah's determination to bring dishonor and calamity upon him and the entire community.

LXII

Despite the vicissitudes of childbirth and political rallies, the inescapable obligations of life on the plantion had come full circle to the Spring plowing and planting. As usual, Elijah and everyone else on the plantation were consumed with the exhausting demands of the season, working long hours to get the new crop underway. Once again, Cincinnati seemed to recede into the distance like a dream in the face of the more immediate challenges confronting them.

After the rally made it clear the climate was growing more and more inhospitable, Elijah was more eager than ever to get the crops planted, so he could at long last fulfill his promise; go up to Cincinnati, and get the new will written. He set himself to working at a breakneck pace, with no let-up. Amy worried he was driving himself too hard, and was afraid the stress would provoke another episode with his heart, but Elijah insisted he was fine and just kept on working relentlessly. At least there had been no immediate repercussions from the political rally for them to contend with, in spite of Dr. Guignard's hopes to the contrary. Nevertheless, they all had the growing sensation that they were sitting on a tinderbox waiting for it to ignite.

It seems, however, that Dr. Guignard and his acolytes were the only ones who associated the ominous threat of abolitionism with some sort of covert plan of Elijah's. Those who had even realized that Elijah had left the rally early did not seem to find it suspicious since it was a planter's duty to look after things at home whether it was his slaves or his family whose health was threatened. Since Elijah was not married and the rest of his relations were there at the rally, most folks simply assumed it was a health crisis with his slaves that had called him away and that he had rightly gone off to deal with it, obliged to protect his investment over all other priorities. So things had calmed down pretty quickly after the rally.

Fortunately, little Savage was thriving, and Amy's recovery from the strains of childbirth had been far quicker than with Eliza. The only thing out of the ordinary seemed to be that the weather was unusually warm and wet for this early in the year. The water standing in puddles, ditches, and marshy areas along the creeks and rivers that criss-crossed the region made for a prolific crop of mosquitos. They were incessantly annoying field hand and household resident alike. Amy noticed that Savage seemed to be a favorite and succulent target of the voracious pests, his tender skin swelling hot and pink with angry bumps from where the mosquitos had gorged on his young blood.

"Momma, do ya'll still have any calendula I can put on the baby's skin? He's scratching himself silly with these mosquito bites!" Amy asked her mother. Momma Celia had learned from her grandmother to make a lotion from marigold flowers that was effective in reducing the pain and itchiness of all kinds of bug bites, rashes and scratches.

"Look over there in the pantry on the top shelf, sugar, on the left where I keep ma medicines." Momma Celia responded, stirring a potful of savory stew. "Matter of fact, I was plantin marigolds out in the garden last week, thinkin I might be needin to make some more lotion, what with all these mosquitos from the wet weather we been havin. Been splittin clumps of lemongrass too- plantin em all around the house, an even the slave quarters!" Momma Celia explained, "They heps keep the mosquitos away. Gilbert told me his wife an children been eaten alive lately! An all the field hands been complainin the mosquitos ain't never been this bad!"

No one realized that yellow fever had broken out that year in New Orleans and had been working its way eastward along the network of rivers that fed into the Mississippi. By the time it reached Georgia, with the unseasonably warm weather, it had jumped to other waterways too, like the nearby Savannah River, whose waters flowed through Georgia and South Carolina to the East Coast rather than towards the Mississipi Delta and the Gulf of Mexico.

The disease was not new to the Americas. It had traveled West from Africa along the slave trade routes for several hundred years. There had been periodic epidemics as far north as New York, Baltimore, and Philadelpha and as far west as the Yucatan Peninsula. Back in 1793, when Philadelphia was still the U.S. capital, the epidemic had taken one in nine of the population, and President Washington and the government had been forced to evacuate from the city.

Yellow fever was not always fatal, however, and it seemed that if you survived it once, you never got it again. There were many Negroes who had acquired an immunity or at least a resistance to it from long exposure- perhaps even before coming to America. Hard to say if they passed it on to their children. The white population seemed not to share as much in that benefit, however, and often died from the internal hemorrhaging, vomiting, dehydration, and liver damage that the disease provoked in its more toxic stages.

Not yet suspecting anything so dire, Amy found the bottle of calendula lotion on the shelf as her mother had directed. "Is this it, Momma?" she asked, uncertain of its contents since it had no label.

"Open it up child. Do it smell like marigolds?" Momma Celia asked, unable to abandon her vigil over the stew lest it burn on the bottom.

"Mmmm, hmmm!" Amy replied, surprised by the obvious.

"Well then, that's the one! Go an put some a that on every bite, and the baby should stop fussin with em," Momma Celia instructed as she tasted the stew to see if it still needed anything.

Amy took the bottle and went upstairs to where Savage lay sleeping fitfully in his cradle. Angry welts covered his chubby arms and legs, and a few on his face were crusted with blood from where his razor sharp little fingernails had broken the skin from scratching. As Amy leaned over the cradle to pick him up, he awoke with a start and began crying, as if in pain. Feeling his forehead, Amy realized he was burning up with a fever, and alarmed, called for Momma Celia.

"Momma! Come here quick! Savage is sick!" she shouted down from the top of the stairs.

Sensing the urgency in her daughter's voice and knowing that after bearing seven children, this was no novice mother getting worked up over nothing, Momma Celia immediately took the stew pot off the fire, took off her apron, and went running upstairs.

When she got there, she found Amy cradling the baby in her arms, patting his back to try to calm him. He was shrieking inconsolably, his forehead beaded with perpsiration, even though his body shivered and trembled, as though from cold. As Amy laid him down to try to examine him he arched his back, his belly distended and rigid, and then proceeded to vomit all over the cradle. Amy looked up at her mother in panic, tears streaking her cheeks in concern for her precious son.

Taking in the situation, Momma Celia tried to reassure her daughter, though her mind was racing. Her grandson's symptoms intuitively triggered an unexpected memory. She had heard of yellow fever, but never seen it before. Savage's appearance, however, somehow reminded her of what she had heard. Her anxiety rising, she suddenly felt out of her league, but she didn't want to add to Amy's fears by saying so.

"Let me take care of this, sugar," she said as calmly as possible. "I need you to go find one of the boys to fetch Elijah- and send Elder on the mule to find Dr. Harley and let him know we might need his hep. Find out if Gilbert's family or any of the others are comin down with fever and chills. And call the girls- I'm gonna need their hep too. Go on now! Hurry up!" she ordered. "I can't run as fast as ya'll, but I can take care a my grandson!"

Amy nodded, still concerned, but somehow comforted by her mother's unruffled authority under pressure. Wiping the tears from her cheeks, she stood up to head for the hallway. As she reached the door however, she turned, by the force of a wave of worry irresitably pulling her like a riptide back toward the cradle. "Is he gonna be alright, Momma? I've never seen any of my babies come down with anything like this before!"

"Good Lord willin, he'll pull through, but we got work to do! Now go on! Do like I told ya!" Momma Celia commanded gently but firmly, not wanting her daughter to see how anxious she was. She had heard of the ravages of yellow fever from a slave she knew who had lived through an earlier outbreak down in New Orleans in 1833. She knew that if she could somehow keep Savage from reaching the bloody vomit stage, he'd pull through.

Momma Celia made a mental inventory of everything she could remember from what her friend had told her about the symptoms of the disease: fever, chills, headache, back pain, loss of appetite, nausea, vomiting, dehydration, and in the worse cases jaundice, internal bleeding, and blood in the vomit. She quickly checked the sour smelling vomit her grandson had just ejected all over his cradle and was relieved to see there was no sign of blood in it. Perhaps she was wrong in her suspicion of the diagnosis, but she knew at least that whatever the nature of it might be, any kind of fever could be bad for a baby. The plantation cemetery had more than a few little graves of slave babies who'd died of some kind of fever or other.

Her mind raced desperately to think of ingredients she might have to make a tea, or some kind of lotion or salve to give her grandson to treat these symptoms. She was worried about the others too, for if they were also coming down with symptoms, she'd need enough of those ingredients for everyone, or the fever might spread.

She realized with a shock that they really had to keep this not only under control, but if possible, a secret. If it was in fact yellow fever, not only could it cause panic if folks in the community found out, but it might require a visit from the odious Dr. Guignard as the town's only other physician! After all the effort they'd made to keep him from finding out about Savage's birth (and obvious parentage), that was the last thing they needed! She shuddered at the very thought of it!

There was a knock on the door, and Clarissa came in. "Momma said ya'll needed my help! She told me Savage is sick. Is he gonna be alright?"

"I hope so, baby, but I need ya'll's hep to make sure. First of all, I need ya'll to fetch me some water and clean towels, so we can clean up this mess. Poor little thing done heaved up his breakfast all over the cradle." Clarissa wrinkled her nose in disgust when she peeked into the cradle and both saw and smelled her mother's curdled milk soaking the sheets and clinging in lumps to the polished wood panels of the sides. She nodded immediately and eagerly ran off to do as she was bidden.

"Tell Julia she's gonna have to take care of Eliza for a while, so's we can take care a Savage!" Momma Celia called after her eldest granddaughter.

Clarissa nodded in affirmation, shouting back "Awright!" as she hurried off to her appointed task.

Turning back to her grandson, Momma Celia said, "Ya'll're truly blessed, little man. Ya'll got sistas and brothas that I can always count on to hep, and ya'll're gonna be just fine, don't you worry! They's too much love in this house for ya not to!" Perhaps it was the conviction in the voice of his grandmother that seemed to soothe him, but his stomach cramps passed, he relaxed, and exhausted, Savage finally stopped his crying and lay limply in his grandmother's arms drifting off to sleep.

By the time Clarissa had returned with the water and towels, Momma Celia had changed the baby's clothes and removed the sheet from the cradle. Clarissa promptly set to washing the vomit off the sides so her little brother could be laid back down to nap.

"I need ya'll to stay with him now, sugar. An if he gets fussy or he starts sweatin, I want ya to cool his forehead with a damp cloth, y'hear?" But keep him covered, cause he gets the chills too, and he's gonna have to sweat the fever out. Meanwhile, I'm gonna go downstairs an find me the ingredients I need to set him straight!" She started for the door and then remembered,

"Oh, be sure to pick him up if he starts to vomit, so he don't choke on it!"

Clarissa looked determined to help, though the thought of the possibility of Savage vomiting all over her was disgusting, and she prayed her little brother would be better behaved than to do such a thing to her- sister or no.

Momma Celia went down to the kitchen to take stock of what she had in the pantry. She needed cayenne, St. John's wort, cranesbill geranium, and shepherd's purse to prevent bleeding; ginger root and peppermint for the nausea; basil and oregano, rosemary, and lavender for the fever – all for the tea; then some witch hazel to rub on him to sooth his skin and cool the fever, and some castor oil to rub on him for the muscle pains.

She found the cayenne, ginger root, some dried basil, witch hazel and castor oil in the kitchen, but needed to go out to the garden to see if she could find some fresh peppermint, oregano, rosemary, lavender and cranesbill for her tea. The shepherd's purse was a weed growing wild. She was pretty sure she could find some near the creek, but was hesitant to go that far from the house until Amy or Elijah, Gilbert, or Dr. Harley were there. She didn't want to leave little Clarissa Ann all alone with the baby for too long.

"God fogive me, I shoulda taught the children bout these herbs sooner! Then I coulda sent them to fetch em for me!' she fretted to herself, resigned that she would just have to make do as best as she could, and trust the Lord to do the rest until help came.

She found everything but the shepherd's purse. She remembered her aloe vera might help too, either as a salve or by adding its juice to the tea. She headed back to the kitchen with her precious harvest. She laid out her herbs, rinsed them, picked off the leaves, and set them to simmer into a tea. "Best add some honey too," she thought, pouring a generous dollop of magnolia honey and a bit of aloe vera sap into the pot and stirring it, "Make it go down smoother, cause they's heat in the cayenne an ginger he might not like too much!" she muttered to herself

When the herbs had simmered to the point that the water had turned a greenish amber, she took the pot off the stove, strained its contents through a piece of cheesecloth so the baby wouldn't choke on the leaves, poured the syrupy liquid into a teapot, and set it aside to cool. As she placed the teapot on the table, she heard footsteps and voices coming from the front of the house and from outside in back as well.

"Momma! Momma!" Amy cried, bursting through the kitchen door, anguish raising her pitch at least an octave. "Gilbert says his wife and children got the fever too! How's Savage?" she asked urgently.

Before Momma Celia could answer, they heard Elijah's, Elder's and Doctor Harley's voices calling from the front hall.

"Amy, darlin! Momma Celia! What's goin on? What's happened to Savage?" Elijah strode into the kitchen, anxiety written all over his face. Dr. Harley and Elder were right behind.

Amy was too worried from Gilbert's news to even speak, so Momma Celia promptly took charge and gave Dr. Harley and Elijah a succinct report, including her concern about keeping the news from spreading to the community if it was yellow fever, and especially to avoid a visit from Dr. Guignard. She also explained in detail the measures she had already taken down to the last ingredient of her tea, which still sat on the table, pale wisps of weakening steam curling slowly upwards and disappearing into the kitchen air as it cooled.

"Well, as usual Momma Celia, I stand in awe. You've done all the right things. How's the baby doin now?" Dr. Harley asked.

"He's upstairs asleep. Clarissa's lookin after him. But he still got the sweats." Momma Celia replied.

"Elijah, Momma Celia's right- we gotta do everything we can to contain this thing so neither the townsfolk nor John Guignard find out about it, if possible. I'm gonna go upstairs first and check on the baby, but I think we need to check on all your slaves too." Joseph Harley's face was lined with concern.

Elijah turned to Amy, "Darlin, is Gilbert over in the slave quarters with his family or out in the fields with the workers?"

"He came in from the fields cause I had Phillip run n fetch him. He's waitin for ya'll in his cabin." Amy replied.

By this time Elleck and Phillip had come to the kitchen door to find out what was happening.

"Boys," Elijah called, "go tell your Uncle Gilbert Dr. Harley'll be by directly to look in on his family. And tell him we need to know if any other slaves on this plantation are feelin poorly."

"- no matter what symptoms they've got!" interjected Dr. Harley, "but especially if anybody's got fever, chills, aches, or vomitin!"

"Go find out for us right away, so's Dr. Harley can examine every last one!" urged Momma Celia.

The boys looked to their mother hestitantly. She nodded her approval, and they ran off to tell Gilbert and find out about the others.

"If this is yellow fever, we need to keep the infected ones in quarantine. Do we even know if anybody here's had it? If they survived an earlier outbreak, chances are they won't get it now." Dr. Harley announced.

"My grandma tole me that some of our people don't get it! She said it's cause we was strong stock back in Africa, and that the white folks genelly got sicker than black folks." Momma Celia informed Dr. Harley.

"Well, I have heard that some Negroes seem to be immune to the disease. Let's hope little Savage has enough of your side of the family in him to keep him from gettin too sick!" Dr. Harley replied.

"My grandma also told me that wherever they's yella fever, they's mosquitos too."

"Lord knows we've had an awful lot of mosquitos this year!" observed Elijah.

"I been plantin lemongrass round the house and the slave quarters, Doctor. Them mosquitos don't like the smell a lemongrass!" Momma Celia confided.

Dr. Harley thought a moment. No one was sure whether mosquitos caused yellow fever, but many had observed that mosquito outbreaks often went hand in hand with outbreaks of the disease. He figured they shouldn't take any chances. "How much lemongrass have ya'll got around here?" he asked.

"Well, I just divided the clumps and transplanted em last week, so they ain't well established yet, but they's enough to cut some if that's what ya'll're thinking." Momma Celia understood Dr. Harley instinctively.

"That's exactly what I'm thinking! I want to ya'll to cut as much lemongrass as ya can without killin the plants. Tie the grass into bundles we can give to each family. Hang the bundles in every window and doorway on the plantation. We gotta try ta keep the mosquitos from bitin folks if we can!"

Momma Celia added, "If ya rub the cut ends of the grass on your skin, the oil'l keep em from bitin ya when ya'll're out in the fields too! An ya can hang a sheet tent-like over your bed to keep em offa ya at night!"

"The other thing is, we gotta try to get rid of any standin water near the buildings." Elijah observed. "You can see the mosquitos growin in the water!"

"Now, how we gonna be able to do that? Been so much rain this Spring, practically the whole plantation's standin in water!" moaned Amy, feeling overwhelmed.

"I can get Julius and Jason to haul over a few wagon loads of sawdust and wood chips from the mill. The boys can make sure all the rain barrels're covered and that they're no buckets, washtubs, or other containers lyin around full of stagnant water, and then we can have em spread the wood chips and saw dust wherever they find puddles and ruts near the houses. At least keep the mosquitos from breedin on our own doorstep!" Elijah explained, his managerial skills once more coming to the fore with all the skill of a general executing a military campaign.

By then Dr. Harley had examined Savage, with Amy anxiously at his side. The baby had thrown up again and seemed to have no appetite when Amy tried to nurse him.

"We gotta get liquid in him so he doesn't dehydrate," Dr. Harley insisted. "When Elder came to get me and told me what was happenin with little Savage, I was he afraid he mighta lost his appetite and not want to nurse, so I brought ya'll something that might help." He pulled out of his black bag an odd looking bottle with what looked like an imitation teat made out of vulvanized rubber where the stopper would be.

"Friend of mine sent me this from up in New York. Seems a fella up there named Elijah Pratt invented it a few years back, but it hasn't really caught on yet. He sent it to me more or less as a joke about what crazy Yankees come up with, but seems to me it might help us get Momma Celia's tea into little Savage. It's worth a try!"

"If it was good enough for one Elijah, maybe it'll be good enough for another!" Amy observed. "How does it work?"

"Well ya just fill the bottle up with the liquid ya wanna give the baby, put the nipple on it, an let him suck on the nipple with the bottle tiltin down, so the liquid comes out into his mouth!" informed Momma Celia intuitively, as if she had been using feeding bottles for years. "Ain't it obvious?"

Momma Celia took the bottle immediately and set to preparing it with her tea, which by now had cooled to room temperature.

"Momma Celia," instructed Dr. Harley, "Be sure you put the bottle in some boilin water first, and then let it cool off before ya fill it. It's important to keep it sterile. And if Savage doesn't take all your tea, keep some aside in the teapot, and reboil both the tea and the bottle before each feed."

Momma Celia nodded in understanding, her face serious as she made a mental note of his instructions, and proceeded to set the bottle in a pot of boiling water on the stove. "Should I boil the nipple too?" she asked.

"Yes, but not for too long. Ya don't want the rubber to soften too much." Dr. Harley explained.

By the time Momma Celia had prepared the bottle with her concoction, everyone was eager to see if the baby would even take it. The whole family traipsed upstairs and surrounded his cradle as Amy picked him up and tried to give him the bottle. Savage looked surprised when he realized the nipple he had in his mouth was not his mother's, and he pushed it out with his tongue before he had even tasted a drop of his grandmother's tea. Amy looked up at Dr. Harley, her distress clearly rising.

"Be patient, my dear, he may take some coaxin. But we've got to get this into him one way or another! So just keep tryin- put your finger in the corner of his mouth, and if he starts to suck on it, pull out your finger and give him the bottle right away."

Momma Celia realized that the crowded room might also be distracting her grandson from his all important task, so she shooed everyone out sayin, "Give the child some privacy- or he gonna get too distracted with ya'll to even try to eat!" Turning to her daughter she added, "Amy sugar, take ya time, and let us know if he drinks it or not. We'll be downstairs if ya'll need us."

As the family returned to the kitchen, the focus shifted from Savage to his aunt and cousins. Dr. Harley went out to Gilbert's cabin and examined his wife and children. They all had fever and chills, and some had vomited, but as yet there was no sign of blood or jaundice.

Calling for Momma Celia to give her medicine to them all, Dr. Harley then asked Gilbert, "What about the other slaves?"

"They's a few feelin a tad poorly- but I don't think any been vomitin yet. Mostly just fever, chills, an aches." Gilbert informed him.

"Elijah, go tell Momma Celia to make as much of that tea as she has ingredients for. If possible, we need enough to dose every man, woman, and child on the plantation, beginin with the affected families. That means you and Amy too! If we get to this early enough, we may be able to prevent it from spreadin." Dr. Harley ordered. "And set the boys to cutting the lemongrass into small bundles. See to it each household gets some to hang in every window and doorway. You'd best get Jason and Julius goin on fetchin the wood chips and sawdust from the mill, too!"

Everyone set to work immediately, all too aware of the double danger of the disease spreading, and Dr. Guignard and the community finding out. By the time they had cut, bundled and hung the lemongrass, hauled and spread the saw dust and wood chips, harvested the herbs, and made a massive batch of the tea, all the slaves had presented themselves for Dr. Harley to examine. More than a few were showing symptoms, some of them severe.

Days passed. Amy had finally managed to get Savage to drink the tea, despite his fussing and grimace of disgust at first taste. She, Elijah, and all the other children drank some too- even Momma Celia and Dr. Harley took some, to be safe. After three or four days, Savage seemed to be on the mend, but not everyone on the plantation fared so well. A few of the slaves went into the toxic state of the fever, vomiting blood, their eyes turning yellow with jaundice, blood seeping even from their eyes and noses. Despite Momma Celia and Dr. Harley's heroic efforts, some even died, including, tragically, Gilbert's wife. Though their relationship had not always been happy, he was devastated by the sheer wretchedness and horror of her death. But he took it stoically, so he could nurse his children back to health. Yet others never even came down with symptoms of any kind, though they'd never been exposed to the fever before this outbreak, making Dr. Harley wonder if some were truly born with a resistance to the dreaded disease.

Mercifully, everyone else in the household survived unscathed. But, as if battling yellow fever were not enough, the cumulative strains of trying to contain the outbreak and keep the public (including Dr. Guignard) from finding out about it, triggered another episode of apoplexy in Elijah. Momma Celia was hard-pressed to keep the slaves and their master supplied with enough of the medicinal teas they needed to restore them all to health. She was running out of fresh ingredients, and was loathe to ask any neighbors for some, for fear of word getting out about what had been happening on the Willis Plantation.

The fact of the matter was, they were all exhausted! Yet the plowing, planting, weeding and hoeing still needed to be done, as always. The cotton and other crops were indifferent to the suffering of men, and time was working against them. Finding the time to go up to Cincinnati still eluded him, as Elijah was forced to rest and recover while simultaneously trying to oversee the operation of the plantation. Amy, recuperating from childbirth, was compelled by circumstance to shoulder more and more of the responsibilities of running the whole operation while Elijah's health still wavered. Dr. Harley had ordered him on bed rest- to which he surrendered about as willingly as if the good doctor had offered to pull all his teeth out with a hammer and a pair of pliers, and not so much as a dose of opium or a swig of whiskey to ease the pain! Amy and Momma Celia, however, were insistent that Elijah obey the good doctor's orders, and placed the children as sentries over him to assure his compliance, willing or not.

LXIII

The numerous setbacks that had befallen them caused Elijah to feel more and more despair of ever being able to get to Cincinnati. Falling into a depression over what seemed to be the insurmountable challenges and dangers they faced, he sought comfort and relief in the bottle. He began to drink even more whiskey than was normal for the average Southern gentleman, for whom whiskey was jokingly referred to as "mother's milk." It was a matter of pride and the mark of a gentleman to be known as a man who could hold his liquor, and Elijah could certainly hold his. But neither consuming nor holding it relieved his pain or anxiety about the future, and he became gloomier by the day. It was as if the whole burden was crushing and defeating him. He became generally taciturn and somewhat reclusive, and found it harder and harder to even derive the pleasure he formerly took in spending time with Amy and the children. As Elijah became more and more despondent, it seemed even his determination to go to Cincinnati to get the new will written was weakening, as was his resolve to liberate all his slaves. Amy was worried.

"Amy, darlin, I just don't know if I can do this anymore!" he told her in exasperation one grey morning, as a late summer rain fell, making the air so oppressively thick that breathing itself, let alone moving, began to feel like an excessively tiresome challenge. "I'm startin to think I should just try to sell everything off, take the money, and take ya'll on up to Cincinnati and be done with it! There's no way I'm gonna be able to take all the slaves up there with us, and tryin to run the plantation long distance from up there in Ohio seems to me doomed to fail. I'm gonna have to sell at least some of em!"

Amy was alarmed at this, but she was also afraid for Elijah's health and didn't dare do battle with him over the emancipation of the others, excepting her family, for fear of triggering another episode with his heart. She knew that the only way to freedom for her and her children was through

Elijah staying alive long enough to get them to Cincinnati. Despite her determination to emancipate them all, her mind couldn't help but ask for a fleeting moment, if it came to that, which ones should be sold? But she said nothing of this to Elijah, preferring to hold to the dream and the plan to emancipate them all.

"Well sugar, I still believe in ya- we all do!" she insisted. "The important thing is for ya'll to recover your health and go get that will written, because if we can get up to Cincinnati once we're freed, even if God forbid, anything should happen to you, I'd have the legal right to free the rest of the slaves, wouldn't I?"

Elijah perked up. "Why, I hadn't thought of that, darlin, but I suppose you would! If ya'll inherit all my property, that would include the rest of the slaves, and you would therefore have the power to bring as many of em as you wanted up to Ohio and free em!" His conscience was hugely relieved at this thought, for the dilemma of what to do about the others had been weighing heavily on his heart.

Yet something in him doubted it could be that simple despite the legal logic, and he thought he should perhaps make some discreet inquiries as to whether there might be any trustworthy prospective buyers for the whole estate, or at least for some of his slaves. He decided, however, to keep that idea to himself for the time being, as he was truly not up to a confrontation with Amy over the subject and knew it would likely upset her. It also occurred to him that perhaps he should ask for Angus Patterson's or John Bauskett's counsel, both as to whether Amy would in fact have discretionary power over the other slaves if his estate passed to her, and whether they thought it advisable for him to go ahead and seek out a buyer, or buyers, for any of his property- including some of his slaves.

LXIV

Summer crept into fall and the harvest season, once again. The wet weather had continued throughout the summer and initially helped the cotton grow prolifically, but now was threatening the harvest with rot. The slaves working the fields, demoralized by the bout of yellow fever, the constant rain, and their master's subsequent depression, were hard pressed to find any enthusiasm to motivate them to be the first to get their crop in to market. Some began to grumble about broken promises and speak ill of Elijah, as if he were deliberately refusing to take them to freedom. As they sat in the barn during a downpour, waiting for the rain to stop so they could go back out into the fields, a bunch of them set to talking.

"I swear we ain't never gonna get off this plantation!" said one of the field hands to a companion. "I think Miss Amy an Mister Elijah been stringin us along just to get us to work harder without complainin!"

"I know what ya mean!" replied another. "Been a couple a years now since Miss Amy let on we might all be set free if we kept quiet. An what do we got to show for it? Nothin!"

"I hear tell they's some of the slaves was there at that rally at Dr. Guignard's, 're thinkin bout tryin to organize some sorta uprisin. Seems listenin to that racist son of a bitch, Robert Barnwell Rhett goin on about how wonnerful slavery is, an how well behaved all the slaves was, got under the skin of more'n a few!" remarked a third.

"I know that's right! Jason tole me it made him mad as a hornet to listen to that fool talking bout us as if we was children, or pets! Said the man ain't done a honest day's work in his life! Been livin off the sweat of folks like us since he was born. I hear tell he wants to reinstate the slave trade and build a new nation on it!" chimed in another.

"Seriously? Man must be crazy!" said one.

"Crazy dangerous! He may be madder'n a pole cat with rabies, but he ain't stupid, and they's more'n a few white folks round here who seem to think the sun shines outa his ass!" commented another.

"Julius tole me all them white ladies was swoonin over him at the rally! Just bout made him wanna puke up that barbeque!" said the first.

"Waste a good barbeque, if ya ask me! They ain't worth it!" said the second.

"They's no figurin out white folks! Maybe bein hateful and crazy's in they blood!" remarked one of the women.

"Now hold on there a minute! Ya'll can't claim all white folks're like that. Mister Elijah ain't never been hateful with us. Nor cruel, neither!" remarked Henry one of the oldest slaves. He was the same slave who had come to Amy and Elijah's defense before.

"Mebbe not, but that don't mean he gonna free us either, and that's its own kinda cruelty, if ya'll ask me!" insisted the first.

"Well I for one, still think the man's doin the best he can. I got no beef with Mister Elijah an Miss Amy- I b'lieve Mister Elijah really wants to free us. Ain't his fault that folks like them people at the rally been makin it harder an harder to do it!" Henry responded.

"Well then, why ain't he gone and writ his new will up in Cincinnati? I heard tell he was gonna free Miss Amy, Momma Celia, and all the children up there, and then come back an fetch the rest of us!" said the second.

"Who told you that?" demanded the first.

"I overheard him talkin to Gilbert out in the barn one day- they didn't know I as there!" he responded.

"Well now, with all that's been goin on- first the rally, then Miss Amy havin her baby, then the fever, then Mister Elijah fallin sick, and the harvest upon us already, how he sposed to get up there to Cincinnati anyway? An he ain't exactly young no mo!" said Henry.

"I spose ya'll got a point, but it don't make it no easier! I just got a feelin it's gonna be a long time b'fo we see freedom, an I spect some of us never will, no matter what ya'll think ya heard in the barn!" insisted the first.

"Well, all I gotta say is, them that's thinkin bout an uprisin best be mighty careful nobody round these parts gets wind a it, or they more likely to see a hangman's noose than freedom! I druther take ma chances with Mister Elijah and Miss Amy any day than get masef lynched!" old Henry replied.

At that point they looked up and saw Gilbert standing in the door listening to them. He made no comment about their conversation, and none of them were sure just how long he'd been there or how much he'd heard. He simply said, "Alright ya'll, no more time for talkin. We got work to do! That cotton ain't gonna pick itself. Come on- get yer bags and get on out there while they's a break in the weather!"

The slaves gathered up the large burlap bags they wore slung over their shoulders to collect the cotton bolls and trudged on out to the fields, wondering how many more seasons they would have to repeat this ritual, or whether there would ever be an escape from it.

LXV

Son! Come on in here, wouldya please?" Angus Senior called from the parlor, his voice steady, reasonable, and dispassionate, as if he were calling a witness in court.

Angus Junior appeared in the doorway, slightly nervous, but trying to keep a poker face so as not to reveal any of his recent escapades to the old gentleman. He knew his father would not agree with the political position he was taking and didn't want to get into a fight over it. He'd made his decision, and was determined to move forward and prove himself independent of his father.

"Set yaself down, son. It seems we need to talk." His father indicated with his cane a place on the settee facing him in his winged-back armchair. Angus Junior meekly complied.

"It's come to my attention that ya seem to have finally made a career choice!" His father's words, as usual, were deliberately ambiguous in their intent, leaving room for doubt in Angus Junior's mind as to whether they indicated approval or disapproval. The young man shifted in his seat uncomfortably and started clearing his throat as if to speak, or at least to prevent his father from going any further. The stratagem failed, of course, and his father pressed on.

"I'm told, in fact, that you and the Willis boys, with some help from Dr. Guignard, actually managed to organize and hold a political rally to launch yaself into the public arena!" There was still no clearly negative judgment in the old man's voice. True to his objective, lawyerly fashion, he was simply establishing the facts of the matter with the lucidity of a mathematician laying out an algebraic problem, before proceeding to solve it. "That's right impressive son, and I'll admit, I didn't know ya had it in ya!"

"Thank ya, sir," Angus managed to mumble in response. This felt to him like a back-handed compliment, for it revealed simultaneously his father's pleasure that his son had accomplished something more complicated than drinking with the Willis boys and his underlying suspicion that despite his recent show of interest in the law, his son was fundamentally too limited to ever amount to much. It was also, from the younger Patterson's experience, the familiar prelude to the inevitable delivery of a critical paternal blow. He found himself instinctively gripping the armrest of the settee, as if bracing himself for its impending impact.

"Public service is a noble callin, son, and the art of politics in that service can be a worthwhile pursuit, despite its many pitfalls, as I know only too well from my own experience. So it comes as no surprise you might want to try ya hand at it and follow in your father's footsteps. Although I truly do applaud ya'll for your perseverance in carryin out such a complex and detailed plan, I have to say, however, that I was sorely disappointed in its purpose!" Angus Senior enunciated this last phrase with ponderous clarity, progressively slowing the delivery of each word. In genteel Southern society, where raising one's voice was considered boorish, a level voiced-delivery of parental disappointment was the devastating emotional equivalent of being severely beaten, and every father's son knew it. There was no ambiguity that the elder Patterson was referring to the racist content of the speeches at the rally and not to the attempt to enter into politics itself.

"Well I'm sorry, Pa, that you don't approve!" Angus Junior said with a mixture of anger and defensiveness. "For once in my life I thought something through, stood up and took a stand, and was applauded by the whole community for it, and I'm still not good enough for you!" he blurted petulantly.

Angus Senior gave a heavy sigh. "It's not a matter of you not bein good enough for me- you're my son, and I love ya. Nothin's gonna change that! It's that you're too good to take the position ya'll took in that rally! It demeans ya and is a dishonor to your upbringin! You do me dishonor by it! I didn't raise ya to hate folks who are different from you! I tried to teach ya to defend and protect em against the folks who abuse em, not guarantee their continued sufferin!" His father's voice was rising with each sentence, his cane thumping the floor for emphasis despite his innate sense of decorum, clearly indicating to his son the enormity of his father's upset.

Mary stood listening outside in the hallway, her heart breaking for both the man who freed her and for the boy she had raised. A large tear etched a glistening track racing down her dark and wrinkled cheek, like a flash flood in a dry creek bed, eventually falling to the floor and leaving a stain where it splattered dully against the polished floorboards.

His longing to be respected and admired left the younger Patterrson torn. The requisites for the respect of his father and for that of his community sprang from contrary views and expectations. His father's present disappointment was just one more in a never-ending series of disappointments in their relationship. The memory of the public's applause at the rally, however, was a new and intoxicating experience that stood in sharp and favorable counter-point to his domestic discomfort. Even though Angus Junior knew he had been manipulated by both Dr. Guignard and by Robert Barnwell Rhett, his thirst for approval overrode the warning signals he had sensed throughout the process of holding the rally. Unable to defend his position with any credibility in his own home, however, and knowing full well his father could see through his dissembling, Angus Junior's only recourse was to flee from his father's withering gaze.

He stood up abruptly, saying, "I never have understood, Pa, how you can claim to care so much about the sufferin of others, and not even see the sufferin of your own son! Ma couldn't understand it either! I think that's part of what killed her!" This last phrase, he blurted out, wanting it to hurt, and then felt ashamed of himself, but realized it too late. The damage had already been done, and the words hung in the air like a poisonous cloud.

Without waiting for his father's wounded response he stormed out of the room, almost knocking Mary over on the way out. One glance at her face made his shame complete. Their eyes met for a moment, and both her love and her pain were unbearable for him. He ran out of the house stifling his gut-wrenching sobs, slamming the door behind him in bitter frustration.

LXVI

John Guignard opened a letter that Sally had presented to him on a silver tray. It was from Robert Barnwell Rhett. It carried the embossed letterhead of *The Charleston Mercury*. Guignard dismissed Sally and sat down by the window to read it on an elegantly upholstered rose-back armchair designed by the famous John Henry Belter.

Robert Barnwell Rhett, Esq.
The Charleston Mercury
Charleston, South Carolina

My Dear Friend John:

I hope this finds you well, despite all the gloomy weather that has lately befallen us. My wife is of the opinion that, if it does not improve soon, we shall have but two choices remaining: either grow fins and gills like a fish, or follow the example of Noah and his Ark!

It must be said that my good wife is somewhat prone to exaggeration. However, I can certainly sympathize with her sentiment, as I'm sure you can too.

Be that as it may, I did want to follow up with you to see what news you might have concerning the list of signatories to the petition your young friends sought to send up to Columbia, and which we duly and proudly published over here in our paper. Specifically, have you been able to pursue any inquiries, or offer any further "persuasion" to those who might have failed to sign? I need not remind you, I trust, that the times are demanding people take a clear stand on this issue, for all our sakes. It is imperative that we of the ruling class present a united front on this matter!

Please provide me with the names of any you feel might be elusive or recalcitrant to our efforts, and I shall be more than happy to offer assistance in

locating the reluctant or undecided and help to persuade them of the rightness
of our cause. You may assure your young friends on my behalf that, once the
necessary follow up has been completed, I shall be more than happy to fulfill
my promise to seek the required sponsorship in Columbia to assure their
petition's passage into law.

Ever the servant of the common good, and your friend,

Robert Barnwell Rhett, Esquire
Owner and Editor
The Charleston Mercury

Dr. Guignard carefully folded the letter, tucked it into his breast pocket, and sat there looking out on the rain dripping off the glossy dark green leaves of the camellia bushes, pondering what course of action he should take. On the one hand, he agreed with Rhett that people needed to take a stand. On the other hand, he resented Rhett dictating terms to him in an implicitly threatening way, for he had no doubt that there would be a public price to pay should he not comply. Rhett was all too eager to decry and defame any who disagreed with him, and had in *The Charleston Mercury* exceptionally powerful and effective means to do so.

Dr. Guignard had been sorely disappointed not to have triumphed over Elijah at the rally, but his keen sensitivity to the cross-currents of local loyalties and the dangers of an open attack on a founding family had made him reluctant to pursue the follow-up that he himself had devised. The fact was, he had never really intended to pursue those who failed to sign. He had hoped that the possible threat of such pursuit would be sufficient intimidation to make it unnecessary.

Dr. Guignard concluded that the best course of action would be one that placated Rhett without implicating himself. It struck him that this would most easily be accomplished through the agency of his young acolytes, so he sat down at his desk to write a letter to the Willis brothers and to Angus Junior, enlisting their support, under the guise of it being a key to their political future.

Gentlemen:

I have recently received a letter from Robert Barnwell Rhett reiterating
his promise to find the necessary sponsorship for your petition to the State
Legislature. The fulfillment of his promise is contingent, however, on a specifc

proviso: that you either pursue those who attended the rally but did not sign the petition, or provide Mr. Rhett the names of such, so that he might provide what he deems the "proper persuasion" to exact their compliance. He actually indicated in his own words- "I shall be more than happy to offer assistance in locating the reluctant or undecided, and helping to persuade them of the rightness of our cause."

Whereas I do not take kindly to his efforts to dictate to us, there can be no doubt that he will hold hostage all chances of your petition being turned into law at least until he is convinced that we have followed through with due diligence in this matter. This is the price you pay for playing politics, so it must be dealt with accordingly.

Although I have no intention of sending Mr. Rhett any specific names at present, I strongly urge you three to consider implementing a plan of pursuit, so that we may honestly assure him that the situation is well in hand, and folks around here are duly in compliance. This represents an opportunity for you. I heartily desire that you three get the credit for doing so, for it will greatly enhance your political prospects for the future.

Please apprise me of your plan and the results of its implementation at your earliest convenience.

Ever your friend and supporter,

John Guignard, M.D.

Dr. Guignard folded, addressed and sealed the letter, and called for Sally.

"Sally!" he shouted impatiently, "SALLY!" his choler rising. "Damn it woman, get in here!" Waiting for her to appear, he muttered to himself about how if he didn't know they were all alike, he'd sell her down the river and get himself a housekeeper worthy of the name.

Sally came shuffling to the door, inured to his habitual abuse by the cloud of depression that surrounded her when in his presence. "Yassuh?"

"Sweet Jesus in Heaven woman, what took ya so long?" he demanded. Without waiting for a reply, he handed her the letter, saying, "See to it that this letter gets to the Willis boys or Angus Patterson Junior right away!"

Sally looked at him blankly, not out of stupidity or ignorance, but realizing that she couldn't have one letter delivered to two addresses. "Yassuh, right away suh, but which address do ya'll want it delivered to, suh? To the Willis's or the Patterson's?"

Dr. Guignard was about to deride her for her stupidity and leave the decision to her, when he thought the better of it, realizing that despite his low opinion of Sally's intelligence, it was in fact an apt question (though he would never acknowledge as much to her, of course). His sensitivity to local social currents being acute, he realized that it would be better to deliver it to the Willis boys, as their parents were fully sympathetic, whereas it might create unnecessary tensions with Angus Senior, which he would prefer to avoid out of respect for the old man. Realizing that the vigilanteism he was promoting might be deemed illegal, he was also aware that enfeebled or not, the elder Mr. Patterson was more than capable of taking legal action against him if he thought it warranted, and he did not wish to sully his own reputation with the taint of any accusatory proceedings, no matter what their outcome.

"Deliver it to James Willis at his store. And make it fast!" he barked.

"Yassuh, anything you say, suh!" Sally answered, backing and bowing her way out the door as if in the presence of royalty, knowing that it pleased his vanity.

Once downstairs and safely away from her master's prying eyes, Sally went into the kitchen. She took a kettle of boiling water off the stove and held the letter over the spout, carefully steaming open the wax seal without disrupting the imprint of Dr. Guignard's signet ring, identifying the sender. Despite her years in his service, Dr. Guignard had no idea that Sally could, in fact, read and write. She had carefully kept the secret from him, not only because he was capable of punishing her for such a violation of the slave laws, but because she knew it might be a skill upon which her own life and the lives of others, could one day depend.

Reading the message, she immediately grasped that Elijah and his family could be in danger. She quickly and expertly resealed the letter and called her nephew. She needed a messenger she could trust.

"Honey, I need ya'll to do an urgent errand for me. Dr. Guignard wants this letter delivered right away to Mister James Willis at his store on the main road outside a town. Take it to him fast as ya can. But they's somethin else that's real important. On yer way back home, I needs ya to stop at the Willis Plantation and give em a message. Ya'll can give it to Mister Elijah, Miss Amy, Momma Celia, or Mister Gilbert- but to nobody else, ya hear?" Her nephew, a serious young man, sensed both urgency and danger in his aunt's demand. He nodded solemnly.

"Tell em that 'The three that held the rally are gonna pursue the folks who didn't sign, and if they don't sign, Mr. Rhett will provide assistance to persuade the folks on the list.' D'ya got it?" Sally pressed him.

"Yes'm," her nephew responded.

"Repeat the message, so I's sho ya got it right," she insisted.

"'The three that held the rally're gonna pursue the folks who didn't sign, and if they don't sign, Mr. Rhett's gonna provide assistance to persuade the folks on the list!'"

Sally nodded with satisfaction, and said in a low voice as she hung a numbered permit around his next to identify him as on his master's business, lest he be stopped and mistaken for a runaway, "That's good, now go on an hurry, child. But be careful! The fewer folks that sees ya goin to the Willis Plantation, the better!"

"I can take a short cut off road past the store, an ain't nobody gonna see me! Then I can loop around back to the main road after I give em the message at Mister Elijah's place, an if Dr. Guignard sees me, it'll just look like I'm comin back from deliverin the letter to the store." He promised.

"Good boy! May the Good Lord bless ya and keep ya'll safe! If any white folks stops ya and asks ya questions, you just tell em ya'll're deliverin a message to Mister Willis for yer master. That'll work for either Willis, and Dr. Guignard won't know which one if it gets back to him, long as ya cuts across the fields to the Willis Plantation and nobody sees ya headin up from the main road to the plantation house. And get back here quick as ya can, so he don't suspect nothin!"

With that, she led her nephew into the foyer toward the front door and called out in a loud voice, in case Dr. Guignard might be listening, "Now go on, boy! Get a move on and deliver that letter! Ya'll know Dr. Guignard don't like no foot-draggin!" Her nephew went briskly out the front door and down the drive to his appointed task, letter in hand, knowing Dr. Guignard would be watching him from upstairs.

Michael, come here! One a Dr. Guignard's nigras got a message for us!" James called to his brother from the front porch of the store. Turning to Sally's nephew he asked, "Did Dr. Guignard need us to send him any response?"

The boy thought a moment. "Not that I know of, sir. I as just told to get this message to ya'll as quick as I could!"

"Well, alright then. Ya'll can tell Dr. Guignard we got his message!" Responded James. The boy stood hesitantly. Michael had by now joined them on the porch.

"Well go on, get on outa here! Ya'll done what you was sposed to do! What ya waitin for, boy? Scat!" said Michael, as if shooing away a pesky dog begging for a bone.

Sally's nephew gave a slight bow, saying, "Yessir, thank ya, sir!" and scurried off down the road, leaving the two brothers to open and read the letter.

"Damn! We gotta go find Angus and show him this!" said James, scanning the letter. "You do realize what this means, don't ya?"

Michael stood looking dully at his brother, waiting as ususal to be enlightened. He shook his head.

"It means, little brother, that one of us is gonna have to confront Uncle Elijah!" explained James.

Michael winced at the thought of it. "Well, it sure as Hell ain't gonna be me!" he swore, "Uncle Elijah scares the shit outa me! We should let Angus do it! He did it last time, and look how good that turned out!"

"I do believe you're right, little brother, we should!" James agreed with a grin. "I don't relish goin out there any more'n you do- and if Uncle Elijah ain't around, I'll be damned if I wanna run into Gilbert instead! We'd best go find Angus and break the news to him!" Closing up the store, they headed into town to find their cohort as Sally's nephew disappeared off road in the opposite direction, heading for the Willis Plantation.

Scuse me ma'am?" Sally's nephew knocked on the kitchen door. Momma Celia came to answer, surprised to see a black boy's face who wasn't from the Willis Plantation. Family resemblance, however, triggered her memory.

"Ain't you Miss Sally's nephew from over Dr. Guignard's?" Momma Celia and Sally had been friends for years, so she was immediately on the alert that something must be afoot for Sally to risk sending her nephew over here. "What's the matter, sugar? Is Sally alright?"

"Beggin your pardon ma'am, but I as told to only speak to Momma Celia, Miss Amy, Mister Elijah or Mister Gilbert. Is you Momma Celia?" asked the boy conscientiously.

"That'd be me, honey, the one an only!" Momma Celia smiled. "Come on in an let me fix ya somethin to eat fa ya troubles."

"Oh, no thank ya ma'am, I gots to get back fast as I can, or Dr. Guignard might suspect somethin. My Aunt Sally tole me to give ya'll a message."

Ignoring his protest, Momma Celia placed a plate of fresh biscuits and a glass of lemonade on the table for the boy. "Well, ya'll can give me yer message, but ya can still take some biscuits with ya to make the trip home go faster!" she grinned.

Ravenous, the boy eagerly snatched a fistful of biscuits and guzzled down the lemonade, mumbling, "Thank ya, ma'am!" between mouthfuls.

"Now what's the message, sugar?" Momma Celia asked, as the boy swallowed the last of his biscuit, wiping the crumbs off the corners of his mouth with the back of his hand.

"My Aunt Sally wanted to warn ya'll that, 'The three that held the rally're gonna pursue the folks who didn't sign, and if they don't sign, Mr. Rhett's gonna provide assistance to persuade the folks on the list!'" he recited, then he added, "I had ta deliver a letter from Dr. Guignard to Mister Elijah's nephews at the store. I come over here across the fields to avoid bein seen!"

Momma Celia immediately grasped the seriousness of the message, but did not want to react in front of the boy. "I surely do thank ya, honey, and you tell ya Aunt Sally that she's in my prayers every day. May the Good Lord bless ya both for gettin us this message! God willin, it'll hep us avoid some nastiness round here!"

"Yes'm," he answered.

"Ya'd best be gettin on home now, b'fo ole Dr. Guingard thinks ya'll been takin too long to deliver his letter. I don't want ya to suffer no beatin for your bravery, sugar! Ya'll're sufferin enough as it is, just havin to live with that man! Go on, now, git!" She hugged the boy in blessing, and handing him a few more biscuits for the road, sent him out back across the fields, hoping he could run fast enough to avoid any penalty for tardiness from his mirthless master. She also hoped he had sense enough to wipe off any more crumbs before Dr. Guignard saw him, lest the man become suspicious, knowing the Willis boys'd hardly be likely to feed a colored messenger boy for his troubles. She heaved a sigh as the boy ran off and immediately went to find Amy, Elijah and Gilbert to give them the warning.

Momma Celia went out back and called out for her grandsons, "Elder! Elleck! Phillip! Come on over here, ya'll! I needs ya hep!"

The boys came running from around the back of the barn. Everyone was a little jumpy these days, so they knew not to dawdle when called, no matter what they were doing, because it could be urgent.

Elijah had been relieved of his bed rest orders on the condition he would take things slowly, and he had started goin back out into the fields, at least to supervise the workers.

"Boys, I needs ya'll to run an fetch Gilbert and Elijah right away! Tell em everything's alright, they's no need to panic, but I gots a urgent message for em they needs to know about, and they'd best come to the house as soon ez they can." The boys nodded and ran off to find their father and uncle. Meanwhile, Momma Celia went back into the house to look for Amy, who she figured would either be upstairs with the baby or in the study, going over the plantation accounts.

"Amy! Amy, sugar! Where you at?" she called out from the hallway by the kitchen.

"I'm in here, Momma! In the study! Is everything alright?" Amy called back. She appeared in the doorway to the study, anxiety creasing her brow as she looked down the hall towards her mother.

"Well, I spose that depends on what ya'll mean by 'everything' and 'alright'!" Momma Celia answered cryptically. Her answer only increased her daughter's anxiety.

"Momma, what's goin on? Is it Elijah? Or the children?" she asked insistently.

"Neither of em yet, but could be all of us soon! Come on in here an lemme splain it to ya."

Amy strode down the hall quickly, saying, "Momma, what in God's name are you talkin about? Ya'll're not makin sense! I don't want riddles, I want to know what's goin on!"

"Set down, child, an lemme tell ya." Momma Celia indicated Amy's habitual seat at the kitchen table.

As she proceeded to tell Amy about the visit from Sally's nephew and the message he delivered from Dr. Guignard via Sally, it was as if a storm cloud had blotted out the sun, darkening Amy's face. Her jaw was set with teeth clenched in determination, but her eyes widened slightly in fear, the whites seeming strangely brighter and making her amber eyes flash. She took a deep breath before speaking.

"Lord help us, Momma! It was only a matter of time! I knew somethin like this was gonna happen!"

Momma Celia nodded with a sigh. "Well, it ain't happened yet, so we needs to keep our heads about us, an see if we can find a way around it. For all their threats, I don't see James and Michael havin the gumption to face down they uncle directly! And Dr. Guignard's not likely to want to be seen attackin Elijah openly, for fear of the other planters' feelins bout the honor of Williston's foundin family!"

"It's not James and Michael that worry me, or even Dr. Guignard, Momma, it's Robert Barnwell Rhett! Rhett 'providin assistance' to 'persuade' folks of how 'right' he is sounds an awful lot to me like vigilante threats, or a lynch mob comin after us!"

The kitchen door opened just as Amy was finishing her last sentence.

"What's this I hear about vigilantes and lynch mobs?" Elijah asked, Gilbert right behind him.

Momma Celia repeated to Elijah and Gilbert everything she had told Amy. Their jaws clenched just like Amy's had, as they contemplated the enormity of what this might mean. Gilbert let out a low whistle.

"Elijah, you gotta get on up to Cincinnati somehow, and get that will writ before it's too late!" urged Gilbert. "Feels like time's runnin out on us!"

Elijah nodded, and sat there pensive for a while. Without saying a word, he got up, walked over to the cupboard, pulled out a bottle of whiskey and a glass, sat back down, poured himself a stiff drink, and took a good swig. Amy was worried and wished he wouldn't drink so much, but didn't dare pressure him on that point at this particlar moment. Finally Elijah spoke up, soberly.

"Well, alright then! We need to work out a plan! Momma Celia's right. James and Michael haven't got the balls to face me down- and still less to face me down with Gilbert by my side!" he grinned at Gilbert. "My money says that it'll be Angus Junior who first attempts to bring me into "compliance" with that jackass Rhett's agenda. Angus is smarter than my nephews, so we should be prepared for some surprises from him, but it may also be possible to get through to him and change his mind about the advisability of any vigilante action. Takin things into their own hands could be the tinder that sets off the whole powder keg around here!" Everybody nodded in agreement. Elijah went on,

"But I'd also bet that Guignard's none too pleased bein made to dance to Rhett's tune- since he can't stand anybody but himself bein in charge, no matter who it is! We may be able to make use of that and play one off against the other, to stall for time."

"What about Cincinnati?" Amy asked.

"Well, Gilbert's right, I do need to get up there soon, but I can't see leavin ya'll to fend off whatever they're planning all alone, without at least having a pretty good idea of what it is they plan on doin!" he proclaimed. "Wouldn't be right or fair, and it might put ya'll in a lot of danger, dependin on how far Rhett's willin to let things go and whether or not Guignard lets him get away with it!" Elijah responded.

"How much time do ya'll figure it'll take before we know what's comin down?" asked Gilbert.

"I imagine it won't be more'n a few days before Angus Junior pays me a visit. The real question is, will that visit be enough to satisfy his masters, and if not, how long will it be before either Guignard or Rhett feels they need to apply more 'pressure?' For that matter, what form will that pressure even be likely to take?" asked Elijah.

"If ya ask me, if Rhett gets his way it'll be offerin ya a pen in one hand to sign the damned petition, or a noose in the other to threaten us all with lynchin!" swore Gilbert, who had taken a visceral loathing to Rhett at the rally.

"Well, maybe so, maybe not." said Elijah. "Funny thing about us South Carolinians is, that we so prize our freedom- our "white freedom" that is- that even if we agree with some firebrand's politics, we don't always take kindly to him trying to tell us how to handle our affairs." Elijah avvered. "I'm bettin there's enough folks around here to stave off a real witch hunt- because decent, well-respected folks like John Bauskett, Joseph Harley, Angus Patterson Senior, and even Will Beazely are not in favor of such purges, and I'm pretty sure would stand up against any mass rush to judgment!"

"Honey, do ya think that all the other planters will side with Guignard and Rhett?" asked Amy anxiously.

"I doubt they all will- some, most probably, but not all. Some of em can't stand Guignard cause he's so arrogant. They see him as a pretentious outsider, a self-centered social climber wantin to be a leader of their society. If he hadn't inherited that plantation of his from his wife, he'd have no standin with the local planters from the older families at all, no matter how much money he has! And what's more, they don't trust Rhett, cause he feels too extreme even for folks around here." Elijah answered. "That bein said, it's more'n likely they all agree that it's best to keep all property in the family- the legal, white family, that is- and would oppose any general efforts to promote emancipation and the leavin of legacies."

"Don't mean none of em've never thought about it theysevs!" interjected Momma Celia. "Mister Martin waan't the only one round these parts wanted to set his family free. Just cause they's all planters don't mean none of em want to leave somethin to the slaves as served em best." She'd never tell anyone, but she was remembering broken promises to that effect from William Kirkland.

"Besides," added Gilbert, "Ya're not advocating general emancipation, ya're only talking about freein your slaves, not everbody else's!"

"You got a point there Momma. And so do you Gilbert!" replied Elijah. "There's a difference in most folks' minds between a general push to emancipation and accepting the emancipation of a limited number of slaves for personal reasons. Many round here see that as within the rights and discretion of the owner on principle, and would resent anyone from outside tryin to tell em otherwise, no matter what the folks up in Columbia say! There's more'n a few planters in these parts who've had families with their slaves, or even who are simply decent, and want to reward faithful service with kindness- like Angus Senior, who freed Mary years ago, before it got so hard to do. I suspect those folks'd be mighty reluctant to start waving any torches if Rhett tries to stir things up to fever pitch!"

"Lord have mercy, let's hope so!" uttered Amy fervently.

An idea suddenly struck Elijah. "I want to read the exact wordin of that petition again. Dependin on how they wrote it, it just might be possible for me to sign the damned thing without violatin my conscience and shut old Guigard up once and for all. After all, if I'm not openly promotin general abolition or the sale of Miz Stowes' book, (even if I think both may be right) then they've got nothin on me! Signin it without a fuss is the very last thing that fool'd be expectin!"

Amy, Momma Celia and Gilbert all looked stunned at first, as if Elijah were somehow betraying his promise and negating his disapproval of the rally in the first place, but, after thinking about it a moment, they seemed to warm to the idea.

Elijah paused and then concluded, "With any kinda luck we'll get a little visit from Angus Junior, manage to persuade him that the Willis family poses no threat to the general white supremacy, and things'll calm down enough to let me get up to Cincinnati at last!"

"Amen to that!" they all answered in chorus.

"May the Good Lord hear ya Elijah, an guide ya safely there!" prayed Momma Celia, to which they all responded, "Amen!"

LXIX

Aw, man! He's ya'll's uncle, not mine! Why do I have to be the one to confront him?" Angus whined in protest. Truth was, none of them relished the encounter with Elijah.

"Because Angus ole buddy, you were so successful in gettin him to come to the rally in the first place it'd be more natural comin from you!" explained James. "If Michael or I did it he'd just figure it was a matter of family jealousy and run us off his property!"

Angus couldn't help but suspect that Elijah would be right on that score, but the die had already been cast and he'd already placed his bet on their future.

"Oh alright! But what happens if he refuses to sign and runs me off?" Angus asked.

"Ain't your problem, my friend! We just tell ole Dr. Guignard or Mr. Rhett and leave it in their hands!" said Michael with naïve conviction.

"It may not be that simple Michael- specially if we just tell Dr. Guignard. After all, he's bent on usin us to do his biddin and ain't likely to let us off the hook so easy," insisted James, quite rightly.

"Well then, we tell Rhett directly. If he wants to send his own henchmen down here that's his bizness. We did what we was asked!" asserted Michael, somewhat defensively, hoping for once to have scored a point on his own.

"If ya'll tell Rhett and don't tell Guignard, Guignard'll be mad as Hell!" observed Angus. "Pissin Guignard off by goin straight to Rhett'd be like jumpin outa the fryin pan into the fire, if ya ask me! No tellin what he might do, but he sure as Hell wouldn't support our political careers if he felt we'd crossed him!"

As always, James recognized Angus' superior logic, and trying to regain control over the conversation he inserted, "Look Angus, we don't know

Uncle Elijah won't sign, so just go talk to him first. If he puts up resistance, we'll put our heads together, and figure out where to go from there! No sense gettin ourselves all worked up over either Guignard or Rhett until we know what Uncle Elijah's gonna do!"

"I suppose you're right," sighed Angus, reluctantly mounting his horse. "I'll talk to him, and we'll see what he says." As he started down the road at a trot toward the Willis Plantation, he called over his shoulder, "Pray for me, y'all!"

James and Michael laughed nervously. "Oh don't you worry, we will! An drink a toast to ya too!" they laughed some more, hugely relieved that Angus had freed them from the need to confront their uncle themselves.

It didn't take Angus long to get to the Willis Plantation, but he slowed his horse to a walk as he turned off the main road and down the avenue of trees to the plantation house to give himself more time to think of what to say. He didn't want to sound weak and pleading, but he knew he couldn't come across as commanding or belligerent either. He decided he'd best play it as cordially as he could, pointing out that the medical emergency that had taken Elijah away from the rally early had not left him time to sign, and asking would he perhaps like to do so now? Angus carried the petition with him, hoping against hope to get the signature and thereby both free himself from further anguish and win the approval of his political mentors at the same time. Remembering James' and Michael's description of Elijah's withering anger last Christmas, however, he was scared that things might go sour and wasn't sure if he could handle it. At six feet tall and a good two hundred and fifty pounds, Elijah was both physically imposing and almost as intellectually intimidating as his father, in his own folksy way.

As Angus was approaching the house, Clarissa spotted him from the upper porch where she and her sisters were playing. She ran into the house to warn her mother that he was coming.

"Momma! Momma! That Mister Patterson's come back again, and he's headin up here to the house!" she called out from the door to the porch. Amy had been nursing the baby, and quickly covered herself and tried to put the baby down, but little Savage would have none of it, and voiced his disapproval with ear-splitting cries. He knew what he wanted, and he simply wasn't finished eating yet! His mother should know better, and in case she didn't, he was going to make sure she got the point. His cries were clearly audible from out in front of the house, where Angus Junior was dismounting from his horse and fixing to knock on the front door. There was no way he could not have heard the baby. The secret was up!

Surrendering to that reality, Amy picked Savage up to stop his crying and went downstairs to greet their visitor.

"Well, Mr. Patterson, what brings you out here? Is your father well, I hope?" Amy said politely, Savage in her arms still fussing and grabbing for her breast, but momentarily distracted by the appearance of this stranger.

Angus looked at Amy, then at the baby, and quickly put two and two together, realizing not only that the baby was Elijah's son, but that his birth had likely been the medical emergency that had called Elijah away from the rally before its completion. Stunned, he was momentarily put off his guard and was at a sudden loss for words.

"Uh, excuse me ma'am, but is, uh, is Mr. Willis at home? I'd, uh, like to have a word with him, if I may?" he stammered.

Amy had decided the best defense was to simply act normal and neither hide nor draw attention to the baby. "He's over at the saw mill, sir, but I can have one of the boys go and fetch him, if ya don't mind waitin. Or if ya prefer, ya'll can head on over there yaself and talk to him. I'm sure he wouldn't mind."

Suddenly feeling acutely uncomfortable realizing that he was witnessing the family reality of Elijah and Amy's intimate relationship, and that but for the color of her skin, it actually felt disturbingly normal to him, he decided it would be better to seek Elijah out at the mill than to remain in that discomfort.

"Well, sorry to have disturbed you ma'am. I don't want to put ya'll to any inconvenience. I think I'll just head on over to the saw mill then, so's not to be a bother."

"Oh, it's no trouble at all Mr. Patterson. If ya'd like to wait, I can have some refreshment brought out to ya on the veranda, or ya'll can go over to the mill if ya'druther." She replied sweetly, as if there was nothing out of the ordinary at all in this encounter.

"Well, I surely do thank ya ma'am, but I think it'd be best if I went over there. Ah, ya'll have a good day now, hear?" With that, Angus tipped his hat, remounted his horse, and set off with relief in the direction of the sawmill on the other side of the plantation, out past the stand of long-needle pine trees.

"Good God A'mighty!" he marvelled to himself. "She acts just like the lady of the house, and there's no doubt that child's father's no slave!" He was not quite willing to face the fact that it had felt natural to him. He thought he should feel scandalized, but in truth he didn't, and that in itself felt scandalous!

By the time Angus made it over to the sawmill and found Elijah supervising some of the workers stacking fresh milled lumber, his mind was in a bit of an uproar. Here he was, approaching a man who had failed to sign a pro-slavery, anti-abolition petition, expecting him to refuse to sign and face the consequences. He knew full well that the man clearly had an emotional involvement with a slave woman by whom he had several children, all of whom were living in his house as if his normal family. Morevoer, to Angus' shock and dismay, he recognized that they both looked and felt like Elijah's real family. What then, if Elijah didn't run him off, but actually signed the petition? But on the other hand, if Elijah didn't sign the petition, Angus knew that directly or indirectly, he himself would then be responsible for some kind of punishment being wreaked on this family that was just minding its own business, not bothering anybody! How in heaven was he going to be able to explain this to James and Michael, or Dr. Guignard? His stomach was tied in knots as he called out in greeting to Elijah,

"Mr. Willis! Mr. Willis! Sorry to interrupt ya, sir. D'ya mind if I have word with ya for a moment?"

Elijah looked up from his conversation with Julius and hardly seemed surprised. He said something in a low voice to Julius that Angus couldn't hear, and then turned to greet his visitor.

"Well, Angus, this is a pleasant surprise! What brings ya'll way out here?" he said affably. Once again, Angus was suddenly struck by how normally everyone was behaving, even though he was certain they all knew how Robert Barnwell Rhett had ranted on about the virtues of slavery at the rally in ways that even Angus found more than a stretch of the truth.

"Uh, well sir, I, uh, I just wanted to show ya'll the courtesy of bringin the petition out to ya to sign, since ya'll got called away on an emergency before ya had a chance to sign it! Miz Wil-, I mean, Miss Amy told me ya'll was out here, so I thought I'd drop on by." Angus cursed himself for almost calling Amy Mrs. Willis, accidentally revealing just how normal their relationship now seemed to him and hoped Elijah hadn't noticed, but of course he had.

"Well, I was truly sorry about that, but I had no choice but to come home to deal with what was goin on here, as I'm sure ya'll'll understand. Now, let me have a look at that petition, as I'm sorry to say I didn't even get a chance to read it that carefully before."

Elijah was sounding unexpectedly reasonable, almost as if he was asking to look at the price of chicken feed rather than a document that, if he failed to sign it, could implicate him in what some might consider treasonous activity with dire consequences.

Angus fumbled for the petition in his saddlebag and finally managed to pull it out without bending or tearing it in the process. He handed it abruptly to Elijah, not knowing what else he could do.

Elijah perused the document leisurely, pausing from time to time with an 'aha,' or a 'hmmm,' leaving Angus Junior as uncertain of his opinion as his own father left Elijah whenever he studied some document. Angus knew all too well that his father was prone to delivering a silent commentary about whatever he was reading in the privacy of his own head, without realizing others were not privy to his counsel. Only in Elijah's case, this was a deliberate ploy, not an absentminded characteristic.

The stratagem was clearly effective judging from the way Angus shifted nervously from foot to foot while Elijah was reading. Finally, Elijah looked up at the young man and smiled disarmingly, saying, "Did ya'll bring a pen and ink?"

Angus was totally stunned. He could hardly believe his ears that Elijah seemed to be agreeing to sign the petition. "Uh, well sir, uh, I, I believe I did, if ya'll'll just give me a moment…" he started fumbling nervously in his saddlebag, suddenly uncertain whether it had ever even occurred to him to come prepared for Elijah to actually sign the document.

"No matter son, come on over to the office in the mill. I've got pen and ink in there." Elijah said in a matter-of-fact way, and strode off in the direction of the office without looking back to see if Angus was following, knowing it would rattle the young man. In something of a daze of disbelief, Angus followed after him, with the petition dangling from his hand almost as an after-thought.

Elijah spread the petition out on the desk in the office, scanned the list of names to apprise himself of those who had and had not signed, grabbed a quill, dipped it in the inkwell, and scrawled his name after the last signatory. He then grabbed a brass-bound blotter with a curved felt bottom, rocked it over his signature to absorb any excess ink, and then blew gently on his name to make sure the ink was dry and would not smear before handing the petition back to his astonished inquisitor.

"Anything else I can do for ya, son? Sorry not to be able to offer ya'll any refreshment out here for your troubles. How's your Pa doin?"

Angus was so disoriented by the entirely unexpected responses from Amy and Elijah that it took him a moment to even respond. As if awakened from a dream he stammered, "Pa? Oh, uh, he's doin alright. His health seems to have stabilized for the moment, and he's holdin his own. You know him, he's a tough ole bird!"

"Well, I'm mighty glad to hear that! Tell him I was askin for him, and that I'll do my level best to drop by and pay him a visit real soon!" Elijah said with total sincerity.

"I surely will sir, and thank ya!" was as much as Angus could think to say before remounting his horse and heading on back to James' store to share the news of this most unexpected response.

LXX

Angus' sense of reality had been deeply shaken by this turn of events. He began to doubt himself, his companions, Dr. Guignard, Mr. Rhett, and the whole presupposition that whites and blacks are fundamentally and irreconcilably different and should never mix. But he didn't quite understand how Elijah could live the life he lived and sign the petition. It seemed like a contradiction to him. He had always admired Elijah, and the last thing he would have ever called him was a liar, yet he signed the petition! He realized that Elijah had read the document carefully, and figured he must have found a way to interpret its wording in a manner that prevented him from commiting perjury. He was much too smart to fall in that kind of trap. For Angus this was distressing, and he felt confused trying to figure out just what the man was up to. Part of him wanted to believe that Elijah was fully within his rights and posed no threat to anyone. Another part of him found Elijah and Amy's living arrangements so disorienting that it just seemed fundamentally wrong- it seemed to contradict and violate everything he thought he knew as true and right.

Much as he wanted to believe that Elijah had done wrong, and that he had been fully justified in either trying to get Elijah to sign the petition or to hold him accountable for not doing so, Angus wasn't really comfortable with the thought of the suffering that might ensue if his mentors wanted to take further action. Yet he felt panic at the idea of abandoning a path that had given him a sense of finally being respected as an adult in his own right for the first time in his life. That sense of self-worth was so rare and precious, and still so unfamiliar, that he couldn't bring himself to recognize it as a house built on the shifting sand of local opinion and political pressures and his own emotional neediness.

Afraid to reveal his distress, and yet equally afraid to be alone with his thoughts, he arrived at James' store in a state of agitation. Both Willis brothers were sitting on the porch waiting for his return. An empty whiskey bottle lay on its side on the floor near James' feet, and another, half full, sat next to Michael.

"Well, hello there Angus! Damn, boy, you look shook up! How'd it go with Uncle Elijah? He run ya'll off at gunpoint?" James called out.

Angus just shook his head 'no.'

"Really?" Michael queried, surpressing a slight hiccup, "That's a surprise!" James poked him in the ribs to shut him up, not wanting Angus to realize they had used him as their scapegoat because of their own fear their uncle would run them off at gunpoint- and might not even keep his finger off the trigger!

Angus, trying to cover his confusion and play it as a victory, replied, "Not as big a surprise as what I got here!" He pulled out the petition and pointed to Elijah's signature at the bottom. Having taken another swig, Michael looked doubtfully at the whiskey bottle in his hand as if he feared it had been drugged, and both brothers proceeded to nearly fall over each other to get a closer look, convinced that their eyes were deceiving them.

"Jesus Christ Our Saviour! Angus, how in Hell did you get him to sign?" asked James in disbelief.

"Damn, Angus, ya'll're either a genius or a goddamn magician! What in the name of God did ya'll tell him to convince him?"

Angus himself shook his head incredulously, saying, "Nothin! I didn't convince him! Didn't even try! He simply up an read the petition and signed it without battin an eye, as if he was signin an invoice in the mill! But that ain't all!"

The Willis boys leaned eagerly toward him for the next revelation. Their world already having been shaken, they were suddenly willing for their entire sense of the possible to be redefined, and pressed him eagerly, "Well, go on...!"

Angus proceeded to tell them about his arrival at the Willis Plantation and his inadvertent discovery of the newest addition to the household- a baby boy with a touch of the tarbrush who looked as much like their uncle Elijah as he looked like his mother, Amy!

"Son of a bitch!" muttered James vehemently. "The man just don't learn! How the Hell can he sign the petition havin just fathered another bastard with that nigra! He's off his head! Plumb crazy! It's the only possible explanation!"

Michael nodded in agreement. "He's unbelievable! I can't figure him out! For the life of me I can't understand what he sees in her in the first place- she ain't no beauty, that's for sure!"

Angus didn't know if he should share his experience of how normal they all seemed. He was afraid to speak up, but he was also uncomfortable with the Willis brother's assertion that their uncle must be insane. Fact of the matter was, Elijah struck him as unusually sane- more sane for sure than Dr. Guignard, or Mr. Rhett, or most of the other folks around Barnwell District for that matter. The conflict must have showed in his expression, because James picked up on it and asked, "What's eatin you? Somethin else happen while ya'll were out there?"

Angus decided to shake it off and keep his own counsel on the matter of what constituted either sanity or normal family relationships. "Naw, I'm just still surprised he signed it, that's all- and with no trace of regret or conflict! At least that should satisfy Dr. Guignard and Mr. Rhett. Tell the truth, I feel kinda relieved. I was not lookin forward to the possibility of any violence or bloodshed over the issue of signin."

James and Michael, despite their inebriation, admitted they were also relieved. In the final analysis, their rancor toward their uncle was less about his personality or his outrageously unconventional lifestyle than it was about the prospect of them losing out on any future inheritance.

"Crazy or not, it is amazin, I'll grant ya that! Last thing in the world I woulda expected!" admitted James.

"At least now we can get ole Dr. Guignard off our backs about Uncle Elijah. That sure is a relief! How many others on the list didn't sign? I spose we'll have to pay em all a visit, won't we?" Michael recognized.

The three of them had been so focused on Elijah that it had not even occurred to them that according Mr. Rhett's directive, he wanted pressure brought to bear on all the folks that hadn't signed! The possibility of violence breaking out over the matter may have been diminished for the Willis family and Elijah's other slaves, but it had not been erased for everyone by Elijah's compliance, for it could still surface elsewhere and be just as damaging to the community.

Angus immediately grasped the potential for disaster in this. "Ya'll realize, don't ya, that we gotta be real careful how we do this? Cause if violence breaks out in one place around here, it's more'n likely to spread like wildfire given the climate these days, and we might not be able to contain or control it!" This was a sobering thought for all three of them.

Angus continued, "We gotta make sure Rhett don't send any men down here, cause the men he sends won't give a hoot about steppin on folks' toes, or hurting folks' feelins, and that might stir up a regular hornets' nest!"

"So what're ya'll proposing, Angus? How we supposed to get everybody else to sign. D'ya'll think they're all gonna go as meekly as Uncle Elijah?" James pressed.

"Probly not," Angus admitted, "But we gotta try to at least see to it that nobody gets seriously hurt in the process. Roughed up a bit maybe, but not seriously hurt, and for sure not killed- black or white!" he insisted pointedly, looking at Michael.

"What the Hell difference does it make if a coupla nigras get killed to show em we mean business? Teach em a good lesson, if ya'll ask me!" Michael, ever the bellicose one, asserted.

"Don't be stupid, Michael!" blurted Angus. Michael, all too accustomed to his brother speaking this way, was taken aback by hearing this from Angus. "What's the most important thing to the planters around here- the absolutely most sacred thing of all?" he asked.

Michael blinked, a blank expression on his uncomprehending face. After a pause, a light flickered back on in his eyes, and he said tentatively, "Bein white?"

Even James couldn't stand an answer that foolish. "Bein WHITE? Are you outa your cotton pickin mind, you idiot?" he said in exasperation.

Angus noticed, however, that James was not offering up a more accurate answer either. Rather than press him on it and emabarrass him, he simply supplied it himself:

"It's property! Property and the right to do with it as one pleases without interference from neighbors, locals, or the government! And slaves are, in most folks' minds, first and foremost, valuable property! You go killin someone else's slaves around here and there'll be Hell to pay, no matter what your politics!" Angus insisted emphatically.

As ususal, James jumped to the winning side of the argument immediately. "Angus is right, Michael. We can't just visit these folks at gunpoint, or with fists raised, we gotta convince em to do the right thing."

These last words rang hollow in Angus' ears, no longer entirely sure of what the right thing was, but he made no comment to the contrary. "I'll tell ya'll one thing, if we're gonna do this, we're gonna do it together. The three of us will go to each of the names on the list. James, you and I'll try to talk sense into them, and Michael, you'll be our back up if we need any enforcement- but ya'll gotta keep that rebel rage a yours under control, y'hear?"

The Willis brothers nodded in agreement. "Sure woulda been nice if we coulda just sent Uncle Elijah's signature back to Dr. Guignard and have done with it, but ya'll're right. Ain't no way he's gonna let us off that light- not with Robert Barnwell Rhett breathin down his neck!" James affirmed. "We gotta do this in a way that gets us off the hook with Guignard, and Guignard off the hook with Rhett!

"Well then, we'd best get to it!" Replied Angus.

The three of them proceeded to go through the list and make a plan of whom to visit. They realized that knowing most folks in the area at least helped them have a better idea of how to approach each one. They consoled themselves that this would be good preparation for running for elective office, and would help them hone their campaigning skills.

LXXI

The Willis brothers and Angus Junior managed to canvass the area with considerable success. Emboldened by their partnership, they began to see themselves as the Three Musketeers of Williston. The unmarried daughter of one of the planters had read the recent novel by Mr. Alexandre Dumas, and romantically projected the dashing heroes of literary fame on their tawdry surrogates in Barnwell District, hoping to be whisked away to the capital and a more glamorous life if any of the three became successful in their political aspirations. After all, a good politician needed a good wife at his side to handle his social life, and any of the three would constitute a good match for a young lady of Williston.

James and Michael and Angus, of course, had no real idea of who the Three Musketeers were or what they were fighting for, but they liked the idea of being dashing young heroes in the eyes of the locals. They now found themselves being invited to parties and even balls, and in their bumbling way tried to rapidly acquire more social graces, as was befitting their political aspirations.

When they presented the petition to Dr. Guignard with Elijah's signature clearly scrawled accross the bottom, the doctor was decidedly impressed and taken quite by surprise.

"Well I'll be damned!" he remarked upon seeing the signature. "I gotta hand it to ya boys, I never thought ya'll'd manage to get this!" he said, pointing specifically to Elijah's signature as if any others were totally unimportant. "It gives me more satisfaction than winnin a horse race with my best horse, and if ya'll know how much I love that, you'll understand how happy this makes me! Congratulations, boys! Well done!"

All three of them grinned at the accolade. Despite the praise, Angus stood there uncomfortable in the knowledge that he knew about little Savage, and that the doctor probably did not. But he decided discretion was, in truth, the better part of valor, and it would behoove them to avoid any mention of that detail, lest the doctor recommission them to launch some sort of new attack on Elijah that could get personally messy for all three of them.

James was of the same opinion, much as he loathed the idea of Elijah having yet another child with Amy. He was afraid that drawing too much attention to the matter might result in Elijah disinheriting them as punishment for their interference- the prevention of which was, after all, the motivating force behind all their efforts.

Of course, neither Angus nor James had thought to school Michael on the matter to assure he would not broach the subject with Dr. Guignard. That proved to be an unfortunate oversight.

"We didn't think he'd ever sign it either, to tell the truth, specially not since he just had another bastard with that nigra woman a his!" gushed Michael, his enthusiasm for the signature blinding him to his indiscretion.

Dr. Guignard's grin froze, and his elation evaporated faster than a dewdrop in a summer morning's sunlight. "What did you say?" he asked, his lethal outrage bubbling just barely under the surface.

Michael looked at him with surprise, still not realizing his faux pas, despite frantic gestures from Angus and Michael standing behind Dr. Guignard, trying to prevent him from doing any further damage. "You mean about how surprised we all was that Uncle Elijah signed?" Michael asked, obtuse as ever.

"No," Dr. Guignard responded coldly. "Did you just tell me that Elijah has had another child with his slave woman?"

Michael suddenly realized he had probably just stuck his foot in a steaming fresh cow pie of trouble. He looked frantically at Angus and James for guidance, but it was clearly too late. Dr. Guignard turned to the others with an acid stare and said, "Is this true?"

They both nodded, too afraid to compound the situation by saying anything they might later regret, convinced that Dr. Guignard would use any and everything he could against them if he felt they had crossed him.

"And how old is this child, might I ask?" Dr. Guignard continued, already suspecting the probable date of birth.

James and Michael looked to Angus, since he alone had seen the child. Angus stammered, "Well, I'm not rightly sure, Dr. Guignard. I haven't been around babies much, so I really couldn't say. I certainly hadn't heard any rumors about another birth, so it kinda caught me by surprise to see the child the other day when I went to call on Mr. Willis, but then, I never have really seen all of the children anyway, so I'm not exactly sure how many there are." he responded. He was hoping his imprecision would not be seen as evasiveness, and would put the issue to rest so that Dr. Guignard would not realize it had been Savage's birth that had called Elijah away from the long planned moment of truth Dr. Guignard felt he had coming to him.

Dr. Guignard turned to the Willis brothers. "Have either of you seen the child?"

They both shook their heads, muttering truthfully, "No, sir!"

Ever prone to playing his cards close to his chest, Dr. Guignard chose not to berate the boys for something that clearly was not their fault. But he was fuming at the thought that Elijah was so incorrigible as to have another child with Amy despite their warnings, and yet signed the petition. Rather than putting the matter to rest, it simply confirmed his fears that Elijah must be up to something, unless, as Robert Barnwell Rhett had intimated in his speech, he was in fact certifiably insane.

Determined to ferret out Elijah's plot, he dismissed the boys so as to have privacy to think. "Well, ya'll done a fine job with the signatures, boys! That at least'll keep Rhett off our backs! But there's gotta be more to Elijah Willis's behavior than meets the eye, and I intend to find out what it is once and for all! That'll be all for now, gentlemen. I'll be in touch soon, once I get this figured out!" He showed them abruptly to the door and went immediately back inside.

As the three mounted up and rode off towards the store, they were relieved at least that, despite his clear upset, Dr. Guignard had not yet lost his temper with them. Angus however, couldn't help thinking to himself, "Oh Lord, what have we gotten ourselves into now?"

LXXII

The Holidays passed uneventfully on the Willis Plantation, a sort of holy respite from the relentless challenges they had faced all year long. To Amy's relief, Elijah's white relations made no effort at the customary forced holiday conviviality, either by inviting Elijah to their home or by visiting the plantation.

Unable to put a finger on any specific plot or plan of Elijah's for the moment, Dr. Guignard also seemed to be lying low, at least until such time as circumstance might reveal some new element for him to investigate. Angus Paterson Senior's health remained stable, sparing the family yet another shock for a time, and they even received a few cards of holiday greeting from folks like Joseph Harley, Reason and Ari Wooley, Will Beazeley, John and Eugenia Bauskett, and a few other long time friends. All in all, it was a Merry Christmas, made poignant by the realization that, God willing, it would likely be their last in Williston, and even in South Carolina for that matter.

Bearing in mind Joseph Harley's insistence that he continue to take things slowly for a while, Elijah decided he would head up to Cincinnati early in the new year, before the Spring plowing and planting, barring any further disruptions. He sat down to write Messrs. Jolliffe and Gitchell to apprise them of that decision and bring them up to date on the circumstances facing them in South Carolina.

Dear Messrs Gitchell and Jolliffe:

I hope this letter finds you both well. I know it has been some time since my last letter, and you must be wondering if I have lost interest in engaging your services after such a prolonged silence. Let me hasten to assure you that is not the case at all! Quite to the contrary. I am most eager to come to Cincinnati and finally, with your diligent assistance, write a new will to emancipate, protect, and endow my family of choice.

Since last I wrote, we have endured a political uprising designed to malign and intimidate me; the birth of a son; the ravages of yellow fever on my plantation; a bout of excessive rain nearly ruining the cotton harvest; and a health crisis of my own- on top of the usual and relentless demands of trying to profitably run a lumber and cotton business in these troubled times. By the grace of God, we have prevailed, and despite my somewhat unpredictable health, financial, and political concerns, I am more determined than ever to make it to your fair city to settle my affairs, so that I may then relocate my family to Ohio with all due dispatch.

My visit will be a brief one, due to obligations and, dare I say, dangers here at home. I do not wish to leave my property or my family unprotected for too long. I expect to be in Cincinnati by the third week in February, as I shall have to return to South Carolina promptly in order to deal with the demands of the spring planting, from which there are no holidays. I shall notify you by telegram of the date of my arrival, and would greatly appreciate you reserving me the necessary lodging at the Broadway Hotel, as you recommended.

A very Happy, if belated, New Year to you both-

Sincerely,

Elijah Willis

Elijah folded, addressed and sealed the letter, and decided to take it to the depot himself for Will Beazely to send off to Cincinnati on the next mail train.

"How do, Mr. Willis?" Mr. Beazely greeted Elijah. "It's been a while! How've ya'll been?"

"Well Will, all things considered, we're not doin too badly. How bout you?" replied Elijah soberly, looking around to see who else might be within earshot. "Any news?" he asked in a low voice.

"Well sir, looks to me like things have calmed down a bit since the rally," Will responded confidentially, "and that petition made the folks who were bothered by Miz Stowe's book an all feel like a point has been made for the record, and they don't have to do too much more about it for the moment. That seems to suit most folks just fine- except for some of the young bucks who're itchin for a fight with someone, just for the fun of it! You know how country boys can be!"

"Yes, I surely do, given that my own nephews are among em! Let's hope it stays calm round here for a good while! I'druther not have to tangle with any self-appointed vigilantes or some would-be politician too big for his britches, if I can help it!" There was no ambiguity as to whom he was scornfully referring.

"Look, Will, I'm gonna be makin a trip up to Cincinnati soon and need to book a train ticket to Louisville," he confided.

"Will ya'll be travellin alone, or with your family this time?" Will asked, clearly referring to Amy and the children.

"Alone for now," Elijah replied. He looked around again to make sure no one was coming. "Will, you and I have known each other for a long time, and I trust ya to keep this in confidence, but I need ya'll to keep your eyes and ears open for me. I may be sellin my place soon, or at least some part of it. I want ya'll to let me know if ya hear of anyone who might be interested in buyin- either land or slaves. Don't tell em I might sell, just let me know who they are, and I'll approach em myself."

Mr. Beazeley was taken aback by this news. "Well, certainly, Mr. Willis, I'll be glad to help if I can!" he paused thoughtfully, "I imagine it must be pretty hard for ya'll with all the anti-abolitionist, pro-slavery agitation goin on- not only from Dr. Guignard and Mr. Rhett and their delegates, but in the papers even up in Columbia and Charleston!"

"That's the God's honest truth, Will! It has, and there's no sign it's gonna let up any time soon. There's always been some around here who've hated the idea of freein any slaves or leavin em any inheritance, but it's gotten worse lately. Seems some folks just can't abide the idea, and feel like they've got a right to stop slaveowners from doin as they please just because they don't agree with their choices!"

Will nodded in agreement. "I do believe you're right, Mr. Willis! I can't ever remember folks getting this worked up about it before! I suspect it's cause the young uns don't much like the idea they'll have to work for their own fortunes, and think everythin outa be given to em by rights! It's a damn shame more of em aren't more hard workin like you, sir!" Will meant this sincerely, for he had always been in awe of Elijah's determination to build his business and take responsibility for those under his care. He'd also had occasion to see James and Michael in action, and did not hold them in high esteem, seeing clearly that they did not deserve a share in Elijah's fortune, and were unfit to receive the admiration their uncle so richly deserved.

Elijah nodded in agreement, and in grateful acceptance of the accolade. "I'm afraid you're right Will! And, sadly there's nothin I can do to change that, at this point. Given my health and my age, I'm worried that the only way I can provide for my family now is to get em outa here! So, much as I hate havin to leave my home and my roots, I think it's best for me to get a fresh start with them someplace else, where they'll be safe."

It was a poignant confession, and Mr. Beazeley felt great empathy for their plight.

"Well, I sure will hate to see you go, sir. You've always been an inspiration to me, to tell the truth. But I can't see how there's any future but slavery for Miss Amy, her Momma, and the children if ya'll stay here," he admitted. "I promise I'll keep an ear out, and let ya'll know if I find anyone interested!"

"God bless ya, Will. I surely do appreciate that!" Elijah shook his hand warmly. "I still need that round-trip train ticket to Louisville for the third week in February, if ya please!"

"Oh, right, a course! Sorry, I almost forgot." Mr. Beazeley wrote out a ticket and left the date open for Elijah to fill in once he decided the exact date he wanted to travel. Elijah counted out the money for the ticket and slid it across the counter to Mr. Beazely, who replied, "There ya go, sir. And I wish ya'll the best of luck! God bless!" He smiled as Elijah placed the ticket in his breast pocket and waved on his way out the door, just as another customer was coming in.

"Well I'll be damned, if it isn't Elijah Willis!" said a gentleman with a grizzled beard, his sad eyes brightening as he bumped into Elijah by accident. "How the Hell are ya?" Elijah was taken aback.

"Ya'll don't remember me, do ya?" the man said in response to the blank expression on Elijah's face. "It's me, Knotts!" the man said.

A flash of recognition illuminated Elijah's face, "Knotts! Can it be? Well bless my soul! I didn't recognize you! My Lord, how long has it been?" Elijah responded, remembering his old friend who he and his childhood companions had known for so long simply by the name Knotts that nobody even remembered his first name was William.

"Too long, old friend, too long! I moved to Charleston more'n twenty years ago- my wife's people were from over there, you remember? Anyway, she passed away last year, and I just figured it might be best for me to come on back home."

Knotts and Elijah had grown up together, but the passage of time had taken its toll on them both. Knotts appeared worn and far older than his years. It was not clear how much of that was due to the loss of his wife or to other events in the intervening years, but Elijah found it sobering that a childhood companion could have suffered such ravages by time. It was yet another reminder of the urgency of his mission to Cincinnati and of his own fleeting mortality.

"Damn, it's good to see you!" he said with unexpected emotion, "Why don't ya'll come over for supper, so we can sit and catch up? There's a lot to talk about!" Elijah was suddenly feeling very alone in the decisions facing him and much in need of an old friend, despite his awareness that Amy might feel some distress at the arrival of a guest who had no idea of her or the childrens' existence, much less their relationship with Elijah.

Knotts hesitated. "Well, I don't know Elijah. I don't want to put ya'll out, especially on such short notice!"

"Nonsense! I'd be offended if you refuse!" he grinned michievously, remembering how they had both joked about the peculiar Southern obsession with matters of honor and offense as young boys, making fun of their elders.

Knotts' defenses duly undone by the memory of their boyhood jokes, he had no choice but to accept. "Well alright then, if you say so," he chuckled, " But I have a few errands to take care of first. How about I meet you out at your place around six o'clock?"

"That'd be just grand!" smiled Elijah warmly, suddenly comforted by the possibility of a sympathetic ear other than Amy's. "I'll be waitin for ya! Ya'll still remember how to get out there, don't ya?" he asked teasingly.

"Hell, Elijah, I may be a bit older and worse for the wear, but I ain't daft!" They both laughed with fraternal pleasure and parted ways until the evening, smiling with anticipation at the prospect of spending a few convivial hours together after each having been through so many trials, and for so long.

Elijah rode home in a better mood than he'd been in for weeks. Amy could see it even from a distance as he rode up toward the house. He seemed to be sitting taller in the saddle, his head no longer downcast as it had been so often of late.

Elijah dismounted out in back, called for Elder to take Beauty to the barn, and went into the house through the kitchen door, where he met Amy and Momma Celia, looking at him with an expression of curiosity.

"Hello there, darlin! Momma Celia!" he smiled and gave Amy a kiss on the cheek, and then gave one to Momma Celia too, shocking her to her core, as he had never shown her any physical sign of affection before.

"Elijah, what in the world is goin on with you?" Momma Celia blurted out, half in amusement, half in fear.

"Ladies, I have a favor to ask. I'd like you to fix a particularly delicious dinnerand set your prettiest table- in the dinin room, if ya please. I have a dinner guest comin this evenin!"

Amy was immediately alarmed. "And who might that be, that we should go to all that fuss?" Aside from Dr. Harley, who ate with them at the kitchen table, there had been no dinner guests for quite some time.

"My old friend Knotts! We grew up here together, but he moved away to Charleston twenty-odd years ago after he got married. Seems his wife passed away last year, and he's come on back home to Williston. He's one of the few people I know I can trust, so I asked him to come to dinner! Literally ran into him on my way outa the depot, just after I mailed my letter to the lawyers in Cincinnati and bought my train ticket to Louisville! Didn't even recognize him at first, but he sure as Hell recognized me!"

Elijah had not told Amy what errand he was on when he left, so this inadvertent news about the letter and the ticket came as a delightful surprise, even though she still was feeling a little wary about inviting anyone into the house she didn't know, given the recent chain of events in the community.

"And will you be wantin us to play slave or be your family in the presence of your friend?" she asked more bluntly than she intended. "How many places should we set at the table?'

Elijah was a little stung by the question, but years of being pressed into a sort of dual role had worn a groove in the pattern of family life, like the calluses built up on the fingers of a guitar player's left hand from pressing the same chords over and again. They all knew they had to dance to that tune when circumstances demanded, but like the guitar player's finger tips it still hurt sometimes, when pressed too hard.

"I want us all there as the family that we are! I need this sugar! There are so few we can talk to openly any more. It felt like a breath of fresh air runnin into Knotts today- especially right after buyin my ticket to Louisville and sendin the letter off to the lawyers tellin em I'm comin to Cincinnati at last!"

"Well, honey, if you're sure this Mister Knotts can be trusted, it's alright with me!" Amy replied, recognizing how lonely it had been for Elijah, and for all of them this past year, since the rally in particular. She gave him a kiss and whispered in his ear, "And God bless ya for mailin the letter!"

LXXIII

By the time Knotts arrived at the Willis Plantation, the children had all been scrubbed and dressed in their Sunday best, and Momma Celia had outdone herself in the kitchen, filling the house with savory aromas of her specialties, each more delicious than the other. The dining room table sparkled with white damask, their best china, spotless crystal, and gleaming silverware. The candles burned brightly even though it was not yet fully dark outside, adding a festive flair to the scene. Elijah felt they needed to celebrate, not just the arrival of his friend, but the mailing of the letter and the purchase of the railroad ticket that committed him to finally making the trip to Cincinnati after so many frustrating set-backs and delays. They all wanted to believe that freedom, not only from legal bondage but also from the oppressive tension of living in fear of local reprisals or vendettas, was truly near at hand.

Elijah sent Elder and his brothers out front to wait for his guest, not knowing if he'd be coming on horseback or by carriage. The boys were eager to see who this friend was. Just as the ormolu clock on the mantle in the parlor was striking six, they saw Knotts approaching the house in a black buggy. He pulled up in front of the house as the boys came forward to greet him. Knotts was immediately struck that these were no ordinary slaves, groomed and dressed as they were.

"Is your master at home?" he asked, suddenly uncertain of how to refer to Elijah. "He's expecting me for supper."

"You're Mister Knotts, ain't ya?" Elder asked. Knotts nodded.

"Yes sir, he sent us out here to greet ya. He's been lookin forward to ya comin all afternoon! Come on in, he's waitin inside!" Elleck and Phillip escorted Knotts into the house while Elder took off the buggy's brake and led Knotts' horse to the trough for a drink before joing the rest of the family.

Amy and the other children were waiting with Elijah in the foyer to greet their guest. As Knotts walked in, before he could even register shock or surprise on his face, Elijah stepped forward.

"Knotts, I'd like you to meet Amy and our children, Elleck, Phillip, Clarissa Ann, Julia Ann, Eliza Ann and the baby, Elijah Junior (we call him Savage). Elder here, our oldest, is the boy who took care of your horse just now," he added as Elder joined them.

Knotts, though certainly caught off guard, was to Elijah's relief, gracious, and greeted each warmly. "Well, ya certainly weren't joshin when ya'll told me that we had a lot to talk about!" he said with a chuckle. "I'm very pleased to meet ya'll," he added sincerely.

The children were dismissed to go help their grandmother with the final touches on the dinner, and Elijah and Amy invited Knotts into the parlor.

"May I fix ya'll somethin to drink Mister Knotts?" Amy asked sweetly.

"Yes ma'am you may, a whiskey if you please, and you may also just call me Knotts. 'Mister' somehow just doesn't ring right – too formal for among friends," he smiled warmly.

Amy quickly took a liking to Knotts and understood why Elijah had been so pleased to see him. It was rare indeed that she felt she could let her guard down when anyone from outside came calling- other than perhaps Joseph Harley.

"Elijah, I gotta tell ya this surely is a surprise, but it's a good one! I always felt bad you had never found anyone- though I couldn't much blame ya, considering the slim pickins of any women worth havin a conversation with round here! And it's clear the children love and respect ya too, that's a beautiful thing!" There was a tinge of remorse or perhaps even envy here that suggested a sadder history clouded the memories of Knotts' own family and past.

Elijah spoke up. "Well, I won't deny I was a tad envious when ya'll got married. Your wife was a fine woman, and I was truly happy for ya, but when ya'll moved to Charleston it kinda narrowed my own options of people I felt truly comfortable talkin to."

Amy realized that Elijah, in fact had been something of a loner even before their relationship had begun, and that lonliness had taken a greater toll on him than she had recognized.

Elijah proceeded to tell his friend of all they had been through and of the plan to relocate to Ohio. Knotts listened attentively, and without interruption. Finally, when the tale had been told and it was his turn to speak, he looked at Amy and Elijah with sympathy.

"When I moved away from Williston, it wasn't just because my wife's family was from Charleston, and she wanted to be closer to her people. It was because this place felt too small- too limited in the ways that people saw each other and treated each other. I'm truly sad to see it hasn't changed much since way back then."

Amy asked, "Well then, why did ya'll come back here?"

"For me, it doesn't matter so much anymore. I'm ready to end out my days in someplace small and familiar. My wife is dead. My children are all grown and have all moved away, and seldom even write. Bout the only thing that holds comfort is bein able to see an hear and smell the sights and sounds and smells I grew up with." He smiled a melancholy smile.

"But I'll tell ya one thing. When I first moved to Charleston I met a remarkable pair of women- the Grimké sisters, Sarah and Angelina. Their father was a highly respected judge in Charleston. Neither of em married and both of em moved away up North not long after I met em, but they left a lastin impression on me."

Amy's curiosity was sparked, for she had heard the Grimké name mentioned but couldn't quite remember what she'd been told. Knotts continued,

"They dedicated their lives to advocatin for the abolition of slavery- and more, for the abolition of the unfair and unequal way that women are treated in our society!"

Elijah muttered, "We coulda done with the both of em round here, if ya ask me! Shame they moved up North! It's no wonder the women here we knew growin up were so borin, when they were never encouraged to think for themselves or learn anything more'n cookin, sewin, settin a pretty table, and havin more white babies!"

Knotss nodded. "Course, there was a whole lotta folks in Charleston who felt the Grimké sisters' father had done em both a disservice, allowin em to read his law books and other materials generally thought unsuitable for young ladies, but I heard em speak on the subject of abolition and women's rights, and I tell ya it sure made sense to me!"

The fact was that the Grimké sisters' writings and speeches caused such a stir that the Episcopal Church to which they belonged in Charleston found them entirely too radical for their liking. Church members began to agitate against the sisters continuing such activities, scandalized that such a well-respected jurist should tolerate activites by his own daughters that could only create a destabilization of Charlestonian society! Both women ended up moving to Pennsylvania and joining the Quakers, where even there they were found to be rather too liberal for the tastes of some. They did not abandon Charleston, however, before making their lasting impression on the awakening social conscience of Knotts.

"I'll tell ya the God's honest truth, Elijah. I can't pretend I was really all that aware of the moral contradicitons inherent in slavery as a young man, much less the unfair and extreme inequalities by which our Southern society created a sort of white equivalent of slavery, discouraging women from learnin or doin much of anything other than raisin children and keeepin house! But the Grimké sisters opened my eyes to a different possibility, and it was inspirin!"

Elijah sensed there was still something more to the story than Knotts was sharing.

"And how did your wife feel about all that? Did she feel awakened and liberated too, or was she threatened by the Grimké sisters' teachin?"

Knotts shifted uncomfortably in his chair and cleared his throat before answering.

"Leave it to my childhood friend to put his finger on an old wound! Ya're right to ask, of course, and I'm sad to say my wife did not undergo any awakening comparable to my own. In fact, she felt quite scandalized by the Grimkés, and it became a bone of contention between us."

Amy could see that there was unresolved pain in their guest's expression that spoke volumes. It also made her suddenly more aware than ever before of how extraordinary Elijah was for having come so far from the confines of his deeply rooted upbringing. Her intuition ever acute, Amy suspected that Knotts' reticence about his children, and his comment that they had moved away and seldom wrote may have been an indication that they shared their mother's sense of scandal and outrage at their father's awakened views, and they had consigned him to oblivion as a result.

"That must have been very hard and painful for you both!" she said with great empathy, immediately endearing herself to Knotts for her understanding.

His eyes welled up with tears and he nodded, only able to muster with a thick voice, "It truly was."

At that point, Momma Celia appeared in the parlor door to announce that dinner was on the table, and would everybody please come on in and sit down. Elijah introduced her to his friend.

"Momma Celia, this is my dear friend Knotts. Knotts this is Amy's mother, Momma Celia. She also happens to be the best cook in Barnwell District, or maybe even South Carolina, so ya'll're in for a real treat for dinner!" Elijah grinned at his mother-in-law.

Knotts bowed politely to Momma Celia, saying, "Very pleased to meet ya, ma'am!"

Momma Celia, unaccustomed to any white man other than Dr. Harley addressing her so formally or politely, just nodded awkwardly in response and gestured toward the dining room door.

As they entered the dining room, in addition to the elegant and festive setting of the table, they were met with a bombardment of delicious smells emanating from a bountiful array of delicacies served up on steaming platters of all sizes. Succulent fricassee of freshly killed capon, slow roasted ham glazed with magnolia honey, green beans with slivered almonds, mashed potatoes with fresh rosemary and garlic, piping hot rolls right out of the oven, countless side dishes of vegetables, fruits, nuts, and various sauces and gravies made your mouth water just to smell them.

The family, including Momma Celia, sat down to table, with Knotts occupying a seat to the right of Elijah, who presided at the head. Amy sat to Elijah's left. Momma Celia sat at the far end, nearest the kitchen door, where she could keep a sharp eye out on her grandchildren and easily exit to the kitchen should anything be lacking or need replenishing.

Elijah picked up his knife and fork, ready to dive in, when a look from Amy stopped him in mid-air. He coughed awkwardly and muttered, "Oh, right. Forgive me!" He then shot glance to the children, who were as eager as he to dig into this impromptu banquet. "Before we begin, I just wanna say how glad we all are to havya here with us this evenin, Knotts. It's not often we can entertain someone who is truly sympathetic."

Amy gave him another look as if to say, "Aren't you forgetting something?"

She picked up from there and added, "I'd just like us to say grace before we eat, to give the Good Lord thanks for bringin us all together like this." The children, on cue, all reverently bowed their heads as Amy prayed,

"Heavenly Father, we thank ya and praise your Holy Name for bringin us a friend this evenin. We ask that ya watch over him and us, that ya keep us all safe from any harm, that ya bring us all to the experience of freedom your Son died for. We also thank ya for this delicious food Momma made, and bless her hands and heart for makin it, and ask ya ta keep everyone on this plantation in your heart and hands. In Jesus' Name we pray." The whole family responded wholeheartedly, "Amen!"

The resonance of the 'Amen' barely silenced, the sounds of servings spoons and forks, cutlery, and the joyous chewing of all filled the air as everyone was served to their hearts' content, and the mouthfuls were interspersed with conversation. The children were asking polite questions about life in Charleston, and such.

The conversation was light and cheerful and punctuated with anectdotes Knotts and Elijah told of each others'escapades as boys, to the particular fascination of Elder, Elleck and Phillip. They were stunned by the sudden realization that Elijah had also been a teenaged boy once, and had done and said carefree and maybe even stupid things that were hard for them to envision in the current atmosphere of perpetual dangers and risks in which they lived. This had the curious effect of endearing both Elijah and Knotts to them all as having felt many of the same things the boys were feeling themselves. Yet it also made them more aware than ever of how different their world was from Elijah's past.

As the meal wore on, little Savage began to fuss, so Elijah held him on his lap and bounced him on his knee, playing horsey to distract him. In the meantime, Amy and Momma Celia and the girls cleared the table. When the last plate was cleared and the candles all blown out, Knotts was lead by hand to his buggy by the girls, as the children chattered affectionately about how much fun they'd had meetin him, and when would he be coming back, as if he was a favorite uncle they had not seen in too long.

"Run along now, children, and get yourelves ready for bed. It's past ya'll's bedtime!" Elijah smiled affectionately as they scampered off back into the house and upstairs to join their mother.

"They're a beautiful family, Elijah. They do ya proud, old friend!"

Elijah gave Knotts a manly hug, shaking his hand and thanking him for his visit. "I'm glad you had a chance to meet em, Knotts. Sorry I didn't warn ya ahead of time, but I figured it was best just to let the truth speak for itself."

"What ya'll're planning to do is mighty dangerous, but ya'll already know that. I do believe though that it is the right and only moral thing ya can do. I just want ya'll to know that if there's anything I can do to help, I'd be pleased and honored to do it for ya. Ya'll can count on me!"

Elijah smiled gratefully as Knotts climbed into his buggy and grabbed the traces.

"God bless ya, Knotts. You have no idea how much your visit has lifted my spirits when they needed liftin the most. This has been a long row to hoe!"

"Well, I could say the same of you, old friend. Comin back here after all these years, I wasn't real sure how I was gonna feel after all I've been through. But whatever the future may have in store, what I feel in this moment right now is thankful, thankful the Good Lord brought us back together again!" With that and a wave, he flicked the reins on his horse's back and the buggy trotted off down the road in the moonlight.

LXXIV

The air was cool and crisp the morning Gilbert drove Elijah to the depot to catch the train for Louisville. Dew lay heavily on the fields and glistened on the leaves of the winter cabbages and turnips in Momma Celia's kitchen garden as Elijah kissed Amy and the children goodbye. It was hard to believe he was finally getting off to Cincinnati after nearly four years of frustrations and delays.

Amy hugged him extra tight before letting him out the door, as if to imprint in the very fiber of his body her love, her faith, and her determination that this trip be a success for him and for them all.

"You come back to me safe and sound, y'hear?" she murmured in his ear as she released him from her embrace.

"I will darlin, I promise! Ya'll take good care a each other til I get back!" he answered, hoping the Good Lord would let him keep his promise.

There was a light mist rising from the ground that created an almost dream-like atmosphere as the carriage trundled down the tree-lined avenue toward the main road. It swirled and eddied behind the carriage wheels like the wake of a rowboat on still waters, tiny whirlpools spinning from each dip of the oars. Once out on the main road into town, Elijah felt a mixture of elation, relief, and anxiety as they neared the depot.

"Ya'll'll keep a close eye out, won't ya, Gilbert? I need to know they'll be safe while I'm away!" he said to his brother-in-law.

"Don't you worry, Elijah. I'll take good care of em. And I can get a telegram sent to ya in Cincinnati if anything happens that ya'll need to know about right away."

"That's a good idea! I'll let Will Beazely know you or Amy can send me a telegram if ya'll need to and make sure he can get an answer out to ya without folks findin out. I'll be stayin at the Broadway Hotel in Cincinnati. And the lawyers' names are Mr. James Gitchell and Mr. John Jolliffe," he repeated for at least the tenth time. "Can ya'll remember that?"

"Yessir, I know. I'm tellin ya, ya'll don't have to worry! Everything's gonna be fine! Besides, ya'll got everybody on the whole plantation prayin for ya, and I believe the Good Lord hears every prayer, even if He don't always answer em when and how we might like!"

Elijah thought for a moment about how bitter that truth was, both for him and some of the slaves, who had no idea they would likely be sold before Elijah could free them all. But that thought simply increased his anxiety, and he had to put it out of his mind for the moment, at least until he could get safely on board and on his way.

They arrived at the depot well before the train, and Elijah went to talk to Will Beazely while Gilbert unloaded his bags onto the platform. Will promised to keep an eye out for any trouble and warn them on the plantation if needed, and to send Elijah a telegram in Cincinnati if circumstances should require it.

As the train pulled hissing and spitting into the station, Elijah and Gilbert looked at each other, aware that other passengers were gathering too. Conscious that prying eyes might raise an alarm if they seemed too familiar for the social norms of Williston, they resisted their instinct to give each other a bear hug for safe-keeping, but their eyes conveyed everything such a hug could, and more.

As Elijah boarded the train, Gilbert had a disturbing feeling that even if Elijah got the new will written and was able to bring Amy, Momma Celia, and the children up to Cincinnati, his own fate might not be so secure. But he tried to smile and wave anyway, sending up a fervent prayer that he was wrong about that. Whatever his own fate might be, he was determind to see Amy to safety and freedom, feeling that if she at least made it the whole family might somehow be redeemed.

Elijah had plenty of time for thinking as the train chugged across the Carolina lowlands, gradually uphill, then across the Smokey Mountains, west of Appalachia to the verdant farmlands and woods of Tennessee and on into Western Kentucky and the eastern edge of the prairies, arriving finally in the bustling metropolis of Louisville.

As Elijah pondered his strategy, he was still torn as to whether to sell off his land and slaves now or wait until the family was safe in Ohio, return to sell them in person, and then bring Gilbert and as many others as he could back with him to Cincinnati. He dreaded the process of deciding whom to save and whom to sell. He had promised Amy he wouldn't die before she saw freedom, and was determined to fulfill his promise. He trusted that God would see him through on that somehow, but he was suddenly less convinced that the promise would hold until all the rest were freed too.

The train's conductor, James Meredith, was a light skinned colored man whose proper carriage and polite demeanor had always impressed Elijah when he had gone on shorter trips through the region on business. They had gotten to know each other a bit over the years, as Elijah was fond of travelling by train whenever possible to avoid the dust and bumps of the country roads throughout the South- there being few highways worthy of the name in that part of the country. An affable man who felt it his calling to put the passengers at ease, and to help the time to pass more smoothly, Mr. Meredith was surprised to find Elijah going all the way to Louisville.

"Nice to see ya'll again, Mr. Willis." Mr. Meredith announced as he was punching tickets for the next stop. "Ain't it a little unusual you goin so far from home, sir?"

In that curious anonymity that sometimes prompts travellers to make frank confessions to total strangers, Elijah replied, "Well, as a matter of fact it is, James, it truly is. But this is not just an ordinary business trip. I'm thinkin a bringing my family up to Ohio to live!"

Mr. Meredith did not know that Elijah was referring to a family of mixed race, due to Elijah never having been accompanied by them on this railroad line. Though he thought it odd a rich, successful white planter would want to relocate to Ohio of all places, he figured that most white folks he had ever known were a little crazy anyway, and there was no telling what might strike their fancy next. He just nodded and smiled politely.

"Well ain't that somethin!" was all he could think to say.

The trip to Louisville was otherwise uneventful. Elijah took a hack from the train station to the riverfront, down Short Street, past a row of modest clapboard houses and store front shops, to the dock. There he could see several steamboats tied up, taking on or unloading passengers and cargo, some headed south to Natchez, others north to Cincinnati. He found the ticket office on the wharf, and bought a round-trip ticket on *The Delta Queen*, a stern wheeled paddle-wheeler plying the river on short runs. Not as grand as *The Jacob Strader* or some of the other newer, more elegant steamboats that doubled as floating casinos, *The Delta Queen* suited his purposes admirably for the moment. "Perhaps," he thought, "when we come back as a family, I'll book us on the *Strader* to celebrate!"

His bags loaded safely on board, Elijah stood pensively by the rail as he watched the crew raise the gang plank and cast off, the steam whistle hooting loudly to announce their departure. As the steamboat pulled away from the wharf and out into the current heading North and East, he could feel the force of the river wanting to pull the boat southward against their will. Even though the surface of the river seemed placid enough, it belied a powerful current flowing southward toward the sea, and the steam engine coughed as it insisted on overcoming the current to take the boat upstream.

Elijah sighed, as if the very opposing forces of river and engine were an expression of the emotional forces with which he himself was struggling. It was not easy to fight the current of generations of family tradition and power, no matter how attractively a life of freedom and opportunity beckoned from Cincinnati. But he knew there was nothing for it but to move forward upstream at this point.

There was a brisk breeze blowing from the west. The air was cold off the water, even though Spring was not far way. As he wondered how much longer it might be before he'd be making the same trip with Amy and the family, Elijah decided to get out of the wind and seek some refreshment inside in the lounge. Though not a gilded floating palace like the Jacob Strader, the Delta Queen was comfortably appointed, and Elijah found a table near a window from which he could watch both the passengers and the river. He bought himself a bottle of whiskey and a glass to pass the time and ponder, yet again, how to construe his Last Will and Testament.

He savored the fiery liquor appreciatively, so smooth on the palate, rising in a heady burst of flavor to the roof of his mouth, then sliding down his throat and warming him as it went. He gave a deep sigh of relief. As uncertain as he felt, given his age and health, about his own ability or even desire to start a new business and household- much less educate his chidren for lives of their own in an area he scarcely knew- he felt convinced that at the very least, Amy, Momma Celia, and the children would be freed. Moreover, they would have enough to make it on their own once he was gone. That was all that mattered anymore. He said a silent prayer as he took another swig, hoping that Messrs. Gitchell and Jolliffe had been a wise choice to represent him, and could be relied upon to see his wishes through in the event that he himself could not.

Having telegraphed his attorneys from Louisville to apprise them of the time of his arrival, he was met by them both at the wharf as he finally debarked in Cincinnati.

"Mr. Willis?" inquired Mr. Jolliffe as he noticed a tall, well-dressed and slightly portly gentleman standing on the dock, looking around as if he were unfamiliar with the place.

Elijah turned and brightened. "Yes sir, I am he. Are you Mr. Gitchell, by any chance?"

"As a matter of fact, I am not. I'm John Jolliffe, but my partner, James Gitchell, has accompanied me. He's just over there on the other side of the gangplank. Since we had no description of your likeness, we agreed to simply inquire of anyone who looked the part of a prosperous Southern planter!" Jolliffe said with a chuckle. "James!" he shouted to his companion, "Over here! I found him!"

From across the dock, James Gitchell looked over and waved, smiling and nodding in acknowledgment, hurriedly making his way through the throng of passengers, porters, and stevedores unloading cargo.

"What a great pleasure to finally meet you face to face, sir!" Gitchell said as he pumped Elijah's hand enthusiastically. "Here, let us help you with your bags!" The two immediately picked up Elijah's luggage without even calling for a porter. It was the first of many moments when Elijah realized how different the culture of Ohio was from South Carolina. Back home it would scarcely ever have occurred to a white man of his status to carry his own, much less another's luggage, especially when there was an ample supply of menials to do it for him. To tell the truth, the contrast was both sharp and satisfying, since Elijah himself had never been prone to being waited on for every little thing, despite his upbringing. That had made him seem odd to his peers, but Ohio, he allowed, might be quite a welcome difference on that score.

The two lawyers escorted Elijah to their carriage, and a Negro coachman jumped down to help them load the baggage onto the back, then asked his employers where they wanted to go.

"Take us first to the Broadway Hotel, Jack," instructed Mr. Jolliffe affably, "But wait for us there until we have gotten Mr. Willis settled, and then we'll all head over to our office!"

"Yessir!" Jack nodded with a smile as he climbed back up into the driver's seat, and with a light flick of his whip he set the carriage rumbling briskly over the cobblestones toward the Broadway Hotel, one of Cincinnati's finest.

A mulato porter and a German immigrant bellhop met them at the door to the hotel and graciously ushered them inside, reminding Elijah once again that he was not in South Carolina anymore. Elijah's room had been reserved in advance, so it was only a matter of moments before he had registered at the front desk, been shown to his room, deposited his bags, and was on his way back out with Messrs. Gitchell and Jolliffe, where their carriage awaited to convey them to the law offices nearby. They settled into the usual social chit-chat on the way.

"I hope your journey was not too fatiguing?" inquired Mr. Gitchell.

"Not at all!" replied Elijah, "Matter of fact, it was quite relaxin, especially the riverboat ride! Actually did me good to get a change of scene and clear my head a bit!"

"That's good to hear," replied Mr. Jolliffe, somewhat distractedly, as impatient as Elijah to get through the social niceties and down to brass tacks. Suddenly remembering himself however, and sensitive to the peculiar circumstances under which their guest was seeking their services, he asked, "Did you wish to send a telegram to your wife to let her know of your arrival? We can arrange to stop by the telegraph office on the way if you'd like?" He chose to refer to Amy as Elijah's wife out of empathy, despite the extra-legality of that status. It was appreciated.

"Thank ya sir, that's real thoughtful of ya, but I think I'druther take care of business first and then let her know, if ya'll don't mind. It'd make for better news than just tellin her I'm here!" He smiled. Both men understood instantly.

"Quite right! Hadn't thought of it, but of course I'm sure that's true! How thoughtless, forgive me. I hope you don't think me insensitive?" said Jolliffe. He felt oddly flustered by having a client who both represented the Southern establishment, and was at the same time victimized by it in such a personal way. Deeply commited as Jolliffe was to the abolitionist cause, he was nevertheless not insensitive to the emotional struggle it must take for his client to break so completely with his own past and his very upbringing, and take such a heroic and monumental step.

"It must be terribly stressful for all of you to be living in such a limbo of uncertainty like this!" Jolliffe continued sincerely, Mr. Gitchell nodding in sympathetic agreement.

"Ya'll have no idea!" said Elijah. "To be frank, I'd become so accustomed to the stress myself that it was not until I boarded the riverboat that I began to realize that I felt distinctly lighter at the prospect of finally accomplishin the goal we set so long ago! I hardly recognized the sensation of relief, it bein so unfamiliar after so many years of the stress weighin on me!"

"I can barely imagine what it must be like to constantly have to watch your back, even in the place you know best!" Mr. Gitchell remarked.

"Not to mention the pain and disillusionment of being attacked by people you'd known all your life!" added Mr. Jolliffe.

"Well now, it hasn't been all that bad, really. At least not yet. I still have a few friends who've been sympathetic and supportive. As for my blood relations, they're just plain greedy and jealous of my success. My no account nephews and niece and her shiftless husband think they were born into privilege and deserve everything without havin done a lick a work to deserve it! My sister-in-law has never given a tinker's damn about me, but surely would love to get her hands on my house and furnishins," he said with a bitter edge in his voice.

Elijah paused as sadness was added to his tone of resentment. "And my brother, though I know somewhere in his heart he still cares something for me, hasn't got the balls to stand up to his wife and children's whinin and complainin about him never bein as successful as I've been. He's never stood up for me once. It's just a royal mess, I tell ya!"

As Messrs. Gitchell and Jolliffe absorbed all this, Elijah added, "My biggest worry, though, isn't about my white relations' discontent. It's about folks in Barnwell District gettin their minds poisoned with fear and hatred, and takin it out on any other folks who see things differently. The whole atmosphere back home seems to be turnin sour." He shook his head. "Seems to me some folks down there're so scared of change they're like a drownin man clutchin at straws, clingin to a system that, as God is my witness, I truly believe can't keep em afloat any more, even though it made me a wealthy man!" Elijah paused before adding insistently, "It just can't end well, that's as clear as day, and I need to get my family out and to safety before the whole damn thing blows up in a war between the states! And if ya ask me," he added, "that time is approachin faster'n any of us care to admit!"

Mr. Gitchell responded soberly, "I'm afraid I believe you're right, Mr. Willis, and it is partly because of that we have been so particularly eager to help you in your plight! I don't mind telling you, both of us are deeply committed to the abolition of slavery, and the opportunity to contribute to that end even slightly by helping you emancipate your family is an honor and a privilege!"

Mr. Jolliffe shot his partner a warning glance for him not to go on at length about his political views, fearing it might put their client off. "That being said sir, rest assured we have no desire to tell you how you should dispose of your property in your will, but only advise you as to what, by Ohio law, you may and may not do." Jolliffe hastened to make clear.

"Well, that suits me just fine, gentlemen, and I surely do thank ya both for your help. Truth is, I've been dreamin about this visit for a long time now, but I'm still feelin a tad torn about some of the details."

Elijah proceeded to share with them his feeling that, much as he might like to free all his slaves, and much as Amy might insist upon him doing so, he was hard pressed to see how it would be possible to pull it off safely. Even bringing Amy, Momma Celia and all seven children up to Cincinnati without mishap was no small order given the current climate, much less bringing an entourage of fifty slaves! He was certain it would alert suspicions along the way and more than likely lead to trouble before they ever made it to Cincinnati.

He elaborated on his thinking that it might be best to sell off some of the slaves before they even moved North, then once he had settled the family safely in Ohio he could return to South Carolina, sell the remainder of his property, and at least bring Gilbert, his family, and perhaps some of the others back up to Ohio with him. He would then have more than enough money for them all to live comfortably, and for him to endow as many slaves as he could emancipate beyond the family circle so that they could live independent lives in liberty.

Elijah also explained that he suffered from heart trouble, and having had several worrisome episodes of apoplexy, he felt a particular urgency to set things up so that should he die prematurely, his family would still be free and have full use of his assets. To that end he also raised the question of whether Amy would have the legal authority to dispose of his property once she was freed, hoping that this might provide a happy solution to the dilemma.

"Were the property in question here in the State of Ohio, and if you were legally married, as your widow she certainly would automatically have such authority. Even as a free person of color she would have discretionary powers once the will had cleared probate," commented Jolliffe. "However, since South Carolina law never sanctioned your relationship, and since a will written here will have to pass probate in both Ohio and South Carolina for her to have such authority beyond the borders of Ohio, it is hard to say." He turned to his colleague and asked, "What do you think, James?"

Mr. Gitchell spoke up, "John's right, Mr. Willis. In theory, Amy would have legal rights over all property you devised to leave her. However, given the fact that your assets are all in South Carolina, and given the obstructionist history of the South Carolina courts on such matters, I think it unlikely she will be able to dispose of it as easily or quickly as you or she might like."

"There's also the question of whether you want to name Amy as legatee with controlling powers or divide the estate into equal shares for all, in which case even when freed Amy would need the consent of all the legatees for her to dispose of any of the property in South Carolina. That could make the legal proceedings even more difficult."

This news elicited a look of consternation on Elijah's face, for he had hoped that merely by declaring his intentions emphatically the legal system would have to comply and that would be that. But before he could respond or pose any more questions, Mr. Gitchell continued,

"It would certainly be better for you yourself to liquidate your assets and, to that end, bring to Ohio as many other slaves as you choose to liberate." He paused and then added, "Realistically, if I were you, I'd be prepared for it to take some time for your will to work its way through probate in South Carolina. However, I don't anticipate it having any difficulty in being approved here in Ohio."

"I see," said Elijah pensively. "Well, it's a shame I can't appoint Amy as executor of my will, she bein still technically a slave, so I suppose I need to find someone here who will do me the honor of servin that function," he said, almost as if thinking out loud.

Impressed with both gentlemen's obvious grasp of the legal and the political complexities of the issues he was facing, Elijah felt comfortable asking them for any help they might be able to provide. He wanted to structure the document in as foolproof a manner as possible, so as to thwart any probable attempt on the part of his white relations to prevent the will's approval in South Carolina, and to prevent them from returning his family to slavery under their control.

Mr. Jolliffe suggested establishing the basic content of the will first and leaving the matter of its execution until later. "As to the particulars of your will sir, might I ask that you first make clear to us whom you wish to name as beneficiaries and specifically with what property you wish to endow them? I gather your lands and business holdings are quite extensive, in addition to the matter of your, uh, slaveholdings." This last word almost caught in his throat, as a matter of distaste.

"Well sir, I've thought long and hard on the matter." Elijah announced. "To tell the truth, when I first started dreamin up this plan I was still considedn parcelin off some of it and leavin a little somethin to each of my many blood relations for tradition's sake. I had already done that in a will I had written back in '46. But the fact of the matter is, since I took up with Amy, my blood relations've all been so despicably mean and rude to her and the children, and to me, that I've decided I don't want any of them to get so much as one thin dime! To Hell with tradition! They don't deserve a damn thing!" he declared vehemently.

"To whom then, specifically, do you want to leave your estate- now that it's clear we are speaking of its entirety?" asked Jolliffe.

"To Amy, Elder, Elleck, Phillip, Clarissa Ann, Julia Ann, Eliza Ann, and Savage (that'd be Elijah Junior) Willis. However, I also wish to emancipate Amy's mother Celia, and her brother Gilbert, and any other offspring they may have in my possession at the time of my demise."

"I see," responded Jolliffe. "Given your health concerns and the social instability of the times, I quite agree that it would be advisable for you to construct the will in such a way as to assure your slaves' emancipation in the event that you were to die before successfully bringing them the Ohio."

"And you should consider adding that any future offspring of any of them would also be free, for future children might be construed as still being rightfully enslaved in South Carolina!" recommended Gitchell, who had clearly done his homework.

"That's a good idea. I'll agree to that sir, but I'd appreciate your advice on another matter too. When I went to Baltimore, it was suggested I set up a trust for Amy and the children, but South Carolina law, I'm told, will not permit settin up any kinda trust to provide for coloreds. So, if I do not surive long enough to see them safely here, I depair of the possibility they might remain financially enslaved forever! What can I do to make sure this'll work, even if I die before I can get em all up here?"

Mr. Gitchell stroked his chin for a moment in contemplation, perked up and said, "It occurs to me there might be another solution! If, rather than trying to bequeath your estate to Amy and the children directly, relying on your ability to bring them all North to freedom yourself, you technically bequeathed it in its entirety to an executor domiciled in the State of Ohio, you could then stipulate that the executor would be obliged to bring them all to Ohio, liquidate all other assets, pay off all debts, and thereafter emancipate and endow the designated former slaves with the remainder of your estate!"

John Jolliffe looked at his partner with admiration, "James, that's brilliant! South Carolina law would not be able to oppose it, for the will's execution would be bound by Ohio law and not just that of South Carolina's! And it circumvents the need for all the legatees to agree to the sale of the property! It could all be handled by and through the executor!"

"Moreover," Gitchell continued enthusiastically, "by Ohio law, if a slaveowner brings slaves into the state with the intent of emancipating them, even if the slaveowner himself does not yet have a residence in Ohio, such slaves are automatically emancipated the moment they set foot on Ohio soil. That would still be the case whether it was you, or the executor of the will who brought them here!"

"Of course, just to be extra careful, to leave no room for any doubt from the South Carolina end, you could also have your executors execute an official deed of manumission through the court upon the slaves' arrival in Ohio, should that not transpire until after your demise. Such a writ might be redundant, but it couldn't hurt!" interjected Jolliffe.

"Once it is legally established that Amy and the children are free persons residing in the State of Ohio, South Carolina law would no longer have any jurisdiction over them, and the disposal of your property would merely be governed by the normal laws of commerce, the race of the out-of-state seller or sellers being irrelevant," clarified Gitchell.

Elijah looked at both attorneys with admiration for their thorough-going intelligence. "If I had my druthers, I'd prefer the executors be you two gentlemen, but if that's not possible, perhaps ya'll know of some other respectable folks of means around here who could vouch for Amy and the children, and help see to it they're never returned to slavery in South Carolina, or anywhere else?"

"I would be honored to serve as your executor, sir!" remarked Jolliffe, without hesitation.

"So would I," agreed Gitchell. "However, strategically it might prove wiser not to have both of us serve, or at least not only the two of us, lest folks suspect us of exercising undue influence, given that our position on the matter of slavery is well known and a matter of public record. We might be able to recommend some highly reputable friends of ours, however, Mr. Ernst and Mr. Harwood, who I'm sure would be more than willing to help in such a worthy cause. With your permission, I shall make some inquiries of them and let you know of their response right away."

"That'd be fine, gentlemen! I surely do appreciate it!"

"Might I suggest that I write up a draft of the will after our midday dinner, and then you can peruse it and make any changes, additions, or corrections you might feel necessary before I draft the final document?" He thought for a moment and then added, "We'll make two exact copies: one for you to take home with you, and another we will keep here in a sealed envelope to be opened only following your demise. That should provide maximum security in the event that any of your white relations try any mischief, attempt to insist your former will is the only valid testament of record, or your copy becomes subject to any kind of 'mishap!'" Jolliffe recommended.

"That sounds just grand! Ya'll have no idea the peace a mind it gives me to know this is gettin settled in a way that'll guarantee my family's safety at last." Elijah's eyes welled up with moisture which he quickly brushed away, not wanting to appear unseemly. After a somewhat awkward pause during which no one was sure quite how to deal with the obvious emotion they all felt, Mr. Jolliffe spoke up.

"I imagine you must be hungry! Why don't we have our dinner at the hotel, and then you could take some rest while we prepare the draft?"

"That will also give us time to contact Mr. Ernst and Mr. Harwood. If all goes well, we may be able to conclude our business by tomorrow and send you back on your way home!" Mr. Gitchell chimed in.

"Excellent, gentlemen, excellent!" responded Elijah enthusiastically. "And if ya'll don't mind, before headin back to board the steamboat to Louisville, I'd like to take ya'll up on that offer to send Amy a telelgram."

"Of course, absolutely! No trouble at all!" affirmed both attorneys, gleeful that they had succeeded in setting up the will in such a way as to be able to guarantee the emancipation of all the slaves Elijah owned at the time of his death. They felt as if they had struck a major blow for the abolitionist cause without ever having to ruffle Elijah's feathers or use any heavy means of persuasion to do so! Not that they were hoping for an untimely demise, mind you, but at least they were hereby assured that if Elijah should depart this world before fulfilling his wishes, they as executors could accomplish such a collective emancipation, and perhaps even more! With that, they went outside and called Jack to take them back to the Broadway Hotel for a sumptuous meal in celebration.

LXXV

Amy's hands trembled as she read the telegram Elijah had sent: "Trip successful. Stop. Solution found. Stop. Be home the 28th. Stop."

True to his word, Will Beazely had even gone to the trouble of delivering it in person, so as not to risk any messenger boy letting slip in town that Amy had gotten a telegram, much less what it's contents might be.

"I truly do appreciate ya'll coming all the way out here to give me this, Mr. Beazeley. Can I offer ya some refreshment for your trouble?" Amy asked graciously, recovering herself.

"No thank ya, ma'am. I'd best be getting back to the depot. There's a train coming in soon, and there'll be hell to pay if I'm not there when it gets here!" he answered. "But I sure am glad it's good news. Ya'll deserve it!" he said with a smile of understanding.

Amy gave a slight curtsey in appreciation. "God bless ya, Mr. Beazely. That's real sweet of ya to say!"

Will Beazely smiled back and said, "I truly mean it, Miss Amy. It's a brave thing Mr. Willis is doin, but in my heart I know it's also the right thing."

Amy smiled back, at a loss for words. She raised her hand to hide her mouth, for fear of crying out loud from the sheer emotion of it. Will seemed to understand, and tipping his hat to her, bade her a discrete good-bye as he headed back to the depot.

Once he was gone, barely able to contain herself, Amy yelled at the top of her voice, "MOMMA! MOMMAAAA! COME QUICK!! HURRY!!!"

Momma Celia came running from the kitchen to the veranda as fast as her old legs would carry her.

"Good God A'mighty child, what's goin on? What is it?" she said breathlessly as she came barreling out the front door. By now the childrens' hurried footsteps could also be heard beating syncopated rhythms in quick time from various parts of the house as they clattered down the front and back stairs, converged in the front hallway and jostled with each other to get through the front door to see what all the fuss was about.

"What is it, Momma? Is Papa comin home?" asked little Eliza eagerly. She doted on her father, and had cried herself to sleep the first three nights he was gone. "What's the news?" "Why're you cryin, if it's good news, Momma?" "Is Papa alright?" the children all started asking in a rush, their questions stumbling over each other like a tangled litter of hungry puppies clamoring to be fed.

Tears of joy ran down Amy's cheeks as she read to the family Elijah's telegram. They all sat in stunned silence, the younger ones not immediately understanding the cryptic import of the message. In explanation, Amy said, "Children, this means we're gonna be free!" she choked up on the last word and dissolved into sobs of relief, as if a floodgate had burst, and an uncontrollable torrent of emotion gushed out. Amy and Momma Celia held each other in a deep embrace of silent, sobbing communion, unable to speak but through the eloquent rivulets of their comingled tears.

The younger children jumped up and down in excitement and then hugged their mother and grandmother repeatedly, as if only by such physical contact could they be sure they weren't dreaming. The older boys stood dumb-founded at first, in incredulous wonder and admiration that Elijah had achieved what had been promised so long ago. After a moment's stunned silence, however, they too started whooping and hollering so loud it brought Gilbert running around from out back to find out what the ruckus was all about.

"Lordy be! Ya'll're hollerin enough to wake the dead! What's goin on?" Gilbert asked, seeing his mother's and sister's tear-stained faces in counterpoint to the children's unbridled jubilation.

Amy still couldn't speak for the emotion of it all, and simply handed her brother the telegram, her sobs slowly subsiding. As he read it, Gilbert slowly crumpled to his knees, as if the energy in his legs had suddenly been drained out of him. He looked up at his sister and mother uncomprehending, as if surprised to find himself kneeling on the brickwork of the veranda and wondering how he got there.

"Amy," he said, her name almost catching in his throat, his voice thick with emotion, "D'ya think the solution means for all of us?" he was almost afraid to ask the question, but this was no time to hold back, and the question had been lying there unspoken for months as Gilbert began to realize what Elijah had already seen: freeing them all might not be possible.

"I don't know, honey, the telegram just says 'solution found.' I'm sure Elijah wouldn't a used those words if he hadn't found a way to make sure we get outa here!" Amy insisted.

Gilbert didn't want to dampen his sister's joy by asking who was included in the 'we,' but he had a sinking feeling the solution did not necessarily refer to all the slaves, and couldn't help but wonder which ones might not make it out. It's not that he didn't believe Elijah's promise to free him and his family, it's just that the logistical reality of it seemed more than challenging, given the growing tensions in the region. He decided he'd just have to wait until Elijah got back to find out the details.

"Well, it says he's comin home on the 28th. That's tomorrow! At least we won't have to wait long to find out the details!" he said with relief.

LXXVI

When Elijah arrived at the train depot the next day, Gilbert went in the carriage to meet him. Amy had realized it would be impossible not to give away their secret if the whole family went to the depot with him, so despite the children's loud protestations, she had insisted they wait for Elijah at home.

Elijah too had realized that caution was still called for, and gave no immediate display of either success or affection as Gilbert met him on the platform, dutifully picked up his bags, and carried them to the carriage, the very portrait of submissive service. Once on the open road however, and away from prying eyes and ears, Gilbert couldn't help but ask eagerly for the details of Elijah's alleged "solution."

"Amy and Momma just bout drowned us all out with tears a joy when ya'll's telegram came!" Gilbert informed Elijah. "I figure ya had ta be mighty careful with the wordin, so's folks round here couldn't find out anything, but I gotta admit the tension a not knowin specifically what the 'solution' actually is has been givin me fits!" He didn't want to press Elijah immediately on who the beneficiaries would be, hoping Elijah would volunteer that information himself.

"Well Gilbert, I gotta admit, there were a few developments I hadn't expected, once the lawyers explained to me how the law up there works and what my options might be." This did not assuage Gilbert's anxiety, but he held his tongue, waiting for more.

"But I do believe I found a way to make sure Amy, Momma Celia, and the children are freed no matter what happens to me." Sensing Gilbert's sudden worry that the liberation might not extend to him and his children, Elijah added, "And I believe it is now set up so that at the very least, you and your children will all be freed too." He was reluctant to go into the details of the possibility that he might have to sell of some of the slaves before the move to Cincinnati for fear of getting Gilbert upset. He was equally reticent to reveal that possibility to Amy.

The carriage rumbled on, as the words "at the very least" hung in the air, suggesting to Gilbert that his suspicions had been correct, and that not all the slaves were likely to make it to freedom. He pondered his own willingness to participate in making the decision of whom to sell and whom to free, deciding he could handle that if he had to. Being as how there were some who were more more ornery and bad-tempered than others, it was gonna be a challenge to decide whether they were more or less deserving of freedom than the cooperative ones. Then too, there were some who had family on neighboring plantations and might not be too eager to move out of state even if they were free, since starting a new life with nothing was not equally appealing to all, especially if they had roots back here. It would be a tough decision to make no matter what the criteria were for deciding. Gilbert said nothing to Elijah about this, as the decision was not yet his to make and perhaps never would be.

By the time the carriage rolled to a stop in front of the Willis Plantation, Amy, Momma Celia, and all the children were waiting eagerly on the veranda to greet them. As Elijah descended from the carriage, he was engulfed in a bundle of hugs and kisses and greetings from them all.

"How're ya'll doin?" he grinned innocently, as if it weren't obvious. "Somethin goin on I should know about?" he teased.

Amy slapped his arm chidingly "Elijah! Come on! Tell us all about it!" and gave him a kiss.

Elijah pretended extreme fatigue, "Aw now, give me time, woman! Can't ya see I'm tired? I need ta rest a spell first!"

"I'll send ya ta your eternal rest if ya don't tell us what happened!" Amy threatened.

Clarissa, always the serious and perceptive one, realized that Elijah was just playing with them and said, "Come on, Papa, stop foolin round! We really want to know all about your trip and the solution ya found!"

Elijah chuckled, "Well alright, if you insist little darlin. But can we at least go into the kitchen, so I can get a cup a Momma Celia's coffee an maybe a biscuit while I tell ya?" He winked at his mother-in-law.

Clarissa nodded gravely, concluding that this was an acceptable compromise, as Julia and Eliza grabbed him by the hand, the boys grabbed his luggage, Amy carried Savage, and Momma Celia led the way to the back of the house and her kitchen, where she had already started preparing some of her specialites to welcome Elijah home.

Gilbert followed behind, aware that there was a subtle line of demarcation in the family relationship that didn't always include him, but feeling entitled to share in the revelation of what had transpired in Cincinnati. Nobody objected, of course.

The aromas wafting from oven, pots, and platters blended together in a symphony of smells that greeted them as they walked in, making everyone feel the deep comfort that Momma Celia's loving hands elicited from any and everything edible, like a conductor coaxing an orchestra to new musical heights to the delight of all. The family ranged themselves around the table where, true to Elijah's expectations, a platter of warm biscuits, a slab of butter, and earthenware crocks of various jams, jellies, and magnolia honey invited the family to savor them.

Momma Celia took a piping hot pot of coffee off the stove and poured some for Elijah, setting it in front of him with a creamer and sugar bowl and a gleaming silver spoon, saying "Nuff of ya'll's excuses, now! Time to tell us what that telegram meant!" she ordered with a smile, holding the coffee pot over him as if she might pour it on his head if he didn't promptly comply.

Before saying a word, Elijah deliberately reached into his coat pocket and pulled out the will, carefully written in a clear hand and signed by him, along with the signatures of W. B. Shattuck, E. Penrose Jones, and James M. Gitchell, the duly required witnesses to make it legal. He unfolded it gently, spreading its pages flat on the table, taking care to keep it well away from the buttery crumbs and sticky dribbles left by the children's eager indulgence in Momma Celia's biscuits.

"Here it is, ya'll!" he said with dramatic flair, "This here is ya'll's ticket to freedom!" It was not a long document, being only a single long sheet of paper, with a title page, but it was densely written and worded, so the family struggled to read their way through the legal verbiage and grasp the essentials of the content.

As they were reading, Elijah proceeded to explain blow by blow what had happened on the trip: the issues Messrs. Gitchell and Jolliffe had raised, the options presented, and the final decisions made. Amy and Gilbert, in particular, listened attentively.

The girls were quickly lost in all the legal terminology, and after eating their share of biscuits contented themselves with playing with Savage on the kitchen floor, while the grown-ups continued to talk overhead. Elder,

Elleck and Phillip, however, were as intent as their mother on listening, and were carefully reading the will even if they had to struggle a bit to understand some of the wording.

"Papa?" Elder spoke up. "I thought you was gonna leave the plantation to us! Says here ya'll're leavin it to the Ex-Ec-U-Tor. What's that mean?" Elder had, of course, touched on the very key of the solution without realizing it.

"Well son, that's a good question. The executor is the fella who makes sure everything in the will gets done the way I want it. Now in this case that means first and foremost he's gotta free you and your brothers and sisters, your Momma, and your grandmother, in case I haven't lived to do it myself." Elder looked at his Uncle Gilbert, suddenly worried.

"What about Uncle Gilbert and the others?" he demanded. There was an uncomfortable shifting in chairs as all eyes turned to Elijah.

"Well, I had to struggle with how to get that done in a way that would be both legal and logistically possible. The law in Ohio wouldn't allow me to leave everything to ya'll outright, cause technically, ya'll're still slaves, and Ohio doesn't allow slavery. That means, ya'll have to be emancipated first before any property can pass to ya- including the rest of the slaves. But ya'll'll get equal shares of everything." Elijah seemed to be dodging the question. Amy looked perplexed as Elijah continued his explanation.

"So by leavin everything to the executor with specific instructions that the executor has to bring ya'll up to Ohio, free ya, and get ya'll set up on a property of your own, means that your Uncle Gilbert and his children will also be brought up to Ohio as soon as possible," Elijah explained. "Hopefully many of the others will too," he added somewhat vaguely.

Elijah could feel that last point hanging heavy in the air, so he went on to tell them that the executor has the power to free whomever was in his possession at the time of his death, and would make sure any children they might have, even in the future, would also be free. The logisitics and timing were the only thing in question, as Elijah still planned to take Amy, Momma Celia and the children to Ohio himself. Since it was simply not practical to try to bring all the slaves at once, both for the cost and for the dangerous likelihood it would cause a ruckus in Barnwell District none of them wanted to deal with. He would then come back to sell the plantation, and then bring Gilbert and the others up too.

Gilbert noticed with disappointment that neither he nor Momma Celia, nor his children were mentioned as legatees in the will. He would have felt better if they had been at least named. He began to make calculations in his head and realized that there was no way Elijah could split everything equally between all fifty slaves and have enough for them all to live on, even if he got top dollar for the plantation's land, livestock, and buildings. If the estate was divided equally only among Amy and the children, that left him, his mother, and his children at the mercy of their collective largesse, even if freed. He didn't want to appear ungrateful, but he had a sinking feeling that freedom alone might be a gift that would cost him dearly, inspite of Elijah's good intentions. He was struggling not to feel betrayed.

Elleck, like his brothers, had been listening carefully, trying to get a clear understanding of what was going to happen. He was worried. "Papa, the way you're talkin, it sounds like ya'll're settin us up on a farm without ya! Ain't you comin with us?" the anxiety in his voice came as a shock to Elijah. He had been so focused on the working out the legalities of their emancipation that he had almost overlooked the emotional attachments they all shared.

"Don't you worry son, I don't want to leave ya- not at all! That's not my intention! God willin, we'll be together for a long time to come, we'll settle together in Ohio on some good land, and ya'll'll get the schoolin I promised, so when ya'll're full grown each of ya'll'll have some property and can make it on your own, wherever life takes ya. But I had to write the will to protect ya'll, just in case I should die before I can get us all up there safely!" The girls in particular looked alarmed. Elijah went on, "Nothin in life is guaranteed, and the Good Lord could take any of us when it pleases Him. He almost took your Momma when Eliza was born, and nearly took Savage too! He's not bound by our desires or hopes or expectations! But I promised your Momma I was gonna free ya'll, and now, dead or alive I know my promise will be kept!" Elijah explained.

Though relieved to have that assurance, Amy's face clouded as she realized the import of the document as it was written in relation to the rest of the slaves. It didn't come as a total shock. Elijah had already broached the subject of maybe having to sell off some of the slaves before they even moved North, but her heart twisted with pain at the thought of having to do so, and dreaded the probable reaction of those who were not destined to be freed. She wanted to talk more to Elijah about this, but sensed that this was not the time or place with Gilbert and the children present. It would have to wait, and she would not for all the world appear so ungrateful as to malign her husband for his efforts when her own freedom in fact had just been guaranteed.

Gilbert too was taking all this in and realizing that there were an awful lot of variables in this equation that didn't necessarily add up to freedom and financial solvency. He sighed deeply, grateful for his brother-in-law's efforts, but fearful that they might not bear fruit for him and his children. He consoled himself with the thought that if Amy at least was freed, she would continue to fight for his freedom too, and her strength and determination were no mean force to contend with.

Momma Celia, feeling the unspoken questions and concerns eddying around the table and recognizing they were all in the same boat, decided to steer the conversation in a different direction before anyone got upset and let the emotional current take them off course. She felt they needed to celebrate what had been accomplished and not let their worries about the future cloud the fact that a white man had done something nigh on impossible for them. After years of living with William Kirkland's broken promises, Momma Celia was deeply moved by what Elijah had done. No other white man she'd ever known or even heard of had done as much. She was not about to let anyone underestimate the importance of that. Her natural caution worried that leaving everything to the executor might result in the executor walking off with a share of the goods, but Elijah seemed to trust the lawyers, and that was enough for her. For the moment, at least, that was all that mattered in the larger light of immanent freedom.

"Well Elijah honey, you done somethin I never woulda believed possible, an I wants to thank ya for it with all my heart! I done fixed ya yo fav'rite foods to celebrate!" She grinned at her son-in-law with genuine affection and respect. "Come on now children, hep me get all this good food on the table. Girls, get ya little brother out from unner the table and make yasevs useful!

There was a general commotion caused by chairs being pushed back from the table, people getting up and moving around, orders being given, and a flurry of activity in response to Momma Celia's initiative. It broke the tension that had been slowly mounting as each pondered the implications of the document still lying spread out on the table. Elijah picked up the will, carefully folded it, put it back in its envelope, and tucked it away inside his breast pocket.

Gilbert gave his brother-in-law a hug in thanks for his efforts, excused himself, and went out the back door toward the slave quarters, brooding on what might be coming down next. He had mixed feelings. On the one hand, like everyone else, he was grateful for what Elijah had done and impressed that it had finally been accomplished. On the other hand, he couldn't shake the distinct feeling of foreboding that his own fate might not be as happy as his sister's. He was also worried about what might happen when the other slaves found out they were not all going to be set free.

LXXVII

That night, Amy wasn't sure whether to be mad or glad. Of course, she was thrilled Elijah had finally succeeded in going up to Cincinnati and writing a new will. She prayed fervently that it would not only pass probate in Ohio but be recognized in South Carolina as well. If it was, then the rest of her concerns could be easily resolved, as, even if Elijah did not survive, the executor, or she and the children would be able to free as many other slaves as possible.

But that was the problem: determining how many that would be, or even could be. After the yellow fever took Gilbert's wife and three other slaves, Elijah still had fifty slaves in his possession, including his immediate family. That meant they had to find a way to emancipate another forty-one slaves counting Gilbert and his children, even once she and the children and Momma Celia were safely in Ohio!

Amy had come around to accept the reality that even Henry Clay had pointed out in his letter to Elijah a few years back: merely freeing the rest of the slaves was not enough. If they could not also be provided for to at least give them a fair start at independence, they could end up far worse off than they were now. If the plantation could be sold outright, and soon, it could bring a good price, but if it lay fallow too long, if something happened to Elijah and the cotton didn't get planted or harvested, or the lumber didn't get cut and milled, the value of his assets would drop and there would simply not be enough to support them all! Much as it grieved her, she faced the fact that Elijah would have to sell off a third to a half of the slaves in order for the rest to be duly provided for.

"Sugar," she said, once she and Elijah were finally alone and the children had gone to bed, "it's an amazin thing you've done, gettin that will written." She wanted to acknowledge Elijah's accomplishment, even if it fell short of her dream. "An I realize it musta been hard for you to make the decision that ya might not be able to fulfill your promise to free all the slaves on this plantation, after all."

Elijah had been dreading this conversation, but knew there was no way he could avoid it any longer.

"God forgive me, darlin, I know I said I wanted to free them all, but I just don't see how it's gonna be possible!" He had deliberately worded the will in such a way that it would be at the discretion of the executor how many of the slaves got freed, but they both knew that discretion would be influenced by how many slaves he had at the time of his demise. In any event, he still had the option of selling some of them before they even went up to Ohio.

"I tried to make it so everyone in my possession at the time of my death could be free, but the truth is, everyone might not be all the slaves living here now. If the goal is not only to free em but set em up with enough so they each have a fair shot at makin it on their own, the fewer slaves I have when I die, the better the chances will be for the ones I free!"

He looked at Amy with an expression of profound melancholoy, desperately hoping she would understand and not merely explode at the violation of their former plan. "I wanna do right by as many as I can, sugar, but the truth is, when push comes to shove, I care more about you and Momma Celia and the children, than about any of the others! If I have to choose between ya'll's well-bein and everyone else's, there's no contest!"

Amy heard his sincerity and couldn't be angry with him for what was a cold logistical and financial reality, much as she hated to have to accept it.

"So what do ya think we should do? Sell off some of em now before we go to Ohio?" she asked. "Or should we wait and you sell some of em when ya come back down here to sell the property and bring Gilbert and the children back up to Cincinnati with ya?"

Elijah sighed deeply. "Well now, I think we need to pray about this some, before we decide. On the one hand, if I sell some of em now, it gives us more cash to work with to get you and the children and your Momma set up right away." Amy could see the benefit to that, much has she regretted having to sell any of them.

"On the other hand," he continued, "havin to tell the rest of the slaves that not all of em are gonna be freed could trigger an uproar that not only affects folks on this plantation, but could spread throughout the other plantations and cause us a whole heap a trouble gettin outa here. I'm just not sure how to go on this, an it's been keepin me up nights!"

"If ya had to do it, who would ya sell off?" Amy couldn't help but ask, pointing out the elelphant in the room that nobody wanted to aknowledge. "What would ya use to decide?"

"Well," Elijah answered slowly, "I've given a lot a thought to that question, and here's my thinkin on it at the moment. There's more'n a few who've got family livin on neighborin plantations. I think I'd try an see if I could manage to sell em to the planters who've already got other family members, so's they'd at least not be alone or feel abandoned." This made sense to Amy, but she did the calculations, and the numbers of slaves with neighboring families didn't add up to enough to solve the financial and logisitical problem they were facing. Elijah, of course, had come up with the same calculus long since.

"And what about the others?" Amy asked, "You'd have to sell more'n the ones with nearby families to make the figures work out, wouldn't ya?"

Elijah nodded soberly, grateful that her business head had already seen the inevitable without him having to spell it out to her. "Well, with Gilbert's and Julius' and Jason's help, I could figure out who the others should be."

He still hadn't really owned up to the possibility that it was tempting to sell the orney and less cooperative slaves almost as a punishment for their behavior, and try and support the ones who had been most hard working. Problem was, some of the hardest workers also complained the loudest!

"Ya'll got any suggestions?" he implored her.

"I dunno, honey. I been thinkin about it too- I thought of usin years of service, attitude, relations, age, probable market value... any number of factors, but what I still come up with every time is that I feel like we're breakin a promise!"

Elijah nodded grimly. "I know. I do too. But no matter how I slice it, it's clear to me that some will have to be sold, either before we head up to Cincinnati, or right after. And the reality is, if anything should happen to me on the way, after might be too late."

There, he had said it. He didn't want to, but he had to, for he knew his heart was like a bomb waiting to go off, and he no longer felt convinced that he could handle the strains they were facing without it having a deadly effect. He knew he was in a race against time, even if he couldn't bring himself to share that conviction with Amy explicitly. He knew she feared it too- it was the unnamed menace threatening the fulfillment of their dreams.

Amy sat there by his side in their bed, pondering the complexities of the decisions facing them. After a long silence she sighed and said, "I think ya should sell em soon!" She lifted a lace edged handkerchief to dab away the tears welling up in her eyes, but her voice was steady and calm, her resolve apparent.

Elijah looked at her with surprise and admiration. He knew how much it hurt for her to have to accept this reality, and how much she had cherished the dream of freeing everyone on the plantation- how hard she had fought for it! He had expected her to pitch a fit and berate him for selling out on the promise, but once again he had underestimated her. She was of stronger stuff than even he had imagined, and that was saying a lot. He put his arm around her and held her to him in silent communion, each by now understanding the other, with no need for more words.

"How do you reckon I should let em know?" he asked, the question searing through their silence. It was, of course, what they both dreaded most.

After a thoughtful pause, Amy responded, "I think ya'll need to get clear how many and which ones ya'll're gonna sell and then start askin around for buyers. Not likely any one will buy em all- and maybe they'll have to be taken outa Barnwell District to one of the slave markets – up in Columbia or over in Charleston perhaps. But if there's any with family near and the family's owner is willin and doesn't have a reputation for bein mean, I think ya'll oughta try your best to sell em to him, or at least settle em somewhere nearby so they won't be too unhappy." She paused, "And don't tell em anything til you got a plan worked out!" she added with conviction.

As ever, Amy's quiet common sense, logic and fairness hit home. It didn't mean it was going to be any easier making the choices, but at least it began to feel like as workable and humane a plan as it could be, under the circumstances.

The next morning after breakfast, Elijah sent Elder to go fetch Gilbert, Julius and Jason to meet him in the barn. He wanted to talk to the three of them together and put it to them straight so there'd be no misunderstandings. He was going to need their full cooperation if this was going to work without causing a whole lot of upset on the plantation or beyond.

The three men came into the barn together. It was clear they were all sensing something of major importance was afoot, but Elijah couldn't tell whether it was because Gilbert had tipped them off, or whether it was just the natural consequence of them being aware he'd been to Cincinnati and back. Not that it really mattered.

"Well boys, I guess ya'll realize I finally made it up to Cincinnati to write a new will. I need to explain the situation to ya to make sure ya'll understand, cause folks'll be askin all kinds of questions, and ya'll need to be prepared to answer em honestly, straight from the horse's mouth."

The three men nodded to Elijah, as if to say, "Go on..." They were not letting Elijah off the hook easily, and there was nothing for it but for him to plow on into the heart of the matter.

"For years now it's been my dream, and Amy's dream, that I could find a way to free every slave on this plantation. Much as it kills me to admit it, I've looked at the matter from every angle, talked it over with several lawyers, and no matter how I calculate it, it doesn't look like that's gonna be possible."

The news, though unwelcome, was not unexpected. The three remained silent, looking to Elijah for a fuller explanation before they dared speak. Jason and Julius were hoping they were not among those to be sold, feeling fairly certain their loyalty to Elijah would not be so unfairly paid, but as life-long slaves, they knew only too well that there were no guarantees of benevolence when the fundamental nature of their relationship to Elijah was inherently unequal, no matter how well they had served him and he had treated them. They shifted their weight from one foot to another, nervously.

Elijah continued, "I promise ya, the three of ya and ya'll's families are in no danger! I have written my will in such a way that, should I not be able to bring ya'll up to Ohio myself, my executor will, and ya'll'll be free. God willin, ya'll'll also get at least a little something in the way of money or property to help ya get a start in lives of your own. I owe ya'll that!" he said with utter sincerity, knowing full well these three had contributed more than anyone else to his ongoing prosperity through their faithful and skillful service.

"But here's the hard part. I'm gonna need ya'll to help me figure out which slaves to sell, and even more, I'll need ya'll's help to make sure things don't get outa hand when they find out. After all these years a thinkin they'd all be freed, it's gonna come as a mighty big disappointment when they find out that's not gonna be the case." Elijah was a realist and had enough empathy to guess rightly that there were some who would be furious and feel they'd been betrayed. There was no telling what they might do and what their reaction might do to the plantation community as a whole, but it wasn't likely to be pleasant.

"How soon ya figure on doin this Elijah?" Gilbert asked pointedly.

"Soon as I can, I suppose. Amy says I should first figure out whether there's any in particular who want or need to stay in this area because of relations on neighborin plantations. Hell, I don't wanna just uproot folks and ship em off, if I can help it!" There was an almost pleading desperation in his voice. "But even figurin some may have relations close by and wanna stay in the area, that don't add up to enough to make it possible for me to free all the others and provide somethin for em."

Julius had a clear idea of which slaves were trustworthy and loyal and which were not. "Mister Elijah?" he asked, "D'ya'll wanna sell the ones who'll get the best price, or you just needin to get rid of some of us to make the figures work out? Cause that might hep us decide who goes, an who stays."

Jason chimed in, "Or do ya'll wanna keep the ones most loyal to ya and sell the rest?" Both men had instantly voiced the most pertinent questions framing the decision that needed to be made. Gilbert, however, said nothing. He was so conflicted from what he had discovered in the past twenty-four hours that he could find nothing more to contribute for the moment.

Elijah sat in silence, perched on a bale of straw. He found himself absent-mindedly kicking a sheaf off a nearby opened bale as he pondered both men's questions. The sweet smell of the straw wafted up from his boot and the barn floor, as if released by the blow that severed its bondage to the bale. It struck him suddenly as an eloquent metaphor for the blows they each were facing: some would feel the sweet smell of freedom, others would feel stomped on like the straw at his feet.

"Ya'll got any recommendations?" he asked almost listlessly, unable to see a clear solution and sensing that any choice he might make was bound to cause someone pain. In his heart, though he knew there were some malcontents on the plantation, he couldn't bring himself to feel any of them deserved to feel stomped upon or remain in bondage forever. How in Hell was he supposed to decide?

Julius spoke again, "Well sir, since no man deserves slavery, ya'll can't decide based on who oughta stay in bondage just b'cause a some bad feelin twixt you an them. An it ain't fair that some get freed an others don't, so fairness don't work as a measure either."

Elijah was all ears, for Julius was expressing his very dilemma, and he was eager to find out where he would go with this line of thinking.

"So seems to me, ya'll ain't got too many choices: Ya gotta figure which ones got the most life left in em, and then decide do ya figure the ones with the least should taste freedom first, or just finish out they days in slavery countin on freedom's reward in heaven? Or should the ones with the most life ahead of em deserve the chance to change they lives and be freed now, or is they better equipped than the others to hold on a little longer, in the hopes that slavery itself'll end some day soon!"

Elijah looked from one to the other, but none of the three men seemed to know the right answer to these questions. He shook his head in despair. "I believe ya'll've hit the nail on the head there Julius, but as God is my witness, I just don't know the answer yet! I'm gonna have to think and pray on this a spell. In the meantime, I know it won't be easy, but don't ya'll tell the others anything about this until I tell ya. It'd be best to have a clear plan in place first, so things don't get outa control when the time comes."

"Yessir," mumbled Jason and Julius quietly. Gilbert simply looked at Elijah poignantly, his lips pursed in thought.

Elijah spoke again. "So for now, as far as any of ya'll're concerned, life on the plantation goes on as usual. It's time to get set for the Spring plowin and plantin. We may be able to bring in one more crop, to help fill the coffers before all this gets done! If cotton prices stay high that could mean freein a few more slaves, so get to it boys!"

Without waiting for their response, Elijah stood up and headed on back to the house, brooding on how he was ever going to be able to make this awful choice. It occurred to him that maybe he should have a talk with Angus Patterson to get his advice. Angus always had a way of seeing through complex situations toward a good solution. Besides, he wanted to let him know the details about the new will and how much the lawyers John Bauskett had recommended had helped him out anyway. A nice visit with his old friend was long overdue, and might be just the thing to help him sort all this mess out.

LXXVIII

Mary came tottering down the hall carrying a tray with Angus Senior's coffee and some biscuits, hoping she could get him to take a little something. He had hardly wanted to eat for days, and despite the fact that he'd pretty much been holding his own for months with no change, Mary was worried sick he was just plain worn out and giving up on life. The cup and saucer rattled and clinked with every arthritic step, and the coffee pot threatened to splash out onto the tray and stain the white linen napkin she had carefully folded by the saucer, but by sheer dint of determination she made it to the parlor, and set the tray down carefully on the table by the old man's armchair.

He had nodded off waiting for her, his head bowed toward his chest, and a peaceful smile on his face. He'd been sleeping a lot these days. The flickering of the firelight played across his features, gilding them softly. The red plaid afghan she had wrapped around his shoulders to keep off the early spring chill dwarfed him, making him appear almost like a little child bundled up by the fireplace. He looked so cozy and peaceful, she hated to have to wake him, but she felt he really needed to eat something, even if it was only a biscuit.

"Mister Angus? Mister Angus? I done brought ya some a that coffee ya'll like so much, and some a my nice fresh buttermilk biscuits! Come on now Mister Angus, wake up for me. Ya"ll're worryin me, not eatin. It ain't like you! Ya always loved my cookin. Don't ya be makin me feel bad that I can't get ya'll to eat, now!" Mary shook the old man's shoulder gently to nudge him awake, but he slumped over, unresponsive. Mary looked closer and realized he wasn't breathing. The reality hit her that, ever so quietly, ever so peacefully, he had gone to his Maker at last.

"Aw now, Mister Angus, why you go an leave without me?" she said plaintively. "I done tole ya I'd take care of ya, even up in heaven!" she moaned, her voice cracking with emotion. She stroked the old man's head as she spoke, as if comforting a child. Her eyes filled with tears and, as the reality fully hit her, her gentle moan built up to a full throated wail of grief that wracked her frail old body with uncontrollable sobs like a winter wind rattling the shutters.

Angus Junior had just come home, having been visiting with James and Michael. Coming in through the kitchen door with a slight stagger after putting his horse in the stable out back, he was alarmed to hear Mary's wail. He shook off the whiskey haze enshrouding his head from his comraderie with the Willis brothers, forced himself to fight though his sluggishness, and came running to the parlor. Somewhere underneath his alcohol induced lassitude, his mind recognized there was only one thing in this world likely to be able to make Mary let out such a heart-wrenching wail.

He ran from the back of the house and stopped, panting in the doorway to the parlor, his befuddled mind struggling to take in the details uncomprehendingly. The cozy fire and inviting tray of goodies stood in sharp contradiction to the image of his father's crumpled body slumping sideways in his favorite chair, Mary's grief-stricken face, wet with tears, and the sound of her discordant sobs interspersed with the cheerful crackling of the fire. It all just seemed wrong.

"Pa!" he shouted, sudden panic driving him to his father's side. He grabbed his father's aged face in his hands, shaking and patting it helplessly, trying to revive him. He looked desperately at Mary, who's rheumey eyes stared back with unbounded pain and love, and simply shook her head as if to say, "It's too late, child, he's gone."

Gently leaning his father back in his chair, Angus instinctively reached out to Mary as he had when he was a little boy, desperately needing the one source of comfort that had been there for him throughout his life, yet knowing that not even her love could make this pain go away. His mind was numb, first from whiskey, then from shock. He found it an effort to even think. His hot tears, rather than sliding docilely down his cheeks, seemed to jump horizontally out of his eyes in eloquent testimony to the raging sorrow and loss he was feeling, but he made not a sound as he wept fiercely, all his love and all his frustration simply boiling over and spurting out of him.

Mary finally composed, disentangled herself from his tight embrace, stood up, sighed deeply and said, "It ain't seemly lettin him sit here all slumped over like this. Ya'll need to lay him out proper in his bed til the unnertaker come to fetch him."

With the calm of her voice some semblance of order was reappearing, cutting through the chaos in Angus Junior's head. It was comforting to have something concrete to do, so he obediently picked his father up and started toward the stairway to carry him up to his bed. It struck him as odd that his father, who had been such a towering presence in his life and in this house, should feel so light. He noted with a mixture of detatched interest and mild surprise, that his father's body was nothing but skin and bones, weighing no more than a hundred pound sack of chicken feed.

His perceptions took on a dreamlike quality, as if everything were in slow motion but somehow more intense, every image clearer, every sound more acute than usual. No sooner had he stretched his father out on his bed, carefully and gently crossing his palms on his chest and smoothing back his rumpled hair, than he heard a knock at the front door, and after a moment the shuffling steps of Mary dutifully going to answer it.

The unexpected sound of Elijah Willis' voice shook him out of his stupor. He heard heard Mary mumbling softly, a new wave of sobs overcoming her and shaking her tenuous composure, and he heard Elijah say with a stunned voice, "Oh my Sweet Lord, no!"

Angus managed to pull himself together and head downstairs to receive Elijah. He realized he had not come to offer condolences, but on some other mission. Ordinarily, that would have raised suspicions and provoked in him an eager curiosity, but it didn't seem to matter any more. The fact was, politics and racial attitudes aside, he knew his Pa had been very fond of Elijah, and Elijah fond of his Pa, so out of respect he had to come down and greet their visitor.

As Angus Junior came downstairs, Elijah looked up at him with disarming affection and empathy. Moving forward to greet him as he reached the bottom stair, Elijah spontaneously gave the young man a fatherly hug and said, "I can't tell ya how deeply sorry I am for your loss, Angus! I had just stopped by to pay him a little visit and cheer him up a bit, thinkin it musta been a long Winter for him, but Spring is on its way...." His voice trailed off, thickening as it went.

Angus forced himself to smile, wanting to be gracious, and replied, "I surely do appreciate that, Mr. Willis, and I'm sure Pa would have too!" His voice choked on the past tense, however, causing conversation to grind to a halt for an awkward moment. Mary continued to sniffle sympathetically in the background.

"I hope you won't think this intrusive but, may I see him please? I'd like to pay my respects." Elijah asked throatily.

"Well, uh, yes, of course sir. He's right upstairs. I just laid him out on his bed." Angus answered. "Mary, can ya'll show Mr. Willis upstairs, please? I'm just gonna slip out for a minute to let the undertaker know we'll be needin his services."

Elijah thought it odd Angus Junior would be so eager to get out of the house- especially to go get the undertaker, but he realized everybody dealt with grief in their own time and way, and maybe that was just Angus' way.

"Take your time, son, and if there's anything I can do to help, you just let me know. There isn't anything I wouldn't do for your father," Elijah commented.

Angus Junior nodded his thanks, recognizing Elijah's sincerity.

Elijah added, as Angus turned to leave, "Tell the undertaker I have some real fine black walnut over at the mill I've been savin. Got beautiful grain. I'd like to offer it for his coffin. He deserves somethin special, somethin better'n pine. I'll have one a my men bring it over straight away."

Angus managed to mutter an awkward, "Thank ya sir, that'd be real nice. I'll surely tell him," before choking up again and feeling impelled to leave, lest he make an unmanly spectacle of himself before his guest.

As Angus rushed out the front door to fetch the coroner and the undertaker, Mary looked after him and said, "He hurtin mighty bad, Mister Elijah, cause he never got to tell his Pa he's sorry."

"Sorry for what, Mary?" Elijah asked.

"For that rally he an ya'll's nephews put together with ole Dr. Guignard and that fool Robert Barnwell Rhett- like about to broke his Pa's heart to see his own son take a stand against freein folks from sufferin." She sighed, "But the boy's as pig-headed as his Pa and couldn't bring himself to ask forgiveness, even though he knew he done wrong, cause he liked folks clappin for him and makin him feel important. Sad thing is, he never realized how important he was to his Pa." Mary shook her head woefully.

Elijah suddenly became worried for Mary, not sure what arrangement Angus had made for her or whether the younger Patterson could be counted on to provide for her, given his political posturing.

"What about you, Mary? You gonna be alright?" he asked.

Mary wiped her tears away with the back of her had and sniffled, "Oh, don't ya'll worry none bout me, Mister Elijah; I'll be fine. Sides, I don't spect it'll be too long b'fo I'll be seein Mister Angus again, like I promised him! I done tole him I'd take care of him, even up in heaven!" The old woman smiled as if this were a simple statement of fact beyond question, or, as Angus would say, "beyond a reasonable doubt!"

Elijah went on upstairs to say his goodbyes to his old friend and counselor, insisting that Mary not strain herself climbing up all those stairs with him. "No need, Mary, I know the way. I'd just like a moment with him alone. I won't be long. Thank ya, anyway."

Mary acquiesced willingly, never eager to climb the stairs, even on a good day. "Yessir, Mister Elijah, ya'll take whatever time ya need. I ain't goin nowhere. I think I'll just set me down by the fire a spell til young Angus come home." She hobbled back into to parlor, straightening up Angus' chair, reverently folding the afghan that had fallen off his shoulders as his son had lifted the body to take it upstairs. She placed the afghan on the back of the chair, patting it gently, as if to reassure it that it was in its proper place, and then sat down on the settee facing it, as though she were having a private chat with the invisible spirit of her liberator and dearest friend.

The late afternoon sun broke through the scattered slate grey clouds of winter's end, and a beam of golden light shone through the window, falling on Angus' face as Elijah entered the bedroom upstairs. It warmed death's pallor just enough to make the old man appear as if he were alive for a moment, and merely napping peacefully, waiting for Elijah to visit.

Elijah pulled up a side chair and sat by the bed. A stream of memories - of countless conversations, of food and drink and laughter exchanged between them over the years- flooded his mind. As he reached out to pat his old friend's hand, his eye caught a glimpse of an open book on the nightstand. It was a law book, and on its open page was a folded sheet of paper with some notes scribbled on it in a spidery hand he knew must have been Angus'.

Drawn by curiosity to take a look, he realized the book was open to a section on manumission and inheritance law. He picked up the sheet of paper and examined it. The outside had some illegible phrases that looked like chicken scratchings, but as he unfolded the paper he saw written clearly, if shakily, "The whole case will hang on proving Amy and the children are free in Ohio." There were a few other cryptic remarks about inheritance law, with what Elijah could only assume were case law references, "Act of 1841," "*Frazier vs. Executors of Frazier*," and "*ut res magis quam pereat*," whatever that meant. It was clear that Angus had been thinking about Elijah's case, right up to the very end. He was deeply moved by that.

Elijah turned toward the body of his friend, still lying with the peaceful smile on his face as if to say, "Go on my friend, that paper's for you!" Though he felt a little uncomfortable just taking it, he also had a pang of anxiety about Angus Junior finding and reading it, prompting him to quickly overcome his discomfort. He refolded the paper and carefully tucked it away in his inside breast pocket. He decided he'd let Mary know before he left, to ease his conscience. Then it dawned on him that he should show this to John Bauskett and see if John could help him decipher it. It might provide him some additional useful insights into what they were facing.

"God bless ya, Angus! You always were a true friend, right to the very end!" Elijah patted his advocate's cold, lifeless hand in farewell. As he came back downstairs, he could hear Mary talking softly in the parlor. When he got to the bottom of the stairs, he looked through the parlor door to find her sitting there alone, facing Angus' chair and speaking her heart to the old man's spirit.

Not wanting to simply leave unannounced, but feeling awkward about interrupting her colloquy, Elijah stood in the door and cleared his throat softly. Mary turned, as if awakening from a dream. She stood up painfully, her joints aching more than her heart for the moment, and slowly came out to the foyer with a serene look on her face. She looked up at Elijah and smiled sweetly.

"He done lived a good life, hepped a whole lotta people, and died a good death, Mister Elijah. He done tole me his soul's at peace. Can't nobody ask for more'n that!" It was not clear whether she meant that this assurance from Angus had come before or after his bodily death. She sighed slightly, and added without uncertainty or remorse, "I sho gonna miss him, but if he at peace, then so am I. It's only young Angus I's worried bout now."

Elijah was worried about the younger Angus too, though for somewhat different reasons. "Well Mary, if there's anything I can do to help, ya'll just let me know," he responded.

Mary nodded. "Mister Angus ain't been much of a church goin man these last years, but I know he set store by the 'Piscopal Church in his younger days. Do ya'll think you could call on the Reverend over there in Barnwell an ask if he could come for a burial service? Mister Angus tole me he wanted to be buried 'Piscopal style."

Elijah didn't much care for the Vicar of Barnwell, but he promised Mary he would be willing to ride over there and speak to the Reverend Mr. Wagner about it if need be. However, he didn't want to seem like he was taking over for Angus Junior, and thought it would be best if Angus were consulted on the matter first.

"You probly right bout that, Mister Elijah, but knowing Angus like I do, I worry he might just run off drinkin with his friends to drown his sorrows, an not take care a his responsibilities! He kinda unpredictable these days, like he fightin a demon in his heart. One day he be all kind an good, next day he be angry, and bitter, and downright mean!"

Elijah nodded, understanding. "Well, now that you mention it Mary, I have a confession to make," he told her. "I found a piece of paper by Mister Angus' bed upstairs- it was lying on an open page of a law book, and it had some notes on it about my Amy and our children. I thought it best to take the paper before it fell into young Angus' hands, not knowin what he might make of it, and wantin to avoid any more trouble. I hope ya'll don't mind?"

"Lawd ha mercy, Mister Elijah! It's a good thing ya'll found it! Mister Angus tole me he was tryin to hep ya'll, and young Angus kept pryin around to see what he was up to. Mister Angus was always mighty careful not to let the boy see his papers, but these last few days I reckon he was fixin to leave an got a little careless. Musta forgot!" Mary admitted. Elijah remembered his own mistake in leaving the letter from Henry Clay, and could only hope that the younger Patterson had not stumbled across his father's notes.

Realizing that Elijah was worried that the Angus Junior might already have seen the paper, Mary quickly added, "But the boy ain't been in his Pa's room for days- I think he been scared he might come in an find him dead, so he just avoided it altogether! You take that paper, Mister Elijah, and the Good Lord willin, Mister Angus' notes will hep ya'll keep safe, and make Miss Amy an Miss Celia an the children free! He'd be right pleased if it did! An so would I," she added with a wistful smile.

Elijah thanked her and, as Angus Junior still hadn't returned with the coroner or the undertaker, he decided he'd head on out, and at least see to it the black walnut planks he'd been saving at the mill got sent over to the undertaker for Angus' coffin.

"Tell young Angus that I'll help with the funeral arrangements or anything else he might need. He can just drop by any time, and I'll be happy to help." He headed toward the door, and turning, added, "I'm gonna head on home now, and send over that wood to the undertaker. So when he comes to fetch the body and measure Mister Angus up for the coffin, you tell him I got something special on the way to send Angus off in style!"

"I sho will, Mister Elijah, an I thanks ya for all ya done. Fact is, I truly b'lieve hepping ya'll added a couple a years to Mister Angus' life, it give him so much joy! He'd almost given up when young Angus' momma died, but ya'll brought him back to life an give him a good reason for livin! The man always loved a challenge for a good cause!" She smiled at Elijah, both with the fond memory of Angus' generosity and enthusiasm for the case, and in genuine affection and admiration for Elijah and his daring plan. "God bless ya, Mister Elijah, God bless all of ya'll." Mary grinned her infectious grin as she let Elijah out the front door, banishing the gloom of death and sorrow for the moment at least.

LXXIX

Elijah wasn't certain whether it would be better to speak to John Bauskett or the Reverend Mr. Wagner first, but he figured he shouldn't wait to get over to Barnwell, in any case. Assuming the undertaker came quickly, he imagined Angus Junior would be expecting a burial to take place soon, before his father's body could decay, as ice was relatively scarce for keeping a body for long. The Reverend would need to be notified promptly. But he was equally eager to get John Bauskett's interpretation of Angus' notes, hoping they would at least confirm the action he had taken in Ohio, and perhaps provide some additional insight he might constructively pass on to Messrs. Gitchell and Jolliffe for future reference.

He rode home quickly, spurring Beauty into a steady canter, to tell Gilbert to take the walnut over to the undertaker and to give Amy the news before heading on over to Barnwell. Since he had set up an expectation that Angus Junior would be consulted at least by Mary before any action was officially taken with the Reverend Mr. Wagner, Elijah decided to go first to visit John Bauskett and then perhaps stop by to pay the Vicar a courtesy visit on the way home, to simply alert him that his services would be needed by the Patterson family.

Amy was upstairs changing the baby when she heard the steady pounding of hoof beats approaching the house, followed by a quick dismount. The sound of rapid, purposeful footsteps crossing over the brickwork of the veranda toward the front door signaled some matter of urgency. Uncertain whether it was Elijah, Amy at least realized that something was provoking the rider to move more quickly than usual. She rushed downstairs to see what was the matter, reaching the bottom of the stairs just as Elijah burst through the front door and started to call for her.

"Amy, darlin! I have some sad news- Angus Patterson Senior just passed away! I went over to pay him a visit, to tell him about the will and ask his help on figuring out the issue with the rest of the slaves, and he had just passed minutes before I got there!" he told her somewhat breathlessly.

"Aw Elijah honey I am so sorry!" she said. "I know how much he meant to ya!" She gave Elijah a comforting hug. She knew he had been counting on Angus to be able to guide him in sorting out the sale of his property and the resolution of the dilemma with the other slaves. The news left her speechless with loss and anxious about their unresolved issues.

"But the amazin thing is," continued Elijah, "seems old Angus had been thinkin about us right up to the very end! When I went up to his bedroom to pay my respects, I found this on his bedside table." He reached into his breast pocket and pulled out the folded sheet of paper he had found. Gently unfolding it, he thrust the paper toward her to read. "Take a look at this!" As she scanned the sheet quickly, he added, "I'm gonna take it over to John Bauskett and see what he makes of it, but I suspect there're some useful bits of information here that might help the lawyers up in Ohio when the time comes!"

Amy scanned the sheet of paper, but other than the sentence referring to proving they were free, couldn't make much sense out of the old man's scribblings. "I think you're right to take it over to Mr. Bauskett, honey. Especially now with Mr. Patterson gone, he's our only local source of reliable legal advice!"

Momma Celia, sensing something was going on and overhearing snatches of the conversation ehoing down the hall, came to the foyer from out back in the kitchen. "Did I hear ya'll say ole man Patterson passed?" she asked Elijah.

"Yes Momma, he did." Elijah answered.

"May he rest in peace, God bless him!" she prayed. "Poor Mary! How's she takin it?" Momma Celia asked. She had known Mary since they were both children, though Mary was older. "She thought the world a Mister Angus. I imagine that even though she's free, she'll stay in that house til the day she dies, just to feel like she's near him. Sides, she bout raised Angus Junior. Maybe if he'll let her stay, she can keep him from goin overboard with all his political foolishness!"

"Well I figure you're right on the first point, but I wouldn't count on the second if I were you. Much as I hate to say it, I'm inclined to think that with his Pa gone it won't be Angus Junior's better side that takes over, especially if he keeps hangin round with my nephews!"

Momma Celia shook her head and muttered, "Mmmmm, mmm, hmmm. Them boys is up to no good, that's fa sho!" She thought for a moment and then said, as if to herself, "I think I'll send a basket a food over so's Mary don't have to cook jus yet. She'n Angus Junior needs to eat while they goin through they loss, but that don't mean Mary gotta cook it!" She headed on back toward the kitchen, lost in thought about her friend.

Elijah called after her, "Momma! I'm sending Gilbert to take some walnut wood over to the undertaker for Angus' coffin. If ya'll can get the basket together quickly, ya'll can go with him and drop it off on your way!"

Momma Celia stopped and looked back at her son-in-law. It wasn't often a white man recognized a colored person's loss like that. She smiled gratefully, "That'd be real nice, sugar. I got plenty a food ready now- won't take but a minute!" She rushed off to the kitchen to put together a basket of goodies for her friend.

Amy looked at Elijah too, touched by his solicitude. "Thank ya for that honey, that was real sweet of ya. Momma and Mary go back a long way. Means a lot to her to be able to help out at a time like this." She gave him a kiss and then said, "You'd best go find Gilbert and tell him to pick Momma up in the wagon before he heads over to the mill."

With that, she handed him the sheet of Angus' notes. Elijah carefully folded it and placed it back in his breast pocket.

"Don't know how long I'll be, darlin. I promised Mary I'd stop by the Reverend Wagner's too, to let him know that Angus wanted an Episcopal burial- so I may be a while. Just ask Momma to save me a plate, and I'll eat when I get home." With that he gave her a kiss on the cheek, handed her a couple of neck permits for Momma Celia and Gilbert to wear just in case, and went out the front door, mounted Beauty, and rode around to the back of the house toward the barn to look for Gilbert before heading over to Barnwell.

It was nearly twilight by the time Elijah knocked on John Bauskett's front door. It being an unsual hour for unannounced visitors, both Eugenia and John Bauskett entered the foyer to see who could be knocking as the housekeeper opened the door.

Elijah took off his hat and nodded toward John and his wife, "John, Eugenia, sorry to trouble ya'll at such an hour, I hope I'm not interruptin your supper or anything, but I wanted to bring ya'll the news that Angus Patterson passed away this afternoon."

Eugenia's hand shot upward to cover he mouth in shock and sorrow. John seemed far less surprised. He nodded and let out a deep sigh. "Well, Lord knows it's been a long time comin. May he rest in peace!"

After a respectful pause, Elijah asked, "John, uh, could I have a quick word with you in private? I won't keep ya but a moment, I promise - I need to get on over to the Reverned Mr. Wagner's before I go home."

"Of course Elijah, come on into the parlor." He turned to his wife saying, "Eugenia honey, why don't ya'll go on into the dinin room and serve, and I'll be along directly." Turning to Elijah he added, "Ya sure ya'll won't stay to supper?"

Elijah shook his head, "No thank ya, John. I appreciate it, but I really do need to be gettin on."

Bauskett nodded and ushered his friend into the parlor while the housekeeper and his wife headed toward the dining room.

Once inside and out of earshot of the others, Elijah drew the folded sheet out of his pocket and handed it to John. "Before ya read this I should tell ya first, I made the trip to visit your Messrs. Gitchell and Jolliffe up in Cincinnati and have rewritten my will in such a way that I believe it is guaranteed that Amy and the children will be freed. God willin, whatever other slaves I have at the time of my demise will also be set free, but that's in the hands of the executors."

John Bauskett responded, "I am aware that you went, for I received a letter from the gentlemen of Cincinnati thankin me for referrin you to em. Of course they didn't reveal any information about the contents of your discussions, due to attorney-client privilege. But I assumed you had met with some sort of success at any rate. Congratulations!"

"Thank ya John. I appreciate that, and thank ya for all ya'll's help. Gitchell and Jolliffe made it clear that the highest priority was my family's emancipation, and that by namin executors in Ohio and by technically leavin the estate to them, the family's emancipation could be assured." John nodded with interest. " Moreover," Elijah continued, "they believe the slaves left on the plantation could also be brought up by the executors and emancipated. Once freed, either the family or the executors could then sell the remainin property and distribute the proceeds among the emancipated as I directed."

Elijah could see John was mentally reviewing the legal arguments, uncertain whether Elijah's argument was fool-proof or not. "Sounds promisin, Elijah.

I don't expect you've got it on you right now, but at some point soon, if ya'll don't mind, I'd like to have a look at the wordin of your will."

Elijah readily agreed, and then, stretching out his hand with the piece of paper from Angus' law book, he said, "I found this by Angus' bedside. I wondered if you might take a look and help me decipher it. I have a feelin it may have information that might be important for us when the time comes."

John Bauskett took a quick look, and smiled, as if Angus had just given him a personal message in code. "Tell ya what Elijah, why don't ya'll drop by sometime next week and bring the will with ya. That'll give me time to look into this. You're right though; there's a whole heap of information here. God bless him, Angus was as smart as a fox to the end, and this paper may just make all the difference someday!"

"That'd be fine John, I most certainly will come! And God bless ya! I'd best be off, now. It's gettin late. Please thank Eugenia for me too, and tell her I'm sorry to keep ya from your supper!" With that Elijah excused himself, and as John waved from the front door, he mounted Beauty and headed off in the direction of the Reverend Mr. Wagner's house.

When he got there, he could see through the window that the Vicar and his wife were just getting up from their evening meal. He knocked on the door, and Mrs. Wagner came to answer, a candelabra in her hand. Being a clergyman's wife, she was well accustomed to visitors at all hours of the day or night, reporting some pastoral crisis or other. Her Christian charity forced her to accept such intrusions, but her pinched face and stiff spine gave the impression that they were more wearily tolerated than genuinely welcome.

Elijah took off his hat and stood in the doorway apologetically.

"Why, Mr. Willis! What an unexpected surprise! Please sir, won't you come in? I'm afraid my husband and I have already finished supper, but I could fix you a tray?" Is everything alright?"

"Thank you ma'am! I'm sorry to intrude on ya'll at such a late hour. I won't be keepin ya but a moment, and I won't be needin any food, though I thank ya for your hospitality. I just dropped by quickly to let the Reverend know that Angus Patterson Senior just passed away this afternoon. He died peacefully at home in his favorite armchair, God bless him. His housekeeper Mary wanted your husband to know that Angus asked for an Episcopal burial. I just thought ya'll should know, as his son may be approachin ya'll about it."

Mrs. Wagner called out to her husband, "Edwin, dear! Mr. Willis is here with some sad news!" The Reverend promptly appeared from inside the parlor.

"Well bless me, if it isn't Mr. Willis of Williston! What's this I hear of unhappy news? Eh? Has some tragedy befallen you, sir?"

Elijah tried to hide his wince at the Reverend's British inflections. He found them strangely grating, but chastized himself for being perhaps a bit mean-spirited about it. After all, the man couldn't help the fact that he was born and raised in England!

"Well, not to me directly sir, though I surely do feel the loss. I was tellin your wife I just dropped by to let ya'll know that my good friend Mr. Angus Patterson Senior just passed this afternoon."

"Oh dear me!" said the Reverend. "What a pity! I'm told he was a very fine man and a first rate barrister! Sorry I never had the chance to meet him personally, though of course I did have occasion to meet his son at the rally they held at Dr. Guignard's plantation. (I thought it a good opportunity to meet more of the local gentry, don't you know)?"

"Well yes sir, he was surely a fine lawyer, a good man, and a whole lot more. He was a true friend. In any case, his housekeeper asked me to let you know he wanted an Episcopal service for his burial. I imagine his son will come to discuss the matter with ya, but as I had business here in Barnwell this afternoon I took it upon myself to let ya'll know ahead of time."

"Well, may God bless you sir for your thoughtfulness! Most generous of you. I certainly do appreciate it! Before you go, would you like to join in prayer for your friend?"

The question, though delivered in tones that struck Elijah as pompous, was in fact sincerely intended, and Elijah felt it. Caught off guard, he realized that he had been so consumed with the possible usefulness of Angus' notes, that he had only prayed they might help, but he had not really prayed for the soul of his dear friend. He felt a slight twinge of guilt and remorse as he stood there awkwardly, his hat in his hand, and he simply nodded, his throat contracting as an unexpected wave of emotion washed over him.

He managed to mumble, "That, uh, that would be real nice, sir. I'd like that!"

Not being blessed with the gift of spontaneous prayer, the Reverend Mr. Wagner ushered Elijah into the parlor where he had attended services with the Bausketts and invited Elijah to kneel. In the flickering candlelight of the stoic Mrs. Wagner's candelabra, he picked up his Book of Common

Prayer and opened it to the Office for the Dead, leafing through the pages until he found the appropriate collect:

Nodding to Elijah and his wife to join him, he bowed his head reverently, intoning in that peculiarly quizzical ecclesiastical sing-song so typical of Anglican clergy,

"Let us pray:

O GOD, whose mercies cannot be numbered; Accept our prayers on behalf of the soul of Angus Patterson, thy servant departed, and grant him an entrance into the land of light and joy, in the fellowship of thy saints; through Jesus Christ our Lord."

Elijah and Mrs. Wagner dutifully responded, "Amen."

Elijah waited a moment, head bowed, wondering if the Reverend was going to say anything more, and glancing up, saw that the Vicar seemed to be communing with the Deity in silence. After a brief pause, he opened his eyes and smiled his simpering smile, as if to convey to Elijah that his mission accomplished, there was no more to be done for the moment. Elijah stood up, not feeling that the Reverend Mr. Wagner's invocation had exactly shaken the gates of heaven on behalf of Angus' entrance therein. He concluded that perhaps, given the cleric's limitations, however, less was more, so he decided not to belabor the point, especially since he was well assured that Angus had no real need of the Reverend's intercessions in the first place for him to gain admittance to his final reward.

"I surely do thank you Reverend," he remarked, as his inborn Southern courtesy demanded. "Now, if ya'll don't mind, I'd best be on my way home!" Eager to make his exit, Elijah nodded to Mrs. Wagner, still standing resolutely holding her candelabra, the hot candle wax dripping onto her hands, dutifully and unflinchingly waiting to illuminate her husband's way upstairs to bed.

"Do travel safely, sir!" said the Vicar. "And God bless you for your troubles in giving me the news. Most considerate of you! Eh, what?"

Elijah thought he was making a clean escape, but the Vicar added, "And I do remember your generous offer for lumber for our new church, sir! You'll be dlighted to know the drawings for its construction are finally complete, so, I'm happy to say, we should be able to place the order soon!" The Reverend smiled with what he, no doubt, thought was an ingratiating smile, though it struck Elijah as simply opportunistic, and a bit insensitive-its timing discordant with the somber nature of the reason for his visit.

Elijah simply nodded, and said curtly, "Well, it's hardly the time to be worryin about that right now, but I'll surely do what I can when the time comes."

He hoped this mild rebuke would not be lost on the Reverend, and tipping his hat, did not wait for a response. He nodded again to Mrs. Wagner, and strode across the porch and down the steps to his waiting horse. As he was mounting Beauty, the front door shut. He looked back through the bevelled glass oval window in the front door, and could hear the shrill voice of Mrs. Wagner upbraiding her husband for his insensitive remark about the lumber for the church, as the light of the candelabra flickered its way upstairs and the Reverend's shadow followed. He couldn't help but smile to himself, thinking, "Maybe she's not so bad after all! I reckon I'd have a pinched face and a stiff spine too, if I had to put up with that pompous bastard every day!"

LXXX

The funeral for Angus Patterson drew quite a crowd, for nearly everyone in Barnwell District, and even neighboring areas, had benefitted from either his legal services or his kindness at some point in their lives, whether white or colored. He was well loved and would be truly missed.

Elijah was there, as were Amy, Momma Celia, Gilbert, and their children-though protocol of course demanded that all slaves stand apart from the whites at a discreet distance from the gravesite. Elijah's white relations were all there too, as was Dr. Guignard, Dr. Harley, Will Beazeley, Reason and Ari Wooley, Knotts, and countless other planters and townspeople, their slaves standing respectfully behind them. John and Eugenia Bauskett had also come, for as it turned out, unbeknownst to Elijah, John was the executor of Angus' will, which was to be read to Angus Junior following the burial.

To Angus Junior's credit and Elijah's surprise, Mary alone among all the coloreds stood by the graveside thoughout the ceremony, though Elijah realized it might be as much for Angus' need for comfort as for any sensitivity on his part to Mary's needs, despite her status as a free black.

The Reverend Mr. Wagner did a credible job of officiating, and was surprisingly attentive and sympathetic to those who were clearly aggrieved by Angus' passing. He had even included a full-throated and heart-felt congregational singing of Amazing Grace, the rich harmonies of Negro voices blending with the white warbling of the melody line. It had been a particular request of Angus Senior that hymn be sung, and Elijah felt his throat choke on more than a word or two, remembering their conversation about its origin, years ago.

The Reverend was also quite rightly solicitous of Angus Junior, promising to be available for him should he need help during his period of grief. The poor man even tried to be sympathetic to Mary, though he clearly felt uncomfortable in relating to people of color, unsure of how to express himself. His efforts were pathetically inept. He erroneously assumed, in his patronizing way, that colored peoples' understanding was too limited and childlike for him to speak to them in the same tones he would to the planters and their families.

Mary, seeing through his ineptitude to his fundamentally good intentions, spared him any further discomfort by simply saying, "Thank ya, sir. I surely do appreciate ya'll doin the service for Mister Angus," and she meant it, not because of the excellence of his performance, but rather because she knew it was fulfilling Mister Angus' last wishes.

The Reverend Mr. Wagner smiled gratefully and quickly moved on to speak to the next mourner.

With the help of Momma Celia and Dr. Guignard's Sally, Mary had prepared a feast of their collective specialities for the many guests who came over to the house to pay their respects following the ceremony. (Dr. Guignard had sent Sally over both in sympathy for Angus Junior's loss and in keen awareness that it would be favorably noticed by the other planters and citizens of stature attending the funeral). There were pies, both savory and sweet, cakes, cookies, salads, soups, ham, fried chicken, biscuits, greens, beans, sweet potatoes, rice, corn pone, fricasees and stews- not to mention copius quantities of rum punch, sweet tea, lemonade, and whiskey. Angus would have enjoyed the party, as people reveled in sharing their favorite stories of his legal victories, his humor, and his genuine kind-heartedness.

It gave Mary great satisfaction to see everyone eat and enjoy themselves- a silent testimony to her indomitable service to the man who had been the center of her life for nearly three quarters of a century. Despite her own decrepitude, she somehow found the reserves to keep herself going throughout the preparation and serving, but was bone tired by the time the guests were offering their farewell condolences to Angus on their way out the door.

Angus, feeling intimidated by the challenge of facing all the mourners without losing his composure and mindful he now had a public image to maintain, had kept himself well-plied with liquid courage, being discreetly brought regular refills of his whiskey glass by James and Michael as the day wore on. But he, and even the Willis brothers managed to keep their composure until the end. He was genuinely touched, and a not a little humbled, by the effusive expressions of appreciation for his father coming from people of all types and conditions.

John Bauskett had sent Eugenia on home- the Reverend and Mrs.

Wagner offering to take her in their carriage- so he could stay for the reading of the will. Even the Willis brothers had gone on home at their parents' insistence, out of respect for Angus' privacy. There was no one left but Elijah, whom John had asked to stay, as, to Elijah's surprise, it turned out he had been named as the legatee of a small bequest from Angus' estate and was therefore entitled to be present at the reading of the will.

This fact caught Angus Junior totally by surprise, as his father had never really spoken to him about the contents of his will. Angus had always assumed that the estate would be divided between him and his older sister, who was married and lived with her husband, a wealthy planter, outside of Charlotte, North Carolina. His sister had not come to the funeral, being too far away to get there in time, so it was just Angus Junior, Mary, and Elijah who remained, awaiting the reading.

As expected, John duly informed Angus that he was heir to the house and land his father had owned. A portion of the land was to be sold, and the proceeds sent to his sister in Charlotte, along with her mothers' jewelry, and a few pieces of furniture and silver her father wanted her to have, but the lion's share of the estate went to Angus, as he was single, the only male heir, and in greater need than his affluent sister.

There was also, not surprisingly, a proviso from Angus for Mary- not a bequest, since the law would not permit it, but a moral injunction upon his son:

"Though the viscissitudes of South Carolina jurisprudence no longer permit the bequest of any financial or material legacy by a white person to any persons of color, no matter how deserving, it is my fervent wish and expectation that my son, Angus Patterson Jr., solemnly commit himself to provide for the material well-being of my housekeeper and dear friend Mary to the end of her days, being already freed, in gratitude for her inestimable service both to me and to him, all our lives. Should he fail to do so, may God reward him accordingly!"

Mary's stifled sobs of gratitude could be heard in the background. Angus turned and looked at her, and simply nodded his reassurance, his eyes welling with emotion before turning back with a shudder to the lawyer, so he could finish the reading of the will. Angus did not doubt for a moment that his father's ghost would haunt him for the rest of his life and beyond, if he were to renege on that promise, the fear of which it was obviously Angus Senior's intent to instill in him.

The only surprise in the reading of the will came with the bequest to Elijah, as John Bauskett read out the pertinent clause:

"And finally, to my dear friend Elijah Willis, I bequeath my entire library of law books and papers, save any files of cases of clients still living, which are to be delivered immediately to my executor and legal colleague John Bauskett, who will be their legal custodian in the event that any of said clients should need further legal assistance, thereby preserving intact the confidentiality of attorney-client privilege I have dutifully honored throughout my career. My remaining law books and papers are to be delivered to Mr. Willis promptly upon my death, hoping he may find them useful."

Elijah was dumbfounded. He had no inkling of such a gift being offered him and did not immediately grasp its import. After all, he was no lawyer, and hardly had either the time or the inclination to sit down and work his way through a mountain of legal minutiae, even as a winter pastime when the crops or his lumber business or his family were not demanding his full attention.

Though registering Elijah's surprise at the announcement, Angus was at first baffled by the bequest, then suspicious, then somewhat resentful. All three emotions registered successively on his face, as John Bauskett concluded the reading of the will with an explanation to Angus of his responsibilities as executor. It was his solemn duty to see that, barring any motion by any party having a legitimate claim to any portion of the estate to contest the will, its provisions should be carried out promptly and to the letter. The will therefore would, he assured Angus, be filed for probate as soon a possible so as to expedite its speedy implementation.

John Bauskett added, "Having (at your father's behest) notified your sister of my status as executor of his estate some weeks before his passin, I have already received a letter from her indicatin that she is amenable to whatever her father's wishes were and would under no circumstances contest any provisions of his will." He produced a letter in Angus' sister's hand in evidence, lest there be any doubt of his veracity.

As Angus scanned the letter quickly, handing it back to the attorney with a nod of acknowledgement; the lawyer continued, "Since the bequest to Elijah was of minor significance, relative to the central matters of the distribution of your father's principal assets, and is not contingent upon the payin of any taxes or filin of any documentation with the government, I see no reason why we shouldn't just bring the books out to his carriage right now, and relieve ya'll and myself of the need to worry about it later!" John shot Elijah a quick glance, warning him not to object.

Angus felt oddly pressured by John Bauskett's suggestion, though he wasn't sure why. His mind not being at its sharpest, however, given the considerable strains and consumption of the day, he nodded numbly in agreement. He was too exhausted to object.

Mary had already realized from Elijah's confession about the notes Angus had left in the book by his bed, that there was likely a lot more information in those volumes that Elijah might need in order to secure his family's future. She also recognized, however, that her new benefactor might be reluctant to part with the books, believing that they might somehow be helpful or even necessary in securing his own political future. She felt with urgency that she had only a brief moment of opportunity to prevail upon Angus to deliver them right away, before her own quasi-maternal influence on him could fade like the waning presence of his father or the alcohol in his bloodstream.

"Angus, honey, put ya Pa's soul at peace, and do like Mister John say. It'd make Mister Angus real proud!" She smiled lovingly at the man she had raised from infancy, as she laid her gnarled hand comfortingly on his shoulder. Ever since he was little, Mary's touch had had a calming affect on Angus and in this moment of vulnerability, despite his uneasiness, he simply sighed and said, "Well alright then, let's do it!"

By this point, Elijah had realized there might be more pertinent information for his family's deliverance, either in the texts themselves or hidden between the pages of Angus' books. So trying not to reveal any eagerness to discover what that might be, he and John and Angus Junior set to carrying the tomes out to his carriage as the will directed. John also went through the files Angus had accumulated in and on his desk, making sure especially to remove any papers identifiable as concerning Elijah and his estate. After numerous trips back and forth, they had finally cleaned out much of the desk and cleared the bookshelves of all their occupants of a jurisprudential, rather than a literary nature. Mary was already trying to clean the near empty shelves with a feather duster, sniffling and coughing partly from the dust and partly from the emotion of seeing such a central element of Angus' life removed as tangibly and definitively as his body had been removed from his bed by the undertaker. There was a crushing, somber finality to it all that struck everyone present.

"Well," said John Bauskett to Angus, after a reverential pause, "I believe we've done about enough for one day, don't you? Ya'll must be exhausted, and I think Elijah and I'd best leave ya both to get some rest. I shall go ahead and file the will for probate in the Court of Equity and let ya'll know if there's anything else needed to see it through." He started towards the door and then turned back, adding reassuringly, "Knowin your Pa, however, I expect I'll find everything needed in his files and there shouldn't be any problem getting the will through probate quickly. Ya'll get some rest now and I'll be in touch!"

Angus shook John Bauskett's hand sincerely, "I surely do thank ya, Mister Bauskett, for all ya help. I know Pa trusted ya'll, both as a lawyer and a friend. Now that Pa's gone, I hope I might at least be able to confer with ya from time to time, as my interest in the law has grown these past few years an I'm sure ya'll's advice would be worthwhile?"

John Bauskett looked at young Angus, slightly taken aback by the request. "Well of course ya can call on me any time! I'd be right pleased to help ya, if I can. The least I could do for the son of my old friend!" He looked over Angus' shoulder to Elijah, whose face registered a slight flicker of anxiety at the request, fearful of what kind of legal advice young Angus might be seeking, and suspecting it had more to do with his misguided political agenda than with his father's estate. John nodded almost imperceptibly to Elijah, as if to confirm he sensed the warning.

Before saying his his own good-byes to his friend's son and heir, (and his own potential nemesis), while John Bauskett was saying his final farewell to the younger Mr. Patterson, Elijah offered his condolences once more to Mary.

"God bless ya, Mister Elijah, an please thank Miss Celia for all her hep with the food today. It was real sweet a her to lend a hand like that!" Mary said sincerely, "I know the good Lord provides- waan't for Him I wouldn't still be standin after all we done today- but it touches ma heart that He keeps on providin through folks I've known since I as comin up, like ya'll's Miss Celia, and Miss Sally over Dr. Guignard's. Gives a body faith they's still plenty a goodness in the world, even when things ain't lookin too good!"

"I'll be sure to tell her, Mary. I know she was more'n happy to do it. She thinks mighty highly of ya- and did it as much for you as for Mister Angus!" This last he leaned forward and whispered to her, wanting her to know Momma Celia had not cooked out of obligation to her own master or to Mary's new benefactor, but only out of love for her and her appreciation for Angus Senior's efforts on the family's behalf.

In gratitude Mary flashed him a dazzling smile, wreathed in wrinkles.

Turning to Angus, Elijah said, "Angus I must admit your father's bequest to me came as quite a surprise, but I am deeply touched by it. I just want ya to know that if there's anything I can do for ya'll, please don't hesitate to ask. I'll be more'n glad to help in any way I can." He meant what he said, remembering both Angus Senior's and Mary's hopes that the right influence would bring out the boy's goodness instead of letting his mean-spirited side win him over.

"I truly do thank ya, Mister Willis. Ya'll have been a great help these last few days, callin on the Reverend, and sendin that nice wood for the coffin, and helpin Mary for the reception an all, an I know Pa thought real highly of ya. I'm sure he'd be mighty pleased to know ya'll an Mister Bauskett'll keep an eye on me! Gives me and him peace of mind just knowing ya'll care." This candid statement struck Elijah as disarmingly honest. Death can often bring the truth out of people that way. Puts life into more proper perspective. He grinned in response, saying,

"Ya'll can count on it, son!" and turning to John Bauskett, who was heading out the door with a sheaf of files under his arm, he added, "Can't he, John?"

John Bauskett answered, "Oh absolutely, Angus! Absolutely!"

With much shaking of hands, pats on the shoulder, and mumbled repetitions of "Good-bye!" and "God bless!" Elijah and John made it to their respective carriages, their coachmen patiently waiting. As young Angus stood in the door to see them off, Mary was urging him to come and eat a little something before going to bed.

"Ya'll needs to take care a yosef, now that you's the man a the house. Your Pa wouldn't wanna see ya fall apart, now! Come on into the kitchen with me, sugar. They's plenty a all that good food left! I know ya'll didn't get a chance to eat nothin, cause ya'll was talkin to all Mister Angus' friends like a proper host should. Ya done a real good job today honey, an I's right proud of ya..." Elijah could hear Mary's voice trail off as she headed down the hall toward the kitchen. Angus seemed only too ready to be soothed and went docilely inside, staggering slightly as he closed the door.

Just as Elijah was climbing into his carriage, John touched him on the arm and said softly, "Don't forget our meeting next week. No need to unload the books until then! Might be useful for our conversation!" he winked before climbing into his own carriage, and the two headed off to their respective homes. As Gilbert had brought Amy and the rest of the family in the wagon and had taken them home after the burial to maintain the appropriate image, Julius was driving the carriage tonight.

"Sho is a lotta books ya'll got back there, Mister Elijah. Didn't know you was such a big reader!" Julius said with a chuckle.

"Me neither, Julius! Me neither! But it seems the Good Lord and my dearly departed friend Angus Patterson think there might be some gaps in my legal education that need fillin! Maybe it has something to do with slavery law, and how to get around it! What d'you think?"

"Could be! Could be!" Julius answered with a smile. "I wouldn't be a bit surprised!"

Though too dark to look at it, his hand lay on a familiar looking book at the top of the pile. Mary had handed it to him as he was heading out with the last load. It was the book that had been on Angus' nightstand the day he died.

LXXXI

Angus Patterson, no longer Junior, awoke feeling like he'd been kicked by a mule. His head hurt from an over-indulgence in whiskey, his body felt listless, his stomach was grumbling with hunger, and his mind was racing.

Why in Hell had his father left all his law books to Elijah Willis? The man was no lawyer and probably didn't even appreciate half the information in those books! And why was John Bauskett so intent on getting the books out of the house right then and there? Something just didn't feel right. He needed to talk to James and Michael about this.

He dragged himself out of bed, still wearing his clothes from the funeral. He made it over to his bureau, on top of which stood a large washbasin and a pitcher of warm water. Next to it lay a fresh towel and a bar of soap, a razor, a shaving mug, and a brush. Mary must've been in recently to check on him, he thought to himself.

The water was welcome. He filled the basin half full, wet his hands and lathered them with the soap, then leaned forward and started scrubbing his face and neck. Pulling his traces off his shoulders, he opened his rumpled shirt, and catching a ripe whiff, he even managed to wash under his arms. Then he lathered up the brush, spread the soap on his face, and began to shave.

Slowly his energy started to come back to him, and his head began to clear of the residual haze left by the 100 proof sippin whiskey he had been imbibing in regular doses throughout the previous day and well on into the evening.

Having completed his ablutions, he changed his clothes into more casual wear and headed downstairs for breakfast. Mary was in the kitchen. She was moving even more slowly than usual, but given Angus' own lassitude, he imagined she must be about as beat as he was, and made no comment about it.

"Mornin, sugar! I done fixed ya some breakfast! Set yourself down and eat while it's still hot!" Mary pulled out a chair from the kitchen table and ordered him into it, placing before him a generous platter of eggs with a savory heap of sausages and a steaming mound of grits, in the center of which sat a melting slab of fresh butter. On the side sat a plateful of toast and a mug of coffee.

Angus almost blanched at the sight and smell of so much food. His stomach was feeling trepidatious at the very thought of eating, but he couldn't bring himself to hurt Mary's feelings by refusing her food. It struck him that this was for both of them the first day of life totally without his father.

"How ya'll doin, Mary? Ya'alright?" he asked, sincerely caring.

"I'm fine, sugar, I'm fine. Just feelin kinda ole an worn today, but I'll get over it." Mary responded with a sigh. "How you? D'ya sleep alright? You was out like a light! I reckon you was all wore out from the funeral too," she observed.

Angus nodded as he tried to chew a mouthful of sausage, forcing himself to swallow. He reached for the coffee and took a gulp, the hot liquid spreading a jolt of energy through his body. His queaseyness passing, he set himself to eating more in earnest, Mary's cooking working on him its restorative magic.

After a long silence, punctuated only by the sounds of chewing and Mary's slow-footed puttering around the kitchen, Angus spoke up to announce, "Mary, I'm gonna go over to James' store. Is there anything ya'll need while I'm there?" Mary knew he wasn't going over there to go shopping, but figured it was hardly surprising he would want to seek out the companionship of his closest friends. She knew he would not get through his grieving alone, in any case. At least it was considerate of him to ask.

"Thank ya, honey, but they's so much food left over from the funeral, I won't be needin nothin for a week! Ya'll go on and see ya friends! It'll do ya good! I think I's just gonna take things kinda slow this mornin." Fact was, Mary had been awake since early morning, from force of habit, bustling about, cleaning up after the reception, but she felt bone tired already and needed a rest.

"You do that, Mary!" Angus replied. "I can manage to get somethin to eat midday with James and Michael, so ya'll don't need to worry about me. I'll see ya'll later."

With that, he finished the last mouthful of grits, sopped up the egg yolk with a piece of toast, washed it down with the rest of his coffee, stood up and headed out back to feed his horse before saddling up and riding over to James' store. Mary watched him go, wondering whether his mourning would make him grow up some and take on the responsibility of the household, or whether he'd run and hide in the bottle with the Willis brothers. As Angus rode off, she clucked and fretted and moaned to herself like a broody hen robbed of her chicks, wishing the boy's father was still around to keep him in line.

When Angus reached the store, he tied up his horse and went inside to find his friends. He found them out in back. James, his bladder filled to bursting from last night's consumption, was standing with his back to Angus, pissing like a race horse off the loading dock. His thick stream of urine formed a foamy yellow puddle that sank slowly into the muddy ground, splashing and dripping off the tufts of grass and a lone spring crocus, glistening in the sun. Michael lay stretched out groggily on a pile of feed sacks, shading his eyes and squinting in the mid-morning light, as if he were somehow confused by the sun's rising so high already.

"Mornin boys!" Angus called out.

James, caught by surprise midstream, turned involuntarily and narrowly missed peeing on his brother. He shook off the last drop and clumsily buttoned up his fly.

"Jesus, James! Watch where yer pissin! Ya almost soaked me!" warned Michael.

Unperturbed, James responded teasingly, "Almost don't count, little brother. Ya want me to try again?" he grinned.

"Fuck no!" Michael replied grumpily, still rubbing the sleep out of his eyes. Remembering Angus, he turned and said, "Hey there, buddy! How ya'll doin? That was some wake for yer Pa yesterday!" He belched, stood up and stretched.

"Was a right proper send-off!' agreed James.

Angus nodded."Yeah, I guess so. Tell the truth, I don't remember too much after the burial, it's mostly kinda a blur," he confessed while rubbing his head, hoping to persuade the ache in it to go away. The Willis boys nodded, as if they could relate to that feeling.

"Say, Angus! What happened after we left, with the readin of the will an all? Don't tell me ya'll don't remember that?" James asked.

"Yeah! How much did yer Pa leave ya?" Michael added on the tail end of James' remark, greedy with anticipation.

"Yeah, I remember alright. He left me the house and most of his property, like I figured he would. Some of the land is to be sold, and the proceeds go to my sister up in Charlotte- along with some of my momma's jewelry and a few pieces a silver and furniture Pa wanted her to have. That's alright by me- Hell, what would I do with Momma's earrings or necklaces, anyway?" he asked. "But the rest goes to me, with one other exception."

The Willis brothers looked surprised and waited, eyebrows raised in curiosity, for Angus to clarify.

Now that he had their undivided and relatively sober attention, he decided to reveal the unexpected twist in his father's Last Will and Testament.

"Only thing that caught me by surprise was that ya'll's Uncle Elijah was named as a legatee in the will." The Willis boys' jaws dropped at this little tidbit.

"No shit? What the Hell did yer Pa leave to Uncle Elijah?" James asked, dumbfounded.

"That's the thing. It made no sense to me at first, but now I think I understand. He left him his entire law library!"

Michael let out a low whistle. "Damn! That's a lotta books! What would Uncle Elijah want with them? He ain't no lawyer- or scholar for that matter! Don't even like to read much!"

"There's more," Angus added before answering Michael's question. "That lawyer friend a Pa's from Barnwell, John Bauskett, is the executor of the will, right? Well, he produced a letter from my sister sayin she would not contest anything, so he insisted we go ahead and load up all the books into yer uncle's carriage right then an there!" he announced, "And Mr. Bauskett took all Pa's files too! Pa said Mr. Bauskett should keep the files to preserve attorney-client confidentiality!"

"Now why d'ya suppose he did that?" wondered Michael out loud.

"The books, ya mean? I dunno. I can see why Mr. Bauskett would take the files- he is a lawyer, and worked with Pa on a lotta the same cases." Angus answered. "But I thought it was a little strange he'd insist on Uncle Elijah taking the books like that, before Pa was even cold in the ground! I mean, why the hurry? But I was so drunk and tired, I couldn't really give a shit at that point. So we loaded em up and off they went. But now I'm startin to wonder." Angus reported.

James furrowed his brow for a moment and then gave Angus a beady-eyed look. "I wonder if yer Pa was trying to send Uncle Elijah a message?

Mighta hid somethin in the books for him to help him with his plot to free his nigra family!"

"Oh, shit!" uttered Michael. "D'ya think? Damn! An I thought maybe Uncle Elijah had learned his lesson from the rally!"

"Oh don't be so stupid, Michael!" James shot a look of disdain at his brother. "Ain't it obvious? Uncle Elijah's been playin us like a fiddle! An now he's got all that legal information at his disposal to figure out how to rob us of our rightful inheritance!" It clearly did not occur to James that Elijah deciding to whom he wanted to give his property was not a question of robbing anyone, but simply a natural privilege and his legal right.

Angus was a little miffed that the Willis brothers seemed so self-absorbed about their own inheritance that they were indifferent to the fact that for him, the real loss was no longer having the legal references to further his own political career. He realized that part of that career was intended to prevent people like Elijah from succeeding in doing what they assumed he was trying to do. He couldn't really blame James and Michael for feeling upset. He just wished he'd looked more carefully at his father's books before they got loaded into Elijah's carriage!

"I dunno, James. Looked to me like ya'll's Uncle Elijah was as surprised as me when Mr. Bauskett announced Pa's legacy to him. He didn't seem to have any idea of why he was given all those books."

"What about Mr. Bauskett?" James asked. "As executor of your Pa's estate, he musta known what was in the will! Did he give away any clues?"

"Not really. Just seemed like he was being real careful to carry out Pa's wishes to the letter for the sake of their friendship. But I do remember askin him if it would be alright if I came to him for his legal advice from time to time now that Pa is gone. He said he'd be glad to help."

"Hmmm!" responded James. "How well do ya think he knows Uncle Elijah?"

"I don't rightly know. They seem friendly enough, in a good ole boys' social kinda way, but not like they're exactly close," Angus replied.

"I wonder if Uncle Elijah's got any ideas to get Bauskett to help him?" wondered Michael out loud.

"I do too, little brother. Have for years. I betcha that's exactly what he's fixin to do! We'd best keep an eye out on Uncle Elijah to see if he goes headin over to Barnwell for a visit any time soon!"

"I suppose I could go over there myself on the pretense of needin some legal advice, an maybe get Mr. Bauskett to reveal whether Elijah's paid him a visit lately!"

offered Angus. "After all, he said I'd be welcome any time!"

"That's a good idea, ole buddy! An me an Michael can keep an eye out on the road too, to see where he might be headin if he comes by here." James announced, revealing that his recognizance efforts became a plausible excuse for not exerting themselves beyond their front porch, masking their fundamental laziness.

"It's a shame ya'll couldn't a hid some of them books before Uncle Elijah walked off with em!" muttered Michael, always prone to deviousness.

"Yeah, it is!" agreed Angus. "I probably would've if I'da known any sooner that Pa had given em all to him! But to tell the truth when Pa passed, lookin at books was about the last thing on my mind!" He suddenly felt a tightening in his gut at even admitting he might have kept them against his father's wishes, fearful his father's ghost had heard and might punish him for it. "But I imagine we can still find out if ya'll's uncle is consultin Mr. Bauskett about em, even if we don't know exactly why."

"Aw, come on Angus, you know damn well why! He wants to deprive us of our inheritance for spite, and free that damned nigra woman and her bastard children!" swore James, clearly fixated on what he perceived to be the gross injustice of it all. "Soon as she got her hooks in him, she ruined everything!"

James and Michael then launched into their usual repetitive diatribe about the conniving evils of Amy, the mental illness of Elijah, the outrage of pickaninnies living in the big house, their mother's and sister's offense at Elijah's rudeness that Christmas when their brother-in-law got harmlessly drunk and started innocently asking Elijah about sex with a black woman… The litany went on and on, in the way that drunkards are prone to ramble. But at least now they had a plan- for the delivery of books to Elijah had rekindled their theory of his conspiracy, giving them something more than whiskey and some vague political pipedream future to live for.

LXXXII

The day for meeting with John Bauskett couldn't come soon enough. Elijah was as eager as a bloodhound on a scent to uncover the mystery of Angus' unexpected legacy. He had already rifled through most of the books in the carriage, and though he found no more detailed sheets with cryptic remarks, he did notice a number of comments penciled into the margins of several tomes, with a few passages even underlined in a shakey hand. He had tried to separate any books with annotations from the rest, so that if John Bauskett asked, he'd be ready to show him what he found.

When he finally rode over to Barnwell a few days after the funeral, Elijah was fairly buzzing with anticipation. He forced himself to breathe deeply, not wanting to trigger another episode with his heart, and managed to calm his nerves before knocking on John Bauskett's door. John had been expecting him and came to meet him at the door himself.

"Mornin, Elijah! Come on in!" exclaimed John eagerly.

"Do ya'll want me to start bringin in the books?" Elijah asked, by-passing the usual courtesies in his own eagerness, uncertain how to proceed.

"Ah! The books! Well, why don't we have a cup a coffee first, while I tell ya'll what I've already deciphered. Then we can get the specific books we need from the carriage." John replied.

Elijah turned and called to Julius, who once again was serving as his driver today. "Julius, would ya'll please hand me that book I set aside before?" He was, of course referring to the one he had found by Angus' bed, and which Mary had handed him just before his departure after the funeral.

Julius seemed clear as to which book he was referring. He climbed out of the driver's seat and opened the carriage door to fetch the requested volume, brought it up to the front stoop, and handed it to Elijah saying enthusiastically, "Here it is, Mister Elijah!" It appeared to John that Elijah had Julius in his confidence and that they had clearly been discussing the contents of the books and the purpose of the visit to the Bausketts.

Elijah thanked Julius and asked him to wait with the carriage. As he went inside, John Bauskett said, "I'll have some refreshment sent out to your man, as this may take a while!" As he called out toward the back of the house, the same Negro gentleman Elijah had seen driving the Bausketts to church appeared in the hallway. John spoke to him quietly, asking him to go to the kitchen and have the cook send out a tray for Julius. The man nodded and looking past his master toward Elijah, grinned saying, "Yes sir, Mr. John, right away sir!" He too seemed to be in his master's confidence his smile implying he suspected what was afoot.

John turned back toward Elijah and gestured toward the parlor door. Inside, a tray with a fresh pot of coffee, cups, cream and sugar, and plate of pomanders- a tasty little confection of fried spiced dough dipped in sugar and cinnamon- awaited them, the inviting aroma of the coffee and sweet spices wafting towards them in welcome. As Elijah smiled back and nodded his thanks to the servant in the hallway, he wondered what John's own beliefs about slavery actually were. He had never asked whether the Negro driver and housekeeper he had seen in his service were slaves or free, and he didn't know if perhaps there were others in the Bauskett's service he had not yet seen. Nevertheless, John was clearly supportive of Elijah and his efforts to emancipate his family and took up the challenge with apparent relish. Life, Elijah concluded, was a series of paradoxes.

Suddenly remembering the tome he was holding, he handed it to John, saying, "This is the volume in which I found the sheet of Angus' notes the day he died. It was opened to a section about manumission and inheritance!"

John received the book eagerly. "Aha! Excellent! This should help give us some additional insight into our friend's thinkin, though I already have a pretty clear sense of where the old fox was directin us!"

As the two men sat down on opposite sides of the tray, John gestured to the coffee pot and said, "Please help yourself, Elijah!" he urged, "And ya'll can pour me a cup too, (cream an sugar, if ya please), while I try to find that section and see what ole Angus was lookin at when he scribbled those notes ya'll gave me!" Elijah appreciated the fact that there was no servant being required for this simple task normally done by slaves, and therefore no risk of breach of confidentiality.

Clearly familiar with the book, after a moment's search John announced, "Here it is!" with a tone strikingly similar to Angus' triumphant cock's crow. He proceeded to peruse the pages, turning them backward and forward to discern their overall context. Then he put the book down and, taking a sip of his coffee, grinned at Elijah.

"Do ya have the will too?" he asked.

Elijah promptly produced the will and handed it over to his friend, who read it carefully, occasionally glancing back at the open book before proceeding. The anticipation was driving Elijah crazy, but somehow he managed not to interrupt Bauskett's reading, for fear of breaking his train of thought. He sipped his coffee to pass the time until his friend was ready to reveal his findings.

Finally, his companion looked up. "Well now, there certainly is a lot for us to talk about!" he said, taking another sip of coffee and helping himself to a pomander. "Why don't ya'll start by tellin me in detail what transpired up in Cincinnati?" He licked the cinnamon sugar off his fingertips and took another sip of coffee, a thoughtful expression on his face. "I'm particularly interested to know what points were made or questions raised by your lawyers up there, before they finally drafted the will. I want to get a sense of their legal thinkin before I start sharin my own views on the matter."

Elijah proceeded to relate to him in detail his encounter with Messrs. Gitchell and Jolliffe. He explained that, since Amy and the children were still slaves and Ohio law did not recognize slavery, he could not simply leave his estate directly to them, for they first had to be emancipated. God willing, that would be accomplished by the mere fact of Elijah bringing them to Ohio with the express intent of manumission, for according to Ohio law, with proof of such intent they would be freed automatically by the very act of setting foot on Ohio soil, with no need for any judicial process to accomplish their freedom.

However, he went on to explain, in the event that he was not able to achieve their successful arrival in Cincinnati in his company as planned, the will needed to be structured in such a way that their emancipation could still take place and subsequently render them eligible for his inheritance. This, the lawyers had explained, could be accomplished by technically leaving the estate to one or more executors residing in Ohio, and therefore outside of South Carolina's jurisdiction, who would thereby be empowered to bring to Ohio any slaves in his possession at the time of his demise- whether Amy and the family, or any others- emancipate them, and then sell his remaining property so as to distribute the proceeds among the emancipated.

John Bauskett sat listening carefully, ruminating on pomanders and washing them down with sips of coffee. When Elijah had finished, he began to pose some questions.

"Did they say anything to you about gettin some sort a declaration of emancipation from the Ohio Court as a precaution?

"As a matter of fact, they did. They recommended that they seek a deed of manumission upon the family's arrival as a safety precaution, in anticipation of my white relations' probable attempts to deny the will's validity and take the family back into their custody as fugitives."

John nodded, "I think that would be wise too. That document would stand in Ohio courts, as a result of the will passing probate up there. That would at least secure the family's safety from the Fugitive Slave Act. You know your family here is not gonna accept lightly the fact that you've cut them out of the inheritance completely!"

Elijah nodded grimly. "I'm sure they won't, but the Devil take em! After all they've put me through, they don't deserve a damn penny!" he responded vehemently.

John nodded again in understanding. He had had the opportunity to meet Elijah's family both at the rally and the funeral, and he realized that Elijah was not exaggerating in his assessment of their attitude towards Amy and the children. He had found James' and Michael's exuberant anti-abolitionism at the rally crude and offensive, and saw immediately that their mother in particular was eager to get her hands on property she felt should be in her husband's hands by rights.

Finally he spoke up, "Well, it appears to me that Messrs. Gitchell and Jolliffe have served you very well. The will is rightly constructed to rebuff any attacks on the part of your white relations. That bein said," he continued, "that's not to also say, however, the plan is totally fool-proof."

Elijah shifted uncomfortably- this was not the news he was hoping to hear. "Where's it's weakness and what can we do about it?" he asked.

"Well, there's no weakness in the will itself- it's clear, straightforward, and legally bindin," John reassured him. "A right masterful job, in fact. I can't imagine there'll be any problem in it passin probate up in Ohio. The trouble will likely come in the Court of Equity here in South Carolina."

He went on to explain that if the will was not approved in South Carolina, even though Amy and the children and Momma Celia would certainly be free in Ohio, and would therefore be beyond the grasp of his white relations claiming rights to them under the federal Fugitive Slave Act, there was still the vexing problem of the inheritance. The executors from Ohio would be helpless to sell any of his property down South- whether lands, furnishings, livestock, or slaves- without the will first being recognized as valid in South Carolina.

Elijah took a swallow of coffee to brace himself. "D'ya mean to tell me that Amy and the children will have no access to my assets or funds until the will is approved in South Carolina?"

"I'm afraid not." John replied soberly. "I would recommend, therefore, that ya'll bring with ya as much cash as ya can when ya bring em up to Cincinnati. That way, should there be any delay in the Court of Equity here, they will not have to suffer loss for their proper maintainance in the meantime." He paused, then added, "Of course, that assumes you will in fact survive to get them up to Cincinnati yourself! If ya do not, it may prove very difficult indeed for your executors to succeed in bringing any of them North, even though the will be approved in Ohio, unless they can come down here and fight their way through the courts to validate the will down here as well."

Elijah gave a slight involuntary groan of distress, then set his jaw firmly and said, "Well then, I'm just gonna have to live long enough to get em up there, aren't I?" It was meant as a rhetorical question, for he had already made up his mind that was his only option. He was certain James and Michael were going to do all in their power to block the will here at home. He couldn't bear the idea of Amy, Momma Celia and the children being free but homeless and hungry in Ohio.

"God Amighty, John, is there anything we can do to prevent my relations from blockin the will down here in Williston?" he implored.

John could feel the depair welling up inside his friend and wanted to try to allay his fears, but he knew that realistically Amy and the children were likely to be in for a long fight before this was over, unless Elijah lived long enough to sell his property himself.

"I think we should prepare for the worst and hope for the best, Elijah." John opined. "I looked at Angus' notes, and there's no question he was right- the entire argument is gonna hinge on provin that Amy and the children are free. Once that has been established beyond any doubt, South Carolina law will not be able to contravert it."

"But that still leaves open the possibility that my relations' foot draggin, obfuscatin greediness and spite will prevent or delay the sale of any property, doesn't it?" Elijah was getting a clear picture of the likely challenges ahead.

"It does," John agreed. "Not only that, but if folks down here succeed in secedin from the Union, that could change the legal landscape too. God forbid we should go to war over it, there's no tellin what might happen to ya'll's property!"

That grim possibility had not seriously occurred to Elijah, and a new wave of anxiety washed over him to even contemplate it.

John continued, "However, I am right impressed by the work of Jolliffe and Gitchell. They seem to have a real good understandin of the probable challenges, and I expect if need be they could come down here and fight this thing successfully. An by the way they structured the will, ya'll have already authorized em to do so!"

"What else did ya'll learn from Angus' notes?" Elijah asked, a bit disappointed that there were no real revelations as of yet. He and Amy had been able to read about the case hinging on proof of their freedom without anybody having to explain that obvious fact to them. He was desperately hoping there might be some other clue, some trick or clause to trump his white relations and thwart any attempt they might make to block the execution of his final requests. He wished he felt confident enough to be assured he would live to free at least Amy, her mother and the children, and sell all his property himself, rendering their possible law suits a moot point. Unfortunately, a nagging, almost subliminal doubt was telling him that might well not happen.

"Well, he referenced a lot of case law," replied John, "both here in South Carolina, and federally. He even referenced British Common law, goin back to before the foundin of the American Colonies." It was clear John greatly admired the thoroughness of Angus' ability to build an argument. "I haven't yet had time to read through those cases in detail" he continued "and some of those materials I don't even have in my own library. That's where his bequest to you comes in! I'm gonna need to read a sizable portion of that collection he left ya!"

Elijah brightened a bit. "I looked through the books to see if there were any other papers and didn't find any. What I did find, however, was a goodly number of marginal notes and passages underlined. I tried to set those books aside from the others to help ya be able to sort through it all!"

John smiled in appreciation. "That's wonderful! I'll look forward to readin em right away! The way I see it, if I do my homework right I'll be well prepared to help out if John Jolliffe or James Gitchell are obliged to come down here and take ya'll's relations to court!"

"Well, I pray to God that won't be necessary, as I still intend to try to see this thing through myself, but I surely do feel better knowin ya'll'll be there for my family- my real family, that is!" Elijah confessed, clearly referring to Amy and the children.

"Ya have my solemn promise Elijah, that I will do everything in my power to see them all safe and provided for, if the need arises!"

"Once again, John, I am ever indebted to ya. I can't thank ya'll enough for ya help."

"It's my pleasure, Elijah," John responded sincerely. "I've promised you, and I promised Angus too, and I'm a man of my word! You know, Angus considered this case a sort of culmination of his legal career- an opportunity to bring all his expertise to bear on what he saw as the noblest of causes. Both for the sake of my friendship with him and with you, I could do no less than see this through, no matter what it takes." With that, he popped another pomander in his mouth and finished his coffee, smacking his lips with satisfaction.

"What say we go get those books outa your carriage, so's I can get to doin my homework?" he said with a twinkle in his eye.

"Well, alright then!" Elijah got up and headed toward the front door to call Julius and ask him to help them bring the books in. "You sure Eugenia's not gonna pitch a fit with us bringin in all those dusty books into her nice clean house?" Elijah asked with a wry smile.

"Well, she might do! But I think I can manage to smooth any ruffled feathers once I explain to her how important they are! Bein as it's for such a worthy cause, I'm sure she won't mind- or at least will get over mindin it right quickly!" John assured Elijah with the chuckle of a husband who had long since learned how to placate his wife's upsets. And with that, they proceeded to unload the carriage of its precious cargo.

"It occurs to me, Elijah," John commented as they carried their respective armloads of books into the parlor, "that there was a double motive in Angus' bequest to you. It seemed odd to me at first, knowing you were unlikely to read or appreciate such a weighty collection of the arcane details of jurisprudence. But I think he was tryin not only to give you tools for your legal battle but send a message to his son too!"

"And what message might that be?" asked Elijah, puffing a bit from the exertion.

"Well, Angus Junior surely knows you and I know each other. And he clearly suspects ya'll are scheming to free Amy and the children, and maybe change your will, though he's got no proof that I know anything about it, and seems unaware that you intend to do far more than he fears," John explained.

"True," responded Elijah, "but what's the message to Angus in givin me the books then?"

"The message is: Beware! Elijah Willis is well-armed, and has the legal counsel you now lack. Don't go lookin for trouble that isn't yours," concluded John.

"Hmmm!" Elijah grunted. "Sounds like Angus! But permit me to doubt his son'll get the message! Even Mary, who's known him all his life, said that he was fightin a demon between his good side and his bad side. Much as I hate to say it, given the amount a time he spends drinkin with my no-account nephews, my money's on his bad side winnin in the long run!"

John could not dispute this assessment, much as he'd have liked to. But he didn't want Elijah to be robbed of hope or to consign Angus to Hellfire and damnation, at least not just yet. He knew hope might be the only thing that could sustain Elijah long enough to see his plan through. "Well, ya'll may be right; I can't deny it, but I keep reflectin on that hymn 'Amazin Grace' an wantin to believe that even your wretched nephews an Angus aren't beyond redemption!"

"Lord forgive me, John, but much as I admire that hymn and much as I believe a conversion of heart is possible by God's grace, I have yet to see any signs in any of em that convince me it's likely to happen for them. The Good Lord may work in mysterious ways, but that would truly be a miracle!"

John's reference to hymnody, however, put Elijah in mind of the passage he so frequently recalled- "You meant it for evil, but God meant it for good". "I guess I'll just have to trust the Lord that He knows what He's doin, no matter what Angus and my nephews do, and that somehow things'll work out alright."

John put an arm around Elijah's shoulders, the last of the books being duly deposited. "Don't lose heart, my friend. Ya'll go on home an reassure Amy. Get some rest. I'll call on ya'll in a few days, after I've had time to look into these cases. I'm sure we can find some useful hints in all this to prepare for whatever battle may be necessary. One thing's certain- no matter whether rich or poor, your family's gonna be free, I swear it!"

Elijah looked in Johns' eyes, and feeling bolstered by his conviction and sincerity, he gave him a hug of thanks, saying, "God bless ya John, and may the Good Lord hear ya too! I guess I'll be on my way then. Please apologize to Eugenia for me and thank her for her indulgence. Friends like ya'll're mighty hard to come by, and I'll never forget all the help ya'll've given us."

With that, he climbed into his carriage and told Julius it was time for them to go home. He didn't notice that just down the road a piece a lone horseman stood facing the Bauskett's house, watching from behind a clump of trees. It was his nephew James.

LXXXIII

Contrary to her hopes, Elijah was less than ebullient when he got home from his visit with John Bauskett. Amy noticed immediately that he seemed troubled by something.

"What is it, sugar? How did it go with Mr. Bauskett?" she asked with concern.

"Well John was very kind and helpful, as ususal," Elijah answered, somewhat evasively.

"I hear a 'but...' in there somewhere," she observed with her usual astuteness. "What exactly did he tell ya?" she pressed, unwilling to let it slide.

Elijah sighed deeply, "Well darlin, there's some good news and then some news that could be troublesome. Fact is, I just don't know what to make of it!" He still didn't want to have to tell her his gut feeling that their freedom might not be as financially solvent as they were planning and expecting.

"Well, for pity's sake Elijah, out with it! I'd rather know bad news ahead a time then get an ugly surprise when it's too late to prepare for it!"

"Alright! Alright! Don't go gettin all upset, now!" he urged her. "The good news is that John thinks the will is real well written and will guarantee ya'll's freedom." Elijah answered, sort of nibbling his way into the meat of the matter.

"Well that's wonderful, honey! Thank you, Jesus! Praise God!" Amy replied. "If that's the good news, how bad can the bad news be?" she wondered out loud.

"Well, John says the will'll pass probate in Ohio, guaranteed. That assures that you and Momma Celia and the children will be beyond the reach of my family, and any attempt they might make to drag you back into slavery under the Fuguive Slave Act." Elijah explained.

"Thank the Good Lord! So what's the bad news then?" Amy asked, perplexed in the face of this long sought reassurance.

"Well, accordin to John the problem may come here in the Court of Equity. If my white relations here succeed in preventin the will passin probate, even though ya'll're free up in Ohio, ya won't be able to sell any of my property here in South Carolina unless and until that changes and the will is validated down here."

Amy listened, as sober as a judge. She was starting to get the picture. "Go on," she urged, hoping for some caveat of relief, "What else did he say?"

"He said that if I didn't manage to bring ya'll up there in person, even though my will in Cincinnati authorizes my executors to bring ya'll up and emancipate ya, my no-account relations're likely to pitch a fit to try to keep that from happenin, and ya'll still bein down here, it'd be real hard for my executors to get ya'll out!"

Amy was almost afraid to ask, "And if Momma and the children an I manage to get up to Cincinnati, but you die before we can get Gilbert and the rest up?"

Elijah's face grew grim, and he sighed again, "Basically John said, unless I can get it done before I die, it's likely gonna be a long battle, and the outcome is not guaranteed! He recommended we bring as much cash with us a possible when we go up to Cincinnati, so that if there is a delay in the courts due to my damned relations' shennanigans, ya'll'll have enough to live on to tide ya over till ya'll can finally sell the house and land."

Amy thought hard about what Elijah was saying and realized that their dream was more than likely to have to undergo some serious modification. Some of this was not news, as they were already aware it would be much better, maybe even necessary, for Elijah to succeed in bringing them himself. Ever the realist despite her ideal, she simply nodded.

"I see," she responded. "Well then, first of all we gotta keep you well, so we can go up to Cincinnati together like we always planned," she declared. "But we knew that already!"

Elijah nodded in agreement. "What worries me is the need for cash. You'd think that with all this property I wouldn't need much cash, but now it seems otherwise. Trouble is, almost all my money's in the land and crops- you know we never have much margin to work with until the crops come in! And then a lot of that has to go back into the land for the next harvest!" He paused in thought for a moment. Then realizing that there was no point in beating around the bush, he pointed out the elephant in the room: "Unfortunately, the one asset I have that is most quickly convertible into cash is slaves!"

Amy's eyes moistened with the disappointment and maddening frutration of facing the inevitable, painful reality that her and her children's freedom was going to depend on perpetuating the servitude of others. She was especially afraid that was going to extend to her brother and his children, it becoming apparent that their prompt reunion in Ohio might not be possible. Her instinct of self-preservation clashing with her ideals, Amy swallowed hard before replying. She wanted to persuade herself that if she, at least were free, Gilbert would still have a chance. Torn between referring to the slaves as "them" or "us," she simply said, "You're gonna have to sell some, aren't you?"

"I'm afraid so," Elijah answered glumly. "I thought up in Cincinnati that this had all been worked out, not realizin that the whole thing could be stymied by the will bein approved up there but not gettin through probate down here!"

"What about the timin, honey? It's plowin and plantin time now- ya sell half the slaves now we can't get the crop in, and there'll be no harvest to cash in on." Amy observed, ever astute to the management of the estate.

"An if I sell em once the crops are planted, but before the harvest, there won't be enough field hands to bring in the harvest!" Elijah realized, thinking out loud.

"So ya need to plan to sell em as soon as ya can after the fall harvest is safely in!" concluded Amy. "That at least'll give us time to work it out as fairly as we can, an not be settin off alarms in the community as to what we're doin."

"I just pray to God none of the others figure this out- much less James and Michael and young Angus! I dunno which of em is gonna be harder to deal with when the moment of truth finally arrives!" uttered Elijah. "And I just don't even know what to say to Gilbert, and Julius, and Jason. I promised them they'd be freed!"

"Well, as God is my witness, if you die before this is done, I will move Heaven and Earth to get my brother outa South Carolina! Ya'll need to tell Mister Gitchell and Mister Jolliffe to be prepared to come on down here for a fight! I will not give up on him! And I will not let your no account nephews steal your legacy!" Amy said with unexpected vehemence.

Having made her declaration she started to cry, her deep sobs shaking her convulsively, as if all at once her pent up fear and frustration were seeking to escape the confines of her body, where they had been so long supressed. Elijah felt as if a cold hand had grabbed his heart and was squeezing it like a sponge. He contracted with pain as he watched her, feeling helpless to relieve her suffering and uncertain whether his own pain was merely emotional, or another "episode." He didn't want to worry Amy more by calling attention to himself, so he struggled to shake it off. Breathing deeply, his pain eased, but Amy's sobs continued.

Elijah didn't want to make Amy false promises or give her false hope, but he also didn't want her to give in to despair- partly because if she did, he himself would lose his own last bastion of defense from a dismay that threatened to cripple his ability to keep fighting. All he could do was put his arm around her in silent understanding, and let her cry until the waves of anguish were purged and she could regain her composure.

"I'm gonna get ya'll up there, darlin, I'm gonna get ya'll up there! I promise!" he kept repeating softly through her sobs, rocking her gently in his arms. All the while he was praying fervently that God would not make him a liar, and would at least grant that he see them safely to Cincinnati.

LXXXIV

James Willis was seething. His suspicions had been confirmed that Elijah was somehow in league with John Bauskett, and he could only assume this was not about mere business matters on the plantation. From the clump of trees where he had hidden, he didn't have a completely clear view of the entrance of Bauskett's house. Elijah's carriage parked in front had blocked the line of sight. He had seen his uncle with his slave Julius and Mr. Bauskett, making several trips carrying something into the house, but couldn't see clearly what it was. However, it was not hard to deduce, after Angus' description of loading the carriage with his father's law books, that the self-same tomes must have been the objects of their efforts.

"Son of a bitch!" he thought to himself, as Elijah and Julius drove off towards home, "Wait til Angus hears about this!" He spurred his horse with a vicious kick and broke into a gallop back toward Williston by a different route, so as not to be seen by his uncle.

On his way, he saw Dr. Guignard coming toward him from the opposite direction in a glistening black carriage drawn by a handsome team of well-groomed horses. A French blue *fleur de lis* trimmed in gold was painted on the door- an affectation of Guignard's French ancestry. The door handles were brightly polished brass.

James slowed to a trot as the Doctor approached. He pondered whether or not he should tell Dr. Guignard what he had discovered, knowing that Guignard had a grudge to settle with Elijah that still was festering ever since Elijah's unexpected signing of the petition took the wind out of the sails of his revenge. However, realizing that his "proof" was still circumstantial, and that Guignard would not take it kindly if it turned out to be false and backfired again, he decided he'd best inform Angus first. Angus had been planning to pay John Bauskett a visit anyway, and James figured he would therefore be in an easy position to verify whether his father's books were now in the lawyer's possession.

"Afternoon, Dr. Guignard!" James called out as they passed.

"Why James! Good to see ya, son! How're ya'll doin?" responded Guignard cheerfully. He smiled and waved, not really waiting for any further response. He left James wondering whether he had heard that Elijah had been named in Angus Senior's will, and what he would make of that- especially if he found out that Angus' entire law library had been bequeathed to his uncle.

James waved back, shouting, "Good to see ya, Doctor. Hope we'll meet again real soon!"

Guignard nodded non-commitally and waved back at James, his carriage rolling on down the road.

Rather than heading back to the store, James decided to drop by Angus' house in town first to see if he was home and give him the news of what his espionage had revealed. When he got there he tied up his horse, climbed the steps to the front door, and let fall the heavy brass doorknocker several times, impatient for an answer.

After what seemed like a long time, he heard footsteps slowly working their way across the foyer, and Mary's aged face looked up at him quizzically as she opened the door.

"Yessir, Mr. James? What can I do for ya'll this afternoon?" she asked politely.

Straining to look past her to see if there were any signs of Angus being home, he asked,

"Is Angus here?"

Mary replied, "No sir. I don't rightly know where Mister Angus is, ta tell ya the truth. Left the house after breakfast this mornin, an I ain't seen or heard from him since. Might be he gone over to ya'll's store to visit ya'll!"

James was mildly annoyed that Angus wasn't there. It pulled the rug out from under his intentions of dramatically delivering his important news. He took his frustration out on Mary. "Tell yer master that I come callin, an he needs to come over to the store right away if he ain't already there!" James said brusquely.

Mary bristled at his tone, and gently but firmly corrected him. "Mister Angus ain't my master, sir! His Pa done freed me more'n thirty years ago- b'fo young Angus was even born! Young Mister Angus is my employer!"

James looked at Mary with disgust. "You getting uppity with me, woman? I don't give a damn if yer a slave or free, yer still a nigra. Just give him the goddamn message!" He stomped off the porch, mounted his horse, and rode off toward the store in a huff, Mary watching his dust as he went, the sting of his rebuke unable to penetrate her leathery hide.

"Hmmm, hmmm, hmmm!" she muttered to herself, shaking her head in pity. "That sorry fool gonna end up in deep trouble one a these days. Ain't nobody gonna put up with his stuff if he don't learn to mind his manners better! God sho to strike him if he go on takin the Lord's Name in vain, cussin like that..." She found herself spontaneously wiping her feet on the carpet, remembering the scripture "And whosoever shall not receive you, nor hear your words, when ye depart out of that house or city, shake off the dust of your feet as a testimony against them." Mary had long since concluded that James and his bellicose brother were not likely to do well on Judgement Day, but they were Angus' friends, so she forced herself to hold her tongue.

James finally caught up with Angus at the store. He was sitting talking with Michael as James rode up.

"Angus! Michael!" he shouted. "I got news!"

The two looked up from their idle chit-chat, their attention suddenly focused on the unknown news and its messenger.

"What's up James? Where the Hell have you been?" asked Angus with mild surprise.

"Where've I been, ole buddy? Where've I been? I've been lookin into the possibility our Uncle Elijah is up to some sort of mischief with John Bauskett and yer Pa's law books, that's where I've been!" proclaimed James.

"Well? Did ya find something, or are ya just trying to sound like ya got off yer lazy ass for no good reason?" grumbled Michael.

"Shut up, Michael! You're no one to talk about bein a lazy ass!"

"I didn't say y'are a lazy ass, big brother, I said ya got off yer lazy ass! he retorted.

"Could you two knock it off please, and let us get on with it?" interrupted Angus impatiently. "If ya'll got some news, James, then spill it! Enough of this 'I know something you don't know' bullshit! Christ, ya sound like ya're a five year old whinin!"

"Well, I was ridin over near Barnwell when I saw Uncle Elijah's carriage headed in that direction and decided to follow it. Seemed odd he was in the carriage, since he usually rides that big mare a his in good weather. Sure enough, it led straight to John Bauskett's place."

"No!" remarked Angus.

"Yessir! I swear to God!" insisted James. "I watched em for a spell from behind a clump a trees, and though I couldn't see clearly what it was, Uncle Elijah and his nigra Julius and Mr. Bauskett was carryin stuff into the house. I bet you anything it was your Pa's books!"

"Damn!" swore Angus and Michael in unison.

"So now what do we do?" asked Michael.

"Well, I thought about tellin Dr. Guignard- I passed him a way back, on my way into town- but I didn't wanna tell him nothin without havin convincin proof. You know how he can get if somebody messes up. He don't take it too well."

Angus was thinking hard. "I'll go over to Bauskett's place! It won't seem invasive, cause I already asked him if I could. I can claim I need help on some detail of Pa's estate. If I see the books over there, we'll know for sure he and ya'll's uncle are up to somethin."

"And what do ya reckon we can do about it?" asked James.

"Well, maybe not much yet. But the more we know, the better prepared we'll be to fight him if he tries to do somethin about freein nigras or givin away any of ya'll's inheritance," answered Angus, ironically thinking like his father, building the case step by step.

"I'm tellin ya, Angus, we're gonna end up havin to take somebody to court before this is all over!" declared James; Michael enthusiastically noddded in agreement, as if that might be fun.

"Well, maybe so- but who and when is the question? Too soon to tell!" Angus' mind was spinning with possibilities- Would it be a suit against Elijah? Against the executors of his estate? Against Amy? It all was going to depend on what Elijah ended up doing. It had not yet occurred to any of them that the drama they anticipated might be initiated outside of Barnwell District or South Carolina altogether!

"Do ya'll think we should let Dr. Guignard in on it?" asked James.

"I don't think so, at least not yet" answered Angus. "I think we need to see how things unfold a little more first, so we have better idea of just what Elijah might be planning and how we can block it. That's where Dr. Guignard's help might come in handy!"

The Willis brothers agreed.

"Damn, but I wish I'd studied Pa's books more when I had the chance!" Angus said, almost to himself. "I know the law doesn't permit emancipation except by petitioning the General Assembly- an pigs'll fly before the legislature grants any such petition these days! But I keep feelin like there might be some way around that- an that's probably the very thing ya'll's uncle and Mr. Bauskett're lookin for too!"

"Why don't we just steal the books back?" asked Michael, his usual penchant for solutions by force coming to the fore.

"What? Are you crazy?" his brother asked. "Nevermind, no need to answer!" he added, his brother's suggestion answering the question for him. "Jesus Michael, we go tryin to steal them books back and we'll be gettin ourselves into a whole mess a trouble!" James reacted, leaving Michael cowed but fuming.

"Hey, I got an idea!" piped up Angus. "Why don't I go over to yer Uncle Elijah's and simply ask if I can borrow some of Pa's books? He won't be expectin that- and would be hard pressed to refuse me. If he can't come up with them, it'll not only be clear that Bauskett's involved, but might even give us a specific idea of which books he's lookin at!"

"Yeah, that's a brilliant idea!" chimed in James. "Then ya'll can go on over to Mr. Bauskett's too, an ask him if he's got any books on emancipation and inheritance ya'll could read- like you was takin an interest in yer Pa's career and thinkin about followin in his footsteps!"

"That'd put em both on the spot, for sure!" observed Angus. "Elijah's not gonna wanna admit he doesn't have the books, and Bauskett's not gonna wanna admit he does, especially after that whole show of loadin em into Elijah's carriage the night of the funeral! Who knows what might slip out in the process?"

"Way I figure it," declared James, "Uncle Elijah ain't got a chance a freein his nigra family if we're prepared to fight! An if he can't free em there's no way they can inherit anything at all!" he smirked with satisfaction. It was inconceivable that Elijah would choose not to leave him and his brother a blessed thing- with or without Amy and the children! Besides, his father had seen the will Elijah had written back in '46, and everything went to his white relations anyway!

"Bring er on!" insisted Michael, eager as a stud bull on a heifer. "That's a fight I'm more'n willin to have!" he grinned maliciously.

LXXXV

Ever since Elijah had come back from Cincinnati and broken the news about the will, he had felt a subtle strain in his relationship with Gilbert. He knew that the uncertainty of their collective future was weighing heavily on his brother-in-law. Ever since he had lost his wife to the yellow fever, Gilbert had become more worried about his children, and was increasingly fearful they were going to remain condemned to a life of servitude despite Elijah's assurances to the contrary. Elijah felt restive about the other slaves too- not only Jason and Julius, but the entire population of the plantation.

When the idea of emancipating Amy and the children had first arisen Elijah had not even seriously considered the fate of the other slaves, but his love for Amy and her concern for them had moved him to see things differently. He had finally come to willingly embrace the dream of emancipating them all. The political and economic reality that this was not going to be possible had been a rude and painful awakening from that dream. Still, he felt a commitment to Gilbert and Jason and Julius at the very least, and was determined to honor it if at all possible. If he could manage to free his family and at least some of the others, he figured he could die in peace. This was the burden he bore day and night, and the stress of it was wearing on him like an old rope on a well pulley- no telling when it might snap under the weight of the bucket, depriving him of the water of life.

In the timeless way of living in the rural South however, Spring seemed oblivious to the concerns of men, insisting that the season inexorably demanded new birth, and everyone best be a participant in that process if they expected to go on living. Nevertheless, as the relentless demands of plowing and planting progressed in their usual rhythm, everyone putting their backs into the inevitable work they demanded, all the folks on the Willis Plantation were feeling a little edgy.

The field hands were grumbling that nothing seemed to be happening to move them any closer to freedom despite the promises, and the rumors of promises they had heard. It was now years since the mention of emancipating them had first been made. Their faith in that promise was faltering in the face of the grinding reality that nothing much had changed other than the rising political tensions in the region that sought to make emancipation and inheritance for coloreds impossible forever!

One Sunday after services, some of the slaves were sitting around outside the slave quarters enjoying a rest in the Spring sunshine, and as usual got to talking. Jeremiah, the young self-appointed but not yet anointed preacher, was still going on about how God had hardened Pharaoh's heart, and no matter how many times Moses told him, "Let my people go" he refused, until Moses and Aaron finally had to lead the Israelites to escape, and God drowned the Egyptians in the Red Sea. He seemed to be implying, due to the years of unfulfilled promises, that Elijah's heart had been hardened against them, increasingly linking Elijah to Pharaoh rather than Moses. The perilous question of leading some sort of uprising was lurking in the background of the conversation like some nocturnal predator, afraid to show itelf in broad daylight but waiting to pounce.

"Jeremiah, I hear the scripture- but I ain't convinced that Mister Elijah's heart is hardened agin us. To me, seems more like folks round here in Williston's got they hearts hardened agin him! Mister Elijah's a good man. He ain't our enemy!" insisted old Henry.

"Well mebbe so, but we still his slaves, ain't we?" Jeremiah shot back in angry frustration.

"Yeah, we are. But we livin a heap better than the Israelites, thanks to him. Ya'll read us that passage bout the Children a Israel bein slaves for a long time before they got free- and even once Moses led em outa Egypt and they was free, life didn't get a whole lot better for em- not for a long time to come!" Henry countered.

"He's right Jeremiah! You actin like all we gotta do is get free and everything gonna be alright. The Israelites was free, but they was wanderin in a damn desert for forty year b'fo they got to enter the Promised Land! Even if Mister Elijah succeed in gettin us to freedom, could be it'll take a long time b'fo we be free to do more'n suffer," responded another one of his companions.

"Not only that! Moses may a been a Israelite, but he was raised like a prince- and had a price on his head for killin that fella that was beatin a slave. Mister Elijah be a prince in this town- part a the foundin family! But hardly feels like a white man sometimes- more like he one a us, the way he relate to us and work with us an all. He go fightin the system here, they might as well put a price on his head too!" insisted yet another.

"Then we all fucked, an ain't nobody gettin outa this mess!" concluded a fourth, heads nodding in agreement to a chorus of "That's right," "Hmmm hmmm," "You know that's right," and "Amen, brother!"

"Mister Elijah getting ole, too. He ain't gonna be around forever. What gonna happen to us when he gone if he don't manage to get us to freedom? God hep us all if we end up in the hands a his brother and nephews! Them boys is jus plain nasty! Meaner n a rattlesnake, an just as poisonous!" worried yet another.

Gilbert had been listening to the entire exchange. He was reluctant to weigh in on the subject, not only because of his peculiar status as part of Elijah's extended family, but because of his own doubts about the viability of Elijah's promise- especially now, since it was clear it would not extend to everyone on the plantation in any case. If he gave that away, the slaves might even turn on him. He felt his gut tighten at the thought of it, for he knew that things could unravel pretty quickly once word got out Elijah was gonna sell any of them off.

His own hurt and rage were tempered by his love and admiration for his sister and his desperate hope that, if she at least were free, he and his children would have a chance. He wanted to believe Elijah would make good on his promise, and though he didn't doubt his brother-in-law's sincerity, he was beginning to doubt that he could succeed in his plan. It seemed the forces of evil were gathering against them.

"Hey Gilbert! You awful quiet! What you think Mister Elijah gonna do? He talk to ya'll more'n to us. What he tellin you?" asked young Elias, who had been so proud of being able to read the envelope of the letter from Henry Clay.

Gilbert shifted uneasily in his seat. "Well, we don't talk much about it, ta tell ya the truth. Most a the time he just talk to me about business- gettin in the crops, cuttin an millin the timber, takin it all to market or the depot to ship off..."

"What about ya sista Miss Amy? She tell ya anything?" asked another.

"Amy? She swear Mister Elijah want to see us free, an I believe her." Gilbert answered truthfully, careful to use 'Mister' so as not to set himself apart. "But wantin it an doin it ain't always the same. God only knows if he gonna succeed!" he couldn't help but add.

Julius and Jason gave Gilbert a look. They sensed there was something more than met the eye behind his comment, but knew he would not reveal it in front of all the others. He avoided their gaze, fearful the others might pick up on it, realizing he had already probably said more than he should have.

"Well, I don't know about the rest of ya'll," stated Jeremiah with defiance, "but if Mister Elijah don't manage to keep his promise, I'd sooner start a rebellion or die a runaway, than the end up bein a slave to anyone in his family!" His statement was met by a mixture of nods, 'hmmm hmms,' 'Yes Lords,' and 'sssshhhhhs!' and "hush yo mouth!" Some agreed, while others were terrified of even mentioning such a possibility.

Gilbert and Julius and Jason all took note of Jeremiah's declaration, and concluded he would have to be on the list of slaves to be sold. They figured he would not be the only one to feel like rebelling or making a run for it, and for his own protection they wanted to try to prevent either. Ironically, selling him might be the only way to do that. They were going to have to think carefully, not only about who should be sold, but what the repercussions might be to those who were not. Hard to predict how folks would react to the news: who would submit and who would resist. Until they had a better sense of just how many slaves Elijah could reasonably afford to free, they had to look at just about everyone on the plantation, outside themselves and their own families, as possible candidates. And even that was not an absolute guarantee.

The last thing they wanted to see, however, was a slave uprising, much as they could understand Jeremiah's point of view. They were pretty well certain that the only freedom to come of that would be the freedom of death, when they all got killed for trying it!

Gilbert finally spoke up, "I heard tell of slaves up in Maryland, or Virginia, or Kentucky runnin away and makin it to freedom, like that story a Miz Harriet Beecher Stowe's, but them slaves didn't have so far to go to get outa slave territory. Down here in Williston, a slave'd have to get all the way through the slave states of South Carolina, North Carolina, Virginia and Maryland, or Georgia, Tennessee, and Kentucky to get even close to a slave-free state, much less to safety in Canada!"

Jeremiah, being young and passionate, and with only a vague idea of geography, was not willing to give up easily. "Well, maybe we could get a boat South and head to the British West Indies, or Haiti! I heard tell slaves there fought they own revolution and kicked out they French masters! Betcha they'd open they doors to a fella refugee from slavery up here!

Julius responded, "That ain't likely to work either! It's too risky! Cuba and Puerto Rico still allow both slavery and the slave trade! If ya'll get blown off course and end up on the wrong island, it could be like jumpin out of the fryin pan an into the fire!"

He remembered that Robert Barnwell Rhett had been talking at the rally about joining forces with the Caribbean nations to build his ideal slave empire. No doubt about it, from where they sat, the odds were clearly against them making a run for it with any reasonable chance of success. It would be suicide!

Jason, remembering the folk tune, 'Keep your hand on the plow,' said, "Ain't no way we gonna find no easy solution, but seems to me it's like the song says bout gettin to heaven, 'Know my robe gonna fit me well/ Tried it on at the gates a Hell/ Keep yo hand on the plow/ Hold on!' It be a kinda Hell bein a slave alright, but I b'lieve if we can hold on long enough, we gonna make it to freedom one way or another!"

Jeremiah felt chastised by looking in the mirror of reality. Like all preachers confronted with failure, he was ashamed of the insufficiency of his faith and the difficulty of trusting in the Lord. All he could think to say was to quote the scripture, "Lord, I believe! Help thou my unbelief!" It pretty much summed up what they all were feeling.

LXXXVI

Angus Patterson rode confidently up the drive to the Willis Plantation, feeling fully prepared to expose Elijah by requesting to see his father's books. Ironically, rather than being like a bee-keeper with a smoke pot that would render the bees docile so he could take their honey without getting stung, the cloud of Angus' self-confidence in fact was befogging his own mind and rendering it unprepared for the fact that the queen bee saw him coming.

Amy was on the upper porch when she heard the hoof beats approaching. As Elijah had gone to the depot to discuss some business with Will Beazely, and then intended to head over to Barnwell to talk with John Bauskett, she knew it could not be Beauty's hooves announcing his return so soon. Her instincts well-honed, she quickly gathered herself to go downstairs and fend off whomever it might be.

Angus dismounted in front of the house, tied up his horse by the trough under the live oak, took off his hat, smoothed back his hair to make himself more presentable, and knocked on the front door. Amy wasted no time in opening it and stepping out onto the veranda, thereby provoking Angus to take a step back to accommodate her. This clever stratagem prevented Angus from being able to look past Amy into the house and pry with his eyes for whatever it was had prompted him to come out there.

"Why hello, Mister Patterson!" Amy said graciously. "Whatever brings you out here today?"

"How do, Miss Amy!" Angus couldn't help but respond instinctively, as if he were speaking to the lady of the house, though once again he cursed himself for his blunder. "Is Mister Willis at home?"

"I'm afraid he's not, sir. He went into town on business. But I'll be glad to tell him ya'll stopped by. Is there anything I can do to help, or a message ya'll'd like for me to give him?" she asked helpfully.

Angus wondered, for a moment, whether he might not be able to get her to let him in the house to look at the books, but then figured that would be going too far. Any wife, or for that matter, any house slave worth her price, would refuse such access without express permission to do otherwise, and he was certain Elijah would have given no such permission for anyone. He also realized it would be unwise to tell Amy his purpose, lest it warn Elijah in the event he should decide to return for a second try.

"Well, thank ya, ma'am, but I guess I'll try to catch up with him some other time. Just let him know I stopped by, wouldya?"

"I surely shall, Mister Patterson." Amy replied, and then diplomatically added, "We're all truly sorry for your loss, sir!" as if assuming the visit was in search of the fatherly advice Elijah had promised was Angus' for the asking should he need it in the days ahead.

Disarmed, Angus nodded his appreciation, muttering, "Thank ya ma'am, that's right kind of ya." After an awkward pause, during which Amy looked at him expectantly, as if to ask, 'Is there anything else?' Angus recollected himself and said,

"Well, I'd best be goin on home, then." He put his hat back on, turned back toward the trough, unhitched his horse and mounted.

"Bye now!" Amy called, waving cheerfully.

Angus tipped his hat, kicked his horse into a canter, and headed back down the drive toward the main road, his mind running faster than his horse "Damn!" he thought to himself, his confidence suddenly deflated. It hadn't occurred to him that Elijah might not even be home when he dropped by. He wondered whether he should just wait for another opportunity, or whether he should head on over to Barnwell and pay a visit to John Bauskett. On the one hand, he thought maybe a visit to Bauskett would tip Elijah off, but on the other, he might be able to gain some useful information. So as not to feel he had wasted his time completely, he decided to head on over to Barnwell and take his chances.

As luck would have it, when he got there John Bauskett was in.

"Well Angus, this is a pleasant surprise! What can I do for you, son?" John Bauskett welcomed him warmly.

"Howdy, Mr. Bauskett! I, uh, I was wonderin if, uh, that is, um..." Feeling suddenly awkward about asking for any books on emancipation, for fear of it being too obvious, Angus found himself dissembling.

"What's the matter son, cat got your tongue? I'm happy to help ya'll if I can, but I need to know what it is ya want!" Bauskett said with a kindly smile.

"Yes sir, thank ya, sir. Well, the thing is, I realized, after Pa died, that I had never fully appreciated all his learnin about the law an all, and I was feelin kinda guilty about it. I was wonderin if ya'll have any books I could borrow to study some. I kinda got a hankerin to learn more about the law. Thought maybe I might give it a try, an see if it couldn't help me make my own contribution down here in South Carolina!"

John Bauskett observed Angus keenly, his lawyerly eye trying to assess the underlying motive for such a request. He thought it odd that, given that his father's law library had gone to Elijah, Angus had approached him for books instead. Did he perhaps suspect that Elijah had brought them over here? Was he prying into Elijah's affairs at the behest of his comrades, or was he simply trying to groom himself for a career in politics and catch up on some belated homework?

"Well son, the law's a mighty big topic. Oceans of ink have been spilled exploring it! Ya'll could fill every room in this house from floor to ceiling and not fit in all the books been written about the law. You got some particular aspect of the law ya'd like to explore?" John Bauskett was no fool. He figured by forcing Angus to narrow down his request, his motives would become more apparent.

Angus could feel the trap being set for him, and shied away. "Oh, nothing in particular, sir. I just want to get a better understandin of legal principles, and how they're all supposed to work." He was, after all his father's son, and was able to think more quickly on his feet than his companions. He was using the same ploy on Bauskett he had used on his father, playing on his legal sympathies in the hopes of gaining his favor.

Recognizing that he had an astute adversary, and perfectly aware that he had buttered up Angus Senior with the same arguments, John Bauskett was enjoying the game of cat and mouse and decided to play along.

"Well then, let me see… I suppose I could find a volume or two I could part with temporarily. Why don't ya take a seat for a minute whilst I have a look." He gestured to a seat in the parlor. Angus complied a bit awkwardly, thanking God he had not been discovered, and hoping that whatever Mr. Bauskett came up with would actually be useful. His father's books were nowhere in sight, to his surprise- John having been discreet enough to remove them to another room so as not to upset Eugenia's insistence on keeping a well ordered parlor for receiving guests. However, the volume Elijah had found by Angus Senior's bed lay closed on the side of the tiger maple secretary near the front window- the same desk where John had stood reading Angus Senior's note requesting his help for Elijah, years before.

As Angus Junior's eyes roamed around the room, waiting for John Bauskett to return with some book or other to lend him, his eyes fell on the volume on the desk. He thought it looked familiar and was fairly certain that it was one of his father's, but the fact was, Mr. Bauskett had any number of books with similar bindings on the shelf, and he couldn't be sure. He noticed, however, that there was a folded piece of paper marking a page, and he was sorely tempted to casually sidle over to the desk and take a peek.

Throwing caution to the wind, he got up and headed toward the desk. Just as he was reaching out his hand to pick up the book and open it to the marked page, John Bauskett returned with a whole armload of books. Angus' hand froze in mid-reach as he found Bauskett staring at him. Bauskett had caught him red-handed, just as Mary had when he was trying to read the letter from Henry Clay, and they both knew it.

"I don't recommend that particular volume, son." Bauskett said calmly. " If had thought it would be helpful, I would already have shown it to ya! What ya'll need is right here…" John said, nodding toward the armload of books. He spoke in a casual, matter-of-fact tone with no trace of reprimand, but carefully steered Angus away from the book containing his father's notes. Angus' gesture of reaching for the book had been sufficient to confirm the lawyer's suspitions about the probable cause of the young man's visit.

Bauskett laid before Angus the pile of books, saying simply, "If legal principle is what ya'll want to know, these'll tell ya most everything ya'll need to learn for a good foundation. The rest just comes from practical experience!"

Angus read the titles on the spines of the leather-bound volumes: The Constitution of the United States of America; the Bill of Rights; The Declaration of Independence; The Federalist Papers of Alexander Hamilton; The Boyleston Lectures of John Quincy Adams; Griffith's Annual Law Register of the United States; the Orations of Cicero and The Collected Works of Quintillian; the Magna Carta; and a compendium of juridical writings by the prolific Supreme Court Justice, Joseph Story; the Scotsman, Hugh Griffiths; George Wycliffe of Virginia; Supreme Court Chief Justice John Marshall of Virginia; Supreme Court Justice William Johnson of South Carolina; and various others. It was a veritable cornucopia of the legal knowledge upon which the nation and its separate states had been founded, going back to British Common Law and the Roman Law of the European Continent.

Angus was overwhelmed. "This here is an embarrassment of riches, Mister Bauskett! It's so much information, I wouldn't hardly know where to begin!"

John Bauskett, having achieved precisely the result he intended, replied, "Well, ya'll don't have to take the whole pile! If I were you, I'd start with the foundation of American Law, the Declaration of Independence, the Constitution, and the Bill of Rights!" he paused for a moment and then brightened, adding, "Oh, and the Magna Carta too! That's kinda where it all began!"

Angus suddenly remembered with embarassment that his father had a framed copy of the Declaration of Independence hanging on the wall in the front parlor, and that he'd never really bothered to read it. He felt unexpectedly humbled that his own ambition had so underestimated the amount of learning needed to really understand the law and the amount of work and time it would take to acquire it! For a moment at least, his focus shifted from political ambitions, racial beliefs, or the desire help the Willis brother's secure an inheritance, to genuinely appreciating the complex structure and genius of the rule of law.

Outside, Elijah Willis was approaching the Bauskett's house, eager to hear what his lawyer friend had learned from looking into Angus' annotations and case references. He was caught by surprise seeing Angus' horse tied up out in front, and pulled Beauty to a halt at some distance. He had to assess the situation and decide whether he should go ahead and knock on the door, or perhaps wait and watch until John's visitor had left. Before he could make up his mind however, the Bauskett's front door opened, and he saw John ushering Angus out of the house with some books under his arm.

Elijah walked Beauty over to the same clump of trees where James had spied on him earlier and simply waited and watched.

"I surely do thank ya, Mr. Bauskett!" Angus was saying. "I'll be sure an read em an get em back to ya'll real soon!"

"That'd be fine son, just fine! I hope ya'll enjoy em. They're a powerful set a documents- almost like Holy Writ to us lawyers! Ya Pa loved those documents, an I'm sure he'd be right pleased and proud for ya to learn em well!" John Bauskett offered a wave of paternal benedicition as Angus carefully placed several books in his saddlebag, mounted up, and with a tip of his hat rode off toward Williston. He did not seem to notice Elijah standing in the shadows nearby.

Once Angus was safely out of sight, Elijah nudged Beauty forward and proceeded to the Bauskett's place. He tied the mare up, climbed the steps to the front stoop, and knocked on the door. John promptly opened it with a smile.

"I saw you out there as our young friend departed!" John admitted. "No need to worry- everything's under control!"

Elijah felt reassured. "Glad to hear it! Did he reveal the true motive of his visit?" he asked, knowing full well it was not a mere social call Angus had been paying.

"Indirectly. He wanted law books- claimed he felt guilty about not studyin em enough while his Pa was livin, and thought maybe he should try his hand at it now, so's he could make his 'own contribution here in South Carolina,'" John remarked.

"That a fact?" asked Elijah rhetorically. "Well, we both know what direction his 'contribution' is headin, and it sure as Hell isn't toward the emancipation of slaves! So what did ya'll tell him- I saw him carryin books out with him. None of his Pa's, I trust?"

"Course not! Fortunately, for the sake of domestic tranquility, I had removed Angus' books from the parlor, so as not to upset the aesthetic and the delicate balance of matrimonial power here at home. (Eugenia does insist on keepin a tidy parlor!) However, I must confess, the book ya'll found with Angus' notes- it was sittin on my desk, and the boy almost got a hold of it! Fortunately, I arrived just in time to deflect him from examinin it and gave him the foundin documents of the nation to study as a primer instead!"

"Thank the Lord! A narrow escape- God must truly love us! Reminds me of the time I accidentally left Senator Clay's letter by his father's chair, and Mary caught him red-handed trying to read it!"

"Well, he knows I'm onto him, as I caught him reachin for the book at the moment I walked in. He froze in mid air before he could even get his hands on it. But I don't think he actually realized what was in the book- meanin either the nature of the text or his father's notes, that is."

"That's good- on both counts!" Elijah breathed a sigh of relief. "From the looks of things, ya'll gave him enough readin material to keep him busy for quite a spell!" he chuckled. "Hopefully that'll buy us some time. The boy's not stupid- he's a heap smarter than either James or Michael- so I don't expect he'll try pryin into your books again any time soon. I'm surprised he didn't come over to my place though, knowin I had all his Pa's books. I wonder if he suspects I brought em over here, or whether he just thinks you an I're in cahoots."

"I figure he probably suspects both, since he came over askin. But that's alright. There's plenty a reasons other than emancipation or inheritance for you and me to be talkin. We can put up a smoke screen easily enough- as your lawyer now that Angus has passed, I could just as easily be advising ya'll on ya business affairs!" Bauskett said with a sly grin.

"That makes sense," affirmed Elijah. "Unless the boy gets some concrete evidence, he'll be wary of tippin off Guignard or my nephews. He's smart enough to try not to get caught in any legal mess himself."

Bauskett nodded, as if that settled the matter for the time being, at least.

"So, have you been able to look into any of the case references of Angus? I'm right curious to know what his thinkin was. He always had a talent for building a case, an I figure whatever he was lookin at must be a part of buildin his argument in our favor."

"True enough- though some of building a case for ya'll requires arguing the case against ya too! That was his way of testin out his hypothesis to make sure it was sound!" John said, with a note of admiration in his voice for the skills of his late colleague. "The reference to the Act of the Assembly of 1841 was clearly the latter- as by that act it became virtually impossible to emancipate a slave or leave a person of color any bequest."

"What about the other references, like that Frazier reference, for instance. What was that all about?" pressed Elijah.

"Well I haven't been able to read up on the entire case, but if I recall correctly, it refers to an attempt to leave an inheritance to someone of color. I need to look into that case again, refresh my memory and understand the details, as I'm certain Angus thought it significant to your situation for some reason."

Elijah took this in and nodded. After a moment's reflection he said, "John, let me ask you something- and I need a straightforward answer- no fancy prevaricatin lawyer talk!" he insisted.

"What is it, Elijah?" Bauskett replied, without elaboration.

"I can't shake the feelin that time is runnin out, and tensions around here are runnin higher an higher. Even if it weren't for Angus and my nephews- we both know things are coming to a boil about secession and the whole slavery issue. If you were in my shoes, how soon would you just go on and head up to Cincinnati with Amy and the children?"

John Bauskett thought for a moment, not as a lawyer exploring a complex and challenging case, but as a man who felt compassion for his friend and the difficult and possibly dangerous path that lay ahead.

"Truthfully? I'd say I agree that things are comin to a boil, and that if I were you I'd want to go ahead an get my family outa here as soon as I could!" He paused reflectively. "Whatever is gonna happen in terms of law suits and court battles, as Angus said, is gonna hang on them bein free, and the best way to safeguard that is to go on and take em outa South Carolina and slave territory altogether, while ya'll still got the strength to do it!"

Elijah sighed and nodded with a melancholy expression on his face. "I've looked at the numbers John, and any way I calculate em, there's no way I can free all my slaves. At best I might be able to free half of em, and leave em each a little somethin to get started."

This came as no surprise to Bauskett, as he had always considered it optimistic to think of freeing the whole plantation. It was not only economically difficult, it would almost certainly cause a major uproar in Barnwell District and could even trigger a violent response. But he understood Elijah and Amy's desire to free as many as possible. If the will passed probate in South Carolina, the executors could free a goodly number of them, but that was a big 'if.'"

"Look Elijah, I gotta be honest with ya. I know you and Amy have a dream of freein as many as ya can- and I applaud ya'll for it. But it seems to me the most important thing for you to do is to get her and her mother and children up to Cincinnati- and worry about the rest later."

Elijah thought for a moment before responding. "Amy and I've talked about waiting until Fall, so we could get one more harvest in- and the cash that would provide- then sell off the slaves we must and take that money up with us to Cincinnati. That way, should there be a delay in the courts down here if anything happened to me, they'd at least have some money to live on until the plantation could be sold. What do you think?"

John Bauskett considered the plan carefully. He knew there were no guarantees, and though if it were he, he would probably go on up to Cinicnnati right away, the financial considerations were significant, and the plan made reasonable sense.

"Well, the way I see it, any course a action ya'll choose is gonna have some element of risk. However, that bein said, I can see reason in wantin to get a final crop to market before ya'll leave, so ya'll have the cash ya need to secure the family's safety for a time," he opined. "But sure as the sun comes up in the mornin, ya'll's white relations are gonna put up a fight, and there's no tellin how long it'll take to settle it. I'll do all I can to help you and them from down here- as I'm certain Jolliffe and Gitchell will from up in Cincinnati- but Amy and the children'd best be as far from here as ya can get em when the fight breaks out, or they may never see freedom!"

Elijah thanked his friend profusely for the promise of help, feeling at least that he and Amy had a powerful legal advocate in their corner here in South Carolina. He felt confident that John Jolliffe would defend his interests as executor, but would need a strong ally down here to help get the will through probate in Barnwell District. Elijah knew he could trust John Bauskett to make the most forceful legal argument possible on their behalf, and felt Amy and the children would at least have a fighting chance of benefitting from the riches he had so diligently and arduously accrued. But if they did not, he knew John was right that if they were free at least, God would somehow provide for their well-being, and he could feel he'd fulfilled his promise.

Realizing that he did not need to know all the legal details of every possible argument in order to trust his lawyer, he said, "Well John, I reckon I should just leave this in your competent hands- knowin that Angus has already given ya'll a solid framework for building the case when the time comes!"

"I'd be a fool to tell ya ya'll got nothin to worry about Elijah, but I can promise ya that I will fight to the very end for ya- and provide Gitchell and Jolliffe any and all the help I can to make sure Amy and the children stay free. God willin, we'll also be able to make sure they get the benefit of all ya'll's hard work to build up your fortune as well!"

With that the two men shook hands, and Elijah started for the door. He turned before he left and added, "If ya'll get wind of what Angus and my nephews're planning to do, I'd appreciate it if ya could let me know. I'd just as soon not have any nasty surprises."

John laughed grimly and said, "Well so long as ya'll expect it'll be nasty, whatever it is, it won't be a surprise! But don't worry, if I find out anything I'll be sure and let ya'll know."

"Alright then!" Elijah nodded again with a sigh and started down the porch steps, mounted Beauty, and headed on home. His heart was heavy, and he felt a little light- headed, as if suddenly exhausted. His thighs, usually instinctively gripping Beauty's flanks, felt flaccid. The mare sensed something was wrong and slowed her pace to a gentle trot, lest he fall.

By the time Elijah got home he had recovered himself somewhat, but Amy noticed immediately that he was not quite himself. He looked pale and unusually worn.

"Sugar, what's wrong? What happened over Mr. Bauskett's? Are you alright?" she asked solicitously, eager for news but concerned by his look.

"I'm alright darlin, just feelin bone weary!" he said, slumping onto the settee in the parlor and propping his feet up on the ottoman. "Pour me a glass a whiskey will ya, sugar? I just need to relax a spell."

Amy reluctantly went over to the side table where a silver tray held a cut glass decanter of whiskey with an elegant stopper and several crystal tumblers. She could see by his mood and behavior this was no time to reprimand him for his consumption, so she poured out a generous dollop and brought Elijah the glass. As he took a good swig and smacked his lips, she asked,

"So what did John say? It's clear somethin's weighin heavy on ya. Tell me what happened."

He proceeded to recount to her the sequence of events from the moment he spied Angus Patterson's horse to the latter's departure with John's books, to the entire discussion of issues with the lawyer. Amy listened intently, only once voicing her alarm when he shared his own concern that Angus was digging for evidence or legal principle to use against them. When he had finished, she simply nodded and said,

"Well, I'm glad ya told me and glad ya asked John's advice. Can't say I'm glad to hear about Angus Patterson nosin about, but I had a feelin he was up to somethin. Fact is, he did come here first, but I had no way of lettin ya know!" she said apologetically. "And though he never mentioned his father's books, I'm certain that's what he was lookin for. He wanted to catch ya for havin taken em over to Mister Bauskett's. I betcha anything he was hopin to walk into a roomful of his Pa's books and be able to report it back to your nephews!" Amy concluded astutely.

"Well thank the Good Lord, the only book of his Pa's he saw at John's was the one I found by Angus' bedside the day he died, but given how many similar books John had of his own, I bet he couldn't be sure it was his Pa's. It was that Amazin Grace again that John caught him red-handed reachin for it, just as he walked back in with an armload of his own books, so the boy couldn't prove it was his Pa's, or see Angus' notes stuck inside!"

Amy groaned that it had been such a close call. "Oh Lordy Elijah, how we gonna make it til harvest time with all this spyin and plottin goin on around us? Do ya really think we can wait that long?" she blurted unexpectedly.

"Well, I asked the same thing of John, and he said if it were him he'd want to get ya'll out as soon as possible, but that the financial considerations were important, because he's certain my white relations're gonna put up a fight to block the will from probate down here, and if anything happens to me ya'll're gonna need as much cash on hand as possible to tide ya over while our case works its way through the courts."

Amy heard the weariness in his voice, and for the first time felt like the "if anything happens to me" was more likely than just prudently hypothetical. It was distressing, but she didn't want to show it, for fear of darkening Elijah's mood even further. She was worried too about Gilbert, whose mood also had darkened noticeably of late. She wondered whether they were going to be able to navigate these perilous waters to safety for all of them, or whether perhaps it was inevitable that some would be lost in the surging rip-tide of political and familial turbulence churning around them.

"Cash is not the only thing we need, darlin. We need you!" This was at once, both a statement of fact and an expression of affection. "So come on now, finish ya drink and let's go on in to supper. Momma's fixed a real good meal for us. An then ya'll need to get some sleep, or all this strain is gonna kill ya- and then where will we be?" This last she meant to sound jocular- a light-hearted teasing, to show her concern was tempered by affection- but was in fact an expression of cold reality, and Elijah could hear it. It was a sobering thought to which he had no choice but to acquiesce.

Elijah finished his drink and standing up, took Amy by the hand and said with a sigh, "Thank ya darlin, I believe you're right! Let's go eat, and go on up to bed." He smiled at her affectionately but couldn't mask his fatigue, and docilely let her lead him by the hand to supper.

Momma Celia took one look at Elijah when he came in to the dining room and felt instinctively that he was on the verge of another episode. As she was serving them supper she said, "Elijah honey, ya'll look a little peaked. I'm gonna make ya'll some a my tea, an I wants ya to drink it up b'fo ya go to bed!"

This was not a suggestion, as Elijah well knew, but a command. Doctor's orders. Fact was, Elijah was feeling enough off that he simply nodded his willingness, and said, "Thank ya, Momma."

Satisfied that her patient was cooperating with her treatment plan, Momma Celia scurried off to mix up a fresh batch of her digitalis tea, muttering a heartfelt prayer, "Lord A'Mighty, keep him with us! Don't abandon us now, when we so close to freedom!"

LXXXVII

A good night's sleep and good dose of Momma Celia's nasty tasting digitalis tea seemed to work wonders on Elijah. He awoke the next morning feeling much more himself. With a clear head, he turned his full attention to the urgency of making certain the crops all got planted in a timely manner to assure as big a bumper crop as nature and the weather would permit.

The slaves even noticed that Elijah seemed to have renewed energy and started to take heart. There he was once again, working with them side by side, urging them to outdo themselves and beat out all the other planters in the region. He seldom went into town these days- preferring to send others on errands and focus his own energy on making the Willis Plantation more productive than ever. Of course, in part he was simply avoiding having to run into his nephews or other relations, or Dr. Guignard, or anyone else who might represent even a remote challenge or threat to his plans. But he was also feeling inspired to outdo his own best performance to assure the biggest cash crop ever, in the hopes that even if it killed him, it would secure Amy and the children's future. He was driven by the well-matched team of fear of impending death and determination to succeed galloping down the road into the future.

The cotton, corn, and vegetables all got planted. Unlike the previous summer, the weather was benign, and the seedlings took quickly. Momma Celia's kitchen garden exploded with kale, collard greens, carrots, peppers, lettuce, spinach, beans, tomatoes, squash, mustard, and a wide variety of herbs, not to mention her marigolds, foxglove, and lemongrass. Once the weather was warm enough, she even managed to root a bunch of aloe vera leaves and plant them. She had to mix sand in the soil of their pots though, to help them drain. They would rot with too much water in the loamy soil.

The lumber mill too was kept busy, and business seemed to be humming right along. Julius and Jason and Gilbert had their hands full keeping the work gangs going full steam ahead, and it wasn't long at all before the first vegetables were already being harvested to take to market.

Elijah's careful husbandry of the various strains of cotton had paid off, and they were seeing a level of production unheard of ten years before. Julius and Gilbert took special pride in this, as their own instinct for breeding and tending the cotton effectively was bearing fruit. Jason, meanwhile, contented himself with focusing on the planting, pruning, culling, harvesting, and milling of timber to ship off down the river or on the railroad for points North and West.

Despite the physical exhaustion that came from hard labor, the frenzy of work had been a kind of analgesic against the emotional and psychological pain of dealing with his plotting relations and their allies. It had distanced Elijah from the daily worry about conspiracies against him and the threat of his family's internecine scheming spilling over into a community uproar. He had been so absorbed in his concerns about that he had not even recognized the warning signals from the slave quarters that an uprising could just as well spring from within the plantation as from without. Fortunately, his own renewed energy seemed to have had a mitigating effect on any possibility that the slaves themselves would stage a protest. The plowing, planting and harvesting grounded him, and seemed to stave off any further episodes with his heart, and restored some normalcy to life on the plantation. Even Gilbert seemed lest restive, the ease of conversation between them having returned, to Elijah's relief.

Nevertheless, Elijah and Amy both knew that the time was rapidly approaching for them to make decisions about the sale of slaves and even to consider finding possible buyers for the plantation itself, without breaking the news to others until it was absolutely necessary.

"Sugar," Amy began one day in late Summer when the cotton was already high and harvest time approaching, "don't ya think it's time we figure out which slaves're gonna have to be sold, and make a plan?"

They had been sitting on the upper veranda on the same porch swing they had shared that summer night years ago, when Amy had told Elijah she was pregnant with Eliza. They were trying to catch a breeze to find some relief from the afternoon heat, and perspiration laid a glistening film over their faces and arms despite the energetic use of palmetto fans and the subtle movement of air produced by the steady rocking of the swing. Their clothes clung to them damply, Amy's skirts hanging limp to the floor, sweeping back and forth heavily as she swung. The oppressive humidity epitomized their dampened spirits and the emotional stickiness of having to face the issue at last. They had both been dreading this moment, but Amy knew it could not be put off any longer.

"Well, I suppose we've got no choice! Won't be long before we harvest the cotton, and then we can go on and sell whomever we must," Elijah answered reluctantly. "Way I figure it, the most I can free is around twenty-five, including you and Momma and the children. That means I'm gonna have to sell the other twenty-five slaves, give or take. We need to figure how many are married or have children- I don't wanna break up any families!"

Amy nodded, her face grim. She started taking a mental inventory and then spoke up, "Gilbert told me he and Jason and Julius thought Jeremiah should be sold, for his own protection. But he's got so much potential!"

Elijah nodded. "He's young and firey and a natural leader, but he's too prone to stirrin things up for his own good."

"What about old Henry?" she asked. "He's mighty loyal to ya."

Elijah smiled. "I'd hate to have to sell him- been with me most a my life. Only thing is, I'm not sure he's got enough strength left in him to start a new life up North."

Amy pursed her lips and sighed, realizing that Elijah's choices all had human consequences that were far more complicated than just being free or not. How in Heaven's name could they judge wisely enough, fairly enough, and humanely enough, when the whole choice was so unfair and so inhuman in the first place? She sighed, "I hate myself for even thinkin this, but I'd almost rather leave this in your hands and not even know who's on the list!" Her voice cracked with emotion mid-sentence.

Elijah grunted, half in sympathy and half in disappointment. He wasn't quite sure how to respond. He hated having to make a choice, but there was no alternative. Amy held in her trembling hand a list of the names of all the slaves on the plantation. A furtive teardrop had slid off her cheek onto the paper, threatening to smudge the names. Elijah reached over, saying,

"Come on, now. Just give me the list." He took it gently from her, resigned to having to just go ahead and decide and have done with it. He scanned the list, considering which slaves knew how to read and write, which had marketable skills, which had families, which were old or ill. He realized that the only freedom there'd be with no skills, no health, or no energy would be the freedom to suffer and die in misery, so he made up his mind on the spot to free the skilled and literate, those with the best chances of survival, and sell the others, hoping at least to find a benevolent owner who would not mistreat them. So long as there were able-bodied workers among them, they should fetch a decent price.

"What if ya can't find buyers around here?" Amy asked, sniffling softly.

The question hung poignantly in the air for a while before Elijah was able to answer. He finally faced what had been lingering on the edges of his awareness for some time, feeding his procrastination in looking for buyers in the first place: that the well-intended complication of trying to find the right "fit" for every slave among the local slaveowners was not only daunting, it was probably impossible.

"To tell ya the truth, I've half a mind to just ship all the ones to be sold off to one of the markets. It's gonna be mighty hard to find enough good buyers around here and parcel em all off to various plantations without folks findin out what our plan is!"

Amy heard the truth, and it was dreadful. She swallowed hard, a cold nausea churning in her belly despite the summer heat. The very thought of the slave markets was traumatic to contemplate. It was impossible to imagine a more degrading environment, where coloreds were treated like livestock, and the auctioneer had little or no regard for their feelings or basic dignity. She knew an auctioneer could be told to sell a family as a single lot, but prices would be better when sold individually- and sometimes there was no one willing to buy a whole family at a time. The whole point of selling them was to get enough money for the rest of them to survive in Ohio, so could they afford not to get top dollar, or to sell any cheap? How in God's Holy Name could they balance compassion and self-interest in the midst of this nightmare?

Despite her inner conflict and her dread and horror at the thought of the slave market, and even though it inspired in her a terrible sense of guilt, Amy realized Elijah was probably right. To try to sell a few here and a few there to local planters in Barnwell- it was not only unlikely he'd be able to find enough buyers for all the slaves he needed to sell, it was almost guaranteed to cause a stir. His reasons for suddenly doing so would make his over-all plan all the more apparent. Not only would his nephews get wind of it, but so would Dr. Guignard, and possibly even that horrible Robert Barnwell Rhett! That was precisely the kind of attention they had been working so hard to avoid all this time, convinced that their safe departure and deliverance depended upon it! They simply couldn't let that happen!

Elijah could see that Amy's noble dream was unraveling as the thread of her idealism got snagged on their dilemma, and was steadily picked and pulled by the reality of conflicting circumstances. It was taking a terrible toll on her. He tried to console her, putting his arm around her damp, shaking shoulders, but she was disconsolate and broke down in uncontrollable sobs of sorrow, pain, frustration and bitter disappointment. This time there was no thunderstorm to clear the air, no relief from a fresh breeze to blow her sorrow away, and no golden moonrise and luminescent mist surrounding them to soften the blow and gild the appearances of these two people thrown into despair. The certainty that their choices were going to cause some people they cared about terrible pain and sorrow, despite their best and noblest intentions, was almost unbearable.

Devastated that he could not console or comfort Amy, but totally sympathetic to her sense of anguish, Elijah spoke to her from his heart. "Darlin," he said softly, "you are the kindest, smartest, most generous hearted woman I know, and I love ya for wantin to free everyone on this plantation! I love ya for makin me want to free em too! This is a rotten, cruel shame we got facin us, no two ways about it! It's the most God-awful decision I've ever had to make, but I gotta make it!" His eyes begged her to understand. "But even if all my slaves can't be free just yet, there's still a chance for a lot of em, and I swore I'd see you, and your Momma, and the children all free before I die. I'm not breakin that promise!"

Amy raised her head, wiping her tears and her runny nose on her sleeve like a little child, her usual poise and decorum having dissolved in the puddle of her tears. She looked through grief-bleary eyes at this extraordinary man, and felt his own sense of pain and loss nearly matched hers. His empathy was enough to pull her back from the lonely abyss into which she felt herself falling, for his promise was like a candle in the darkness of her desperation, giving her a tenuous, still flickering hope: a golden, shining point of focus to reorient her and break her fall.

On the pretext of making arrangements with Will Beazely at the depot for the shipment of his cotton crop Elijah saddled up Beauty and headed into town. As he approached the depot he surveyed the area, looking further down the road towards town as well as along the platform and into Mr. Beazeley's store, to assess how many people might be around within earshot. He needed to speak to Mr. Beazely privately and could not risk anyone eavesdropping.

He slowed Beauty to a casual walk so as not to look conspicuous, and rode her up to a hitching post on the road side of the platform between the depot store and the train tracks. As he dismounted, a few ladies from town were exiting the store with their purchases. He tipped his hat to them and bade them a courtly good morning and then proceeded on in, once satisfied that they were each well on their way home and out of hearing range.

"Well hello there, Mister Willis! Long time no see! What can I do for ya sir?" Will Beazely called out cheerfully as Elijah approached the counter.

"Mornin Will! Nice to see you too!" Elijah's automatic response seemed a bit distracted, not realizing that Will had only implicitly remarked that it was nice to see him. He was looking around the depot to make sure no one else was there before continuing.

"Will, I need to speak with you confidentially about some decisions I've come to." Elijah lowered his voice and immediately had Will's undivided attention. Having already asked him to keep an eye out for buyers for his property and slaves, the stationmaster had a pretty good idea of where Elijah was heading.

"Of course, Mister Willis! How can I help ya?" he responded immediately.

"Well Will, ya know how I asked ya'll to keep an ear and an eye open for possible buyers for some of my slaves and property? It's time you knew that I'm gonna be takin Amy and the family up North and resettle there real soon, but I need to raise some cash before I do. I'll most likely come back and sell my plantation later, but I want to get them to safety first."

Will listened attentively nodding his understanding. "I understand, sir. What can I do to help?"

"Well here's the sad truth of it. I was hopin to free all my slaves, but I can't afford it and still have enough money for Amy and the children's support if anything happens to me. So I'm gonna have to sell about half of my slaves as soon as the harvest is in. I thought about tryin to find em good homes around here, but I can't see how I could sell enough of em without raisin all kinds a suspicions, and that could make it harder for us to get up to Cincinnati."

Will continued to listen, as always admiring Elijah for his business acumen and clarity of financial analysis. "So do ya still want me to try to look for possible buyers for ya, then?" he asked for clarification, uncertain as to what Elijah's thrust was going to be.

"As a matter of fact no, though I appreciate your willingness to try."

"So what is it ya'll need me to do then, Mister Willis?" Will pressed.

"I've decided the best way to handle this is gonna be to send the whole lot off to one of the slave markets somewhere outside of Barnwell where they won't be known and where tongues won't immediately start waggin about me." Elijah answered.

"That shouldn't be any problem sir, as long as you or some other white man accompanies them on the train. The railroad won't allow any shipment of unattended coloreds- even free ones need permission." Will responded.

Elijah's brow furrowed and he pursed his lips. He wished he could delegate this task to someone else, but there was no one he could trust to do so. "Alright, I can do that, but I want to do it with as little commotion as possible. I'druther folks around here not see me haulin that many slaves off on the train."

"Well sir, if ya'll caught the earliest train outa here there'd more'n likely not be anyone here to see ya'll loading em on board. There's a train to Charleston rolls through about five in the morning, an another that heads out toward Georgia bout an hour later. Since ya'll don't have to drive through town to get here from your place, shouldn't be too hard to avoid bein noticed," Will assured him, "unless ya'll're makin a lotta noise!" he added.

Elijah suddenly envisioned a wagonload of slaves possibly wailing in grief at their departure and felt his anxiety level rise despite Will's assurances. He would have to try to keep them quiet and might need to enlist Gilbert's, Julius' and Jason's unenviable help to do so. He didn't want to have to resort to the threat of punishment, but he might not have a choice.

"Good point, Will. We'll have to do the best we can about that, but it won't be easy," he acknowledged. "This is about the hardest thing I've ever had to do!" he muttered, as much to himself as to Will. Then, as if asserting his conclusion, he addressed the stationmaster, "I'll need round trip fares for me and possibly two or three others, plus one-way fares for about twenty-two."

Will let out a low whistle at the realization of how many slaves would be travelling. "Alright Mister Willis, ya'll can count on me to make the necessary arrangements. Just tell me the dates and destination of your travels, and I'll see to the rest. Lemme just remind ya that if ya'll take em outa state to sell, ya'll'll be checked at the state line to be sure ya have the legal right to do so. But you must remember that from when ya'll went up to Baltimore a few years ago." Will said helpfully.

"Yes I remember Will, but thanks for remindin me. Once I get the cotton crop in, I'll figure this out an let ya know. May be that I can ship the slaves with the cotton an make it look more like they're helpin, so's not to raise suspicions along the way..." this last he sort of muttered under his breath. He was thinking out loud and realized it.

"Sorry Will, just tryin to find the best way to do this. But please God, don't tell anybody about this or all Hell could break loose, and we can't afford to let that happen! Not after all we've been through!"

He began pondering which market would be the best place to sell them. Charleston was the most profitable, but with Robert Barnwell Rhett and his paper located there, there was a risk he might get wind of it and publicize Elijah's sale. That would be a disaster. He remembered that the Charlotte, Columbia and Augusta Railroad line passed right through Hamburg, just this side of the Savannah River and the Georgia line. There was a slave market there. He might be able to sell them there and not have to cross out of state. Moreover, he'd be far away from the prying eyes and ears of Robert Barnwell Rhett in Charleston. He would have to give more consideration to the matter before he actually booked his tickets.

A coffle of slaves could be marched overland too, but he didn't have the heart to subject his slaves to that indignity and add insult to their injury. It was bad enough he'd have to chain em at all. And a march would take more time. He couldn't afford to be away from the plantation for long, as he was uncertain how the remaining slaves would act once half of their companions were shipped off. There was a need for speed to accomplish this once everything was set in motion. It occurred to him he might even be able to contract a trader to come take delivery of the slaves here at the depot, so as not to have to accompany them to the market himself. That would save him time away (and save him the agony of seeing his slaves on the block too).

"Hold on a minute, Will. Do ya'll know of any reputable traders come through here? If a trader could meet me here at the station and take delivery of the slaves, it'd make things a whole lot easier- save me some time and a few fares as well."

"There's a fella comes by from time to time on the run from Charleston to Atlanta. I could try an contact him for ya, you know, discreetly," Will suggested.

Elijah thought about the risks of involving anyone else in his plan and the chances of word leaking out. "I don't know Will- it may be too risky. I'm gonna have to think about this some more. If you could at least get the fella's name and a way to contact him, I'd be grateful. But don't tell him about me, or my plan. Just make it like a general question on behalf of local planters who might want to know. Not another word, swear?"

Will Beazely understood the intensity of the dilemma Elijah was facing, even if he didn't know all the details. He had already promised his help and discretion. There was no question of his compliance. "Ya'll have my word, I won't tell a soul!"

Outside, Elijah could hear a carriage arriving and the voice of someone approaching. Taking that as his cue to depart, he shook Will's hand gratefully and started heading out of the depot just as John Guignard entered, ordering his coachman to wait for him outside. Guignard's tone was customarily brusque and contemptuous. Seeing Elijah, his expression immediately changed from a scowl to a toothy grin, like a chameleon changing its color to adapt to his environment. It may work for a chameleon, but it couldn't really hide Guignard's malice. His two-faced nature was transparently clear to both Elijah and Will Beazely. No doubt it was equally and onerously clear to his coachman as well.

"Well bless my soul if it isn't Elijah Willis! Been a long time!" Guignard said in his usual oily way. "What brings ya'll into the depot today?" he asked, his sociability thinly masking his habitual suspicion and invasive curiosity.

"Oh, nothing much John. Just talkin to Will about shippin rates an all. Got quite a crop a cotton and lumber to be shipped this year!" Elijah smiled, as if he hadn't a care in the world and business was booming.

"That a fact? Well congratulations!" Guignard responded insincerely.

"What about you John, what brings you here?" Elijah shot back.

"Well as a matter of fact I'm lookin into shippin a couple a my thoroughbred mares up to a stud farm in Kentucky for breedin! Ya'll know how fond I am of a good race! I'm bettin on breedin my mares and improvin my stock, so's I can cash in at the racetracks all over Carolina!" he chuckled gleefully.

Guignard's lust for gambling and his pretensions to rivaling the fastest horses in the Bluegrass had inadvertently tipped Elijah off to a possible danger. He had to make sure not to ship his slaves or his family on the same train as Guignard's horses, or his whole plan might get blown! He shot Will a cautionary look, and Will caught his eye with a slight nod of recognition. He had already seen the same perilous possibility.

"Isn't it a little late in the year for breedin, John? I heard up in Kentucky they like their mares to drop foal around March. With an eleven month gestation period, that means prime breedin time would be in April, not the Fall!" Elijah may not have raced horses, but he knew more than a thing or two about breeding them, and Beauty was the proof of it.

"Well, true enough, Elijah, but I figure sendin a few mares up to Kentucky to winter'd give em time to adjust and be in their prime, grazin on that bluegrass when breedin time rolls around! They say up there it's the limestone in the water makes the grass such good pasturin- makes the horses' bones stronger for runnin!" Guignard shot back, trying to impress Elijah with his superior knowledge. He was slightly miffed that Elijah had the presumption to challenge his understanding of horse breeding, since he deemed himself the area's foremost expert.

"Well best a luck to ya John! You plannin on accompanyin your mares up to Kentucky, or do ya'll have someone to handle it for ya?" Elijah probed, suddenly aware that the answer could make a difference in his own plans.

"Matter of fact, I do intend to go along with em! I have friends outside a Lexington. I couldn't let my babies travel all alone, and there's not a nigra in all a South Carolina I'd trust to take em even if it were legal! Either they'd mishandle the horses or try to run away- and we can't have that now, can we?" he said with a cautionary edge, as if to warn Elijah against the foolishness of the insufficient supervision of blacks.

"Heavens no!" answered Elijah mockingly. "That'd be a terrible threat to your investment!"

"To both of them, actually- whether in my four legged livestock or the two-legged variety!" Guignard smirked, showing his disdain for slaves as mere chattel. It made Elijah want to bash his smug face in, but he restrained himself.

"Well I surely do admire your gamblin spirit John, even if ya haven't won all your bets! Nobody ever does!" Elijah said with a wink, as if to warn Guignard not to count on beating him.

The two men smiled from their faces, not from their hearts, only slightly masking their mutual loathing. Elijah tipped his hat to Guignard and bade him farewell, as Guignard moved forward toward Will Beazeley to make his shipping inquiries. Will noticed that the veins on Guignard's temples were pounding and his neck was flushed above his white starched collar, belying his seething rage and contempt for Elijah. It was a timely reminder of the caution he needed to exercise to assure Elijah's plans were not revealed, even if this arrogant fool tried to wheedle some tidbit of information out of him.

Having overheard the entire conversation, as Elijah mounted Beauty outside and rode away Will asked, "So Dr. Guignard, when did ya'll want to ship your horses?"

"So did ya catch Uncle Elijah givin yer Pa's books to Bauskett?" James asked Angus, eager for news confirming his conspiracy suspicions.

"As a matter of fact I didn't." Angus confessed to James' and Michael's great surprise. "I went over to your uncle's place to see if I could look at the books, but he wasn't home. So then I went over to Barnwell and paid Mr. Bauskett a visit. I was wary a givin away too much, so I just asked if I could borrow some books to learn more about legal principles... Figured it'd be too obvious to ask about manumission or inheritance law."

"D'ya'll mean to tell me Bauskett didn't have yer Pa's books! I'd swear that's what Uncle Elijah an his nigra were bringin in the other day!"

"Well, I only saw one book in the parlor that might have been Pa's- but then again it might not. Bauskett's got a heap a law books of his own, bein a lawyer himself. I'd seen em before, that time when Pa asked me to take him a message a few years ago." Angus was reluctant to reveal he'd gotten caught red-handed attempting to look at the book, so he sort of glossed over some of the details of his visit.

"An what did Bauskett say?" pressed Michael, eager to get to the crux of the matter.

"Well, he said that book would not be of any help to me and proceeded to give me a stack a books to read- the Constitution, Bill a Rights, Declaration a Independence and the Magna Carta. Said all the legal principles I needed to know were in em, and I should study em hard."

"Shit!" swore James. "I was sure you'd be able to catch Uncle Elijah's trickery and call him out on it. But the fact you didn't see the books don't mean he don't got em! Betcha he's hidden em away!" James clearly felt it was downright inconsiderate of John Bauskett not to simply fess up and invite Angus to peruse them all at his will. He was determined to get at them somehow.

Michael, for once not resorting to the ham-handed solutions of a ruffian, offered, "Well if Angus studies up on the law, won't he be able to keep Uncle Elijah from pullin a fast one and take him to court? I mean Hell, his Pa was a real smart lawyer, maybe Angus could be too! At least some of his Pa's smarts might a rubbed off on him!"

James was still fuming about not catching his uncle out with the books. "That's why we need those books, damnit!"

Angus tried to calm him down. "Take it easy James! It really doesn't matter! Michael's right. Maybe we been focusin on the wrong thing. If I can learn enough about the law, I can face your uncle in court no matter what he tries to pull! Bauskett may have actually given me the key by givin me those foundational books ta read!"

Michael, thrilled to be affirmed for a change by the smarter Angus, added, "Hell James, we don't even know what Uncle Elijah's pullin yet, least not in any particulars. But no matter what it is, if it frees any nigras or leaves em any property it ain't legal here in South Carolina. Angus can prove it in court, and we'll win!"

For Michael the issue seemed like him, uncomplicated and simple. From a certain perspective he was actually right about that. Any will or devise Elijah might have written could not go into effect without court approval. That's where the battle would be fought and won. And neither Elijah's nor John Bauskett's libraries were the only sources of legal information available to them. There were other lawyers in the region who would be more than sympathetic to their cause. It was time they started expanding their horizons beyond the confines of the small town Lowlands.

"I'm gonna read those books a Mr. Bauskett's, by God! No matter what ya'll's uncle tries, I'm gonna find a way to fight it!" Angus promised.

"Well then get to it boy, cause I got a feelin whatever he's gonna do it's gonna be soon! So ya'll best get crackin on learnin all ya can about how the law's supposed to work! We don't have all the time in the world ta get this taken care of! I don't intend to have to wait til I'm old to collect on my inheritance, just cause a some damned court battle!"

James' selfishness and impatience all too apparent, Angus thought to himself that he was being very small-minded not so see that committing to study the law went way beyond being the means for securing his possible inheritance. Angus realized it could be much much more. He was willing to let the Willis brothers think he was doing this just for them, but already his mind and ambition were looking beyond the Willis brothers' self-serving goals to a much bigger picture of shaping and using state laws himself. He realized he wanted to be able not only to understand the laws, but to also help make them. Elijah's breach of social norms might just be a stepping stone to writing new laws that would not only prevent emancipation and the leaving of inheritance to coloreds, but could even criminalize having mixed-race families in the first place, so that no other whites would have to be faced with the insulting possibility of being forced to share their birthright with any colored usurpers again.

"Don't get yer nuts in a twist, James! I'm gonna read those books, don't you worry! My Pa always said, in a nation a laws like ours, the biggest battles are won in the courts, not on the battlefields. I intend to be a winner!"

The cotton harvest had been the best ever. The gangs had worked in shifts non-stop and brought it in in record time. There had been a feeling of anticipation, a sense that this was more than just another harvest, that something big was afoot. Seeing Elijah's determination had inspired the field hands and they had worked extra hard thinking that it would thereby so endear them to their master that he would finally act on the promise of emancipation at last.

The dark truth was that Elijah and Amy were feeling tormented. They couldn't make up their minds whether it was better to be straight with the slaves and tell them what was going to happen outright so they'd be prepared, or keep quiet until the very last minute, possibly even tricking them into thinking they were going on a trip rather than being sold. That way there would be little or no chance of word getting out about what was going on, and their own departure for Cincinnati might thereby be made easier and safer. They agonized over it day and night, despite Elijah's convincingly upbeat demeanor out in the fields.

Elijah was not being totally duplicitous, for he was genuinely enthusiastic about the success of the crop and proud of his workers for achieving it. He had always taken pride in working hard and making his plantation productive. Knowing this would be the last time he would oversee the harvest had given it an almost nostalgic quality, and he had actually enjoyed the hard work as a sort of crowning effort. All the more so because it would purchase the crown of freedom, at least for Amy and his children and hopefully for some of the others as well.

He figured with any kind of luck he could get between ten and twenty-thousand dollars for the slaves, and add to that whatever the cotton, corn, and lumber brought in. He could take a chunk of that with them up to Ohio and leave the rest with Gilbert to cover expenses down here in Williston until he could get back, sell the plantation, and bring the rest of them up to Cincinnati.

"Amy sugar, the way I see it it'd probably be best for me to take the slaves over to Hamburg to be sold." Elijah informed her one evening after supper when the children had already been sent off to bed. "I won't have to cross the Georgia line, and it's a goodly ways away from nosey eyes and ears here in Barnwell District. Safer than goin to Charleston too, with our friend Mr. Rhett always on the prowl around there for anything he can report about the evils of abolition or improprieties with the coloreds!"

Amy listened thoughtfully, her lips in a scowl of dismay mixed with determination. She barely trusted herself to speak on the subject for fear of coming undone again, so she nodded her reluctant assent silently.

"What I still can't decide is how or when to tell em!" This of course was the heart of the matter emotionally- the bitter moment of truth, the possible responses to which had given both of them nightmares for weeks.

"Do I just line em up and put em in chains and say, 'Sorry ya'll, but I gotta sell ya'- an march em onto the wagons to haul em away to the depot? Or do I try an explain?"

Amy looked at Elijah in deadly earnest and said, "Elijah, no explanation is gonna take away their pain- an it could just make it worse. They gonna feel betrayed, hurt, angry and scared, no matter what ya say to em."

She had been pondering this scenario for months, and had come to the conclusion that trying to handle it nicely was impossible since there was nothing nice about it. As a slave owner Elijah really didn't owe any explanations to anyone, for he had the right to dispose of his property as he chose. As only his unofficial spouse she didn't owe them any explanations either for she, like they, technically lived at her master's pleasure and had no legal right to intercede on their behalf. What Elijah chose to do to her and the children was really no concern of the others, no matter what their jealousies or hopes might be. She had no responsibility for what was about to happen- it was entirely in Elijah's hands. That was both depressing and oddly liberating, for it relieved her own feeling of guilt a bit.

But no matter how abhorrent the situation, she could not simply let herself be bitter either - least of all toward the man who had given her four beautiful children and for nearly five years had been trying to move heaven and earth to set her, her mother, and her children free. Trying desperately to find some seed of grace in this nightmare, she remembered the passage

Elijah kept quoting from Genesis, "You meant it for evil, but God meant it for good." She felt compelled to remind Elijah of it, adding,

"I'll admit I can't see how, but I wanna believe that even for those who are sold, God is with em and can lead em home! Truth is, we got no way a knowin how all this is gonna play out- either for them or for us, but the Lord has led ya this far, an I gotta believe His grace will lead us all home sooner or later. Just go do what ya gotta do sugar, and let the Lord take care a the rest!" she said, resigned to the uncomfortable reality of an uncertain fate.

The reminder was helpful. After all, Joseph had been sold into slavery and even imprisoned, and yet he became the Pharaoh's vizier and saved all the people from the famine- his own people and Egypt's as well. Elijah figured the slavery of the mind was a whole lot worse than slavery of the body- and it wasn't up to him to determine whose minds were more enslaved.

"Well then, I guess I'd best go into town in the mornin and book passage on the first train out to Hamburg. When I come back I'll tell Gilbert, Julius and Jason to get ready to round up the slaves on the list and take them to the depot the following morning before dawn, so they won't be likely to be seen by folks in town." He yawned, exhausted.

Amy sighed, "Whatever ya think is best, sugar…" She pulled the covers up around her as if to comfort her from the impending sorrow, and stifled a yawn. "Best get some rest now. Tomorrow's gonna be a hard day."

Elijah couldn't fall asleep easily. His mind was churning about how to handle the dismissal of the slaves with a minimum of pain for all of them. He figured he'd let em each take whatever clothing and personal items they could easily carry. In fact, he thought he'd have Gilbert tell them all to dress in their best, figuring it would give them more dignity, and, at the same time make a better impression with the buyers, and maybe even fetch a better price if they did.

"Tell your momma to cook up enough for several baskets to send em on their way. I don't want em goin hungry," he added though Amy, half asleep, barely heard him, only grunting in response. As he heard the comforting sound of her soft snoring by his side he too felt himself drifting off to sleep at last.

The next thing he knew he heard a chorus of moaning and wailing from outside in front of the mansion. Sitting bolt upright in alarm, he dressed hurriedly and ran downstairs to see what was the matter; Amy pulling on a dressing gown followed close behind him.

He opened the front door and found Gilbert, Julius and Jason were out in front, facing the house with their families and some of the others. The sky was just beginning to lighten before the dawn, so it was hard to see them clearly. Elder, Elleck, Phillip, Momma Celia, the girls and little Savage were out there with them- twenty-seven slaves, including women and children. As they saw Elijah open the door and spotted Amy behind him, they started gesturing to her to come and join them. Hesitating a moment, Amy gathered her dressing gown around her, stepped past Elijah, and ran to her children. Elijah looked at their faces and saw tear tracks streaking their cheeks like silver slashes reflecting the growing light. The children were sobbing, their mothers moaning with despair. The men looked at him with angry glares, white teeth clenched in silent rage.

Elijah looked more closely and noticed each wore a heavy iron collar, through the hasp of which was threaded a long chain connecting them all. Behind them stood a tall, unshaven white man with a rifle and greasy hair, shouting, "All right you niggas! Come on, get movin!" Another, with a surly expression, held one end of the chain and started yanking it, making some of the slaves stagger backwards away from the house. Amy and the children reached out towards Elijah desperately, uncomprehending, their eyes pleading, their mouths open in silent, terrified screams.

Down the drive, Elijah spotted a shiny black carriage with a French blue fleur de lis trimmed in gold on the door. John Guignard leaned out the window and gave Elijah a smile of triumph. "Get that coffle movin boys!" he barked to the slave traders. Elijah suddenly realized the two traders were his nephews, James and Michael!

"Don't worry, Elijah, I'm gonna sell your slaves for ya- just not the ones you were intendin!" He laughed a cruel laugh as James and Michael joined in, and with that the carriage headed down the drive with two pregnant thoroughbred mares tied to the back of it. Michael was holding the chain on horseback, dragging the slaves behind him, a light of sadistic pleasure in his eyes as he watched his cargo stumble and wince. He was followed by James with the rifle, threatening to shoot any stragglers. He seemed to take particular delight in poking Amy in the back with the rifle as she brought up the rear with Momma Celia and the children.

Elijah felt his heart racing. He let out a yell from the very depths of his soul, "AAAAAMMMMYYYYY!!!!" A jolt hit his chest like the kick of a mule and knocked the wind right out of him. He lay there panting, wide-eyed, drenched in sweat, wondering if he had been shot, Amy hovering over him with a worried expression.

"Elijah! Elijah sugar, you alright?" she asked, urgency written all over her face.

It took him a moment to respond. He was so disoriented, he wasn't sure exactly where he was or what had happened, whether he was dreaming now or had been dreaming when he saw Guignard haul off his family and everyone else he was trying to free. All he could do at first was look up at her bewildered. He couldn't seem to manage to speak. Finally the horrific image of the coffle of slaves shuffling down the drive, their heavy chains clanking ominously with every step and groans and sobs being interspersed with rude orders shouted by the traders, faded away. He was baffled to discover that he was lying in his bed, in his room, in his house, with his wife anxiously attending him.

"What happened, darlin?" she asked. "You were moanin and groanin and crying and shoutin in ya sleep, and then ya sorta flopped in the bed like a catfish outa water, or like you'd been kicked in the chest! Must a been some awful bad nightmare!" Amy was hoping and praying that was all it was, but Elijah was so pale and sweaty she had called Momma Celia right away and told Elder to saddle up the mule and fetch Dr. Harley, just to make sure.

Elijah mumbled, "Terrible, horrible dream..." He was still half-way between sleep and wakefulness, and uncertain of his perceptions. He tried to move his arms but they felt heavy as lead. A slight tingling ran down his left arm and side. Even his face felt odd. His head finally started to clear and he said, "Thank God you're here! I thought I'd lost ya!" His voice sounded strangely weak to him, and like his tongue was thicker than usual. He noticed Amy leaning closer to hear better.

"What's that, sugar? You thought you'd lost me? Honey I'm the one who was afraid I was gonna lose you!" Amy was worried that Elijah wasn't making much sense, and felt increasingly that this had been more than just a dream that beset him.

Momma Celia came in and pulled Amy to the side so she could get in close and examine Elijah. She noticed a slight drooping of the left side of his face. She held up his left arm and asked him to hold it up on his own. It was a struggle, and soon it dropped to his side, but he was able to move his arm, his hand, and his fingers. The color was coming back into his face, and he had stopped sweating. Momma Celia took his wrist and felt for his pulse. She could feel a slight flutter in the beat.

"Are ya havin any pain, sugar?" she asked solicitously. Elijah thought for a moment, taking a quick inventory of his body, and concluded he did not.

He shook his head "No."

"Do ya feel numb or tingly anywhere, like pins an needles was stickin ya?" she asked.

"A little on my left side," he answered with a slight slur, "but it seems to be gettin better."

"Well, honey, I'm gonna mix up some more tea for ya, and we just gonna wait an see what Doctor Harley say, but seems to me ya'll had what they calls a stroke. Ya'll're lucky, cause some folks lose all they movement an can't even speak. God was good to ya, lettin ya keep movin and talkin, but you ain't gettin out a this bed befo Doctor Harley say you can, ya hear?" she looked at him with an expression that would not take "no" for an answer.

Elijah nodded and found himself drifting off to sleep again, suddenly extremely tired.

It wasn't long before Dr. Harley returned with Elder and came straight upstairs. Momma Celia shared her clinical observations with him, and the two talked quietly in the corner of the bedroom away from Elijah's bed, first one nodding, then the other. Elder stood in the corner, frightened by Elijah's pallor and feeling helpless to do anything but watch. Amy sat anxiously stroking Elijah's hair and wiping his brow with a cool, damp cloth, saying, "It's alright sugar, ya're gonna be alright."

The coolness of the cloth seemed to rouse him and he opened his eyes, immediately sensing someone was there. Dr. Harley then came over to the bedside.

"Joseph! What are you doin here?" he asked. He thought his confusion stemmed from his bizarre and disturbing dream, but it didn't explain the presence of his friend in his bedroom. He looked to Amy, "What in God's name is goin on?"

Amy was thrilled that Elijah was not only speaking, but speaking clearly. Momma Celia joined Joseph Harley immediately at his bedside. They were both looking at him like he was some sort of exhibit in a museum. By now Elijah was feeling slightly annoyed and struggled to sit himself up in bed, though he still felt surprisingly tired.

"Elder, give me a hand here son. Help me sit up will ya?"

Elder rushed over to his father's side, happy to be able to do something more than fetch the doctor. He helped his father sit up, fluffing the pillow behind him and gently laying him back against it.

"You alright, Papa?" he asked solicitously. Elijah smiled affectionately at the boy. Elder noticed that Elijah's smile was a little lopsided. It just didn't look right.

"I'll be fine son, don't ya'll worry. I'm just feelin a little weak for some reason."

He turned back to Joseph Harley and repeated his question, "Well, what are ya doin here? Ya'll didn't need to come out here just cause I had a bad dream for God's sake!" Elijah didn't realize his speech was slightly slurred.

"Well, that's a good question Elijah, and to tell the truth I'm not quite sure what's goin on. Seems you had a nightmare of some sort, and that it triggered in you a stroke too. What do you remember of what happened?"

Elijah proceeded to recount his recollection of falling asleep, and then he started to recall bits and snatches of the dream. He slowly pieced them back into a cohesive, dark and frightening narrative. Amy and Momma Celia looked deeply disturbed by the images but kept silent throughout Dr. Harley's inquiry.

When Elijah finished describing his hideous dream, Dr. Harley reexamined him, repeating Momma Celia's test of his movements, this time on both sides. He also looked into his eyes, asked him to follow his finger movements up and down, left and right, without moving his head; stick out his tongue, move it from side to side, raise his eyebrows, close his eyes tight, hunch his shoulders, pull and push against the doctor's hands, and squeeze his fingers. He touched him on both sides of the face, both arms and both legs simultaneously asking, "Do ya feel that? Does it feel the same to ya on both sides?" to which Elijah nodded "Yes."

Satisfied that his examination had been thorough, Dr. Harley informed Elijah, "You have a little weakness on the left side, and some loss of coordination. The good news is that no serious damage seems to have been done, but this was a close call. You were lucky!"

He then turned to Momma Celia, "Momma Celia, do ya'll have any willow bark in your collection of medicines downstairs?" Joseph had been reading about recent developments in Europe extracting salicylic acid from willow bark as an analgesic, but had heard it could also be a blood-thinner useful to prevent clots too.

"Yessir! I makes a tea with it that can take down swellin!" she replied.

"Exactly!" Dr. Harley responded, "I'd like ya to go make Elijah some, please- it might help restore his energy and strength and help prevent another attack."

Momma Celia willingly scurried off to fulfill Dr. Harley's request, taking Elder with her to help, and once they were out of the room, Joseph turned to Elijah and said, "I know ya'll're under an awful lotta stress these days, and that doesn't help. Was anything in particular goin on last night before ya fell asleep?"

Elijah owned that there had been, as he and Amy were agonizing over the realization that they had to sell off half the slaves in order to have even a prayer of freeing the other half. Elijah explained their decision, the timetable he'd set, their agony over the pain it would cause, and their realization that they had no other choice. He also mentioned running into Dr. Guignard in the depot as he was inquiring about shipping the slaves to Charleston or Hamburg.

Joseph Harley listened with his customary attentive compassion. When Elijah had finished, he said, "Clearly your pain over these terrible circumstances and the awful decisions they require of ya triggered the dream- but they triggered the attack too! As your doctor and your friend, I'm tellin ya ya'll're in no condition to go into town tomorrow, much less to handle the strain of partin with half the population of this plantation! Ya'll need to postpone it until ya can get back on your feet again safely!"

Elijah surprisingly did not put up his usual resistance. The fact was, this attack had really scared him- almost as much as the nightmare. His prevouious episodes he had been able to shake off- even the one after Savage's birth didn't seem too dangerous to him. It had been more of a prolonged and annoying inconvenience. This time he saw not only Amy's dream of freeing the others crumbling before his eyes, he was now afraid the same would happen to his solemn vow to free her and the chidren. He simply must not, could not let that happen!

"How long d'ya think it'll take me to recover, Joseph?" he asked softly.

"Hard to say. Ya're a tough old buzzard, but these episodes a yours take a cumulative toll. If ya'll don't get a good long rest, ya might not survive the next one!"

Amy was listening to this exchange, feeling torn between the urgency to get to Cincinnati as soon as possible and her fear of losing Elijah forever- whether freed or not. Trying to boost his spirits, she said, "Well look at it this way honey ya just got in the best cotton harvest this plantation has ever produced. Folks'll be expectin ya to relax some now anyway. So you just take whatever time ya need, and we'll get through this!"

At that moment Momma Celia came in with her willow-bark tea and a biscuit.

"Ya'll drink this up now!" she said, handing him the teacup. "Eat the biscuit too though, cause sometimes the tea can trouble ya innards a bit- specially if they's empty. The biscuit'll help ya keep the tea down so's it can do its healin."

Joseph Harley nodded in agreement. "I want ya take a cup a this tea every mornin and every evenin for at least a week or two. I also want ya to rest- ya don't have to stay in bed all the time, but no work, no ridin, and no climbin up an down stairs too much. I need ya'll to take it real easy until I say otherwise, an I'm gonna set Momma Celia on ya like a watch dog, to make sure ya obey the doctor's orders!" he winked at Momma Celia, knowing it was a toss up as to which doctor he was referring to, for they both had the same orders in mind.

Amy and Momma Celia nodded in agreement, Amy adding, "And don't be thinkin ya'll can sneak around Momma, cause I'm gonna be watchin ya like a hawk too!"

Elijah sighed in acquiescence. "Alright, alright! I got the message. I'll be good, I promise!" he said, like a schoolboy grudgingly accepting detention, and not for the first time.

Satisfied that the patient would be compliant, they told Elijah to go lie back down and try to sleep. They closed the door on their way out as if to underscore they weren't fooling. Joseph Harley walked downstairs with Amy and Momma Celia. When they got to the bottom of the stairs, Momma Celia announced she was going to go over to the creek and collect some more willow bark since she was going to need to make a good bit more tea. Amy asked Joseph if he'd care for a cup of coffee before heading home.

"That's kind of ya, my dear, but I really must be goin. But before I do, there's something ya need to know. I didn't tell Elijah cause I didn't want to add to his stress just now, but given the imagery of his dream I think ya'll need to hear it."

Amy was immediately alarmed. "Whatever is it, Doctor Harley?"

"Well, I was called to tend to a sick slave over on the Kirkland plantation the other day, and in the course of tending to her I happened to overhear some of the Kirkland slaves whispering to each other. I imagine you and your Momma may know some of em from before." He was discreetly acknowledging that they had formerly lived on the Kirkland plantation themselves. It dawned on Amy for the first time that Joseph Harley might even know of her birth and her mother's relations with William Kirkland. She admired him all the more for never showing any sign of judgment towards them for it.

"Seems they know somethin's afoot over here, and they were speculatin about some folks bein freed an some folks bein sold. It would be unfortunate if that gossip reached other white ears, if ya know what I mean. I'm just sayin…"

Amy listened to this with grim resignation. It felt like their tortured road to freedom had more twists and turns than the hills and hollows of the Smokey Mountains, and was just as likely to lead to nowhere!

"Well, thank ya for tellin me Doctor. I don't know as there's much of anything we can do about that at this point, except pray! Fact is, I'm almost as worn out as Elijah from all this, and my fear is if we don't get up to Cincinnati soon, we may never get there at all!"

"I understand, and God knows I feel for ya'll. I wish there was more I could do to help, but right now I can't stress enough how important it is for Elijah to rest and eat right. If ya can try to keep him as stress-free as possible, he should regain his strength enough to be able to travel." Dr. Harley advised.

"How we supposed to keep him stress free when everything about our life right now is stressful?!" blurted Amy. "Ya'll got no idea the fits it's given him havin to accept the necessity of selling off half the slaves in order to even try to free the other half. Do ya know what it's like to play God with people's lives like that, choosin who stays and who goes? It's just awful!"

Sadly, Dr. Harley was all too aware of how glibly some of the planters did just that, with no twinge of remorse or compunction for the suffering they caused simply because they persuaded themselves they were dealing with livestock rather than human beings, to spare their own consciences. Of course he found such callousness monstrous and indefensible, but he refrained from commenting any further on it, knowing that in fact Amy's question was merely rhetorical.

Amy's pent up anxiety was now overflowing, her outpouring of words like a dam bursting under the pressure of torrential rains. "An I feel guilty cause I made him promise he'd free em all, and now he feels he's breakin his promise to me and to God, an he's so upset he's not sleepin, an he's drinkin too much, an I'm afraid he's gonna die on us an I just don't know what to do!!!" she fretted, her voice catching in sobs. "I try to take care a things on the plantation, but I got no authority to sell slaves- he's the only white man here, and is the only one can both make that decision, and act on it too."

Her dilemma was not imaginary. They truly were in one hot mess of a predicament. She went on, "An then there's his nephews and relations, and that evil Dr. Guignard, an young Angus Patterson, an that madman Robert Barnwell Rhett, an God knows who else, plottin and spyin on us! I tell ya, Doctor, it's like about to put me six feet under too! That nightmare a his sounded too close to the truth- scared the livin daylights outa me to hear him tell it!"

Her diatribe finished, she fell silent, and smoothing back her hair, took a deep breath. She was suddenly aware that she had been far too personal, and despite her trust in Dr. Harley, was afraid she'd been inappropiate.

"I'm sorry Doctor, I, I didn't mean to go on so, it's just been real hard lately!" She said, embarrassed by her outburst.

"No need for apologies my dear, I truly do understand. Fact is, I have great admiration for ya both in the way ya'll have been handlin this God-awful situation! I'm not surprised it's given Elijah nightmares! But if Elijah doesn't rest what will follow will be an even worse nightmare for you and your Momma and the children too. I'm not foolin!"

"I know Doctor, I know," she reassured him, "and we'll all make sure he gets plenty a rest. Thank ya for comin, an please pray for us!" she squeezed his hand urgently in farewell.

"You know I do and I shall, my dear, I do and I shall." Doctor Harley actually leaned forward and gave Amy a hug of comfort. She was overwhelmed, as the only other white man who had ever touched her with compassion had been Elijah.

"God bless ya Doctor Harley! An I promise I'll let ya'll know if anything develops."

"Be sure ya do, now. I'll stop by in a day or two to see how he's doin. In the meantime tell ya Momma she can give him any tea she thinks he needs. I trust her completely!"

"I sure will Doctor, and thank ya!"

Joseph Harley left honestly wondering to himself if his friend was going to make it to Cincinnati or not. He was amazed that the stroke had not done more damage, but he knew they were playing with fire. It wouldn't take much to trigger another possibly fatal attack, and given the bad blood between Elijah and his nephews, John Guignard's overweening pride and resentment toward Elijah, and Angus Patterson's political ambitions throwing in with the anti-abolitionists and secessionists, it'd take a miracle for Elijah to remain stress-free long enough to fully recover.

As Amy climbed the stairs to go check on Elijah, she thought to herself, 'Well, maybe bein sick will give a believable excuse for sellin off some of the slaves, since he's not allowed to do any more work... We could say that because of his health he's gonna just focus on the lumber business, since he needs less men to operate the mill than to plant and harvest cotton...' She was worried that a long convalescence would complicate their departure. Now that she'd come to terms with its necessity she still wanted to sell off the other slaves soon so as to have the necessary, resources for the trip since Elijah was able to travel. The only question was how to get it done without adding to Elijah's stress? She couldn't help but reconsider Elijah's idea to have a trader come and take them off to Hamburg, much as she loathed the heartless scum that chose to make their living delivering slaves to the block.

News of Elijah's illness did not take long to reach the slave quarters. His conspicuous absence after working with the field hands side by side every day throughout the harvest was indication enough. But the worried faces of his children and the sight of Momma Celia running around the whole plantation cutting herbs and looking for any kind of root, leaf, bark, fruit, nut, or plant that might have healing properties made it abundantly clear that all was not well in the big house.

"Lord ha mercy! What we gonna do if Mister Elijah don't get better? I heard Momma Celia talkin to Gilbert, sayin it was a close call," said one field hand.

"Mmmm, mmmm, mmmm! Sho is a shame! The man was workin lika a hoss in harvest time. Mebbe it was just too much on him. After all, he gettin ole!" said another.

"Yeah, that's true, but ole Henry here kep on workin an didn't fall sick, did ya Henry?" commented a third.

"Me, nossir! I kep right on workin to the end!" Henry chuckled with pride. "But I'll allow as how I'm all tuckered out now!" he admitted. "Reckon Mister Elijah is too!"

"Hey Henry, how ole is you anyway?" asked the first.

"Don't rightly know. My momma tole me I as born the same year George Washington was elected President of the U-nited States of America. He the first one! So I don't know how ole that make me, but I's older than Mister Elijah!" Henry replied.

"Damn, Henry! I didn know you was that ole!" said the second.

"Anyway, whether Henry ole an tired or not ain't the point! Mister Elijah got a right to be tired! Gettin the cotton harvest in, overseein the lumber mill, takin care of Miss Amy and the children- an all a us too- that's a heap a responsibility for one man! Mebbe it's getting to be too much for him!" explained the first.

"An don't forget him havin to deal with all them white fools round here tryin to stir up trouble against the colored folks! Like about to give me fits just thinkin about it, an I ain't got ta deal with it like he do!" offered Henry.

"Yeah, but if Mister Elijah up an die on us, we all gonna be in some deep shit! Even Miss Amy and Momma Celia an his children! Just cause they his family, don't mean the white folks're gonna treat em right. They all slaves in the eyes a white law! The white folks can't stand the thought of em bein anything more than that!" remarked the second.

"If he dies before freein us, I say we make a run for it! Ain't no way I'm gonna let his nasty nephews or their sorry ass father lord it over me! I'druther die runnin than under their whip! An you best believe they'd use a whip too! Not like Mister Elijah!" said the third.

"I hear that! Never could understand how they got so mean, but I'd sooner pet a rattlesnake than have to deal with the likes a them!" remarked the second.

"Me, I'm gonna pray Mister Elijah gets better so's he can keep his promise and somehow set us free, cause anything else is gonna end bad!" concluded Henry.

"Amen to that brother! Amen to that!" the others agreed.

Fall passed into winter and Elijah was still feeling weak and sluggish. Christmas had come and gone almost without notice- Amy and Elijah exchanged some simple gifts with the children- new clothes and some candies Elijah ordered all the way from Charleston. The girls were delighted with their new dresses, and the boys looked a little awkward dressing up like young gentlemen but were secretly proud to have such finery. Elijah had even ordered luggage for the whole family in anticipation of their travels. He wanted his family properly outfitted so they would not feel or look like slaves when they finally set foot on Ohio soil as freedmen.

Elijah procrastinated through the Holidays about selling any slaves, not wanting to dampen further what was already a fairly somber Christmas. Much to his surprise, his brother paid him a visit at the New Year without his obnoxious family in tow. Amy discreetly left the two in the parlor to talk amongst themselves.

"How are ya brother?" Jimmy asked Elijah with apparent concern.

"Well if it isn't James Willis Senior! Hello there brother! Hope ya'll're here in a friendlier spirit than your sons James an Michael, an that drunken Polack son-in-law a yours! I'm holdin up I guess. How bout you?" he responded diffidently.

Jimmy Willis knew that the slap at at the younger generation of Willises was well deserved, but still, it was not appreciated. Elijah and his brother were dancing around the issues that separated them like two magnets with the wrong poles facing each other, yet some sort of bond had clearly prompted Jimmy to visit, and to do so unaccompanied by Elijah's nemeses. Bond or no bond, Elijah was wary of revealing too much about his health or other concerns, uncertain of his brother's real motives for the visit.

"I'm doin fair to middlin I guess," Jimmy responded. Elijah nodded, as if something substantive had actually been communicated.

"So what brings ya out here Jimmy? Been a long time since you and I talked one on one. Ya'll got somethin to say, or are ya just keepin up appearances for the sake a tradition?" Elijah pressed a bit bluntly, losing patience with the endless avoidance in which they had been locked for years.

His brother looked annoyed but then spoke up, "Aw Hell, Elijah! I'm your brother for God's sake! I just came to see how ya are!"

"Ya mean, ya wanted to see if I'm fixin to die?" Elijah answered.

"No! I came because I'm worried about ya! Ya'll're runnin yaself ragged! Just look at ya! Why don't ya'll go on an quit this nonsense an finally enjoy your earnins?"

It was not clear as to what specific 'nonsense' he was referring. Elijah suspected it was not his hard work but rather what the family had always deemed the nonsense of taking up with Amy and living with her as though she were family, and it made him bristle. But he also saw an opportunity to plant a seed with his brother that might ease any suspicions about their departure.

"Well maybe ya're right, Jimmy. I've been thinkin it might be nice to get away for a spell- go on a good long trip that wasn't just business for a change."

"I think ya should! Ya'll been working so hard for so long- what the Hell's the point of makin all that money if ya can't enjoy usin some of it in your old age?"

"Who said anything about getting old?" Elijah objected. The more aches and pains he felt in a day the less he appreciated anyone telling him he was getting old, as if by sheer dint of will power he could forestall the inevitable process of aging. He was proof that denial is not a river in Egypt!

His brother sighed in exasperation. "Well alright then ya stubborn son of a bitch- enjoy it while ya *can*, if that makes it easier for ya to hear!"

Elijah concluded that his brother actually meant what he was saying, uninfluenced by the insidious presence of his avaricious children or his shrewish wife. That being the case it dawned on him that he might be able to make the sale of the slaves no longer suspect by using his brother's own argument. He might thereby get his brother to call off the dogs- James, Michael and Angus- from sticking their noses into his business trying to catch the scent of trouble.

"Maybe ya're right, Jimmy. On the one hand my success at breedin and harvestin good cotton is an achievement I'm right proud of, and I'd hate to give it up. But on the other hand the lumber business takes less workers to run, and less of my time an energy to make profitable. Maybe I should retire from the cotton fields and just live off the rest?"

Elijah's brother was surprised by this, given Elijah's competitive passion for getting his cotton crop in ahead of all the other planters in the area, but it also made instrinsic sense. He could see his brother aging, and despite all their differences, really didn't want to see Elijah work himself to death.

"I think that's a fine idea Elijah! Jesus, ya'll been workin this land for more'n forty years. Why not take it a little easier?" his brother agreed.

"Well I suppose I could, but then I'd probably have to sell off some of the slaves. No point in feedin all those extra mouths if I'm not plantin cotton any more!" Elijah announced.

Jimmy thought about this and nodded. "Hell, I betcha ya'll could get a pretty fair price for em over in the slave market in Hamburg!" he suggested, figuring that even if Elijah sold them he wouldn't spend all the money, so there'd still be plenty left as an inheritance. Jimmy was of course unaware of the new will, and was assuming he and his boys were still legatees, so he felt he could afford to be magnanimous. He decided to avoid the subject of Amy and the children, knowing they would not be among those that Elijah decided to sell. He figured that if Elijah died they'd decide what to do with Amy and her children later.

"I hadn't thought of that, but that's not a bad idea!" Elijah responded, hoping to sound open to this as a new possibility. Unfortunately, he immediately regretted his word choice.

"What d'ya mean 'ya hadn't thought of that?' How could ya have? I just suggested it a minute ago! Are you tellin me you'd already thought about this?" Jimmy pressed, suddenly wondering whether he was being played.

Trying to cover his blunder quickly, Elijah responded, "Well, I guess it'd crossed my mind once or twice, but I never took it seriously until you come by! I gotta admit, as good as this year's cotton crop was it nearly did me in to get it all harvested. Truth is, I'm tired Jimmy!"

"Well nobody's gonna hold it against ya if ya decide to take a break! The land's not goin anywhere- ya'll can skip a year, let it lie fallow, and plant again next year if ya wanna!"

"Why would I do that? If I sell off some of my slaves and then decide to plant again, I'd just have to go buy me some more- and then go through the Hell of trainin em to do things the way I like em done. No sir. If I sell the slaves it'll be because I've decided to retire from the cotton business!"

Jimmy thought about it, and nodded. "I suppose ya're right about that. But that's alright! Ya'll got a right to retire whenever ya want. When ya die, there's others that can work the land!" Jimmy hadn't meant to let that slip out, but it was too late.

"So ya are thinking about me dyin!" Elijah blurted, feeling wounded again. Seemed like every time he had a conversation with his brother that felt like it might heal the rift, something happened to pick the scab off the wound and make it bleed all over again.

"Come on now Elijah, don't be like that! I didn't mean it that way! I'm just sayin this land is good land- always has been an always will be in the future too- but just cause it's good land doesn't mean you gotta be the one to plant it!" Jimmy was digging himself a deeper hole.

"An I suppose you think ya'll can do better?" retorted Elijah.

"Christ Almighty Elijah, I'm just tellin ya ya'll need to let yaself enjoy the fruits of your labors and not worry about farmin the land any more! Period. No other agenda. Get it through yer thick skull!"

Just as Elijah felt his blood pressure rising Amy walked in with a tray of holiday cookies and coffee. She had been listening from out in the hallway and felt an intervention was called for to avoid the brothers coming to blows. She discreetly set the tray on the table and nodded politely to Jimmy before exiting the room. On her way out she managed to shoot Elijah a quick glance of warning, as if to say "Watch yaself- don't get yaself all worked up! Doctor's orders!"

Recognizing that her timing was far from accidental, Elijah forced himself to calm down before responding to his brother.

"Well I appreciate the advice brother, and I'll take it into consideration," he answered tersely.

"Well good! Glad ta hear it! It'd be a first!" Jimmy snapped. It was clear that at heart both brothers wanted to make peace, but there were so many wounds unhealed on both sides that everything they said came out with an edge. Jimmy grabbed a cookie and started munching on it, hoping to prevent any further outbursts by the distraction.

Elijah resisted the temptation to get in another blow and started munching on a cookie himself. It felt like they were little kids again who, though trying to stay mad at each other, couldn't even remember what they were fighting about given the magic of Momma Celia's molasses and spice cookies, which had an almost supernatural power to instill a sense of delicious well-being in the eater.

The two men, suddenly uncomfortable with the unfamiliar feeling of mutual acceptance, shook off their cookie-induced reverie, rose from their respective seats and faced each other.

"Well, uh, thanks for droppin by, little brother!" Elijah managed to say gruffly. Jimmy nodded.

"Ya'll take care of yaself, hear?" he responded. Elijah also managed to nod his acceptance. "I guess I'd best be on my way then. Happy New Year to ya!"

"Ta you too!" Elijah responded as Jimmy headed out to the door. He couldn't bring himself to say 'send my regards to your family,' and neither could Jimmy, for it would have felt hypocritical. Jimmy seemed to understand and just turned and said, "Bye now!" and walked out to his horse. Elijah could hear the hoof beats slowly receding down the road as Amy came back in to the parlor.

"Well that was unexpected!" she commented.

"What- that he came, or what was said?" Elijah asked, still feeling slightly ruffled by his brother's visit.

"Both, actually. But I believe the Lord's hand was in it when ya told him ya might sell off some slaves and quit plantin cotton! Could be God just gave us a free ticket outa here without havin to worry about an ambush from your nephews on our way!"

"Well truth be told, that's what I was feelin too! Even Jimmy suggestin I send em over to Hamburg, when that's what I'd been figurin, seemed Providential. It could turn that nightmare a mine into a better dream!"

"The pain of sellin slaves, rather than freein em, still feels like a nightmare to me," Amy said pointedly, "but I know what ya'll're sayin. Be a whole lot worse if we had ta sneak em outa here for fear a James an Michael catchin wind of it and stirrin up trouble!"

"Exactly! Now Jimmy'll tell em I'm retirin from plantin cotton and figure on sellin off some of my slaves, cause I won't need such a big work force. They won't be able to object. An him suggestin I go on a nice trip, it shouldn't raise so many eyebrows when I decide to take ya'll along with me- specially since I already did it when we went up to Baltimore!"

"Well, the coast may be clear for us to head up to Cincinnati, but there's one detail ya haven't resolved yet," Amy reminded him.

"What's that?" Elijah asked, unsure as to what she was referring.

"Why, your health, of course! Just cause ya may've managed to get your nephews off your back doesn't mean ya can just go galavantin off to Cincinnati without Joseph Harley's approval! A promise is a promise!" Amy announced with finality.

"My health is doin fine, sugar. All the better now, if I don't have to worry about tryin to sell the slaves without anyone findin out about it, or bein stalked or pounced on by James and Michael and Angus!" Elijah began to sound upbeat for the first time since his stroke.

"Well that may be- an I surely am glad to hear ya get some spark back in ya- but that don't mean ya can go saddle up Beauty and gallop over ta Barnwell, much less manage to get all of us up to Cincinnati just yet!" Amy insisted.

Elijah could tell when he was confronted with a non-negotiable proposition. He sighed with feined frustration, but smiled at her affectionately. "Alright, darlin. But could we maybe at least invite Joseph over to give me a good lookin at? If I have ta stay in this house much longer without gettin out, I'm gonna end up too crazy to take ya'll even to the depot, much less to Cincinnati!" he responded, only half in jest.

Amy allowed as how that might be possible, but insisted that Momma Celia was gonna have to weigh in on the decision as well. She was not about to take any more chances on him getting so worked up that he had another stroke, or worse, and now made it her mission to preserve his life, so he in turn could preserve theirs. All in all, it was not an unreasonable proposition, and Elijah realized he had no choice but to comply.

Joseph Harley happened to stop by the next day to offer them all best wishes for the New Year, and to check on his patient.

"Well now, howya feelin, Elijah?" he asked with a cheerful smile.

"I'm doin better Joseph, truly I am!" insisted Elijah.

"Hmmm, hmmm." Dr. Harley responded distractedly, as he focused on analyzing his patient's motor skills, strength, speech, and balance. Not content to take Elijah's word for it, ever the empiricist, Dr. Harley began to give his patient a thorough exam- repeating many of the same diagnostic tests he had used the day Elijah had the stroke. Elijah was humbled into silence as he awaited the verdict of the assessment.

"Well?" Elijah asked with impatient expectation, as Dr. Harley was putting his brass trumpet stethoscope back into his black medical bag.

Joseph Harley looked at Elijah sternly. "First of all, may I remind ya of ya'll's promise to obey the Doctor's orders, no matter what?" Elijah knew this did not sound like the introduction to the promising news for which he was hoping, but nodded his assent nonetheless.

"Well, matter of fact, I agree with ya that ya're doin much better!" Joseph announced to Elijah's great relief. "However," came the caveat, "ya're still not well enough in my opinion, to undertake the challenge of the sale and transfer of slaves, or the relocation of ya family!"

"But Joseph!" Elijah began to protest. Dr. Harley held up his hand to stop him from going any further.

"Let me explain. Though your speech is markedly clearer, I still detect a slight slur. Though your pulse is stronger and steadier, I still detect a slight irregularity in the beat, and though you're a heap stronger than you were, ya still have some weakness on the left side and lack of balance in your gait- ya're favoring one side."

"So what does all that mean- and what am I supposed to do now?" Elijah pleaded.

"Well, it means ya're not yet fully recovered, and until ya are, over-exerting yaself could provoke a relapse or worse. As for what can ya do, I actually want ya ta start gettin out some. Go on walks, maybe even an occasional ride (no gallopin or canterin- just a gentle trot). Fresh air and light exercise'll do ya'll good, and help speed up your recovery."

Elijah, relieved that he was to get at least some reprieve from his confinement, nodded his acceptance but felt there was something more Joseph wanted to say. He looked at him and waited to see what else his friend might offer.

"As for the sale of the slaves that triggered the upset that caused your stroke…"

Elijah interrupted, "I think I have stumbled upon a solution that would make that unhappy event far less stressful than I was anticipatin." He proceeded to recount his conversation with his brother Jimmy, and the realization that it might be possible to ship the slaves openly and leave for Cincinnati on the pretense of taking a long and recreational journey to celebrate his retirement from the cotton business.

Joseph replied with sober realism, "Well, that certainly would be somewhat less horrible than than your original proposal! But I know ya Elijah, and I know damn well it's still gonna be emotionally wrenchin for ya to part with half the population of this plantation after all these years of feedin, trainin, healin, carin, and workin with em. Ya don't have it in ya to be the cold hearted type like John Guignard, who feels no compunction or empathy and is indifferent to all sufferin but his own!"

Elijah knew it was true, but slightly resented Joseph bursting the bubble of what appeared to be an easier solution with the sharp, penetrating fact that he was still dreading having to sell any of them.

After a pause of solemn reflection, he spoke up, "So what, exactly, is it that ya recommend I do, Joseph? I can't just put it off forever! I need to get my family up to Cincinnati, and I need to do it soon!"

Jospeh Harley knew his friend was also right, but the medical facts and the emotional realities of the situation seemed to clash. He sought a happy medium that would give the best patient outcome, assuring both Elijah's immediate survival, and the ultimate emancipation of Amy, her mother, and the children.

"Look Elijah, I appreciate the urgency ya'll're feelin about this, I truly do. But as your doctor and your friend, it'd be irresponsible of me to just tell ya 'go ahead an go now!' when I have good reason to believe ya might not make it! And I don't want that to happen, for any of ya'll's sake!"

Elijah knew Joseph was not just being overly cautious, much as he wished it were no more than that. He felt on an almost subliminal, but nonetheless powerful level, that death was standing nearby, patiently waiting for the opportunity to take him to his Maker.

"How much longer d'ya think I need before it's reasonably safe to try?" he asked, wanting to cut to the chase but knowing there were no guarantees.

"Well sir, given that it's winter up in Ohio, and Ohio is a damn sight colder than South Carolina," Dr. Harley pointed out, "if it was me, I'd wait until spring. Go up in the good weather, after the April rains. By then ya'll should be pretty fit, provided ya don't try an overdo things in the meantime! Eat right, get lots a sleep, avoid upsets as much as possible. Be a nicer trip for the family then too!"

Though a longer wait than he was hoping for, this actually made sense to him. Elijah had not actually considered the weather, so intent was he to avoid the emotional storminess of Williston. Amy hated the cold, and Momma Celia was not likely to do well with it either, given her arthritis. Grudgingly, he had to admit this made sense. At least now he had a viable plan and a concrete goal to work for.

"Alright, Joseph. I trust ya- even though I wish this were all over! When I first spoke to ya about this five years ago, I never dreamed it could possibly take this long or be this hard. But it's in God's hands, and as long as I can keep my promise to Amy and the children, I can die in peace."

"Ya'll've been through a lot in these five years! I can't tell ya'll how much I admire ya for your strength, your courage, and your perseverance. Just be patient a little longer, and I believe the Good Lord'll answer ya'll's prayer at last." Joseph spoke from his heart, and his words encouraged Elijah.

"I don't know how we could've gotten through some of this without ya, Joseph! There aren't words enough ta thank ya. Ya have my word, I'll do as ya say, but by May I'm gonna take my family outa here come Hell or high water, even if I have ta take me a pine box along as luggage just in case!"

Joseph Harley chuckled in appreciation. He could understand Elijah's feeling that sooner or later he'd just have to make the leap of faith. "Fair enough, my friend, fair enough! But until then behave yaself, y'hear?"

"I will Joseph, I promise," Elijah responded, "I druther die at the hands of the Lord than at the hands of Amy and Momma Celia, if they catch me disobeyin ya!" He grinned. The image of mother and daughter getting on Elijah's case was not hard to visualize!

"Well, alright then. If I were in ya'll's position, I'm sure I'd feel the same way!" he allowed. The two men shook hands, Joseph giving Elijah a pat on the back in encouragement as he left. "And remember, light exercise does not mean plantin the South twenty instead of the South forty!" he reiterated on his way out.

As if there were any doubt of Elijah disobeying, as fate (or complicity) would have it, Amy and Momma Celia were waiting out on the veranda to say their good-byes. Needless to say, Dr. Harley reiterated his diagnosis and instructions to them both, lest Elijah accidentally forget any details! Amy nodded her understanding, giving Elijah one of her "don't even think about doin otherwise" looks as the good doctor climbed into his buggy, flicked the reins, and rumbled away down the road.

Sit down, ya'll!" Gilbert ordered them. "Mister Elijah's got something he's gotta say to us." Gilbert deliberately said 'to us' rather than 'to ya'll,' not so much out of self-protection as out of the realization that whatever Elijah was going to say, it truly was going to impact all of them. Matter of fact, not even he knew exactly what Elijah was going to say, even though he had a pretty good idea of where it was heading.

Elijah had thought about what to say for a long time and decided he owed his slaves at least a clear explanation of what was about to happen, no matter how hard it was to hear or how hard it was to deliver. He stood before the entire gathering of slaves on the Willis Plantation. They were, after all, a community: every one of them an integral part of the place they all called home. He was in a sense as much the patriarch as the master of those assembled, and his paradoxical relationship with them was lost on no one.

As the sky was overcast and looked like it might rain, they had all gathered in the barn. Anxiety was written on their faces, clearly suspecting there was important news, but not sure what it was or how it would affect them. Elijah had had the habit of gathering them all together periodically over the years- especially before planting time- to encourage them to work well and to promise them rewards for doing so. But this gathering felt different.

"I called ya'll together cause I want ya'll to hear this from me directly so there're no misunderstandins." The slaves shifted uncomfortably in anticipation.

"Ya'll know my health has not been too good lately." Several slaves nodded in recognition of this indisputable fact. They had watched Elijah's slow recovery, first after the yellow fever outbreak and then after the stroke. The subtle changes in his gait and smile, despite his improvement, still recorded the impact of his last attack in his every movement.

"My doctor tells me that I cannot keep workin the way I always have, or it's gonna kill me." He told them bluntly. "And, as ya'll can imagine, the prospect does not appeal to me- neither the prospect of quittin nor of dyin, that is!" A few chuckled.

"So I've come to one of the hardest decisions a my life. Proud as I am of ya'll and the work we've all done makin the Willis Plantation one of the best cotton-producin plantations in South Carolina, the production a cotton on this plantation is gonna have ta stop. I just can't keep it up any more!"

This was not what they were expecting to hear! Some had been expecting him to announce some plan for their emancipation at last, others were afraid he was going to tell them the opposite, but nobody had ever thought that the plantation would stop producing cotton!

Before anyone could start to question his decision, or suggest that Elijah could stop working without the plantation having to stop, Elijah pressed on.

"I've come to a stage in my life where I've been persuaded to take some time off and rest from my labors, for the sake of my health. My doctor says I should even take a trip and get away from the cares of the plantation for a while. So I'druther suspend production now- after our best crop ever but before it's time to plant a new crop- than try an keep it goin without my supervision and have the reputation of the plantation suffer in my absence."

Elijah was sort of clutching at straws, trying to present a plausible argument for why he had to sell some of them off without wanting to make it sound like he didn't care about them. Never having been prone to flaunting the Willis reputation in the past, however, it seemed odd he should do so now. He wasn't sure they were buying it, but he continued anyway.

"So much as I hate to admit it, I've gone over the books, and I realized I can't afford to keep all of ya'll if we're not plantin cotton anymore. It pains me more'n ya'll can possibly know- it's kept me up nights, and Doc Harley even thinks it triggered my last attack- but I'm gonna have to sell half of ya'll in order to keep the plantation afloat with just the lumber business and enough food crops to keep us goin."

There was a deafening silence as the reality of this news sank in, broken only by the sound of the wind outside. There was a portentious chill in the air that felt like approaching rain.

"Now I know this is gonna be hard for all of ya," Elijah continued. "Some of ya'll have been born and lived here all ya lives. And it's been a mighty hard choice to decide who'll stay and who'll go." His voice started to waver as he looked at the crowd, some sitting on the floor, others on bales of straw, some even dandling little children on their knees. All eyes were on him, from aged Henry's to the firebrand Jeremiah's to the smallest child's. He saw parents clutching their children with panic in their eyes, and stifled moans and sobs started to pass through the crowd in concentric circles, like the ripples on a quiet pond after a stone has been thrown into the water.

"I wont break up families- I promise ya. And I want ya'll to go wearin ya best Sunday Go to Meetin Clothes, so ya look good and feel proud of yaselves, as ya should. And I'm gonna send ya'll off with baskets of Momma Celia's good cookin to tide ya over on your journey. God knows, I'd free all of ya, if I could, but South Carolina law won't allow it. I know it's not fair, cause ya'll've done nothing wrong to deserve this..." his voice was catching in his throat. He managed to add huskily, "But I simply got no choice!"

Elijah signaled to Gilbert to come over. He handed him a list of names to read out of those who would be going to Hamburg. He felt his pulse fluttering and wanted to leave, but couldn't bring himself to go just yet.

"I want ya'll to know that this was never what I wanted. I pray that the Good Lord will keep ya'll safe, find ya good masters who'll treat ya the way ya'll deserve to be treated, and hope that we all meet again in a better place." There were mutterings of "Amen!" and "Yes, Lord!" and "Hear us, Sweet Jesus!" mixed with sniffling and sobbing.

Elijah could no longer hold back his emotions, and several tears ran down his aging cheeks in spite of his attempts not to break down before them in an unmanly fashion. It was not that he was embarrassed by his feelings or ashsamed of them, but rather that he wanted to inspire to bravery those who were being sold, so they would face what was coming with dignity. He had always tried to set a good example for them, and they had admired him for it.

As Gilbert read out each name a fresh chorus of moans and sobs broke out, first here, then there, as families and friends embraced each other desperately, trying to comfort each other in their loss. Some of the younger ones, especially the men, struggled between sorrow and rage, feeling that for all of Elijah's nice words, they had been betrayed- cheated of the promise of freedom held up by Amy years ago. But they also knew freedom was not Amy's to promise, for she too, in the final analysis was a slave like them. Some felt compassion for Elijah, knowing he had always been good to them and believing that this was a hateful decision for him too. Some merely felt numb from shock and disbelief.

When all the names had been read off, Elijah announced, "I will not clap ya'll in neck irons and rob ya'll of ya dignity, but ya'll will have ta be tied together. Ya can take whatever personal items and clothin ya can easily carry with ya. An I won't make ya'll march in coffles to the slave market either! Ya'll'll be taken to the depot in the wagons, and then take the train straight to the market in Hamburg. The train leaves pretty early in the mornin, so ya'll best get yaselves ready quickly, so's ya can have some time together and say your good-byes."

For his own emotional self-preservation, having delivered the awful news with as much compassion as he could, Elijah got up, heavy hearted, walked out of the barn, and headed back to the mansion. The tears, now that he was out of sight of the others, ran hot and fast down his cheeks. As if in sympathy for his sorrow, the skies opened up in a spring rain that soaked him before he could reach the house. Behind him, the wails and tears of the slaves in the barn blended with moaning of the wind in the trees and the splashing of the raindrops, in a funeral dirge.

It was April 6, Good Friday. Elijah remembered going to church as a boy and hearing an interminable sermon on Jesus' Seven 'Last Words-' the various things He was supposed to have said from the cross at his crucifixion. It struck Elijah as ironic that, out of all of them, the phrase that he suddenly found himself muttering as he walked into the house was, "It is finished!" He couldn't help but wonder however, how many of those on the list were experiencing, "My God, My God, why hast Thou forsaken me!" instead.

"Lord help me, and help us all!" he thought to himself. He found it hard to imagine Jesus having the strength to say, "Into Thy hands I commend my spirit," when he himself was finding it so hard to accept that this was God's will.

He heaved a heavy sigh as Amy silently met him at the door with a towel, and Momma Celia poured him a cup of one of her teas. She made him sit down near the stove to drink it, so he wouldn't catch a chill from the rain.

"You alright, sugar?" Amy asked quietly, concerned for his health and certain this meeting had taken a toll on him.

Elijah nodded morosely. "Bout as alright as I can be under the circumstances, I guess," he sighed. "Hardest thing I've ever had to do in my life!" he attested, his face haggard.

Amy did not press him for details. She knew he needed to just be. He'd talk about it when he was ready, and there was no sense rushing him. She hugged him around the shoulders as he sat, and giving him a kiss on the cheek reminded him reassuringly, "You're a good man, Elijah Willis!"

She had been unable to bring herself to attend the meeting for fear of breaking down in front of the others, so under the pretext of helping Momma Celia bake and cook the provisions for the slaves' journey to the market in Hambug, Amy had stayed in the plantation house with the children. A somber pall seemed to be draped over everything and everyone that afternoon, and like the devastating emptiness and sense of abanandonment of the Good Friday liturgy, there was nothing for it but to surrender to the gloom of the Calvary experience, hoping that by the miracle of grace, after this agony on the cross there would in fact be a resurrection and a new life.

The following morning Gilbert, and Julius, and Jason went from cabin to cabin to gather the slaves being sent to market. They assembled everyone in the barn again, as the ground was still damp from the preceding night's rain, and Elijah didn't want them getting their good clothes all muddy. His three lieutenants held long coils of thick hemp rope in their hands, and once everyone was gathered, they quietly set about tying them all together, heartfelt apology in their tearful eyes. They tried not to tie them too tight or hurt them, but they needed them to be sufficiently bound that they could not easily escape. Elijah was doing the head count to make sure all had been accounted for. He realized old Henry was missing.

"Jason!" Elijah called. "Go see what's keepin Henry!"

"Yessir!" Jason responded, relieved to be spared from the onerous task of tying up his companions.

A few minutes later he came running back. "Mister Elijah! Mister Elijah!" he said in a low, urgent voice, so as not to call attention, "Come quick!"

Shaken from the grim census taking, Elijah looked up at Jason surprised, a sense of foreboding seizing him. He went with Jason over toward Henry's cabin and froze with alarm as Jason pointed toward the door. There on the threshold lay Henry, a small bundle of possessions tied neatly in a large bandana by his side, his eyes big and sorrowful in a fixed stare.

"Oh, dear God!" moaned Elijah, kneeling by his most faithful of slaves. He was suddenly filled with remorse. He felt guilty that his decision to sell Henry, rather than put him through the ordeal of starting a new life at his advanced age as a freedman without strength or marketable skills, had killed this good and gentle man whom he had known most of his life.

"Help me pick him up, Jason!" The two men lifted the old man carefully, and carried him inside. They laid him gently on the rope mattress of his bed, crossing his arms over his chest. Elijah reached forward to try to close the old man's eyes, but they wouldn't close, rigor mortis having set in. He pulled his hand back from the old man's face as if stung, and turned his own gaze away, unsettled, afraid to see reproach in those old eyes confirm his guilt.

Jason looked at Elijah with a mixture of sorrow and pity.

"What ya'll wanna do, Mister Elijah?" he asked.

Elijah realized that announcing Henry's death would just upset everyone else all the more. "Keep this quiet for now, till the others have left. When we get back from the depot, we can gather the rest of us for prayers, and we'll give him a proper burial. No need to upset everyone else with this right now- they've got enough sorrow for one day as is."

"I reckon ole Henry just decided he was too ole to start over, an he'druther go in peace here at home, so's he wouldn't have to miss us all so!" Jason observed philosophically.

His poignant remarks actually helped relieve Elijah's anguish a bit, preferring to think that it was simply Henry's time, and that the old man had just wanted to go to his Maker from where he called home. Elijah hoped he wasn't just placating his own guilty conscience by thinking so.

Elijah and Jason returned to the barn, and so absorbed were each of the slaves in their own sorrows and in the trauma and discomfort of being tied together, nobody even seemed to have noticed they had been gone, or that Henry was missing.

"Alright ya'll!" announced Gilbert once they were all tied together, "Time to go!" With grunts and groans, and sobs and moans they all stood up, unaccustomed to being bound, and clumsily started shuffling out the door toward the wagons, some stumbling and catching each other as they went. Being used to working in gangs however, they quickly mastered the challenge of moving as a group. The men went first, with the women and children bringing up the rear.

Elijah would have preferred to just have Gilbert take them off to the depot and stay home himself, not having to witness any more of their agony than he already had, but he knew he must go too, for he had to sign them over to the trader he had arranged to have meet them at the depot. He had already paid Will Beazely for their passage, so it should be a fairly straightforward and quick transaction, in any case.

He debated about riding to the depot in the carriage, where he would not have to see the slaves, nor they see him during the trip, but he thought that was unfair and disrespectful to them, and a bit cowardly of him to want to avoid them. It would also necessarily require the use of a driver, whose efforts were better spent overseeing the slaves in the wagons, so he had asked Elder to saddle up Beauty for him. It had been a long time since he had ridden her, due to Dr. Harley's orders. But this would be no cross-country gallop, so Amy and Momma Celia had granted their permission as the good doctor's proxies, trusting he would ride at a safe and sedate pace.

Elder, Elleck, and Phillip had all been witnessing the preparations with solemn faces and morbid fascination. Though they had spent most of their lives with Elijah, they still had a few memories of their early childhood on the Kirkland plantation and how hard it had been to leave where they were born. They could feel the pain of the other slaves, and had mixed feelings of relief and guilt as to why they should be spared and the others not. It was hard to talk about their feelings with their parents, especially because of Amy's fears of triggering any more episodes with Elijah, for lately emotional strains and upsets seemed to abound, in spite of her efforts to avoid them.

"Hey Elder!" Phillip asked his brother, "D'you remember when we were little, and Mister William told Momma Celia and Momma he was sellin us?" Elder had been only about ten years old, and Phillip about six.

"Yeah, I remember," his brother said somberly, not immediately offering up any additional details.

The brothers had seldom talked about their life on the Kirkland plantation or their memories of their biological father. He had been a hard man, struggling against his bondage and taking it out on his family in impotent rage. His temper and violent outbursts against Amy and the children had not endeared him in their memory. As painful as their sale had been at first, fact was life had gotten a whole lot better for them all, once they moved to the Willis Plantation and away from their father. The boys had genuinely accepted Elijah as their father now, remembering Momma Celia telling them, "It ain't the man who makes the babies is the father, but the man who cares for em." They had never felt their biological father had really cared for them at all, and were secretly relieved to see him sold off to a different owner rather than being sold to Elijah with the rest of the family. It had been William Kirkland's one redeeming act of kindness to atone for his betrayal of Momma Celia.

"Well, why are Uncle Gilbert an Julius an Jason tyin everybody up like that? We didn't get tied up, did we?" Phillip asked. The situation was confusing, for though he knew they were slaves, he actually had little experience or memory of suffering from that fact. Other than the game of playing slave when white folks came to the plantation, and experiencing the loathing of Elijah's white relations or occasional stares and comments from people on the rare occasions they left the plantation, his life had been pretty comfortable. And since Elijah did not resort to cruel or abusive treatment, he didn't see the other slaves suffering that much either, though he understood they all lived in an unfair and unequal world. But this- the fear and sorrow on the faces of the people he had grown up with- the loaded silences as his uncle tied them together with that thick rope, the winces as the rough hemp chafed against their ankles- he had not been prepared for this, and it was frightening!

Elleck weighed in on the matter, saying, "That was different. Papa bought just us, and we didn't have far to go." This simple observation seemed to suffice for Elleck, but it left Phillip wondering why having further to go required tying people up.

"So, just cause they got further to go than we did, they all gotta be tied up? That seems dumb!" Phillip declared.

"It's so's they don't run away, stupid!" interjected Elder, exasperated that his younger brother didn't seem to fully grasp what was going on.

"But why would they? Where could they go without gettin caught? Better to be fed, clothed, and housed on another plantation than runnin barefoot in the woods and swamps, with nothin to eat and no place to sleep, if ya ask me!" Phillip responded.

"Well no one is askin you!" fired back Elder, who was deeply disturbed by what he was seeing and was struggling to reconcile his love for Elijah with the appearance that this suffering he was seeing was caused by the man he called Papa.

Elder stood holding Beauty by the bridle, waiting for his father, his brothers watching by his side. Gilbert and Julius and Jason helped everyone get loaded on to the wagons with their belongings. It was crowded and uncomfortable, and the looks of anguish and fear on their faces seemed to burn themselves into the boys' memories like a branding iron, marking this moment on their souls forever.

Elijah came up to Elder, and taking Beauty's reins in his hand, swung up into the saddle. He leaned over and put a gentle hand on the boy's shoulder, saying, "Thank ya, son." He felt Elder flinch and recoil at his touch, and looking him in the eye said, "Don't hate me for doin this. I know it's hard. Is for me too. But it's got ta be done so you, your Momma, your grandmother and your brothers an sisters can all go up to Cincinnati and become free!"

Elder looked past Elijah at the wagonloads of misery, and then looked back at his adoptive father, his eyes brimming with raw emotions too complex for him to even identify. He managed a nod and released the bridle from his grasp.

Elijah looked at his sons wrestling with this tragedy. "Boys, I want ya'll to go find your Momma and your grandmother and keep em company. They'll be needin your comfort too. Tell your Momma I'll be back soon as I can." He gave Beauty's flanks a slight kick and she started off down the drive at a stately pace, the mournful wagons following like hearses at a mass funeral.

The remaining slaves stood silently by, gathered together in a grieving cluster, a few waving to friends one last time as they disappeared down the road, knowing they would never see each other again. Amy and Momma Celia stood side by side on the upper veranda, each with an arm around the other for comfort, watching Elijah lead the wagons off toward the main road and the depot. Finally, once the wagons were out of sight, Amy collected herself and went down the outside stairs, the boys meeting her at the bottom. No one said anything, they just hugged each other fiercely, their dark fingers pressing pink into each other's shoulders, as if by squeezing the stream of sorrow welling up from within could be shut off.

After a moment Amy shook them off, smoothed back her hair, and headed toward the slave quarters. She knew emotions there would be running high, and she felt the need to help keep things calm. She hoped her presence would be a comfort and not an aggravation, but she wasn't entirely sure what to expect.

A sudden shriek and wail from inside one of the cabins shook her resolve, and she broke into a run to find the source of the lament. It was coming from Henry's cabin, but it didn't sound like Henry- and as far as Amy knew, Henry was supposed to be on one of the wagons with the others, heading off to Hamburg.

When she got to the open door and looked in, the cabin was dark, but she heard deep sobs and, looking over toward the bed in the corner, realized what had happened. One of the slave women who had always in on Henry to make sure the old man was alright, knelt by the bedside where Henry's body lay. Amy assumed the woman had laid him out, not knowing that it had been Elijah and Jason who had found him and brought him inside.

The woman looked up, her face bathed in tears, "Oh Miss Amy! Miss Amy!" she sobbed. "Poor ole Henry done lef us! Broke his heart Mister Elijah decide to sell him afta all these years! Why he have ta do that, Miss Amy? Why he wanna sell ole Henry?" the woman asked uncomprehendingly.

Amy felt overwhelmed with the woman's grief and with her own. The cumulative sorrow of everyone on the plantation and in the cortege going down the road to the depot seemed too much to bear!

"When did ya find him, and who helped ya lay him out?" Amy asked, rather than attempting to answer woman's questions.

"Didn't nobody hep me lay him out- I found him like this a few minutes ago, afta the wagons lef!" she answered.

"Well then, how'd he get laid out all dignified like this?" Amy asked herself. No sooner were the words of the question formed in her mind, however, than she realized what must of happened and what a blow it must have been to Elijah to find Henry dead in the midst of what was already such a stressful event. She was both touched by his efforts to lay Henry out and by his courage in going ahead with the plan anyway. But all this was too complicated to try to explain.

"Well, whoever laid him out musta loved and respected Henry, that's for sure! That was a real kind thing to do." Amy was trying to assuage the woman's anger at Elijah without having to actually defend him outright, hoping she'd come to see for herself that Elijah was not a villain in this scenario, but a fellow victim.

"Yes'm, it was." sniffled the woman.

Amy knew that grieving folks needed to have something to do to keep the grief from weighing too heavy on them, so she turned to the woman and said, "I want ya to go let all the others know that Henry has passed and that we're gonna give him a proper burial as soon as Mister Elijah gets back," she ordered adding, "Henry would like that."

The woman wiped her nose on her sleeve, nodded in obedience with a mumbled "Yes'm," and still sobbing, left the cabin to tell the others. Amy could hear a series of gasps and wails denoting a fresh flood of tears moving with the news down the line of cabins, like sluice gates opening the successive locks of a canal. She wondered if a day could get any gloomier, or a sadness any greater. It weighed on everyone like a physical thing, bearing down on them and making it hard to breathe.

"Oh Lord!" Amy thought to herself, "If I'm feelin so much strain, dear God, Elijah's gotta be feelin even more! Protect him Lord! Don't let this take him from us too!" She looked down at poor old Henry and for the first time noticed his open eyes. Like her husband, she too found herself unable to look for fear of seeing blame in them. She shuddered involuntarily and left the cabin quickly to go tell Momma Celia what had happened, passing the other cabins and barely noticing the stunned silences, the blank stares, and the lethargy that seemed to have taken a chilling hold on everyone.

Somehow, in the catatonic blur of collective grief numbing the memory and dulling the senses, Elijah managed to sign over the slaves to the trader waiting for him at the depot. Once the slaves were safely loaded onto the baggage car and out of his sight, he felt a liberating finality intermingle with the bitterness of his remorse, knowing that despite the heavy emotional price paid he was but a few steps away from finally being able to leave for Cincinnati with Amy and the children.

The return home with Gilbert, Julius and Jason in now empty wagons would have felt like coming home from a funeral if it weren't for the fact that they knew they still had to bury Henry as soon as they got back. None of the four of them spoke to each other on the way, each trying to simply deal with their own emotions, but there was some sense that the grief was truly shared by all. Neither Gilbert nor Julius nor Jason felt blame toward Elijah, seeing him clearly suffering from the ordeal. In fact Gilbert, knew that the saga was not yet over, and was concerned about the impact this strain might have on this man who was both his brother-in-law and master (and hopefully soon his liberator). He watched closely for any signs Elijah was having heart trouble, ready to get him off Beauty and lying down in a wagon to rest, if necessary.

When they got home, even before Elijah went to preside over Henry's burial, Momma Celia made him drink some of her digitalis and willow bark tea. Despite a grimace of distaste he willingly acquiesced, shaken as he was by the whole sequence of events and much in need of Momma Celia's tonic remedies to get him through the ordeal of the burial still awaiting him.

The remainder of the community duly gathered in a spot near the creek at the edge of the clearing where they worshipped on Sundays. Julius and Jason dug the grave straight and true under a live oak where Henry would sometimes sit of a summer evening and regale the others with tall tales and legends he remembered from his Yoruba grandmother, who was the daughter of a chieftan in Benin. It only seemed right he be buried in a place he loved so much and that brought everyone on the plantation such happy memories of him.

Most everyone shared a kind word or a loving memory of Henry, including Elijah, who memorialized Henry with genuine affection in several anecdotes from his own boyhood on up to the present.

Elijah led them all in reciting the Lord's Prayer and the 23rd Psalm. The words "He maketh me to lie down in green pastures, he leadeth me bedside the still waters, he restoreth my soul…" seemed particularly vivid and comforting in the green of the clearing with the soft babble of the creek behind them. When Henry was finally lowered into his grave dressed in his Sunday best as Elijah had ordered, Elijah felt his own throat choke with sorrow that faithful and obedient to the end, it was as if Henry had gotten himself ready for his own funeral so an undertaker wouldn't have to.

Once the last shovelful of dirt had covered him, Gilbert hammered into the ground a wooden cross he had fashioned at the head of the grave. The slaves joined in reverently tamping down the soil with their palms in blessing, leaving their handprints in the fresh dirt like a flutter of angels' wings to carry Henry's soul heavenward. Momma Celia stuck a blooming branch of bright magenta azalea in the dirt at the level of Henry's heart and watered it, praying it might take root as a living testimony to a beautiful soul. Everybody sang a few hymns, passed the peace, and in silence each solemnly headed back to their respective cabins, exhausted from the emotional intensity of the past twenty-four hours, and feeling the emptiness of their departed companions, both living and dead.

Elijah walked back to the plantation house with Amy, Momma Celia, and the children. Gilbert too, gathered his children closely around him, as did all the others who had spouses or children. There was little or no small talk as they went to their respective dwellings, each keeping their own counsel, trying to process the emotional upheaval of this sequence of events and preparing for the many changes to their lives that would ensue as a result of it.

James Willis couldn't resist trying to spy on his Uncle Elijah; the fear of him depriving the Willis brothers of their hoped for inheritance was like a festering wound that gave him no rest. He found himself passing by his uncle's plantation just to see if anything was happening out of the ordinary. It was plowing and planting time, but James didn't see the usual flurry of activity in his uncle's fields. It looked like only some of the slaves were working, and they seemed to only be plowing where his uncle usually planted some corn and vegetables. None of the cotton fields had been plowed yet, and it was getting late to get started! This was not like his uncle, who was always eager to get the crop in early. Convinced this was further evidence of a plot, he went to his father to report his nefarious observations.

"Settle down, son. It's alright!" his father counseled him. "Seems your Uncle Elijah has finally taken my advice for once in his stubborn life!"

James was caught completely off guard by his father's remark, unaware that he and his uncle had spoken at all. "Whatcha talkin about, Daddy? What advice did ya give Uncle Elijah- and when did ya talk to him? I thought ya'll weren't even on speakin terms ever since he came an ruined our Christmas!" The fact that several Christmases had passed since that unhappy encounter had done nothing to dim the memory of his uncle's rebuke to them.

His father coughed to clear his throat and said, "Well, fact is I went over to see him, man to man, at New Year's. I didn't take ya'll with me, figurin I might be able to get through to him without him just gettin riled up about you all again."

James felt a twinge of embarrassment mixed with surprise and curiosity that his father had managed to actually communicate with his problematic brother. "Well, what dya'll talk about then?" he pressed.

"I told him I was worried bout his health and thought he should stop workin so hard. He looks ten years older, and I heard he's hardly been seen outside since the cotton harvest ended."

"Yeah? An what did he say to that? He send ya'll to Hell like he usually does?" commented James cynically.

"As a matter of fact, he didn't. Almost worried me more than if he had, ta tell the truth! He agreed to just keep the lumber business goin and stop plantin cotton. Said he was worn out."

"Well, what's he gonna do with all those slaves if they ain't workin?" James asked, ever mindful of his uncle's assets.

"Well, he realized he couldn't afford to keep em all if he wasn't plantin cotton, so he sold off about half of em- shipped em off to Hamburg," his father announced, to James' astonishment.

"He what? he asked, incredulous.

"You heard me! I told him he should get a pretty good price for em in the slave market over in Hamburg, and he took my advice and sent em over there." His father seemed pleased as punch that his brother had listened to reason for once, but James was unconvinced that reason was the driving factor.

James was stunned. This did not fit his expectations at all. He wasn't sure whether he was madder that they had been sold- thereby diminishing the potential windfall he was counting on inheriting- or that Elijah's sale of the slaves seemed to disprove that his underlying motivation was social disruption by emancipation and abolitionism. This was about as confusing as when he signed their petition after the rally.

His father went on to say "I told him with his health so poor, he should go on a good long trip somewhere- get away from the worries of the plantation for a while and enjoy some of the fruits of his labors for a change!"

"I bet if he does, he'll take that nigra woman an her pickanninies with him!" swore James.

"Hell, son, so what if he does? They're his property, he can do with em as he pleases!" His father didn't want to get into that go-round about Elijah's insulting improprieties again. He'd come to accept his brother's choice even though he disapproved of it. They were too old to keep fighting over it at this point.

"It don't matter, since he's leavin the estate to all of us, anyway! Ya'll just leave your uncle alone! He's old, he ain't well, he's probably gonna die soon, and then all this nigra-loving hoopla'll be over and done with!"

James said, "Well alright Daddy, but if ya ask me there's still something ain't right about all this!"

"Well I ain't askin ya, I'm tellin ya! Back off, the both of ya! Go an tell your brother an your friend Angus that he'd best back off too. Ya'll can say a lot about Elijah's choice a women, but he's the best goddamn planter around these parts, and has made our family name famous for it. Let him finish his days without ya'll harassin him, and ya'll'll get your reward before long!"

James knew his father's word on the matter was final. "Yessir!" he answered, not wanting to cross his father. He didn't relish delivering that message to Michael and Angus, but he knew he had no choice.

When he got back to his store, Michael and Angus were sitting around talking as usual.

"Where the Hell you been?" asked his brother. "You look like you just drank curdled milk. What's goin on?"

James proceeded to recount his discovery while reconnoitering the Willis Plantation, and his subsequent conversation with their father.

"Damn!" uttered Michael in mixed astonishment and admiration. "Daddy actually managed to get a word in edgewise with Uncle Elijah?"

"More'n a word, apparently. An the amazin thing is Uncle Elijah took it!" affirmed James.

"So who cares if he sold off half his nigras anyway? Whatever money he gets for em and doesn't spend'll still be part of the estate too. And even if he takes a trip and takes them with him, ain't no way he can spend it all! It's the land that matters most, an we can always get or breed more nigras to work it!" Michael laughed a coarse laugh- his solutions always reliably simplistic.

Angus had been listening attentively, his mind racing to process this unexpected information. "Did your Daddy give any indication of where your Uncle Elijah might go on a trip?" he asked.

"Nope. No idea. Don't even know for sure he'll go on a trip- it was just Daddy's recommendation," answered James. "Why, does it matter?"

"Maybe it doesn't. Just curious. I was just wondering what would happen if your Uncle should die while on a trip with his nigras?" speculated Angus.

Michael offered his usual simple solution. "Why we'd go fetch him back home for burial, and be the proud new owners of a bunch a nigras!"

James realized Angus had posed a question that might well not have such a simple solution. "The Fugitive Slave Act would give us the right to bring em all back here, wouldn't it?" he asked, hoping Angus had done enough of his homework to know the answer.

"In theory, yes." Angus affirmed, "That was the whole point of passin that Act."

James could hear the unspoken "but..." in Angus' reply. Angus, just like his father, being uncertain of the precise legalities outside of South Carolina's jurisdiction, did not choose to articulate the implicit "but...," and considered paying John Bauskett another visit to further his law education before stirring that pot any further.

"Well then, we got no worries!" offered Michael cheerfully, already imagining what he might do if he ended up owning Amy and her family.

"Let's hope not!" affirmed James, unconvinced and ever suspicious. "But best not count our chickens before they hatch. Uncle Elijah's full of surprises."

The three nodded their agreement, once again with a swig of the whiskey that so often sealed the bond of their friendship, and each indulged in their own speculations of what might happen once Elijah was finally dead and buried. For the first time, given Jimmy Willis' assessment of his brother, it seemed this event might be more imminent and probable than the more Macchiavellian machinations of emancipation they had so feared. Whereas James and Michael tended more toward fantasies of being served by Elijah's slaves- and especially his humiliated "family" nigras- Angus perceived that there might be some unexpected legal challenges to face before that could happen, and figured he needed to do some more homework, so he'd be ready if there were.

A few weeks later, Elijah received a brief letter from John Bauskett:

My Dear Elijah,

I just wanted to let you know that Angus Patterson, the Lesser, has paid me another visit in pursuit of legal knowledge: specifically, concerning the Fugitive Slave Act and the conditions for emancipation in the Northern States. The boy has some of his father's intelligence- especially in his ability to sniff out an issue- though lamentably little of his father's compassion and high moral character.

I think it would be wise, if your health now permits it, to make arrangements for your trip to Cincinnati as soon as possible, before young Angus' line of inquiry inspires him and your unfortunate nephews to some new preventive mischief.

As ever, I promise you and Amy all the legal support at my disposal should the need arise, but I suggest you also apprise Messrs. Gitchell and Jolliffe of the date and time of your arrival in Cincinnati, post haste, so as to be as well prepared as possible for all eventualities.

Eugenia and I wish you Godspeed, and pray you keep in touch.

Your friend and legal counsel,

John Bauskett, Esq.

Elijah read the letter carefully. Will Beazeley had actually come out to the plantation to deliver it in person, as he suspected its import and had already noticed that the Willis brothers seemed to be prowling around the depot again as if looking for clues to Elijah's plans.

"I surely do thank ya Will, for comin all the way out here to deliver this. It looks like the time has finally come to book those tickets to Cincinnati! Seems young Angus might be suspectin that if I get the family up to Cincinnati myself, they could finally be free from the reach of the Fugitive Slave Act and of my nephews' greed!"

"Oh Lordy, Mister Willis, d'ya think they'd try to keep ya'll from goin?" Will said with alarm.

"Can't rightly say, but I wouldn't be surprised if they tried! I've had enough of their nonsense- just can't put up with it any more! So I want ya to book us tickets for May 15- for me, Amy, Momma Celia and all the children- that'll get us up to Louisville- and then I want ya to book us tickets on the Riverboat *Jacob Strader* from there to Cincinnati. That should get us there on the 24th. Send a telegram to my lawyers, Messrs. Gitchell and Jolliffe in Cincinnati, announcing our arrival date and time once you've booked the tickets. I'll come in to the depot and pay ya for em ahead a time- I've got to tie up some other business in town before I go, and wanna make sure Gilbert's got all the provisions he'll be needin to keep things goin til I get back."

"Yessir, Mr. Willis, I'll book em right away for ya. Sure am gonna miss ya'll though. Ya'll've been a real inspiration to me- not to mention my best customers!" Will smiled.

"Why thank ya, Will. I'm gonna miss you too. Haven't been many around here I could trust to help me in all this, so I truly do appreciate all ya've done. May the Good Lord bless ya for it, cause we surely do!"

As Will departed, Elijah called out to Amy, "Sugar! Come here a minute, would ya? There's something I want to show ya!"

Amy came out from the study, where she had been going over the plantation accounts and making note of any debts owed by or to Elijah in anticipation of their departure. She wanted to make sure everything was in order, and that they had ample cash on hand whenever they were finally able to leave. She also knew that Gilbert would need funds available to take care of any purchase of supplies that might be needed to sustain the others until Elijah could get back down to the plantation to sell the place and bring the rest of them up to Ohio and freedom.

"What is it, honey? Did I hear Mister Beazeley's voice out here?" she asked.

"Ya did. He came by to deliver me this!" He handed John Bauskett's letter to her. As she read it, worry on her face, he continued, "I told him it's time to book the tickets for Cincinnati! I asked him to book the train up to Louisville for the 15th, and then book us tickets from Louisville to Cincinnati on the Jacob Strader! If we're gonna go, we're gonna go in style!" he grinned.

Amy looked up from reading the letter, as if she hadn't quite heard or didn't trust her ears. "D'ya really mean it? We're finally goin? Oh my God, Elijah, I can't believe it!" the excitement surged through her like a freight train out of control.

"MOMMAAAAA!!!!" she yelled, fairly jumping with excitement. She threw her arms hurriedly around Elijah, gave him a kiss, and ran towards the kitchen, in the door of which her mother had appeared in alarm.

"What in the Name a Sweet Jesus you hollerin about, Amy? Like about to skeered me to death, child!" Momma Celia scolded.

"Momma, Momma! We're finally goin to Cincinnati!!! We leave on the fifteenth! Oh Momma, I can hardly believe it! Elijah told Mister Beazeley to go ahead and book the tickets! It's finally happenin!"

"Lord ha Mercy!" Momma Celia replied softly, shaking her head in stunned disbelief, her voice redolent with the emotions of a lifetime of servitude nearly completed. "Baby, that's wonderful news!" she looked past her daughter to see Elijah smiling at them, and her eyes filled with tears of gratitude.

"God bless ya, Elijah, God bless ya!" was all she could manage to say before the emotion overwhelmed her, and she and her daughter locked in a cathartic embrace, tears of joy flowing freely.

The children had also heard their mother shouting for Momma Celia and came running to see what was the matter. The girls clattered and thumped down the front and back stairs in a race to the kitchen, the boys flung open the back door, running in from the barn and the chicken coop, and all converged around their mother and grandmother who were still locked in a tight embrace.

"What's goin on, ya'll? asked Elder and Elleck simultaneously.

"Papa, why're Momma an Momma Celia cryin, an you smiling?" asked Julia, not yet understanding the nature of their tears, and confused by the contradictory signals of joy and sorrow.

There was a general outburst of questions gushing from all the children, forcing Amy and her mother to release each other from their embrace. Amy blowing out a deep sigh of relief and cheerfully wiping her cheeks, said,

"Children- we have wonderful news! We're finally leaving for Cincinnati! Your father's asked Mister Beazely to book us tickets for the 15th!"

Expecting comparable shouts of elation from the children, she was taken aback that they seemed almost subdued. The older boys looked to Elijah for confirmation. Elijah nodded. The girls responded with a mixture of excitement and worry.

"Will I be able to take my dolly?" Eliza asked anxiously.

"Of course ya can, sweetie pie," assured her mother.

"What about the kittens?" asked Julia- the cat out in the barn had just had a litter and the girls were captivated by their cuteness and took turns holding and cuddling them.

"The kittens'll have to stay here at home with their momma. They're too little to go on a long trip," explained Elijah, "but maybe when we get settled up in Cincinnati we can get ya'll a new kitty."

Julia pouted at the news she could not take the kittens with her, and was not mollified by the thought of replacing them with another cat. "Aw Papa, can't you bring up these when ya come back with Uncle Gilbert?" she insisted, not willing to accept some unknown cat as a replacement for the fuzzy personalities she had already attributed to the litter in the barn.

"Well maybe we could do that, we'll see." Elijah said placatingly, hoping to avoid thereby a tantrum from his middle daughter.

Clarissa was more excited than the other girls. Her experience helping deliver Eliza had matured her, and she had dreams of becoming a midwife- dreams that seemed unlikely to be fulfilled staying on the Willis Plantation. So the thought of a big city like Cincinnati struck her as a thrilling adventure, that would open up new horizons for her future.

Elder, Elleck and Phillip were torn. They had tasted the attractions of city life briefly up in Baltimore, and it had whetted their appetite for more. But the memory of the wagonload of slaves being hauled off to Hamburg to make that possible for them also weighed on their consciences. They felt the pull to stay with their cousins in the familiarity of the world in which they had grown up, uncertain whether the move was going to be an adventure or just another painful separation.

Momma Celia, sensing her grandchildren's mixed emotions, tried to comfort and encourage them. "Chillun, I know ya'll're feelin kinda worried bout this move. But ya Papa has done somethin I don't think ya'll can fully appreciate yet- somethin few white men've tried, and fewer still succeeded at doin. Whatever we gonna have to face up in Ohio, we gonna face it free!"

The children listened to their grandmother with solemn attention, even the youngest realizing that she seldom spoke of such things, and that this was an important moment in their lives they'd best remember.

"Why freedom so important, Momma Celia? We got a good life here!" offered Phillip. He knew he should feel overwhelmingly grateful for what was about to happen, but given his generally benign experience of his status, sheltered as he had been under the wings of Elijah's kindness, it was hard for him to see why this was such a big deal.

Momma Celia sighed a deep sigh, and said, "Child, ya'll've been blessed livin here- no doubt about it- but it's a precarious blessin that could turn to hardship in the blink of an eye!" Momma Celia was a realist and, though she didn't want to frighten the children, she did want them to grasp why this was so crucial to their future. "Your Papa knows that, and knows that because we all his slaves as well as his family, the day he dies, that family protection dies with him, and we all just be somebody else's slaves to do with as they please. Ain't likely we'd find such comfort an love again."

The boys took this sobering reality in. They had been dealing with the fear of Elijah's death ever since his first attack at Christmas time years ago, but to them it was more a fear of losing someone they loved, for the parental compansionship, guidance, wisdom and laughter he shared with them. Only now were they fully realizing what could happen to them if he were to die without having managed to set them free.

Amy had had enough of serious talk. Contemplating the horrifying possibilities that could await them should Elijah die before their arrival in Cincinnati was just too depressing, and she grew annoyed that it was dampening the mood of what should be a joyous celebration. They had been through enough dark days since Elijah's stroke that she felt a great need to keep things in a positive light, and move forward.

"Come on ya'll!" She interrupted. "We got work to do to get ready! We gonna have to pack up all ya'll's clothes, for one thing- an I want em all clean an pressed before ya pack em. Papa's bought ya your own valises, and we got that big new steamer trunk too…. An Momma's gonna need ya'll's help too!"

Everyone shaken out of the questioning and doubts for the moment, Amy started organizing the move like a military campaign. Momma Celia went off to the pantry to start figuring what she would need to take and what she could afford to leave. She started by going through her medical supplies, insisting that her ingredients be carefully packed, as she was pretty well certain she'd be needing them, and wasn't sure which of them, if any, were also available up north in Ohio.

Elijah, meanwhile, went to go find Gilbert to give him the news. He wanted to reassure his brother-in-law that he fully intended to come back and bring him, his family and all the others up to Ohio as soon as he could get Amy and the children settled.

He looked for Gilbert in the barn and in the slave quarters, but he was not to be found. No one seemed quite sure of where he was- one thought he might be over at the mill, another thought he was supervising the planting of the corn fields. Elijah saddled up Beauty and headed out to find him.

Gilbert wasn't in the fields, and he wasn't in the mill. Perplexed by this unusual behavior, on a hunch Elijah headed over toward the clearing by the creek. From a distance he spotted Gilbert kneeling by Henry's grave.

As he gently poured water around Momma Celia's azalea shoot, the fresh green of new leaves now sprouting from where the blossoms had wilted and faded, Gilbert was wondering whether he would ever put down roots in soil of his own, or like Henry be fated to stay rooted only in another man's land.

Elijah dismounted and walked quietly over to the live oak, not wanting to interrupt what seemed to be for Gilbert a moment of prayer. His foot stepped on a twig as he approached, and the crack alerted Gilbert to his presence. He got up slowly, brushed the dirt off his knees, and joining his brother-in-law, the two men walked over to a large log by the bank of the stream and sat down on it, silently watching the water slowly flow by.

"Water's kinda like time, ain't it?" commented Gilbert after they'd been watching for a spell. "Sometimes seems to flow fast, sometimes slow, but sooner or later carries everything away."

Elijah could sense his brother-in-law's deep emotion- was it sorrow, resignation, bitterness? He wasn't sure, but it was clear that Gilbert was feeling the cumulative weight of the recent series of events, and it was heavy on his heart. A brief memory crossed his mind of the hymn "O God, Our Help in Ages Past" "Time, like an everflowing stream, bears all its sons away..." Gilbert's observation seemed particularly poignant. Rather than try to answer it, however, Elijah decided to just go ahead and break the news.

"I came to tell ya the time has finally come. Got a letter from John Bauskett today, urgin me to make arrangements to head on up to Cincinnati as soon as possible. Seems Angus Patterson may be figurin out our plan at last, an we need to get outa here before he an my nephews have time to stir up any more trouble for us."

Gilbert felt both a rush of excitement and of anxiety, as he knew he would not be accompanying his sister and mother and the children, and would have to hold down the fort here in Elijah's absence. They both knew that Elijah's nephews were just as capable of stirring up trouble after Elijah left as before, and it was not a comforting thought.

"When ya'll leavin?" he asked, his mouth feeling kind of dry.

"The fifteenth. Should reach Cincinnati around the 23rd or 24th . Once we're settled up there I'll let ya know. I'll come on back to fetch ya'll as soon as I can. Will Beazely's promised to give ya the message himself so's ya won't have to worry about dealin with any of my damned relations!"

Gilbert nodded, deep in thought. After a moment he spoke up, "Elijah? It's an amazin thing ya'll're doin. I want ya to know how much I admire an respect ya for it." His voice was thick with emotion.

Elijah could feel Gilbert's sincerity, but he also sensed a twinge of doubt, and he knew it was not because he didn't trust Elijah's word but only that he didn't trust Elijah's health. There was an unspoken fear they shared that despite their best efforts, God would take Elijah before he could see his plan fulfilled. Amy felt it too, but there was nothing any of them could do about it but try their best to keep body and soul together and move forward with the plan.

"Look Gilbert, I know we're takin a leap a faith here, an a whole lotta things could still go wrong before this is all over, but as God is my witness, I won't ever give up on ya- an neither will Amy! I'm gonna get ya'll outa here and free if it's the last thing I do!"

"Well, I pray the Good Lord hears ya, but I tell ya one thing. I've had plenty a time to set with this an think it over, an I promise I won't blame ya or hate ya if God's plan an ya'll's turn out not to be the same. Whatever happens, ya'll deserve nothing but praise for tryin so hard to do right by us all!" His voice choked on this last phrase, and he fell silent.

The two men continued to sit pondering life's twists and turns, watching the creek flow by in its own meandering course. Its gurgling sounded alternately like tears and laughter, as if blending both extremes of human emotion into a single current that would sooner or later carry each of them away to what they prayed would be a better life, perhaps in some Heaven where hatred and fear were unknown.

A breeze freshened, rustling the leaves of the live oak behind them, the willows on the bank swishing softly in reply, reminding them they had much to do.

"Well, alright then!" said Elijah, standing up a little stiffly. "Guess I'd best head back to the house. Ya'll want a ride with me?" he offered.

Gilbert shook his head, "Thank ya, I think I'd like to walk if ya don't mind. But I'll be back directly. I guess I'll need to know exactly what ya'll want me to do while ya're away to get ready to sell the place?"

"We'll talk later about all that. I still got some paper work to do- bills to pay and all- and need to take stock of provisions so's ya'll have enough to get by. But we'll figure it out, and I'll leave ya with some cash too, in case ya'll need somethin before I get back. Will Beazely'll help make sure ya'll can buy what ya need without havin to resort to my nephews' store and deal with the likes a them! Best steer clear of all the Willises if ya can!"

With that Elijah mounted Beauty, nudged her in the ribs, and cantered off toward the plantation house, leaving Gilbert to ponder what might be lying ahead until such time as Elijah could return for them.

The fifteenth of May dawned bright and clear. A warm breeze made the bright green of the willows flutter in welcome, the Spanish moss in the live oaks waving back in cheerful greeting.

"This is a perfect day for travelin!" announced Elijah as he came into the kitchen for breakfast. "God is smiling in His Heaven today!"

"Well He may be smiling in His heaven, but ya'll're gonna be frownin in this earth if ya don't hurry up an eat ya breakfast so's I can wash up before we gotta leave for the train!" Momma Celia was not about to leave her kitchen in disarray, even though she'd never cook in it again!

"Take it easy Momma, we got time! An the children'll all lend a hand so ya'll don't have to get yaself all in a snit!" Elijah teased her.

"Chillun ain't got time to hep me wash up when they got theyselves to get ready. Now come on, eat ya breakfast!" she chided him, not willing to be easily appeased. The closer the time came, the more nervous she was getting. The fact was, the very thought of actually leaving and finally being free was giving her fits of anxiety.

"Momma, maybe it's time for ya'll to be the one drinkin one a your nasty-tastin teas!" Elijah laughed. "Ya'll gonna give yaself a fit if ya're not careful!"

Momma Celia glared at her son-in-law with pursed lips and a slight shake of the head, and then with a snort set to rummaging around in one of her boxes, looking for some mint or chamomile to brew up to calm her nerves.

Word had gotten out in the slave quarters that their master was leaving with Miss Amy, Momma Celia, and the children, and the entire population of the plantation was torn between fear and excitement that at least some of them were about to reach freedom, with a promise that the rest of them would soon follow.

As Amy marshaled the forces in the house to get all the bags packed and downstairs, and Momma Celia fussed around in her kitchen, trying to decide if Northern folks had sense enough to have the right kind of skillets and pans, and fretting about which ingredients she should take and which she might safely trust to find in Yankee territory, Elijah went out to speak to the rest of the slaves. Gilbert had gathered them all out in front of the house rather than in the barn, so as to give Elijah and Amy a proper send-off.

"Mornin ya'll!" Elijah said cheerfully.

"Mornin, Mister Elijah!" they mumbled back in staccato chorus, some happily, others with worried expressions on their dark faces.

"Well, I guess ya'll know now what's goin on?"

There was a chorus of "Yassuh," "Hmm hmmm," and "Sho do," punctuated with nods and a few sniffles. The remaining slaves were experiencing high anxiety about their master leaving. This was not like other trips he had made. There was a finality in this that they were not emotionally prepared for, despite Elijah's efforts to secure their well-being in his absence.

"I want ya'll to know that I'm leavin Gilbert, Julius an Jason here in charge til I get back. If ya'll have any problems, bring em to them. They can always get a telegram to me if need be- an I can get Will Beasely or John Bauskett over here to help out, if needed. I hope it won't be too long, but I gotta get Momma Celia an Miss Amy an my children settled first, then I'm comin back to fetch the rest of ya'll and sell this place."

He paused for a moment before going on. "I promised Amy, ya'll, and God I'd do this- an ya'll know the price we all paid for it! I hope you can forgive me that I couldn't set everyone free, but this was the only way to free ya'll and be able to give ya'll something to get started in your new life too. Just didn't seem fair or right to free ya'll an then leave ya with nothin." The crowd rippled with nods and a few low moans at the heartbreaking memory of the two wagonloads of friends and co-workers trundling off down the drive toward Hamburg and an uncertain fate.

"While I'm gone," Elijah continued, "it's real important ya'll keep this plan a secret from anyone and everyone outside this plantation. No exceptions! Not relations or friends on other plantations- nobody's to hear of this, or the whole plan could go up in smoke! So if ya'll wanta be free, ya'd best keep your lips sealed like a tomb til we can get ya'll outa here, ya hear?" He didn't feel like threatening them with punishment if they broke their promise- and from the looks of worry on the assembled faces there seemed little likelihood anyone would risk it.

A chorus of "yassuhs" rippled through the crowd, punctuated by fervent nods of assent and anxious looks exchanged.

"I just wanna say, ya'll have earned my utmost respect. I know white folks don't tell black folks such things, but it's true nonetheless. Ya'll've always done right by me, and as God is my witness, I'm doin everything in my power to do right by ya'll. We're in this together!"

"Yassuh," "Amen to that!" "That's right!" and other such expressions rippled through the crowd with nods.

"Well, alright then," Elijah concluded, "Ya'll take good care a each other til I get back now, y'hear? As far as folks outside this plantation know, I'm just goin on a pleasure tour with my family, so ya'll gotta keep this place up and lookin like we'll be back shortly, and it's business as usual. Understand?"

Everyone nodded in agreement. As Elijah concluded his speech, Amy, Momma Celia and the children appeared on the veranda, dressed in their finest.

"Come on ya'll!" Elijah called to them, gesturing for them to join him, "Time ta say your good-byes! God willin, ya'll'l be seein each other again real soon, UP IN OHIO!" Elijah tried to sound rousing, but fact was it sounded a bit forced, and there was an uneasiness that everyone seemed to be experiencing now that they were faced with the reality of their departure. Everybody exchanged hugs all around, the children embracing their uncle and cousins with particular fervor. There weren't many dry eyes in the crowd, and Elijah felt his own welling up, to his dismay. He did not want to cave in to his emotions at such a time. He felt he needed to present a strong and confident image to the others, so they would feel encouraged and manage to keep things together until he could get back.

He called Gilbert and Jason and Julius to him one more time for some final instructions before they left.

"There's three people have my complete trust around here- besides you three, that is- Dr. Harley, Will Beazeley, and John Basukett. Don't let anyone else into the house under any circumstances unless one of those three're with em! Gilbert's in charge, but I want you two to help him keep everybody calm while I'm gone. Work the fields and the mill just as if I were here."

The three nodded in agreement saying, "Don't worry, Mister Elijah, we'll take care of a everthing- and everyone!" they added.

Elijah nodded his approval. "We need to look to everyone on the outside like we're just doin business as usual- except for the cotton. My health is already the excuse for that, and it was my own brother's suggestion I stop plantin cotton so's I don't work myself to death! I'm sure he's let that be known around town already." Elijah chuckled at the irony of his brother's unwitting complicity. "And remember that, God forbid, anyone tries to rob us or take anything off this land, by South Carolina law ya'll got the right and duty to defend the plantation- even against white folks! There's a couple guns up in the house and enough ammunition to help ya defend it, if necessary. Gilbert knows where they are."

The three nodded their understanding, each hoping fervently it would never come to a shoot out, as much for the disquieting fear that they might enjoy killing their assailants as for fear they themselves might get killed. Elijah dismissed them, and turned to say his own farewells, insisting on speaking to each of the assembled slaves, from the oldest to the youngest.

While Elijah and the family said their good-byes, Julius had brought the carriage around, and he and Jason had gone into the house with Momma Celia to bring out the luggage and load it on board. As the last of the luggage was being loaded onto the back of the carriage, Gilbert noticed his mother had not come back out of the house. He went in to look for her and found her sitting in her kitchen, a forlorn expression on her face.

"What's the matter, Momma?" he asked, knowing perfectly well the answer.

"I know it sound strange bein a slave, but I hates to leave this place! This house is the first white man's house I ever been in that made me feel welcome. Sho am gonna miss it!" she quietly sniffed back a tear.

"I know Momma, but what made it welcomin was Elijah, and ya'll goin with him- ya just gonna make another kitchen up North smell an feel as good as this one do here down South! That's all!" he said to comfort her.

Momma Celia looked up at her son with moist eyes. "God bless ya baby, ya always did know how ta make me feel better!" she wiped away a furtive tear. "Sho am gonna miss you, too!" she said, no longer trusting her voice not to crack.

"There now, Momma, don't be gettin all sad on me now. Ya'll're goin to freedom, pavin the way for the rest of us! Just think Momma, in a week or so you'll no longer be anybody's but God's! Won't that be somethin!?" Gilbert too was desperately trying to keep a cheerful face on for their departure, but he couldn't shake the fear it might be a long time before he saw his mother again, if at all!

"Momma!" Amy's voice called from the foyer. "Gilbert? Ya'll in there? Come on! Time to go! We're gonna be late for the train if ya'll don't hurry up!"

Momma Celia got up with a sigh, patting her son's muscular arm. "Yes honey, that truly will be somethin!" she forced herself to smile through her tears and headed out her kitchen door to the veranda without another look back, her son following behind her.

Gilbert's children ambushed their grandmother with hugs and tears on her way out the front door. She gave each of them her blessing, admonishing them "Ya'll behave yaselves now, hear? I don't wanna hear no reports of ya'll misbehaving, unnerstand?" She waved a scolding finger at them with a fierce scowl that quickly broke into a toothsome grin. "Come on now, gimme some sugar one mo time befo I go- cause it's gonna hafta tide me over with enough sweetness til ya'll get up to Ohio!"

Elijah joined them on the veranda and gave his brother-in-law a bear hug, saying,

"Ya'll take good care a each other til I get back now, hear?"

Gilbert nodded, unable to trust his voice, and turning said, "Go on now children, let ya grandmother get into the carriage. We gotta go! I'll be back soon as I get em all on the train."

With that the cluster on the veranda broke up, some heading toward the carriage, the others joining the rest of the slaves assembled as a going away party.

The wave of sorrow and attachment passing, the family felt a surge of excitement as Gilbert climbed up on the drivers seat, Elder and Elleck on either side, and flicking his whip sent the carriage rumbling on its way as Amy and the girls waved to everyone through the windows. Only Elijah and Momma Celia refrained from looking back, not trusting their own emotions to stay under control, and refusing to risk a collapse.

Momma Celia reached into the picnic basket on her lap and pulled out a mason jar filled with an amber liquid. It was not sipping whiskey. She offered it to Elijah and said, "Ya'd best drink some a this. Can't be havin ya getting palpitations at a time like this!" She smiled encouragingly.

Elijah accepted the beaker gratefully and took two generous gulps before puckering his lips in distaste and handing it back to her with a sigh. "I'd best save the rest for later!" he said. She sealed the jar without complaint, replacing it in her picnic basket.

"Sho do wish I coulda said goodbye to Doctor Harley befo we left." Momma Celia commented. "Hardly seems right, afta all he done for us. Only doctor I ever saw treat the person instead of just the disease. I'm gonna miss him!"

"Well, as a matter of fact Momma, I figured that, so ya'll're gonna get to say ya good-byes at the train station. Joseph's gonna meet us at the depot." Elijah announced.

Momma Celia grinned her gratitude, her mood suddenly lightening.

"Now listen up, ya'll!" Elijah ordered, once they were out on the main road and the plantation house was out of sight, "You two up with Gilbert in the driver's seat listen too!" he insisted loudly, "When we get to the depot, we still got ta play master and slave- ya'll aren't free just yet! As far as anyone around town knows, we're just goin on a pleasure trip and're plannin to come home soon. Understand? We can't risk ya'll getting so excited ya let slip anything about freedom, or it could stir up trouble- especially for your Uncle Gilbert and the rest of the folks back on the plantation, ya hear? Not a blessed word!" He looked fiercely at the girls in particular, as they were far more prone to babbling their excitement than the boys were.

The children all nodded their understanding, the girls looking suddenly frightened.

Amy spoke up, "Come on ya'll, everybody clasp hands! We gotta say a prayer together! Boys- ya'll can hold on to ya Uncle Gilbert's hands while he's drivin!" she called.

The whole family joined hands, and Amy nodded to Momma Celia, as the family elder, to lead them in prayer.

"Sweet Lord Jesus," she began, "Watch over this family and all the folks back on the plantation too! Keep us all safe! Let Elijah fulfill his promise to ya, to free us at last, that we may show our love for ya in freedom, and help others to do the same! In your Holy Name we pray!" Everyone uttered a heartfelt "Amen!"

Amy, feeling confident they had duly "put on the armor of Christ," settled back in her seat and took a deep breath. She smiled at Elijah, her love and admiration glowing in her eyes. He smiled back, feeling relieved they had weathered the farewells without his heart going into palpitations, and hoping the rest of the trip would proceed as favorably.

When they got to the platform at the depot, both Jospeph Harley and Will Beazeley were waiting for them.

The boys helped Gilbert unload the luggage while Amy and Momma Celia unloaded the rest of the children, keeping them close by for safety and so as not to draw any undue attention to them. Elijah went over to talk to Will Beazeley.

"Here're ya'll's tickets, Mister Willis- an the confirmation of ya'll's passage on the *Jacob Strader* like ya asked."

"That's great, Will, thank ya kindly. Did ya remember to telegraph Messrs Gitchell and Jolliffe?" (He chose not to reveal any more information for fear of unknown ears eavesdropping).

"Yessir I sure did, and got a confirmation they'd received the message!"

"Perfect! I've left some cash with Gilbert in case he should need to pick up any supplies while I'm away. You'll be sure an help him out, won't ya?"

"Ya'll can count on me, sir. I'll be happy to help."

While Elijah was settling accounts with Will Beazeley, Joseph Harley approached Amy and Momma Celia. Ever the gentleman, he doffed his hat to them, saying,

"Mornin ladies! Surely is a fine day to take a trip!" He too was being cautious lest any onlookers overhear, but the coded message was easily understood by them both.

"It really and truly is, Doctor Harley!" affirmed Amy, her voice charged with affection and excitement.

"God bless ya, Doctor Harley. Sho is nice of ya to see us off!" said Momma Celia, wanting to say a lot more but fearful it might be overheard and give them away.

"Well, it's nice to see you all too! Makes me feel good knowing they got you goin with em, Momma Celia. Almost like travelling with their own private physician!" he smiled at her and winked with a chuckle that some onlooker could take as mocking, but Momma Celia knew was a genuine compliment. "Ya'll have a good trip now, hear?"

Joseph Harley waved to them cheerfully as he strode across the platform to where Will and Elijah were still finishing their transaction.

"God bless ya, Joseph! Ya'll don't know how much it meant to Momma Celia to be able to say good-bye to ya!" He uttered in a low voice.

"I trust she's brought her apothecary with her?" Joseph asked quietly.

"She'd a brought a whole wagonload if I'da let her, but yes, she's well supplied with the essentials." Elijah affirmed with a chuckle.

"Good! Make sure ya take her teas every day, and watch what ya eat-stay away from our good Southern fried cookin, and learn to eat Yankee potroast! And boiled potatoes!" he said with a laugh, as Elijah grimaced at the thought of it.

"I'll do my best Joseph, but some foods may just be worth dyin for!" he said, only half joking.

"Well, I expect I'll be hearin about it if ya don't follow ya doctor's orders, so try an behave yaself!"

"I will, Joseph, and Amy and I can't thank ya enough for all ya've done!"

"Think nothin of it, my friend. It's been my pleasure and my privilege. Ya'll take care now. Safe journey to ya!" he gave Elijah a hug just as the train whistle blasted the announcement of its arrival.

"Alright ya'll! Everybody ready?" Elijah called to his family as the train slowed to a halt in front of them. He hated that they would still be relegated to the baggage car, but he promised to visit them frequently along the way and reminded them that at least they'd be together on the Riverboat to Cincinnati, he having reserved a suite, insisting that his personal slaves attend him throughout the journey.

Gilbert helped them all on board, handing the boys the luggage to stack inside. The children all gave him hugs in turn, even the boys. Momma Celia grabbed him by both arms and held him at arms length, looking up into his eyes, saying softly, "Ya'll take good care a each other now. We'll be waitin for ya, sugar!" she pulled his face down to where she could reach it and gave him a kiss of blessing. "God bless ya, son."

Amy, in turn threw her arms around her brother fiercely, whispering in his ear, "We're gonna get y'll out, I promise!" Gilbert hugged her right back and then pulled away.

Only Elijah was left standing on the platform, and the conductor was already callin, "All Aboard!"

The two men looked at each other intently, volumes passing unspoken between them. "Well alright then," said Elijah in a husky voice, "Take care of everyone til I get back!"

Gilbert nodded, muttering "Yessir" to keep up appearances. And then, just as the conductor was waving to the engineer to start the engine, Elijah threw caution to the wind and gave Gilbert a quick but heartfelt hug just before climbing into the Pullman car, leaving Gilbert both stunned and deeply touched. He looked around quickly to see if anyone had noticed, but to his relief there was no one else around but Will Beazeley and Dr. Harley.

As the steam engine shrieked and hissed and roared like an iron dragon taking flight, announcing the train's departure to everyone for miles around, Will Beazeley, Gilbert, and Joseph Harley stood on the platform and waved, each one praying that the iron beast would land its passengers safely beyond the reach of the dark forces gathering in South Carolina. Amy and the children couldn't wave back, as there were only a few high windows in the baggage car, but Elijah, sitting by a window in the Pullman car, raised his hand in blessing and farewell as the train surged forward, carrying them toward the fulfillment of his promise and their peculiar destinies. He couldn't see that from a nearby field, bordering his own plantation, his brother Jimmy sat astride his horse, watching the train carry them away, wondering whether they would ever meet again.

Amy awoke to her mother's gentle shaking. She had fallen asleep in her seat. The shaking felt like she was still sitting on the train, the wheels clacking rhythmically over the joints in the rails as she contemplated the joys of freedom that awaited them at long last.

"Amy, sugar!" Momma Celia shook her shoulder, again. Amy knit her brow in annoyance, not wanting to interrupt her dream. As she opened her eyes, however, she realized, with a shock that she was no longer on the train.

"Wake up honey! The unnertaker's here ta talk with ya bout Elijah's funeral!" insisted Momma Celia, looking care worn. Amy's head cleared immediately as she looked over and saw Elijah's body laid out beside her, and the uncertain reality of her newly gained freedom struck her full force.

A tall Negro gentleman in a black cutaway jacket, waistcoat, starched butterfly collar and black silk bowtie stood before her with a sympathetic smile, flashing very white teeth.

"Miz Willis?" he asked. "My name is Leroy Johnson, ma'am. I've come over here, at the request a Mister John Jolliffe to offer ya'll my services for your husband's burial arrangements," he announced.

Amy smoothed back her hair, stood up, and held out her hand graciously. "Pleased to meet you, Mister Johnson. Do forgive me, I must look a sight!" she worried, as she straightened her skirts. "I surely do appreciate ya comin so quickly."

"Yes'm. My pleasure ma'am. Happy ta oblige! First, let me just say how truly sorry I am for ya loss. This must be a terrible shock to ya'll." Mr. Johnson did not sound as if he were rattling off the perfunctory condolences his profession demanded. Amy wondered how much he had been told by Mr. Jolliffe, but realized he might also simply be inferring the complexity of the situation by seeing a white man lying there next to a recently arrived colored woman from South Carolina. The Dumas family were not the only free blacks in Cincinnati accustomed to helping the formerly enslaved.

"Now Miz Willis, Mister Jolliffe told me ta give your husband a right proper burial in our Negro Cemetery here in Cincinnati. We're happy to offer our help. Specially seeing as how ya'll don't know nobody here in town, it's gotta be real difficult for ya! So ya'll don't have to worry about a thing! Mister Joliffe said to just send the bill to him, and he'll settle with us later."

Amy was so emotionally drained from the trip, the trauma of Elijah's death, and her recollection of what had brought them to this juncture that she could barely think to protest or to ask the undertaker any questions. He was rambling on about the various kinds of caskets they had available- pine, oak, even mahogany- but all Amy could think about was how was she going to keep the eight of them fed, clothed and sheltered without Elijah there to help? She knew they could not afford to use all the money on hand to buy even a small farm, for they would have nothing left on which to live, and it would take time to make a farm productive. It struck her they would have to be frugal, but she wouldn't skimp on Elijah's funeral. He deserved the best they could manage. Her mind was now racing with all the challenges, questions, and necessities facing them.

"Miz Willis?" the undertaker was asking, "Miz Willis?"

"I'm so sorry, Mister Johnson, do forgive me! I'm afraid I'm just a bit overwhelmed right now- all this is so sudden."

"Yes'm, I understand. I was just askin which of the coffins ya'd prefer for Mister Willis- the knotty pine, the white oak, or the mahogany?"

Amy forced herself to concentrate. "The mahogany would be fine, Mister Johnson. Thank ya."

"Yes'm. A fine choice. Real dignified." Mr. Johnson said, delighted she'd chosen their most expensive one without him even having to persuade her.

"Now did ya want, wooden, iron, or nice brass handles on it, ma'am?" he pressed on smoothly.

Amy was beginning to lose patience. She felt a bit guilty, but the truth was she just wanted him to take Elijah's body away so she could go lie down. "Oh, whatever ya'll think is appropriate, Mister Johnson. I don't mean to be rude, but I'm terribly tired!"

"The brass handles it is, then, Miz Willis- that'll look right dignified, like your husband here!" he concluded. "I'll be happy to take your husband to the funeral parlor now, unless ya'll care to say any more goodbyes before I

A Complicated Legacy

go? Mister Jolliffe and Mister Gitchell told me to bring him to the cemetery tomorrow round about noon. Is that alright with you, ma'am?"

"Yes, fine, that'll be fine." Amy responded impatiently. "Now if you'd just give me one more minute alone with my husband, I'll get outa your way and let ya'll get on with your business." Amy dismissed Leroy Johnson with a look that left no room for further questions. He discreetly backed out the door with a smile that was as content with his sale as expressive of true sympathy, closing it as he went to provide her some privacy. Amy could hear the man offering his condolences to Momma Celia out in the hallway and shuddered in disgust at his unctious opportunism.

She turned to Elijah, the grim reality of his passing now unmistakable as his cheeks began to shrink in the pallor of death. Remembering that wrenching look of apology on his face as he died, Amy said to him,

"Elijah honey, don't you ever think ya failed me! Don't you ever! I don't know how ya managed it sugar- cause I know ya were sicker than ya wanted to let on and livin in fear we wouldn't make it, but we did! By God, and by you, we did! An whatever your white relations try to do, and no matter how long it takes to fight em in court, we gonna be alright- all of us. I'm just so sorry ya can't be here with us to really see it's true, but fact is we were free before ya died, baby, just like ya promised!"

Amy leaned over and kissed her husband one last time, the coldness of his forehead leaving an odd sensation on her lips. Choking back her tears, she patted him gently on his now immobile chest and said, "That ole heart a yours was mighty big to take on such a heavy burden when nobody else woulda, an mighty strong to put up such a fight for so long! We'll always love ya for it, so you rest in peace now!" With that she turned and opening the parlor door, informed Mr. Johnson that she was ready for him to take her husband to prepare him for burial.

The following morning, James Gitchell and John Jolliffe arrived at the Dumas House promptly at nine. Amy, Momma Celia, and the children had already dressed and were eating breakfast, knowing they had the ordeal of Elijah's funeral ahead. The lawyers found them in the dining room, just finishing.

"Good morning my dear! Did you and your family manage to get some rest, I hope?" Asked Mr. Gitchell solicituously.

"Good morning to ya both, gentlemen!" replied Amy, nodding to each in turn. She signalled her mother to take the children and finish preparing for the funeral so she could speak more privately with the lawyers. "Yes we did, thank goodness. I'm afraid I may have been a bit abrupt with your

Mister Johnson from the funeral parlor. I was just so weary, I couldn't really think to answer all his questions."

"That's quite alright my dear, no need to apologize. We've just come from Mr. Johnson's establishment, and everything is in order. We are to meet him there by the hearse at the entrance to the cemetery at noon, from whence we shall proceed to the gravesite. I've taken the liberty to engage a very fine clergyman, the Rev. Dr. Lyman Beecher, the President of our Lane Theological Seminary here, to preside. I thought he'd be able to say something appropriate on your husband's behalf, for he is an ardent advocate of abolition, as are all his children. Perhaps you've heard of his daughter, Harriet?"

Amy looked blankly for a moment, wondering how he would think she might know some Yankee woman in Cincinnati when she'd never even been here before, and then it hit her, "Harriet Beecher Stowe, the woman who wrote Uncle Tom's Cabin? She asked in astonishment.

"Yes indeed! I imagine she and her husband Calvin may also accompany her father and her brothers- all of whom are fine preachers in their own right. We wanted your husband to have a proper send-off, as frankly, to us he is a real hero."

Amy was overwhelmed. "I'm deeply touched, gentlemen, by such an honor. And I must say, I agree with your assessment of my husband, for I've known no braver nor more steadfast man, white or black, in my entire life. Ya'll do him credit, sirs, and my family an I truly thank ya!" she found her efforts at formality inadvertently waning, as her heart prompted her to simply speak in her Carolina drawl without pretense or self-consciousness.

John Jolliffe then spoke up. "May I call you Miss Amy?" he asked, "Mrs. Willis seems too formal for someone whose life story is now so intimately known to us."

Amy nodded her aquiescence. "Certainly, sir."

"Miss Amy, I'm sure your husband informed you of the contents of his will, did he not?"

Amy nodded, reminding him that it had also been read by the lawyer, Mr. Ball, the day before, at the coroner's inquest.

"I am well acquainted with its entire contents Mister Jolliffe, as I am with the legal principles and probable challenges that may govern its acceptance in probate. My husband and I often discussed these matters, takin the counsel of our late friend Angus Patterson Senior and his colleague John Bauskett, with whom I believe ya'll've been in correspondence."

Once again impressed by Amy's keen intelligence and quick grasp of the issues, Jolliffe smiled and said, "Excellent! That's wonderful! And yes, we have been in touch with Mr. Bauskett. I gather he had promised your husband to serve as our proxy in South Carolina, should the need arise?"

"That's right sir, he did, and my husband and I have every faith in his diligence to do so." Amy responded, unconsciously still speaking of Elijah in the present tense.

"Fine, fine!" responded Jolliffe, relieved that there would be no need to cajole her into permitting such a possible collaboration, as he was certain it was going to be necessary.

"I would like to know, gentlemen," Amy inquired, "if there is any doubt as to our current legal status? It was my understandin from my husband that if a slave owner brought slaves into Ohio with the express intent to emancipate them, since Ohio does not permit slavery except for recognizin that status among slaves who may be accompanyin their masters to or through Ohio for a limited time, those slaves become free upon settin foot on Ohio soil. Is that correct?"

"It is!" concurred both attorneys simultaneously. "You and your mother and children are officially, in the eyes of the law in the Great State of Ohio, now and forevermore, free!" they proclaimed exultantly.

Hugely relieved by this news, Amy reverted to her more informal dialect, "Elijah had mentioned ya'll might need to go ta court to get some deed a manumission, just as a precaution against his white relations. Is that right?"

James Gitchell responded, "Well it's not actually required, and in any event, could not be done before the will goes through probate, since the estate now passes to the executors as custodians, but they cannot take action on the distribution of property until the will passes probate. It's a pity, in a way, that your husband couldn't have written the will after he got here- in which case you would have had no need for a custodial executor, and it could have passed directly to the lot of you. But that is clearly a moot point."

Jolliffe, trying to prevent his colleague from engaging in a lengthy and enthusiastic discourse on the legal minutiae of her situation, interceded.

"As executor of your husband's estate, I think it would in fact be wise to seek a deed of manumission from the court, just as a safety precaution, as soon as the will passes probate here. In fact, we can apply for both the probate and the deed at the same time. That way there can be no claim over any of you on the part of Elijah's white relations, not even under the federal Fugitive Slave Act, no matter what happens with the will in South Carolina!"

Amy took all this in thoughtfully. "And how long do ya'll expect it will take for the will to pass probate here in Ohio?" she asked.

"Not long at all, I shouldn't think!" exclaimed Gitchell. "There is no ambiguity about your husband's intentions- they're spelled out quite explicitly in the will- he was clearly of sound mind when the will was written, and our credibility as his executors will go unchallenged here. It will be done in a matter of days at the most!"

"The court battles, if there are any, will surely not come here, but rather when the will is presented for probate in South Carolina. As I'm sure Elijah must have made clear to you, until it is approved there we will not have access to or control over any of his assets, except possibly for the purpose of paying off any outstanding debts on his estate. Even there, we would not be permitted to sell any of his property to raise cash for such payments so long as the case remains unresolved in the South Carolina Court of Equity, especially should a copy of his previous will surface!" explained Jolliffe. That was a thought that had never occurred to Amy or even Elijah, as far as she knew! It was one of several disturbing factors facing her.

"I assume that also means that my brother and his family, and the remaining slaves on the plantation, will not be able to be either sold or even brought here until such time as the will is accepted down in South Carolina?" she asked, dreading their confirmation.

"That is correct, I'm afraid."

"Well, fortunately my husband and I were careful to pay off all our outstanding debts before we left, and as I told you, I have notes for the sum of three thousand dollars of monies due him from various clients, as well as over $500 in cash here with me. I may need ya'll's help to collect on those debts, but if they're duly and promptly paid, we should have enough money to live on in reasonable comfort until ya'll can get the will through probate down home."

"I certainly hope we shall be able to collect on them for you right away! But if there is any delay, please be assured that we shall find you whatever support you may need, until such time as you can finally liquidate your late husband's assets," affirmed Jolliffe.

"And," insisted Gitchell, "we will charge you nothing for our services unless and until we can successfully settle the case!"

John Jolliffe looked at his partner in surprise at this, but found himself agreeing in spite of the fact that they had not previously discussed the matter. Looking at his watch he said, "Dear me! Look at the time! We really should be going to the cemetery! We can certainly continue this conversation later, however. Please know that you may ask us any questions you may have at any time. We promised your husband we would do whatever might be necessary to provide for your needs, and are happy and honored to do so."

"I'm mighty grateful to ya both, gentlemen. It's a comfort to know we have good legal counsel, as I'm certain Elijah's relations will try to block the will from probate in South Carolina once they discover the existence and contents of the will ya'll helped him write last year." Amy responded. "I was struck however, when ya'll mentioned the possible influence of a previous will on the probability of a court battle. I don't know if Elijah mentioned to you the contents of his former will?"

The attorneys nodded that he had. "And he was quite specific about not wanting so much as a penny to go to any of the formerly named legatees!"

Amy smiled, as if she were hearing Elijah fulminate about his no-account greedy nephews in particular.

"Ya'll's mention of the earlier will makes me all the more certain they will try to use it to discredit this one."

"More than likely they will, my dear. However, they will have no solid legal ground to stand upon to do so, for it is entirely legal, and not at all uncommon for wills to be changed in the course of a man's life, for many good and valid reasons." Gitchell announced.

"His white relations thought he was crazy, just because he loved me! With their hatred of colored folks and greed for his land, they just couldn't imagine the possibility of such a thing for any other reason than madness. Why, I wouldn't be surprised if they accused me of bewitching him with some sort of African magic!" she laughed a scornful laugh.

Jolliffe made mental note of her comments, so he could take specific measures to counter them if Elijah's relatives did in fact attempt such arguments to discredit his ability to make a new will with sober judgment and sound reason.

At that point, the attorney's coachman Jack appeared and announced to his employers that two coaches were awaiting them outside to take them to the cemetery.

"It's time, my dear," said Mr. Jollifffe gently. Both attorneys stood to escort her to their carriage.

Amy nodded, got up from the table and said, "I'll go fetch Momma and the children, I won't be a moment!" She excused herself and went to their rooms to call the family together and make sure all the children were properly combed and dressed. She wanted to make sure they looked diginified for the occasion out of respect for Elijah, and for the unexpected notables who whould also be attending.

Momma Celia had already checked each grandchild, from Elder looking like a full grown man, standing proud and serious in his new suit, down to little Savage who had cried at having to put his shoes on, and chafed and fussed under his collar. The girls all wore the new dresses Papa had bought them at Christmas, even though Clarissa Ann had already nearly outgrown hers, and they had bought them large!

Having passed muster, Amy spoke to them, "Children, I need ya'll to not break down cryin and moanin at the cemetery even though ya'll're sad. There's a white preacher gonna preach the eulogy, and a bunch of white folks're comin from here in Cincinnati who're workin to abolish slavery everywhere. It's real important ya'll behave and make a good impression on these folks, cause we may need their help to get settled, y'hear?"

The children uttered their chorus of "Yes'ms," and Amy nodded to Momma Celia to lead them on downstairs to the awaiting carriages, bringing up the rear, standing tall and straight and proud, mindful that now she was a free black woman, no more a slave. She would not allow herself sentimental indulgences on this, her first foray in public in Cincinnati, for she wanted to show Mr. Gitchell and Mr. Jolliffe, and all their friends, that she and her family deserved their freedom, and would be a credit to the new society in which they now found themselves.

C

It was not a terribly long drive to the cemetery. Amy had chosen to go in the carriage with Mr. Gitchell and Mr. Jolliffe, bringing Elder, Elleck and Phillip with her. Momma Celia followed in the second carriage with the three girls and little Savage. When they arrived at the cemetery they were surprised to find a cluster of white folks, men and women, and a few free blacks eagerly awaiting their arrival, standing at the crest of the hill, silhouetted against an overcast sky.

Mr. Leroy Johnson was also there, decked out in a silk top hat and white gloves added to his ensemble of the previous day. Momma Celia, not appreciating Mr. Johnson's emulation of formal white attire, took one look at him and muttered to herself, 'Who that fool think he is, the King a England? All fancied up like that- Hmmm mmmm mmm!" She shook her head in disgust.

Mr. Johnson tipped his hat gallantly, smiling a toothy grin to Amy and her mother saying, "Good mornin to ya, ladies. I hope ya'll were able to get some rest last night?"

Momma Celia responded with a "hrumpf!", but Amy greeted the undertaker as cordially as she could, eager to overlook the peculiarities of his dramatic flair in the interest of getting on with her husband's burial.

"Is everything in order, Mr. Johnson?" she inquired.

"Yes'm. We got flowers by the grave sent by the American Colonization Society and from Lane Seminary, and a bouquet from Miz Stowe an her husband- they's a lotta folks here in Cincinnati heard bout ya husband's death, an're feeling ya'll's loss!"

Amy nodded her acknowledgement. Remembering Elijah's discovery of the mixed motives of some of the supporters of the American Colonization Society when they were in Baltimore, she was feeling uncertain as to whether the Society meant their flowers as a suggestion the family were now free to go back to Africa, or as an acknowledgment of Elijah's efforts at their emancipation. She chose to take it as the latter and asked, "Is the preacher here yet? I should like to meet him before the service begins, if I may?"

"Yes'm, he's here. He's right over there, talkin with Mister Jolliffe an Mister Gitchell."

Mr. Johnson pointed to a tall, elderly, white gentleman with a long, craggy face and a mane of white hair, wearing a black Geneva gown over a black cassock with starched white preaching tabs at the neck. The total affect was less benign than she was expecting. The only other white clergymen she had ever met were the occasional circuit preachers Elijah invited to lead services for the slaves, or the Rev. Mr. Walker in Barnwell, with that curious mixture of pomposity and bumbling affability. This was a far more fearsome and intimidating personage, looking as stern as an Old Testament prophet.

Amy thanked Mr. Johnson and moved toward the gentlemen gathered near the gate to the cemetery.

"Ah! Miss Amy!" proclaimed Mr. Gitchell. "Allow me to introduce you to the Reverend Doctor Lyman Beecher, President of Lane Theological Seminary, and a great advocate of the abolition of slavery!"

"It's an honor to meet ya, sir!" Amy nodded with a slight curtsey.

"On the contrary, my dear," said the Reverend sincerely, "The honor is mine!"

Amy cleared her throat, hesitant to apprise the good cleric of her concern, but even more averse to the possible consequences of her failure to do so. Drawing the celebrant aside to speak more privately, she said,

"Forgive me Reverend, if I seem inappropriate or unappreciative of your services in my request. I do not wish to offend, and am unfamiliar with the custom here. But I should like the focus of your words for my husband not to be on the evils of slavery, but rather on his bravery in eschewing them." Amy paused hesitantly before continuing, insistently, "I would not have his funeral become merely a platform for the promotion of abolition, but rather a testimony to the goodness of a heart who, though an owner of slaves, never resorted to the lash, or chains, or any of such cruelties, as I'm told were so well proclaimed by your daughter in her book. My husband loved me and all our children, and fought long and hard to make us free. That he literally gave his life to do so should be his eulogy."

Upon hearing what could have been Elijah's most eloquent epitaph, there was an awkward silence between the preacher and the two attorneys, who had in fact been hopeful that the city's leading cleric would stir the crowd with a clarion call to abolition, knowing that the press would soon report it.

"And I'd also like to request, if ya'll don't mind," Amy added, "that the burial be a private one, as my family and I are so lately arrived here, we'd like to do our grievin without the urgency of social interaction with those whom we do not know, no matter how well-meanin they surely must be."

John Jolliffe, though taken aback with the unexpected boldness of Amy's request, was filled with admiration for her forthright spirit and her refusal to make her husband's burial an occasion for others to appropriate to the larger cause of general emancipation.

Overcoming a twinge of embarrassment that his partner was somewhat prone to doing just that, he said, "I quite understand my dear, as I'm sure we all do," giving both the Reverend and his colleague a stern look that discouraged disagreement.

The Reverend too, though unaccustomed to others dictating the content of his sermons, recognized that a woman of exceptional integrity and intellect stood before him, instantly earning his respect.

"Mr. Gitchell and Mr. Jolliffe, as well as their friends who have been considered for the honor of being executors of your husband's will, have already apprised me of Mr. Willis' excellence of character, his bravery, and resolve, my dear. Fear not that I shall speak of him in glowing terms, though I had not the pleasure of meeting him," the Reverend proclaimed.

"I do thank you most sincerely, Reverend. I hope I have caused ya'll no offense by my requests- it's just that my Elijah was not one for bein made a fuss over. He lived a private life, and woulda wanted a private burial."

"Absolutely, Mrs. Willis!" Gitchell responded, desperate to salvage something of his hopes to further their cause. He did not want to insult those they had gathered by summarily sending them away. He thought it both impolite and impolitic to do so, given that he considered prevailing upon them for the family's financial support, should there be undue delays in the South Carolina courts impeding access to Elijah's assets. Offending them at the funeral would not likely inspire them to open their purse strings wider!

"But might I request," he interceded, "that since as you can see, a goodly number of those in our community -who would do him and you all honor for your courageous departure from South Carolina- at least be allowed to express their condolences to you following the ceremony? They would of course keep at a respectful distance to assure your privacy in the interim!"

Amy did not want to offend her hosts- especially since they were her only source of information and support in Cincinnati and had already been instrumental in assuring that they were not returned to their bondage in Williston. So despite her uneasiness about Elijah's burial becoming some sort of occasion for publicity in the name of a political cause, she gave her consent, and Mr. Gitchell hurried off to inform the others of her request.

Such obstacles to its fulfillment being now removed, the funeral party duly proceeded towards its sepulchral conclusion. Mr. Johnson had enlisted the services of Messrs. Gitchell and Jolliffe and their companions Mr. Hargood and Mr. Ernst as pall- bearers who solemnly accompanied the hearse into the cemetery, past the assembled well-wishers and on-lookers at the gate, to the gravesite. The Reverend Doctor Beecher led the procession, exuding gravitas, and Amy, Momma Celia, and the children followed behind the catafalque.

As the procession drew to a halt near the burial site, Amy sent the three older boys to join the pallbearers to help carry Elijah's casket to the grave. Since Elijah was a big man and the mahogany dense, the casket was heavier than they had expected, and the pallbearers suppressed their grunts, puffing as they staggered slightly unloading the casket, until they found their footing over the uneven ground.

With much waving of his gloved hands and exhortations to be careful not to fall in, Mr. Johnson orchestrated the placement of the coffin on the planking spaced over the grave, on top of which lay two long ropes stretching across the gaping pit to lower it to its final resting place. As the pall-bearers stepped back from the tomb and the Reverend began the service, the sky seemed to lighten- the sun shining white-hot through the shroud of thinning clouds.

Truth be told, in the numbness of their grief, Amy and the children barely heard what was said. The preacher did in fact refrain from grandstanding about abolition, and kept his words to the point of Elijah's kindness, bravery, love, and perseverance in freeing his family. He rightly extolled the great and noble thing Elijah accomplished, fulfilling his vow to God and his family. Prayers were then said for Elijah's soul and for the comfort of those he left behind, and then to Amy's surprise, the Reverend broke into a warbling rendition of Amazing Grace. The tune was a little different from the way they sang it back home, but Amy and Momma Celia felt moved to join in.

There was an echo of the verses coming from the cemetery entrance, where Amy spied the gaggle of very straight-laced looking white women, dressed in black taffeta from head to toe, their ruffled bonnets flapping in the May breeze. They were belting out the hymn, slightly off tempo with those at the graveside, the occasionally shrill tones of their discordant voices displaying more fervor than musicality.

Out of the corner of her eye she noticed Momma Celia looking with raised eyebrows toward the ladies by the gate too, shaking her head and muttering something about "white folks" between verses. Amy felt a hint of a smile stretch the corners of her mouth for the first time since Elijah had dropped at her feet. Fortunately, the Reverend's eyes being closed, he was so absorbed in intoning the final verse- 'there'll be no less days to sing God's praise, than whe we'd first begun-' that he didn't seem to notice Momma Celia's critique or Amy's surreptitious smile.

As the coffin was lowered into the grave, the boys and other pallbearers took turns shoveling in the dirt, and the girls stepped forward on Momma Celia's cue to leave bunches of daffodils by the still unmarked headstone, little Julia unable to suppress a sob but recovering herself quickly, remembering her mother's admonition before leaving the Dumas House.

The Reverend Doctor Beeecher seemed unexpectedly moved by the tenderness and sincerity of the gathering, and his stern face softening, gave heart-felt condolences and offers of spiritual comfort in their bereavement to each of them. He then started to stroll toward the cemetery entrance where his daughter and son-in-law, and several others, awaited.

When Amy reached the gathering of white supporters, she tried to smile graciously and shake the hands of each as Mr. Gitchell and Mr. Jolliffe introduced them one by one, presenting her mother and children in turn. These Prebysterian worthies, with their pinched faces and ramrod straight backs, weren't like Southern white women and their famous charm. But they struck her as sincere and honest folks. And she realized from their comments and condolences they weren't there just for show, but because they had been inspired by Elijah's heroism and the family's bravery. She was unexpectedly touched by that, and hoped it boded well for their adjustment to this new place and new life.

When she was introduced to Harriet she said, "Miz Stowe, it's an honor ta meet ya, an I'm sure your book's gonna help move a whole lotta hearts, and maybe change some minds." She wasn't about to mention Elijah signing a petition to prohibit its sale in South Carolina as a tactical necessity, even though they had discussed its contents and largely agreed with the author.

Harriet Beecher Stowe smiled and said, "That's very sweet of you, Mrs. Willis."

Amy noticed that she had respectfully chosen to call her Mrs. Willis, and felt encouraged to continue, "But I hope ya understand that the evil of slavery isn't really about bein beaten an abused. I'm sure plenty a white folks have suffered such things too. It's about bein told ya don't count, ya don't matter, and ya got not right to speak up for yaself. That can kill your spirit! That's the real evil- killin your God-given soul! It doesn't just offend us, it insults our Creator!"

Amy looked Harriet right in the eye and added, "My Elijah was not like the slave owner ya'll wrote about. He was good, and kind, and generous, and wanted to do right by all of us in spite of awful opposition at home, even from his own relations. So ya see, Miz Stowe, it's more complicated than simple right and wrong."

Harriet had not been prepared for such a candid encounter, and though taken aback, was also humbled by this woman who had been through more than she could rightly imagine. She was at a loss for words, so simply nodded thoughtfully in response.

Amy felt a tug at her skirt and looked down to see Eliza saying with a whine of exhaustion, "Momma, can we go now?"

"Yes sugar, we can go now! Go run an tell Momma Celia to get ya'll into the carriage, and I'll be along directly!" As Eliza ran off to give the news to her grandmother, Amy excused herself from Harriet, and looked to catch Mr. Jolliffe's eye. He came over promptly, seeing the children heading toward the carriage with their grandmother, and realized how drained the family must feel, clearly eager to return to their lodgings.

"I do beg your pardon, my dear, I was just expressing my thanks to the other mourners for coming to share this sad occasion with us. You must be worn out. Please, go on ahead to the carriage, and Jack will drive you home. I must speak with a few others before I go, but I don't want to detain you."

"I truly do wanna thank ya for all ya'll've done for us, Mister Jolliffe, and on such short notice too! I appreciate your understandin and the trouble ya'll took to get the Reverend and the others out here. I hope ya don't mind if I head back to Dumas House now?"

"Of course not, not at all!" he assured her. "I shall let you rest, and then we can meet in a day or two to discuss the practical details of what comes next. We shall prepare to enter the will for probate, as well as draft a deed of manumission to be enacted by the court immediately."

Amy nodded in agreement and smiled in gratitude.

He then continued, as if just remembering another important detail, "Mr. Gitchell will also look right away into the collection of the monies owed your husband in the notes you brought with you, and we shall consider how to proceed in settling you and your family more permanently as soon as possible. There will be much to discuss, but we don't have to do it all in a day! Please take some rest. If there is anything you or the family needs in the meantime, please don't hesitate to let me or Mr. Gitchell know."

"Thank ya sir, and God bless ya!" Amy responded with a curtsey, and turned to enter the carriage, leaving Mr. Gitchell and Mr. Jolliffe to circulate her gratitutde among the gathered crowd and to discharge the obsequious Leroy Johnson, waiting expectantly by the now empty hearse.

With the finality of Elijah's burial complete, the two carriages seemed to head back to the Dumas House with a brisker pace than they had come. Amy felt the vertigo of rushing into the uncertainties that awaited them, and wondered to herself, "How would Elijah have handled this?"

Thanks to the due dilligence of Messrs. Gitchell and Jolliffe, the Probate Court of Hamilton County in the great State of Ohio moved to prove the will valid. Moreover, the court promptly issued a deed of manumission, leaving no doubt whatsoever as to the free status of Amy and her family before the news of Elijah's death had even reached South Carolina.

"I have good news for you, my dear!" John Jolliffe announced to Amy. "Mr. Gitchell had the foresight to file Elijah's will for probate the very day Elijah was buried. He started preparing it right after the inquest. We've just returned from the Court House, and the probate court has proved Elijah's will valid and in force! Moreover, the court has issued the deed of manumission just as we petitioned! You are all now officially and irreversibly free!"

"Well I'd say that's doubly good news, Mister Jolliffe!" Amy exclaimed.

"Indeed it is my dear, indeed it is! Congratulations!" exulted James Gitchell. "We are so pleased for you! This is truly a great victory!"

"The victory is surely as much yours as ours, sir! And we are most grateful to ya for seein it properly done!" insisted Amy.

"I need to tell you that Messrs. Ernst and Harwood opted not to serve as executors in the end, we having mutually decided that it might make things less complicated to have a single executor deal with the courts of South Carolina. Therefore, as sole executor of the will my dear, with the aid of your friend John Bauskett I shall now enter it for probate in South Carolina as well!" Jolliffe announced.

He looked at Amy frankly and paused, reluctant to dampen her spirits with sobering reality and feeling his own elation tempered as well, but he knew it was his responsibility to shepherd her through the remaining legal challenges. He continued,

"As great and lasting a triumph as your freedom surely is however, I must remind you to prepare yourself for what may be a difficult time in fully realizing your dream of emancipation for your brother and the rest of the slaves still on your plantation, not to mention your ability to sell the property and reap its rewards."

Amy was of course not unaware of those challenges- she'd been living with the fear of them since before they ever left Williston. She nodded gravely. "So, what do we do now sir?" she asked him outright.

"Well, James and I have already been preparing our arguments on your behalf, citing both Ohio State and Federal law to support them. Mr. Bauskett is doing the same, keenly aware of the nature of the probable challenges from the perspective of South Carolina law. For the moment we can do no more, until such time as we either get a ruling from the Court of Probate or are apprised of any challenges mounted against your case."

"And if Elijah's relations oppose the will?" Amy pressed, certain that they would.

"Much will depend on the legal grounds upon which they attempt to do so. Once we learn of those grounds we shall be in a better position to fight them and if need be, appeal any adverse ruling the court might issue against you," explained Mr. Gitchell.

"So all we can really do is wait and pray?" Amy concluded.

"More or less, I'm afraid so. But fear not, we shall not remain idle, passively waiting for attack! I assure you we shall diligently search any and all pertinent case law that might be brought to bear in your support. We are confident that though it may take some time, ultimately the law is on our side and you will prevail!" affirmed Mr. Jolliffe.

Amy took all this in thoughtfully. "And may I inquire as to any news of success in collecting on my husband's debtors?"

"Sadly we have not as yet had time to pursue them fully, having only issued letters requesting payment so far. We have not yet heard any response but assume we shall in the near future," Mr. Gitchell informed her.

"Well gentlemen, I surely do thank both of ya'll for your efforts. Ya'll've been most kind, and I feel guilty about prevailin upon ya for further assistance," Amy acknowledged. "I am concerned, however, that the cash I have available may not be sufficient for our maintenance, and I'm wonderin if it might not be more economical for us to rent a house somewhere so we can cook our own meals rather than eatin expensive hotel fare." The argument was not soley economic of course, for everyone in the family preferred Momma Celia's cooking to the hotel's and they were missing it terribly!

John Jolliffe had already foreseen such a need, and agreed that it was not desireable for them to become long-term residents of the Dumas House. "I have been giving that matter some thought, and I quite agree that we shall need to find you more appropriate and affordable lodgings," he reassured her. "Mr. Gitchell and I shall make some inquiries on your behalf as soon as possible and see what we can find. Once he has gotten the expected responses on your husband's notes we shall be able to budget your maintenance accordingly."

Amy expressed once again her gratitude for their help and decided to broach another subject while she had the opportunity. "In the event that there is a delay in liquidatin my husband's assets and the cash raised from the notes should prove insufficient for our needs, I'd be interested to know what manner of employment we might expect to find to help support ourselves? Momma is an excellent cook, and Elder and Elleck are certainly old enough to work, being already well accustomed. They're both strong and intelligent and I'm sure could learn a trade quickly if need be…"

John Jolliffe admired Amy's practical grasp of necessities and her keen administrative sense of how to marshall her resources to good advantage. He did not want to alarm her with the reality that employment in Cincinnati for free blacks in general, and for women in particular, was limited and the pay generally poor. He was hoping to dispense with the legal challenges quickly and sell the plantation so as to be able to establish her and the children on a farm as per Elijah's wishes, knowing she would thereby have a much better chance at self-sufficiency. Whether out of cowardice or tact was hard to say, but he chose not to go into the matter in detail at this particular moment.

"Well, let's not put the cart before the horse here shall we? I know it was your husband's intent that a farm be purchased for you and your family, and that continues to be our primary objective once we can liquidate his assets in South Carolina," he reassured her. "Let us not deflect our attention from that noble goal by trying to create alternative scenarios that hopefully may never come to pass! The question of your possible employment is surely premature and should be a subject for discussion only at a later date in the event that our main objective proves unattainable!"

Amy was not completely convinced, as she had always lived by the motto "prepare for the worst and hope for the best." Nor was she entirely comfortable being passively dependent upon the two lawyers despite their good intentions. She was unaccustomed to having nothing to do and did not like the experience, for it left her with too much time on her hands to worry. However, it was clear that neither Mr. Gitchell nor Mr. Jolliffe intended to go into the matter any further for the moment so she simply nodded and said, "Well, perhaps ya'll're right. It would certainly be wonderful if we could fulfill the rest of Elijah's dream and find us a farm somewhere in the area. That way when my brother and his family and the others join us, we'd be in a better position to support them!"

Her vision for their future clearly articulated, her attorneys accepted the challenge and bade their farewells, vowing they would dedicate themselves to the task of fulfilling it. In the meantime Amy went to talk to her mother and let her know that God willing, they should at least be able to find a place to live where she could cook, before she died from the frustration of eating what she considered the tasteless Yankee food in the Dumas House dining room. She also needed to talk to all the children. They were growing restive in the hotel, missing not only their father but also their life on the plantation, since they now had nothing constructive to do to pass the time.

Now that the funeral was behind them they were in that limbo of mourning where life seemed flat most of the time; flickers of joy and pleasure would resurface for brief periods and then be swept away by unexpected and random waves of sorrow. Amy knew they would all have to simply take things one day at a time, trusting that eventually they would get through the darkness and life would once again feel hopeful and happy.

Will Beazeley opened the weekly shipment of newspapers he received from various cities around the region and the country. He had always prided himself on providing folks with up to date information on both local and national news- even though his readership was small (sometimes he himself being the only one to actually read the papers). But since he had never travelled, it was his way of feeling like he knew something about the wider world. He had always enjoyed hearing the stories of those who came and went from Williston, for he could see the places they visited in his mind's eye and feel like he was somehow a participant in a bigger life than he actually had down home in Barnwell District, South Carolina. Every time a train left Williston depot he'd imagine himself on it going somewhere interesting.

As he scanned through the papers, starting with the local *Palmetto Sentinel,* and then moving on to the others- from Columbia, and Charleston, Charlotte and Richmond, and even up in Washington, he came across a copy of *The New York Times.* Leafing through its pages to see what folks up North were considering newsworthy, he was stunned to read a headline dated May 25, 1855, from Cincinnati, Ohio: "*Sudden Death of Slaveholder, Twenty-Five Slaves Emancipated.*"

"Oh my God!" he said to himself, as he read the article describing Elijah's death on the wharf, "Poor Mister Willis! And Miss Amy! And her Momma! And the children! What a tragedy!" As he read the article further, he learned of the will Elijah had written in Cincinnati that effectively freed his family. It gave him joy in his sorrow that Elijah had at least succeeded in that, at long last.

Just as he was finishing the article, James Willis and his brother Michael came into the depot.

"Mornin, Will!" James called out cheerfully, Michael smiling and nodding to Will in conjunction with his brother's greeting.

Will, still moved by the news and not thinking, responded, "I am so sorry for your loss, boys!"

Of course, the Willis brothers had absolutely no idea as to what he was referring. "What d'ya mean, loss? Whatcha talkin about, Will?"

"Well your uncle Elijah's passin, a course! I thought ya'll knew!" Will said, assuming the family had somehow been notified.

The brothers looked as if forked lightening had struck them both simultaneously.

"What the Hell're ya'll talkin about, Will? What makes ya think Uncle Elijah is dead? Daddy told us he just went on a trip to get away for a spell, even watched him leave! But he's comin back soon!"

"I know about his trip- he bought the train tickets here! But accordin to this article right here in *The New York Times*, he died up in Cincinnati on May 23rdth! Dropped dead on the wharf just after getting off the riverboat!" (Will refrained from mentioning that he was accompanied by Amy, Momma Celia, and the children).

"Give me that!" James grabbed at the paper in disbelief. When he saw that twenty-five slaves had allegedly been freed by this subterfuge, he started swearing a blue streak. "Son of a BITCH! That old fool's not gonna get away with this!!!! He can't fuck with us like that! I'll go up there and drag his nigra whore back here in chains myself, if I have to! And the rest of the slaves down here- ain't no WAY they're goin up to Cincinnati!" he fumed. "They're ours now!" This last he said with a particularly vicious edge.

Michael, seeing the look of shock on Will's face at the stream of expletives pouring out of his brother's mouth, jabbed James in the ribs to quiet him down, realizing it was unseemly in the extreme to show no grief whatsoever for their departed uncle- especially in a place where word of their insensitivity could travel so quickly. It would not endear them to the folks in Williston and could even hurt their political aspirations.

"Hush up, James!" he hissed under his breath. "This ain't the time or place for all that!" he insisted.

James turned to look at his brother, as shocked out of his tirade as if he had been slapped in the face. Rather than blasting his brother however, as he normally would, he realized with a jolt that Michael was right- he had committed a huge mistake blurting out his diatribe in front of Mr. Beazely.

"Uh, sorry Will, I, I didn't mean to go off like that!" he stumbled, trying to cover his blunder.

Harboring no illusions as to the Willis brothers' motives, Will simply responded, "Grief can make folks do and say surprisin things sometimes! In any event, please give my condolences to your Daddy!"

Will having put James in his place, the Willis brothers forgot the reason they had even come to the depot in the first place and after a brief silence muttered, "Uh, yessir. Thank ya sir. Uh, we sure will!" and then promptly left to go find Angus and see what legal steps they would need to take to prevent this catastrophe from being fully enacted.

As they left Will blew out a deep sigh thinking, "How is it possible that such a good man could have two such low-down, good-for-nothin nephews?"

Will prided himself on getting along with everyone in town, but James' stream of greed and hate-driven invective without so much as a nod of acknowledgment or a brief flash of sorrow over their uncle's death, had truly shocked him to his core. He now understood fully why Elijah had gone to such lengths to keep them at bay. He could well imagine that with their vestigial respect -or fear- of Elijah now gone with his passing, they would launch an all out war to deny Amy and the children and all the others their freedom. He shuddered to think of the abuse and suffering that would await them should the Willis boys succeed, and shook his head in disgust. "What a couple a sorry, mean ass sons a bitches!" he muttered.

While Will was bemoaning the sad state of the Willis family and their dynastic intrigues, James and Michael were high-tailing it into town to Angus' house to break this horrible news and get him to help them make a plan of legal action to prevent the tragedy from being implemented. The tragedy to them, of course, was the loss of property (including slaves) they had been counting on inheriting- not the sudden death of their miscreant uncle. How could they mourn a man who had insisted upon ignoring the good of his family and community out of selfishness and lust for some slave?

Fairly leaping off their horses in front of Angus' house, they both bounded up the front steps and banged furiously on the door. Mary, who had nodded off in her chair in the kitchen while a big, fragrant pot of her spring lamb stew was slowly simmering, was startled awake by the racket.

Worried that some catastrophe had occurred, she heaved herself up out of her chair, and painfully started rushing toward the front door. Of course rushing in her case was a relative term, for her arthritic pace was akin to that of one of those giant tortoises Mr. Charles Darwin had recently discovered in the Galapagos Islands off the coast of South America. Consequently, her delay in reaching the front door resulted in a second round of furious banging which, rousing Angus from a deep sleep upstairs, sent him galloping down the stairs, unkempt and disgruntled, to see what was the matter. He nearly bowled Mary over as they both reached the bottom of the stairs simultaneously.

"Sorry Angus, honey" Mary apologized, "I tried to get there, so's not to disturb ya, but ya'll know these ole bones don't move like they used ta…"

Angus brushed her aside impatiently, not interested in her excuses and annoyed he had been so abruptly awakened. "I told ya to call me 'Mister' Angus, Mary. I'm the head a the house now, and deserve that respect!" he whined.

Mary felt stung, but mumbled, "Yassuh 'Mister' Angus," to placate him, realizing the boy was trying to be the man his father was and had a long way to go yet.

Somewhat mollified, Angus opened the front door and saw James and Michael standing there, dancing nervously on the porch in eagerness to spill out their disturbing story.

"What the Hell're ya'll doin, bangin on my door like that? Tryin to break it? What's goin on? Ya'll look like ya're either dancing on hot coals or gotta piss somethin awful!" Angus admonished them.

"Angus, can we come in?" urged James. "We got some awful, terrible news to tell ya, an we need ya'll to help us deal with it!" he blurted excitedly, as the obsessed often do, subconsciously thriving on crises. This was awful news, but it was also awfully exciting to have an occasion for a good fight to liven things up in sleepy Williston, where nothing much ever happened!

"It's about Uncle Elijah! He's dead!" chimed in Michael, eagerly letting the cat out of the bag.

Mary's hand shot up to cover her mouth in shock and dismay. Her distress was compounded by the clear lack of sorrow or remorse on the part of Elijah's nephews. Her heart sank, already suspecting what kind of "help" the Willis brothers were seeking.

"No! Where? When? How?" Angus answered, shocked by the unexpected news. Much as he had disagreed with Elijah's living arrangements and views on emancipation, he had actually liked and respected the man, and felt saddened by the news.

"Well can we come in, or ya'll gonna make us keep on standin out here?" James reiterated impatiently.

"Oh yeah, sorry, a course! Come on in!" Angus replied, "Mary, can you fetch us all some coffee an maybe some biscuits or somethin? We'll be in the parlor." Without waiting for Mary's reply he led his companions into the parlor and sat down in his father's favorite armchair. Already realizing their questions would be legal, he was hoping it would infuse him with his father's judicial wisdom to speak *ex cathedra* to his friends' legal needs.

"Come on then! Tell me what in Hell happened! How did ya'll find out, anyway?" Angus asked.

James proceeded to recount their visit to the depot, Will's unexpected offering of condolences, his reading of *The New York Times* article reporting Elijah's death and the emancipation thereby of twenty-five slaves, including Amy, Momma Celia, and all seven children.

"Damn!" Angus replied, astounded and unable to think of anything more to say at first.

"Well, so what can we do about it?" demanded Michael. "It just ain't fair!" he whined. "Daddy told us Uncle Elijah had a will that left everything to the family- to his real family. Now we get word in the goddamn Yankee newspaper he wrote another will and left us nothing. That's just plain wrong!"

"An worse- he gave it all to that nigra woman a his, and her bastard children!" fumed James, outraged. "He can't do that! It's against South Carolina law!"

At that point Mary came tottering in with the coffee tray, a few spills puddling around the coffee cups. She tremulously set it down in front of Angus, apologetic. Angus saw the spills, but could not bring himself to chastise her for them, knowing she was doing the best her frail body could. Before excusing herself and returning to the kitchen, she gave him a look that was filled with with concern. Angus shifted uncomfortably, realizing it was meant as a commentary on his choosing to help the Willises fight Elijah's apparent victory in emancipating his slaves. It was almost as if she were his conscience- or his father's proxy- warning him to watch out. Still desperate to assert his adult independence, he resented the warning, showing himself to be still more the child than the man.

"That'll be all for now, Mary," he nodded dismissively for her to leave, trying to sound all grown up and in charge, but she knew he had gotten her message despite or perhaps because of his uncustomary rudeness.

She shuffled back down toward the kitchen secretly rejoicing that Elijah had made it safely to Cincinnati with Momma Celia, Amy and the children, even if it had so tragically cost him his life. "He was a mighty good man to do that!" she muttered to herself, feeling both joy and sorrow at the news. She couldn't help but think too, "Your Pa'd be mighty happy to know they's free! Yassuh, ole Mister Agnus'd be pleased as punch!" she smiled to herself with satisfaction, dispelling for a moment both her grief for Elijah and her worry about what the boy might be getting himself into.

Back in the parlor the three companions were trying to figure out their options. The Willis brothers were peppering their dialogue with a series of salty expletives, obscenities, and declarations of where Elijah should now be and where his Yankee lawyers could go to join him, as well as a variety of creative suggestions as to where they might duly relocate some of their body parts in the meantime.

Angus, however much he sympathized with their sense of loss, injustice, and outrage, nevertheless felt constrained to point out some potential legal pitfalls facing them.

"James, ya can't just go gallopin off to Cincinnati to recover fugitive slaves if they weren't fugitives! It's clear yer uncle took em with him on purpose, and it's now equally clear from the newspaper report that he did so with the intention of emancipatin em! Whether that stands up as legal or not is gonna depend on whether the new will he wrote is deemed legal by the courts!"

"An what if it is?" asked Michael, worried.

"Well as I see it, there're really two issues that need decidin," answered Angus. "One is whether the slaves he took with him are legally free now. The other is whether they have a right to inherit the plantation- which would include the rest of the slaves the newspaper article claims have now been freed."

"Which includes that bitch's brother and his children, don't it?" grinned James with a sudden malicious gleam in his eye, as if considering using Gilbert as bait to recover the others.

"Hey! That's right! It does!" agreed Michael, always ready to jump on the bandwagon of malfeasance toward people of color in general, and toward Elijah's preferred slaves in particular.

"Maybe we can use that! Hey Angus, don't the will have to be accepted here in South Carolina too?" asked James.

"Exactly!" answered Angus. "And that's the one way we may be able to block this thing. If the will isn't proved here, ya'll'd only be out nine slaves-seven of em children! Miss Amy and her family might be free, but they could never set foot in South Carolina again without returning to their slavery, or get a hold of any Willis property down here!"

"Includin her own brother?" Michael asked.

"Includin her own brother!" Angus affirmed.

"Well alright then!" exclaimed James, rubbing his hands together gleefully. "Whadda we have ta do to block the probate?"

"Well as far as I know ya'll can petition the court to throw it out, but ya gotta have legal grounds to do so."

"Ain't keepin nigras from getting their filthy hands on white property legal grounds enough?" asked Michael, as if the answer were obvious.

"Not if yer uncle's concubine and her brood're deemed his legal heirs," answered Angus. "First, ya'll'd have to prove that yer Uncle Elijah either didn't intend to free em, or couldn't free em. That would mean rejectin the new will's validity. If the court ruled that it was invalid, then they'd still be slaves and the distribution of the estate would be determined by the terms of the old will instead."

"An how could we prove the new will wasn't what Uncle Elijah intended?" pressed James.

"Well, I'm pretty sure ya'd have to be able to prove that either he was not of sound mind when he wrote it, or that he was somehow forced to write it through what they call 'undue influence,'" Angus explained.

"Well Hell, that shouldn't be hard to prove! I bet every judge an jury in South Carolina'd agree he was downright crazy to write that will! And I bet we could claim that whore a his just pressured him into it. The old fool was just plain pussy-whipped!" James insisted.

"Or bewitched by some Voodoo spell a hers!" echoed Michael in agreement.

James looked down at the coffee tray in disgust. "Shit, Angus- ain't you got anything better ta drink than coffee? What about that good sippin whiskey ya Pa always bragged about? I need a drink!"

Angus looked around the room, feeling keenly the loss of his father's law books, wishing he could look things up right then and there. His eyes fell on the decanter of whiskey on the side table. He was reluctant to open it, knowing that James and Michael were more than capable of finishing it off in a sitting. As it was the last whiskey his father had sipped, he was not eager to part with it just to let them indulge.

"Damn, James- it's ten o'clock in the mornin! There'll be plenty of time for drinkin later! We need to focus on gettin a petition together to fight the will in probate court. And I don't know enough yet about the law to do it alone. We need to get some legal help, here!" Angus insisted.

"Well Hell, I don't know any lawyers, other than Mr. Bauskett." complained James.

"We can't use him- cause he'll claim conflict of interest, as ya Uncle Elijah was his client. We're gonna have ta find somebody else. Who do we know who could tell us who ta ask?" Angus replied.

"What about Dr. Guignard?" offered Michael.

"Brilliant, little brother! I'm sure Dr. Guignard will know of someone! Come on boys! Let's go pay him a visit!" affirmed James.

The three agreed this was a good idea, and set off immediately for the Guignard plantation.

John Bauskett was sitting having a late breakfast with Eugenia when his housekeeper presented him with the day's mail. It included a large envelope from Will Beazely containing a recent copy of The New York Times, and a note scrawled across the top of the masthead saying, "Thought you should see this!"

John opened the paper, and out of its folded pages fell a letter from the Law Office of Gitchell & Jolliffe, in Cincinnati. He placed the letter to the side, and had just picked up his cup of coffee to take a sip when he discovered the circled headline. He immediately put his cup down with a clatter, the coffee slopping onto the saucer with a splash.

"Oh dear God! Eugenia! Elijah Willis has died!" he exclaimed.

Mrs. Bauskett had been raising her napkin to her mouth to wipe off the crumbs of a biscuit she had just finished, and pressed it to her lips to stifle a wail. "Oh John!" she cried, "Did they make it to Cincinnati, or were they still in slave territory when it happened?" For all Eugenia's plump sweetness she was no fool, and more than thirty years as a lawyer's wife had given her a legal education well attuned to the issues behind Elijah's case.

John read on in silence for a moment and then reported, "It was just as they arrived in Cincinnati, thank God! They had all landed safely on Ohio soil just moments before!" he affirmed as he read through the rest of the article. "Seems some folks tried to force the family back on the riverboat and even threatened to kick Momma Celia into the river, but Amy stood her ground, and got them all to their boarding house safely.

"Dear me, John, how tragic! What's to become of them now? Do ya think the will'll be proved in Ohio at least?" Eugenia asked with concern.

"I'm certain of it! But I'm also certain that the Willis boys will do all they can to prevent it from getting through probate here!" John answered.

Eugenia shook her head in dismay. "I don't have a good feelin about this John. I saw those boys at the rally and then at Angus' funeral. They're heartless and greedy- and drunkards to boot!" she declared emphatically.

"I'm afraid you're right, my dear. Elijah's battle is surely not over yet- even if he did, by the grace of God, manage to get Amy and the children to freedom!" John concurred.

"That's no small feat considerin the climate around here these days!" insisted Eugenia.

"No, indeed it isn't- but I imagine that's not as comforting a fact as Amy might have expected, given the possibility they may face a life of poverty instead of the comfort that Elijah intended and they deserved- that is at least, if the Willis boys succeed in blockin the probate," John commented. He paused for a moment, reflecting, then continued,

"Amy and her mother and the children are not totally without resources. Elijah told me he was takin a decent amount of cash with them to tide em over until he could get back here and sell the plantation," he informed her. "But my fear is for the long haul! If the Willises succeed in blockin the probate and it has to go to appeal, it could take years before the property can be sold!" As that sobering thought sank in he added, "If it isn't proved here, what happens then all depends on whether the whole will is deemed invalid or only certain parts of it- as Elijah was certainly within his rights to change his previous will."

Eugenia was taking all this in. "What's that letter there?" she asked, reminding him to open it and hoping it might provide some useful insight.

"It's from those two lawyers I referred Elijah to up in Cincinnati- the ones that helped write the new will," he told her as he took his knife and slid it under the seal. He opened the letter and began to read it over, commenting, "They're informin me of Elijah's death and askin for my help to shepherd the will through the probate process down here. Seems John Jolliffe is the sole executor in the interest of simplicity- that'll make things easier to coordinate! He tells me Amy and her mother and children are all safe and well, but deeply concerned about her brother Gilbert and the other slaves, as well as about gaining access to the assets here in South Carolina!"

"Well thank goodness they're alright at least! It must be something awful, all of em bein in a place they've never been an havin to go through such a loss- an under such precarious circumstances!" sighed Eugenia with sympathy.

"John!" she exclaimed with sudden alarm, "Ya'll don't think Angus Junior'll try to get your legal advice to help him fight this, do ya?"

"I don't think so- I think he's smart enough to realize I wouldn't give it- and couldn't, even if I wanted to, on the grounds of conflict of interest, as I'm representin Elijah and his estate. If he's fool enough to ask however, I will obviously tell him 'no!' But he's surely smart enough to realize he's gonna need a lawyer, an I expect he'll ask John Guignard's advice on that point since he'd sorta taken him and the Willis boys under his wing!"

"Whom do ya suppose he'll recommend?" inquired Eugenia.

"I imagine he'll send em over to Aldrich or Owens. No doubt their politics would agree, and they'd be happy to represent a case so near an dear to their own hard hearts!" John Bauskett was clearly no friend of Messrs. Aldrich or Owens. Having represented other cases on issues of manumission, he had a pretty clear idea of where the loyalties of all the area lawyers lay, and held the both of them in low esteem. "But, at least I'd know what I'm up against. I've dealt with em before- they're long on bluster but short on legal skill."

"Well honey, don't take anything for granted! Ya'll know perfectly well that with the attitudes around here, bluster can easily win the day over intelligence! There's no dearth a gullible fools here in Barnwell District!" Eugenia observed sagely.

"Too true, my dear, too true. I appreciate your admonition! In any event whomever they choose, I intend to be ready and well prepared to fight this- all the way to the South Carolina Supreme Court if necessary!"

"Pray God ya'll don't have to take it that far!" uttered Eugenia fervently. "That would guarantee it'd take years! Ya know how slow they can be- and a case like this might be one they'd prefer to drag their feet on, seein as it's such a touchy subject! That'd be awful hard on Amy and the children!"

"You may be right sugar, but I guess we'll just have to find out. I'll enter the will in probate as soon as Mr. Jolliffe sends me a copy, and then we'll see what happens!

Angus and the Willis brothers rode over to the Guignard plantation. It was late morning. As they rode up toward the house past the white fenced paddocks, they spied Dr. Guignard leaning against a fence carefully observing a chestnut mare that was sporadically nibbling the bright spring green grass of the paddock. She was clearly with foal.

Angus pulled up near the fence and greeted Dr. Guignard.

"Mornin, Dr. Guignard! Sorry to bother ya sir, but could we have a few minutes of your time? We have an urgent matter that we need your advice about!"

"Mornin, boys! Ya'll've caught me at a busy moment- I'm tryin to assess the potential of my best mare and the foal she's carryin. The sire's a thoroughbred stallion up in Kentucky. I just brought her back from up there outside a Lexington. I want to make sure she's not off her feed after the trip- the noise of the train kinda spooked her an if she doesn't eat right, it'll affect the foal's development. I just can't have that happenin!" Dr. Guignard turned back to watching the mare, clearly not feeling terribly inclined to permitting any distractions from his focus on the object of his passion.

"Yessir, that's a mighty fine looking mare, no doubt about it! An I can appreciate your interest in her well-bein- after such an investment a time and money in shippin her up to Kentucky, payin the stud fee, and shippin her back an all." Angus affirmed appreciatively. "But the thing is, we are in urgent need a some legal advice concerning the estate of Elijah Willis and we didn't know who else to turn to."

The mention of his nemesis got Guignard's one-pointed attention immediately. "I'll tell ya what, boys. Why don't ya'll head on up to the house then, an I'll meet ya'll up there in a few minutes, soon as I tell the groom what I want him to do with the mare. Tell Sally I said she should bring ya'll something ta drink while ya wait."

Without waiting for an answer he started walking toward the stables, flicking a riding crop against his thigh as he went and calling out for his groom, who came running. He was accustomed to the painful consequences of any failure to respond immediately when called, and was well aware that the riding crop could be just as easily used on him as on a horse.

Angus and his companions headed on up to the house and knocked on the front door. Sally opened the door with her usual sullen, disgruntled expression.

"May I help ya'll?" she asked.

"Mornin Sally! Dr. Guignard sent us up here and said for ya ta bring us somethin to drink while we wait for him to come back up from the paddock!" James announced.

"Yassuh, come on in, then." She opened the door wider and stood aside for them to come in, gesturing them toward the parlor. "What d'ya'll want to drink?" she asked out of disinterested obligation.

"Coffee'd be fine Sally. Thank ya." Angus replied. James shot him a look of annoyance- still craving the bottle- but Angus shook his head to indicate this was not the time or place to indulge. James pursed his lips and snorted in annoyance, but held his tongue.

Sally lumbered off toward the kitchen to prepare a tray for them while the three comrades sat down on Dr. Guignard's elegantly upholstered settee and armchairs to wait.

Just as Sally was returning with a tray laden with coffee, cream and sugar, and a mouth-watering plate of piping hot crullers, Dr. Guignard opened the front door and came striding in. He took one look at the tray and then at James, and said,

"Damn it gal! What're ya doin servin these boys coffee at a time like this? Take that away and come back with a proper drink a whiskey, an four glasses. Go on now- hurry it up!"

Angus looked wistfully at the disappearing plate of crullers, as Sally tried to keep from frowning and took the tray away. He was wishing she could at least leave the crullers, but he said nothing.

"Well now, boys, what's all this about Elijah's estate? Has he finally crossed the line an tried to emancipate that woman a his? Cause he should know South Carolina law won't let him, and won't let him leave her a dime either!"

"Well uh, as a mater of fact sir, he literally did cross the line- the State line, that is- and took her and her family up to Ohio! But the thing is, seems Mr. Willis dropped dead as soon as he got there!" recounted Angus.

"An what's worse, he wrote a new will up there, not only freein that whore an her pickaninnies but leavin everything he owned to them!" James chimed in, giving vent to his outrage.

Just as James delivered this invective, Sally reappeared bearing a tray with a decanter of whiskey and four cut crystal tumblers. She silently poured out four drafts and passed the tray to Dr. Guignard and his guests. James grabbed his glass eagerly, downing it in a single gulp. Dr. Guignard gestured impatiently to Sally to refill it. Once she had done so, she set the tray down and exited the parlor, smiling secretly to herself at the news that her old friend Celia and at least part of her family had made it to freedom.

As she headed out into the hallway she could hear her master offering his condolences and knew with a certainty that he was glad Elijah had died- and probably believed God had struck him dead as punishment for trying to free his slaves. "All depends on how ya look at it, though! Maybe God just kept Mister Elijah alive long enough to make sure he got em to safety!" she mused.

"Well! That's certainly unexpected news!" Dr. Guignard said, genuinely caught by surprise. "I had no idea he'd passed away. His brother Jimmy told me he'd decided to stop plantin cotton and focus on his lumber business- an so he'd gone on a trip. But it sounded like he was just takin some sort a pleasure cruise!" he said, almost as if thinking out loud. "Sorry for your loss, boys" he added, addressing the latter to James and Michael as gentility required.

Michael responded petulantly, "For which one? Uncle Elijah, or his estate?"

Dr. Guignard was taken aback by Michael's bluntness, but it certainly went straight to the point of their issue. "Well both, I suppose!"

"Doctor Guignard- we're gonna need to fight this thing in court! If the will doesn't pass probate here, then that woman and her children can't get their hands on any of the Willis property! But we're gonna need a lawyer to help us do it! We can't go to John Bauskett, cause he sorta inherited Elijah as a client from my Pa when Pa passed away, so he'd be bound by conflict of interest. Ya'll got any recommendations?" Angus insisted.

Guignard thought for a moment, calculating who might be best among the many whom he knew who were opposed to micegenation, emancipation, and leaving any inheritance to people of color.

"Well boys, I think I'd recommend Mr. Aldrich and Mr. Owens. They're a couple a good ole boys who have the ear a Judge David Wardlaw, whom I'm sure would want to rule in ya'll's favor." Guignard advised.

"Oh that's perfect!" enthused James. "If we can get the judge on our side, that bitch'll never be able to get her hands on Willis land!"

"Or free that brother a hers!" added Michael, relishing the thought of finally getting the upper hand over Gilbert, who had always intimidated the Hell out of them both.

"We sure do thank ya for the recommendation, Doctor Guignard!" Angus declared.

"It's my pleasure, boys! After all, we gotta stick together on this issue! It's about protecting not only ya'll's rights, but the rights of all the future generations a whites too!" Dr. Guignard proclaimed with passion. "We can't let a case like this set a precedent that opens doors for nirgra-lovin to run rampant and destroy everything our ancestors've worked for, now can we? I'll send a letter a introduction to both Aldrich and Owens to alert them to the problem ya'll're facin. I'm sure they'll be happy to help out."

"That's mighty kind of ya, Doctor. We surely do appreciate it!" The Willis brothers answered in chorus, finishing off their drinks.

"Well boys, I tried to convince your uncle to give up his perverted ways, to keep from sullyin the good Willis family name! Sorry to say he didn't heed my warnin, and insisted on bringin this shame on ya'll! But perhaps by helpin ya'll now, I can make some small contribution to restorin the family dignity, for the sake of both the town and its foundin family! It'd help put things back in their proper order!"

John Guignard arose from his seat after this disingenuous proclamation, clearly indicating their audience with him was now over. The three young men also arose, smiling and thanking him repeatedly as they headed out the front door. Their host meanwhile went upstairs to the desk in his room, which afforded him a view of the approach to his mansion, from which he could carefully observe all who came or went from the plantation. He watched the three companions mount up and head off down the road and clucked to himself, "It's a damn shame about Elijah- but the fool shoulda known better! I'd best get that letter off to Aldrich and Owens right away- we need to put a stop to this immediately!"

James Gitchell was opening the morning mail- the usual motley collection of bills, client petitions and inquiries, occasional payments, lawyers' requests for discovery, and the like. Amongst the jumble of envelopes and circulars piled on his desk he found one post-marked Barnwell, South Carolina. Recognizing John Bauskett's elegant hand, he opened it immediately.

To James Gitchell and John Jolliffe, Esquires
From John Bauskett, Esq., Attorney at Law
Barnwell, South Carolina

My Dear Gentlemen and Esteemed Colleagues:

I received on Thursday last your sad announcement of the passing of my dear friend and client Elijah Willis, coincidentally in the same mail as a copy of The New York Times recounting the details of his death. My wife and I were sorely aggrieved by the news, yet we rejoice that through the grace of God and your good offices Amy and her mother and children are safe and sound up there in Cincinnati- and free at long last!

In the following post I also received a copy of Elijah's Last Will and Testament as drafted by you, and will duly enter it into probate in the court here as per your request. I am frankly not optimistic it will be proved, for it is clear to me that with the help of Angus Patterson Junior (the unfortunate heir of the good lawyer who had originally counseled Elijah), various members ot the Willis family (principally among the younger generation most distressed by the loss of a long-expected inheritance) will protest the probate and do all in their power to discredit the more recent will in favor of his previous one in which they were named as legatees.

Should that occur, as is most likely, I may well need one of you- and preferably Mr. Jolliffe as the executor- to join me here in Barnwell to help appeal the case to a higher court. Rest assured you would have no expenses for your stay, as my wife Eugenia and I would be only too happy to have you as our guest for the duration!

I shall keep you apprised of things as they develop. In the meantime, please let Amy and her family know our prayers go with them, and while we give the Good Lord thanks for their deliverance into the open arms of freedom, we are deeply saddened by their loss- which is also ours- and we pledge to do all in our power to assure that justice is rightly and swiftly done!

Do not hesitate to inform me of any significant developments on your end that might prove useful in pressing our case. I would also appreciate your views on how to manage the plantation and its remaining resident slaves in the absence of a court decision, for I have some concerns as to the possible incursions of local family members into the plantation's affairs, and would prevent such if at all possible. As Elijah's lawyer, I may be able to seek a court injunction to such effect, and will in any case journey to the Willis Plantation tomorrow to inform Amy's brother Gilbert, the de facto foreman of the estate, of the sad event and its possible consequences.

Awaiting your further instructions and advice for securing Amy and the children's legacy, I am,

Most sincerely your servant and theirs,

John Bauskett

"John!" James Gitchell called to his colleague, "John Bauskett, Elijah Willis's lawyer in South Carolina, is presenting the will for probate but is doubtful it will be proved. He's certain the family will try to block it in favor of the earlier will, and says he's likely going to need your help in the event of an appeal."

He passed the letter over to his colleague, who reading it looked up and peering over his glasses said, "That is just as we expected! The question is only on what grounds do they intend to oppose it? I will make you a gentleman's wager of a five dollar gold piece that they will attempt to discredit his sanity, and probably also allege undue influence by Amy!" John Jolliffe asserted.

"I'd be a fool to take that bet and part so quickly with my money, as I heartily concur that is their most likely line of reasoning," responded Gitchell. "So how shall we prepare the defense?"

John Jolliffe thought for a moment. "We'll need to collect testimony from as many people who knew Elijah as possible- testimony as to his character, his standing in the community, his demeanor and observable state of mind over a prolonged period." He insisted. "Moreover, we ourselves can testify, as can the other signatories on the will, that he came here of his own accord without Amy, over a year before his demise, which should go far to disprove the 'undue influence' theory."

"We can ask Amy for the names of people she thinks would be sympathetic witnesses. I believe she mentioned a Dr. Joseph Harley as someone who had been supportive. A doctor's testimony as to Elijah's sanity would be a powerful aid in disproving any allegations of mental incapacity! I'm sure there must also be others who knew him well and could verify his soundness of mind too."

"Excellent idea, James! By all means, let's meet with her right away so as to begin gathering material for discovery. We can send it to John Bauskett and ask that he interview the list of witnesses himself if possible, or at least lay the groundwork for me to do so when I get down there!" John Jolliffe agreed.

Content that they had established an effective plan to address the issue, they called for Jack to bring the carriage around so they could go pay Amy a visit and bring her up to date on the developments. Once the carriage arrived, they promptly set off for the Dumas House, remembering they had promised Amy to begin looking for more suitable lodgings and feeling slightly embarrassed that they had not yet done so.

When they arrived at the Dumas House they immediately inquired after Amy. The bellhop went to find her, leaving them to wait in the same parlor where Elijah's body had so recently lain. A few moments later Amy appeared in the doorway. Though well-groomed and dressed, she seemed more care-worn than they had expected.

"Good mornin, gentlemen. To what do I owe the honor of your visit?" Amy extended her hand in greeting, as each attorney shook it in turn.

"Good morning, my dear," replied John Jolliffe. "We come with news, and a request. We have just received a letter from John Bauskett apprising us of the fact that he is entering Elijah's will into probate in the court in Barnwell. However, he is virtually certain that Elijah's white relations will try to block the probate, so we need to ask you for a list of persons whom you think might testify on Elijah's behalf."

"We suspect his relations will attempt to allege either that he was of unsound mind when he wrote the new will or that he did so under your coercion, so the references you give should be people you are well persuaded could refute shuch erroneous allegations- people who have known you both and seen the manner in which you lived together, but people who are also known and respected in the community," James Gitchell clarified.

"In the event that the probate court refuses to prove the will and we need to appeal the case, I will go down to South Carolina myself to assist," Mr. Jolliffe explained. "But in the meantime, John Bauskett can take the affidavits of probable witnesses to prepare the defense. We won't know entirely what's needed, however, until we get some sort of response from the court and see how that response is worded."

Amy listened thoughtfully and heaving a sigh responded, "I was afraid this would be the case. Do ya'll think they're likely to succeed in blockin the probate?" she asked, her voice weary with the cumulative effects of the recent strains.

"I wouldn't be a bit surprised," replied Jolliffe.

"Nor I," agreed Gitchell. "In fact, I think it more than likely."

"And how long do you suppose the appeal process might take?" Amy asked.

"That is difficult to say, I'm afraid. If it is rejected in the probate court, it would then pass to the Court of Equity, and if that appeal fails, we could have to take it to the South Carolina Court of Appeals, which, if I'm not mistaken, would be a jury trial, or even take it to their Supreme Court. I fear we could be talking about months, or even years."

Amy suppressed a moan. She was worried. "Gentlemen, is there nothing we can do? I am fearful for my brother and his family, still on the plantation- and worry that Elijah's relations may attempt to seize the property. If they do, it will surely mean great suffering for my brother, as they have always feared and resented him and will likely take out their vengeance on him in my absence." Amy painted a vivid picture of the probable consequence of any Willis incursions onto the property.

"I fear too for my children here," she continued. "They've been accustomed to runnin free on the plantation, and havin numerous chores and tasks to keep em busy and entertained. Bein cooped up here with nothin to do is sorely wearin on em, to the point a tryin my last nerve! Can nothin be done?" Amy's slipping from her more formal language into her vernacular was a clear indication of her unmistakable exasperation, not to say her disillusionment with the alleged benefits of freedom. This was not what she had been hoping for at all!

"As to your first question my dear, as we told you, John Bauskett has already anticipated the probability that Elijah's white relations might attempt to take over the plantation. He is prepared to get a court injunction to prevent any such seizure, pending the definitive outcome of the courts as to whether and how much of his Last Will and Testament may be valid. That should buy us some time. He has also gone to the plantation to inform your brother of the unhappy sequence of events that have led us to this juncture. I'm sure he will make every effort possible to secure the safety of the property and its remaining residents."

"As to your second question," Gitchell intervened, "having been so occupied with the legal details of getting your case settled here as well as in Williston, we have been remiss in not yet finding you alternative housing that will permit you greater freedom of movement and activity. We sincerely apologize to you all for that unavoidable reality. Though I originally had envisioned you living here in the city, I am now persuaded that even if we cannot yet access the necessary assets to purchase a farm for you as Elijah had intended, perhaps we could find you lodging in one of the local nearby farms- either renting a property or perhaps finding employment for you on one."

Amy was not thrilled at the prospect of working as a domestic servant for some white family much less working as a field hand after living as the lady of the house for years on Elijah's plantation. But she understood that she might have to do so in order to keep her family fed, clothed, and sheltered- at least until she could access the assets in South Carolina. She could only hope that if it were necessary, the treatment of domestic employees by Northern whites would be significantly better than the frequently abusive treatment colored slaves received by their owners in the South. She gave an involuntary shudder of dread before continuing,

"I am prepared to do whatever is necessary gentlemen, for the sake of my family," she avowed stoically.

"We promise we shall look into housing options for you and your family right away. But in the meantime, if you would be so kind as to provide us the names of those whom you think would likely be effective witnesses to testify to Elijah's good character and sound mind, we'd be terribly grateful. We shall send the list to John Bauskett on the next post," John Jolliffe affirmed.

Amy began to take a mental inventory: "Dr. Joseph Harley, our family physician, Will Beazely, the Williston postmaster at the depot, John Bauskett, our lawyer, Eugenia Bauskett, his wife, William Knotts, a long-time friend of Elijah's, Ari and Reason Wooley, our neighbors, the Reverend

Mr. Wagner, the Vicar of Holy Apostles over in Barnwell… would all be supportive, I believe. Dr. Guignard, a man determined to accuse Elijah of immorality because of his relationship with me, Mr. Frederick Matthews, his lapdog, all of the Willises, and Angus Patterson Junior would all of em surely oppose us." Amy informed them.

"What about any others- for example, you mentioned a gentleman you had met on the trip up here, a Mr. Callum or Cullum, I believe? Was there anyone else on the train, or on the *Jacob Strader* who could attest that Elijah had intended to emancipate all of you? It will be important to corroborate the terms of the will with eyewitness testimony if possible."

"Well yes, Mr. Cullum and his wife, I should think. He saved Momma from bein kicked into the river, and she was the one who whispered to me to clean out Elijah's pockets before any authorities could get there" Amy agreed. "Oh, and the conductor of the train! I believe his name is James Meredith. He had known Elijah from his various business trips- and even from when Elijah had to send some of his slaves to market in Hamburg. In fact, he wondered if he was taking us there, though we were too well-dressed for that! Elijah told him we were his family, and he was takin us up to Cincinnati."

"Excellent! That's very helpful, my dear! I shall inform John Bauskett right away and ask that he start gathering testimony from your suggested candidates!" Jolliffe enthused.

"We shall certainly keep you abreast of any developments as they unfold. In the meantime we shall explore the options for finding you more suitable housing," Gitchell assured her.

"I do thank ya both- an I hope ya'll don't think me unappreciative of ya'll's efforts. It's just that I'm startin to see there's a difference between freedom in the eyes of the law and the feelin of freedom we thought would accompany it! It's a harder difference than I was expectin!" Amy said with apologetic candor.

"Have no fear my dear, we understand. And though only the Good Lord can assure us real and lasting freedom from suffering, we certainly pledge to do our part to make sure you suffer no more than the normal lot in life, at least due to the legal machinations of Elijah's white relations," Mr. Jolliffe assured her."Please give our regards to your mother and children and assure them their well-being is of utmost importance to us. God willing we shall see you safely and comfortably resettled soon!" reiterated Mr. Gitchell.

The two gentlemen bade Amy farewell and took their leave, so as to deliver to John Bauskett the list of witnesses Amy had suggested and look into possible alternative lodgings for her and her family.

As they departed Amy sighed deeply, wondering, "Dear Lord, what's to become of us now?" She prayed, "Please God, don't let the Willises rob us of our inheritance and leave us stranded here!" She shuddered again at the thought of becoming a domestic servant after all she'd been through, but having already fought continuously for five years with constant set-backs and frustrations before her freedom was granted, she knew that the Lord's time-table and her own were not necessarily going to be the same.

CVI

When James and Michael learned of Elijah's death and informed Angus of it, Angus had recognized from the outset that they would need to present the earlier will for probate immediately, figuring that that would prevent the new will from being proved and implemented. As they returned home from their visit to Dr. Guignard, Angus pointed out the urgency to them, lest it be lost on either of his companions.

"I imagine it'll take some time for your Uncle Elijah's lawyers to present that new will for probate down here. They'll have to get it through probate up in Ohio first. I suspect, therefore, that nobody down here even knows about the new will yet- exceptin probably for John Bauskett. So we need to get the first will registered right away!"

"We'll have to talk to Daddy an see who's got a copy. If the only copy is on the plantation we'll have one helluva time getting it- cause I'm damn sure Uncle Elijah told Gilbert and the others about their right an responsibility to protect the property. I for one don't fancy tryin to face Gilbert down on that score! I think a couple a our uncles were appointed executors, so surely someone in the family must have it tucked away safe an sound somewhere!" exclaimed James.

"Well whoever it is who's got it, we need to get it, take it over to the Probate Court in the Barnwell District Courthouse, and register it as fast as we can! If it gets registered first, maybe it'll prevent, or at least delay that new will getting through probate down here."Angus informed them.

"We'd best go talk to Daddy and break the news to him! That way we can find out where the old will is!" commented Michael.

"Then we'll let ya know and figure out what we need to do about it," added James to Angus.

"Alright then, let me know, but don't dawdle! This needs doin quickly if we're gonna beat John Bauskett to the punch. I imagine he's already been informed of Elijah's death by now and may even have received a copy of the new will himself, to enter into probate. While ya'll're talkin to your Daddy, I think I'll go pay a visit to the lawyers Dr. Guignard told us about an alert em that we need to get this done right away. We can meet back at my place this afternoon."

"That's a good idea, Angus! We'll see ya later then!" confirmed James.

The three friends parted company, Angus riding off to introduce himself to the lawyers, the Willis boys heading over to their father's place to break the news to him of his brother's death.

"Hi Ma!" James greeted his mother, "Daddy home?" he asked.

"He's here, but he's in the privy, honey- " she answered. "been bound for days!" she added in a stage whisper meant to be a confidential tone. "What brings ya'll over here at this time a day? Everything alright?"

"Well, we got some important news to tell him- and some questions for him too." James said somewhat evasively. He preferred to tell his father first, rather than spill the beans to his mother.

"It's about Uncle Elijah!" Michael confided, knowing it would shift his mother's attention to him. James gave him a fierce look not to say any more.

Mrs. Willis looked piercingly at both her sons. "What's goin on here, you two? Why all the mystery?" She was about to wheedle something out of her younger son- always more easily manipulated than his brother- when her husband appeared, pulling a pair of suspenders up over his shoulders, but not looking particularly relieved from his sojourn in the privy.

"Answer your mother, boys! What brings ya'll over here in the middle of the day without it bein mealtime?" their father asked, with a slight dig at their tendency to show up more for food than for "family feelin."

"Daddy! We just found out Uncle Elijah's dead! Dropped dead up in Cincinnati! An he took that nigra woman a his an her mother an children up there with him to free em! Seems he wrote a new will up there leavin everything to them- so we gotta get Uncle Elijah's real will an enter it into probate right away to prove we're the real heirs, and he can't violate South Carolina law like that!" James said in a breathless torrent.

"Oh my Lord, Jimmy!" Mrs. Willis blurted to her husband, "He can't do that, can he?"

James Willis Senior did not miss the fact that his wife's first comment was focused on his brother's legal move, not on her husband's bereavement or loss.

"Good God, woman! Ya could at least show a little respect for me losin my brother before worryin about his estate!" he said, acidly.

His wife demurred immediately, "Oh Jimmy honey, ya know I didn't mean it like that! I was just so shocked by what James here blurted out I just couldn't think straight! A course it's a tragedy Elijah dyin so suddenly, right when he finally went on a trip to take a rest after workin so hard all these years!" She shot a look to both of her sons visually demanding they follow suit out of respect for their father.

"We're real sorry about Uncle Elijah, Daddy!" James and Michael avowed. "It's just that we want to protect the Willis family honor, as he clearly intended in the will he showed you," assured James.

"This other will- he musta been crazy from drinkin an whorin with that nigra woman when he wrote it! I bet she forced him into it!" swore Michael.

"We just think we all need to stand up to it and make sure the court doesn't think it's real!" clarified James. "For the sake a your good name, Daddy- ya'll're the head a the Willis Family now, an deserve that respect without Uncle Elijah's immorality sullyin your reputation!"

Jimmy Willis heard his family's proclamation, and though he didn't really disagree with their reasoning, his heart felt the blow of Elijah's death in ways the others did not. He held his tongue however, and turned his attention to the very real matter at hand.

"Well, Elijah appointed our sisters' husbands as executors- he figured bein married into the Willises rather than bein blood relations gave em a little more distance to be objective, I guess. I reckon we'll have to pay em both a visit an let em know what's happened. Truth is, I'm not rightly sure which one of em actually has the will itself, but I know one or the other does," Jimmy announced.

"We realized we'd need some legal help with this, Daddy, so we asked Dr. Guignard for some advice on who should best represent us. Angus went over to talk to a couple a lawyers he recommended- a Mr. Aldrich an a Mr. Owens- to let em know what'd happened and how we need to fight this thing," James informed his father.

James was hoping his father would be proud of them for taking such initiative, but instead his father scolded them, "Now why the Hell did ya'll go runnin off to Guignard like that, without even consultin me? Who do ya'll think ya are, anyway? I'm the head a this family, an I'll decide whether we need a lawyer and who it should be, d'ya hear me? Damn fools! Bringin in a stranger into our family's business like that without my permission- I thought I'd raised ya'll better than that!" Jimmy was furious.

"Sorry, Daddy! Truly, we were just tryin to be helpful! Don't go gettin all worked up over it!" begged James.

"It was Angus' idea, Daddy! He just wanted to warn us of the possible complications if we didn't get Uncle Elijah's first will entered into probate before John Bauskett enters the new will, that's all. Honest, Daddy! We meant no disrespect!"

"I'll handle this! If I need ya'll's help, I'll let ya know- but you let me do the talkin here! I'll get the will and we'll take it over to the Courthouse." Jimmy was in no mood to argue with his sons. He was truly aggrieved by the death of Elijah, their fraternal differences notwithstanding, and it pained him to see his wife's and children's indifference to that fact, their greed for his property masked as attachment to the family honor, taking precedence over any emotional pain at the loss.

James and Michael, cowed by their father's displeasure, mumbled their assent, realizing that this would put a crimp in their intentions to meet with Angus that afternoon to further their plan of legal attack. Not having the will in hand for Angus to examine the wording was an inconvenience- but they could at least discover what he had learned from the lawyers Guignard had recommended. Deciding that discretion was in truth the better part of valor, they decided not to push the issue any further with their father for the moment, and had to content themselves with waiting on the results of his conversation with their uncles.

John Bauskett did not relish the task of breaking the news to Gilbert. As he drove up the lane to the Willis Plantation, the late-blooming azaleas had finished flowering and were in the raggedy-looking stage of not having yet dropped the wilted brown vestiges of their floral splendor. The magnolias, though thick with buds, had not yet bloomed. Bauskett thought the juxtaposition was oddly symbolic of the condition of the human crisis now unfolding. He pondered how strange it was that everything seemed so perfectly normal when in fact tragedy had befallen the plantation and its residents.

His carriage kicked up dust along the road. Julius, who happened to be near the house at the time, spotted it and immediately ran to fetch Gilbert- uncertain as to who was coming and feeling the need for them to be prepared to defend the place against anyone nosing about, with both Elijah and Amy away.

Gilbert and Julius stood in front of the veranda, protectively expectant, as John Bauskett's carriage rolled to a stop and the lawyer climbed out.

"Mornin Gilbert!" John said cordially, remembering him from the rally. "I expect ya'll remember me, I'm John Bauskett, Elijah and Amy's attorney."

Gilbert relaxed, seeing it was a friendly face, but was struck by Bauskett's choice of words- "Elijah and Amy's attorney-" never having heard anyone claim to represent the interests of a colored person, much less a slave before.

"Yessir, Mister Bauskett- I remember ya from the rally- and from what Elijah an Julius here told me about all the help ya'll have given us. What can I do for ya today, sir?" Gilbert asked, his stomach tightening in the realization that a message was coming from the lawyer rather than directly from Elijah or Amy themselves, and uncertain whether that boded well or ill.

"Well Gilbert, I'm afraid I have some very sad news for ya. Elijah Willis dropped dead of a heart attack in Cincinnati the moment he set foot on

Ohio soil with his family!"

Julius let out a groan of anguish. Gilbert felt as if he'd been kicked by a mule in the chest. His mouth went dry and he struggled to speak for fear of the response to his question, "And Amy, Momma, and the children?" he asked, anxiety thickening his voice and moistening his eyes to the brim.

"Thankfully, they all made it to safety and are well. James Gitchell and John Jolliffe, the attorneys who helped Elijah draft his new will, have taken them under their wing. Jolliffe is the executor of the will, and as such is now ya'll's legal owner until he can sell the plantation and try to free the rest of ya," Bauskett explained. "As for Amy, your Momma, and the children, they are all now legally and permanently free! Jolliffe has gotten the will through probate up there in Ohio, and had a deed of manumission issued by the court to confirm their freedom just in case the Willises tried to take em back!"

"Oh, Thank the Good Lord for that!" Gilbert and Julius both said fervently, relieved at least to hear they had not been shipped back in chains. "So what happens now?" Gilbert asked, aware that no matter what Elijah's new will said, it might not be implemented right away.

"Well sir, that's a good question! It all depends on gettin the new will through probate down here in South Carolina. The reason I came out here was to warn ya, in case any of the Willis relations try to come out here and take over. They can't do that- at least not yet- so if they try, I want ya'll to try to get word to me right away."

Gilbert knew that no Negro could just go riding all the way over to Barnwell without raising suspicions, and maybe even being stopped, even if he was wearing a permit. "An if we can't get anyone all the way over to ya'll's place in Barnwell, what d'ya want us to do?" he asked astutely.

"Hmmm, that's a good point. Do ya think ya could get a message to Will Beazeley at the Depot?" Bauskett asked, thinking out loud about how to circumvent unwanted incursions onto the plantation.

"Yessir, that'd be no problem- it'd just look like we was doin plantation business as usual," replied Gilbert, Julius nodding in agreement.

"Good! Then you get a message to Will and have him get the message to me however he thinks best."

"And if anyone comes on the property tryin to snoop around?" Julius asked.

"Well, ya'll have the right and obligation to defend the property. Ya'll can be polite and civil and ask em nicely to leave, explainin ya're operatin under legal orders. If anyone objects, ya'll can send em to talk to me." Bauskett paused in thought for a moment. "Do ya'll have any firearms on the property?" he inquired.

"Yessir- Elijah provided us with a couple a shotguns, a few pistols, and some ammunition, just in case!" Gilbert affirmed.

"Good! Don't use em unless ya have to- but ya'll're legally entitled to use force to protect ya master or his property- so don't worry about gettin into trouble if ya have to stand ya ground. I don't imagine even the Willis boys'd relish riskin sheddin their own blood over this, so hopefully it won't come to havin ta use force!"

Julius paused, uncertain of how much to say or ask Mr. Bauskett, but as he had helped carry Angus Patterson's law books into the Bauskett's house, he felt emboldened to speak up.

"Scuse me, Mister Bauskett, but if the Cincinnati will don't get through probate here, what happens to the likes a us?"

"That's a good question, Julius. I wish I had a definitive answer- but truth is I don't. We'll appeal it in court if the will is rejected, and it probably will be, given the Willis boys' fight to keep their uncle's property. But Mr. Jolliffe up in Cincinnati is willin to take it all the way to the Supreme Court of South Carolina if necessary, to secure Amy's rights to the inheritance."

"That sounds like it could take a goodly length a time to get worked out," observed Gilbert, his face grim.

"I'm afraid it could," admitted Bauskett, "But we are already workin on gettin testimony in support of Elijah from all the folks around here who knew him, to prove he wasn't either crazy, or forced to write the new will. Once we prove that, we'll be on solid ground to secure the inheritance- even if it takes time to get it all through the courts." Bauskett explained. "The Willis boys can't protest the will just because they don't like it or because they hate colored folks! They'd have to be able to prove it was legally invalid- and there are just no grounds for them to do that."

"It's a shame they won't allow colored folks to testify!" said Julius. "They'd be plenty a colored folks round here who'd speak up for Mister Elijah!"

John Bauskett was struck by the comment. "It's true Julius, ya'll'd be able to put things in a whole different perspective! But unfortunately, we both know that's not a perspective most white folks are willin to hear. Sad thing is, even if you were free, most states still wouldn't allow ya to testify in court!"

"So who has control of the plantation now? How we supposed to run it if they's no white man in charge?" Gilbert pressed.

"That's a good question too, Gilbert. For the moment, as Elijah's lawyer, I'd put you in charge- since ya'll've been runnin the place all along anyway. Do like ya'd always do, for now." He paused, as if running through a mental check-list of considerations.

"Did Elijah leave ya'll any money for supplies an such?" he asked.

"Yessir, an I got it stowed away safe too," affirmed Gilbert.

"Good! I'm gonna be enterin the new will for probate in the Barnwell District Courthouse tomorrow- an I honestly don't know if the Willises have already done the same with the earlier will. Guess I'll find out when I get over there. If they have, we'll contest it immediately, and the court will schedule a trial to present the contendin cases. As Elijah's lawyer of choice, my word concernin the runnin of the plantation for now should have precedence at least until the case is settled. So sit tight for now, and make sure ya'll let me know if anything unusal happens!"

"Yessir Mister Bauskett, we will! May the Good Lord keep ya, an help ya save us all!" Gilbert hoped ardently.

"Amen to that!" agreed Julius.

"Alright then boys, ya'll take care now, and keep me posted if ya'll have any trouble. I'll get back to ya as soon as I know anything more!" John Bauskett affirmed. With a tip of his hat he climbed back into his carriage and signaled to his driver to head on home. The driver, who had overheard the entire conversation in the unobtrusive, virtually invisible way that servants had all learned to do, gave a look to both Gilbert and Julius that spoke reams. It was full of hope and full of concern for their fate. He nodded in a knowing way, and they both nodded back in mutual recognition- as if conveying a silent code among brethren facing challenging times.

CVIII

When John Bauskett reached the Barnwell District Court House, he went directly to the office of the Registrar of Wills in Room 108, to discover whether or not Elijah's will of 1846 had been filed. He was hoping it had not, thinking it might give him the tactical advantage of "first strike." If he could get the Cincinnati will registered first, it would then be incumbent upon the Willises to demand a trial.

"Mornin!" he greeted a sleepy-looking clerk.

"Oh, morning Mr. Bauskett! What can I do for ya, sir?" the clerk perked up, recognizing the attorney.

"Well, I'd like to register my client's will if I may."

"Yessir, I'll be gald to help ya'll. What's the client's name and place of residence?" the clerk inquired.

"Elijah Willis of Willis Plantation, in Williston, Barnwell District, South Carolina." John announced.

"Oh! Mr. Willis? He's already got a will registered here, Mr. Bauskett-dated 1846. Is the will ya'll're registering a more recent one?" the clerk inquired.

"It is. It was written in February of 1854." He replied.

"Hmmm. Is it an ammended form of the 1846 will, or are there substantial differences?" the clerk asked.

"There are significant differences, and the will was written up in Cincinnati, Ohio."

"Well sir, then if the will ya'll want to register contests the content of the will the Willis family registered, there'll have to be a court rulin as to which is the valid will."

John Bauskett, though disappointed to find the Willises had beaten him to the punch, was not particularly surprised. "Please advise the Court accordingly, and let me know as soon as the date and time for the hearing is set," he requested.

"Yessir, I sure will sir. I expect it'll be Judge Wardlaw hearin the case, just so ya know," the clerk informed him.

John Bauskett thought to himself, "Just my luck! It would have to be the most secessionist judge on the South Carolina bench! Damn! More'n likely he'll rule against us, and we'll have to appeal."

"I surely do thank ya, and I'll look forward to gettin that trial notification right quickly!" John Bauskett bade the clerk good-bye and headed on home to map out his plan of attack. He'd need to start interviewing right away everyone on the list Messrs. Jolliffe and Gitchell had sent him.

Angus Patterson and James and Michael Willis stood nervously outside the Court of Equity chambers in the Barnwell District Court House on Main Street in Barnwell. They were accompanied by their new-found lawyers Messrs. Aldrich and Owens, both of whom had eagerly agreed to represent the Willises in their petition to block the probate of Elijah's Cincinnati will. Along with them were two of Elijah's brothers-in-law, Mr. Fanning and Mr. Phillips, who had been appointed executors of the original will Elijah had written back in 1846.

John Bauskett entered the Greek Revival building carrying a sheaf of papers with the names, addresses, professions, and affidavits of a list of witnesses testifying for the defense. He had already shared them with the opposing counsel as discovery, of course, so he showed neither shock nor dismay at seeing the Willises there gathered, for he was prepared for their assault.

The bailiff opened the courtroom door, announced that the consideration of the Last Will and Testament of Elijah Willis was to begin, and invited all interested parties to enter. Both John Bauskett and Messrs. Aldrich and Owen proceeded to take their seats at opposite desks facing the bench, the Willis brothers, their uncles, and Angus sitting directly behind Messrs. Aldrich and Owens.

John had asked his witnesses to attend too, just in case, though he was fully expecting that there would be a continuance granted to allow the judge time to consider any petition the Willises might present before ruling. Joseph Harley, among others, had been alerted, and sat at a discreet distance behind John Bauskett. John saw that the Willises had notified their witnesses too, some of whom with carefully worded questioning might be used for either the prosecution or the defense- including Dr. Guignard and Frederick Matthews.

The bailiff disappeared for a moment through a side door behind the bench to the left and then returned shortly, announcing, "All Rise! Hear ye Hear ye! The Court of Equity of Barnwell District, in the Great State a South Carolina is now in session, the Honorable David Lewis Wardlaw presidin!"

Judge Wardlaw was a man who exuded gravitas much like the Reverend Dr. Beecher, yet without the aura of sanctity of that austere cleric. His face was angular and square-jawed, with deep-set eyes and dark heavy eyebrows, his short hair was the color of salt and pepper. Though not quite gaunt, his cheeks were somewhat sunken and clean-shaven. He cut an imposing, even intimidating figure in his judicial robes as he swept into the chamber and ascended the steps to the bench. Looking out over the assembled group and sizing the situation up quickly, he took his seat.

"Please be seated ya'll," he said with the affability that comes only from one completely in control and on his own turf. "Bailiff, what've we got here?" the judge asked, feigning ignorance of a case of which he was already well aware. The tactic was carefully honed to keep the lawyers on their toes and uncertain, assuring he could thereby turn the conversation at will.

"Your Honor, this case, Jolliffe v. Fanning & Phillips, is concernin the Last Will and Testament of one Elijah Willis, of Williston, Barnwell District, South Carolina." The bailiff was a stickler for including the formal details in proper order.

"I see," responded Judge Wardlaw, matter-of-factly. "That sounds like it's concernin a lotta wills to me- will, Willis, Williston..." joked the judge. "And who is representin the deceased?" He was going through the formalities of recording what was already known.

"I am, Your Honor, on behalf of Mr. Jolliffe, executor of the more recent will!" John Bauskett announced.

David Wardlaw nodded in acknowledgement to Bauskett. "Nice ta see ya, John. Ah, for the record counselor, would ya please state your name and place of residence?"

"Yes, Your Honor: John Bauskett, Esquire, Attorney at Law in Barnwell, Barnwell District, South Carolina."

"Thank ya, John," replied the judge.

"Are there any petitioners who would contest the will ya'll're presentin?" the Judge then inquired, knowing perfectly well that there were, or there would be no need for a trial.

"There are, Your Honor!" Messrs. Aldrich and Owens, in their eagerness announced loudly in unison.

"I'm not deaf, counselors! I don't need ya'll talkin in chorus- one of ya is quite sufficient," chided the judge.

"Yessir, Your Honor, sorry sir," apologized Mr. Aldrich, giving his colleague a look to keep quiet.

"And am I to assume ya'll are representin the petitioners, uh, Mr. Phillips and Mr. Fanning, is it?"

"And several other family members too, yessir, we are Your Honor."

"Very well, state your names and places of residence for the record then."

"James Aldrich, Esquire, and Clyde Owens, Esquire, Attorneys at Law in Barnwell District, South Carolina."

"Thank ya, gentlemen," the Judge resumed. "Now, what is the point of contention concernin this will, John?"

"Well Your Honor, in February of 1854, my client, the testator, Elijah Willis wrote a will in Cincinnati, Ohio, as was his legal right, completely overturnin a previous will written here in Barnwell District back in 1846. The Ohio will seems to be in perfectly good order. It was drafted by James Gitchell and John Jolliffe, attorneys at law in Cincinnati, and signed by the testator and two reputable witnesses from that city." Bauskett deliberately avoided focusing on the contents of the distribution of the will, knowing that Judge Wardlaw was a secessionist at heart and not wanting to intentionally cloud the situation with political overtones.

"Do ya'll have a certified copy of the will present?"

"Yes, Your Honor!"

"Approach the bench. May I see it please?

"Certainly, Your Honor!"

As John Bauskett approached the bench, the Willis brothers were fairly chomping at the bit to introduce their petition to reject the probate, their attorneys signaling them to keep quiet.

Judge Wardlaw put on a pair of spectacles and began to read the copy of the will proffered by John Bauskett. With furrowed brow and stern visage, he handed it back to Bauskett. "Thank ya, counselor, please take ya seat, sir. Mr. Aldrich! What d'ya'll have for me?" he addressed the petitioners.

James Aldrich approached the bench with a copy of the 1846 will and handed it over to the judge. Judge Wardlaw scanned the earlier document and returned it to Mr. Aldrich, saying, "Ya'll can return to your seat too, counselor."

After a thoughtful pause, the Judge announced, "Gentlemen, I have read the discovery ya'll presented in preparation for this case, and have carefully considered the law governin this matter. It's clear to me that the newer will is not only in contradiction to the previous will, but also to the laws of South Carolina. Therefore, in the matter of the Last Will and Testament signed and dated by the deceased Elijah Willis in February, 1854 in the City of Cincinnati and the State of Ohio, it is the rulin of this court that enterin this will for probate is denied, on the grounds that is in violation of the Act of 1841 of the General Assembly of the State of South Carolina and therefore invalid. Case dismissed!"

Judge Wardlaw brought down the gavel. Everyone stood nearly dumbfounded that there was to be no discussion or presenting of arguments for or against either will. Seeing no one look like they were fixin to leave, the judge added, "That'll be all, gentlemen!"

The bailiff announced, "All Rise!" Everyone in the courtroom promptly got to their feet, upon which Judge Wardlaw pushed back his chair, smiled, and left the bench for his chambers. John Bauskett thought he detected a slight nod and a wink from the judge to Messrs. Aldrich and Owens. It all seemed to be over almost before it had begun, without a single witness being called or a shred of testimony given!

Michael Willis let out a rebel yell of jubilation, hugging his brother and pounding him on the back in triumph. There was much congratulating and shaking of hands going around among Messrs. Aldrich and Owens, the Willis brothers, their uncles, and Angus Patterson.

James Willis looked over to John Bauskett and nodded with a smug smile, in acknowledgment.

John Bauskett responded by approaching the petitioners' attorneys. "Well gentlemen, I hope ya'll realize this is not over yet, it's just beginnin," he said in a matter-of-fact tone. "We will most certainly file an appeal to this initial foray immediately, as this decision clearly ignores both the facts, the law, and due process."

"I figured you'd say that, John," responded Aldrich. "Go right ahead! Ya'll won't win, but if it'll make ya feel better, be my guest!" he added with the arrogance lawyers sometimes use to try to intimidate their opponents- especially when they are on uncertain ground and hoping to bluff their way out of it. He was implying that Judge Wardlaw's opinions on matters of race and politics being what they were, the ultimate opinion would necessarily be weighted in their favor as a foregone conclusion, rendering Bauskett's objections futile. He didn't consider that to be judicial bias, of course- it was merely the common sense, normative position of the views shared by the ruling class., and therefore inherently just.

John Bauskett was not easily fooled by the ploy, being certain the rejection of the probate was legally unfounded. Moreover, he was well persuaded John Jolliffe would share his opinion and be only too happy to come down to South Carolina to argue the facts before a jury in the Court of Appeals, to which the case would now be deferred.

"Just tell your clients not to count their chickens before they hatch! There's a whole lot more lawyerin gotta be done before this thing is settled!" he said with confidence.

Angus Patterson was eavesdropping on the conversation between Aldrich and Bauskett, figuring it was a good way to further his informal legal education. He pulled James aside saying, "Listen up, James! The fact that the new will did not pass probate yet doesn't mean it can't still be approved, either in part or in whole, upon an appeal. Bauskett's just told Aldrich he's filing an appeal right away! This ain't over yet, so don't think ya'll can just waltz onto Willis Plantation and take charge! The court won't allow it, unless and until the case is settled!"

"Jesus, Angus! Are you serious?" replied James, the grin of elation quickly fading from his face. He had assumed the judge's ruling was all that stood in the way of his family taking possession of the plantation- and he was expecting he and his brother would be instrumental in implementing the takeover.

"Dead serious!" responded Angus. "If ya don't believe me, go ask Aldrich yourself!"

"Go ask Aldrich what?" inquired Michael, butting into the conversation after loudly congratulating his uncles, and thanking Mr. Owens for their victory.

James turned to his brother and informed him, "Angus here says Bauskett's gonna file an appeal of the case immediately on the grounds of a mistrial, an fight us on this! He says we can't just go onto Willis Plantation and take charge of anything until the issue's settled in court!"

"Damn, Angus! Are you sure about that?" Michael answered, crestfallen.

"Like I said, if ya'll don't believe me, go ask Aldrich yaselves!" insisted Angus.

The Willis brothers accosted Mr. Aldrich saying, "Mr. Aldrich! Angus here says Mr. Bauskett's gonna contest Uncle Elijah's original will and that till it's settled, we can't take over the plantation! Is that true?"

"I'm afraid it is, boys! It's unclear as to who has custodianship, because there are purportedly two wills with different executors. The newer will passed probate in Ohio before the older will was proved here, and until the legitimacy of one is proven over the other, ya'll have no rights to control your uncle's property in any way unless a court appoints someone to oversee it," he explained. "The court'd not likely appoint any possible legatee as overseer, since it is their right to inherit that is in question and under consideration by the court in the first place!"

"So what're we supposed to do in the meantime?" asked James.

"Well sir, we'll have to wait til it goes to trial, that's all," responded Mr. Aldrich.

"Damn!" swore James under his breath, his frustration and disappointment abundantly clear. "How long's that supposed to take?" he asked.

"Hard to say, exactly. First thing is the Court has to give us a date- and that date'll depend on which judge is assigned to hear the case, and how full that judge's calendar is with other cases. As soon as we get a court date set, the lawyers for both sides'll have to identify any witnesses they intend to call, interview each one, and share with each other the information each witness offers in testimony, so each lawyer knows what to expect, and can figure out how they want to mount their arguments." Aldrich explained. "Some a that, a course, we've already done- and Mr. Bauskett has too."

"And then?" Michael asked.

"Then we'll get to court, and the judge'll take us through the jury selection process. Once a jury's chosen the trial'll begin, and it'll take as long as it takes to present the arguments, rebut them, and deliberate a verdict. The judge'll ask for the jury's verdict- and then may have his own comments to make before issuin a rulin." Mr. Owens chimed in, having by now joined the conversation.

"Sweet Jesus!" uttered James in disgust. "All that, just to decide what everybody knows- that Uncle Elijah was crazy an had no right to leave his plantation to that nigra? Shit! I thought it was clear South Carolina law doesn't allow slaves to inherit!"

"Well, it doesn't! But what this case'll hang on is first- whether the will ya uncle wrote up in Ohio is, in whole or in part, a valid will that supercedes the one he wrote back here in '46. Then, if it is, the court'll have to decide whether the nigras he supposedly freed are in fact free; and then if they are, whether they have any right to inherit down here in South Carolina! So ya see son, it ain't quite as simple as it seems!" Mr. Owens explained.

"Aw Hell! Sounds to me like this could drag on for months!" swore James.

"For months or even longer- years maybe- dependin on what the outcome is! Even if the judge rules in ya'll's favor, Bauskett could appeal it up to the Supreme Court if he wants ta. Course, the high court'd have to agree to hear the case, an even that could take a while. So ya'll'd best keep calm and be ready for the long haul, cause this case could take quite some time to settle!" Aldrich informed them.

"Angus! Ain't there anything else we can do to get through this faster?" James asked his friend in desperation.

"Not really! Just pray that the court rules in ya'll's favor from the outset. Bauskett can demand a retrial, but the Judge doesn't necessarily have to grant it. We'll just have to wait an find out which judge we get and then see what happens," Angus answered.

The Willis brothers were fuming, but there was nothing for it but to surrender to the process. They were determined not to give up, for they were both convinced, as were their uncles, that the original will was more valid than the new one, and therefore protected what they had always considered their God-given rights to the property. After all, they thought, the whole purpose of having a plantation in the first place was to pass wealth from generation to generation in the same family- and blacks simply couldn't count as part of a white family, it was that simple.

John Jolliffe opened the letter from John Bauskett with some trepidation. He was eager to know what had transpired with the probate of the will, but he was not optimistic it had been proved without a contest. Of course, his suspicions were well founded, as he soon discovered from Bauskett's careful account of the proceedings.

My Dear Mr. Jolliffe:

It is my sorry duty to inform you that, just as we anticipated, Elijah's will did not pass probate. The Willis family members mounted an attack, insisting the original will was the only valid one, and Judge David Wardlaw, upon reading both wills, simply ruled the Cincinnati will could not even be entered for probate, as it violated the terms of the Act of 1841 of the South Carolina General Assembly, rendering it invalid.

Needless to say, I filed an appeal immediately, as I felt the judge's ruling clearly violated both the facts and the law. We have been scheduled a jury trial in the Court of Appeals for the Fall Term of 1856. The wait is maddening, but they claim the case load is so full that that is the soonest the case can be tried. Fortunately, however, the Honorable John Belton O'Neall will be presiding.

That is a good thing, as Judge Wardlaw is a well-known sympathizer with the secessionist movement, and has always upheld the positions espoused by the planters. Judge O'Neall, however, is much more balanced in his judicial approach. Not having been raised among the elite himself, he is more sympathetic to the realities of the lives of others. That should work to our benefit. That being said, however, as this will be a trial by a jury of Elijah's peers, there is certainly the possibility that social biases down here may trump judicial wisdom. We shall just have to play it out and see.

I feel, therefore, that as sole executor of Elijah's estate, (at least according to the terms of his most recent will), it is incumbent upon you to press the case in person as the plaintiff. I shall keep you apprised of any developments in the meantime, but suggest you begin to prepare to spend some time down here with us in South Carolina in the near future!

I have informed Amy's brother, Gilbert, of the situation, and instructed him to keep careful guard over the plantation. By South Carolina, law he is both entitled and required to protect his master's property- no matter who his master ultimately is determined to be.

Please inform Amy and her family of these developments, and assure her we are doing everything possible to expedite the legal procedures to arrive at a just and swift conclusion. That being said, however, she must also be urged to exercise the utmost patience and not give in to despair or frustration due to the ponderous pace with which the judicial process is often known to move. Given that lawyers sometimes look at precedents going back centuries, the term "swift" being linked with "justice" is of a decidedly more relative nature in matters of the law than in its more common usage!

In the meantime I have set myself to the task of interviewing witnesses for discovery and gathering affidavits where necessary, so that when you do arrive we shall be able to analyze their content and determine the best strategy for presenting their testimony.

If there is anything else you or Mr. Gitchell would have me do in preparation for the trial please do not hesitate to contact me at your earliest convenience.

Collegially yours,

John Bauskett

"Well James, it seems I am to make a journey to South Carolina! Just as we anticipated, Elijah's family moved to block the probate of the will and an initial hearing refused to even submit it for probate on the grounds that it violates the Act of 1841 of their South Carolina General Assembly." Jolliffe informed his partner, handing him the letter for his perusal.

"Daniel into the lions' den, eh?" mused Gitchell. "I'm sure they're salivating at the very thought of getting their paws on a bona fide Yankee Abolitionist lawyer!"

"No doubt they are!" Jolliffe agreed, with a chuckle, "But let's just hope they also remember that by the grace of God Almighty, Daniel triumphed in the end!"

"And so shall we, my friend. As, by that same grace of God, we must! Let us analyze their Act of 1841 for starters. No doubt Mr. Bauskett can provide us a copy and summary with case law references as to the history of its application," Gitchell insisted. "It's good he has also begun interviewing witnesses. We have a few here whose affidavits we could also provide- Ernst and Harwood, and the others who were willing to serve as executors, at the very least."

"I feel I should go inform Amy and her family so they are prepared and feel they have a grasp of what is happening. She may also help provide some additional insight that will be useful for our preparation." Jolliffe announced.

"Excellent idea! While you do that, I shall compose a letter to John Bauskett, requesting the contents of the Act of 1841, and any other documentation he might deem useful, as well as confirming that you will certainly travel to South Carolina to represent Amy's interests in person for the both of us." Gitchell confirmed with relish, eager to engage in what he considered one of the signature cases of their career.

"You do realize, John, that should we win this case, we may be setting a precedent that will empower future victories against the entire slave-holding establishment and perhaps even help hasten its abolition altogether?" Gitchell declared enthusiastically.

"God willing, my friend- we shall triumph not only for Amy and her family but for the countless others still in thrall of men whose own consciences should accuse them of so heinous a crime against humanity!" Jolliffe, in private, tended to wax eloquent on the high morality of their goal with no less enthusiasm than his partner. He was just more circumspect in declaring it publicly.

Having agreed to their respective tasks, Jolliffe then left his partner to his correspondence and set out to pay Amy a visit to bring her up to date on these recent developments.

When he reached the Dumas House he was informed by the desk clerk that Amy and her family were not there. They had gone out together that morning, and the clerk was under the impression from overhearing their conversation, that they were looking for someplace to settle down. Seems they had hired a hack to take them around in their search.

John Jolliffe felt a pang of guilt that he and Mr. Gitchell had still not managed to find the time to help Amy and the family relocate to more acceptable housing. He was worried she might have difficulty trying to negotiate lodging on her own, but he had to admire her determination not to remain dependent upon others, no matter how well meaning they might be!

He asked the clerk for pen and paper, and wrote a note to Amy to let her know the recent developments.

My Dear Miss Amy:

First let me say how sorry I am not to have stopped by sooner to assist you with your search for alternative lodging. The clerk informs me you and your family have embarked on your own search. I sense your urgency and feel ashamed I have not been prompter in my response to your daily needs, so consumed have James and I been in pursuing your legal ones. Please forgive us.

I shall be more than happy to assist in making the necessary arrangements, or vouch for you, should you find anything to your liking.

I stopped by today principally to bring you up to date on recent news from South Carolina. I would prefer to speak in person, but wanted to at least give you a basic outline of the situation as it currently stands.

As we expected, the will did not pass probate on the first try. It was denied admission for probate in a decree pro forma, on the grounds that it violates the Act of 1841 of the South Carolina General Assembly.

John Bauskett has filed an immediate appeal, certain that the ruling is in violation of both the facts and the law. I will go join him in South Carolina to press the case before the appellate court. We are awaiting a specific court date, but are told it will not be until the Fall Session of the Court in 1856 due to the heavy case load of the court. That is an onerous period to have to wait, but alas, we are at the court's mercy in this matter and have no recourse to insist on an earlier date!

In the meantime, Mr. Bauskett is interviewing the people you identified as potential witnesses in preparation, as well as reviewing pertinent case law and specifically, the text of the Act of 1841 upon which Judge Wardlaw based his original ruling against the Cincinnati will.

Your brother Gilbert has also been informed of the situation, and Mr. Bauskett has authorized him to protect the plantation- by force if necessary (God willing it won't be).

I shall keep you apprised of any further developments. In the meantime, please let us know how your housing search has gone and what we can do to assist you.

Most Sincerely,

John Jolliffe

When he finished the letter, he carefully folded it and wrote Amy's name on the outside. "Please be sure to give this to Mrs. Willis as soon as she returns. It's very important that she get it right away," he instructed the clerk.

"Yessir, Mr. Jolliffe, don't you worry, I'll make sure she gets it as soon as she comes in!"

With that Jolliffe bade him farewell and left for his office, so as to give his partner some assistance in setting up the interviews of the witnesses available in Cincinnati. He assumed the South Carolinians would attempt to impugn Elijah's character- and probably his very sanity- so he wanted to make sure from the outset that they addressed in their discovery all questions of his mental state and demeanor in a straightforward way.

Oh Lordy! Momma! What're we gonna do?" Amy moaned, having read her mother the letter from John Jolliffe."We can't just keep goin on here in this boardin house! The boys are climbin the walls for want of somethin to do, the girls are fussin more an more- even little Savage is pitchin fits, bein cooped up in this place! They're all pesterin Mr. Dumas to the point a him losin patience with em! And poor Gilbert must be fit to be tied. This is gonna drag on an on!" Amy was sinking into despair, seeing that all her cherished dreams of freedom- bringing Gilbert and the others up from South Carolina, settling on a nice farm in Ohio, being self-sufficient, and educating her children- seemed to be going up in smoke.

"Was I a fool, Momma, to push Elijah so hard to bring us up here?" she asked plaintively, "I was thinkin we'd be so much better off, an here we are with no Elijah, no income, nine mouths to feed, no home of our own, livin at the mercy of a coupla white lawyers, and no guarantee we'll ever be able to sell the property down home!" Amy said, full of self-recrimination. "Not only that, how we gonna be able to free Gilbert and his children and the others if we can't get the will through probate? He an Julius and Jason and their families must think they've been abandoned, stuck down there in Williston!"

"The Good Lord knows it ain't your fault, child, things turned out the way they did! And no, ya wasn't no fool to fight for freedom! Woulda been a fool not to!" Momma Celia reassured her daughter. "Things may not feel better right now- we ain't livin high in a plantation house an all like we was- but just think about how bad things woulda a been if Elijah had died back home with all of us there and his wicked relations swoopin down on the plantation like a bunch a buzzards, wantin to punish us for spoilin the family name!" She gave an involuntary shudder of horror at the very thought of it. "Them fools'd probably blame us for his death, all the while they was rubbin they greedy hands together over gettin his property, an they'd a took it outa our hides too! Mark my words!"

Momma Celia's stoic clarity was both sobering and comforting. It was just the tonic Amy needed to snap her out of spiraling downward into a deep depression and wallowing in self-pity. She could almost hear Elijah reminding her of Joseph saying, "You meant it for evil, but God meant it for good!" She heaved a heavy sigh, wiped the tears streaking her cheeks, nodded, and smiled at her mother.

"You're right Momma, things could be a whole lot worse! Elder and Elleck are old enough to get jobs now, and you an I might be able to find some ways to bring some money in too. There're a few colored owned businesses here in town I might be able to find work in as a clerk, or somethin. After all, I ran a very profitable plantation down South- I oughta be able put that knowledge to work somehow!"

"You plenty smart, sugar, but don't count on no business hirin ya. They don't know ya and might not trust ya – not just cause ya colored, but a woman to boot! But ya'll got one big advantage- ya know how to read and write and work with numbers! I don't know how many of the colored folks up here know how to do that since back home it ain't legally allowed. Maybe it ain't allowed up here either, or at least not too common. We was lucky Elijah supported his slaves gettin a education in secret. Served him well, but it served us too." Momma reflected, ever the realist.

"You may be right Momma, but I'm gonna have to try to find work, if only to keep from goin stir crazy sittin in this damned boardin house all day! Elder told me he heard they were lookin for workers over in the brickyard. He wants to see if they'll take him an his brother on. Said there's a mulatto fella, Manuel Ash, runs the place. Might be he could also use someone to help keep their books!"

"Could be, honey. Ya ain't got nothin to lose by askin, cause if ya'll ask me, settin round here just waitin for the wheel of white folks' law to turn our way might be a mighty long wait!" Momma Celia said philosophically. "Phillip may be young, but he's like his uncle Gilbert- big and strong. No reason he can't work with his brothers too! If you an the boys can get work, I can take care a the girls and little Savage. I'm too ole to go lookin for work- sides, somebody's gotta do the work a takin care a this family!"

Amy began to see a way out of the pit she felt they were stuck in, now that it was clear that they couldn't simply sit passively and wait for the plantation to be sold as their source of financial well-being, no matter how many lawyers they had working away at making that possible. They would have to start exercising that freedom they'd just won and start building a new life for themselves- with or without the benefits of Elijah's hard earned assets or a couple of white lawyers to support them! Time to stop mourning and start working!

The more she thought about it, the better it actually felt not to wait on Messrs. Gitchell's and Jolliffe's largesse- as kind as they had been. For it was also clear to her that both of them saw her situation as part of a larger story of emancipation and the abolition of the entire institution of slavery. It was a cause to which they were deeply and sincerely committed, but which so consumed them that they sometimes overlooked the more mundane daily necessities confronting her and the children. At times she felt almost like a pawn in that game. Not that she wasn't proud to take part in that struggle- but she was frankly more focused on her family's immediate survival than on making any grand political statements at this point.

Amy now realized that work was not only something they needed for essential income to make ends meet, they needed it for their psychological well-being too. After all, slavery may have taught them many harsh lessons, but hard work was no stranger to them and nothing they feared. In fact, they were so long accustomed to it that the possibility that they themselves, rather than someone else, might reap its rewards was something they eagerly embraced. They had not wanted to be free so they could be indolent, like some of the planters she knew and loathed. She wanted all of them to exercise their God-given abilities to build lives of their own choosing instead of the choosing of someone who claimed ownership over them, even with love! She decided she would like to pay this Manuel Ash at the brickyard a visit herself and see if she couldn't find a way to start building that new life after all. It was both oddly exhillerating and somewhat frightening to even realize this was a choice she could make without anyone else's permission.

On May 22, 1856, exactly one year after Elijah Willis's death in Cincinnati, South Carolina Representative to the United States Congress Preston Brooks entered the Senate chamber and savagely beat Massachusetts Senator Charles Sumner, actually breaking his heavy gold knobbed cane over Sumner's head and causing him such severe damage that he was unable to resume his seat in the Senate for a full three years! The assault had been provoked, according to Brooks, by the outrageous and libelous speech given by Sumner calling for the immediate admission of Kansas as a slave-free state. Sumner, according to Brooks, committed the unforgivable sin of criticizing and dishonoring the Kansas Act's sponsors, Brooks' relative and fellow South Carolinian Senator Andrew Butler, and Illinois Senator Stephen A. Douglas as immoral for their promotion of slavery.

The Kansas Act had permitted the Kansas Territory to determine for herself whether or not slavery would be permitted within her borders. To the Northerners, and especially the pro-abolitionists, this was anathema.

Sumner said in his speech,

"The senator from South Carolina has read many books of chivalry, and believes himself a chivalrous knight with sentiments of honor and courage. Of course he has chosen a mistress to whom he has made his vows, and who, though ugly to others, is always lovely to him; though polluted in the sight of the world, is chaste in his sight -- I mean the harlot, slavery. For her his tongue is always profuse in words. Let her be impeached in character, or any proposition made to shut her out from the extension of her wantonness, and no extravagance of manner or hardihood of assertion is then too great for this senator."

Sumner speaking thus of the bill authored by the Congressman's relative as embracing the harlot of slavery, raping a virgin territory and forcing it into its polluting embrace cut too close to home for Mr. Brooks. He knew full well how many white planters forced themselves upon their slaves with impunity as their sort of *droit de seigneur*, and it made him apoplectic to have their dirty laundry publicly aired with such Yankee sanctimony.

The responses to this outrage were widespread and unambiguous. The Cincinnati Gazette said,

"The South cannot tolerate free speech anywhere, and would stifle it in Washington with the bludgeon and the bowie-knife, as they are now trying to stifle it in Kansas by massacre, rapine, and murder."

William Cullen Bryant of the New York Evening Post, asked,

"Has it come to this, that we must speak with bated breath in the presence of our Southern masters?... Are we to be chastised as they chastise their slaves? Are we too, slaves, slaves for life, a target for their brutal blows, when we do not comport ourselves to please them?"

As a measure of the times, despite this Yankee outrage, rather than Brooks being severely chastised for the beating, he was lauded by Southerners everywhere. So much so, that he was inundated by the gift of hundreds of gold knobbed walking sticks to replace the one broken over Senator Sumner's head- some even bearing inscriptions like *"Beat him again!"*- lest he ever run out of weapons in time of need! South Carolinians rejoiced that one of their own had literally and metaphorically struck such a blow for their sacred values.

When the probate of Elijah Willis's will came up for appeal before the court in Barnwell District, a few months after this notorious beating, the region was still resonating to Mr. Brooks' bold act, and it was abundantly clear that the climate would not look favorably on Elijah's cause.

The Barnwell District Court House had seldom seen such a crowd gather. Word had gotten out that there was to be a trial to determine whether Elijah Willis had the right to free his enslaved family and leave them his plantation, or whether his white relations had sole intrinsic rights to the inheritance. Folks came from miles around, partly because the trial promised to include some lively debate and might be right entertaining to see. But they were also drawn to come because the subject touched on the lives of a great many more white folks in the area than most would openly acknowledge. The vested interests of the ruling class being what they were in Barnwell District, the potential implications of the case's outcome were a matter of keen interest and the utmost importance to nearly everyone- especially the younger generation of whites who stood to win or lose the most, according to the verdict. More than a few were hoping to serve on the jury; some of them to make sure things went the right way!

John Jolliffe had made the trip from Cincinnati a week before and had been the houseguest of John and Eugenia Bauskett. His visit had provided both of them an opportunity to pore over the case law enshrined both in John's books, and in the collection he had inadvertently inherited from Angus Patterson Senior via Elijah as well. It had also allowed Mr. Jolliffe the opportunity to meet a junior colleague of John Bauskett's, Mr. Bellinger who would be assisting, as well as a chance to meet most of the witnesses. Together, the three lawyers had been able to take all the necessary depositions to build their case for the trial.

"Well John, ya'd best be prepared for how things're done down here in Carolina," Bauskett prepped his colleague as they drove to the courthouse. "The judge may seem informal in some manners a speakin, but don't let that fool ya. He'll be expectin ya to mind your p's an q's- especially cause ya're a Yankee!" Bauskett cautioned.

"Now I've been in touch with Owens and Aldrich, the lawyers for Mr. Fanning and Mr. Phillips- Elijah's brothers-in-law, who were assigned as executors of his previous will. But it's really Jimmy Willis's sons, James and Michael, who're driving this whole fight," Bauskett digressed.

"Owens and Aldrich're planning to claim not only that your Cincinnati will's invalid on the grounds of the Act of 1841, but also they're gonna claim Elijah was insane, an alcoholic, and subject to the undue influence of Amy's coercion to write the will in the first place! They'll want to paint that as fraud too!" added Bellinger.

"In other words, they're clutchin at straws for anything they can think of that might make the judge discredit Elijah and nullify the will," concluded Bauskett.

"Just as my colleague Mr. Gitchell and I expected," affirmed Jolliffe. "I think we are fully prepared to meet this challenge on all points, gentlemen!" he added with confidence.

"The one wild card in this hand is gonna be the jury," Bauskett cautioned. "The oligarchy of white planters down here is dead set against abolition or even emancipation on an individual basis- even though more'n a few of em have their own colored mistresses and children. The legal arguments are gonna have to be well constructed and carefully worded to persuade a jury of Elijah's social peers that he could give his plantation to Amy and her children, which to them is a much bigger threat than freein em in the first place!"

Jolliffe knew he needed to be discreet even with Bauskett and Bellinger, not wishing to offend. He was not entirely sure how sensitive they were to criticism of the institution of slavery, being as how they were surrounded by it and of necessity had to deal with it on a daily basis. He assumed they could not sanely do so if all they felt was anger and opprobrium for it.

"I imagine it must be a challenge for you gentlemen to seek justice for those to whom justice is in part at least, constitutionally denied," Jolliffe commented.

"Well sir, it surely can be. But the thing is, when ya're livin in this world ya begin to see things a little differently. It's not easy to deal in theoretical absolutes down here, no matter whether ya're for or against the condition of slavery. There are a lot of good folks down here who don't like slavery, especially when they see some slaveowners abusin their slaves and makin em suffer somethin awful, but they still see it as a necessary evil, without which the entire economy would collapse," Bauskett explained.

"There are others, though- some of whom you may see in the courtroom today- who are sincerely convinced that the Negro is a fundamentally and irrevocably inferior creature, little better than livestock and incapable of either thinkin or feelin as we do, and that slavery is a genuinely positive good for the slaves as well as for their masters!" insisted Mr. Bellinger. "Of course, sincerity is not a measure of truth and never has been- folks can be, and often are, sincerely wrong!" he added.

"True, but they may still win the day with their delusion if their sincerity is shared by the majority of their ilk, or by the judge!" cautioned Bauskett. "Therein lies our challenge in court!"

As the carriage drove up to the courthouse entrance, the three lawyers looked out the window and immediately realized they would have quite an audience listening to their arguments on Elijah's behalf, including more than a few free blacks and even some slaves who were accompanying their masters. Both Angus Patterson's housekeeper Mary, and Dr. Guignard's housekeeper Sally and her nephew were to be seen climbing the stairs to the segregated Negro seating in the gallery.

The three attorneys couldn't help but wonder how many of the crowd filing into the courthouse would be persuaded by Elijah's kindness, honesty, and forthright reputation. How many, on the other hand, would look no further than the words 'manumission" and "inheritance" and slam the doors of their minds shut, admitting no further entrance to any ideas that might shed a new and different light on the subject?

Messrs. Owens and Aldrich shepherded Mr. Fanning, Mr. Phillips, James, Michael, and various other Willis relations into the courthouse with imperious gestures as if escorting royalty, expecting the crowd to part and cede passage to the protagonists of this judicial drama.

The crowd, of course, consisted not only of planters and their wives, but also of townspeople, merchants, and various friends and acquaintances of Elijah's who were there to serve as witnesses. It didn't help the planters' cause that many of those attending still had a fairly dim view of James and Michael as drunken ne'er do wells, though that impression had been somewhat mitigated by them joining forces with the well-spoken Angus Patterson Junior in the rally a few years back. Still, the planters showing up in force easily overrode such negative impressions, if not by conviction then at least by their presence having an intimidating effect on many townsfolk, who feared the possibility of being looked down upon by the ruling class for any support they might give for the opposition. The impetus toward the imperative of white solidarity may not have cut completely across lines of class distinction, but it damned near did.

The lawyers contesting the Cincinnati will made no attempt to socialize with their opponents, preferring to engage in affable conversation not only with their clients, but with various and sundry members of the audience, clearly courting their favor, knowing that some might serve as jurors. John Jolliffe caught snatches of their remarks, generally whispered with a grin:

"I know we can count on ya'll to stand up for our cherished values," or,

"I hope ya'll'll feel free to defend the rights upon which our proper society is built down here!"

Messrs. Aldrich and Owens were careful not to actually suggest specifically what position folks should take, lest the judge disqualify them for jury duty upon questioning or accuse the lawyers of tampering, but the way they worded their remarks left nothing to the imagination of the locals as to what they were referring. Some nodded and grinned back, others seemed slightly uncomfortable being approached. It was hard to tell whether the strategy would be effective in shaping the ultimate outcome of the jury selection, much less the jury's verdict.

Both John Jolliffe and John Bauskett watched the responses carefully to get a sense of which way the prevailing winds of opinion might be blowing. The truth was that despite the anti-Negro, racist sentiments enshrined in public policy, there were subtler forces within white society that constituted potentially powerful cross-currents to the simplistic rejection of all rights for blacks. The sacred cow of this quasi-feudal planter society was the individual planter's rights to self-determination and to the freedom to use his property in any way he saw fit. Most planters resented anyone- including other planters- telling them what they could or couldn't do with their own property, whether land or slaves. Consequently, some saw Elijah as simply exercising his God-given rights, even if in a way of which they might personally disapprove. The important thing was to stand up for his right to do so, lest they themselves end up forfeiting their own right to do the same. Solidarity was then not simply a black-white issue, but a class issue in which notions of individual rights and privilege played an enormous role.

As he and John Jolliffe were watching their opponents' lawyers working the crowd, John Bauskett spotted Joseph Harley and signaled for him to come over as they headed toward the front of the courtroom.

"Joseph, this is John Jolliffe, the Cincinnti lawyer whom Elijah named as executor of his current will. John, this is Dr. Joseph Harley, of whom we spoke earlier." Bauskett introduced the two. "Joseph, your testimony as Elijah's physician may be key here, as I'm certain the Willises are goin to attempt to claim he suffered from insanity, and maybe alcoholism too."

Dr. Harley nodded to Jolliffe and shook his hand warmly saying, "Pleased to meet ya, Mr. Jolliffe, I've heard a lotta good things about ya, sir." Then, turning to Bauskett he answered, "Don't worry John, I'm fully prepared to declare I saw no evidence of insanity or mental instability in him at all."

The bailiff by then was asking folks to take their seats, so Bauskett, Jolliffe and Bellinger excused themselves and headed on up to their table facing the judge's bench. A gated fence at the end of the aisle indicated the legal line of demarcation between the public and the principal parties much like a communion rail separated the sanctuary and the altar from the nave of a church. The architectural parallel was probably not accidental, as the judge and lawyers considered the courtroom a virtual temple of justice, with the judge serving as the celebrant, and the lawyers, bailiff, and clerk as his deacons and acolytes, the jury occupying the place of the choir.

The excited chatter of the crowd slowly died down under the bailiff's stern and expectant gaze, and he finally announced with clarion voice, "All Rise! The Court of Appeals of Barnwell District, in the Great State of South Carolina, is now in session! Judge John Belton O'Neall, presidin!"

Judge O'Neall made his entrance with rather less drama than Judge Wardlaw. Sixty-three years of age, he was tall and lanky with a shock of white hair combed over to one side of a high, intelligent forehead. His face was long and craggy, but not severe. There was a warmth and kindness in his large eyes and an unassuming air in his stance that inspired trust. Unlike many on the South Carolina bench who had risen to prominence more as a result of social connections and privilege than personal merit, O'Neall had been raised in humbler circumstances, and like Henry Clay and other notable frontier lawyers and legislators of the beginning of the nation's first century, he had earned his law education by hard work, personal charisma, and undeniable ability. This had won him the respect of the rich and poor alike.

Taking his seat, Judge O'Neall brought down his gavel and called the court to order. "Mornin, ladies and gentlemen! It is my understandin that this court is called into session to deliberate the validity of a will and its acceptability for probate. The will was written by the testator Elijah Willis, of Williston, Barnwell District, South Carolina, in Cincinnati, Ohio on the 23rd of February of 1854, of which the plaintiff, John Jolliffe, Esquire, a lawyer of that city, is named sole executor. Mr. Willis had written an earlier will here in South Carolina, of which Mr. Fanning and Mr. Phillips, the late Mr. Willis' brothers-in-law, were named executors, in 1846. The Cincinnati will was proved in the probate court of Hamilton County, Ohio on May 23rd, 1855. The earlier will was admitted into probate here in South Carolina shortly thereafter, on June 12th, 1855, and the more recent Cincinnati will was refused probate by the Ordinary here in Barnwell District. Mr. Jolliffe and his able colleague, our own Mr. John Bauskett, entered an immediate appeal, hence we are here today. Is this also ya'll's understandin?" Judge O'Neall asked the counselors.

Each responded in turn, "It is, Your Honor."

"Well, alright then," answered the judge. "So, before we proceed to hearin the arguments for and against the respective wills, I must inform ya'll that this is to be a jury trial. Therefore, we must first proceed to the task of selectin the jury members." The audience shifted expectantly in their seats, many hoping to serve, others dreading the possibility.

"Now the law of South Carolina places some constraints on who may or may not serve on a jury," Judge O'Neall went on to explain, "and though our ancient precedents in British Common Law, as well as our United States' Constitution and Bill of Rights, secure the right of all citizens to a trial by a jury of their peers, this of course excludes the testimony of slaves, and in South Carolina, restricts the jury selection to white male citizens." He let this last phrase hang in the air with apparent irony- implicitly recognizing that such jury candidates were, by dint of exclusive race and gender, inherently not the peers of all possible litigants in the justice system.

"Now then, before we go to the actual selection of the jury, let me ask ya'll how many of you folks here today have been asked by any of the lawyers here, or their representatives, to serve as a witness in this trial?" A goodly number of hands were raised.

"Alright then, I must instruct those of ya that raised ya hands, none of ya'll may serve on the jury!" Judge O'Neall announced. "Counselors, has the clerk a the court provided ya'll with a list of potential jurors?"

"He has, Your Honor," they all agreed.

"And do ya'll see any of your witnesses on that list?" Judge O'Neall continued to ask.

The lawyers scanned the names on their respective lists, and nodded. "Yessir."

"Well then, I'm instructing ya'll to strike from the list any names either party has identified to this court as a potential witness," the judge ordered. The lawyers dutifully complied.

"We'll go through the list of whoever's left in alphabetical order. When I call your name please stand, identify yaself, and answer the questions ya're asked. Understood?" The remaining potential jurors variously nodded or mumbled their assent, and the tedious process began.

The lawyers for both sides, needless to say, were jockeying, trying to get the jurors they thought might be most sympathetic to their cause. This meant that Messrs. Owens and Aldrich sought to select a jury composed almost exclusively of planters, presuming they would be innately supportive of the Willis family complaint. Messrs. Joliffe and Bauskett, on the other hand, wanted a more balanced group comprised of merchants, townsfolk and planters- preferably people without intrinsically preferential connections to the white members of the Willis family. Unfortunately, some of their best choices were excluded because they were more urgently needed as witnesses.

Eventually, after several hours of questioning a full complement of jurors was reached. Judge O'Neall announced, "Alright, ya'll! Now let me tell ya how this works! You folks who are now on the jury- each of ya has a number from one ta twelve. We've also chosen three alternates, who will participate in the trial and sit with ya'll, but will not join in the final deliberations on the verdict unless one of the twelve of ya is indisposed at the time a deliberation. Ya'll're not allowed to discuss your deliberations outside the jury room with anyone, not even your wives or sweethearts, until after the verdict has been delivered. I don't know yet how long this is gonna take, but ya'll are bound by oath ta keep showin up every day until the job is done. D'ya'll understand?"

The band of jurors and their alternates all confirmed, "Yes, Your Honor."

"Well alright then, Bailiff- swear em in!" O'Neall ordered.

The bailiff stepped forward and instructed the jurors "Raise your right hands. Do ya'll solemnly swear to faithfully and honestly discharge your duties to this Court, as instructed by Judge O'Neall, so help ya God?"

Each of the jurors answered, "I do!"

The bailiff then stepped aside, and Judge O'Neall instructed the jurors, "Alright then folks, take your seats in the jury box accordin to your designated number. Juror number one will serve as your foreman- he'll be the spokesman for the whole lot a ya. And might I remind ya, ya'll'll remain under oath until this is all over. Understood?" He was met with a bobble of nods.

James and Michael, already bored by what they considered the unnecessary tediousness of the proceedings, turned to Angus and said in a stage whisper clearly audible to Judge O'Neall, "Jesus, Angus! How long is this nonsense gonna take?"

Judge O'Neall glared at the Willis boys as Angus tried to shush them. "Counselors!" he barked with a stentorian voice, "I recommend ya'll instruct your clients not to go interruptin this trial or my courtroom with their comments about 'this nonsense,' or they'll be held in contempt a court! Do I make myself perfectly clear?"

Mr. Aldrich immediately responded with abject apology "Yessir, Your Honor! Sorry, Your honor, won't happen again, Your Honor!" while his partner, Mr. Owens turned to stare fiercely at the Willis brothers and whispered under his breath, "Keep your damn mouths shut if ya'll wanna win this thing, boys, or there'll be Hell to pay!"

Judge O'Neall went on to give instructions to the lawyers, the court clerk, the bailiff, the sherriff, and the general public about the do's and don't of court procedure, and what was to be expected of each of them, respectively. This took quite a while. By the time he had completed his preparatory instructions it was midday, so he called for a recess.

"Bailiff, take the jurors to the jury room! Ya'll'll remain sequestered there throughout the day when court is not in session. Ya'll are free to discuss the trial amongst yaselves durin your sequestration, but ya may not solicit votes or attempt to sway any other juror's opinion, so's each of ya can make your own decision as to the truth of the matter. If any of ya need to answer a call a nature while sequestered, notify the sheriff, he can get ya a thunder mug or lead ya to the privy," the judge instructed them.

The bailiff ordered the jurors to rise and follow him, and the sheriff led them out a side door to a large room supplied with a dining sized table and chairs. Several ladies of the town had sent in food baskets to provide them sustenance, and they all settled down to take an impromptu lunch while the bailiff returned to the courtroom.

Satisfied that the jury had been duly sequestered, Judge O'Neall brought down his gavel and announced, "Court adjourned for lunch. We'll reconvene at two o'clock this afternoon!"

The bailiff once again ordered, "All Rise!" after which Judge O'Neal left for his chambers, and the crowd started filing out to go home, or to the one hotel in town that had a dining room, or to picnic in the open space next to the courthouse where the platform had been laid for a big new vertical sundial. Everyone was intent on getting something to eat, to build up their resistance before returning to the courthouse to endure the afternoon session.

"Good God Almighty!" exploded James, once they were outside. "That was the longest, most borin goddamn mornin I ever spent in my entire life!"

Mrs. Willis was following behind her sons, and overhearing James' expletives, smacked him fiercely on the arm with her fan, making him wince. "Hush your mouth, James Willis Junior! Shame on you! I'll not have you blasphemin in public! D'ya hear me?" she hissed in warning. "This trial is about our family honor and reputation! Bad enough one Willis has besmirched it! I'll not be havin you or Michael add insult to injury with foul language and inappropriate behavior! Do I make myself clear?" she scowled at both her sons, defying them to contradict her on pain of a punishment implicitly worse than death.

"Sorry Momma!" James whimpered, duly cowed.

"Yes'm!" echoed Michael, immediately, secretly reveling that it was James, and not he, who had received the rebuke, for a change. "But ya'll gotta admit Momma, it was awful borin!"

While the Willis clan was bemoaning the tedium of due process in front of the courthouse, John Jolliffe and John Bauskett remained inside, talking quietly in the corridor outside the courtroom.

"Well John, what do ya think of our justice system down here in South Carolina?" Bauskett asked his northern colleague, enunciating the words "justice system" with a slight trace of sarcasm.

"Well, I'd say your warnings about misleading appearances and the rigors of court propriety on Judge O'Neall's part were right on the money. But I also sensed a genuine fairness in the man- something I'd hoped for but had not dared actually expect, truth be told."

John Bauskett smiled, recognizing that his colleague was an astute observer of character and had read the judge well. "Very perceptive of ya, counselor! I quite agree! The issue here won't be Judge O'Neall's fairness but the jury's! I gotta tell ya, that line- up this morning was about as impartial as a pack a coonhounds lustin for blood an catchin a scent. The judge can instruct em all he wants to on how they're not to show partiality- but it's like instructin a huntin dog not ta eat meat. Most of em are here cause they're ready for the chase, and expectin to eat their fill when they finally run their prey to ground!"

The graphic analogy was not lost on Jolliffe, despite his urban sensibilities.

CXIV

Elder, Elleck, Phillip and Amy set out from the Dumas House for the brickyard, leaving Savage and the girls in Momma Celia's watchful care. They could see the chimneys of the brick kilns from a distance, and soon came upon the yard itself. Countless pallets of baked bricks were stacked haphazardly on one side. On the opposite side, under long shed roofs with removable tarpaulins to both let the sun in and to keep the rain off, as the situation demanded, sat rack upon rack of molds filled with wet clay. They were in various stages of drying before being stacked for firing in the two huge coal-fired ovens at the back of the yard. Along the front side of the yard, to the left of the big double gates through which wagons came and went to carry in their the coal and clay and carry out their cargo of bricks to local building sites, sat a low shed where the brickyard office could be found.

They opened the office door, and the four of them entered. Sitting behind a desk piled with crumpled and smudged invoices and various miscellaneous orders- for bricks, for clay, for coal for the ovens- sat a middle-aged, clean-shaven mulato man in an open shirt somewhat stained with red clay dust. His braces crossed a muscular chest, his sleeves partially rolled up, revealing strong, sinewy arms. A row of large, dusty windows and a door behind him gave onto the brickyard, from whence he could keep an eye on the workers in all parts of the establishment.

The man seemed flustered with the paperwork, as if it was the last thing in the world he wanted to be doing. From the looks of him, he was more naturally inclined to the production of the bricks than to handling the minutiae of marketing the finished product.

As the four strangers entered the office, he looked up. Noticing that one of them was a woman, he quickly rose to his feet in greeting.

"Are you Mr. Manuel Ash?" Elder asked.

"That's me, son, what can I do for ya?" Ash replied.

"Well, sir, uh, we heard ya'll might be lookin for workers to help out at the brickyard. Me an my brothers here need a job and thought maybe you might be willin to let us work for ya," Elder explained, eager to make a good impression and prove his maturity. "Oh, and this here's our Momma," he added.

Manuel Ash's eyes met Amy's, and he was immediately struck with the realization that this woman had a presence unlike any of the colored women he knew in Cincinnati. Unconsciously, even a little nervously, he smoothed back his hair and with a ready smile lighting his face, stretched out his hand saying, "Pleased to meet ya, ma'am!" He then shook hands with the boys as well.

Amy, appreciating his manners and looks, decided to speak up and tell him something of their plight. His large brown eyes were lively and sympathetic, and she decided to take a chance on trusting him. "Mr. Ash, I don't mean ta trouble ya, but we're recently arrived here in Cincinnati. I just lost my husband a year ago, and now we find ourselves in need of employment. Fact is, I ran a large plantation for my husband. He was a planter dealin in cotton and lumber down in South Carolina before he brought us up here. My poor Elijah died the day we arrived, but he'd kept his promise we'd be free! I can read an write and keep accounts too! So I was wonderin if maybe ya might wanna hire some help for the office as well as hirin my boys here for the labor?" She looked pointedly at the messy desk with a sweet smile and slightly raised eyebrows, as if to underscore that this was as much a rhetorical question or statement of fact deserving his acknowledgment as a request requiring his consent.

Manuel Ash was quite taken by Amy, and given her description of her skills and experience, was no longer wondering why she had such a presence. "I'm sorry to hear of your loss, Miz…?"

"Amy, Amy Willis," she replied, suddenly flushed.

"Miss Amy, then!" he flashed his smile. "To tell ya the truth Miss Amy, I wasn't expectin to hire quite so many at once, but as I guess ya'll can tell, though I can't pay ya much, I really could use some help both in the yard and with the paperwork!"

Amy smiled back at him, feeling encouraged and relieved that her first real foray into the world as a free woman had met with some success. To earn anything for themselves at all for the first time in their lives would be an amazing experience, and would surely help them survive. And, she told herself, there was still the chance that the lawyers would settle the estate soon. Then either Mr. Jolliffe or she could ultimately sell the plantation. She considered the brickyard no more than a temporary possibility to tide them over until the legal battle was won.

Focused as she was on the fulfillment of the dream she had envisioned with Elijah, it was simply too soon to willingly modify or exchange that dream for another one, or to fully accept the reality that God might have other plans. And though she was flattered by Manuel Ash's attention and felt an unexpected pleasure when he flashed her his smile, she was most definitely not yet ready to face the possibility that the charming Mr. Ash might in time come to be more than her or her sons' employer. Still, if she worked in the brickyard with him, she thought, the twinkle in his eye might make the time pass quicker. It just might help save her from the loneliness of the limbo in which she felt they were suspended, while white lawyers hundreds of miles away were arguing over subtle points of law upon which her and her family's future seemed to depend.

The afternoon session of the trial began with the lawyers laying out their arguments for and against the validity of Elijah's second will. In his opening statement, John Jolliffe insisted that the will had been voluntarily written by Elijah in proper legal form under the direct supervision of legal counsel, and in duplicate- one copy being kept by the testator and the second copy being kept in the safe of the law office of Messrs. Gitchell and Jolliffe, of which he was a partner. He also attested to the fact that both copies of the will were duly signed not only by Elijah Willis, but also by two prominent citizens and men of property, serving as witnesses in the City of Cincinnati. He further pointed out that Mr. Willis had come to Cincinnati alone and unaccompanied for the express purpose of drafting the will, after discussing the matter extensively with the Cincinnati attorneys by letter for more than a year before his arrival, showing that this decision was clearly premeditated and carefully considered.

John Bauskett also took the floor and informed the jury that by Ohio law, if a slave owner brought slaves into Ohio with the express intent of emancipating them, they would become free immediately upon setting foot on Ohio soil with no need for any further legal procedures or documentation other than proof of the express will of their master. As the will in Amy's possession at the time of Elijah's death in Cincinnati matched verbatim the will brought to the coroner's inquest at the Dumas House by Mr. Jolliffe, there was incontrovertible proof that it was, in fact, Elijah Willis's intention to emancipate Amy and her children in Ohio. That they had all disembarked onto Ohio soil minutes before the untimely death of the testator was evinced not only by the coroner's inquest and death certificate issued by Dr. Menzies, but even by the article in the New York Times dated May 25, 1855, describing the event. Moreover, Bauskett claimed, following the probate of the will in the Hamilton County Courthouse in Cincinnati, a deed of manumission for Amy, her mother, and seven children had been secured from the Court by Mr. Gitchell, leaving no further doubt as to their legal status as freed blacks. A certified copy of the deed of manumission was entered into evidence at Judge O'Neall's request.

The opening remarks of Mr. Aldrich, on the other hand, claimed that Elijah Willis was a degenerate man, fallen under the dual influence of drink and his Negro slave mistress, who was likewise dissolute. The moral depravity of the conditions in which the testator lived had, according to the lawyer, become a cause of great shame to him, provoking him to seek ever more refuge in the bottle, to the point that he was chronically depressed, withdrawn from society, frequently drunk, and mentally unstable. It was in this condition then, according to Mr. Aldrich, that the wicked Amy pressured him to take her, her mother, her Negro children by a former relationship, and the bastard children she had borne Mr. Willis, up to Cincinnati to emancipate them. It was further alleged that the will was written under false pretenses in an attempt to defraud the testator of his considerable property which he had already previously bequeathed in 1846 to his next of kin- the numerous relations of the extended Willis family living in Barnwell District- as tradition and propriety would expect.

Mr. Owens then took the floor to insist that the Act of 1841 of the General Assembly of the State of South Carolina specifically forbade the emancipation of slaves by will or devise, and furthermore prohibited the leaving of any material inheritance whatsoever to a slave. He claimed that the residence of a slave was determined not by the temporary location of either the slave or the master, but by the permanent domicile of the slave owner, which in the case of Elijah Willis, remained the Willis Plantation in Williston, Barnwell District, South Carolina! Moreover, the Act insisted that the only means of manumission possible in the State of South Carolina was via the petitioning of the General Assembly. No subsequent legislation had been enacted to date that might overturn all or part of said Act, so it was presumed to remain the law of the land, and in full force. As Amy and her children were all indisputably identified in the text of the will as slaves at the time the will was written, and no petition to manumit them, Mr. Owens hastened to point out, had ever been filed by Elijah Willis with the General Assembly, it could only be concluded that the slaves in question remained slaves, and could not be emancipated through this spurious and fraudulent will written in Cincinnati, nor be the legatees of any property whatsoever.

When the attorneys had all finished their opening remarks, Judge O'Neall spoke up. "Thank ya kindly, counselors, ya'll did a right good job a layin out the basic parameters and issues concernin this case. Seems to me, if I may clarify, that we do, however, have a number of issues to decide here. Now you gentlemen a the jury," he interrupted himself, "I want ya'll to pay close attention to what I'm sayin, so it'll guide ya'll in your deliberations!" The judge gave a stern look to the jury members, some of whom were looking glassy-eyed and befuddled from the lengthy barrage of juridical jargon and labyrinthine legal arguments.

The jury members shifted uneasily like school children caught napping by the teacher and sat up straighter in their chairs, duly chastened by the judge's exhortation.

"Now then, where was I?" Judge O'Neall wondered out loud, "Ah, yes!" he remembered. "First, ya'll gotta decide whether the will written in Cincinnati is a legal will. Then if it is, ya'll need to determine whether any of it is invalidated by the Act of 1841. Then ya'll gotta decide whether the Negroes Mr. Willis took with him to Cincinnati are slaves or free. Then ya'll need to figure out whether, if they're free, they are entitled to inherit any property here in South Carolina."

"In order to do all that," Judge O'Neall went on, "ya'll're also gonna have to wrestle with the matter a Mr. Willis's physical and mental health, and whether he suffered from any condition that would fundamentally impair his judgment. It will require ya'll ta put your own moral preferences aside to determine whether there is any legal evidence of fraud or coercion on the part of the Negro slaves allegedly liberated by Mr. Willis, or on the part of anyone else, for that matter! This isn't a trial about Mr. Willis's morality, but only about the legality of his actions and the strength of the evidence for or against em. Now let me make clear that the standards of evidence require it to be 'clear and convincin, beyond a reasonable doubt,' not mere hearsay!" he underscored.

Jolliffe, Bauskett, Owens and Aldrich were all furiously scratching notes as the judge elucidated his expectations of them.

Finally Judge O'Neall announced, "I think we've done about enough work for one day- I can see some of our jurors are lookin like they wished they'd paid a little more attention to their studies when they were comin up!" he chuckled. "Well that's alright! I promise ya, if ya'll pay attention, ya'll'll get quite an education here and learn a whole lot about the law in this trial!" He smiled at Jolliffe and Bauskett. "One more thing before we go to recess- I just wanna remind you jurors ya'll're still under oath, and the rule against discussin the trial outside the jury room extends to home or anywhere else ya'll might feel like goin when ya'll leave here this evenin!"

He brought down the gavel and announced, "Court adjourned until ten o'clock tomorrow mornin!"

The bailiff went through his ritual, "All Rise!" Judge O'Neall descended from the bench and exited to his chambers. Upon his departure the courtroom promptly broke into a hubbub of chatter as townspeople, slaves, planters, lawyers, witnesses and litigants all began talking to each other at once about the day's events, while people gathered their belongings and headed out of the courtroom to their respective dwellings.

"Well!" John Bauskett exclaimed, "at least now we know where the battle lines've been drawn!"

"It would seem so," agreed Jolliffe. "It looks to me like some points will be easier to defend than others. That the will is legal should be no problem to prove, nor should the allegations of fraud or insanity bear any weight, as the testimony of the affidavits we took from Ernst and Harwood as well as the testimony of people here like Dr. Harley, should make clear."

"True, but the issue of domicile could be a stickier matter. We'll need to take a close look at the case law on that point and determine whether legal domicile of the slave owner even applies in this situation!" Bauskett pointed out.

"Well, Ohio law doesn't say the slave owner must move his domicile to Ohio in order for his slaves to be emancipated, only that he bring the slaves themselves to the State with the express intent of freeing them!" Jolliffe explained.

"Good point, John! That will be very useful in arguin the matter before the jury!" observed Bauskett.

"How do you see the allegations of immorality bearing on the jury's opinions?" asked Jolliffe, rightly perceiving that more than a few jury members, as well as a significant number of those in the audience, showed visible signs of disgust and disapproval at the descriptions of Elijah's and Amy's illicit relationship proffered by Messrs. Aldrich and Owens.

"Well, let's just say hypocrisy isn't exactly a new phenomenon in these parts! Ya'll're right to note the distaste many feel concernin the whole subject of miscegenation, but bear in mind that some of those who appear to be most vociferous on the subject could easily get caught in the lie of it if anyone started questionin em under oath about their own experiences of interracial relations!" observed Bauskett wryly.

"That might not be a bad strategy to use if things look like they're going against us," commented Jolliffe.

"Well perhaps, but we need to exercise caution in not overplayin our hand, cause it could backfire and just make the jurors angry- especially if it's a Yankee doin the questionin!" Bauskett cautioned.

"Understood. But if you think it needed, do you feel you could put questions to the witnesses in such a way as to box them in, without them having to plead the fifth ammendment?" Jolliffe pressed.

"Maybe so, but we'd need to do so in such a way that it doesn't elicit sympathy for them from the jurors. We shall see," answered Bauskett.

Down the hall near the courthouse entrance, Aldrich and Owens were exulting, "We got em on the run! Even if the insanity don't stick, the domicile will!" crowed Aldrich, feeling proud of himself for arguing that point.

"Yeah, I could see old John Bauskett gettin right nervous as we laid out that piece," agreed Owens enthusiastically.

"Once we get Dr. Guignard in there testifyin that Elijah was depressed and ashamed, we'll have the jury eatin outa our hands!" claimed Aldrich.

"Mr. Aldrich?" James and Michael had made their way through the departing crowd to catch their lawyers while their uncles met up with their respective wives outside.

"Hello there, boys. What can I do for ya'll?" Aldrich responded.

"Well sir, we were just wonderin how ya think the trial's gonna go, an how much longer ya'll think it'll take til we're finished and can take possession of the plantation?" Michael asked.

"Well son, as to your first question, I think it's goin right well! I don't believe your uncle's lawyers are gonna be able to wiggle their way outa the facts of the Act of 1841, so I expect we're gonna win! As for how long it'll take, that depends on how many witnesses get called to testify, how long it takes the jury to come to a decision, and what the judge ultimately rules." Aldrich announced.

"An as we told ya'll before, Bauskett and Jolliffe could try to appeal that rulin- which would mean it'd go to trial all over again up in the State Supreme Court, so I wouldn't count on movin in any time too soon!" cautioned Owens, almost as if he relished the possibility of proving their case before the High Court as well.

"Damn!" James swore. "This is one stinkin hot cow pie of a mess!" Turning to Michael and Angus, who was then approaching them as he wove his way through the crowd, he said, "I told ya'll we needed to push harder on our petition and on gettin the General Assembly to write some more laws to prevent this kinda foolishness! We oughta get Robert Barnwell Rhett to cover this trial in his paper- that'd shake things up a bit!"

Angus replied, "Come on now, James, ya'll know it's not that simple!" he said placatingly, "I'm startin to understand why my Pa was so insistent on the details of the law, cause that's where ya might find a way oughta the problem. We gotta be smart about this- not just loud!" More and more his father's son despite their different views on race, Angus had rightly perceived that Judge O'Neall would not tolerate trying to get the crowd or the jury worked up in a pro-slavery fervor. They needed to use and respect the law, not abuse it!

Outside the courthouse, Dr. Guignard's housekeeper Sally and her nephew were greeting Mary, Angus's housekeeper, as they waited for their master to come out. Dr. Guignard was still busily lobbying the others inside, wanting his views to be well noted in hopes of somehow swaying the jury by popular opinion against Elijah's will- a sort of post mortem attempt to get in one final blow against his nemesis. Truth was, he had only allowed Sally and her nephew to come in the first place to teach them both a lesson that fighting slavery was a lost cause!

"How ya'll doin, Mary?" Sally asked her old friend.

"Well I'll tell ya, seem like the years're finally catchin up with me! Some days I gets up with aches in mo places than I thought I had places!" the old woman replied with a smile of resignation and a chuckle. "But long as I can still move, I thank the Good Lord for all He done for me an just keep on goin! How bout you? Ya nephew here sure growed up!" Mary acknowledged Sally's nephew with her generous smile, and he smiled timidly back at her, a little embarrassed, but pleased to receive some recognition of his existence, given his general invisibility in the eyes of his master.

Sally smiled a weary smile and sighed, "We doin alright, all things considered." She nodded back in the direction of Dr. Guignard, clearly indicating the relativity of her well-being. Then she lowered her voice and said, "Sho would like to see Miss Amy get that plantation! Just knowin she an Celia an the chillun're free give my ole heart a lift it ain't had in years! But to actually win this case! Hmmm, mmm, mmm! Now that really would be somethin!"

Mary nodded, "It sho would! Mister Angus'd be right proud to see it happen too! I just wish I could get Young Angus ta unnerstand. Pains my heart somethin awful he's put in with the Willis boys an their lot. But I can't leave him after all these years- even though I's free. I done promised Mister Angus I'd look after him, an I'm gonna keep my promise. It's the least I can do, after all he done for me! 'Sides, more n likely my time'll be over soon enough!" she sighed in acknowledgment that she really was feeling her long life would soon be coming to an end.

Sally looked at her old friend and said, "God love ya, Mary! I sho do admire yo spirit! They be days when I just don't know how I can go on livin with the misery of Dr. Guignard, but thinkin on you give me hope! I wanna thank ya for remindin me that being black don't have to mean feelin worthless an havin no hope at all!" Sally's eyes began to tear up.

Mary patted Sally on the arm comfortingly and said, "Hush now, ain't no cause for despair! Lord loves ya, and so do I! God knows ya'll've had it awful hard, but He gonna save yo soul, don't ya worry none bout that! Look what He done to His own Son! An yet Jesus got the Victory in the end, an won! We will too! Jus hold on, now!"

Mary was about to say something more, but at that moment Dr. Guignard appeared at the door of the courthouse, looking around for Sally. The two women hastily parted company, Sally and her nephew hurried to join their master, as his ownership demanded.

"There ya are! I saw ya'll lalygaggin around! It's about time ya got here!" Guignard exclaimed with his usual tone of impatient displeasure. "Well, I hope ya'll saw in court today that there's no point in fightin slavery! The law is clear, and slavery is here to stay! I just figured ya'll oughta see for yaselves, lest ya get any ideas!" Guignard looked at the two of them with a cold satisfaction, as if certain that Amy and her family would lose the case, and feeling secure that their loss would send a clear message to all the slaves in the region that their fate was sealed beyond any hope of redemption.

Sally and her nephew hung their heads and muttered obediently, "Yassuh, Dr. Guignard," but they would not let themselves be convinced that Amy's cause was lost, for to give up hope for Amy was to abandon hope for themselves and for all the other enslaved folks- and to be truly hopeless would be worse than death. Mary looked on from a distance and, seeing their submissive gesture, caught Sally's eye. She lifted her chin slightly, as if to say, "Chin up, gal, don't ya let him beat down yo spirit!"

"Counselor, call your first witness." Judge O'Neall ordered.

"Thank ya, Your Honor. Counsel calls Col. Johnson Hagood to the stand," John Bauskett announced.

Col. Hagood was not originally expecting to testify on behalf of Elijah, but rather on behalf of the Willis relations. The announcement seemed to have caught him a little off guard. After being sworn in, Mr. Bauskett proceeded to question him.

"Colonel Hagood, sir, would you please state your occupation and title, for the benefit of the jury?"

"Colonel Johnson Hagood, Commissioner of Equity for Barnwell District, South Carolina."

"Thank ya, Colonel. Now, did you at any time know the deceased, Elijah Willis, of Williston, South Carolina?"

"Yessir, I did," Hagood replied.

"And did you, or did you not sign a document attestin to his good character?" asked Bauskett.

"Yessir I did, back in June of 1852, if I recall correctly," Hagood replied again.

"And what, sir, was the occasion of you signin such a document?" demanded Bauskett.

"Well sir," Hagood explained, "Mr. Willis was fixin on makin a trip up to Baltimore and takin some a his Negroes with him- said he wanted to settle em in trades up there- so he needed a letter for the authorities in case he was questioned about em."

"And was it your opinion that Mr. Willis was a man of upright character and sound judgment?" Bauskett queried.

"Yessir it was. He always had a fine reputation for havin a real good head for business and for bein a right successful planter," Hagood insisted.

"And was that document you signed also signed by Angus Patterson Senior, a lawyer of Williston, attesting to Mr. Willis's unimpeachable character?" Bauskett pressed on.

"Yessir it was, and by several others too, all of em upright citizens, as I recall!" Hagood agreed.

"Thank ya, Colonel, I have no more questions," Bauskett concluded.

"Mr. Alrdich, do ya'll have any questions for this witness?" asked the Judge.

"No sir, Your Honor," Aldrich responded.

"Colonel, ya'll can step down now, if ya please. Mr. Bauskett, do you by any chance have that document in your posession?" asked the Judge.

"Yessir Your Honor, I do, and if it please the Court, I'd like to enter it into evidence," Bauskett replied.

"Thank ya, counselor, so ordered," the Judge responded, as Bauskett handed the document to the clerk of the court. "Call your next witness," O'Neall then ordered.

"Your Honor, I call Dr. Joseph Harley to the stand," announced Bauskett. Bauskett and Jolliffe were systematically calling any and everyone they could who could attest to Elijah's sanity and good character. They knew Guignard would speak against Elijah, though he would probably pretend to have a friendship with the deceased. As a physician, his word therefore might bear weight with the jury, so it was important that they establish that Joseph Harley had a closer and more frequent relationship with Elijah and his family than Guignard, and that he was therefore better qualified as a physician to assess Elijah's mental and physical health. Once Dr. Harley was sworn in, Bauskett resumed his questioning.

"Doctor Harley, could you please tell the jury what the nature of your relationship was with the deceased, Elijah Willis?"

"Certainly, sir. I was his physician for many years."

"And did you ever have occasion to attend to any of the Negroes living either in his house, or on his plantation?"

"Yessir, many times. I assisted at the birth of several children born to Amy, and attended her and all her children, as well as all the other slaves on the plantation."

"Did you, in the course of your long and intimate connection to Mr. Willis, ever have concerns for his mental or physical health?"

"Well sir, I did, on several occasions over the last few years, treat him for apoplexy, which I am well persuaded was the condition that ultimately took his life in Cincinnati. But as for his mental health, other than understandably despairin of bein able to free the Negroes livin in his house, I saw no signs of mental instability or illness whatsoever. On the contrary, I found him to be of very sound and disposin mind, well ordered and thoughtful in all his affairs," Harley answered pointedly.

"Thank ya, Doctor Harley. I have no further questions, Your Honor," Bauskett replied.

"Counselor, you may cross-examine," Judge O'Neall addressed Mr. Aldrich.

"Yes, Your Honor, thank ya, sir," Aldrich responded. Turning to the witness he began, "Doctor Harley, did you at any time have occasion to see Mr. Willis consumin alcoholic beverages?"

"Well yessir, I did," answered Harley.

"And did you have any concern that Mr. Willis was consuming an excessive amount, from the standpoint of his health?" pressed Aldrich.

"If by that ya mean do I think he was an alcoholic or a drunkard? I'd say no sir, I do not," Harley said firmly.

Aldrich was disappointed at not being able to extract some implication that Elijah was overly prone to drink, for he was hoping to use the doctor's testimony to convince the jury that Elijah was depressed and under the influence often- which might well have affected his judgment.

"Doctor, it has been reported that Mr. Willis was frequently in a melancholy state, prone to depression, and fond a drink. Would such things possibly affect his clarity of thought or judgment?"

"Well, sir, if by fond a drink ya mean did he appreciate good sippin whiskey, I'd say yes he did- like most of the gentlemen here present!" there were chuckles of recognition throughout the courtroom and even the jury box. "But if ya mean do I think he was overly fond, or addicted to drink, I'd have to say no. As for melancholy or depression, I would say he was often frustrated and saddened by the difficulties that confronted him in fulfilling his desire to emancipate Amy and the children, but from a medical standpoint I do not find that either unnatural, or indicative of mental imbalance."

Aldrich decided he was not likely to extract from Dr. Harley anything more to support his thesis, and would have to resort to Dr. Guignard's testimony to do so instead.

"Thank ya Doctor Harley, I have no more questions at this time," declared Aldrich.

"The witness may step down. Thank ya Doctor Harley!" Judge O'Neall smiled graciously.

The questioning went on for hours and included friends, neighbors, business associates and various townspeople who had known Elijah. Knotts was questioned, so were Will Beazeley and both Reason and Ary Wooley, as well as several others who knew Elijah from a business standpoint. All of them basically attested to him being of sound mind and high integrity, and having genuine affection for Amy and the children in the household. Much as Angus Junior had wrestled with his unexpected reaction to Amy as if she were truly Elijah's legal wife, despite his moral objections to entertaining that possibility- all of the witnesses painted a picture of Elijah's domestic situation as being not unlike that of any family, despite its racial peculiarities.

When Dr. Guignard took the stand therefore, Aldrich was especially eager to get him to paint a convincingly negative picture of Elijah, which of course Guignard was more than willing and eager to do.

John Bauskett knew that Guignard and Matthews had visited Elijah to express their disapproval of his living arrangements and to pressure him to return Amy and her children to the slave quarters, as in their opinion befitted them. He also knew that Elijah had been extremely annoyed by this attempt and had unceremoniously sent the two gentlemen packing. However, he knew this from Elijah- who could no longer testify-and from Amy, who likewise was not able to testify, so he and Jolliffe were hard-pressed to refute Guignard's version of what transpired as more than hearsay.

"Dr. Guignard, did you ever have occasion to offer medical care either to Mr. Willis or his Negroes?" Aldrich asked.

"On a few occasions. The Negro woman Amy miscarried once, not long after her arrival at the Willis plantation. I did not ask about the parentage of the child, nor was I told, though given the subsequent birth of children claiming Mr. Willis as their father, I suspect he may even then have been involved with the woman! I was in attendance at the miscarriage, as Dr. Harley was indisposed at the time. Mr. Willis seemed unusually grieved for a slave owner who had just lost a Negro baby. As for Mr. Willis, I had occasion for concern about his drinkin, but was not actually called upon to treat him for that, or any other condition." Guignard inserted, knowing full well it was not an answer to the question asked, but hoping that once heard by the jury it would make a lasting impression on them, planting at least a seed of a reasonable doubt, anyway.

Guignard went on, under Aldrich's tutelage, to describe Elijah's profound melancholy state, alleging his deep shame at the condition into which he had fallen and the humiliation it had caused his family, and his propensity to drown his sorrows in whiskey.

Upon cross-examination by Bauskett, a slightly different picture emerged.

"Dr. Guignard, did you and a Mr. Frederick Matthews pay a visit to Mr. Willis some years ago to address your concerns with him?"

"Well uh, yes sir, we did."

"And, to the best of your recollection, please describe how and where ya'll were received, what the nature of your concerns were, and how Mr. Willis responded."

"Well, uh, as I recall, we met on the veranda of the Willis Plantation. We both acknowledged our respect for him as a planter, a businessman, and a member of the foundin family of Williston. Then we told him, in the nicest possible way, that we were concerned that his livin arrangements with his slave woman were ruinin his and his family's reputation. We urged him, outa Christian charity, to return em all to the slave quarters where they belonged, as propriety demanded!"

"It's an interestin notion of Christian charity ya're describing, Doctor, given the penchant of Jesus Christ to protect the poor an the marginalized of society, but I'll let that pass for now- bein as it's more the province of a theological discussion, not directly pertinent to our question at hand. Did Mr. Willis seem receptive to ya'll's importunate visit?"

Guignard bristled under Bauskett's challenge of his supposed Christian virtue but bit his tongue, realizing that to do open battle with the attorney would undermine the thrust of his argument against Elijah, and deflect attention from pressing his case.

"He most certainly did not!" Guignard sufficed to say. "He told us he appreciated our intentions to save what we construed his family's honor to be, but said he 'found it more honorable to respect and care for those whom he loved, and who loved him back, than to worry about the opinions of people who've got nothing better to do than gossip about others, and whose affections for him had never been more than superficial in the first place!' Then he thanked us for our time and bid us good day, and just stood up and walked away! Just like that!" Guignard could not resist sharing the full affront to his dignity, his voice almost trembling with the remembered outrage, hoping it would elicit sympathy from the jurors.

"Thank ya Doctor, for that illuminatin description! On a slightly different subject, Dr. Guignard, do you, as a slave owner yaself, believe slave owners basically have the right to determine what to do with their own property, without interference from others?" Bauskett knew he had Guignard on the run now, for Guignard was well known for his views on the absolute rights of slave owners.

"Yessir, I do, but…" he wanted to add a justification, but Bauskett cut him off.

"Thank ya, Doctor. And, in your strictly medical opinion, Dr. Guignard, did Mr. Willis's resistance to ya'll's allegedly charitable intent seem to ya an indication of insanity or merely a significant difference of personal opinion, based on him standin up for his inherent rights as a slave owner?" asked Bauskett pointedly, remembering Angus Patterson Senior's admonition to his son that the kind of answer you get was often determined by how you put the question.

Knowing he'd been caught out, and before Mr. Aldrich could voice an objection for leading the witness, Guignard mumbled, "A difference of opinion, I suppose."

To drive the point home for the benefit of the jury, Bauskett said, "I'm sorry Doctor, I didn't quite catch what ya said, could ya please speak up a little louder so the judge and the jury and all the rest of us can hear ya, sir?"

Judge O'Neall suppressed a slight smile of appreciation for the learned counsel's adroit line of questioning. Frustrated yet again in his attempts to punish Elijah by confirming his degraded condition, John Guignard squirmed in his seat and said almost petulantly, "It was a difference of personal opinion, I suppose."

"Thank ya, Doctor Guignard, that'll be all. I have no further questions," announced Bauskett. The witness was dismissed, fuming, and there was a ripple of mumbling throughout the courtroom. Some were feeling glad that Bauskett had put the arrogant Dr. Guignard in his place, others were feeling put out that the court seemed to be indulging those who would undermine their sacred values, rather than supporting the majority view of the planters.

When all the questioning was finished at long last, the attorneys made their closing remarks. Jolliffe and Bauskett contended that the will was clearly legal in form and therefore valid, and consequently deserving of probate. They insisted that there could be no question of fraud, as Elijah Willis had corresponded extensively with Gitchell and Jolliffe for more than a year before visiting them in Cincinnati to draft the will, had several witnesses present during the drafting and signing of the will, and was unaccompanied by Amy. Moreover, it was clear the will was written more than a year prior to his death, and the testator had ample time to amend it in any way he might have chosen, but failed to do so. It was also certain that the will was in the testator's and Amy's possession at the time of their arrival- that was confirmed by the reading of the exact copy brought to the inquest by Mr. Jolliffe- so there could be no question of undue influence or coercion in the writing of the will.

Jolliffe and Bauskett furthermore contended that the will being valid, having been proved in the Probate court of Hamilton County, Ohio, and Ohio law having both de facto and de jure already endorsed the freedom of Amy, her mother and children by setting foot on Ohio soil with their master's consent and indisputable intent, as evinced by the matching copies of the will, by the testimony of numerous witnesses that he wished to free them, and by a deed of manumission issued by the court, there could be no further question as to their status. Therefore, they insisted, if free and not slaves, they should necessarily qualify as legatees of the rest of the estate.

Aldrich and Owens attempted to insist that because Elijah had not changed domicile from South Carolina to Ohio, and there was no definitive evidence he intended to stay in Ohio and change his own domicile, the slaves in his possession were consequently also legally domiciled in South Carolina and therefore subject to South Carolina law. According to the Act of 1841, no slave in South Carolina could be emancipated by will or devise, nor receive any material inheritance whatsoever. The only possible means of emancipation being by petition to the General Assembly, and no such petition ever having been filed by the late Elijah Willis, the only possible conclusion to draw was that Amy, her mother and children, though perhaps physically now in Ohio, by South Carolina law were technically still slaves and therefore not able to inherit the plantation or any of Elijah Willis's assets.

Judge O'Neall thanked the lawyers and the witnesses for their participation, and then gave his charge to the jury.

"Gentlemen, before I dismiss ya'll to deliberate this case and come up with a verdict, I need to remind ya'll what ya are and what ya are not asked to decide here:

"First: Is the will Elijah Willis wrote in Cincinnati in 1854 legal, in full or in part, and therefore legally deservin of probate in the State of South Carolina; and does it therefore effectively supercede the terms of the will written here in 1846?

Second: Whether now legally free or not, were the Negroes brought by Elijah Willis with him to Cincinnati free at the time of his death?

And third: If then free, does their freedom entitle them to inherit the remainder of Elijah Willis's estate, or not?

I need to remind ya'll that what is at stake here is a purely legal matter, devoid of moral judgments or preferences concerning Mr. Willis's lifestyle or choice a partner. We're not here to judge the deceased on the righteousness or immorality of his private life, but only on the legality of his actions as they pertain to the will and its terms. Ya'll're not to let your personal opinions on that subject cloud the clarity with which ya deliberate the weighty matters of the law and the respective rights of the parties in question!"

There was such a crescendo of grumblings and mutterings and even shouts of opinions among the public in in the courtroom that the judge became annoyed and, banging his gavel, called,

"Order in the Court! Order! If ya'll don't quiet down now, I'll have the bailiff march ya'll right outa here! This here is a court a law, not a court a public opinion!" Judge O'Neall demanded. "And you gentlemen of the jury, you are to ignore any attempts by the public to sway ya one way or the other, d'ya'll understand?"

The courtroom quieted down and the jurors all voiced their assent to the judge's instructions, upon which Judge O'Neall ordered the bailiff and the sheriff to escort them to the jury room, where they were to remain until they came up with a verdict. The court was then adjourned until such time as the foreman of the jury indicated to the sheriff they had reached a verdict, and the court would then reconvene.

"Lord Almighty!" said James in exasperation. "This damn trial's wearin on my last nerve! The jury's gotta see this whole plan a Uncle Elijah's was just plain wrong!"

"Well, maybe they will and maybe they won't," replied Angus. "Just cause it may a been morally wrong don't mean it was illegal! The judge was pretty strong on that point. Remains to be seen whether the jury'll take it that way!"

"Ole Dr. Guignard was squirmin like a nightcrawler on a fish hook! Did ya'll see how he kept tryin to turn this into a debate on morality?" commented Michael. "An Mr. Bauskett wouldn't let him!"

This surprisingly astute observation of Michael's set them to arguing about whose testimony was most credible, and what the jury was likely to make of it.

Down the hall Elijah's lawyers were discussing quietly their assessment of the day's events too, and were speculating on the probable reaction of the jury to their respective closing remarks.

"Well John, I think you did an admirable job of questioning the witnesses and making the case for the will's legality, free of allegations of insanity, fraud or undue influence. I sensed that Judge O'Neall was inclined to agree with you, but I didn't get the feeling that the jury did," commented Jolliffe astutely.

"Well thank ya, sir, for the acknowledgment, and I'm afraid I agree with ya on the probable opinion of the jury. These folks have been so imbued with the prejudice of slavery as both a fundamental necessity and a basic right of the rulin class, that I think it'll take more than this to convince em," Bauskett admitted.

"Well, if the jury is hung or rules against us, but the judge is inclined to agree with us, what do you suppose he'll do?" asked Jolliffe.

"Well, I imagine he could distinguish between the parts of the case pertaining to the issue of probate and those that pertain to the issue of administration, and sorta separate out the issues by court jurisdictions. If he decides some of the legal issues are beyond the scope of this particular court, he could order a new trial, and send it on up to the State Supreme Court, I suppose, but there's no guarantee he will!" Bauskett surmised.

At the opposite end of the hall, Aldrich and Owens were also closeted in analysis of the events so far.

"Damn! That John Bauskett's a cagey one!" Aldrich said with a mixture of exasperation and admiration. "I was sure I was gonna get the jury behind Dr. Guignard, but John Bauskett was right clever in his questionin and managed to make Guignard look a little foolish in his responses."

Owens nodded in agreement and commented, "And I was surprised he called on Col. Hagood right at the start! Havin that letter of good character entered into evidence right from the get go didn't help us, especially mentioning that Angus Patterson Senior had also signed it!"

"Well, maybe not, but folks seemed plenty outraged by the images of that Amy woman bearin Elijah Willis's children and livin in the big house! They were none too pleased by Guignard's report of Elijah bein rude to him and Frederereick Matthews in response to their efforts to save his reputation, either!" offered Aldrich hopefully.

"The jury hears that, and it's gonna stick in their minds, cause they'll put themselves in Guignard's and Matthews' shoes and identify with their upset, no matter what the judge instructs em to do!" swore Owens.

People outside the courthouse were as deeply engaged in discussion as were those on the inside. The planters were all, of course, siding with the partisans of the 1846 will, and were declaiming loudly about the importance of enforcing the Act of 1841. Some of the townspeople, however, knowing both Elijah and Amy, were considerably less sanguine on the subject of the Act of 1841, and were prone to supporting Jolliffe's claims that Elijah had been acting fully within his rights. There seemed to be a pretty clear line of demarcation between how people felt about the matter of the emancipation of Amy, her mother and children on the one hand, and the matter of them inheriting the estate on the other. For most, the emancipation of a handful of Negroes- especially now that they were no longer in the area to cause any trouble, was of relatively little consequence. Most, in fact, seemed inclined to indulge the follies and caprices of old man Willis on that score, however morally questionable they might be, as they no longer had any direct impact on the community.

The issue of inheritance, however, was quite another matter, for the entire white population tended to define themselves in terms of the property they amassed, and the wealth they could pass down to successive generations to thereby secure their family's name for all posterity. They followed such matters with a dedication and zealous attention to detail worthy of Burke's Peerage, the definitive compendium of British nobility that had been published yearly since 1826. It was one of the paradoxes of South Carolina planter society that prided itself on its independence and its patriotic defiance of the British Crown in the Revolution, yet aspired to the very nobility that War had officially spurned as undemocratic and anti-American!

And then there were the discussions outside and out back of the Courthouse among the slaves and free blacks who had been attending the trial. They were unanimous in their support of Elijah's Cincinnati will, whether they knew Amy and her mother personally, or not. Every person of color present knew that if Amy won, even if they themselves remained enslaved, a precedent would have been set for an alternate possibility, and that would give them all something to hope for.

When the court was finally reconvened and the judge ordered the sheriff to bring the jury members back from their deliberations in the jury room, everyone present was feeling the suspense.

Addressing the foreman of the jury, Judge O'Neall asked, "Mr. Foreman, has the jury reached a verdict?"

"We have, Your Honor!" the foreman announced.

A palpable tension ran through the crowd no matter whether they favored or opposed the will, for everyone agreed that much hung in the balance of the verdict. As the foreman opened a folded sheet of paper in preparation for reading the verdict, everyone seemed to hold their breath in anticipation.

"Your Honor, the jury rules against the probate of the will of February 23rd, 1854, on the grounds that it violates the Act of 1841! Though the will be written in legal form and constituting a legal will superceding the will of 1846, and its appointment of Mr. Jolliffe as executor is found legal, its terms being in violation of the Act of 1841 renders the distribution of property indicated by the testator inoperable. Moreover the jury feels the Negroes taken to Cincinnati are still bound by the domicile of their owner and thereby still in a condition of slavery."

The foreman handed the written verdict to the bailiff, who in turn handed it to the judge. Judge O'Neall looked visibly disappointed. The crowd collectively exhaled and then broke into a raucus expression of reactions both for and against the verdict. There were shouts of exultation and of despair, including some moans and wails from the Negroes up in the gallery. The Willis family fought to control their elation, but the brothers hugged each other fiercely, grinning triumphantly as Judge O'Neall began to pound his gavel again demanding order.

"Order in the Court! Order! That's enough ya'll! This trial isn't over til I say so, so ya'll best quiet down an pay attention, or the bailiff'll have to take all a ya'll outa here, so I can deliver my opinion to the lawyers!"

It took a few moments for the crowd to finally calm down so the Judge could speak. After reading through his notes, the judge asked the respective attorneys for and against the will to stand.

"Counselors, I have been listenin carefully to your arguments for and against this will. I've listened to the testimony of all your witnesses, and I've considered carefully the jury's grounds for refusin the will for probate. So this is my considered opinion:

On the grounds of the weight and sufficiency to impeach the will, on grounds of insanity of the testator, I find insufficient evidence.

On the validity and sufficiency of the provisions of the will in general, it is the opinion of the Court that a clause in a will, void under the Act of 1841 because it directs certain slaves of the testator to be taken beyond the limits of the State and there emancipated, does not vitiate the will upon question of probate.

On the validity and sufficiency of the provisions of the will in general, it is the opinion of the Court that a will is not invalid upon a question of probate just because it contains a devise and bequest for the benefit of slaves, such devise bein void under the fouth section of the Act of 1841.

On the question of fraud and undue influence in general, it is the opinion of the Court that there is insufficient evidence to impeach the will on the grounds of fraud and undue influence.

On the question of determinin in probate proceedins the validity or construction of the will, the inquiry is whether there be a valid will, in whole or in part; if only so much be valid as revokes prior wills and appoints executors, it is the opinion of the Court that it still must be admitted to probate.

And finally, on our ability to determine in probate proceedins as to the validity or construction of certain provisions of the will, it is the opinion of this Court that whether clauses in the will directin certain slaves to be taken to Ohio and there emancipated and makin provision for such slaves out of the other estate of the testator are void under the Act of 1841, is a question which belongs to a Court of construction and administration, and not to a Court of probate.

Consequently, with all due respect to our good citizens servin on the jury, and with my sincere thanks to em for their diligent efforts to come to a verdict in this matter, the law actually obliges me in this situation to set aside their verdict, and order a new trial!"

With that, Judge O'Neall brought down the gavel and adjourned the Court. The Bailiff ordered "All Rise!" as Judge O'Neall left for his chambers, and there was a stunned silence.

Michael and James looked to each other, to Angus, and to their lawyers in total confusion and bafflement.

"What the Hell did that mean? What just happened?" protested James.

"I thought the jury ruled against the will, and that settled it!" protested Michael. "Can Judge O'Neall do that?"

"What's the point of havin a jury if the judge is gonna ignore their verdict?" complained James. Turning to Aldrich and Owens he shouted, "Why the Hell don't ya'll do somethin? Ya just gonna stand there like a coupla ninnies gapin at the bench? Damn it all, why the tarnation're we payin ya'll if ya can't get this thing settled?!" James was apoplectic.

Angus, on the other hand, stood in awe of Judge O'Neall, realizing he had just witnessed a masterful piece of judicial skill at work in parsing the fine points of the law. He also realized that Judge O'Neall was quite right in his analysis.

"Listen, ya'll, the Judge may've taken us by surprise, but accordin to the law he's right, so we'll just have to get ready to fight this in the new trial, and learn from our mistakes in this one! We can forget about wastin time tryin to make out that your uncle was crazy or was tricked into writin that will. We need to focus on the Act of 1841, residency requirements, and the like, and leave aside the question of his immorality and the rest!"

Aldrich and Owens were struck by Angus' clarity of thought and quickly agreed. "He's right boys, this ain't over yet, and we may still be able to snatch victory from the jaws a defeat if we play our cards right!" Obviously both lawyers had an investment not only in placating their clients, but also in continuing the battle- if not to win the case, at least to win the commensurate fees the case would demand for their services and the enhanced reputation that would accrue to them for arguing it before the high court!

During their conversation the crowd had once again erupted in lively discussion of this unexpected development. John Jolliffe and John Bauskett looked at each other and smiled with relief.

"Of course we'll file immediately for the retrial. Now the race has clearly narrowed to the issues of the Act of 1841 as it pertains to the validity of the specific clauses of the will concerning the distribution of the estate," John Bauskett proclaimed. "With the will accepted for probate as Judge O'Neall clearly ruled it must be, you cannot be removed as executor in favor of Fanning and Phillips, which is crucial for the future of Gilbert and the others! Even though ya'll may be the sole executor, however, what remains to be decided is whether South Carolina law will permit ya to remove any more slaves to Ohio. At least there's a chance! So the issue hangs on whether Amy and the children were not only free at the time of Elijah's death, but are thereby free to inherit as well!" Bauskett concluded.

"No doubt they're going to argue that the remaining slaves must stay as collateral against debts and the like, but if the Court rules that Amy and the children are free and entitled to inherit, thereby obviating my executorship, we should be able to get them free at least eventually!" Jolliffe opined.

"True, but ya do realize, don't ya, that it might be years before the High Court actually hears this case?" advised Bauskett.

"I know, and I dread breaking that news to Amy and her family, but there is nothing we can do about it, is there?" replied Jolliffe.

"I'm afraid not," agreed Bauskett. "Especially given how politically heated this whole issue has become down here. That alone may make the court want to drag its feet on dealin with the matter!"

When John Jolliffe returned to Cincinnati, he and James Gitchell sent their carriage to fetch Amy to their office, telling their coachman to tell her it was on urgent business. Amy didn't know whether to be excited or alarmed, but quickly gathered herself together and climbed into the carriage, hoping Jack the coachman might have some clue as to what this was all about.

"I can't rightly say, Miss Amy. All I know is Mister John and Mister James seemed mighty intent on talkin to ya right away!"

The ride across town to their office seemed interminable. When they finally got there, Amy could feel her stomach doing flip-flops with anxiety and her pulse was racing. It crossed her mind that she might end up needing some of that digitalis tea her mother used to make for Elijah to get through all this!

Gitchell and Jolliffe met her together at the door and ushered her to a seat, offering her their own tea to calm her nerves.

"What's this all about, gentlemen? You've given me quite a fright! What news do ya bring back from South Carolina, Mr. Jolliffe?" Amy said, her anxiety making her voice rise to a higher pitch.

"Well to tell you the truth, the news is mixed! First let me say however, to reassure you, that your brother and his family are all well, as are all the other slaves remaining on the plantation, and they send their love to you all. Gilbert told me he is still counting on you to get them to safety!" Jolliffe announced.

Amy realized that Mr. Jolliffe's choice of words about whom Gilbert was trusting to free him could be an indication that Jolliffe, as executor, might not be able to accomplish that task himself, as was originally planned and as Elijah had dictated. She felt her stomach tighten as she continued to listen.

"And as for the court proceedins?" she asked, her voice trembling slightly.

"Well, there is both good and bad news on the legal front. The bad news is that the jury ruled against admitting the new will to probate, confirming Judge Wardlaw's earlier decision. Until the legality of the provisions of the will is established, Mr. Jolliffe cannot yet sell any of the property or free any of the slaves remaining there," explained Gitchell.

Amy swallowed hard and took a deep breath. "That is indeed bad news-the worst imaginable! If the will is not accepted there, we are all ruined! What, then, could the good news possibly be?" she asked, having a hard time imagining what good could come out of that decision.

"The good news is that the Judge disagreed with the jury and decided to set the verdict aside and order a new trial, on the grounds that some points of the case were beyond the legal scope of a court of probate to answer. He found the will itself to be legal and worthy of probate, but determined that the legality of its provisions were beyond the scope of a probate court to determine. This means that the case will now be tried before the Supreme Court of South Carolina!" Jolliffe announced.

"Not only that," Gitchell explained, "Just as we had predicted, the Willis boys tried to prove that Elijah was insane, was an alcoholic, led a dissolute life, and that the will he wrote here was done under your coercion to defraud Elijah of his property. The judge deemed there was insufficient evidence to justify any of those charges!" He then added with satisfaction, "That means that the most emotionally charged opinions were discarded and the case was pared down to a narrow issue of the interpretation of the Act of 1841, and whether you and your family were or were not already free at the time of Elijah's death!"

"I am confident we shall win on that score," Jolliffe hastened to reassure her. "The only real question is how long it will take before the high court is willing to hear the case. Mr. Bauskett is of the opinion that there could be considerable foot-dragging on the matter, due to the volatility of the current political climate in South Carolina over this very issue," he advised.

"So where does that leave us, gentlemen, in terms of prosecutin the case to its conclusion?" asked Amy pointedly. She maintained her grace and charm, but was beginning to lose both her patience and her hopefulness of a happy conclusion, the 'good news' of the retrial initially struck her as just one more delay in an interminable process whose solution seemed to elude them.

"Well, since the judge ruled that the grounds for refusing probate of the will itself were unfounded and all that was in question were some of the specific provisions of the will, that de facto means that Mr. Jolliffe here must be considered the sole executor unless and until the Court rules otherwise," explained Gitchell. "However, since the specific provisions of freeing slaves and selling the property have yet to be resolved, he cannot act on such provisions until the case is retried. There is however, at least one benefit of this, for it prevents Mr. Fanning or Mr. Phillips from assuming executorship and trying to take over the daily operations of the plantation!"

"Well that is some small comfort at least, though I doubt my brother Gilbert will be so greatly consoled by it that he will feel he need not continue to be ever vigilant against Elijah's relations, just the same!" announced Amy, a tinge of complaint, or perhaps mere sarcasm, in her voice. "Do ya'll have any indication of how long it might be before the case is finally heard?"

Gitchell and Jolliffe shook their heads. "I'm afraid not, my dear," replied Jolliffe, "and it truly grieves me that you and your family remain in this hellish limbo of uncertainty because of it." They then shared with her in detail the testimony offered- especially by Elijah's friends- hoping it would build her confidence in an ultimately beneficial outcome.

"All I can attest to" concluded Jolliffe, "is that we- James, myself, John Bauskett and his colleague, Mr. Bellinger- shall do everything possible to pursue this case to the very end, and protect your rights to the best of our ability. I recognize of course that it must surely seem to you to be a test of Biblical proportions to have to endure such travail!"

Amy was once again unexpectedly reminded of Elijah's epiphany about the story of Joseph's many trials while enslaved in Egypt before he became reconciled with his brothers. She sighed in resignation and thanked the attorneys for their diligence. They in turn assured her they would keep her apprised of any and all developments in the meantime, as they would be in regular correspondence with John Bauskett.

While the lawyers' coachman Jack drove Amy past the brickyard on her way to the small house she and her sons had by now managed to rent nearby with their earnings, her thoughts turned to Manuel Ash. Working for him part time had proven not to be an onerous experience. He was kind, well mannered, and appreciative of her help. If he was at times a bit flirtatious he at least had never attempted to force himself on her in any way. Though she had avoided his advances so far, she was suddenly feeling that perhaps she should reconsider, as it was clear there was no reliable or definitive solution to their legal issues in sight and even once resolved there was no guarantee the court would rule entirely in their favor. They might never reap the financial rewards they had counted on, and that represented a serious challenge to their collective well-being, especially if Amy was to manage to also educate her children! She would be forced to find some alternative means of security. What had looked like a temporary measure, working for Manuel to tide them over for survival's sake seemed to be stretching out into the future with no clear end visible on the horizon.

She was shaken out of her reverie by the carriage slowing to a stop. Jack announced, "Here ya are, Miss Amy!" He even climbed down from the dirver's seat to open the carriage door for her.

To her surprise, as Jack deposited Amy at her doorstep, bade her good day and drove off, Elder met his mother at the door with a worried look on his face. Though she had not expected him home from work so soon, she assumed it was merely his concern for news about the trial that was troubling him. That assumption however, was quickly shattered.

"Momma! Come quick! It's Momma Celia!" Elder demanded.

Her heart in her throat, Amy rushed into the house to find her mother lying on the shabby settee one of Mr. Gitchell's friends had provided to help them furnish their modest dwelling. Momma Celia's breathing was shallow and rapid, her eyelids fluttering nearly shut, trance-like, her face looking drawn, and a grimace of pain flickered across her lips.

"Momma! Momma! What happened? What's wrong?" Amy could never remember seeing her mother sick with anything in her life, so to see her lying so enfeebled was truly alarming. She felt her mother's forehead for any signs of fever but found none.

Momma Celia finally opened her eyes, turned and looked at her daughter as if coming back from a great distance. She smiled and took Amy's hand, patting it reassuringly.

"I'll be alright, baby," she said "It just come over me all of a sudden!" she explained. Of course her explanation did nothing to allay Amy's fears, or even clarify what had happened.

"What d'ya mean Momma? What came over ya?" Amy pressed her mother.

Momma Celia was silent for a long time, her lips moving voicelessly almost as if having a conversation with someone else while her daughter and grandson nervously waited for an answer. Amy shuddered involuntarily and repeated, "Momma what's goin on? Ya're scarin me!"

Momma Celia seemed to have finished her conversation with her invisible visitor and now breathing more calmly, turned again to her daughter.

"I seen a vision, child! It was a fearsome sight, set my heart to racin! They was soldiers on our plantation dressed in grey. They was stealin our chickens and hogs and most everything they could. Trampled my garden into the mud! They stomped through my kitchen an all over the house with they muddy boots, makin an awful mess! Then other soldiers came dressed in blue, and some of em was colored! They chased away the soldiers in grey- they was shootin and killin an blood an sounds a pain an fear everywhere!"

Amy found her mother's vision almost as alarming as the sight of her lying on the settee panting. It seemed to her however, that there was more to the vision than her mother was revealing.

"Was there anything else Momma? Where were Gilbert and the others?" Amy pressed.

Momma's faced clouded over again and she fell silent, as if listening to a voice from somewhere else. By and by her face relaxed, her color returned, and she spoke to her daughter once again.

"Everthing's gonna be alright sugar! God done tole me ya'll're gonna win ya inheritance in due time. Be some mo dark times to go through yet, but ya'll're gonna win!" She smiled confidently, her face radiant, as if the matter was now settled and it was simply a matter of time to wait for the fruition, just as Elijah had planned.

Unnerved by her mother's vision and less prone to trusting in supernatural communications than Momma Celia, Amy pondered the images her mother described and felt a chill run through her whole body. There had been talk of secession by South Carolina from the Union for years but no one she knew of had ever proposed a war! What could her mother's vision mean? Was it prophetic of things to come, or merely the result of their cumulative fears playing tricks with her aging mother's mind? Yet Momma Celia had always been extremely lucid, with the memory of an elephant. Dementia seemed an extremely unlikely explanation! And then there was her mother's word choice "ya'll're gonna win-" as if she were not included in that victory.

Was she going to die? Was God calling her home? Amy remembered stories her mother and grandmother had told her when she was little about how her people back in Africa had been gifted with the ability to know things- to receive messages from spirits and the like- and how sometimes they'd have visions shortly before they died, like they were gaining access to another dimension to which they would soon belong. Was her mother suddenly turning into a visionary with the second sight, or had she been one all along and just kept it secret for fear the white folks would brand her a witch woman? The whole situation was decidedly disturbing.

She was so unsettled by this unexpected event that even once her mother seemed to have returned to her usual state, Amy almost forgot to tell Momma Celia of the most recent news from South Carolina. Feeling reasonably assured at last that her mother had suffered no illness and was back to normal, she finally informed her.

"Momma- I just came from Mr. Jolliffe's and Mr. Gitchell's office. There is news from home." She caught herself using the word home and realized that was no longer the right word, however revealing of her affections it might be. "From South Carolina, I mean," she corrected herself.

"The jury rejected the will in the Court of Appeals. James and Michael and their lot tried to make out Elijah was a crazy drunk, and that I forced him to write the will to steal his property, but - God be praised - the judge found insufficient evidence for any of those charges. He decided that even if the will itself was legal, some of what was in it might not be, and that the court was not legally permitted to decide whether Elijah freein us and leavin us the plantation was legal in a court a probate, so he ordered a new trial!"

"I done tole ya, God's gonna make everything work out! I saw it in my vision!" Momma Celia insisted with a beatific smile, almost as if frustrated that Amy should even doubt it.

"Well, ya'll may be right Momma! At least for now, Gilbert and the others are still safe and Elijah's in-laws can't take over, cause Mr. Jollife is considered the sole executor at this point, even though he can't sell any a the property or free any a the slaves- at least not yet!"

"Praise Jesus for that, honey, praise Jesus for that!" Momma Celia's words sounded oddly hollow, almost distracted, as if at the mention of Gilbert's name another memory from the vision had reinserted itself into her awareness. Whatever it was, she was clearly not inclined to share it and chose to keep her own counsel on the matter.

Amy couldn't help but wonder if her mother's thoughts weren't far away with her son and other grandchildren. Would they ever see each other again?

Manuel Ash could not deny he had feelings for Amy. He had grown up free in North Carolina, but had left for Ohio because the atmosphere was so inhospitable, leaving behind the memory of the only woman he had ever loved. She was a slave whose freedom he had tried to buy from her master. The master refused, and locked her away. Manuel had continued to try for years to free her, in vain, and then finally got word she had died from wounds inflicted by her master in a rage. Devastated, he decided to set out for Ohio and start a new life. He had managed to create a decent life for himself in Cincinnati, but it had been a lonely one, and the day Amy walked in the brickyard door was the first time he had ever actually felt that cloud might lift and the sun of love might actually shine on him at last.

Amy had gradually revealed bits and pieces of her relationship with Elijah and her earlier life in the course of casual conversation. She felt a growing trust and comfort with Manuel, which was a welcome respite from the very small circle of mostly white contacts she had here in Cincinnati. But at the same time she felt cautious, wary of involvement or of revealing too much about her family's situation. She didn't want any man thinking that he could just ingratiate himself to her and then hope to profit from the outcome of the trial. She also worried that it might somehow dishonor Elijah for her to admit to her emotional and physical needs as a widow. She wasn't quite sure she was even ready to love anyone again, and even though her older boys were nearly grown, she was also concerned how the children would feel about another man in her life at this point. Her feelings for Elijah had been complicated, and the thought of choosing a spouse in freedom, or being chosen in freedom, was almost disorienting to even contemplate as a possibility.

"I can't, Manuel, I'm sorry." Amy was gently rebuffing him one day at the end of work when Manuel had tried to take her out to dinner. But

Manuel felt like there was a glimmer in her eye and a warmth in her smile that didn't really mean 'no,' at least not a permanent 'no.'

"Come on now, what you afraid of?" he teased her. "I ain't gonna bite ya!" He flashed his dazzling smile. "It's just dinner! Ya'll don't have to worry bout the children. Your Momma's there to look after em!"

Amy felt her resistance wearing down, but wasn't quite ready to give in.

"Ya know what I think? I think ya'll're still so caught up with the memory of your old identity that ya're afraid to create a new one!" His comment hit home. She knew he was right about that, though it didn't seem so simple a matter to her.

"I got a idea! Instead a callin ya Amy, I'll call ya Mary! Yeah! Try that on for size an see how it fits ya! Even though nobody uses it, your full name is Mary Amy, ain't it? So why not just use Mary instead a Amy? Be like you gettin a fresh start, but still bein you. That way ya'll can let yaself be in your new life without feelin like ya're sullyin your memories of your old one!" He laughed a gentle laugh and coaxed a smile out of her. She was impressed at the subtlety of his understanding. Of course, she still didn't go to dinner with him that night, but she knew she would eventually. Manuel didn't press her any further because he knew it too, and that was enough for him.

At the same time the matter of the Last Will and Testament of Elijah Willis was being considered in the Probate Court, the Court of Equity, and the Appellate Court in Barnwell District, South Carolina, another case was being argued up in Washington in the Supreme Court of the United States that wrestled with issues that might have a bearing on the outcome of the South Carolina case.

Dred Scott was a Negro slave born in Virginia, but taken by his owner Peter Blow first to Alabama, then to Missouri. Following the death of his master in 1832, he was sold to Dr. John Emerson, an army surgeon who travelled on Army business up and down the territories east of the Mississippi: North to Illinois, then up to Wisconsin, then down to Louisiana, then back to Missouri. In short, Scott accompanied his master to several free territories where slavery was either not permitted or the slave issue had not yet been decided. Ever willing to profit from his investment, on several occasions Dr. Emerson hired Dred out to work for others as a slave while he was away, effectively introducing slavery into a free territory. This was in violation of the law.

During these travels Dred Scott married Harriet Robinson, another of his master's slaves, and they had a daughter, Eliza, born on a riverboat in free territory while traveling down the Mississippi River en route to Louisiana. Eventually Dr. and Mrs. Emerson moved back to St. Louis with their slaves, where Scott and his wife continued to be hired out. Dr. Emerson died and upon his master's death, Scott tried to buy his and his family's freedom, but his master's widow refused to grant it.

His petition for freedom having been refused by Mrs. Emerson, he took her to court. Determined to be free, Scott sought the help of abolitionists and attempted to sue his mistress for freedom in the Missouri court. His claim was based on the grounds of having been brought into free territories and residing there at length and on the grounds that his late master and current mistress had violated the law by hiring him and his wife out as a slaves in non-slave holding territories. Moreover, Scott's daughter being born on the Mississippi in free territory, he claimed, made her free by birth.

In 1847 the Missouri Court threw out the case on a technicality, for Scott had failed to produce proof that he was owned by Mrs. Emerson, but then the court decided to retry the case. In 1850 it was retried, and the court ruled in favor of Scott- declaring that he and his family were free.

Two years later, however, Scott's former owner appealed the case and the Missouri Supreme Court overturned the earlier decision, placing Scott in the custody of the St. Louis Sheriff, who himself continued to hire Dred and Harriet Scott out and put their earnings in escrow, pending a final decision on their status. Mrs. Emerson then transferred ownership of the Scotts to her brother, John Sandford, and moved to Massachusetts. In the meantime, Scott's new master himself moved to New York, leaving Scott and his family in Missouri still in the custody of the St. Louis sheriff.

With the help of abolitionist lawyers, Scott then fought the court's decision in federal court, on the grounds of diversity jurisdiction. The principle of diversity jurisdiction allowed federal courts to hear civil cases in which the parties were citizens in different states or territories. Scott and his lawyers took their case all the way to the U.S. Supreme Court. In what would rapidly become the most infamous, and arguably worst decision ever pronounced by the U.S. Supreme Court, however, the Court ultimately ruled against Scott.

It was an election year, and the winning presidential candidate, James Buchanan, who was counting on Southern support, seemed to have closeted himself with at least one high court justice to persuade him that if Scott's appeal were granted, it would cause such a political uproar as to put the Union's very survival at risk!

Whether through political pressure or simple collective self-interest (most of the justices being pro-slavery), the Court decided that no individuals of African descent, whether slave or free, could be considered American citizens. Consequently, they had no right to sue in a federal court. But even worse, the Court claimed quite illogically that the federal government had no power to regulate slavery in the federal territories that were acquired after the creation of the United States but had not yet achieved statehood. This overturned the terms of the Missouri Compromise and the Compromise of 1850, which had divvied up the territories as slave holding or slave-free in an attempt to prevent national schism.

Scott and his lawyers had continued to insist that his having lived in free territories in the absence of his master rendered him rightfully free, and that hiring him out as a slave in free territorires was an illegal and unconstitutional attempt to introduce slavery into such territories without the consent of the people. The problem was, even if true, the issue hung on the presupposition that Scott was in fact a citizen- whether of a state or territory. Only as such could he even press his case. The Court decided otherwise, denying his citizenship, and therefore his right to sue at all!

Chief Justice Tanney, perhaps somewhat naively, thought his decision was a masterful solution to the slavery issue that would appease the Southern block and thereby preserve the Union. Instead, it inflamed the Northerners and made the divisions between slave and free states all the more volatile. Some felt it pushed the matter beyond the point of no return toward schism, and possibly even war.

Ohio, being the hotbed of abolitionist sentiment that it was, had been keenly sensitive to what they deemed the spurious reasoning behind the Supreme Court decision. To prove their disagreement with it, in their confidence in the power of States' rights to make their own decisions on such matters Ohio therefore automatically granted slaves such freedom as Scott had presumed should be his. Initially they did this on the mere indication that the owner had permitted the slave to enter the state. Under political pressure however, the practice shifted to require not only proof of permission to enter but also proof of the owner's intent to emancipate when the slave was brought to Ohio. Amy worried whether the political furor over the Dred Scott decision would reinforce the implementation of that precedent and preserve the freedom of people like her and her family, or would they by some cruel twist of fate and polticial pressure be forced back into a state of permanent bondage?

There were of course other sober minds in both North and South also considering the matters raised by the Scott decision, even in the sleepy backwaters of Barnwell District, South Carolina. Judge John Belton O'Neall for one, read the reports of the Supreme Court decision with keen interest. Having recently ordered a new trial in the matter of the Last Will and Testament of Elijah Willis, he pondered whether this federal ruling might have any bearing on the legal issues at hand, and was loathe to schedule a new trial until he was more certain of the implications of this ruling. He decided to wait for the popular furor to die down a bit before scheduling the case. Unfortunately, the furor continued to build rather than go away, though that was not immediately apparent to the judge.

As he contemplated the details of the Dred Scott decision, O'Neall could forsee that the proponents of Elijah's earlier will might want to cite it to reinforce their argument that Amy and her family were not really free, and perhaps could not even appeal to the South Carolina Court at all, as they were not deemed citizens- diversity jursidciton thereby being rendered inapplicable to her case.

He quickly concluded however, that would be a specious argument, for the Scott decision was based on whether or not the plaintiff should be granted freedom from an owner who chose to deny it to him, and whether as a resident of free territory he was thereby automatically a citizen entitled to sue in federal court.

The Willis case, though touching on some of the same themes vis à vis the mechanism of granting freedom through residency, had nothing to do with whether Amy and her family could be emancipated, but rather whether they might already be legally emancipated in Ohio by duly constituted Ohio law. The slavery issue had long been settled in the State of Ohio by both common law precedent and state constitution- even if such emancipation, as the federal Supreme Court now claimed, could not grant them full citizen status or the right to seek justice in the federal system. Amy and her family were not appealing to the federal court, in any case, but only to that of South Carolina. Moreover it was not even Amy and her children themselves who were appealing the court decision at all, but rather John Jolliffe, the white executor of the will! Nobody would even question his citizenship or right to sue! Taking all this into consideration, O'Neall recognized that the heat and smoke generated over the Scott case should not be allowed to cloud the issue for the Willis case.

Will Beazeley was still receiving newspapers both from around the region and the North. John Bauskett had even prevailed upon him to supply him some in the hopes that being well informed of the legal arguments posited around the country might help him and Mr. Bellinger better craft their arguments in favor of Elijah's will in even more persuasive terms, for they were well aware of the political developments at hand.

The Southern papers were nearly unanimous in praising the Dred Scott decision, for it clearly protected and even promoted the vested interests of the ruling class of planters. Northern views were obviously quite different. *The Evening Journal* of Albany, New York, Bauskett read, roundly denounced the Dred Scott decision in unambigious terms. The paper deemed it an egregious offense to the principles of liberty upon which the nation was founded and an ominous victory for slave states over the free states:

"The three hundred and forty-seven thousand five hundred and twenty-five Slaveholders in the Republic, accomplished day before yesterday a great success — as shallow men estimate success. They converted the Supreme Court of Law and Equity of the United States of America into a propagandist of human Slavery. Fatal day for a judiciary made reputable throughout the world, and reliable to all in this nation, by the learning and the virtues of Jay, Rutledge, Ellsworth, Marshall and Story!

"The conspiracy is nearly completed. The Legislation of the Republic is in the hands of this handful of Slaveholders. The United States Senate assures it to them. The Executive power of the Government is theirs. Buchanan took the oath of fealty to them on the steps of the Capitol last Wednesday. The body which gives the supreme law of the land, has just acceded to their demands, and dared to declare that under the charter of the Nation, men of African descent are not citizens of the United States and can not be — that the Ordinance of 1787 was void — that human Slavery is not a local thing, but pursues its victims to free soil, clings to them wherever they go, and returns with them — that the American Congress has no power to prevent the enslavement of men in the National Territories — that the inhabitants themselves of the Territories have no power to exclude human bondage from their midst — and that men of color can not be suitors for justice in the Courts of the United States!"

That editorial ended with a clarion call to war:

"...All who love Republican institutions and who hate Aristocracy, compact yourselves together for the struggle which threatens your liberty and will test your manhood!"

Bauskett and his colleagues read such words with concern. The Dred Scott decision had maintained that the Missouri Compromise was unconstitutional, interpreting Article IV of the Constitution's granting to Congress the power to acquire territories and create governments as being restricted to the Northwest Territories. Missouri had been acquired through the Louisiana Purchase and according to the Court was therefore not subject to the same application of law. Bauskett and his colleague could just imagine Henry Clay, Daniel Webster, and Angus Patterson Senior turning over in their graves- and John C. Calhoun jumping up and down for joy in his!

Given that seven of the nine Supreme Court justices had been appointed by pro-slavery presidents and five of them were from slaveholding families themselves, Bauskett was not surprised the Court would rule so. He was not being cynical in his assessment, merely realistic. But it raised new issues about the future of slavery itself, seeming to reinforce it universally rather than curtail it, despite rapidly intensifying opposition to it in the North and in many of the Western Territories. Both Bauskett and Bellinger worried that if the Union collapsed under these pressures as folks like Robert Barnwell Rhett had been advocating, the entire validity of jurisdictions and court rulings between Ohio and South Carolina might have to be radically redefined, and that would seriously complicate their efforts on behalf of Amy and her family. It would most especially affect their ability to get Gilbert and any of the other remaining slaves out of South Carolina to freedom!

It was unthinkable that centuries of American jurisprudence and comity, first between the American colonies and then between the states and territories, might thereby be cast by the wayside! Yet reason and logic seemed to be increasingly rare in the heat of debate, rendering common sense a misnomer and a commodity in unusually short supply. Nothing, they concluded, was to be taken for granted.

The politicians and the journalists continually ranted and raged about their competing notions of justice, and abolitionists and slave owners fulminated about who and what was right, as they were ever wont to do. In the meantime, quietly and at first unnoticed, the sons of Peter Blow, Scott's first owner, who had grown up with Scott as chidldhood friends and had been helping him defray his legal expenses throughout the ordeal, bought Scott and his family their freedom on May 26th, 1857. It was less than three months after the Supreme Court announced its decision. Sadly, Dred Scott died nine months later, but he was at long last truly a free man.

The Blows' purchase of his freedom was a moving testimony to the calibre of Dred Scott as a person, and a reminder that even those who had participated in the institution of slave holding were not all devoid of conscience, compassion, or humanity. Once discovered, the Scotts gaining freedom quickly became national news and was celebrated in northern cities.

As tensions continued to rise between North and South, however, in what the abolitionists considered an unholy alliance, Steven A. Douglas, Senator of Illinois, decided to run for the presidency. Bending over backwards in what the abolitionists deemed a most unseemly manner,

Douglas tried to appease the South. He was creative, but disingenuous in his attempt to justify the Supreme Court decision and its peculiarly self-contradictory implications for the matter of states' versus federal rights in the territories that had not yet achieved statehood. It was reported by some that Douglas was well financed for his pains by wealthy slave owners throughout the South in his bid for the White House. Some anti-slavery Northerners deemed this tantamount to treason.

Douglas' opponent, Abraham Lincoln, warned of the dangers of the arguments posited by Douglas and their probable consequences in a speech at Springfield, Illinois on June 16, 1858:

"Put this and that together, and we have another nice little niche, which we may, ere long, see filled with another Supreme Court decision, declaring that the Constitution of the United States does not permit a State to exclude slavery from its limits. ... We shall lie down pleasantly dreaming that the people of Missouri are on the verge of making their State free, and we shall awake to the reality instead, that the Supreme Court has made Illinois a slave State."

As did Harriet Beecher Stowe, her husband, father, brothers, and most folks in Cincinnati, John Jolliffe, and James Gitchell also read the newspaper accounts of these momentous events avidly. While Amy was languishing in despair of their case ever finally being even heard in South Carolina, much less that the high court might grant her appeal, her lawyers nevertheless held on to a glimmer of hope that things might ere long turn in their favor.

Bauskett had reported to Jolliffe and Gitchell that there were rumors in South Carolinian legal circles that Judge O'Neall might soon sit on the bench of the high court himself, which would unquestionably be a blessing in their favor. Could it be, perhaps, that was why they still had not been given a date for the trial?

The situation was decidedly worrisome regardless of such rumors. The abolitionist John Brown, who had been active in Cincinnati a few years earlier, had finally turned to violence as the necessary means to the definitive elimination of slavery. He resorted to the use of the bludgeon and the Bowie knife to elicit an overthrow first in Kansas, then in Harpers Ferry, Virginia. There, after killing five men at a federal armory and attempting unsuccessfully to start a slave rebellion, he was captured, tried for treason against Virginia, and hanged. This further inflamed the sentiments on both sides of the slavery issue and folks felt more and more like the powder keg they'd been sitting on for years was finally about to blow sky high. Short of Divine intervention or some unexpected outpouring of grace to calm the turbulent waters, this real and immanent danger seemed increasingly inescapable.

Amy too had been hearing the news, and it worried her sick that measures might be taken to deprive them of their long sought freedom, even up here in Ohio. Those fears nearly overrode her concerns about the court case in South Carolina, causing her sleepless nights and more than a few anxious conversations with Messrs. Jolliffe and Gitchell on the subject. Despite their reassurances that such a thing would not and could not happen, Amy felt that they were steadily being swept up in the larger issue of general emanicipation far more than she had ever expected or wanted.

Though not totally unfounded, her fears would soon be somewhat assuaged. News came from South Carolina that John Belton O'Neall, the conscientious and thorough master of jurisprudence, was not only appointed to the bench on the South Carolina Supreme Court but was appointed its Chief Justice! It spoke volumes of his high moral character and the great respect in which he was held that this should occur despite the allegations of some that he was a crypto-abolitionist, and the fact that many of his views on the subject of race and slavery were extremely unpopular among the planter elite. It would also bode well for the outcome of Amy's petition.

John Jolliffe was not ignorant of the arguments presented to the Supreme Court in the Dred Scott case. In fact, in 1856 as the Dred Scott case was being heard, he had represented a Negro slave from Campbell County, Kentucky who had crossed the Ohio River for a few hours to fetch a doctor. In the case of Anderson v. Poindexter argued in the Ohio court, by Ohio law the enslaved Mr. Poindexter was free because he came to Ohio with the consent of his owner despite the fact that he then returned to Kentucky and served his master for several years.

"John, I am certain we shall prevail before your High Court. The issue here is clear. If Amy and her family are free, then they are entitled to inherit. Period. To rule otherwise would be in total contradiction of the settled law governing inheritance." Jolliffe insisted to his colleague and now co-counsel, John Bauskett.

"What if, as in the Dred Scott case, Aldrich and Owens attempt to argue she cannot inherit because she is not a citizen, even if free?" questioned Bauskett.

"It doesn't matter!" Jolliffe declared. "One doesn't have to be a citizen in order to inherit. There are many families of British extraction who have left legacies to family members on both sides of the Atlantic. We simply have to hammer home the reality that the will found on Elijah incontrovertibly establishes his intent to manumit and that all nine of the slaves in question had debarked from the Jacob Strader before Elijah dropped dead on the wharf."

"And if they argue that because Elijah never changed domicile to Ohio himself, that somehow precludes him from emancipating them?" challenged Bauskett, already knowing the answer but rehearsing for the probable need to defend the point.

"As I told you before, my friend, Ohio law makes no mention of the slave holder having to change domicile to Ohio in order to manumit in Ohio. Nor does the brevity of the master's soujourn in Ohio invalidate the manumission. It requires only the permission for the slave to enter the state and the declaration of an intention to emancipate."

"So your seeking the deed of manumission was in truth entirely unnecessary?" asked Bauskett.

"It was rather gilding the lily I suppose, but I felt it might be useful in providing documentary proof so as not to leave the slightest shadow of a doubt that by Ohio law they were free, and if free, then able to inherit!" smiled Jolliffe. Clearly, he had built his reputation on the basis of arguing these matters many times with great success.

"We shall have to underscore the issue of comity here too, reasserting that the laws of one state must be respected by another lest they attempt to argue that because of the Act of 1841 Ohio law becomes a moot point, insisting that Amy and her family are still thereby enslaved." reflected Bauskett.

"I am certain Justice O'Neall would be quick to knock down any such attempt. I'm telling you John, we are going to win this, I am certain of it!" Jolliffe proclaimed.

"Manuel, please!" protested Amy, pushing him away with a coquettish smile. "Not in front of the children!"

Manuel had joined Amy and her family for dinner and had leaned over spontanteously to give her a kiss. The children stared with mixed feelings. The older boys were distinctly uncomfortable. It had been hard adjusting to see Elijah as their father when they had moved from the Kirkland to the Willis plantation, but they were much younger then and in need of a father. Elijah had admirably met that need and they felt a deep loyalty to him because of it. Now Elder was already grown, and Ellick and Phillip were nearly men. They were no longer looking for a father figure, and were having trouble enough adjusting to freedom and trying to make their way in life. They were also aware of their own male urges, and had been looking with new attention at all the colored girls they met. Their social circle was extremely small and they had little opportunity to see or meet any white girls, but their natural impulses rising like the spring sap, they were open to all possibilities- except facing the reality that their mother might have urges of her own.

It's not that they didn't like Manuel or appreciate him giving them a job and all, or even that they begrudged their mother his friendship. It had been a Godsend, and had given them all new confidence that they could stand on their own, but already the boys were hoping for more, and the brickyard was getting too small to contain their dreams. Manuel's advances just made them think all the more about setting out on their own.

The girls and little Savage on the other hand were a lot younger and still very much in need of a father figure. Savage could barely even remember Elijah, his memories being more a rehearsal of stories he'd been told than his own recollections, and most of Eliza's memories were of the events surrounding her little brother's birth and then his falling sick with the yellow fever. Elijah's subsequent depression and prolonged withdrawal had also blurred Eliza's memories of him. Clarissa was perhaps the most torn. She remembered Elijah with great love, but could also feel her mother's loneliness after Elijah's death and saw how she had lit up and come back to life when in Manuel's presence. Little Julia also picked up on the lightness in her mother's voice and the twinkle in her eyes when Manuel teased her.

"Momma, are you and Mister Manuel gonna get married?" asked Julia innocently, watching Manuel's advances and seeing the smile on her mother's face even as she pushed him away.

Amy blanched, suddenly becoming flustered and nervous, and Manuel just grinned and turning to Amy raised his eyebrows quizzically. This of course flustered her even more. "Why Julia honey, what makes ya think Mister Manuel would want to marry a widow woman like me?"

Momma Celia weighed in on the situation. "It ain't no dishonor to the dead to love the livin," she remarked with a smile, insightfully putting her finger on the source of Amy's conflict as only a mother could. Manuel looked at her with quiet gratitude but said nothing. He knew Amy well enough not to push her, for she could be stubborn as a plow mule once she got her back up about something. This situation required patience and diplomacy.

"I admit it children, I love your Momma- I love all of ya'll in fact. But marriage is not somethin to enter into lightly and it's not somethin we've even discussed." Manuel replied, deciding it was better not to be dishonest about his feelings, since the children could see through such subterfuge clearly. But he also didn't want to put Amy in a compromising position, knowing she needed time to come to such a decision. Though they hadn't openly talked about it, it was true; his interest was unambiguous, leading to a logical conclusion that marriage figured into his plans for the future.

Amy looked at him thoughtfully and then clearing her throat said, "Like he said, it's not somethin we've ever discussed, but if we ever do we'll let ya'll know."

Manuel was dying to ask the children how they would feel about him marrying their mother, but decided discretion was the better part of valor and refrained. He did feel suddenly hopeful however, for Amy had clearly not closed the door on the subject. He concluded it was a discussion they should finally have, and soon.

"That's not the kind a discussion a man and a woman have in front of others in any event. Wouldn't be proper. An ya Momma's a proper lady!" he offered, clearly implying that the conversation would take place but in another setting.

Realizing that the diplomatic thing to do at that point would be to excuse himself, Manuel then added graciously, "Momma Celia, I can understand why ya had a reputation for bein the best cook in Barnwell District. Shoot- I haven't had a meal this good since I came to Ohio, so I could say the same about Cincinnati! Dinner was truly delicious an I surely do thank ya for it!" He smiled broadly at Momma Celia and pushing back his chair, stood up.

"It's getting late. I should head on home." Resisting the temptation to give Amy a good-bye kiss he simply smiled at her warmly, and thanking everyone again bade them all good night and left.

After dinner, when all the dishes were done and everyone had gone to bed, Elder and Phillip lay awake.

"Hey Elder?" whispered Phillip, not wanting to wake the others. "You awake?"

"Yeah." Elder answered softly.

"How do ya'll feel about Manuel takin up with Momma?" Phillip asked.

"I dunno," Elder responded, his tone flat. "How bout you?"

"I dunno." Phillip replied. "It kinda makes me uncomfortable to see em sorta flirtin like they do."

"I know what ya mean. Specially him bein younger than Papa. Makes me look at Momma different. Feels kinda strange." Elder couldn't quite put into words the implicitly sexual content of what he was feeling.

"Yeah, it does," agreed Phillip. After another pause, his brother asked, "Do you ever think about gettin married?"

There was an awkward silence before he answered, as if he were debating how much to open up to his brother. "Well yeah, I guess. There's a gal works in the dry goods store- Alice- sho is pretty. I met her when Momma sent me to pick up something she'd ordered there. I woke up wet from a dream bout her the other night!"

Phillip shifted in his bed. "You have those kinda dreams too?" He sounded relieved. "I been havin sticky dreams too- was almost at the point a askin Momma Celia if there was something wrong with me, but couldn't quite bring myself to do it. I was afraid she'd tell Momma."

Elder laughed quietly. "Everybody has them dreams. It's about bein a man. The preachers say it's about sin, but I can't figure it that way- feels too good!"

"But it ain't sin if ya're married, right?" asked Phillip for clarification.

"No. It's alright if ya're married. Guess that's why folks wanna get married in the first place- so's they can feel good in at least somethin in they lives!" There was another pause while both brothers pondered the matter.

"But Elder, Momma and Papa wa'nt legally married. Does that mean they were sinnin when they had Clarissa an Julia an Eliza, an Savage too?" The thought was disturbing. Phillip had come to accept and love Elijah, and it didn't seem like a man who would try so hard to set them free and give them a good life could be the kind of sinner the preachers talked about.

"I don't reckon so. Momma always said she felt like she an Papa were married in the eyes a God- it was only the eyes a white folks couldn't see it. They thought it was a sin for Momma and Papa to be together at all, but that's just stuff n nonsense." Elder affirmed.

"So what ya'll gonna do. You gonna ask Alice ta marry ya, so's the devil don't take ya for yer sticky dreams?" Phillip asked, teasing.

"Could be," answered Elder, seriously considering the question. "Could be!"

"Way I figure it, if Manuel marries Momma, might be time for us to move along too!" speculated Phillip. "I just don't know if I could live under the same roof knowing they was sharin a bed. Know what I mean?"

"Yeah. I kinda feel that way too. But I don't wanna hurt Momma after all we been through. Don't know how she'd feel about us movin out on our own." Elder commented.

Sleep was finally overcoming Phillip. He yawned and muttered, "If Mister Jolliffe and Mister Bauskett can win our case we might actually be able to afford to move out an get married!"

"Hmm mmm," mumbled Elder also drifting off, hoping to dream another sweet dream of Alice.

The fact that John Belton O'Neall had been appointed Chief Justice was surely comforting, but hardly a guarantee of the outcome of the trial. There were other notable jurists on the bench, one of whom was both particularly formidable in his knowledge of the law and in his distaste for Negroes and their emancipation: Justice Francis H. Wardlaw. Coming from a distinguished family of South Carolina lawyers hailing from Abbeville, including the Judge David Wardlaw, who had first ruled against the Cincinnati will; Justice Wardlaw was a force to be reckoned with. Well aware of his political views, his keen intellect, and his encyclopedic knowledge of the law, neither John Bauskett nor John Jolliffe intended to be caught napping with Justice Wardlaw's watchful eye upon them.

They came prepared. In addition to the copious testimony of people who had known Elijah- Wooley and Ary Reason, William Knotts, Joseph Harley, Will Beazeley, John Howard, Jonathan Pender, and all the others who had already testified in the Apellate Court, they were armed with depositions from people outside of Barnwell too. James Meredith the train conductor, William Cullum who had travelled with Elijah on the *Jacob Strader*, Robert S. Duming the clerk of the *Jacob Strader* who booked Elijah and his family's passage; all attested to Elijah's confession of his unambiguous intention to emancipate his family in Ohio. So did the depositions of Messrs. Ernst and Harwood, who had originally offered to serve as executors of Elijah's will.

Lest there be any doubt on the matter, Jolliffe and Bauskett came equally armed with legal reinforcements in the form of depositions from a passle of lawyers from Ohio. All of them attested to the established principle of automatic emancipation via entrance into the State of Ohio and the utter absence of any State legislation to the contrary. In addition to a deposition from James Gitchell, there were corroborating depositions taken from Thomas Ewing Jr., Alexander H. MacGuffey, Charles Cist, and William C. McDowell, all lawyers practicing in Cincinnati. McDowell claimed an additional distinction, being of a family who had married into the family of Henry Clay himself, and sharing the late stateman's views on the rightness of emancipation. McDowell even went so far as to insist that by Ohio law a slaveowner need not even express the intent of manumission. The mere act of permitting the slave to enter the State of Ohio was sufficient to achieve such status.

As was to be expected, the questioning by the justices was pointed and sometimes intense. The debate meandered through centuries of law and policy, Justice Wardlaw in particular frequently citing British law on the slavery issue and the deliberations resulting in the Act of 1841 with great erudition. As the debate wore on however, it seemed to Jolliffe that the arguments against Elijah's will were gradually crumbling.

Justice Wardlaw and Mr. Alrdich spent considerable time questioning Elijah's intentions. They indulged in a great deal of speculation about whether had Elijah not died, he might have changed his mind about emancipating the family, citing as precedent the fact that he had taken Amy and the family to Baltimore and yet brought them back to Williston. Justice Wardlaw in particular took great pains to rehearse the history of manumission and inheritance law going back to colonial times, and even in the British legislation that had abolished the slave trade, yet always with an eye to the preservation of property and the State's right to determine policy on the matter.

O'Neall, on the other hand, distinguished between policy and law, and insisted upon the need to separate politics and popular opinion out of the matter. Moreover, he argued that if a will be legal in form, and the content that controverted South Carolina law were inapplicable because it only applied to slaves, and that the freedom of the Negroes in question were proved by Ohio law, it would be a contradiction to acknowledge their freedom and then deprive them of their rights to property.

Aldrich duly presented their case in favor of the heirs in law- Elijah's next of kin. Bauskett and his colleagues clearly presented the case of Jolliffe on behalf of Amy and her family. Volumes of testimony were presented to the justices as well as copious citations of case law to back each party's arguments. Nothing more could be done now but wait for the justices to deliberate and then reconvene to announce their ruling.

"Goddamnit!" swore James Willis to his brother and Angus, exasperated. "If I'd a known it was gonna take this long to go through the courts I never woulda gotten into this mess! Probably shoulda shot the lot of em when we went up to Cincinnati to see Uncle Elijah's grave!"

"Jesus, James! Great solution! Get yaself arrested for murder instead? I'll admit it's aggravatin, but what about our political plans? Was that all bullshit to you? We can't just ignore the courts! If it doesn't go our way we can still help enact new laws!" Angus exclaimed.

James looked skeptical.

"Maybe the first petition wasn't so effective because it didn't drive the real message home. This isn't really about the dangers of abolitionism- it's about the dangers of miscegenation!" Angus insisted.

"Angus is right, James. Hell, you always been the smart one, but now ya act like ya wanna quit! Forget about whether they can be emancipated. I say we get up a new petition for the legislature to prohibit white men from havin families with black women at all!" offered Michael.

"Prohibition ain't gonna be enough!" insisted James, eager for some satisfying possibility of redeeming their cause. "There's gotta be some kind a punishment for whites pollutin our race and undermining our economy and our society just cause they can't keep it in their pants with some nigra!" James said with a mixture of vindictiveness and vehement self-righteousness.

"Hold on now boys!" cautioned Angus. "We don't even know what the justices're gonna decide yet! Let's not go puttin the cart before the horse! No point in puttin up another petition until we know their decision, cause it could influence how we word any petition we might wanna enter!"

"Well it can't hurt to go ahead and write it up now. It'd give us a way to let off steam while this thing gets decided. We can always edit it later if we need to," insisted Michael, with James nodding his agreement.

While the Willis brothers were fuming and plotting their revenge in preparation for the possibility that by some cruel aberration of the judicial process the court might actually rule in Elijah's favor, Jolliffe and Bauskett were having a very different kind of conversation.

"If the court decides in our favor we must act swiftly to help Amy emancipate Gilbert and the others!" warned Bauskett. "I'm frankly more fearful every day that the preservation of the Union hangs by a thread and war may become inevitable all too soon! If war breaks out it will be far more difficult and dangerous to get them out of South Carolina!"

"Indeed, my friend, I quite agree. Should that transpire I'm afraid the value of the plantation is also likely to plummet. No one in their right mind would buy such a vast tract of land in the middle of a war!" agreed Jolliffe. "Amy may be disappointed in what of Elijah's assets she is ultimately able to recoup, but such things are well beyond the scope of our control."

"I suspect that as long as she can get her brother and the others out safely, she'll cut her losses. She's a formidable woman and a resourceful one!" commented Bauskett.

"She is indeed! Quite contrary to my own expectations, she took it upon herself to find suitable lodgings for the family and employment for her and her older boys. They now live modestly but freely in Cincinnati. Jack our coachman even tells me our Miss Amy has a suitor! A mulatto gentleman from North Carolina who works in a brickyard!" Jolliffe announced.

John Bauskett was mildly surprised at this last piece of news, wondering whether Amy felt this a lowering of her expectations, but upon reflection recognized that it was understandable enough that a man of her own race might be attracted to her. She was after all an impressive woman- charming and intelligent and strong, and even potentially wealthy. He assumed anyone she might consider marrying must know of her law suit, and was a bit concerned that the suitor not be an opportunist hoping to cash in on her inheritance- especially since its ultimate value lay very much in question, given the political climate! But he had confidence in Amy's strength of character. He doubted after all they'd been through with her fighting for their rights with the ferocity of a lioness, that she would permit herself to be used by any suitor, even in exchange for the alleviation of the loneliness she must have felt at the loss of Elijah. He smiled in appreciation of Elijah's choice of spouse. "The man was no fool!" he thought to himself.

Chief Justice John Belton O'Neall called to order the session of the South Carolina Supreme Court for the Fall Term of 1860. The attorneys for both parties stood in respectful anticipation before the assembled justices as the members of the bench settled into their seats and looked out at the lawyers and their clients. It was more than five years since Elijah Willis had dropped dead on the wharf in Cincinnati leaving the nine Negroes who had accompanied him in a precarious situation, uncertain of their future or their freedom. For five years they had fought for what they had been told by their lawyers were their rights. For five years Elijah's erstwhile relations in Williston had contested those rights at every step. For five years South Carolina and the nation had been edging steadily closer to seeing their differences over the very issues of this case as being irreconcilable, the only resolution for which would be an all out war. So when those gathered in the courtroom stood waiting for the justices' decision, they did so with a heightened sense of the importance of the verdict. This was no mere squabble over land or property. It cut to the core of the values and the self-identity of all present, no matter which party they chose to support.

"Please be seated!" ordered the Chief Justice, his tone more formal than usual given the solemn nature of announcing a decision from the bench.

The rendering of a Supreme Court Decision was not what one might consider a brief announcement, but rather a detailed review of the legal questions put to the bench and their considered evaluation of them, pro and con. All this must transpire before the announcement of the Court's ruling and whether there were any minority dissenting opinions expressed by the sitting justices.

"I advise ya'll to make yaselves comfortable, as this may take a while," O'Neall informed those assembled.

He then launched into a lengthy and detailed, but eloquent explanation of the circumstances that had prompted the trial, the legal issues they raised- both state and federal- and the legal principles that governed their resolution. He detailed the precedents in the case law of similar issues previously tried, and he systematically reduced the question upon which the entire case hung to a single point: were Amy and her family legally free at the time of Elijah Willis's death, or not?

"The elaborate decree of my brother Wardlaw (while a Chancellor) is in many of its parts, entitled to the commendation of every well-informed mind. Yet there are parts which have not met the concurrence of this Court. One, a very material part, on which the whole case depends, has not been satisfactory to a majority. Indeed, on it we have come to a conclusion entirely antagonistc to the decree," announced O'Neall.

With that Jolliffe and Bauskett heaved a huge sigh of relief- for whatever might follow by way of explanation, it was clear they had won.

Across the aisle Mr. Aldrich sat clenching his jaw and pursing his lips, clearly struggling to restrain himself from any outburst. He too knew that the Court had beaten him and his clients, though his clients had not yet realized this.

O'Neall, in his delivery of the Court's decision, walked a finely balanced line. He clearly did not pander to abolitionist sentiment, making oblique reference to John Brown and his ilk who disregarded the law in preference for what they deemed a more righteous cause. Nor did he cotton to the locally racist popular preference.

"I should feel myself degraded if, like some in Ohio and other abolition states, I trampled on law and constitution, in obedience to popular will. There is no law in South Carolina which, notwithstanding the freedom of Amy and her children, declares that the trusts in their favor are void. As soon as they were acknowledged to be free one moment before the death of Elijah Willis, they are capable to become the cestui que trusts under his will." O'Neall explained, his archaic French legal term indicating Amy's legally confirmed status as beneficiary.

Refuting Aldrich's contention (supported by Justice Wardlaw) that the case hung on Elijah's unknown intentions after he reached Ohio- allowing for the possibility he might again change his mind as he had in Baltimore- O'Neall pointed out the futility of ruling based upon an unknowable.

"We can only judge of that by what occurred before. We know what he intended up to the moment when he reached Cincinnati. What did he intend when the boat reached the wharf? He might possibly then have remained on the boat with his slaves and returned to South Carolina, but he did not do that, he made the act of freedom absolute by landing within the territorial limits of Ohio. This showed that he intended to confer freedom by making Ohio their home. He had told Amy "when we get out of South Carolina you should never return". The act made his words good. For he could not, if he had desired it, have again reduced her to slavery," O'Neall insisted.

Deeming the efforts of Aldrich and Wardlaw to overwhelm the Court with superfluous erudition and historical precedents that did not speak to the real issue of the case, O'Neall concluded,

"I have not undertaken to review many of the cases of the Chancellor, as in the able argument of the case here. For the case turned upon a very narrow point; in which lights of authority could only help to the general principle that if the act done was in consequence of the intention previously expressed, it was enough for the case.

"This has been proved to be so on review of the whole law and facts, and the result is that the woman Amy, and her children, were free at the death of Elijah Willis, and were capable to become the cestui que trusts of the executor.

"The Chancellor's decree is reversed, and the bill is dismissed."

Justice Johnstone announced, "I concur in the result."

Justice Wardlaw announced his dissent, justifying it yet again with a rehearsal of his opinion. He concluded with a complaint and whine of disgust, not to say a rather florid excess of rhetorical drama that fell petulantly and hollow on the ears of Bauskett and Jolliffe,

"My bretheren seem more inclined to adopt the extravagance of the Irish orator, which revolts most men of sober mind and correct taste, and declare as the law of South Carolina:

"The first moment a slave touches the sacred soil of Britain (or Ohio) the altar and god sink together in the dust; his soul walks abroad in her own majesty; his body swells beyond the measure of his chains that burst from around him; and he stands redeemed, regenerated, and disenthralled by the irresistible genius of universal emancipation."

Jolliffe muttered to himself with satisfaction, "Amen! Quite so!" taking Wardlaw's contemptuously mocking citation of an abolitionist speech delivered to the British Parliament as a legal triumph and confirmation of their cause.

After the Chief Justice had brought down the final gavel and the Court was adjourned, John Bauskett and John Jolliffe grinned at each other. "Counsellor, I'd like to invite you to partake of a victory libation with me!" Bauskett then produced a bottle of fine sippin whiskey. "This was a gift from Elijah to me just before he left for Cincinnati the last time. I believe it is Kentucky Bourbon he acquired during his first visit to Cincinnati. Seems only appropriate we drink a toast to him and to Amy for achievin somethin truly remarkable, don't ya think?"

Jolliffe smiled broadly. "I gratefully accept your invitation sir, and heartily concur! After all, though distance may separate us geographically, we are united by the waters of Elkhorn Creek that flow from Kentucky into the Ohio River – for they are the source of some of the best sippin whiskey in the world!"

Outside the Courthouse, James and Michael were fuming. "I can't fuckin believe it!" raged James. "This is horse shit!"

"We oughta march right over to the General Assembly an demand they take up our petition! This is just plain wrong!" Michael fulminated.

Angus, however, kept his own counsel. He was struck by the masterful use of the law by Justice O'Neall and, just as his father had always insisted, the devil was in the details of the case. He saw how Justice Wardlaw had attempted to overwhelm with details and legal trivia and thereby effectively cloud the issue from being resolved by the clear light of truth. He also saw how Justice O'Neall had seen through the strategy and refused to let it obscure the clarity of his vision. It had been a truly admirable and illuminating performance.

"Hey ya'll, I'm starvin! I can't take any more of this right now! Let's go get a drink and somethin to eat, and then we can figure out what comes next! The General Assembly's supposed to rule on our petition any day now. The battle may be lost, but the war ain't over yet!" he said, almost prophetically.

Up in Cincinnati John Jolliffe and James Gitchell were exuberant. They had informed Amy of their victory and already had her, as the current proprietor of the Willis Plantation, sign documents ordering Gilbert and his family to be brought North by John Bauskett immediately.

"Gentlemen," Amy said, her voice cracking with emotion and sheer relief, "I just can't find words enough to thank ya'll for all ya did for us- an for Elijah!"

"My dear, it was a pleasure and a privilege! I never despaired that we would triumph in the end, but it has been an ordeal for all of us! We can thank the Good Lord and his Grace that it is now behind us and you are free to move ahead with your lives! Congratulations, by the way- Mr. Gitchell tells me that you have remarried! I hope you and your husband will be very happy together!"

Amy smiled through her tears of gratitude, and, discreetly dabbing them away with her ubiquitous lace handkerchief answered, "Thank you, sir. I struggled over the decision to remarry, until my mother made a comment that struck me to the core: 'It ain't no dishonor to the dead to love the livin,' as you say," she smiled, " it is time to move ahead with our lives, whatever freedom may bring!"

Jack drove her home with great pleasure. "I sho am happy for ya, Miss Amy. Ya'll deserved to win! It kinda feels like a victory for all of us, ta tell the truth!"

Amy smiled as Jack helped her out of the carriage. "Thank ya Jack, that's mighty sweet of ya. God bless ya for your support! You bein here from the beginnin helped us remember we weren't alone. That's meant a lot to all of us."

"My pleasure, ma'am. I remember when Mister Elijah come up here, an I thought to myself, 'He's a mighty fine man.' Then when ya'll come up I realized just how good he really was. Ya'll truly deserved to win this, so go on an enjoy it Miss Amy, and God bless. Ya'll take care now, y'hear?" Jack said as he climbed back up into the driver's seat and grabbing the reins, headed back across town to his employers.

When Amy entered the house, elated to share her wonderful news, she found Manuel and all the children gathered around with serious faces. She instantly sensed something was wrong.

"What's the matter? Why ya'll standin here with long faces? No need to worry about what the lawyers said!" She assumed the reason for their mournful expressions. "I got wonderful news! We won! The South Carolina Supreme Court ruled in our favor! Can ya believe it? It's over at last!" she told them excitedly. "I've already sent for Gilbert and the others!" Amy suddenly realized her mother was not in the crowd. Her heart sank.

"Manuel, where's Momma?" she asked, panic welling up inside her.

"She's upstairs, baby. But she's not doin so good. She fell right after ya left for the lawyers' office. She was clutchin her chest, so we called the doctor right away. Doctor came and said it was her heart. It ain't good. She been callin for ya." Manuel stepped aside as Amy rushed upstairs to her mother's room.

Momma Celia lay motionless on her bed, her breathing shallow and rapid.

As Amy rushed in she opened her eyes and seeing her daughter, weakly reached a gnarled hand out toward her.

"It's alright child. Don't ya cry now! I already tole ya, God's gonna take care a everything!" Momma Celia's voice was weak, but her eyes were clear. "Tell me, what did the lawyers say?"

"Oh Momma, you were right- we won! We own the plantation and the entire estate! Mr. Jolliffe is afraid that South Carolina's about to secede from the Union, so he insisted I sign an order as proprietor, that Mr. Bauskett bring Gilbert and the others up here right away! Mr. Jolliffe couldn't do it as executor, but I can as proprietor! Isn't it wonderful? Momma we did it! Elijah fulfilled his promise to me and to God!" Amy gushed, as tears trickled down her face and dampened her mother's hand.

"Hush child, hush! Go call the others in here. I got somethin to say an I don't have much time to say it," Momma said with a quiet urgency that cut through Amy's emotionl indulgence.

"Manuel! Children! Come here quick! Momma wants to talk to ya'll!" Amy called from the door as the others promptly climbed the stairs and respectfully filed in around their matriarch's bed. Amy returned to Momma Celia's side, sitting on the edge of the bed and stroking her mother's wiry gray hair and wizened cheeks, and patting her hand almost as if to reassure herself her mother was still there and could not leave.

Momma Celia winced in pain, struggling for breath, and then her face relaxed. She looked at each of her grandchildren and at Manuel, and at a pretty girl named Alice clinging to her oldest grandson's side. She smiled gently in blessing to all of them.

"Love's a beautiful thing. But it ain't always easy! Sometimes it seem like it take you into some mighty hard times and dark places, but even if you give up on it, it won't give up on you! It'll see ya through them hard times to the other side!" She smiled a luminous smile, as if her very presence were proof. The children all nodded in agreement, unable to speak. The girls were already sniffling and choking back tears. "I want ya'll to promise me somethin! Don't ya'll never stop lovin each other, even when ya might not feel ya'll're lovable. God don't don't make no mistakes, and God made all of ya'll, an He'll always love ya too! Love Him, love yaselves, and love each other! That's His legacy to us all! An it's a complicated legacy! Ya'll gotta have faith in Him, and faith in yaselves to do it! I got faith in both, so I know it works! Now come on an give me some sugar, so's I can give ya'll my blessin."

From the smallest to the eldest, the children bent over to kiss their grandmother as she laid her hand on the head of each in turn. Manuel and Alice had held back, out of respect. Momma Celia said softly, "Come on ya'll, you part a my family too!"

Alice and Manuel also came forward for her blessing and then stepped aside for Amy.

"Amy sugar, I am so proud a you! I never doubted the Lord would see ya to this day! But ya gotta tell Gilbert somethin for me!" She panted, "Tell him he'll always have my love and my blessin no matter what he decides." Her voice grew weaker. "But tell him if he ever puts on a blue uniform an fights in South Carolina, he'd best be careful he don't get shot by nobody wearin a grey uniform. I seen it in my vision!"

Her voice had grown so weak, this last phrase was barely a whisper. Amy had to lean close to make out what she was saying.

"Don't worry, Momma, he'll be here soon. Ya'll can tell him yaself!" She tried to assure her, unwilling to accept that her mother's departure was imminent and desperately wanting to celebrate their victory with all the family reunited. Momma Celia's eyes had closed and she seemed to have dozed off. A sweet smile lit up that wise, gentle old face, and even her wrinkles seemed to suddenly disappear, her cheeks becoming as smooth as a baby's, as if she had been strangely rejuvenated. Perhaps it was just that she felt relaxed, having given her blessing to all those whom she loved. But a sudden loud snore from her was followed by a still silence. Uplifted and unshackled by the love of her family, Momma Celia had passed on to her own ultimate freedom.

On November 29, 1860 the South Carolina House of Representatives' Committee on Colored Population reported on the petition signed by Michael and James Willis, A.P Bogecki, Col. Hargood, the Barnwell Commissioner of Equity, and forty-odd others who were outraged by the South Carolina Supreme Court's ruling on the will of Elijah Willis. The committee members determined that regarding the issue of miscegenation and a need for its severe punishment, "the evil complained of cannot be prevented by legislation" and that they could not therefore recommend any additional legislation thereon. On December 17, 1860 the petition was tabled. Three days later, on December 20 South Carolina became the first state to secede from the Union. On February 4, 1861 The Confederate States of America were proclaimed an independent Southern nation. On April 12 Confederate forces fired on the U.S. federal Fort Sumpter which controlled the entrance to Charleston harbor, making outright war a *fait accompli*. The following year, the Willis Plantation was seized by the Confederacy on the grounds that its owners were not "true Southerners"- a euphemistic attempt to ignore the laws of proprietorship in the name of a white supremacist nationalism that could not tolerate colored ownership of any property befitting the planter class. On January 1, 1863 President Abraham Lincoln issued the Emancipation Proclamation. On April 8, 1864 the United States Senate passed the Thirteenth Amendment. On on January 31, 1864 it was passed by the House of Representatives. On April 9, 1865 General Robert E. Lee surrendered the Armies of the Confederacy to General Ulysses S. Grant, ending the Civil War. On April 15, 1865 Lincoln was assassinated by a Confederate sympathizer John Wilkes Boothe, and on December 18, 1865 the Thirteenth Amendment to the Constitution was formally adopted, ending slavery for all time.

After the war, Amy Willis, by then known as Mary Ash, demanded an accounting of the Willis plantation from the Barnwell District Probate Court, where she and her children were listed as owners, and between 1873-1878 she succeeded at long last in selling off various parcels of land through her agent, John Bauskett.

POSTSCRIPT

This is a true story. Well mostly true, anyway. All of the characters named herein with both a first and last name are historically accurate, with the exception of a few spouses, a Mr. Stoddard, purveyor of whiskey, Leroy Johnson, the Cincinnati undertaker, and the first name of the lawyer, Mr. Owens. The opinions and actions attributed to the characters are based on the known facts of the case. Other than Amy, her mother and children, her brother Gilbert, and Manuel Ash, the names, personalities and actions of all the other people of color are fictitious. But the general sweep of the story and its conclusion, in the context of the momentous social changes leading up to the Civil War, are accurate. They take on a freshness and urgency in the light of the current political environment in America, echoing many of the same attitudes more than a hundred and fifty years later.

I first heard of the story of Elijah and Amy Willis from a mixed race colleague of mine at the Johns Hopkins Hospital in Baltimore, where we served together on the Diversity Council of the Department of Human Resources. Her former husband was a descendent of Elijah Willis. We both agreed it was a remarkable story that needed to be told. Though we considered a collaboration, we decided that our styles and voices being quite different, it would be better for each to go our separate ways, free to write as our hearts dictated.

I debated whether to abandon the project, but the more I researched it, the more it caught a hold of me and simply would not let me go. The clincher was the improbable discovery that Elijah Willis had consulted my own paternal ancestor, Henry Clay, on how to emancipate his slaves. Consumed with curiosity sparked by this distant family connection, as I got deeper and deeper into the story I became fascinated with the psychological and emotional complexity of the issues and the multi-dimensional relationships they spawned. Having to recount some of them in a believable voice, however, took me well outside of my own comfort zone.

The writing of this book in many ways is the result of my own ongoing confrontation with these issues, and my good fortune of living through the cultural sea change of the 1960's. I was a middle class white boy, born in Kentucky before the Supreme Court decision on Brown v. The Board of Education. Growing up in the Civil Rights era, I was educated in New England at Exeter and Yale. I remember watching Dr. Martin Luther King Jr.'s "I have a dream" speech live on TV, and listening to Mahalia Jackson sing. I remember seeing the news coverage of the faces of African Americans and whites weeping together at the passing of President Kennedy's funeral cortege, that sad day the whole nation mourned. I lived in Franco's Spain for a year, and upon returning, I was an eyewitness to Dr. King's last Sunday sermon and the race riots that set Washington on fire four days later, in the wake of his assassination. I was also an eyewitness to Yale University shutting down for the only time in its long history for the Bobby Seale Black Panther trial in New Haven. I began my teaching career teaching inner city children in Barcelona and then in New Haven. I led a multi-cultural congregation for fourteen years, and deal daily with the inequalities of health care delivery to the needy in my current job as a medical interpreter.

These issues of racial and socio-political inequality are hardly academic or merely historical to me. They are an integral and formative part of my own life. I hope that addressing them, not from a simplistic black/white perspective, but rather from a mixed-race one of both love and hate, might shed some new light on a subject that is all too prone to stereotypes- from our textbooks in school to the movies we watch and the jokes we tell.

I know from my own experience that giving a name and a face to the "other-" telling and listening to our personal stories- changes our perceptions and experiences both of who "they" are, and who we ourselves are as well. I am convinced that however painful the story might be, telling it is better for us all than keeping silent, no matter how we define "them and us." I find it uplifting to plumb the depths of human experience, to give a name to and recognize the roots of our common humanity. This is, in fact, a commitment that continues to motivate me.

It was a revelation to me, as I researched this story, that the matter of white men having families with women of color in the Ante Bellum South was hardly restricted to Mr. Jefferson and Sally Hemings. It was so frequent, in fact, that it posed a serious threat to white hegemony. Growing up in an era where Civil Rights and Anti-war protest was a liberal badge of honor for American youth, it was disturbing to find that it was actually the younger generation of whites that fought for more stringent prohibitions against emancipation and the leaving of inheritances to those they deemed usurpers, even though they shared the same blood. I did take some liberties with the facts- according to the *New York Times* article about his death, Elijah made his fortune from lumber. There was no mention of him raising cotton, but I thought it made sense to add that element without risk of stereotyping, as it was a central element to the economy of the region and of the State of South Carolina. It provided an additional element of plausibility for his financial motivations in going to Baltimore as well, and to the logic of selling off some of his slaves before the move to Cincinnati.

Though I was unable to find specific correspondence between Elijah Willis and Henry Clay, despite references by Chief Justice O'Neall to their contact in the trial transcripts, I attempted to construct the probable content thereof in voices as faithful to the two men as I could muster. Clay's letter to Elijah is basically a summary of his known views on the matter of the emancipation of slaves. Details of Henry Clay's life and politics, his last days in Washington, his death from tuberculosis, and his mansion in Lexington are accurate down to the description of his card table- which is a family heirloom in my own possession. Even the account of his manservant Levi running away to Cincinnati and then returning unchastized is, surprisingly, a matter of historical fact gleaned from Robert Rimini's definitive biography of Clay. Equally true are the details of his eccentric and flamboyant cousin Cassius Marcellus Clay, who later became Lincoln's ambassador to the Court of the Czar of Russia and urged Lincoln to follow the Czar's example of freeing the Russian serfs.

The names of George Brown and his father Alexander, in Baltimore, are well known in the local financial world of that city- Alex Brown & Sons still being a premier financial institution. *Mattchett's Baltimore Director* is a real document, and with its list of businesses, places of worship, maps, and the names, addresses and professions of Baltimore's residents, is a goldmine of historical information about its people in the 1850's. The Admiral Fell Inn on the plaza on Fells Point, is still operating as a hotel today- though for a considerably more refined clientele than was the case in Elijah Willis's day. William Dorsey was a real lawyer who really did live at 3 Fayette Street in Baltimore at the time of Elijah Willis's visit, and was in fact a supporter of Henry Clay's, though I have no evidence of either him or George Brown ever meeting Elijah Willis.

As Dorsey is also a family name of mine- my maternal grandmother's family had come from Maryland- the genealogical information William reports to Elijah is in fact genuine. Toward the end of the story, William C. McDowell, the Cincinnati lawyer referenced, may or may not be related to the McDowell who married Henry Clay's granddaughter Ann Clay, and to her great-great-grandson, my father, William McDowell Stucky. However, geographical proximity to Lexington makes it likely in the smaller world of mid-nineteenth century America.

The descriptions of the Willis Plantation house, *The Affleck Plantation Journal and Account Book*, the invention of a baby bottle with a vulcanized rubber nipple by Elijah Pratt in New York, the plant based remedies for atrial fibrillation, yellow fever, the healing of scars and other maladies, the Barnwell Courthouse and it's eventual perpendicular sundial- are all easily found by an internet search. The information about the Grimké sisters and Harriet Beecher Stowe, her family, and the publication of Uncle Tom's Cabin is accurate, though Harriet's father presiding at Elijah's funeral was my own artistic invention. The names and descriptions of the *Jacob Strader*, the Powhatten Packet Line, The Old Bay Line, and the *North Carolina* are easily verified by a search online, replete with photographs, although the *Delta Queen* is a steamboat of more recent construction still in operation. William Law Olmstead, the architect of New York's Central Park, was known to disapprove of slavery and had in fact made a Southern Tour with his brother right at the time of Elijah's trip North with his family to Baltimore- but the possibility of them travelling on the same ship with Elijah and his family was artistic license.

The Reverend Edwin Wagner, Vicar of All Saints Episcopal Church, was in fact an Englishman, and a church was built on his property next to his home in Barnwell in the "Timber Gothic" style in the late 1850's. Robert Barnwell Rhett was an extreme secessionist with delusions of forming a trans-Caribbean slave empire, and the Willis brothers and Angus Patterson Jr. did spearhead an unsuccessful petition against miscegenation to the General Assembly in 1860, but the "Proper Order Party" and their rally at Dr. Guignard's were my own invention.

The details of the death of Elijah Willis were taken directly from the *New York Times* article published the week he died. The descriptions of the deaths of Henry Clay and Daniel Webster, citations from their speeches, Lincoln's eulogy of Henry Clay in the Illinois Statehouse in Springfield, the Northern reactions to the Dred Scott decision, are all historical fact just as reported. So too, the report of the caning of Senator Sumner by Congressman Brooks. The quotes of the rulings of Dred Scott Decision and the South Carolina Courts themselves are accurate- even if the descriptions of those present at the trials and their reactions are products of my own imagination. Chief Justice O'Neall's final ruling, however, is straight out of the trial transcripts.

It appears that Amy Willis did in fact marry a man named Manuel Ash, who was a mulatto from North Carolina working in a brickyard in Ohio. Her name appears as Mary Ash in some documents, but her story as Mary matches precisely that of Amy, down to the place of birth and the names and number of her children. Though *The New York Times* article named her as Mary Amy Turner, I found no other documentation referring to her as such, so the explanation for her name change is my own conjecture.

All the events and dates reported in the Epilogue are straight historical fact as matters of public record, with no interpolation whatsoever on my part.

Sudden Death of a Slaveholder—Twenty-five Slaves Emancipated.

From the Cincinnati Gazette, May 22.

Over a year since, Mr. ELIJAH WILLIS, of Williston, Barnwell District, S.C., came to this city and executed, in the office of JOLIFFE & GITCHELL, a will, bequeathing to his wife and her heirs and assignees, all his property, real and personal, to the value of $150,000, consisting of two plantations well stocked, and from forty to fifty negroes. His wife, MARY AMY TURNER, and children, six in number, are mulattoes, and were held by WILLIS as slaves. Mr. WILLIS agreed with Messrs. A. H. ERNST, EDWARD HARWOOD and JOHN JOLIFFE, whom he made his executors, that they should be manumitted, and that the executors might dispose of the remainder of his slaves at his death as they deemed best. Mr. WILLIS returned to his plantation.

Yesterday morning he arrived from the South on the *Jacob Strader* with his wife, her mother, and six children. After securing a hack to convey the family up to the Dumas House, Mr. WILLIS, with a daughter held by each hand, approached the carriage, and was in the act of stepping in, when he was seized with a palpitation of the heart, to which he was subject, and falling backwards, expired in about five minutes. Coroner MENZIES held an inquest over the body, and the jury returned a verdict in accordance with the above facts. Mr. WILLIS was about 60 years of age, a very respectable old gentleman, and has been married to MARY AMY about thirteen years and always manifested towards her and the children a warm affection.

He has been in bad health several years, and his relatives, who reside in the Barnwell district, have frequently importuned him to give up his business and travel with his family. He left home about four weeks ago, not, as they supposed, to make said trip, but to come to this State, free his family from slavery, and provide them with comfortable houses on free soil. Having done this, it was his intention to return to South Carolina, settle up his affairs, and live the remainder of his life free from all care and anxiety. Bad health for several years was an additional inducement for him to pursue this course.

The remains of Mr. WILLIS, accompanied by the family, were taken to the Dumas House. The family appears to be deeply afflicted by Mr. WILLIS's sudden death. They are kindly cared for. His last will is in the possession of FLAMEN BALL, Esq., counsel for the wife of WILLIS, who will attend to her business, and see that she obtains that bequeathed to her. The funeral of Mr. WILLIS will take place to-day.

Those who affect to believe that the abolition of slavery would lead to universal amalgamation at the North, will please make a note of the above case.

From the Cincinnati Columbian, May 22.

On the 23d of February, 1854, a fine-looking, corpulent gentleman, apparently about sixty years of age, came to this city in search of Dr. BRISDANE, from whom he wished advice as to the proper course to pursue to effectuate the manumission of a number of his slaves. Not readily finding Dr. BRISBANE, he obtained the advice of JOHN JOLIFFE, Esq., and had duplicate wills drawn up. One of these he took with him, and the other he deposited with Mr. JOLIFFE, to be used if he should die suddenly, and the will in his possession be accidentally or purposely destroyed. He stated that one of his brothers had died very suddenly, and that he himself, being subject to palpitation of the heart, was liable to be also summoned to another world at a moment's notice.

ELIJAH WILLIS—that was his name—staid only a few days in Cincinnati, but his bright, benevolent countenance and manly frankness were not soon forgotten by those whom circumstances had thrown into contact with him.

Returning home, he drew up a complete inventory of all his property, and making two of his neighbors his confidants, he deposited this inventory with them, to be used in case of his sudden death, at the same time making them pledge themselves not to make it public previously.

He was largely engaged in the lumber business, and raised no crops except what were necessary for the support of the twenty-nine full grown slaves, and the numerous slave children that he owned. The lumber got out by his slaves was rafted down the Edisto River. In this business Mr. WILLIS had amassed a large estate. He was noted for the kindness with which he treated his slaves, who were never driven with the whip, nor shut out by a lock from the stores of provisions. They ate in the kitchen part of the same food that Mr. WILLIS ate in the parlor.

A number of the relatives of Mr. WILLIS, who are all in comfortable circumstances, lived near him, but seldom visited his residence. His housekeeper was a dark but very shrewd mulatto woman whom he purchased with her mother, brother and sister, about thirteen years ago. This housekeeper's name was MARY AMY ELMORE TURNER. Her father, who was owned by another master, had deserted her mother, and for this was sold to a cotton planter in Alabama.

AMY, as the housekeeper, was ordinarily called by Mr. WILLIS, while the slave of a former master, a Mr. KIRTLAND, had a colored husband by whom she had three children before he was sent South.

This woman, by her faithfulness and shrewdness, soon acquired great influence over Mr. WILLIS, by whom she had three children. She watchfully superintended his domestic affairs, attended to the wants of the slaves, and advised as to the business.

Mr. WILLIS, feeling concerned for the future welfare of his children, and urged thereto by AMY, at last determined to free her, her mother, her six children, her brother and her sister. When he came to Cincinnati, one year ago, and had his will written, it was to carry out this intent.

After his return home, he arranged all his business as rapidly as possible, and taking notes for outstanding debts due him, made preparations for disposing of his entire estate and moving to Ohio, where he proposed to locate on a farm, with AMY, her mother and the children. Finding that the expense of bringing AMY's brother and sister and their families would be considerable, and that there might be some difficulty in at once securing a home, Mr. WILLIS concluded finally to come North with AMY, her mother and the children, and having secured for them a residence, return to close up the business and bring the others.

On last Tuesday week, they left home as thus proposed. On reaching Louisville, they got on board the steamer *Jacob Strader*, and reached here at 6 o'clock yesterday morning. Soon after the boat touched the wharf, Mr. WILLIS and his company went on shore, and he called a carriage, when, just as he went to reach one of the small children into it, he breathed heavily. AMY asked him if he had another attack of palpitation of the heart. He nodded affirmatively, gave two or three heavy breathings, and then fell dead.

Just at this moment some one asked where they came from; Amy's mother did not answer, and was threatened with being kicked into the river. Some one urged Amy to go on board again, and she refused. By the advice of a friend she at once secured the money (about $530) in Mr. W.'s possession, notes and due-bills amounting to three thousand dollars, a gold watch and other valuables. She was taken with the trunks and the body of Mr. Willis to the Dumas House.

Dr. Menzies being called in, held an inquest, when a verdict was returned in accordance with these facts.

Mr. Ball, of the legal firm of Chase & Ball, being called in, the will of Mr. Willis, found on him, was opened and read, when it was found that he had willed his entire estate to Amy and her children, and had appointed John Joliffe. A. H. Ernest and Edward Harwood as executors. This will is a duplicate of that left in the care of Mr. Joliffe, which has not yet been opened. If the property is obtained, each of these colored children will have a fortune of $25,000 or $30,000. The body of Mr. Willis will be buried to-day. The executors of the will are all residents of this city.

The New York Times

Published: May 25, 1855
Copyright © The New York Times